The middle of the crowd quickly parted to form a narrow aisle along which two armed guards half-led and half-dragged a naked man through the deep snow.

Lionstone gazed down at him thoughtfully. 'This pathetic object is Fredric Hill, head of Starport Security. This man let the rebels in. We have therefore decided that an example shall be made.'

She looked back at the Grendel, and after a moment everyone else did too. It stood calm and relaxed behind the throne, a living nightmare. The yoke around its armoured neck suddenly gave a little chime, and then the alien surged forward more quickly than the human eye could follow. One moment it was standing just behind the throne and the next it was towering over the cringing Security head, its great clawed hands on his bare shoulders. The courtiers nearest it surged back as far as the pressure of the crowd would allow, but the Grendel paid them no heed. Its claws sank deep into the man's flesh, and thick runnels of blood coursed down his colourless flesh. He began to scream.

SIMON R. GREEN

DEATHSTALKER REBELLION

First published in Great Britain 1996
as a Vista paperback original

This edition published in 2001 by
Gollancz
An imprint of the Orion Publishing Group
Orion House, 5 Upper St Martin's Lane
London, WC2H 9EA

Second impression published in Great Britain
in May 2002

A catalogue record for this book is
available from the British Library.

ISBN 1 85798 337 8

Typeset by CentraCet, Cambridge
Printed and bound in Great Britain
by Cox & Wyman Ltd, Reading, Berks.

Deathstalker.
It's not just a name, it's a destiny.

PROLOGUE

In the beginning was the Empire, and all was well. It was the great adventure of humanity, springing out from its home-world, pressing on into the endless dark in search of new worlds and wonders. It was a time of heroes and marvellous deeds, as humanity spread from world to world and the frontier pressed remorselessly outwards. A thousand worlds, with a thousand civilizations, blazing so brightly against the dark. The Empire.

It took four hundred years for the rot to set in.

Parliament became corrupt, the Company of Lords grew increasingly powerful on the profits from plundered worlds, and the Emperor ruled over all with an iron fist from his Iron Throne. Technology produced human clones and espers, declared them nothing but property, and institutionalized slavery. It was still a great Empire, but only if you were rich, or of noble birth, or had connections in the right places. Everyone else worked hard, kept their heads down and tried not to be noticed.

And so it went on for nine hundred years.

By the time of Owen Deathstalker, the Empire was ripe for rebellion. Owen had never wanted to be a hero. Despite his Family's martial history, he always saw himself as a scholar rather than a warrior. But when the Empress Lionstone XIV had him outlawed and put a price on his head that had his own people scrabbling to kill him, he had no choice but to run for his life and reluctantly grasp his destiny. He fell in with fellow outlaw Hazel d'Ark – pirate, bon vivant and ex-clonelegger – and together they fled to the rebel planet

Mistworld, where they encountered Jack Random, the legendary professional rebel, Ruby Journey, the female bounty-hunter, and Tobias Moon, an augmented man from lost Haden. Together the companions travelled to the planet Shandrakor, with its boiling jungles and endless carnage, and at the mansion known as the Last Standing of the Deathstalker Clan they discovered Owen's ancestor of some nine hundred years earlier – Giles Deathstalker, first Warrior Prime of the Empire and creator of the terrible Darkvoid Device, capable of extinguishing suns. He took them to the Wolfling World, where they met the last Wolfling, sole survivor of his genetically engineered kind. The companions passed through the Madness Maze and were changed, emerging much more than they had been.

Together they would inspire and lead the greatest rebellion the Empire would ever know.

From her palace of brass and steel, set within a massive steel bunker deep below the surface of the planet Golgotha, reigned the Empress Lionstone XIV, the beautiful and adored, whose word was law and at whose whim blood flowed and people died horribly. At her side was the Lord High Dram, Warrior Prime and Consort, called by some Widowmaker, though never to his face. Under her command were loyal subjects like Captain John Silence and Investigator Frost, of the starship *Dauntless*. At her feet, the Families jostled and conspired to win her favour, and hunted down her enemies without mercy. Lionstone had strengths and surprises of her own, and would not easily be brought down.

And, watching from the sidelines, waiting to see which way the wind might blow, were many who might be swayed one way or the other. Valentine, head of Clan Wolfe, favoured and powerful; a dandy and a user of drugs in legendary proportions. Kit SummerIsle, head of his Clan, called by some Kid Death, the smiling killer. Cardinal James Kassar, fanatic and rising star of the Church of Christ the Warrior.

In the shadows, the clone and esper underground fought their losing battles and dared to dream of freedom. They had allies in the cyberats – computer hackers and by choice nonpeople – and also in restless younger sons who knew they would never inherit the Family name and riches. And just occasionally a hero would come to them, such as Finlay Campbell – once known as the Masked Gladiator, unconquered champion of the Arena – and Mater Mundi, Our Mother Of All Souls, uber-esper and unfathomable mystery, powerful beyond hope or sanity.

All the players were in place. The stage was set. All that was necessary now was for someone to strike the first blow. Owen Deathstalker, that reluctant hero, headed for Golgotha with Hazel d'Ark on a strange golden ship run by the Hadenmen – augmented men once known as the Enemies of Humanity – and, though posterity has no access to his thoughts, they were probably: 'Why me?'

CHAPTER ONE

Golgotha: Opening Gambit

Why me? thought Owen Deathstalker as he headed for the toilet yet again. He knew he wouldn't really need to do anything once he got there, but his bladder wasn't listening to reason – not for the first time, it had ideas of its own. He was always like this when the pressure was on and he had too much time to think. The afternoon before he'd made his first major speech at the Imperial Historians' Convention he'd spent so long in the toilets that they'd actually sent someone in to ask if he were all right.

Owen stepped inside the starship's single toilet and pulled the door shut behind him. It wasn't much: just a small steel cubicle with a gleaming steel bowl. Owen unzipped, and aimed carefully. He didn't want the others to think he was incredibly nervous. It was the waiting that got to him. He was hardly nervous at all during a fight – usually because he was too busy trying to keep himself from being killed to have time to worry. But beforehand his imagination always insisted on picturing all the ways things could go horribly wrong. And his current mission – heading for Golgotha, the most closely guarded planet in the Empire, in a golden ship built by non-human beings – had never struck him as being that sane an idea in the first place.

Even if it had been *his* idea.

Nevertheless, the Hadenman ship was the best choice open to the nascent rebellion. His own ship, the *Sunstrider*, had been one of the fastest in the Empire, but he'd had to leave it where it had crashed, deep in the deadly jungles of Shandra-kor. And the Last Standing had been ruled out very early on:

a huge stone castle with a built-in stardrive was many things, but inconspicuous wasn't one of them. The sleek golden ships of the Hadenmen, however, were everything the rebels needed, and more – incredibly fast, powerfully armed, and so tightly cloaked there wasn't a sensor display in the Empire sensitive enough to pick them up. In theory, anyway. The Hadenmen had been out of things for a while.

The one thing the starship hadn't had was a toilet. Apparently augmented men didn't need such things. Owen hadn't inquired further. He didn't think he really wanted to know. When Owen had discovered that he and Hazel d'Ark had been volunteered to represent the rebellion on this mission, he had argued long and loudly against the decision. And, when he had lost the argument, as he'd always known he would, he had stated flatly that he wasn't going anywhere with the Hadenmen until they installed a toilet. However fast and powerful the Hadenman craft might be, it was still a long trip to Golgotha, and Owen knew only too well what his nerves were going to be like.

So they'd added this cramped little cubicle especially for him and his nerves. There was no washbasin, no rug around the base, no seat to lift. There was no toilet paper either, but Owen had already decided very firmly that he wasn't going to think about that. He looked at his reflection in the steel wall before him: a man in his mid-twenties, tall and rangy, with dark hair and darker eyes. Not exactly soft, but not the kind of person you'd be scared of meeting in a back alley. He sighed deeply, finished what he was doing, zipped up again, and left the toilet with as much dignity as he could muster.

Minimalist though it was, he preferred the look of the toilet to the interior of the Hadenman ship. Its layout had not been designed with human comforts in mind, like sense or logic, and some of its aspects were positively disturbing. He concentrated on getting back to Hazel, who was sitting cross-legged on the deck between two enigmatic protrusions of Hadenman machinery. She was busy dismantling and cleaning her new projectile weapon, and she spared Owen only a scornful glance as he approached. Hazel d'Ark had never been bothered by nerves. Give her something destructive to play with and she was happy as a pig in muck. Owen sank down beside her, being very careful not to touch anything.

There were no seats or rest-stations anywhere in the ship. Instead, unfamiliar nonhuman technology filled the interior from stem to stern, with Hadenmen plugged into it here and there as needed. The augmented men were part of the ship, or it was part of them, and they ran it with their thoughts. Owen and Hazel fitted in where they could, and tried not to look too directly at the incomprehensible machinery – because it made their eyes hurt. Lights of painful brightness and unfamiliar hues came and went, and the angles of the larger shapes were disturbing, as though trying to lead the human eye somewhere it couldn't or wouldn't follow. Owen settled himself as comfortably as he could on the unyielding steel deck, and hugged his knees to his chest. The ship intimidated the hell out of him, and he didn't care who knew it. He looked at Hazel, who was completely absorbed in what she was doing.

A tall, lithely muscular woman in her early twenties, Hazel always looked as though she were about to explode into action at any moment. Green eyes peered challengingly out at the world from under a mane of long ratty red hair, and her rare smiles came and went so quickly they were often missed.

As usual, she'd loaded herself down with weapons. Her disrupter hung in its usual place on her right hip, in its well worn leather holster: the standard energy pistol was powerful enough to blast through steel plate as long as its crystal was fully charged. The trouble was that you then had to wait the two minutes it took for the crystal to recharge. Her sword – heavy enough to do real damage, without being so long as to be unwieldy – hung on her left hip, the chased metal scabbard stretching out across the deck. Scattered before her were the component parts of her projectile weapon. Actually, it looked as if there were enough parts to make *several* weapons. Owen had had no idea the things were so damn' complicated.

He had ambivalent feelings about the antiquated projectile weapons his ancestor Giles had provided from the Last

Standing's armoury. They weren't nearly as powerful or as accurate as energy weapons but, when they were pumping out several hundred bullets a minute on full auto, they didn't need to be. There was none of that nonsense about waiting for two minutes between each shot, either. Hazel had all but fallen in love with the new (or, more strictly speaking, old) type of weapons, and sang their praises at every opportunity. She'd taken to carrying several of the guns, plus enough ammunition to bulge every pocket she had. Owen remained unconvinced. He carried a projectile weapon in addition to his disrupter, but he thought he'd wait and see how the gun performed in a continuous firefight before he made up his mind. Personally, he thought the only reason Hazel liked her new toys so much was because they had lots of separate pieces she could play with.

When push came to shove, he still believed in cold steel as the answer to most problems. A sword had no parts to go wrong, never ran out of ammo, and didn't need to recharge for two minutes between use.

'You keep squeezing it dry like that, you're going to flatten it,' Hazel said casually. 'Never known anyone to spend so much time in a toilet. Check your guns again. It's very comforting.'

'No it isn't,' said Owen. 'There isn't a single comforting thing anywhere in this unnatural ship, and that very definitely includes you.'

'You never cease to amaze me, aristo. I've seen you fight appalling odds, and go charging into situations I wouldn't tackle for all the credits in Golgotha's Treasury, and you come from one of the greatest warrior Families in the Empire, but every time we have to wait around for a bit you get jumpier than a nun at a dating agency.'

'I am not a warrior,' said Owen determinedly, not looking at her. 'I'm a historian who is temporarily, and under extreme duress, being forced to act as a soldier of the rebellion. Personally, I can't wait for the rebellion to be over so I can go back to being a minor scholar again, of no importance to anyone but myself and with no pressures apart from the occasional symposium. I still don't see why I was volunteered for this mission.'

'Because it was your idea in the first place,' said Hazel. 'Serves you right for being a smartass. If anyone shouldn't be here, it's me. I'm still not convinced any of this is going to work.'

'Then what are you doing here?'

'Someone's got to watch your back. Besides, I was getting bored just sitting around. A complete lack of human comforts, far too much talking, and no action of any kind. I need to be doing something or I get cranky.'

'I'd noticed,' Owen said dryly. 'Trust me, the plan will work. It's been discussed from every angle and subjected to intense analysis. Even the Hadenmen liked it. This mission is just what we need to start the rebellion with a bang – something to make the whole Empire sit up and take notice.'

'Oh, sure. They can all tune in their holos and watch us getting our ass kicked in living colour. Probably repeat it in prime time, with extra slow motion for the gooey bits.'

'I thought *I* was the nervous one?'

'You are. I'm just practical.'

'So am I. That's why this plan represents the best way to announce the rebellion's presence. We can't hope to win a head-on fight. They've got far more men and guns and ships than we have. So instead we launch a lightning attack and hit them where it really hurts – in their pockets. With the Hadenmen's help, we'll slip right past Golgotha's defences unobserved, sneak our way into the main Income Tax and Tithe Headquarters, perform our little act of economic sabotage, and be gone before anyone even knows we were there. It's very elegant, when you think about it. We transfer a whole bunch of credits to our pre-prepared Rebel accounts, and then erase and scramble everything else. Thus we not only kick the Empire and Church where it really hurts and give a major boost to Rebel funds, but we also make a lot of friends among the general populace, when they realize the Empire won't be able to tax them again until they've got all the records sorted out and re-established. Which could take years. Hazel – could you at least *try* to look interested in what I'm telling you? You managed to avoid most of the strategy sessions, but you need to understand what we're going to be doing down there.'

'No, I don't. Just point me in the right direction and turn me loose. If it so much as *looks* like an Imperial guard, it's dead meat. I was good in a fight before we went through the Maze, but I'm hell on wheels now. I've got all kinds of abilities I never had before, and I can't wait to try them out.'

Owen sighed. 'We're not fighters any more, Hazel. Like it or not, we've become important figures in the rebellion. People will look to us for inspiration on how to strike back against the Empire, and they'll join the rebellion in droves. The underground on Golgotha are committing a lot of their people and resources to help us in this, just because they believe in us. By surviving everything the Empire sent after us, we've become the hope of everyone who ever dreamed of being free.'

'If we're their only hope, they're in big trouble.'

'Maybe,' said Owen, 'but, whatever the truth of the matter, we have responsibilities now. We're not just doing this for us. If we pull this off it'll be a sign the rebellion has a realistic chance of succeeding. The people might believe in us, but the cold facts are that rebellions are extremely expensive to mount. Starships and bases don't come cheap. Remember how Jack Random had to deal and compromise and make questionable promises to questionable people to get funding for his wars? And he was the professional rebel. He had to compromise. With the credit we'll be lifting, we won't have to.'

'All right,' said Hazel. 'Assuming, for the sake of argument, that we bring this off without being killed in horrible ways, what then? Turn pirate, and pick off Empire ships between planets? Last I heard, the Empire was handing out some really nasty punishments for piracy.'

'Didn't stop you being one.'

'I'm not exactly noted for my career choices. So what's the

16

current version of the master-plan, Deathstalker? I can tell you're just bursting to tell me.'

'That's because it's such a good plan. As you'd know if you'd attended the strategy sessions like you were supposed to.'

'Nag, nag, nag. Get on with it.'

'We start small, picking our fights carefully, and build success on success until we're a viable force within the Empire. Then we call on the people to rise up against Lionstone. They've never dared, in the past. Quite rightly, they fear reprisals. They also value their comforts too much. They think they have too much to lose. Unless their noses are rubbed in it, they don't like to think about where those comforts come from, and who suffers to produce them. Our task is to change the way people think – the way they see the Empire. First we educate them, then we encourage them to rise up, and then we help liberate them. Classic strategy. If the Empire really understood the lessons that can be learned from history, they'd ban it.'

'You're getting into this, aren't you, Deathstalker? You've come a long way from the amateur scholar who just wanted the world to leave him alone.'

Owen smiled briefly. 'The world insisted on being heard. I can't go back to being what I was, much as I might like to. I've seen too much, done too much. But don't ever see me as some kind of warrior or hero. I might have to play the part for the rebellion, but don't confuse *me* with *the role*. I'll fight when I have to, and that's it. When it's all over and the fighting's done, I'll be only too happy to climb back up into my ivory tower and kick the ladder away. I've spent most of my life trying to be the scholar I wanted to be rather than the warrior my Family expected. Circumstances may compel me to act the hero, but circumstances change, and the moment I'm no longer needed I'll become a historian again so fast it'll make your head spin. People watching will suffer from whiplash.'

Hazel sniffed, fitting her gun back together with calm,

practised fingers. 'It's fighters, not dreamers, who make things change.'

'I know what you want,' said Owen testily. 'You think all of us who went through the Maze should use our special abilities to cut a bloody path straight through the Empire to Golgotha, so that you could strut right into the Imperial Palace and take on the Empress head-to-head. Well, you can forget that. The moment we step out into the open, Lionstone will stomp on us, hard, even if it takes half her Fleet to do it. We're not gods or superhumans. We've been given a few extra abilities, that's all. Very useful abilities, but only if used in the right ways at the right times.'

'You're no fun,' said Hazel. 'What did the others think? I suppose they all wanted to pussyfoot around, too?'

Owen frowned. 'Giles wanted to spend the next few years gathering data from a distance and developing hidden power bases throughout the Empire before we risked catching Lionstone's attention. If we'd listened to him, we'd still be sitting on our asses twenty years from now, wondering if it was the right time yet. He hasn't been the same since he killed Dram. He's gone all cautious and non-committal. Jack Random wanted to raise an army on the strength of his name, and fight the Empire world by world, like he used to. He had to be reminded rather forcibly that his way hadn't worked then, and wouldn't work now. Ruby Journey just wanted to kill someone, as soon as possible. And the Wolfling . . . wanted to be left alone. So I've been making most of the decisions, of late. Everyone else was too busy sulking.'

'Maybe I should have got more involved, after all,' said Hazel.

'We all asked you, at one time or another. You didn't want to know. You were always off on your own somewhere, preoccupied with your own business – whatever that might have been. Target shooting with your new toys, or trying to seduce a Hadenman, probably.'

'I was busy experimenting with the abilities the Maze gave us,' Hazel said hotly. 'You might be afraid of the changes it made in us, but I'm not. We're all stronger, faster and fitter than we were, but there's more to it than that. There's a connection between us now, a mental link on some deep, basic level. It's not esp. I can't read your mind, or anyone else's. But we're . . . joined now, in some new, primal way. Mind to mind, body to body, soul to soul. Anything you can do, I can do, and vice versa. For example, I can boost now, just like you.'

Owen looked at her sharply. Boost was both the gift and the curse of the Deathstalker Clan. For short periods he could become all but superhuman – inhumanly fast and strong, unbeatable with a weapon in his hand. A combination of mental training, gengineered glands and secret chemical caches deep within the body, boost was a jealously guarded Clan secret. It was also more seductive and addictive than any drug could ever be. Owen had learned to use it only sparingly. The candle that burns twice as brightly lasts half as long. Too much boosting would quite literally burn him up.

Hazel knew some of that, but not all, and not nearly as much as she thought she did. Owen kept his voice carefully calm and even. 'You must be mistaken, Hazel. The boost isn't some esper phenomenon: it's the result of inherited characteristics, physical changes in the body, and a hell of a lot of training.'

'And I've got it.' Hazel smiled triumphantly. 'I've been practising with it. You never told me it would feel so good, Owen. I hadn't thought about physical changes being involved, but you're probably right. So what? It just means my body has adapted itself as necessary. Interesting. I wonder what other changes I could make in myself, just by thinking about it . . .'

Owen leaned closer, so he could look her right in the eyes. 'You're heading into dangerous waters, Hazel. We don't understand enough about what's been done to us just to experiment wildly. You're jumping off the edge with no idea of how deep the drop is. We need to take this one step at a time, under carefully controlled conditions.'

'You're just frightened of the possibilities!'

'Damn' right I am! So should you be! The Maze was an alien artifact, remember? Designed by alien minds for alien purposes. The last people to go through it ended up creating the Hadenmen. Every time you experiment blindly you're risking your very humanity. It's important we take this very slowly, very carefully.'

'There isn't time, Deathstalker! The rebellion needs us now. You're the one who says we have responsibilities, who keeps going on about how important this mission is. If we're going to survive it, and the ones that follow, we're going to need every advantage we can get our hands on. If you're not prepared to lead us, stand aside for someone who is. Don't you worry, aristo: once I've reached my full potential and I'm the superhuman you're so afraid of becoming, I'll take over the rebellion and you can go back to your books. Despite what I said earlier, you're right. You actually *are* too soft to be a real warrior, Deathstalker. You always were. You still dream about that kid you crippled on Mistworld, don't you? Let it go. She would have killed you without a second thought.'

'That doesn't matter,' said Owen, still meeting her gaze. 'She was a child, and I cut her down without thinking, without caring, because I was caught up in the thrill of battle. I won't do that again. If I have to be a fighter, I'll be the kind of fighter I choose to be, not the kind my Family or you might prefer. And I won't give up my humanity in the name of necessity. I'm making the decisions in this rebellion because I'm the only one who's studied the wars and insurrections of the past, and understood how they've been won and lost. We'll fight the Empire through sabotage and subterfuge, and by winning the hearts of the people. No innocents will ever die at our hands. And, if you think people will flock to follow some strange, superhuman leader, you're wrong. They'd scream for the Empire to hunt you down and kill you, just so they wouldn't have to be afraid of what you might do. We're going to attack the Income Tax and Tithe Headquarters as planned. It'll be the signal for a new kind of war, a new kind of rebellion, where no one has to die unnecessarily.'

'Like I said: soft. And still far too prone to lecturing people.

I was hoping the Maze might have cured you of that, but apparently not.'

'Then why are you here, Hazel?'

'I told you: someone's got to watch your back. Otherwise, damned if I know, Deathstalker. I was hoping I was in for a little excitement, but it seems I was wrong about that, too. Doesn't matter. This is the start of the rebellion, and I'm not missing out on it. And, if things do go wrong in your carefully worked-out plan, I'll be there to save your ass with my superhuman powers. Fair enough?'

'You don't understand, Hazel. I'm not afraid of the abilities themselves – just of the price we might have to pay for them, further down the road.'

Hazel looked at him expressionlessly. 'You're a fine one to talk. You were quick enough to take that new metal hand of yours from the Hadenmen. They may have built all kinds of hidden surprises into it, and you'll never know until they activate them.'

Owen glanced down at the gleaming golden artifact that had replaced the left hand he had lost fighting a killer alien the Empire had brought to the Wolfling World. The new hand was perfect in every detail, and responded to him just as readily as had his real hand . . . though it always felt subtly cold.

He looked back at Hazel, and shrugged uncomfortably. 'It's not like I had a choice. I needed a new hand, and you know I can't trust regeneration machines any more – not after my treacherous personal AI programmed the last one with control words the Empire could use against you and me.'

'That AI – Ozymandias – is gone, Owen. You destroyed him.'

'Doesn't make any difference. Who knows what further surprises might be lying in wait for us in any other Empire machine we trusted our bodies to? I don't trust the Hadenmen completely – I'm not a fool – yet right now they're the lesser of two evils. They can mess with my hand, but not with my mind. Besides, they did a really good job on this hand. Full sensory analogues, and far more powerful than the original. And I don't have to trim the nails on this one.'

'It's still a product of the Hadenman laboratories,' said Hazel, 'and I don't trust anything that comes out of them further than I could spit into a hurricane. The last time the Hadenmen took on the Empire it was as Gods of the Genetic Church, bringing transformation or death: become a Hadenman or become extinct. Remember? You must have read about it in one of your precious books. And now they're born again and so polite and helpful and reasonable it's downright spooky. I want to jump out of my skin every time one of them approaches me. I keep waiting for the other shoe to drop.'

Owen nodded. He knew what she meant. They both looked silently at the augmented men running the golden ship. There were twenty of them, connected to their strange machinery by thick lengths of cable plunging into their bodies or immersed in gleaming technology like a man half-submerged in water, their inhuman minds communing directly with their unfathomable technology on a level no human mind could understand or appreciate. Each Hadenman had a specific function aboard the ship, and performed it perfectly for as long as required. They did not suffer from boredom or fatigue, from inspiration or original thought – at least, not while they were working. Perhaps, off-duty, they were real party animals, but Owen rather doubted it. From what he had seen of the Hadenmen as they'd gone calmly about rebuilding their strange and unsettling city deep below the frozen surface of the Wolfling World, the augmented men had no attributes that were not strictly logical and functional.

The only Hadenman whom Owen and Hazel had known at all well was Tobias Moon, who'd travelled with them for a while, but he'd spent so long among humans that he'd acquired a surface gloss of humanity, or at least a very good copy of it. He'd worn out most of his energy crystals down the years, losing many abilities and functions along the way, and had freely admitted he was only a pale version of the real thing. Still, it had to be said that even on his good days he'd been a disturbing son-of-a-bitch. The glowing eyes and

22

inhuman buzzing voice hadn't helped, but it was in his mind that the real differences lay. Tobias Moon thought differently, even when he tried not to.

The augmented men who'd emerged from the Tomb of the Hadenmen, after Owen had released them from their long restorative sleep, had moved like living gods. Their eyes had blazed like the sun, their movements had been perfect and graceful, and they had seemed not so much nonhuman as *more* than human. They still scared the shit out of Owen, even after the past few months of getting used to them, and he kept his hand near his gun whenever one of them approached him. They called him their Redeemer, and were always quiet and deferential to him, but Owen knew better than to warm to them. He'd studied the old records of their attacks on humanity. He had seen holos of the sleek golden ships running rings around the slower, clumsier human vessels, blowing them apart with perfectly aimed weapons, had seen the tall shining figures stalking through blazing cities, killing everything that lived, had seen what happened to the humans the Hadenmen had experimented on, the living and the dead, in the name of their Code of the Genetic Church. When you no longer had to worry about human emotions or restraints you could do anything, and the Hadenmen had. They had created abominations, seeking always for an inhuman perfection of man and machine, a whole that would be greater than the sum of its parts.

They would have won the war had there been more of them and fewer of humanity, but in the end they had been thrown back, their golden ships outnumbered and blown apart, and the scant survivors had fled back to the safety of their Tomb, hidden deep within the endless night of the Darkvoid, beyond the Rim of Empire. But they had come very close to wiping out humanity and replacing it with something horrible. Yes, Owen remembered what he'd seen in the records, and all the politeness in the world wouldn't make him forget what the Hadenmen had done, and might do again.

But none of that mattered for the moment. He needed

them. The rebellion needed them. And, if he were to go up against the Empire, there were going to be times when he'd require an army of trained fighters to meet Lionstone's troops. That was where the Hadenmen would come in – assuming they could be controlled, or at least persuaded to follow orders. Owen was under no illusions about the danger he'd reintroduced to the Empire. Given time, the Hadenmen might become a worse threat than Lionstone could ever be. He tried not to think about that too much, for the time being. It helped that he had so many other problems to worry over.

'Let's talk of other things,' he said determinedly. 'Assuming we get past Golgotha's defences as easily as the Hadenmen have promised, this will be our first chance to make real contact with the underground. They're practically the only organized rebellion left in the Empire. Mostly clones and espers, as I understand it, but with a great many useful fellow travellers – some of them quite influential. We need them on our side. Hopefully, kicking the crap out of the Income Tax and Tithe Headquarters will make a good first impression, and convince them we're a force to be recognized. Jack Random's name should open a few doors. He's given me the details of some people he swears we can trust, but that information could be years out of date. He betrayed a lot of people when the Empire mind-techs were working on him in their interrogation centre, which is not going to make him very popular in some quarters. His name could work against us as much as for us. Same with my ancestor Giles, the original Deathstalker. Having a living legend on your side is very useful in recruiting people, but there's always the chance those same people will be disappointed when they meet the reality rather than the legend.'

'Assuming he really *is* the original Deathstalker,' said Hazel.

'There is that, yes,' said Owen unhappily. 'For someone who's supposed to have been in stasis for the past nine hundred years he does seem to know a hell of a lot about what's been going on recently.'

24

'So, if he isn't who he says he is, who is he? An Empire plant? A clone? Some madman with delusions of grandeur?'

'Those are certainly a few of the possibilities,' said Owen. 'But I had something rather more disturbing in mind. There's always the chance he could be a Fury.'

Hazel looked at him for a long moment, struck dumb by the very thought. The Furies were terror weapons created by the rogue AIs on Shub to act as their agents in the world of men. Creations of living metal within cloned flesh envelopes, identical to humans as far as the naked eye could tell, they were unstoppable killers and merciless opponents, capable of appalling havoc and destruction. Luckily espers could spot them easily, and disrupters didn't care how strong the Furies were. But there was always the possibility that there were some around, undetected, living their fake human lives, reporting back to Shub and waiting for the order to destroy humanity from within.

'Do you have any reason for thinking Giles might be a Fury?' Hazel said finally.

'Nothing specific. It just seemed a little odd to me that, with so many factions appearing to take part in the rebellion, Shub is the only one we haven't heard from. Not that I'd have given them the time of day if they'd contacted us, but if I were them I'd have an agent or two planted in the Court and the underground. Shub has a vested interest in knowing when the Empire is weak.'

'You're right,' said Hazel. 'It's a disturbing thought. If you have any more like it, feel free keep them to yourself. If you're that worried, why haven't you said anything before?'

'I haven't any proof. Besides, I wasn't entirely sure of who might be listening. Or who I could trust. Personally, I've decided to think Giles is exactly who he says he is.'

'Why?'

'Because you have to trust someone.'

'Yeah,' said Hazel. 'That's what's been bothering me.'

Owen sighed once more. 'Life never used to be this complicated. There was a time when my most arduous decision of the day was which wine to have with my meal.'

Hazel smiled suddenly. 'And you want to give up all this excitement, just to return to that, and your dusty books?'

'Damn' right I do. I want my old life back. It was perfect then. The best wines, first-class meals, every whim indulged, waited on hand and foot every minute of the day and night . . . No worries, no responsibilities I couldn't safely delegate to somebody else, and absolutely no chance of being suddenly and unpleasantly killed. I'd go back like a shot, if I could.'

'And leave behind all your friends?' Hazel batted her eyes at him coquettishly. 'And what about me?'

Owen winced. 'Please don't do that. It looks almost unnatural when you do it. You needn't worry that I'll abandon you, or the others. I've already said I'm aware of my obligations as a leader of this rebellion. And I've seen too much of the suffering and injustice the Empire is built on to be able to turn a blind eye to it any more. Millions of people bled and died and were enslaved so that I and a few others like me could have our lives of comfort. I have sworn upon my blood and upon my honour to put an end to that, and I will see it through or die trying. I just don't have any illusions about myself, or about how I came to be doing this. I'm nobody's hero, Hazel: just another poor soul caught between a rock and a hard place.' He paused. 'Let us change the subject yet again. Was there anything new from Mistworld before we left?'

'Nothing helpful. Ruby and I knew a few useful people in Mistport, and of course Jack Random came up with some extra names, but they're all still very suspicious of us. We didn't make any friends on our last visit, and they've learned the hard way down the years to trust no one but themselves. They're waiting for us to commit ourselves first. They want a sign – something bold and audacious and, above all, successful.'

'Fair enough,' said Owen. 'This first strike against Golgotha should impress the hell out of them . . . assuming nothing goes wrong and we don't foul up. We have only one chance at this, and we've had no chance to practise. I've done my best to stop thinking about all the things that could go wrong

. . . it just makes my head hurt, and does terrible things to my bladder. As I keep saying, I was never meant to be a warrior, no matter what my father wanted.'

Hazel looked at him for a moment. 'Owen, you think about your father too much. You've told me how he tried to manipulate you all your life, through his schemes and intrigues and hidden agendas, but he's dead now. It's all over. Let it go. You're your own man these days.'

'Am I? He's still pulling my strings, even from the grave! This is just the kind of magnificent heroic gesture he always believed in. I'm becoming exactly the kind of man he wanted, the kind of man I've struggled all my life not to be – a bully with a sword.'

It was Hazel's turn to sigh. He could tell she was wondering how many times they were going to have to change the subject before they could find something they could both safely talk about.

'This Stevie Blue who's supposed to be meeting us dirt-side,' she said. 'Know anything about her?'

'You've read the same reports I did. Apparently she's an esper clone, in fairly high standing in the Golgotha underground. Assuming we manage to find her, she'll come back with us to be the underground's voice in our planning sessions. Reading between the lines, I get the feeling she's a bit of an anarchist, but it takes all sorts to make an Empire. Or a rebellion.'

'What do you expect to happen after we've won, and it's all over?' Hazel said suddenly. 'We've never really discussed this, any of us. We've spent a lot of time talking about bringing Lionstone down, but none at all on what we're going to replace her with.'

'It's all rather moot at the moment,' said Owen. 'The odds are stacked against us surviving, let alone winning. But if we do depose her . . . Well, I suppose Parliament and the Company of Lords will put forward suitable candidates, and together we'll choose someone new to become Emperor and begin a programme of reforms. Clean up the corruption, work in a little more democracy here and there, and of course give a pardon to all rebels past and present. Then we can get back to leading normal lives again.'

'To hell with that!' Hazel said hotly. 'We're not going through all this just to settle for the same old set up, but with some pretty new window-dressing! The whole system is corrupt from top to bottom, and our only chance for real justice is to tear it down and start again. No more Emperor, no more Lords, liberation for all clones and espers, full democracy and freedom for everyone!'

'Everyone?' said Owen, aghast. 'Clones, aliens, espers . . . *everyone*?'

'Damn' right. It has to be for everyone. That's what freedom means.'

'Sounds more like anarchy to me. Not to mention total bloody chaos. If no one knows their place, how can you achieve anything?'

'I have never known my place, and I've achieved quite a lot. You'd be surprised what people can do, given a chance.'

Owen looked at her thoughtfully. 'Hazel d'Ark. The d'Arks used to be nobility, not all that long ago. Do I detect just a little over-reaction here? By someone just a bit ashamed of their aristocratic roots? Surely, Hazel, you must feel some loyalty to the Iron Throne?'

'Not one damned bit. The only soft spot I would have for the nobility would be a massive quicksand big enough to swallow the lot of them. I was never an aristo. I wasn't born a d'Ark: I stole the name when I was on the run and needed some false papers in a hurry. Mainly because I liked the sound of it. I didn't want to risk my family finding me again, or my being sent back to them if I were rounded up.'

'You never talk about your family,' said Owen. 'Don't you miss them?'

'No, I bloody don't,' said Hazel. 'If I never heard from them again that would suit me just fine.'

Owen chose his words carefully. 'Did they . . . abuse you in any way?'

'Oh, no. Nothing like that. They were just so bloody boring and nice I couldn't stand them. Their idea of a wild party was a wine and cheese tasting where you spat the wine out. I had to get away, see the universe, taste some life before I got old and grey like them. You know how it is.'

'Yes,' said Owen, 'I suppose I do. But I never had a chance to leave my Family. Too many duties and responsibilities. In the end they all left me, dying one after the other while I just stood by helplessly and watched it happen. There was never anything I could have done, but it didn't stop me feeling I should have done something. Of course, the boost killed a lot of them while they were still children. Only a few in every generation survive its first onslaught. It's the price of our genetic gift. Which is why I am all that remains of the sons and daughters of my father's line – in fact, I'm pretty much all that's left of the Clan now. Apparently they found some distant cousin to take over the Lordship in my place, but I'm the last of the direct line. When I die, my line dies with me. I'm not sure whether that's a good thing or a bad. Seems to me we did as much harm as good down the years, but then I suppose that's true of most of the Families. And, above it all, my father, sacrificing me and everyone else to his endless intrigues . . . I never had a life of my own, ever since I was a small child. This mission is the nearest I've come to running away – to doing what *I* want to do instead of what my father wanted. It feels very . . . liberating.'

He smiled suddenly. 'You're right. I do tend to lecture people, don't I? One of the more socially acceptable vices of the scholar, I'm afraid. What were we talking about? Oh, yes, universal suffrage, even for the unpeople. I really don't think you've been thinking this through, Hazel. If all the clones and espers were to be freed and enfranchised, the Empire itself would collapse. Its whole economy is based on the exploitation of clones and espers. They turn the wheels that keep things moving. Without them, everything would just fall apart. Food and power distribution would be disrupted, businesses would be in chaos . . . civilization itself could be threatened. Billions of innocents would suffer.'

'No one's really innocent if their lives of comfort are based on the suffering of others. If we have to rip civilization apart

29

in order to put it back together again in a more just form, then that's what we'll do. Remember how horrified you were at how people lived on Mistworld? The appalling conditions and the short, brutal lives? Think how bad the lives of clones and espers in the Empire must be, if they're prepared to risk death just for a chance to flee to Mistworld. They're not second-class citizens, they're not even slaves. They're just property. Worked until they drop, because there are always more to replace them. When I said we should tear it all down, I wasn't kidding. Anything would be better than what we've got now.'

'I guess I can't argue with that,' said Owen after a moment. 'I spent most of my life ignoring things I didn't want to see. I won't do that any more. But there's still the problem of the aliens. There are at least two new alien species Out There somewhere, plus whatever created the Madness Maze, all of them with a level of technology equal to our own or higher. Weaken the Empire too much, and they might just walk in and exterminate us.'

Hazel shrugged. 'We can't afford to think about all the possibilities, or we'd go mad. There'd always be some good reason why we should put things off. Lionstone has to fall if the people are to be free, and if you and I are to live in safety. All we can do is take things one step at a time. We'll worry about the aliens as and when they make an appearance. They don't have to be enemies, you know. Anyway, you're a fine one to talk: you're the one who woke a whole army of Hadenmen from their Tomb. The only reason the Hadenmen aren't still the official Enemies of Humanity is because the AIs on Shub are worse. I suppose you'll be suggesting we team up with *them* next.'

'I would rather cut off my head with a rusty saw,' Owen said firmly. 'The Hadenmen are a calculated risk. Shub, on the other hand, will settle for nothing less than the extermination of the human species. I may be reckless, but I am not stupid.'

They both looked up sharply as one of the augmented men approached them. Hazel surreptitiously turned her reassem-

30

bled projectile weapon so that it tracked the Hadenman's progress. Owen casually let his hand drift closer to his disrupter. The augmented man loomed over them, his movements inhumanly graceful, his eyes blazing so brightly Owen and Hazel couldn't look at them directly. His face held nothing that could be recognized as a human emotion, and when he spoke his voice was a harsh, grotesque buzzing.

'We have left hyperspace and are currently in orbit over Golgotha. The ship's computers have made contact with the orbiting security satellites and persuaded them that our presence here is entirely natural and unthreatening. Our cloaking device will conceal us from passing ships and planet-based sensors as we descend towards the surface. There will be no difficulties. You may prepare yourselves for the drop.'

'Thank you,' said Owen politely, but the Hadenman was already walking away. They didn't go in much for small talk. Hazel pulled a face at the Hadenman's departing back, and then looked at Owen.

'So, are you ready for the drop, or do you need to disappear into the toilet again?'

'I don't think you could get any more out of me if you used a syphon. Let's go on down to the cargo bay. It's time we got this show on the road.'

'Damn' right,' said Hazel.

They made their way through the hulking alien machinery, climbing carefully over it when there was no clear path around it. The gleaming metal felt uncomfortably cold, and some of it shimmered uncertainly, as though it weren't always there. Owen and Hazel gave the machines as much room as they could and kept their hands strictly to themselves as they descended floor by floor to the empty cargo bay. The vast steel cavern was lined with thick ribbed cables that curled around and over each other in eye-numbing confusion, but the only bits of equipment set out in all the empty space were two standard gravity sleds and a small package of carefully prepared code disks to be fed into the Income Tax and Tithe computers. Owen and Hazel checked the sleds over thoroughly, just in case, and then settled down to wait. It wouldn't be long now.

The sleds were really nothing more than a flat surface – disturbingly like a coffin lid – with an antigrav motor, a set of controls, two built-in disrupters, and a force shield to protect the rider from the wind. Pretty basic, but all they'd need. If nothing went wrong.

Owen hefted the disks in his hand. A very small package, to do so much potential damage. Rather like Hazel, in fact. He smiled at the thought, and looked across at her. She had her sword out and was polishing the blade with a filthy piece of rag. Owen was never entirely sure what to make of her at any given time. He respected her, certainly, and her skill with weapons . . . she was one of the finest fighters he'd ever fought beside. And he certainly admired the fire in her voice when she spoke of freedom and justice, even if he didn't always agree with her solutions. She'd come barging into his life like a runaway horse, saving him from almost certain death, and then proceeded to shake up and question everything he thought he believed in. And somewhere along the line, quite against his will, he'd fallen in love with her.

He hadn't told her, and wondered if he ever would. He was everything she claimed to despise, a naive aristo with more ancestors than sense. He liked to think she regarded him highly as a fighter – she'd said so, after all – but beyond that he had no idea what feelings she held for him. Besides, as a Deathstalker he had a duty to marry someone of his own station. Except . . . he wasn't an aristocrat any more. Lionstone had publicly declared him an outlaw and stripped him of every rank and privilege, which meant he was free to do as he liked. And Hazel was brave and true, with a great smile, and eyes to die for. Pity about her hair . . . She was smart and quick, and determined not to take any shit from anyone, least of all him.

He loved her, in a way that made him realize he'd never really loved anybody else. Cathy had been his lover for several years, but she had been his mistress, which was really just another kind of servant. She'd also been an Empire spy, and she'd tried to murder him when he was outlawed. He'd killed her without hesitation. And there'd never been much love in his Family, particularly from his father, who was always busy somewhere else, so he'd learned to live without love. But then Hazel had burst into his life, and everything had changed. Sometimes he couldn't look at her without catching his breath, and his heart quickened when she spoke to him. Her infrequent smiles could put him in a good mood that lasted for hours.

To be honest, he could have done without love. It complicated their relationship and distracted him from more important things. But he didn't seem to have any choice in the matter. He loved her, despite all her many faults, or perhaps because of them. Even if he could never tell her. At best she'd laugh at him, or tell him to go to hell. At worst, she might be kind and understanding as she said 'No', and he didn't think he could stand that. He understood nothing of love or lovers, but he did know hope was better than disillusionment.

An alarm sounded quietly through his comm implant, and he saw Hazel's head snap up as she heard it too. She put her sword away and climbed aboard her gravity sled, ready for business as always. Owen slipped the computer disks into an inside pocket, zipped it shut, and powered up his sled. A view from the ship's sensors appeared before his eyes, patched in through his implant, showing the main landing pads stretched out below. There were ships everywhere, of all shapes and sizes, growing steadily larger as the Hadenman vessel descended at speed. There wasn't room anywhere for it to set down, but that was all right. It wasn't intending to land.

Owen grinned. The plans called for the Hadenman ship to drop its cloaking about now. Then things should get really interesting.

They were almost on top of the starport control tower when the cloaking device shut off. People stopped believing their sensors, took one look at the huge sleek golden craft hovering right above them, and launched straight into a mass panic. There was a lot of screaming and shouting, and a great deal of running round in circles. Owen didn't blame them. The last time Golgotha had seen any Hadenman ships this close they'd been coming in force as the Enemies of Humanity, to wipe out the homeworld's defences. And they'd nearly – uncomfortably nearly – succeeded.

The visual feed cut off, and Owen smiled across at Hazel, who grinned back. In this much chaos and confusion, who would see two small gravity sleds? Owen gripped the controls of his sled firmly. Only a few more moments and he wouldn't have time to be nervous any more. He hoped Hazel was feeling as confident as she looked. It would be nice if one of them were.

The alarm sounded briefly in his ear again, and the great cargo bay doors cracked open below them. The temperature in the hold dropped sharply, and Owen could see bright sunlight through the widening crack. He raised his sled slightly, so that it was hovering just above the floor. Hazel lifted hers, too, and moved in beside him. The doors opened wider, and now they could see the landing pads below. It looked a long way down. Owen took a deep breath and directed his sled through the doors. Hazel followed close behind, and together they dropped out of the belly of the huge golden ship and plummeted towards the landing field.

The bay doors slammed shut behind them, and the Hadenman vessel shot away, already pursued by half a dozen Imperial attack ships firing everything they'd got. The golden ship's force shields flared briefly here and there, but never even looked like going down. No one noticed two tiny sleds heading silently for the ground.

The plan was very simple. The Hadenman ship would hang around, drawing attention to itself, while Hazel and Owen got on with their mission. It would take some while for the starport to come up with anything big enough to worry the golden craft, by which time the mission should be over and the ship could return to pick Owen and Hazel up again. They would then depart at great speed, drop back into hyperspace, and be gone before the Empire could get its act together.

A very simple plan. Owen believed in simple plans. The

more complicated a plan was, the more chances there were of something going wrong. He wasn't worried about anything happening to the Hadenman ship. The strength of Hadenman force shields was legendary, and the ship itself was bulging with all kinds of weapons, some of which Owen hadn't even been able to recognize. He'd made the augmented men promise to use those weapons sparingly, and only in self defence – it wouldn't do to start the rebellion with a bloody Hadenman massacre. It would give entirely the wrong impression, and first impressions were important. The augmented men had nodded very politely, and said 'yes' and 'no' and 'of course' in all the right places, and Owen had crossed his fingers and hoped for the best.

The sled's force shield snapped on automatically, protecting him from the rushing wind. He dropped like a stone. Speed was all that mattered at the moment – to get away from the starport's airspace and disappear into the crowded city before he and Hazel could be spotted. The pastel towers of the city loomed up before him, and he slowed a little so he could duck and dodge around them. The force shield snapped off, to conserve power, and suddenly the wind was whistling past him again, cold and bracing, blowing tears from his eyes. He narrowed his gaze, and concentrated on bringing up the image of the map he'd memorized earlier. It wasn't that far, but the route was tricky, particularly if you weren't intending to follow the established traffic paths.

He flashed past a floating red light and tucked in close beside a tower to avoid an oncoming tour bus. He had a brief glimpse of open-mouthed faces from windows on both sides, and then he was through and in the clear again. He grinned and activated his comm unit on the shielded channel.

'Still with me, Hazel?'

'Damn' right I am. You'll have to do better than that to shake me.'

'I thought you said you hadn't had much practice on a gravity sled before?'

'I haven't. Half the time I feel like I'm riding a crashing elevator. But I can follow anywhere you lead, Deathstalker.'

'Wouldn't doubt it for a minute, Hazel. We're almost there, so stand ready to protect my back. Remember, they stripped these sleds down to basics for extra speed, which means we have only minimum shields. One good hit from a disrupter and they'll go down faster than a back-street whore. So I'm counting on you not to let anybody shoot us. On the other hand, please remember we're supposed to be the good guys here, so try not to kill anyone except Imperial Guards. It's important we make the right impression here.'

'Details, details,' Hazel said airily. 'You concentrate on your map and leave the fighting to me. That's how we work best.'

Owen felt a strong answer to that rising up in him, but he forced it down. He was going to learn to be polite and charming to Hazel if it killed him. He pressed on through the city, whipping back and forth between the towers and fighting the sudden updrafts.

Still wrapped in early morning light, the city was only just waking up. The sky was a bloody red, painting the pastel towers with crimson shadows. There was hardly any air traffic yet, but that would change in a hurry once the sun was up and the business day began. The plan called for Owen and Hazel to get into the Income Tax and Tithe Headquarters, do what they had to do, and then get the hell out while the skies were still comparatively uncrowded. Owen piled on the speed, and the force shield snapped on again, giving his watering eyes and numbed face a break. He and Hazel were on their own until they could land and make contact with the underground, and right now he felt very alone and vulnerable.

He could feel Hazel crowding close behind him. He didn't look back to make sure. He didn't need to. All of those who'd passed through the Madness Maze were linked to each other now, in some deep fundamental way that none of them yet understood, but that none of them doubted. It was a kind of low-level esp, an unquestioning certainty as to where the others were at any given moment. And, as Hazel had shown, whatever gifts or talents one possessed, the others had too, as if they'd always had them. Owen could *feel* Hazel's presence at his back. It was reassuring. He whipped around a tower, so close he could have reached out and trailed his fingertips across the windows flashing past, and then there, right before him, exactly where it was supposed to be, was the Income Tax and Tithe Headquarters, in Tower Chojiro, the tallest and ugliest of the immediate towers, a gleaming monument of glass and steel, the Clan colours and signals clearly marked. It was undoubtedly bristling with hidden weapons and other nasty surprises.

Owen grinned fiercely and again opened his secure comm channel. 'Almost there, so brace yourself. And, Hazel – don't use the boost unless you have to. There are things about it you don't know. It's . . . unwise to use it too often.'

'Nag, nag. You always were a bit of an old woman, Deathstalker.'

Owen decided he wasn't going to answer that one either, and made himself concentrate on Tower Chojiro as it loomed up before him. He cut his power and slowed steadily, but kept the force shield up. The Hadenmen had assured him on more than one occasion that his and Hazel's sleds had been carefully adjusted to that they would slip past the tower's defences unmolested, but of course there had been no way to test this in advance.

It was a bit late to be worried now. Either it would work, or he and Hazel would end up splattered across the tower's energy fields and the rebellion would have to start somewhere else. Oddly, he discovered that he didn't feel particularly nervous. He took a firm hold on the controls, braced himself, and headed the sled straight for the top floor. The windows came flying towards him at incredible speed, and Owen just had time to realize he must have safely penetrated the tower's force shields before the sled slammed through the toughened steelglass window as though it hadn't been there.

The sled screeched to a halt some twenty feet past the shattered window, and its force shield switched off. Owen released his death grip from the controls and stepped down, a little shakily. He looked quickly about him but the top floor of Tower Chojiro was deserted, just as it should be. There was a little furniture scattered here and there on the thick carpeting, all of it designed to within an inch of its life, and just the occasional small painting on the walls – originals, of course. Clan Chojiro was famed for its minimalist approach. Owen hoped it applied to their security systems as well, but he rather doubted it. His and Hazel's entrance had to have set off all kinds of alarms, and, since the interior weaponry hadn't instantly finished them off any more than had the exterior force shields, the odds were that a large number of heavily armed men were currently on their way up to find out what was going on. Of course, they'd have to start at the bottom and work their way up floor by floor to make sure everything was secure, which should take them some time – more than enough time for him to deal with the computers and leave. Theoretically. He drew his disrupter and activated the force shield on his wrist. The oblong of glowing force formed instantly on his arm, its familiar low hum distinctly comforting.

Hazel moved in beside him, a gun in each hand. 'Taxes and Tithes is four floors down, right? Elevator or stairs?'

'Stairs, of course. The elevators can be over-ridden by the tower's central computers.'

Owen led the way out of the empty room and on to the stairwell, which was narrow and brightly lit and looked as though it had last been whitewashed sometime in the previous century. After all, who used stairs any more, except in emergencies? Everything was deathly quiet, apart from the racket Owen and Hazel made clattering down the bare steel steps. No doubt the tower's defences were sounding all kinds of alarms, but that would be on the tower's private security channel, and Owen didn't have the time to search out which particular channel they were using that day. No doubt Security changed it regularly. He would have.

Hazel checked the lock at the bottom of the stairs, a simple combination mechanism, and whistled disparagingly. 'On Mistworld this wouldn't stop a ten-year-old. I'll have it open in a few minutes.'

'No,' said Owen. 'Let me try.'

He bent over the lock, studied it carefully, and then entered a short series of numbers. The lock clicked open. He straightened up and smiled at Hazel. 'You got the boost from me; I got breaking and entering from you – somewhat improved by the Maze's influences. Wonder what else we've got that we don't know about?'

'This is getting spooky,' said Hazel. 'At this rate we'll end up with more augmentations than a Hadenman.'

'Now that is a disturbing thought. But it'll have to wait. When I open this door, everyone in the room beyond is a target. We don't have the time to deal with prisoners.'

'Suits me,' said Hazel. 'Never did like tax collectors.'

Owen put his shoulder to the heavy steel door, and it swung inwards with surprising speed. Five technicians looked up, startled, and barely had the time to draw breath to cry out before Hazel picked them off with separate shots from her projectile weapon. Owen quickly swung the door shut behind them, and there was silence in the computer room. He was glad he hadn't had to use his disrupter to back Hazel up. Firing an energy weapon in a confined space full of delicate equipment was rarely a good idea. He holstered his gun and leant over the nearest body to make sure it was dead. He grimaced. Projectile weapons got the job done, but they were extremely messy. There was blood all over the floor, and holes in the bodies big enough to stick his fist into. Disrupters tended to be much neater, and cauterized their own wounds.

'Marvellous weapons,' Hazel said happily, studying the damage she'd done. 'Don't you just love them?'

'Check these people are all dead,' said Owen flatly. 'I don't want any surprises while we're working.'

'Oh, sure,' said Hazel. 'You have a bash at the machines, and I'll stand guard. What I know about reprogramming computers could be engraved on my left thumbnail.'

'It shouldn't be that complicated,' Owen said hopefully, studying the terminals before him. 'Jack Random and the Hadenmen worked out the programming between them. All I have to do is load the disks and let them run. If you'd like to cross your fingers at this point, feel free to do so.'

He pulled up a chair and sat down before the massive bank of computers that covered the wall in front of him. These were the computers responsible for setting and collecting the many taxes of the entire Empire. Trillions of credits came and went at their commands every day. Decisions made here could be questioned by no one lower than the Empress Lionstone herself. The computers distributed the wealth of the Empire, with contributions from the lowest and the highest. Even the Families paid taxes, through their business interests. It took a lot of money to run the Empire and keep Lionstone in the manner to which she'd become accustomed. That the Church of Christ the Warrior, quite possibly the most paranoid religion of the time, trusted these computers to run their tithing system as well spoke volumes for the machinery's efficiency and security. *Everyone* trusted the computers implicitly . . . but they'd never come up against Hadenman technology before. Few had. Owen grinned broadly. The entire financial base of the Empire ran through this room, and he, a despised outlaw, was about to bring it all crashing down in ruins.

He entered the necessary codes, then removed the package of disks from his hidden pocket and slotted them into place one after the other. He paused, just to savour the moment, and hit the final entry key. Nothing obvious happened. The machines hummed on as before. But, deep within the database, changes were being made. First, extremely large sums were being diverted from the Empire coffers into previously prepared Rebel accounts – billions of credits, soon to be chasing from one short-lived bolthole to another until their provenance was hopelessly lost and confused. It seemed only fair and right to Owen that the Empire should fund its own destruction.

And, once it had completed that little task, the programme would set about erasing or at the very least hopelessly scrambling every scrap of data in the computers. No record would remain of who had paid what, or when – in short, there would be utter chaos. For security reasons there was no copy of the records anywhere else. Lionstone believed very firmly in centralization: having things in one place made them easier to control. And who would ever have thought that the mighty Clan Chojiro's extensive security systems could be defeated by two lowly individuals on gravity sleds?

So, once the news got out – and it would get out eventually, whatever the Empire did – a great many lesser people would suddenly find they were far better off than they had been, courtesy of the rebellion. The Empire, on the other hand, would not only find itself suddenly short of working funds but have to spend even more credits and man-hours just trying to put together a picture of how badly off it was. It would be years before Lionstone could raise taxes again. And, while the Empire was thus preoccupied, the rebellion could get on with more serious projects.

'How long is this going to take?' said Hazel.

Owen looked back at her and shrugged. 'Beats me. I did ask but, since no one's ever done this before, no one knows for sure. Basically, we hang around here until the computer spits out the disks, and that should be it. Let's just hope it doesn't take too long. Clan Chojiro's security forces are undoubtedly following standard procedure and working their way up the Tower floor by floor even as we speak. They'll stop to secure each floor as they go, but even so it won't be that long before they come hammering on our door. Hopefully the disks will have done their stuff – and Stevie Blue will have made contact with us – a comfortable amount of time before that happens. Otherwise, we are in deep shit.'

'I love it when you talk technical,' said Hazel.

They both stopped and looked sharply at the closed metal door. They hadn't heard anything yet, but they sensed something. The awareness was another gift from the Madness Maze. Owen moved quickly over to the door, eased it open a crack, and listened intently. From not all that far away came the sound of massed booted feet crashing on steel steps. It was drawing steadily closer. Owen let the door close silently, and backed away from it.

'Company's coming,' he said, not looking at Hazel. 'Lots of them. Either they're not bothering to secure every floor or

41

there's a hell of a lot more of them than we were led to believe.'

'I knew this was going too smoothly,' said Hazel. 'Well, let them come. I could use a little exercise.'

'Not for the first time, you're missing the point,' said Owen. 'If the security forces are already this close, how is Stevie Blue supposed to make contact with us?'

'Tricky,' Hazel agreed. 'I suppose we'll just have to kill all the security people, won't we?'

Owen looked at her. 'You've become altogether too cocky since we survived the Maze. We're a lot more than we used to be, but we're not unbeatable.'

'Speak for yourself, Deathstalker. We're stronger, faster and sharper than any damn' security guards. We can take them. It doesn't matter how many of them there are. You worry too much, Owen.'

He shook his head sadly. 'Cocky. Definitely cocky. Unfortunately, since we can't leave here yet, we have no choice but to let them come to us. Try not to get yourself killed, Hazel. I'd hate to have to start training another partner.'

Hazel glared at him. 'First, we are not partners. Second, if there's any training going on here I'm the one who's doing it. If it weren't for me, you'd have been killed a dozen times over. I'll do the fighting – you watch for those disks to reappear. Once they're out we're gone.'

'And Stevie Blue?'

'Can save her own ass. Serves her right for being late.'

The sound of tramping feet was very close now. Hazel hefted her two guns and stood facing the closed door. Owen hauled the dead technicians to one side so that he and Hazel would have room to manoeuvre, if they needed it. He got blood on his hands and sleeves, and wiped them thoroughly on the front of his jacket – he didn't want his hands to be slippery if he had to use his sword.

Feet crashed on the floor directly outside, and then the door slammed inwards as three guards put their shoulders to it. The men paused a moment in the doorway as the took in Owen and Hazel and the blood on the floor, and that moment

42

was all Owen needed to aim his disrupter and fire. The energy beam blasted a hole right through the first guard's chest, and took out the man standing behind him as well. Hazel got the other one, her disrupter beam neatly separating the man's head from his body.

The rest of the guards came crashing in, convinced their opponents' energy weapons would be useless now for the next two minutes. Owen and Hazel ducked down behind their personal force shields, and energy beams ricocheted around the room. Various pieces of equipment exploded and burst into flames. The guards put away their exhausted guns and pressed forward with drawn swords.

Hazel lowered her force shield and opened up with her projectile weapon.

Explosive bullets tore through the men in the room, ripping them apart and throwing their bodies aside. Blood flew on the air. The roar of the gun was deafening in the confined space. The security men had no force shields – too expensive – and relied on numbers instead. But they could get through the door only half a dozen at a time, and the projectile weapon cut them to shreds while they were still struggling in the opening. All too soon Hazel's gun ran out of bullets and fell silent. She swore briefly and holstered the weapon. More guards came thundering in, and this time Owen and Hazel went to meet them with cold steel in their hands.

Swords rang on swords but, though the security men outnumbered the outlaws a dozen to one, it was still no contest. They were confused and demoralized, with so many of them already dead, and Owen and Hazel both had the boost. Owen's smile stretched into a death's-head grin, blood roaring in his veins and thundering in his head. His enemies seemed to be moving in slow motion, and he cut them down easily, glorying in their deaths. He'd always been fast when boosting, but the Maze had made him superhumanly fast. The guards fell quickly, butchered like so many helpless animals in the slaughterhouse.

And suddenly there were no more targets, only unmoving bodies on the bloody floor.

Owen checked the room was empty apart from himself and Hazel and the corpses, peered out the door into the empty corridor, and then dropped out of boost. He shuddered helplessly as the reaction hit him. For a few fleeting moments he had been almost a god, and now he was only human again. It hurt. His muscles ached from the strain he'd put them through, and his movements seemed unbearably slow and sluggish. He breathed deeply, concentrating, as he'd been taught, and his senses quickly returned. The Deathstalker Family had spent generations perfecting the surge of strength and speed that was the boost, but even so the human body could stand it only for short periods. It burned up the nervous system with a remorseless appetite, and afterwards there was always this price to be paid.

Hazel hacked at the dead bodies before her, laughing breathlessly, her face slick with sweat. Her eyes were wide and feral, fixed on some inner Valhalla.

Owen called to her but she didn't hear him. He moved towards her and she spun towards him, sword at the ready, her grin terribly eager.

He sheathed his sword, switched off his shield, and held out his hands to her, so that she could see they were empty. Her head cocked a little to one side as he spoke to her soothingly.

Owen took another step closer, and she lunged forward, her sword flying towards his gut.

Owen tapped his boost for just a moment or two – just long enough for him to sidestep so that her sword flashed past him, missing his side by less than an inch.

He clamped his arm down hard so that the sword was held in place, and hugged Hazel to him. She fought him fiercely, and he knew he couldn't hold her for more than a few moments.

Owen held her blazing eyes with his and reached out to her through the mental link they shared, the Maze-given connection of the undermind. He couldn't reach her with words or thoughts, only the simple truth of his presence, and of who and what he was. Her mind was bright and dazzling, darting

44

like quicksilver, sharp and deadly, but slowly she responded, calming gradually. Her eyes slowly cleared and he felt the first faint stirrings of her feelings before a barrier slammed down between them as Hazel cut off the link and dropped out of boost.

She almost collapsed as her legs shook. Owen held her trembling body close to him until she had enough strength and control to push him away and stand alone. She took a deep, shuddering breath and nodded to him brusquely. He knew this was the only acknowledgement he'd ever get of what they'd felt and shared for a moment.

Hazel's hands were almost steady as she wiped the sweat from her face with the same filthy rag she'd used earlier to clean her sword.

'That . . . was something else,' she said finally. 'I've never felt anything like it, and I've tried a lot of things in my time. I was so alive . . . I would have killed you, if you hadn't stopped me. Is the boost always like that?'

'Mostly,' said Owen. 'You never really get accustomed to it. That's why I only ever use it when I have to. Take it easy for a few minutes. It takes time for your body to replace the energy the boost burns up.'

'And you've lived with this most of your life?' She looked at Owen with new respect. 'You're a harder man than you look, Deathstalker. I was once a plasma baby, addicted to Wampyr Blood, but the boost is stronger than any drug I ever knew. How do you stand it?'

'By using it only when I absolutely have to,' said Owen. 'And, remember, I've had training you haven't. It gets a little easier in time, though not much. I did try to warn you.'

'Yeah, you did,' Hazel turned away and looked at the corpses scattered across the room. The floor was awash with blood, and she shuddered briefly before she was back in control. 'You suppose that's all of them?'

'I very much doubt it. This was just the first wave, sent in to check out the situation. Look at the bodies – they're all wearing short-range sensors. Their superiors know exactly what has happened here – which means that, not only can we forget about having the advantage of surprise, we can also expect a heavily armed, much larger second wave. The experienced fighters. Things are about to get really interesting.'

He broke off, and they both looked at the closed door again.

Someone was coming. They could feel it.

Owen pulled the door open and stepped out into the corridor, his now-recharged disrupter at the ready. Behind him, Hazel was quickly reloading her projectile weapon. Owen moved slowly towards the stairwell. Someone was climbing the stairs; the unhurried footsteps were loud and echoing in the quiet.

Hazel moved in beside Owen, nudged him to get his attention and mouthed: 'One man?' Owen shrugged, and they both crept forward to look down the stairs.

The newcomer took his time on the last flight of stairs, and then came to a halt at the final corner, looking impassively up at Owen and Hazel. He was a tall, blocky man, with thick slabs of muscle and a patient, brooding face. His skin was dark, his close-cropped hair was white, and his cold eyes were a startling green. He wore no armour, only a long green kimono of the Chojiro Clan, decorated with stylized dragons. He carried a long curving sword in each hand.

'Oh, shit,' said Owen, feelingly.

Hazel looked at him. 'You know this guy?'

'Unfortunately, yes. This is ex-Investigator Razor. Used to work for Clan Campbell as their pet killer and intimidator, but, given the Campbell's downfall and that extremely tacky dress he's wearing, I can only assume he's taken up a similar position with Clan Chojiro. If you know any good religions, now would be a good time to start praying.'

'He doesn't appear to have any guns. Why can't we just shoot him from a safe distance?'

'One, he undoubtedly has a personal force shield. Two, it might annoy him.'

Hazel put away her guns and drew her sword. 'So we get our hands dirty.'

'Hazel, Investigators are killing machines – the best there are, with any weapon you care to name.'

'So what do you suggest we do?'

'If it were anybody else I'd suggest surrendering, but Investigators don't take prisoners. So we're going to have to fight him. *Oh, shit.*'

'Will you stop saying that! He's just one man. I'll take first crack at him.'

'No you won't. I will. You still haven't recovered from boosting.'

'I can take him! Really!'

'Excuse me,' said the Investigator.

'You be quiet,' said Owen. 'We'll get to you in a minute. Hazel, I'm taking first crack, and that's all there is to it.'

'Since when were you in charge of this mission? If I want to take him, I'll take him!'

'Hazel, this is really not a good idea!'

'Excuse me,' said the Investigator firmly.

'Shut up!' said Owen and Hazel, glaring at each other.

Investigator Razor shrugged, and surged up the last few stairs impossibly quickly, his two swords swinging in shimmering blurs. Owen and Hazel stood their ground, swords at the ready, and went into boost. Razor hit them like a thunderstorm, his swords like lightning. The air was full of the ring of steel on steel as Owen and Hazel were driven back, unable to meet the sheer ferocity of his attack.

Razor left the stairwell behind him, moving implacably forward, until Owen and Hazel bumped up against the corridor wall and there was nowhere else to go. Owen and Hazel separated and attacked him from two sides at once. Razor held his ground and stood them both off, his blades moving too fast to be seen. Owen ducked at the last moment, and a flashing sword cut a groove into the wall where his head had been. Hazel lunged forward, hoping to catch Razor momentarily off-balance, and then had to hurl herself sideways as a waiting sword leaped out to meet her. She hit the floor rolling and was quickly back on her feet, breathing hard.

Blood soaked her left sleeve, but she ignored it, cushioned from pain and shock by the boost.

Owen had already realized they couldn't beat Razor on their own. The Investigator had been trained to the peak of perfection in all the killing arts, and Owen didn't have the expertise to match him. Neither did Hazel. But they did have the boost, and what the Maze had done to them. He reached out to Hazel through the mental link, the undermind they didn't have to understand to use, and their consciousnesses touched. They threw themselves at Razor, attacking in perfect synchronization, two swords wielded by one concerted will. Razor fell back a step, and then another, but that was as far as he would go. Even joined, Owen and Hazel could be his equal, but no more.

There was no saying which way the fight might have gone if Razor's kimono hadn't suddenly burst into roaring fires. He threw himself to one side, rolling on the carpeted floor to try to crush the flames, but they just blazed the brighter. The blaze was already licking up around his face as he lurched to his feet and ran off down the corridor, but he never made a sound.

He disappeared around the corner, still burning, and was gone. All they could hear were the echoes of his feet.

Owen and Hazel dropped out of both boost and mental link and hung on to each other as they waited for the reaction to pass. The cut on Hazel's arm had been messy but minor, and was already healing itself. Nevertheless, neither of them stopped trembling for a while. At last their breathing began to return to something like normal.

When they finally let go of each other and looked round, they found themselves facing three women who had the same face, smiling sardonically at them from the top of the stairs. *Clones*, Owen thought immediately. Presumably from the underground. They looked tough enough.

All three of the clones were wearing battered leathers adorned with brightly polished lengths of steel chain, over T-shirts bearing the legend *Born To Burn*. They seemed to be in their mid-twenties, but their faces were somehow older, more harshly used. The women were short and stocky, with bare muscular arms, and their long dark hair was full of colourful knotted ribbons. There were splashes of colour on their faces, too, perhaps to disguise how pretty they might have been were it not for their cold eyes and determined mouths.

'Can we help you?' said Owen politely, not lowering his sword. He had a suspicion he was smelling strongly of sweat, but decided he wouldn't bring it up if they didn't.

'The seagulls are flying low tonight,' said the woman in the middle, meaningfully.

Owen looked at her, and then turned and looked at Hazel, who looked back at him.

'The seagulls are flying low tonight,' said the woman in the middle again, this time with extra emphasis.

'Sorry,' said Owen. 'Didn't quite catch that. The seagulls are what?'

'Hold everything,' said Hazel. 'Seagulls. That was part of the contact phrase, wasn't it?'

'I don't know,' said Owen helplessly. 'I can't remember. It's gone right out of my head.'

'If I don't start hearing an answer sometime soon, I am going to start shooting,' said the woman on the left.

'Angels!' Owen said quickly. 'Something about angels!'

'Something something angels in the moonlight,' said Hazel. 'I think.'

'Oh hell,' said the woman in the middle. 'That's close enough. Be here all day otherwise.'

'We're your contact,' said the woman on the left. 'Sorry it took us a while to get here, but there are security guards everywhere, and we didn't want to kill them all. It would only have attracted attention.'

'Fair enough,' said Hazel. 'But . . . where's Stevie Blue?'

'We're here,' said the one in the middle.

'Right,' said the one on the right.

'All three of you?' said Owen.

'Got it in one,' said the Stevie Blue on the left. 'I'm Stevie

49

One, this is Two and Three. Don't get us mixed up. We're touchy about it.'

'I take it you're also espers,' said Owen, putting his sword away. Hazel reluctantly sheathed hers, but kept her hands near her guns.

Owen gave the Stevie Blues his best diplomatic smile and vowed silently to do something unpleasant to whoever had got Stevie Blue's personal details wrong. 'Nice work on the Investigator. I think he was prepared for everything except a sudden flash fire – next time please reduce him to a pile of smouldering ashes. All right, let's get down to business. The program's in the machine and running. All we have to do is keep the hostile natives at bay until it's finished, and then we can leg it. We've got a ship coming back to pick us up. It's a Hadenman ship, but don't let that panic you. They've been very reasonable. So far.'

The three Stevie Blues smiled, in unison. 'Anyone annoys us, they're toast,' said Stevie One. 'We're pyros. And we're also elves – from the Esper Liberation Front.'

'And you're the underground's idea of diplomats,' said Hazel. 'You're going to be very popular at strategy planning sessions. I might just start attending them again.'

'The cyberats are running interference to keep this tower isolated,' said Stevie Two. 'No one from outside will know anything's happened until it's all over.'

Owen frowned. 'Computer hackers aren't exactly noted for their reliability.'

'You can trust these,' said Stevie One. 'If only because they know we'll kick their asses if they screw up.'

'Right,' said Stevie Three.

Owen and Hazel suddenly turned away and looked thoughtfully at the stairs.

Hazel drew her guns, and Owen turned back to the clones. 'Visitors are on their way,' he said.

'You espers or something?' said Stevie One.

'Something,' said Owen. 'The Investigator must have put himself out and alerted his people. Any minute now we're going to be hip-deep in security guards.'

'That's not all,' said Stevie Two. 'They've got an esp-blocker with them. I can feel my powers fading as it gets closer.'

'Wonderful,' said Hazel. 'Can anything else go wrong?'

'Quite a lot, if we just stand around here waiting for them,' said Owen. 'May I suggest we get the hell back to the computer room?'

'Too late,' said Stevie Three. 'They're here.'

The three clones drew their swords with the same quick, professional motion, and moved to block the head of the stairwell. Owen and Hazel stepped in beside them, guns at the ready, just in time to see a single tall figure come into sight at the last corner of the stairs below. He was dressed in jet-black robes and battle armour, seemed to be in his early thirties, and was handsome in an unspectacular way. His dark eyes and slight smile were utterly cold; just standing there, hands empty, he looked calm and confident and very dangerous.

Stevie Two whistled softly. 'The Lord High Dram, his own bad self. We should be honoured. He normally murders espers only from a safe distance.'

'He can't just blast and burn the tower this time,' said Stevie One. 'The Empress would have his nuts if he let the Tax computers be destroyed.'

Owen and Hazel stared at each other.

'That man is quite definitely dead,' said Owen. 'I saw the body.'

'So who's this?' said Hazel. 'A clone? Does anyone at Court know? Or was the one we saw die a clone?'

'Are we supposed to understand any of that?' said Stevie One.

'I'll explain later,' said Owen, 'assuming there is a later. For the moment, just believe me when I say things have suddenly got a lot more complicated. Dram – the Widow-maker – could be a major rallying point for the Empire, one we hadn't counted on. We have to get this information back to Rebel HQ.'

'I've got a better idea,' said Hazel. She raised her projectile

51

weapon and let Dram have it point-blank. The stairwell echoed to the roar of the gun as bullets hammered into the steel walls over and over, but Dram's cold smile never wavered. His holo image shimmered slightly, but was otherwise unaffected.

'You didn't really think someone of my quality would come in person to deal with Rebel trash, did you?' said Dram calmly. 'The lower floors of this tower are now blocked off and occupied by my troops. There's no way out, and nowhere for you to go. Surrender, and at least you'll live long enough to stand trial.'

The Stevie Blues glared at him fiercely. Stevie One spat on the floor. 'What makes you think we'd trust treacherous scum like you? You came to us pretending to be someone else, a man called Hood, and we trusted you. In return, you betrayed us to the Empire forces. Hundreds of good men and women died that day just because they happened to be espers or clones. We'll all die before we surrender to you.'

'Suit yourselves,' said Dram, and his holo image disappeared like a popping soap bubble.

The steel stairs shuddered in the distance as another large body of armed men came lumbering up them. Owen fired his disrupter down the stairwell, but the energy beam ricocheted away from an advancing force-shield wall several floors down. The espers concentrated, and boiling flames filled the well. But the force wall just kept coming, pushing back the flames, which were already beginning to die out as the esp-blocker drew nearer.

The Stevie Blues looked at Owen and Hazel.

'Don't stare at me,' said Hazel. 'I'm right out of ideas. How much longer does the programme have to run, Owen?'

'Can't be long now. A few minutes at most. But we can't afford to be cornered in the computer room with it.'

'And we don't have a few minutes anyway. How about setting up a barricade?'

'Couldn't hurt,' said Owen. 'See, you *can* come up with ideas, when you have to. Stevies, if you'd care to lend a hand . . .'

They dashed back into the computer room, grabbed everything blocky that wasn't actually welded in place, and manhandled it out into the corridor. Between them they manoeuvred the heavy equipment over to the top of the stairwell and launched it down the stairs. The way was immediately completely blocked, and the enemy advance came to a sudden halt. Force shields were excellent at stopping energy blasts or bullets, but they had real problems coping with three hundredweight of assorted wedged office equipment. The security guards stopped to discuss the matter. Dram snarled at them acidly from below. Owen and Hazel grinned at each other and at the esper clones, and then they all spun round at an unexpected sound behind them. It was the bell that signalled the approach of the elevator.

'That shouldn't be possible,' said Stevie One. 'The cyberats were supposed to have cut off the elevators.'

'Never trust anyone who has an unnatural relationship with his softdrive,' said Stevie Two.

'Right,' said Stevie Three.

They spread out before the elevator door, guns and blades at the ready. It was very quiet in the corridor. Owen's hands were sweaty, and he wished he had time to dry them. The elevator chimed again, and the doors slid open to reveal a man of medium height, impeccably dressed, with a heavily lined face and long, carefully styled white hair. He smiled at them all engagingly, and the Stevie Blues let out their breath and lowered their weapons.

'We should have known,' said Stevie Two. 'If anyone could slip past an entire army of guards and just waltz in here, it would have to be you.'

'You know how it is,' said the newcomer in a deep, resonant voice. 'I do so love to make an entrance. Now be a dear and introduce me to your friends. Guns make me nervous.'

'This ageing reprobate is Alexander Storm,' said Stevie One. 'Long-time rebel, adventurer, and gadfly by appointment. Hero of the rebellion, professional clothes-horse and a general pain in the ass. We only put up with him because he's so good at making the Empire forces look like prats.'

'Right,' said Stevie Three.

'Couldn't have put it better myself,' said Alexander Storm. He stepped out of the elevator and clapped Owen firmly on the shoulder. 'I'm an old friend and comrade-in-arms of Jack Random. I've been semi-retired for a while – you know how it is – but, once I heard Jack was back in the thick of things, I knew I had to join him. It'll be just like old times, fighting shoulder-to-shoulder again. I haven't seen the dear fellow since Cold Rock. Not one of our better showings, I'm afraid. Still, it's the thought that counts. Anyway, I contacted the underground, pulled a few strings, and here I am. The Stevie Blues will represent the clones and espers, and I shall speak for the other parts of the underground. Delighted to meet you at last, Deathstalker. Word of your exploits has spread far and wide. Everyone in the rebellion is delighted to see you following in your father's footsteps. He'd be so proud of you. But then "Deathstalker" has always – well, almost always – been an honourable name. Great things are expected of you, my boy. You are the hope of humanity.'

Owen became aware of a dangerously quiet, fuming figure at his side. 'This is Hazel d'Ark,' he said quickly. 'I'm sure you've heard of her, too.'

Storm smiled at her dazzlingly. 'Of course. The rebellion can always use another canny fighter. Tell me, Owen, how is Jack Random these days? Last I'd heard, he'd taken a hell of a beating at the Empire's hands.'

'He's . . . better than he was,' Owen said carefully. 'Try not to look too shocked when you see him. He's been through a lot.'

'Are we going to stand around here chatting all day?' said Hazel, ominously, 'or is someone going to check whether the program's finished running yet?'

The barricade filling the top of the stairs shifted suddenly as someone underneath tried to move it, but it just settled itself more comfortably.

Then an energy beam tore right through the mass of equipment, scattering fragments of molten metal in the air. The rebels ducked back and covered their heads with their arms. The security forces began dismantling what was left of the barricade.

'Let's save the official getting-to-know-each-other session for a better time,' said Owen hastily. 'I'll check the program. Until I get back, shoot at anything that moves.'

He sprinted into the computer room and saw with relief that the disks had finished their task and ejected themselves. He grabbed them, pressed their self-destruct, and watched with satisfaction as they were consumed in smoky flames. Wrinkling his nose at the smell, he dropped the burning disks to the floor. Now, even if he or any of the other rebels were to be captured, there would be no way the Empire could reconstruct what the program had been.

He ran back to the stairwell and found Hazel spraying the disappearing barricades with bullets, to no obvious effect.

'Time to go,' Owen said briskly. 'The program's taken care of, and we have more than outstayed our welcome. Grab anything that might be useful and head for the roof. There are gravity sleds waiting there.'

'We can use the elevator,' said Storm. 'The cyberats have control of it.'

'We'll use the stairs,' said Hazel. 'The cyberats' commands could get over-ridden, and it'd be a damn' silly way to get trapped.'

She headed for the stairs without looking back to see if the others were following. Storm raised an eyebrow at Owen, as though surprised he wasn't taking charge – he was, after all, the hope of humanity. Owen shrugged sheepishly and hurried after Hazel. Storm and the Stevie Blues followed behind. Owen kept his gun trained ahead of him, just in case, but there was no one lying in wait on the stairs, and they reached the top floor without incident. The gravity sleds were waiting where they'd been left, for which Owen was very grateful. This would not be a good time to have to walk home. Hazel was already aboard hers, powering it up. Owen took Storm on his sled while the three clones insisted upon crowding on to Hazel's.

The sleds rose into the air and headed for the shattered

windows by which they'd entered. Energy beams stabbed the air around them as Dram and his people burst into the top floor, firing wildly. Owen and Hazel pushed the sleds to full speed and shot away between the pastel towers, dodging and diving erratically to throw off the guards' aim. The Stevie Blues hung on grimly to Hazel's bucking vehicle and fired back at their attackers. More guards appeared, some at the windows of other towers, and opened fire. Dram must have got the word out. Owen and Hazel darted the craft in and out among the towers, fighting updrafts and dodging unexpected protrusions. The energy beams came at them from every side.

A disrupter hit the front of Owen's sled a glancing blow, blasting it off course. White-hot metal spattered across his hastily flung-up cloak as he struggled to regain control. The cloak burst into flames. Storm pulled it free from Owen's shoulders and threw it overboard. It fell away, burning brightly, finally disappearing into the long drop. Owen fought the sled back under control but its speed had dropped by half.

Hazel fell back to keep pace with him. Owen gestured for her to go on but she shook her head stubbornly.

He activated his comm implant. 'Hazel, will you please get the hell out of here! Dram will be putting sleds into the air any time now.'

'Exactly,' Hazel said calmly. 'You're going to need someone to look after you. We can't let you die. You're the hope of humanity, remember?'

He would have argued more but then they whipped around the side of a tower to find themselves facing rows of armed guards waiting for them on top of the next one. Owen and Hazel cursed simultaneously and threw the sleds into a dive. Energy beams slashed past them, and one hit Stevie Two squarely in the back. The force of the blast threw her over the side of the sled. The other two Stevies screamed in unison as the burning body plummeted towards the distant ground.

Owen sent his sled plunging after her, pushing its speed well past the recommended safety limits. The engine whined in protest, but he ignored it.

He overtook the falling body, swept the sled underneath, and then surged up to catch Stevie Two. The burning body slammed on to the sled's deck. Storm wrapped his cloak around her to smother the flames.

Red warning lights glared all across the sled's controls, and Owen snarled back at them. He'd saved a life – he hoped – from the Empire's venom, and that was all that mattered.

Hazel's sled swept in beside him. Stevies One and Three were firing Hazel's projectile weapons at the guards, driving them back under cover. Hazel gestured back over her shoulder and Owen glanced briefly in the same direction.

Imperial gravity sleds were coming up behind, closing the gap fast.

Energy beams continued to flash past the rebels' sleds from behind and ahead – warning shots, to show the guards had got the range.

Owen caught Hazel's eye and pointed upwards. She nodded, and the two sleds darted straight up, leaving the sheltering towers behind.

Owen activated his comm unit again. 'This is Rebel One to Golden Boy. I can't come to you, so you'll have to come to me. Lock on to my signal and get your ass here fast.'

There was no answer, but he hadn't expected one. The two conscious Stevie Blues were firing down at the pursuing Empire sleds, tears for their sister streaming down their cold, set faces. When their guns ran out of ammunition the espers dropped the projectile weapons to the deck and grabbed two more from Hazel's belt. They opened up again, and one of the pursuing sleds suddenly erupted into flames, and fell spiralling between the towers like a burning leaf.

Owen and Hazel sent their sleds whipping back and forth over the towers, their Maze-accelerated reflexes enabling them to pull off evasions their pursuers couldn't hope to match. But still the Empire sleds came on with their superior speed, remorselessly closing the gap.

Suddenly, right before them, the great golden ship of the Hadenmen appeared out of nowhere as it dropped its cloaking shields, filling the sky, gleaming brighter than the sun. The pursuing sleds took one look and did everything but throw themselves into reverse. A few fired useless shots at the huge ship, but most just settled for shuddering to an unruly halt in mid-air.

Owen glanced back over his shoulder and saw Storm looking up at the ship, his mouth hanging open. Even the Stevie Blues had stopped firing at their pursuers. Owen grinned, and flew up into the open cargo doors in the ship's belly. Hazel came through behind him.

'Get the hell out of here right now!' yelled Owen in the general direction of the cargo bay. 'Go, go, go!'

The belly doors slammed shut and Owen and Hazel landed their sleds. Owen slumped over the controls, exhausted, but made himself turn around as Stevies One and Three ran over.

Storm was bending over the unmoving body of Stevie Two. He looked up as the esper clones reached him, and shook his head sadly.

'I'm sorry. She must have been dead from the moment the beam hit her.'

Owen wanted to say something, but couldn't.

Stevie One nodded stiffly to him. 'You risked your life to save her, even though she was just a clone. It's not your fault she didn't make it. We'll never forget what you did, Owen Deathstalker. Wherever you lead, we'll follow.'

'But now there are only two of us,' said Stevie Three quietly.

Stevie One put her arms around her, and hugged her hard. After a while she let go, and the two Stevie Blues walked off to be by themselves for a while.

Hazel came over to join Owen and Storm. 'Nice flying, Deathstalker. Maybe you *are* the hope of humanity, after all.'

'You're never going to let me forget that, are you?' said Owen.

'Listen, aristo,' said Hazel, 'you need me to keep you honest. If you're the hope, we are in deep shit. Hey, Hadenmen! Any chance of showing us what's happening outside?'

A viewscreen appeared, hovering on the air before them. The planet was falling away below them, but half a dozen starcruisers were in pursuit. The vessels were unusually large, bulky ships of a kind Owen didn't recognize. He looked at Storm, who was biting his lower lip and frowning.

'The Empress's new Fleet,' Storm said quietly. 'E-class, all with the new stardrive. Reputedly even faster than the legendary Hadenman ships. It would appear we're about to find out whether that's the case.'

The Empire ships opened fire. Disrupter cannon fired in sequence so that the starcruisers could maintain a constant onslaught. The golden ship fired back, but the Empire ships were rapidly closing the gap. Owen assumed the Hadenman's shields were still holding, on the grounds everyone on board would have been breathing vacuum by now if they weren't.

And then the ship's engines roared, and the viewscreen disappeared as the Hadenman craft dropped into hyperspace. Owen let out a long, low sigh of relief, and Hazel slapped him on the back.

'Told you we'd make it, aristo. Personally, I was never worried. Not for a minute.'

'Then you should have been,' said Owen. 'If those new ships are typical of the E-class, we are all in real trouble. Think of a fleet of ships as fast as my old *Sunstrider*. We've been relying on the Hadenman ships to give us an edge, but it would appear they're not Number One any more. Which means, if we're going to go head-to-head with the Empire, we too have to have ships with the new stardrive.'

'What the hell,' said Hazel. 'We can worry about that later. The mission was a success. The Income Tax and Tithe computers are gone, and we got most of our underground contacts out alive.'

'We lost one,' said Owen.

'It wasn't your fault,' said Storm. 'You tried. These things happen. I'll go and have a word with Stevies One and Three. Offer them some comfort and a friendly shoulder to lean on.'

He bowed formally, and moved away. Hazel watched him go. '"These things happen!" He's going to be a real comfort.'

'I think we could both use a drink and some rest,' said

Owen. 'Perhaps you'd care to join me, Hazel? Or we could have a meal together. Would you like that?'

'Not really, no,' said Hazel. 'No offence, Deathstalker, but let's keep our relationship professional, OK?'

She smiled at him briefly and then strode over to Storm and the two esper clones, gesturing for them to follow her. Owen watched them go. He was sure he must have been turned down faster than that at some time in his past, but he was damned if he could think when. Things like that weren't supposed to happen. He was a Lord, after all. And the hope of humanity.

'Nice try, though,' said the AI Ozymandias through his comm implant.

'Shut up, Oz,' said Owen. 'You're dead.'

CHAPTER TWO

Up to Gehenna and Down to Golgotha

Captain John Silence of the Empire starcruiser *Dauntless* was going home to die, and was trying hard not to give a damn. After all, he'd merely failed in his mission and got most of his people killed. He looked at the brimming glass in his hand and pulled a face. The trouble with sustained heavy boozing was that, after a while, your tongue went numb and you couldn't tell what you were drinking. Though, given exactly what it was he was pouring down his throat in such great quantity, this wasn't necessarily a bad thing. The food synthesizers could produce alcohol and flavourings, but the combinations, like the quality, were strictly limited. It was supposed to be red wine, but all the 'red' part did was turn his teeth pink. Still, for a wine whose vintage was under ten minutes, it wasn't that bad. Not that it made any difference – he would have drunk it anyway.

His head hurt, his hands were shaking and his stomach lurched this way and that when he moved. He'd been drinking steadily for almost three days now, taking time out to eat and sleep when he absolutely had to. He didn't drink much normally, and he was finding getting drunk and staying drunk harder work than he'd expected. But he kept at it. There was nothing else to do. He was a failure, going home to report that fact to an Empress who'd kill him for it.

And all those good men lost . . .

He was heading back to Golgotha with bad news and worse, and, although the Empress Lionstone had pardoned him once in the past for screwing up, she wouldn't put up with it a second time. He'd been sent to the Wolfling World on a straightforward mission. Accompanied by a contingent of trained adjusted men plus the Wampyr and the Empress's lover and right-hand man, the Lord High Dram, he'd been commanded to arrest and execute that most renowned traitor, Owen Deathstalker, and all with him, and then return to Golgotha with the rebels' heads and the secrets of the legendary Wolfling World. They'd even given him the single Grendel alien ever to be subdued and controlled – an extraordinary and so far unique specimen. The mission should have been a walkover.

Instead, Dram's body was down in the cargo hold, the Grendel had been killed – which was supposed to be impossible – and the three Wampyr who hadn't died fighting the rebels had been detained by the newly risen Hadenmen . . . John Silence didn't want to think what for. He took another drink.

The Hadenmen. Once the Enemies of Humanity: defeated long ago in a fierce and bloody war, they were supposed to be extinct, or at worst sleeping endlessly in their hidden Tomb. But Owen Deathstalker had found and woken them, and now they sided with the rebels. God help the Empire. The walls were falling, and the wolves were running loose among the flock.

He downed another drink, and another. He wasn't looking forward to explaining to the Empress that the Wolfling World was in fact also Haden, home of the Hadenmen. Which meant the rebels now had access to the legendary laboratories of Haden, and all the wonders and horrors they had produced in the past. Science beyond reason and weapons beyond any hope of resistance, and all of this to be aimed at the Empire. By his failure he'd signed the death warrant of civilization, and quite possibly humanity was well.

No, he had nothing but bad news to lay before his Empress, and she would kill him for it . . . if his own men didn't do it first. All the people he'd taken down into the caverns deep below the frozen surface of the Wolfling World had died there, facing weapons and horrors they could not have anticipated. And, instead of taking vengeance, Silence had been forced to return to his ship and run. His crew didn't understand what he'd seen down there – why it was vital he abandon everything and flee, to be sure the Empire would get advance warning of the threats to come.

So now his crew despised him. Many hated him. If Investigator Frost hadn't stood by him and made it very clear she would personally avenge him if he died, he wouldn't have had to worry about facing Lionstone: there would have been a sudden, regrettable accident, and it would all have been over . . . which might have been kinder, really, but you couldn't expect an Investigator to understand that. Investigators were trained from childhood to hunt and kill aliens, and the subtleties of human behaviour often escaped them.

So Captain John Silence left the running of what had once been *his* ship to his Second-in-Command, and sat alone in his cabin, drinking. To pass the time as much as anything else.

There was a knock at the door and he looked up blearily. He knew who it would be, who it had to be. Only one person ever came to see him these days. He thought about getting up to open the door himself, but decided against it. He didn't trust his legs. He worked his numbed tongue around his slightly slack mouth and said, 'Door: Open,' with as much authority and clarity as he could manage.

The door indeed slid open, and Investigator Frost stepped into his cabin. She nodded to him, gazing unhurriedly about as the door closed behind her. Silence didn't look. He knew the place was a mess. He'd never been particularly tidy, but normally his batman took care of things like that. He hadn't seen his batman in five days, and he found it faintly surprising just how bad things could get in five days when you didn't give a damn any more.

He did sneak a quick glance at himself in the mirror on the wall opposite, and winced. A tall, lean man in his late forties, with a lined face that could use a shave topped by a distinctly receding hairline, he looked rumpled and badly used, like the unmade bed he was sitting on. His uniform was a disgrace. He'd been sick down it twice, and the left sleeve had never really recovered. The Investigator, by contrast, looked utterly immaculate in her tight starched uniform, complete with brightly polished buttons, as though she were just about to step out on to a parade ground. Tall and lithely muscular, she was in her late twenties, though her eyes were much older: they were cold and blue, burning fiercely in a pale controlled face. Her auburn hair was cropped close to the skull. She wore a gun on her hip, despite shipboard regulations; a long sword hung down her back. Just standing there at her ease she looked ready and willing to take on a fair-sized army all by herself. She was handsome rather than pretty, and it would have been a brave men who even smiled at her without a direct invitation. Frost smiled only when she was killing something.

Now she pulled up a chair, removed and discarded a dirty shirt with thumb and forefinger, and sat down facing Silence. He raised an eyebrow. Frost was usually impeccably formal, even in private.

'What are you doing here, Investigator?' he said tiredly, pleased his voice was still steady, if a little slurred.

Frost sniffed. 'I thought we'd agreed you were going to stop drinking.'

'You agreed. I just got tired of arguing.'

'It won't help, Captain.'

'It can't hurt, either,' Silence said reasonably. 'Things are already as bad as they can get.'

'There's always the chance they might improve unexpectedly. We have to keep our wits about us, Captain – be ready to take advantage of any opportunities that might arise.'

'*You* take advantage, Investigator. I'm too tired, and I really don't care that much any more. No matter what happens, our mission is still a mess, civilization is still doomed, and my men are still dead. They were good men. They followed me into the Madness Maze because I ordered them to . . . because I told them it would be safe. And, not content with that, I ended up sending the survivors into a head-on confrontation with Hadenmen. It would have been kinder to have shot them all in the back . . . except that's what I did do, really.' He sighed as the familiar guilt and pain washed over him again. He'd lost men before, but never like this. Failed before, but never like this. 'Now, if you'll excuse me, Investigator, I have some serious drinking to attend to.'

He looked down at his glass, to give her a chance to leave with dignity, but when he raised his eyes again she was still there, staring at him coldly.

'I can feel your distress,' she said evenly. 'No matter where I am. Ever since our experiences in the Madness Maze, you and I have been . . . linked, in some strange way. Not quite telepathy, but close. I chose to disregard it, as did you. We didn't want to be taken for espers. Since then the link has become stronger. And unavoidable, when it wants to be. If I concentrate, I can feel what you're feeling, sense what you're sensing. Sometimes it comes whether I concentrate or not. It's really very annoying. For an Imperial officer, your mind is extremely disorganized. Your feelings are as undisciplined as your thoughts, and my mouth is currently full of the taste of whatever garbage that is you're drinking. It has to stop.'

'I can't sense *your* mind,' said Silence. 'But then I wouldn't, would I? You're an Investigator. You don't have any feelings.'

'My mind is disciplined,' Frost said calmly. 'Unlike yours. Is that why you're trying so hard to climb into a bottle and drown?'

Silence glared at her. 'In case it has escaped your attention, Investigator, the *Dauntless* is carrying us back to inform the Empress that, not only was our mission shot to hell, not only is her lover and Warrior Prime dead and cold, but a major rebellion – complete with an army of reawakened augmented men – is in the offing. She is not going to be pleased with us. Not at all. If we're lucky, she'll just kill us both on the spot. But we haven't been particularly lucky so far, have we, Investigator?'

'So why are we going back?' said Frost.

The words hung in the air between them, refusing to let Silence ignore them. He looked into his glass, but it had no answer for him. He breathed out heavily, and made himself meet the Investigator's cold blue eyes.

'Because it's my duty. I may have screwed up everything else in my life, but I still know my duty. The Empress must be warned. I swore an oath upon my honour to serve and protect the Empire to the last drop of my blood, and I still believe in that, irrespective of whoever happens to be sitting on the Iron Throne. The Empire is worth preserving, for all its many faults. Every alternative is worse – from barbarism and mass starvation on a thousand worlds if the system breaks down to all kinds of petty dictatorships if the Empress's authority is broken. The rebellion is a threat to civilization itself. I don't even want to think of what might happen if those damned AIs on Shub seized the opportunity to attack while we were preoccupied with a rebellion. And what about the aliens? You saw that thing on Unseeli, with its half-living ship. Lionstone must be warned, and made to understand the urgency of the threat. She won't want to believe me, so she'll order a mind-probe; she'll have to believe *that*, whether she wants to or not. So I'm going back. Because I must. But you don't have to, Investigator.'

He took a long drink. His throat was dry.

Frost shook her head. 'I have to go back, too. The Empire trained me to be an Investigator, and I don't know how to be anything else. And I wouldn't want to be, even if I could. I like being what I am. It's direct and uncomplicated. But only the Empire has any use for an Investigator. So I'm going back, and I just hope that between now and then something happens to get us off the hook.'

'And if nothing does?' said Silence. 'If I did run, afterwards . . . would you come with me, Frost?'

'No. I can't. I have to be what they made me.' She looked at him for a long moment. 'I can warn the Empress. It doesn't need both of us. And it certainly doesn't make any sense for both of us to die.'

'I can't leave you to face the storm alone.'

'I'd leave you to, if I could.'

'I know that.' Silence smiled at her, and wasn't bothered

66

that she didn't smile back. She was an Investigator. And, though she was supposed to be nothing more than a cold, calculating killing machine, Silence thought he understood her, even in the things she didn't, or couldn't, say. He didn't need the link for that.

'How's Stelmach?' he said finally. It was as good a way to change the subject as any.

Frost snorted. 'Still sulking, because we had to leave his precious alien pet behind on the Wolfling World. Apparently he learned to control the Grendel only by accident, and isn't at all sure he can recreate his success again with another subject. Still, you can be sure he's already got some story worked out, to make him look good and us very bad.'

'Undoubtedly,' said Silence. 'I swear he was closer to that bloody alien than he ever was to anything human. Mind you, if I'd been christened Valiant and ended up as a mere security officer, I'd be hard to get along with too. Whatever report he turns in, you can be sure his main motive will be to stab us in the back.'

'Of course. That's what security officers are for.'

'The point is that he'll be more interested in looking out for his own interests than in convincing Lionstone of the Rebel threat. Just another reason why I have to go back. Dammit.'

'We could always kill him,' said Frost. 'Hard to stab anybody in the back from inside a coffin.'

Silence thought about it. 'No. It would only complicate things further. He doesn't know enough to really hurt us. He doesn't know about the link.'

They'd never told anyone. The link wasn't esp, as far as they could tell, but it wouldn't prevent the Empire treating them as espers, if word ever got out. And espers were second-class citizens, little better than clones. Certainly it would be the end of their careers as captain and Investigator. They'd end up as lab animals, specimens to be quarantined, studied and quite probably vivisected.

'Have you heard anything from your daughter recently?' said Frost.

Silence shook his head. His daughter Diana was an esper.

She'd been with them when everything went to hell on Unseeli. She'd gone through a lot – enough to break anyone else. But Diana had survived, and had emerged stronger than she'd been before. Strong enough that, when they'd returned to Golgotha from the Unseeli mission, she'd jumped ship and disappeared into the clone and esper underground. Silence hadn't seen her since, or received any word from her. He was glad of that. He would have hated having to turn her in. Diana was his daughter, his only child, and he loved her deeply; but he knew his duty. Which was probably why she'd had the sense not to contact him.

He hoped she was well, and happy.

'What's happening with the crew?' he said. 'Anyone offering you any trouble?'

'They wouldn't dare,' said Frost. 'A few of them tried giving me the cold shoulder, so I slapped them around a bit to teach them some manners. They'll be fine once they get out of the Infirmary. In the meantime, everyone else is being very polite and obedient, as long as I'm around. I don't know what they're griping about. So we lost a few people. Sometimes, that's part of the job.'

'But we lost an entire away team,' said Silence. 'And all the Wampyr.'

'Trust me, Captain. No one gives a damn about the Wampyr.'

'But they were the last battle-trained adjusted men in the Empire.'

'That's like saying they were the last cockroaches. Everyone on this ship is glad they're gone.'

'They were still my men,' said Silence. 'I was responsible for them. And I just stood there and watched as the Hadenmen led them away.'

'There was nothing you could have done. We were outnumbered.'

'They'll be dead by now. Cut apart to see what makes them tick – pieces in neatly labelled jars in some Hadenmen laboratory.'

'Best place for them,' said Frost. 'I never trusted them.'

'They fought beside us,' said Silence. 'And most of them died doing it. Doesn't that mean anything to you? No, of course it doesn't. I was forgetting again. You're an Investigator. All you've ever cared about is killing the enemy. And, God, I wish I were like you.'

He lifted his glass, but it was empty. He reached for the bottle and Frost put a hand on his arm.

'Please. Don't.'

They looked at each other for a long moment, and then a chime sounded suddenly in their ears. Silence raised an eyebrow. It had been some time since anyone had contacted him on the command channel. He activated his comm implant, and paused a moment to be sure his voice was calm and steady.

'This is the captain.'

'Bridge here, Captain. Communications officer. I think you and the Investigator had better come up to the bridge immediately.'

Silence frowned. There was something in the man's voice – something more than concern. 'What's the problem?'

'A signal has come in, Captain. I think you're going to want to hear this for yourself.'

Definitely something in the voice. Something had shaken the communications officer right down to his socks . . . which was why he'd come running to his captain.

Silence smiled grimly. 'All right, I'm on my way. Go to Yellow Alert, and prepare all battle stations. Captain out.' He broke contact and looked thoughtfully at the Investigator. 'Must be something really unusual, or dangerous, if they want both of us on the bridge. Could be an alien contact.'

Frost stood up and pulled at her uniform here and there to ensure everything was as it should be. 'I told you something would come up, Captain. Something always does.'

'That's what worries me,' said Silence. 'The way my luck's been going, this could turn out to be really nasty.'

'Good,' said Frost. 'Maybe I'll get the chance to kill something.'

Some twenty minutes later Captain Silence and the Investigator strode on to the bridge of the *Dauntless* and headed straight for the communications station. Silence had taken an emergency purge and was feeling very sober. He also felt like he'd just run a marathon. His legs were shaking, as were his hands when he forgot to clench them into fists. He'd shaved and climbed into a fresh uniform, but he still felt like death warmed up and allowed to congeal. He bent over the communications station and studied the board. Nothing seemed obviously wrong. The communications officer leaned away a little, and Silence realized his breath must still be foul. Tough. He made himself concentrate on what the communications officer was saying.

'We dropped out of hyperspace just inside the Rim, so we could re-establish contact with the Empire. Our signals still won't cross the Darkvoid ... since comm signals travel through hyperspace it shouldn't be possible for anything to interfere with them, but that's the Darkvoid for you. Anyway, the minute we reappeared in normal space, my station began operating normally again. And the first thing we picked up was a signal in emergency code. No visual, just a voice. It's from the Empire base on Gehenna. I looked it up. Gehenna's an unpopulated world, right out on the edge of the Empire. A nasty place, by all accounts. The base is a scientific research lab, with a hundred and seven personnel. They're calling for help. The emergency code they're using is Top Priority. I think we actually have to be at war to use a higher code. Officially, standing orders say we're supposed to head straight back to Golgotha, to report in person on the outcome of our mission, but I thought you ought to hear this, in case you wanted to over-ride.'

'Quite right,' said Silence. 'Let me hear the signal.'

He listened intently to the whispering voice coming from the comm station. It was barely audible, despite everything the communications officer could do to boost the signal. Silence looked at Frost, who was frowning thoughtfully, but she just shook her head. Silence turned back to the communications officer. 'What do the computers make of it?'

'Not a lot, Captain. It's a beacon, repeating a recorded message over and over. The only clear parts are the origin of the signal and the plea for help. We've tried contacting the base directly, but there's no reply.'

'If it's a beacon, how long has it been sending?' said Frost. 'And why hasn't anyone else picked it up?'

'Unknown, Investigator. But the signal is very weak and this *is* the Rim. Strange things happen out here. Perhaps the only reason we picked it up is because we're right out on the Rim. What are your orders, Captain?'

Silence looked at Frost again. 'We should ignore this – go straight to Golgotha. The beacon could have been repeating its message for ages. Whatever happened on Gehenna, it's probably over by now.'

'Of course, Captain,' Frost said solemnly. 'But those people could still need our help, and we are the only ship out here.'

'Precisely,' said Silence. 'So our duty is clear. Helmsman: set a course for Gehenna. Investigator: we'll discuss this further in private. Second-in-Command: let me know when we get there. Otherwise, I don't wish to be disturbed.'

His Second sniffed audibly, contempt clear in the sound. Frost spun on him, her hand dropping to her sword, but Silence stopped her with a hand on her arm. He strode over to the command chair, gripped the Second by the throat with one hand, and lifted him effortlessly out of the chair. The Second's eyes bulged and his tongue protruded from his mouth. He scrabbled at Silence's hold with both hands but couldn't budge it. He drew his disrupter and Silence slapped it out of his hand. The gun skidded across the floor until Frost stepped on it. The rest of the bridge crew saw the look on her face and sat very still at their stations. Silence let go of his Second's throat, and the man dropped back into the command chair, gasping for breath. Silence leaned forward, so his face was right before the Second's, and locked eyes with him. 'You show disrespect for my rank again, boy, and I'll fire you out of one of the torpedo tubes, in your under-wear. Now get on with your business, and leave me to mine. Is that clear? Good. I'm glad we had this little talk. Feel free

71

to come to me again if you need anything else explained to you.'

He turned and left the bridge. Frost fell in beside him. As he passed the comm station the communications officer murmured, 'Good to have you back, Captain.' Silence had to hide a smile.

The door slid shut behind him, and he let out his breath in a long sigh. He stopped and leaned back against the corridor bulkhead. His head ached sickly, and his hands were shaking again.

'I need a drink,' he said tiredly.

'No, you don't,' said Frost.

'Look, whose hangover is this?'

'You didn't need any help hauling the Second out of his chair,' said Frost calmly. 'And with only one hand, too. I'm impressed.'

'So am I,' said Silence. He pushed himself away from the bulkhead and strode off down the corridor. Frost came alongside him again, and they didn't say any more until they were safely back in his quarters. It was no secret that Security Officer Stelmach had the whole ship bugged from stem to stern. Silence debugged his quarters on a regular basis, and, since he had access to better tech than Stelmach, he was just about keeping ahead.

He sank into his favourite seat, and Frost pulled up a chair opposite. Silence looked thoughtfully at the half-empty wine bottle, and then looked away. Maybe later.

'So, Investigator, it would seem our short time in the Madness Maze changed us more than we realized. For a moment there the Second seemed to weigh nothing at all. I could have ripped him apart with my bare hands. And part of me wanted to.'

'I wonder if I'll get stronger too,' said Frost. 'Or perhaps there are other surprises in store for me. I wonder what we might have become, if we'd made it all the way through the Maze . . .'

'You can always ask the rebels, if we ever get another bash at them. They did go right through.'

'Either way, I think this is something else we should keep strictly to ourselves, Captain.'

'I couldn't agree more, Investigator. Let us talk of safer things. What do you think could have happened on Gehenna that their only call for help was an automated beacon? Under normal conditions, all they had to do was call on an open channel and an Empire starcruiser could have been there within hours. That's standard, no matter where in the Empire you are. Of course, we *are* right out on the Rim, but even so . . . Could it be the first rebel attack?'

'I doubt it, Captain. First, the rebels didn't look anywhere near organized enough to mount a major attack. Second, I don't think they've got the resources to mount anything major yet. And third . . . I've got a bad feeling about this. To take out a planetary base so quickly and so thoroughly that they had time to fire off no more than a beacon would require weaponry of immense power. Perhaps greater power than either the rebels or the Empire could muster.'

'So what are we talking about here? The Hadenmen? Shub?'

'Perhaps. But I can't help thinking that the last time a base fell silent we ended up on Unseeli.'

'Where we discovered a crashed alien starship, of a technology unknown to the Empire and quite possibly superior to anything we have, and a base full of dead people.' Silence scowled thoughtfully. 'You think it could be those aliens again?'

'Could be,' said Frost. She smiled briefly. 'And I'm in just the mood to kick some alien ass.'

'I've never known you when you weren't, Investigator. Personally, I'm just glad of a good excuse to put off our return to Golgotha. Possible alien attack is one of the few acceptable excuses we could come up with. But I have to say that I don't like the idea of our losing another planetary base. It leaves the Empire vulnerable to all kinds of things. And there's always the chance this is some kind of trap, designed to pull in unsuspecting ships.'

'Then we'd better get there first,' said Frost. 'We are, after all, expendable.'

The *Dauntless* dropped out of hyperspace and settled into orbit around the planet Gehenna, the world of eternal fires. It burned like a blazing coal in the dark – with continent-wide flames leaping and flaring but never dying down. Long ago something had set light to the surface of the planet and, through some kind of chain reaction, the fire had spread until it had covered all the world. The poles had melted and the oceans had evaporated, and all that now remained was the flames. The surface burned, consuming itself slowly but inexorably. There was evidence that Gehenna had once been inhabited by an alien civilization, but no trace remained of the aliens or their works, aside from a handful of strange stone bunkers, huge and impressive but utterly empty, buried deep in the bedrock, away from the all-consuming fires. If they held any secrets those remained a mystery. No one knew what had happened to the aliens – whether they'd been destroyed by some outside force or whether they did it to themselves, whether the fire had come first or was just an after-effect of whatever had destroyed an entire species so thoroughly that not even a hint remained of what it might have been.

The Empire was, of course, very interested in something that could set an entire planet alight: it would make one hell of a weapon, and Lionstone wanted it. So she had given orders for a base to be established here, right in the heart of the flames, protected by the strongest force screen the Empire could provide. According to the *Dauntless*'s records, the scientists in the base had been working there for nine years and had been no nearer finding any answers.

Silence led the away team himself – partly because, if the base had been compromised, he needed to be right there on the spot making decisions, but mostly because he didn't want to go. He still felt like shit, his crew were still sneaking sidelong glances at him when they thought he wasn't looking, and he wasn't at all sure he was up to making command decisions when people's lives might be on the line, but that was why, in the end, he had to go. If he didn't, he might as well resign his captaincy, and he wasn't ready to do that just yet. So he led the team and prayed he was up to it.

Frost accompanied him, of course, as the ship's Investigator. More surprisingly, Security Officer Stelmach insisted on coming along as well – probably because he didn't trust the other two out of his sight. The rest of the team consisted of six marines chosen by lot, plus Communications Officer Eden Cross, who'd worked at Gehenna Base briefly, two years ago. He didn't seem at all happy to be paying the place a return visit.

Cross was of average height and average weight, dark-skinned and tight-lipped. He hadn't been one of those who conspicuously ostracized the Captain, but anyway he rarely had much to say outside his duties . . . although he'd become almost eloquent when it came to trying to find reasons why he couldn't or shouldn't be part of the away team. Silence approved of that. He didn't want mindlessly loyal people with him in dangerous situations. He wanted people who were scared, on their toes: survivors. Cross hadn't been a communications officer very long. He'd been passed from one position to another, usually at his own request, apparently because he just got bored after a while, no matter what he was doing. He was an overachiever in a Fleet where uniformity was prized above all. He'd either make captain before he was thirty or burn out early.

Silence made him pilot of the pinnace that would take them down to Gehenna's surface. Cross would get them down safely or die trying. It wasn't in his nature to do any less.

Silence gripped the arms of his seat tightly as the pinnace dropped towards the planet below. He accessed the pinnace's sensors through his comm implant, and temperature readings sprang into life before his eyes. He watched blankly as the figures rose in sudden spurts, starting high and then moving rapidly up to unbelievable. He cut them off: they made him nervous. The long slender ship slammed through the overheated atmosphere, rocking and leaping as it plunged into the roaring flames that leapt miles above the endlessly burning surface. Silence made himself let go of the seat's arms. The pinnace's outer hull would protect them against any temperature to be found on a solid world, and there was always the force screen. The vessel could handle anything Gehenna might throw at it.

Theoretically.

Silence wasn't entirely convinced about this. There were already too many unanswered questions about Gehenna, of which the emergency beacon was only the latest. He tried to stir uncomfortably in his seat, but his hard suit wouldn't let him. Like everyone else, he'd put on the protective suit before getting into the pinnace. He wouldn't need it until the pinnace landed, but clambering into a hard suit was difficult enough at the best of times, and almost impossible for a crew of ten to manage in the cramped confines of a pinnace. He and the others would put the helmets on later.

A hard suit was part-spacesuit, part-armour and part-weapons. It was designed to keep the bearer alive, no matter how inimical conditions got. Once all the systems were connected, the suit guaranteed to keep the wearer cool and calm, no matter what was happening outside it. The suits tended to be slow and awkward and about as subtle as a flying half-brick, but they got the job done. They'd been pretty much superseded by portable force shields and screens, but they still had no equal when someone needed to make hands-on investigations. Radiation-proof, environmentally secure, harder than steel and able to withstand practically anything except a point-blank energy beam, they'd originally been intended as combat armour for extreme field conditions, but they were too clumsy and slow for that, so the Fleet had inherited them as go-anywhere do-anything suits.

Everyone else on the pinnace seemed to be moving easily and confidently within the suits' limits. Silence felt as though he'd been dipped in congealing tar.

Sweat was beading his face, but he couldn't lift his armoured arm high enough to wipe at it. He shouldn't be feeling so hot. The pinnace's life-support systems automatically maintained a comfortable interior temperature. But you couldn't think about the impossible heat outside and not feel something, even if it was only in the mind. The six marines were trying to pass a bottle of something back and forth, and spilling most of it as they over-compensated for the suits' servomechanisms. Silence wished they'd pass the damn' thing his way, but he couldn't ask. It would look bad. Weak. It was important he appear strong and confident before his men – particularly after what had happened the last time he'd led an away team down to a planet . . .

He turned his head to look the other way. Stelmach was sitting by himself, a quiet, nondescript man, anonymous as any civil servant, staring straight ahead, clearly wishing he were somewhere else. Anywhere else. Frost was frowning slightly, her gaze remote. Times like this were what she lived for. That, and the promise of a little mayhem. Gehenna Base promised a fascinating deductive problem and the possibility of killing something. Any happier and she'd probably explode. It occurred to Silence that she might be studying what was going on outside the pinnace; he patched into the ship's exterior sensors through his comm implant, so he could see too.

His vision was immediately filled with roaring flames as the pinnace bulkheads appeared to become transparent. No matter where he looked, there was always fire. Now and again he thought he caught a glimpse of the dark, hard-baked surface far below, always burning, somehow never completely consumed. There was nothing else down there but the base. Nothing born of Gehenna survived, as far as anyone knew, and the only remaining structures were deep underground. That would have been the most sensible place for the base, too, but Lionstone had insisted it be constructed aboveground – it had been a matter of principle to show that the Empire could build and preserve a base right in the heart of hell, where no one else could. The base could still be intact behind its force screen. And, if the screen was still up, the base personnel ought to be intact, too. The screen could take anything this world could throw at it. Even if the screen had fallen for some reason, the base had been built specifically to withstand Gehenna's heat. Yet Gehenna was an unforgiving world, waiting always for the smallest mistake or oversight. Silence tried to feel optimistic, but it was hard work.

'Coming in for landing, Captain,' said Cross. 'Hold on to your seat harness. It's been a while since I had to land a ship here.'

Silence cut off the sensor input, and the pinnace's walls snapped back into being around him. He felt hotter than ever. He realized the others had turned in their seats, as far as their suits would allow, to look at him, waiting for some last and hopefully reassuring word from him. He took a deep breath, and when he spoke his voice was calm and casual.

'Power up all systems, and get ready to put on your helmets. Remember, a hard suit can keep you alive for up to a week down here if necessary, but, even so, take things carefully. Keep your eyes open, and watch everyone else's back as well as your own. This place will kill you if you give it the slightest opening. And if you have to use your guns, watch the readings of your energy crystals: hard suits can soak up a lot of power in combat mode.

'The moment we're down, the Investigator will exit the craft first. She'll make an immediate assessment of the situation and decide whether the mission can proceed. Assuming we haven't dropped into an actual war zone, the marines will disembark next and set up a defensive perimeter. Then Cross, Stelmach and I will bring up the rear. Remember, people: this is a rescue mission, not an invasion. You shoot anyone you don't absolutely have to, and I am going to be annoyed with you. I want survivors with answers, not bodies with holes in them. All right, that's it. Secure helmets. Cross – take us in.'

Silence picked up his helmet from his lap. The featureless steel helm fitted perfectly on to his shoulder yoke. There was a moment of utter darkness as the suit's connections linked up, and then the helmet's sensors kicked in, patching into his comm implant to give him a 360-degree view. It was as though his helmet had suddenly disappeared. The rest of his team looked blind in their blank helmets, which made Cross at the controls appear particularly worrying.

And then the pinnace slammed down on to the planet's surface and skidded along, barely slowing. Silence and the others clung desperately to the arms of their seats, only their heavy-duty seat harnesses keeping them from being flung into the aisle or smashed against the walls. The ship shook them back and forth, and then lurched to a sudden halt as though it had hit something.

Silence hit his seat-harness release with a steel fist and rose jerkily to his feet, the whine of servomechanisms loud in his ears as they translated his body movements into suit responses. He stomped down the aisle to the inner airlock door, where Frost was already waiting for him. Her suit bore the colours of her uniform, just as his did, but he would have known it was her anyway. Only Frost could have got to the door that fast – most of the marines were still trying to get out of their seats. Silence waited for Cross's raised hand, and then smacked the inner-door release. The door hissed open. Frost stepped inside the airlock, and the door closed behind her.

There was a pause, and then Frost's voice sounded calmly in his ear.

'Outer door open, stepping out on to the surface.' Another pause. 'No problems, all clear. No sign of anything but dirt and flames. Not unlike walking into a crematorium, actually. Come on in – the inferno's lovely this time of year.'

Silence smiled despite himself, opened the inner airlock door and waved the marines past him. It didn't take long for everyone to cycle through. Silence himself stepped out on to the surface of Gehenna with only the slightest of hesitations.

At first all he could see were the flames: a blazing sea of scarlet and gold, leaping high up into the air. Vague shadows moved in the fire around him, and then the hard suit's computer enhancements kicked in, boosting the helm's sensor images until the shadows came into sharper focus as the members of his team. He looked down and around, and could only just make out the ground he was standing on. It was baked black, broken apart here and there by deep crevasses from which flames belched forth in sudden jets, mixing with the constant glow around him. The temperature readings displayed in his helmet had gone beyond unbelievable to impossible.

Welcome to hell, thought Silence. *Welcome to the broken lands, and the fire that never dies. When the Empress finally has me executed, at least I'll know where I'm going.*

'Captain, this is Cross.' The communications officer's voice sounded loudly in his ear. 'If you're ready I'll get us moving. I've locked on to the beacon; the base is only a few minutes' walk from here.'

'Of course,' said Silence. 'Good piloting, Cross. Lead the way. Everyone else, power up your weapon systems, but remember what I said about unnecessary firing. I'm all for making a dramatic entrance, but I don't want to end up accidentally killing the very people we're here to rescue. Are you listening to me, Investigator?'

'Relax,' said Frost. 'I kill only people who need killing.'

'I'm sure we're all very relieved to hear that, Investigator,' said Cross dryly. 'Pay attention please, everyone. Follow me in single file, your hand on the shoulder of the person in front of you. Take your time and don't get distracted. It's only too easy to get lost here. If you do lose contact with the team, your suit will automatically lock on to the pinnace's beacon. Go back there, and stay put until we return. Have I forgotten anything, Captain?'

'No,' said Silence. 'You're doing fine. Carry on.'

He waited patiently while the team formed itself into a single line, and then put his hand on the shoulder of Stelmach, in front of him. He could see his steel gauntlet resting on the security officer's shoulder, but he couldn't feel it, and as the line moved off he realized what Cross had meant about how easy it would be to get lost. Inside the hard suit, the only sense he had left to him was sight. The sole sound on Gehenna was the constant roar of the flames, and he'd automatically turned that down to protect his ears and to be able to hear his team-mates over the comm. The hard suit cut him off completely from the world. It had to, to protect him.

He trudged on after Stelmach, and the fires raged impotently around him. Sweat was dripping off him again, despite the cool air circulating inside the armour. Time passed slowly, with no landmarks to show any progress. Cross had said the base was only a few minutes away. Surely much more than a few minutes had passed already? Or had Cross lost his bearings, and begun to lead them in a huge circle? Silence hadn't thought to check the time before they started . . .

The answer to his dilemma suggested itself almost immediately, and he was glad the others couldn't see him blushing. He switched the comm to the emergency channel, and the base's beacon sounded out, loud and reassuring. His sensors placed the base straight ahead, in what would have been plain sight on any other world. He stared hard into the flames, pushing the computer enhancements to their limits, and a huge dark shape slowly formed before him.

Its image grew sharper on the inside of his helmet. It was only then that he realized he shouldn't have been able to see it this close. The base's raised screen should have stopped them before now. He called for Cross to halt, and then walked carefully down the line, shoulder by shoulder, until he was standing next to Cross and the Investigator. At this range he could clearly see the cracked and broken walls of the base. The outer wall had been designed and built to withstand everything from a sustained barrage from disrupter cannon to earthquakes and a nuclear firestorm, but something had cracked it open like an eggshell. Wide jagged rents crawled up the walls from top to bottom. The main doors were open, with only darkness beyond. Silence bit his lower lip. One thing at least he could be sure of. This wasn't the result of any earthquake or natural force. Something must have hit the outer walls again and again until they broke apart and whatever was responsible for the attack could get in.

'This isn't supposed to be possible,' said Cross's voice in his ear. 'I know the specifications for the outer walls. This base was designed to survive intact even if the screen went down. It was ten times tougher than any other base has ever been. And why would they lower the screen anyway?'

'You're missing the point,' Frost said calmly. 'Something did this. Something unknown. And, to be able to do it, this unknown force must have had a technology not only equal to our own but quite possibly superior. So where is this "unknown force"? Still inside the base? Or, if it's not inside, where has it gone, and is it coming back any time soon?'

'Good questions,' said Silence. 'But you're missing something, too, Investigator. The force screen is down and the walls are broken in so many places they might as well not be there. So why hasn't the whole base gone up in flames along with everything else on this infernal planet?'

'Only one way to find out,' said Frost, and Silence didn't need to see into her featureless helm to know that she was smiling.

'Lead the way, Investigator,' Silence said calmly. 'But remember: answers, not bodies.'

'Of course, Captain. Of course.'

She moved past Cross and strode forward through the open doors. Silence moved after her, with Cross's hand on his shoulder, and the marines and Stelmach followed. The security officer was being very quiet, but Silence doubted this would last long once they got inside. A place like this was bound to be full of sensitive material that lowly captains and lesser ranks weren't supposed to know about. Silence didn't give a damn. If there were answers here he was going to find them, no matter where he had to look.

He stepped carefully through the gaping doors, his gaze sweeping back and forth, but everything seemed quiet. It was dark, and Silence turned on his suit's exterior lights, mounted on his shoulders. More illumination pushed back the darkness as the rest of the away team turned on their own lights, and the foyer slowly formed around them. The first thing he noticed was that it was raining . . . it took him a moment to realize the sprinkler system was still, somehow, operating. But the water should have evaporated in this heat. He checked the external temperature on his suit's sensors, and the figure appeared immediately, low down on the inside of his helmet: it was only a few degrees above standard, despite the broken walls and open doors. Which should have been impossible. With the screen down and the walls breached, there was no way the base could be maintaining a standard temperature.

'Investigator, check your sensors. What temperature do you have?'

'Same as you, Captain. Standard, near as dammit. I'd swear there was an energy screen still protecting us, but nothing registers on my sensors. What we have here is standard gravity and a breathable atmosphere, but don't ask me what's maintaining them. We could survive here without our suits, if we had to.'

'Don't even think it,' Silence said quickly. 'Don't take your helmet off. Since we don't know what's maintaining these conditions, we can't be sure they won't be cut off at any moment. Also, I want full quarantine procedures followed. Suit integrity is to be preserved at all times. Is that clear, everyone?'

Quick affirmatives came back to him from the rest of the team. Frost just grunted, but that was to be expected.

Silence glared around the deserted foyer. 'Marines, move out and set up a defensive perimeter. Investigator, don't wander too far away just yet. Stelmach, don't touch *anything*. Cross: you've been here before. First impressions?'

'The place is a mess,' said Cross. 'Whoever came through here really wrecked it. I can't tell anything from this.'

Silence had to agree with his communications officer: the foyer looked as though a grenade had gone off in it – maybe several grenades. Furniture had been overturned and scattered everywhere, much of it reduced to little more than kindling. The main reception desk, a huge slab of ironwood, had collapsed in the middle, as if something extremely heavy had sat on it. None of its built-in instruments were functioning. There was no trace of life anywhere. The hellish glow of the fires outside could be seen through the wide cracks in the walls but, strangely, the bronze light didn't penetrate far into the darkness. The sprinkler rain had touched and soaked everything, forming pools and little lakes here and there.

'No blood and no bodies,' said Frost, from the far end of the foyer, 'but somebody put up a fight. There's damage to the walls and ceiling from discharged energy weapons. No sign they actually hit anything, though.'

Silence looked up at the jagged holes in the ceiling. Trust Frost to spot something everyone else would have missed.

'Why the ceiling?' said Stelmach suddenly. 'How big were their attackers?'

'Let's try and keep an open mind,' said Silence. 'We don't have any hard evidence yet that there *were* any attackers. This could turn out to be just another bad case of cabin fever. Unlikely, I'll admit, but we have to consider all possibilities. Frost, run an energy scan on these disrupter holes. See how old they are. Stelmach, see if you can find a working terminal somewhere in this mess that'll let you access the base computers. The commander's log might give us a few clues. And, Cross, how come the sprinklers are still working? Surely they should have run out of water long ago?'

'The sprinkler systems feed off an underground lake,' said Cross. 'It's a long way down, but there are millions of gallons down there. It could rain forever in here, on a planet of eternal fires. It's like a miracle.'

'Don't start getting religious on us,' said Frost. 'I'd hate to have to puke inside this helmet.'

'Over here,' Stelmach said suddenly. 'I've found someone.'

'Stay put,' said Silence sharply. 'Don't touch anything. Investigator, check it out.'

The security officer was crouching beside the collapsed main desk.

Frost moved quickly in beside him, and studied the situation for a long moment. 'It's a hand, Captain. Human. Unprotected. No obvious booby-traps attached, according to my sensors. Help me move the desk, Stelmach.'

They moved awkwardly round the desk in their clumsy suits, and Cross and Silence went forward to help them. A colourless hand protruded from under one side of the desk.

Working together, the four of them used the power of their suits' servomechanisms to lift the massive lump of ironwood and put it carefully to one side.

They all looked at what they'd uncovered. It had been a woman once, but most of her was missing. The bones were still there, piled loosely together, but so devoid of flesh they seemed almost polished. The only flesh left was on the side of the face they could see and on part of the arm attached to the hand they'd found. Most of her long hair was present, but something had cracked open the back of the skull and removed the brains. Sprinkler water pattered down on the head, and ran over the staring face like tears.

'Picked clean,' said Frost. 'And, judging by the ragged end of the remaining arm, I'd have to say this was brought about by teeth rather than any blade or sharp instrument. Same with the back of the skull: brute force did that, not a cutting tool. I wonder why they left the face and one arm . . .'

'Perhaps it, or they, were interrupted,' said Cross.

'What could have done this?' said Stelmach, his voice thick with nausea. 'What kind of creature . . .?'

'Move away and take some deep breaths,' said Silence. 'Vomiting inside a hard suit is not a good idea.'

'I'm all right,' said Stelmach angrily. 'I can handle it.'

'It was a good question, though,' said Cross. 'What kind of creature would feed like this?'

'Practically anything,' said Frost, 'if it were hungry enough. The thoroughness is interesting, though. They didn't just go for the fat and the muscle: they took everything. That's unusual. More commonly, different species feed off different parts of the body . . . Maybe the attackers killed her first, and then something else came along afterwards and fed off the body.'

'There are no living things anywhere on this planet,' said Cross. 'Maybe the assailants brought something with them.'

'Still think this was cabin fever, Captain?' said Stelmach.

'I'm not ruling anything out yet,' said Silence calmly. 'This is looking more and more like an alien attack, I agree, but we still have no hard evidence that anything other than humans

were ever here. Remember, too, the Hadenmen are loose
again. And there's always Shub, and its Furies. Investigator,
could the tissues taken from this body have been intended for
study rather than food?'

'Quite possibly, Captain. It would explain the
thoroughness.'

Silence decided. 'This can wait. I want the whole base
checked out, floor by floor. There'll be time for questions and
hypotheses after we're sure this place is secure.'

He gestured sharply to the marines, and with Frost in the
lead the party moved on deeper into the base, weapons at the
ready.

Things grew worse the further in they got. There was
destruction everywhere, and more partial corpses. Doors had
been torn out of their frames, holes punched through walls,
instruments wrecked and the pieces scattered to no apparent
purpose or pattern. Every room had been torn apart, but
nothing obvious had been taken. The number of bodies
mounted steadily. The amount consumed or taken varied,
but the heads were always left intact apart from the brains,
leaving so many silently screaming faces. Silence felt a slow
core of cold anger building within him. This hadn't been an
attack, it had been a slaughter; and he swore silently to every
new dead face that he would take a bloody revenge for them
all.

Frost just seemed increasingly interested, but she was an
Investigator. Cross said very little, except to comment in a
choked voice on the increasing destruction and identify the
occasional face. Stelmach had nothing to say, but kept very
close to the others. The six marines maintained their defensive perimeter, checking, weapons trained, every open doorway and every turn of the corridor. Tension built inexorably
as the away team moved on through the darkness, their only
light being what they had brought with them. Shadows
loomed and danced. The only sounds were their own increasingly harsh breathing and the dull thuds of steel boots on the
floor. No one felt like talking much. There was still no trace
of any alien dead, but broken swords lay here and there

shattered on something harder than steel, and everywhere there was damage to walls and floors and ceilings from discharged energy weapons. In some places great holes had been punched through the thick steel walls by some incredible force. The last creatures Silence had seen that were capable of such a feat had been the genetically engineered aliens he'd discovered sleeping in the Vaults on Grendel. The thought disturbed him, so he kept it to himself.

And, everywhere they went, the water came down in an endless rain, as though trying to wash away what had happened.

On the second floor Frost stopped suddenly and knelt down, shining her lights on to something on the floor. The others crowded around her, adding their lights to hers. The Investigator studied a pool of dark liquid thoughtfully, and then stirred it slowly with a steel finger. It was a thick, sticky fluid that tried to cling to her finger when she pulled it away. She had to shake her hand hard to get it free.

'What is it, Investigator?' said Silence finally.

'Too early to say, Captain. I've seen smaller splashes of it here and there. There's nothing to suggest what it is or where it came from. But it looks organic.'

'Alien blood?' said Cross.

'Maybe,' said Frost, noncommittally. 'I'll take some samples, and the *Dauntless* labs can run tests on it.'

'Follow full quarantine procedures,' said Silence. 'Just in case.'

'Of course, Captain.'

Of course. She knows what she's doing. Let her get on with her job. Silence took a deep breath and let it out slowly as he straightened up. He looked about him, and scowled inside the safety of his helm. It wouldn't do any good for the others to see how frustrated he was getting. They'd ended up in one of the main control centres on the second floor, and it was even more of a mess than everywhere else, if that were possible. Most of the instrumentation had been ripped out of its settings and partially dismantled – as though the dismantlers had never seen anything like it before. Perhaps they hadn't. Not for the first time, Silence remembered the alien ship he and Frost had found crashlanded on Unseeli, with its strange and unnatural biomechanical systems. A ship that had been grown as much as made. The single alien from that ship had killed every human being in Unseeli's Base Seven, and transformed the base itself in horrid alien ways. Hopefully, that wasn't what they had here. The signs were different.

'Stelmach, try and find a computer terminal you can access. I need the commander's log.'

'I'm doing my best, Captain. There are some working systems still on-line, but reaching them's the problem. Whatever came through here really trashed the place.'

I want results, not excuses! Silence nearly snapped, but held it in. 'Do your best, Stelmach. We won't leave here until you've exhausted every possibility.' He looked round as Cross came over to join him. 'Anything new?'

'Not exactly, Captain. There's something wrong here, apart from the obvious. There aren't enough bodies.'

'Explain.'

'Given the size of the contingent running this base, we should have encountered far more bodies than we have. Unless they're all piled up somewhere we haven't found yet, I'd have to say as many as seventy to eighty per cent of the base personnel are missing. Which suggests to me that the invaders may have taken the survivors with them when they left.'

'As hostages.'

'Or specimens.'

'But there is a chance they could still be alive?'

'Unknown, Captain. They could have been taken to the alien craft for . . . study.'

That was an interesting choice of word, Silence thought unhappily. It could mean anything from observation to vivisection. Either way, it was a complication he could have done without. He had come to Gehenna to investigate what had happened at its base, not go chasing blindly off after missing personnel. But he couldn't just ignore them. Not if there was a chance, however small, that some of them might still be alive. He scowled, indecisive about what to do for the best. His duty was clear: discovering what had happened in the base had to have top priority. Whatever had wrecked the base so thoroughly could be a threat to the Empire itself – just at the time when the last thing it needed was another threat. But he couldn't abandon people to death or worse. He couldn't. He made himself stop frowning. His head was beginning to ache again. Facts. He needed hard facts, to help him make his decision.

'Stelmach . . .'

'All right, all right! I think I've got something . . .'

Silence and Frost moved over to join Stelmach and Cross beside a comm panel that didn't seem quite as ruined as the others. It looked pretty bad, nevertheless, and from the way Stelmach and Cross were fiddling with its innards there was clearly still a lot wrong with it.

'Bear with us for a moment, Captain,' said Stelmach without looking up from what he was doing. 'I've cobbled together parts from a dozen panels, and if we're very lucky it might just condescend to work for us.'

'I helped,' said Cross.

'All right, I was going to tell them. This man's wasted in communications, Captain. He knows more about the inside of comm tech than I do, and I thought I knew everything. Ever thought about a career in security work, Cross?'

'Save the recruiting speeches for later,' said Frost. 'What have you got?'

'If we're extremely lucky, access to the security systems. There are surveillance cameras throughout the base, and their files are kept separate from the rest, hidden away, for obvious reasons. Apparently the aliens didn't dig deep enough to find them.'

'Yeah,' said Silence. 'Right. That sounds like Security.'

'You'd better hope I'm right, Captain,' Stelmach said stiffly. 'Whatever happened here, it's over. The attackers are long gone. These security files could be the only records of what actually happened here.'

'We'll applaud later,' said Frost. 'Get on with it.'

Stelmach sniffed loudly, just to let them know his feelings were hurt, and then he and Cross made the last few connections. The information in the security files downloaded directly through their comm implants, so that visions from the past played directly on the insides of their helmets. They were patchy and incomplete, flashes of sight and sound, a swift succession of scenes from throughout the base, but taken together the story they told was clear enough – the story of what had happened the day the aliens came to Gehenna Base.

They were insects and spiders, of all shapes and sizes. Bugs and praying mantises and yard-long centipedes, scuttling and crawling in an endless tide. They varied in size from less than an inch to bigger than a human, and everything in between. There were horrid combinations of dull carapaces and shimmering wings, too many legs and eyes, and all of them moving incredibly quickly in sudden darting movements. They snapped and stung and tore at human victims with clawed limbs. Some had clacking mandibles big and strong enough to rip a man's head from his shoulders with an ease that was almost obscene.

Silence's skin crawled with instinctive reaction. There was something awful and unnatural about insects this big, this organized. He watched with mounting horror as the creatures swarmed through the base, crawling over all the surfaces, running along the walls and ceiling, jumping up at and dropping down on the base personnel, biting and tearing without pause or mercy. Blood splashed everywhere, and the smaller insects licked it up. Disrupters and cold steel took their toll on the invaders, but there were so many insects, thousands of them, and they never stopped coming, eating their own fallen as they went. And men and women died from poisoned bites and stings, or lay shuddering on the floor while smaller insects burrowed in their flesh. Huge bugs, like living armour, tore human limbs away with horrid ease and waved them like dripping banners. People screamed and fought and died, and still the insects pressed on.

'Interesting,' said Frost quietly. 'I've never seen so many apparently different and unconnected species acting together. Could be a mass consciousness, a *Gestalt*. Or maybe they're all drones, following orders from some hidden and protected Queen. I can't be more certain without specimens to examine. But I'll tell you one thing for sure, Captain. Those big bugs aren't natural. Insects don't get that large. Body structure won't allow it. Which implies they were genetically engineered, constructed and adapted for various functions. Maybe all of them were, even the smaller ones. Which in turn suggests a level of biotechnology well in advance of anything we have.'

'How can you be so calm?' said Cross angrily. 'Those bastards slaughtered men and women and tore them apart, and you sound as though this were nothing more than a training session!'

'All part of the job,' said Frost.

'Damn you, those were real men and women!'

'She knows that,' said Silence. 'But she's an Investigator. She's seen worse. Now be quiet and watch the records.'

'I think this new file shows the beginning,' said Stelmach. 'It's the last intact one.'

The base's force screen had shut down suddenly, for no reason anyone in the base could understand. It was supposed to be impossible. The personnel weren't too worried at first. The base itself had been designed to protect them from the heat of the fires, even without the screen. And then the insects came, cracking the base open like an eggshell – the image recurred in Silence's mind – to get at the unprotected flesh within. The base called for help with increasing desperation, but the comm systems were useless. Jammed. Which was also supposed to be impossible.

Finally, one by one, the cameras stopped recording, as the insects discovered and destroyed them. After that, there was only darkness.

The control-room surroundings reappeared on the insides of everyone's helmets as the security file came to an end, and the members of the away team stood quietly for a long moment.

'There was a pattern to the invasion,' said Frost. 'The larger insects broke things, the medium-range ones attacked people and investigated human tech, and the smaller ones cleaned up after them, sucking up blood, carrying away machinery and eating the fallen, whether human or insect.'

Silence closed his eyes, but he could still see the images of screaming men and women struggling helplessly, crying out for help that had never come. He was glad he'd seen only glimpses of the carnage. He didn't think he could have stood witnessing the horror of it in real time. He opened his eyes and breathed deeply to clear his head. He had to be cold and centred if he were to have his revenge on the bugs.

'They were specialized by function.' Frost was still speaking, and Silence made himself pay attention. 'Designed for specific purposes. But what did they want here?'

'What aliens always want,' said Stelmach. 'To destroy humanity.'

Silence swallowed hard, his mouth dry. 'It isn't usually that simple, Stelmach. We know what happened here, but not why. And, without the why, we can't hope to predict what they'll do next. They could be anywhere inside the Empire by now. There has to be a reason for all this destruction and slaughter. Investigator: you said the insects appeared to have been designed for specific tasks in this assault. That implies there was an aim to be achieved, and end to be reached.'

'Yes,' said Frost. 'Almost certainly. I get the impression they were after information as much as anything. They certainly seemed to pay special attention to the computer records. People were mostly killed or attacked when they got in the way or tried to interfere with the search. I think the insects were looking for something.'

'What could they have wanted here?' said Cross. 'Gehenna is the furthermost planet in this sector of the Empire. There's nothing beyond here but the Darkvoid.'

'And they couldn't have come even this far through the

Empire without being noticed,' said Stelmach. 'So they must have come from . . . *outside* the Empire.'

'Nothing lives in the Darkvoid,' said Frost, 'apart from the traitors on Haden.'

'Then maybe they came from the Darkvoid's other side,' said Silence slowly, 'and this was the first human outpost they discovered. But why just attack? We always try to communicate first, if only to find out what we're getting into. Did the base have something the aliens wanted? Something they knew the base personnel wouldn't give up voluntarily?'

'I think we're speculating a bit too far here,' said Cross.

'Of course we are,' said Frost. 'It's all we've got. Now, unless you've got something useful to say, shut the hell up. We're thinking. So, they took tech apart, killed people, in search of something. Information. What did they want to know that no one would tell them?'

'Weaknesses,' said Stelmach. 'Defence stations, weaponry, secrets . . .'

'The location of the homeworld!' said Silence. 'Destroy Golgotha, and the whole Empire would be crippled!' A shudder ran through Silence as his thoughts raced ahead of him. 'You believed this might be a trap, Investigator, but it isn't. It's a decoy – intended to keep us occupied here while the aliens head for Golgotha! Heads up, everyone. We're leaving.'

'Oh, come on,' said Cross. 'This is really stretching . . .'

'No,' said Frost. 'It feels right. It's what I'd do.'

'But what about the missing personnel?' said Cross. 'What if they're being kept somewhere here on Gehenna? If we go chasing off after a theory, they could die here! What if we're wrong about this?'

'Then we're wrong,' said Frost. 'Now move. Homeworld must be protected, at all costs. No wonder you keep being transferred, Cross. You talk too much.'

'We're leaving, people!' said Silence. 'Investigator, lead the way. Cross and Stelmach, stick with me. Marines, bring up the rear. If anything moves, shoot it. We don't have any friends here any more.'

They made their way back out of the base, breasting the endless sprinkler rain like swimmers in a race. It was hard to run in the heavy, clumsy hard suits, but they did it anyway. There was no telling what kind of advance the aliens had on them. The attack on the base couldn't have happened long ago. What was left of the human bodies hadn't had time to corrupt much – that meant a few days, at most. So everything depended now on what kind of stardrive the alien ship had, and whether it was the equal of the *Dauntless*'s own new drive. The *Dauntless* was supposed to be the fastest thing in the Empire, but Silence and Frost knew something the others didn't. The amazing new stardrive was based on the one Silence and Frost had found in the alien ship crashlanded on the planet Unseeli. Which meant there was no telling how fast this latest alien vessel might be. Especially if it had crossed the Darkvoid from one side to the other, something no Empire ship had ever dared attempt.

Usually the Empire found aliens and made decisions about their future. The aliens could join the Empire, be subjugated, or die: no other choices were available. This time, something had found the Empire. And all Silence could do was hope the *Dauntless* got back to Golgotha in time to give a warning. Before the aliens arrived, and started making decisions about humanity.

The *Dauntless* dropped out of hyperspace and plunged into orbit around Golgotha, all weapons systems charged and ready, and immediately began broadcasting warnings on all channels. Sensors raked the darkness for signs of the alien ship, and only then did they discover that the homeworld's defences were in a complete shambles.

The *Dauntless* homed in on the main starport only to find everyone was shouting at everyone else, and no one was listening. Cross ran through all the comm channels, but the chaos had spread even to the most restricted emergency frequencies.

'What the hell is going on down there?' said Silence. 'Did the alien ship beat us here?'

'No sign of anything on the sensors,' said Frost immediately. 'But that's not all that's missing. There are supposed to be six starcruisers constantly on patrol, orbiting Golgotha, as the Empire's last line of defence. I can't find a trace of any of them.'

Silence looked across at the comm station. 'Cross, are our warnings getting through?'

'Impossible to say, Captain. The channels are such a mess that priority's a joke.'

'Let me try,' said Stelmach, moving in beside Cross. 'I have access to security channels that most people don't know about.'

'Go ahead,' said Silence. 'Frost, use the long-range sensors. Get me some pictures of what's going on down there.'

Frost grunted something, preoccupied with her instruments, but after a moment the viewscreen suddenly flickered into life. The starport and its landing pads had been systematically destroyed. Smoke rose from blazing buildings, and broken starships lay scattered across the wrecked pads like so much shattered crockery. The steelglass control tower was cracked so much it looked like a jigsaw, and everywhere fires blazed out of control Emergency services were doing what they could, but things had obviously got out of their control long ago. There were bodies everywhere.

'The alien vessel got here about six hours ago,' said Stelmach. 'It launched its attack while the control tower was still trying to identify it. It blew up the ships on the pads, and then made dozens of strafing runs, raking the port and the city with energy weapons of an unfamiliar type. Force fields and screens were no protection – they either failed or the energy weapons blew them aside. Known casualties are in the hundreds of thousands. As yet the Empress is in no danger; she's safe in the Imperial Palace, deep below the surface. We can only hope the aliens don't know she's there.'

'This is insane!' said Silence. 'How could one ship have done so much damage without the defences taking it out?'

'It appears the aliens got a lucky break,' said Cross. 'As far as I can make out, the rebel underground launched some

95

kind of sabotage attack only a few hours before the alien ship arrived. The rebels made their escape on a Hadenman craft, and the six starcruisers took off after it. Security were busy chasing their own tails trying to sort out the extent of the sabotage, and got caught napping.'

'It wasn't Security's fault!' Stelmach said quickly. 'The rebels apparently crashed nearly all of the computer defences. We were helpless.'

'Forget about placing the blame and get me some information I can use,' said Silence. 'Where's the alien ship now?'

'On the far side of the planet,' said Frost. 'It's on its way back here. Two, three minutes tops, depending on whether it stops to blow something else up.'

'What are you going to do, Captain?' said Cross.

'Blow it to shit,' said Silence.

'No,' said Frost immediately. 'Normally I'd agree with you, Captain, but for now we need answers more than revenge. We have to know more about them, where they come from. If this ship really did cross the Darkvoid to find us, who knows what else might be following them? We need prisoners to interrogate, and the ship as intact as possible, to study.'

'Any other restrictions you want to lay on me?' said Silence.

'There's also the case of the missing base personnel,' said Cross stubbornly. 'If they're being held on the alien ship . . .'

'Then they're expendable,' said Silence. 'I'll save them if I can, but I'm not making any promises. Same to you, Investigator. Stopping the attack comes first. Homeworld must be protected. And, if it comes to blowing the alien ship apart rather than letting it escape, that ship is dead.'

'Understood,' said Frost. 'You'd have made a good Investigator, Captain.'

'Thanks a lot,' said Silence. 'Cross, where is it?'

'It's coming,' said Cross. 'Should be in visual range any time now.'

'Red Alert,' said Silence. 'All shields up, everyone to their battle stations. Power up all weapons and tie in fire-control systems. Cross, download our log so far, along with any other useful information concerning the aliens and what happened at Gehenna Base, and launch the files in an emergency buoy. If anything should happen to us, the information can be retrieved later by whoever survives this mess.'

'I have the ship in my sensors,' said Cross. 'Its speed is incredible.'

'Put it on the viewscreen,' said Silence.

The scene on the screen changed to show the great glowing curve of Golgotha and the darkness and the stars beyond. One of the stars was moving rapidly towards them, growing in size in jumps as Cross increased magnification. The alien ship finally sprang into clear view, and Silence leaned forward in his command chair. The vessel appeared to be a huge ball of sickly white webbing, tied and tangled together. It reminded Silence of a wasp's nest or a cocoon. Insect imagery. The ball had no details of shape or structure, and no recognizable technology.

'How big is it?' Silence said finally.

'About two miles in diameter,' said Cross. 'I'm listening on all channels, but I'm not picking up anything from it.'

'Sensors indicate mainly organic material,' said Frost, 'presumably protected by some kidn of force shield, but the few energy readings I'm getting make no sense at all. No identifiable drive, or weapons, or . . . anything, really.'

'Try talking to them,' said Stelmach. 'Maybe we can negotiate.'

'Unlikely,' said Frost. 'Even the best computer translators take months to produce a working language – you should know that. Besides, I'd say they've already made their intentions clear.'

'Damn' right,' said Silence. 'I don't negotiate with butchers. Anything else on the sensors?'

'Getting some high-energy readings as they come closer – nothing familiar. Wait a minute. Something's happening. Those readings are building . . .'

Flaring energy leapt out from the alien ship, crossing the intervening miles in a moment, and crackled across the *Dauntless*'s force shields, testing, searching for weak spots. Alarms went off all over the *Dauntless* as slowly, inexorably, the crackling energy tore through the shields, seeped through the outer hull and burst into the ship's interior. Blazing light leapt out of work stations on that side of the ship, incinerating crew members where they stood. More alarms sounded every moment, and fires burned unattended in a chaos of screams and shouted orders. Emergency systems were bypassed and the energy spread.

'Evacuate that section!' said Silence. 'Get out as many as you can, and then isolate the section and seal it off. Set up a series of force shields in the corridors. See if you can slow it down, at least. Frost, talk to me. What is that stuff? What is it doing to my ship?'

'Sensors indicate pure energy, Captain,' said Frost calmly. 'But it also has definite physical properties. Possibly some form of plasma energy in suspension, but don't quote me. It's ignoring everything we throw at it. And, if these readings are to be believed, the energy has begun to infiltrate our instrumentation in that section – subverting it and taking it over.'

'We just lost sectors H through K,' said Cross. 'They're no longer responding to central control or auxiliary backups, Life-support systems are shutting down in those sectors.'

'Is everyone out?' said Silence.

'Most of them,' said Cross. 'Those that didn't get out won't last long.'

'Evacuate the adjoining sectors,' said Silence. 'Seal them off with as many interior force shields as we can generate. Any injured are to get themselves to the infirmary. Everyone else is to stay at their posts. Investigator, any recommendations?'

'Our shields won't hold back the energy for long, Captain. Defensive measures are strictly temporary. This would seem to indicate the need to take the offensive. If the alien ship has any force shields, my sensors can't find them. It's looking more and more like our best bet is to hit them with everything we've got and see what happens.'

'I was hoping we'd have something else we could try first,' said Silence. 'I don't like playing our main hand this early. But needs must when the devil drives. Gunnery officer, target the alien ship. Hit it until its shields go down and we start inflicting actual damage, and then break off and stand by for new orders.'

The *Dauntless*'s disrupter cannon opened fire sequentially, maintaining a constant barrage of destructive power. Strange energy fields suddenly flared into being around the alien ship, shimmering fiercely. The disrupter cannon pounded away at them, but they held firm. Within the *Dauntless*, the strange crackling energy spread slowly but inexorably from one section to the next, still infiltrating essential systems as it went. Life support was going down sector by sector. Crew members died at their posts, or running for their lives.

A work station on the bridge exploded suddenly, throwing its operator lifeless to the floor, his clothes and hair burning ferociously. Weird energies danced on the air like heat lightning. Silence yelled for people to back away from the blazing work station, but for everyone else to hold their posts. Fires licked along one wall, hot and blazing.

The *Dauntless*'s disrupter cannon were still firing and firing, when suddenly the alien ship's fields went down. Chunks of the sickly white webbing were blown away into space. And, just as suddenly, the strange energies infesting the *Dauntless* disappeared. Surviving work stations returned to normal, emergency systems began taking care of fires, life support was re-established, and the attack was over.

Silence ordered the disrupter cannon to break off, but to stand ready to resume the attack if necessary. The fires were put out, the injured were helped, and the dead were dragged away. When the last alarm turned off, it was eerily quiet on the bridge.

'All right,' said Stelmach. 'What do we do now?'

'We board the alien ship,' said Frost. 'We've done them some damage, but we have no way of telling how much, or how long it'll take them to make repairs. So we'd better strike now, while they're still weakened.'

'Agreed,' said Silence. 'Now that it's no longer a danger to Golgotha, I want that ship taken intact so Empire scientists can pull it apart and see what makes it tick – especially the shields and the weapons. We might have to face those again. But, given the state of the *Dauntless*, I can't authorize more than a small boarding party. You, Investigator, myself, and a dozen marines.'

'Sounds good to me,' said Frost.

'You can't leave the ship now, Captain,' said Stelmach. 'There are damage reports coming in from all over.'

'Then you deal with them. I'm needed in the boarding party, if only because I'm one of the few people here to have faced aliens and lived to tell of it. Cross, you work with the security officer. See he has all the support he needs.'

'Yes, Captain,' said Cross. 'But I do feel I should point out that Regulations clearly state . . .'

'All right, you've pointed it out. Now forget it. With all the trouble I'm in, a few more broken Regs are the least of my worries. You don't need me here, Cross. This ship is currently dead in the water. Just watch over her, and don't let Stelmach get too carried away with his new responsibilities. Anyone calls, you know where to find me. Let's go, Investigator. I want a close-up look at the kind of ship that can trash an entire city and starport and almost took out an Imperial starcruiser.'

'Right,' said Frost. 'And with a bit of luck we'll get to kill some aliens too.'

'There's always the chance they're playing possum,' said Stelmach.

'Then they'll soon be dead possums,' said Silence.

The *Dauntless* manoeuvred carefully, with the little power she had left, to set herself alongside the alien craft, which made no move to acknowledge her presence. Sensors picked up no energy readings or life signs. Silence lay quietly in his hard suit inside the torpedo tube, listening to the various reports over his comm implant. He didn't place too much reliance on the sensors. He had a strong feeling the alien ship was still perfectly capable of keeping its secrets to itself. Uncomfortable, he shifted as best he could. He was lying face-down, the shoulders of his hard suit brushing against the steel walls of the torpedo tubes; he barely had room to twitch his fingers, never mind attend to the itch that was building up with slow malevolent intensity between his shoulderblades. Normally he had to wear a hard suit only half a dozen times in a year, and this was the second time in a day. He sighed deeply and ran through his suit's built-in diagnostics again. Anything to keep his mind occupied. As soon as the *Dauntless* got close enough, he was going to be fired out of the torpedo tube towards the alien ship, and he wasn't looking forward to it one bit, even if it had been his own idea. The alien vessel had no entry port he could fly a pinnace to, and blowing a hole in it big enough to dock a pinnace might have had all kinds of unpleasant consequences. That just left climbing into a hard suit and knocking on the door the hard way.

Silence sighed again, and wished he'd made time to visit the toilet first. The suit's facilities were efficient but primitive. The inside of his helmet had nothing to show him but the inside of the torpedo tube and whatever displays he felt like calling up. It felt like he'd been stuck in the tube for hours, but the suit's timer, blinking officiously low on his left, insisted it had been barely twenty minutes. Silence wondered idly if this were what the inside of a coffin looked like, and then rather wished he hadn't.

'Captain, *Dauntless* is in position,' said the Second-in-Command's voice suddenly in his ear. 'Launching now.'

Silence had an almost overpowering urge to say *No, stop, I've changed my mind,* but then pressure exploded around him and he was shot out of the torpedo tube and into space.

The stars were very bright. They whirled around him in dizzy arcs, then settled down as the hard suit oriented itself and its computers locked on to the alien ship. The rocket pack on his back kicked in, nudging him towards the alien craft with a series of carefully considered bursts. The huge white ball hung silently before him, blank and ominous. This close, the tangled strands of webbing looked more like thick twisting cables. It all seemed disturbingly organic. Alive. And quite possibly not nearly as damaged as it was pretending to be.

He could see the blistered areas increasingly clearly as he drifted closer. They were jagged pits in the sickly white surface, going deeper than his suit's augmented vision could follow. The ragged edges of the broken cables hung limply, unmoving – or were they? Silence frowned, and studied them closely. He kept thinking he saw some of them twitching just on the edge of his vision, but, when he looked at them straight, they were still.

Frost came into view beside him, and his sensors told him the dozen marines were spread out around him in a narrow curve. Their presence was immediately reassuring, and he began to breathe a little more easily. He hadn't spent much time in open space since his cadet days at the Academy, and he'd forgotten how cold and lonely it could be. Golgotha lay below him, great and golden and giving him at least a sense of up and down, but the sheer size of space was horribly intimidating, and, lovely though the stars were, they were a hell of a long way off. And, if anything were to go wrong with his suit, he could end up dying in a variety of unpleasant ways.

But nothing *was* going to go wrong. The suit's diagnostics said everything was fine, and its computers would get him to the alien ship far more safely than he could have managed on his own. At which point he would no doubt encounter some really disgusting alien lifeforms, more than ready to kill him in even worse ways. Join the Imperial Navy and see the universe. He smiled despite himself. He'd still rather be here than stuck helplessly back on the bridge, worrying about what Frost and the marines were getting into.

He concentrated on the alien ship as it grew steadily larger. It filled space before him, expanding like a small planet as he drifted towards its surface. The white cables were thicker than a landing craft and impossibly long, stretching away in each direction, and pocked with small and large holes, as though something had been gnawing on them. Silence found that thought disturbing. What the hell could the alien craft have encountered, in its long travels through the Darkvoid, that had actually tried to eat it? He put the idea out of his mind and concentrated on his landing.

Silence, Frost and the marines drifted down on to the surface of the alien ship like so many seeds settling on a forest floor, and collected on the edge of one of the holes the *Dauntless* had blasted in the outer surface of the ship. It was a good thirty feet across and went down at least a hundred feet. There was no telling how much deeper it went: the hard suits' sensors couldn't follow that far, though they should have been able to. Silence checked his other instruments. No ambient heat from the hole, no radioactivity, no magnetic fields, and only low traces of gravity – maybe one-tenth homeworld level. Whatever secrets the alien ship possessed, it was keeping jealously to itself.

Silence activated his comm implant. '*Dauntless*, this is the captain. Do you hear me?'

'Loud and clear, Captain,' said Cross immediately. 'Sensors are locked on your position, and we have full telemetry on your hard suits. Wherever you go once you're inside the alien craft, we'll be able to follow your movements and advise you.'

'I feel safer already,' said Frost. 'Keep your guns trained, Cross. Whatever happens, this ship is not to be allowed to escape. You will prevent such an escape with all means necessary, whatever the cost. Is that clear?'

'Captain?' said Cross uncertainly.

'Do as the Investigator says,' Silence said harshly. 'She's the expert here. If it comes down to the bottom line, we're all expendable – the Investigator and I perhaps a little more so than the others. We're going in now.' He addressed the away team. 'Let's all stick together, people. And, whatever we find inside this ship, don't get distracted. I want information, not dead heroes. Investigator, if you'd care to lead the way, we can get this show on the road.'

'Of course, Captain.'

Frost stepped off the edge fo the pit and began to fall slowly down into the great hole the *Dauntless* had made, helped on her way by short bursts from her backpack. Silence followed

103

her, and one by one the marines came after him, in a long line of slowly falling bodies. The shoulder lights on their hard suits pushed back the darkness as they fell, but there wasn't much to see. The inside walls of the pit were composed of the same thick white cables, pressed and twisted together. The controlled fall seemed to go on for ages, and then the floor of the pit loomed suddenly up beneath them. Frost touched down first, got her balance, and looked quickly about her, built-in weapons at the ready. Silence joined her a moment later. The massive cables, bulging around him like waves in a frozen sea, didn't give beneath his feet at all. The marines drifted down around him, dropping out of the gloom like great silver snowflakes. They landed easily, with casual skill, and moved out to form a defensive circle around Silence and the Investigator, who was thoughtfully studying the floor of the pit.

'Interesting,' she said finally. 'We hit this ship with everything we had. When its shields went down, the outer skin of the hull, or whatever the hell this stuff is, took the full brunt of disrupter cannon firing at virtually point-blank range. Solid steel would have melted and run like water, where it didn't immediately evaporate. But I can't find any trace of heat or structural damage.

'Self-regenerating?' said Silence, and the Investigator shrugged.

'Maybe. If it is, it's far beyond anything we've got. And why just repair the walls? Why not seal over the hole?'

'Because they knew we'd be coming, and they wanted to control where we landed,' said Silence. 'The word "trap" suggests itself to me. Ideas?'

'Blast a way to the interior,' said Frost. 'I brought enough shaped charges to blow a path through a small moon. Once we're inside, we'll see if anyone comes to complain about the noise.'

'If you're going to start messing about with explosives, I am getting myself and my men out of here,' Silence said firmly. 'I never met an Investigator yet who understood the concept of subtlety when it came to explosives.'

Then he broke off to look sharply at the wall beside them.

Two of the thick white cables were twisting slowly apart to form a tunnel leading deeper into the ship. Frost leaned in cautiously, her suit lights illuminating the tunnel as far as they could. It seemed entirely empty. Silence tried his suit's sensors, but they weren't picking up anything: as far as they were concerned, the tunnel might not have been there.

'Silence to *Dauntless*. You picking up anything your end?'

'We're patched into your suits' comm signals, Captain,' Cross murmured in his ear. 'We can see everything you can. But long-range sensors have nothing to add. I can say we're not picking up any life signs yet. We've heard from Golgotha starport; they're still too busy putting themselves back together to be able to offer us any help. The good news is that the six starcruisers that went chasing off after the Hadenman ship apparently lost contact with it. They're on their way back. Should be here in just under an hour.'

'Well, that's something, I suppose.' Silence turned to Frost. 'Your call, Investigator. Do we go in?'

'Into a possible trap, maybe crammed with murderous aliens? Of course, Captain. Nothing to be gained standing around her.'

'I had a feeling you were going to say that. All right; lead the way. Marines, stay close behind us. Be ready to fire at a moment's notice, but exercise caution. There's always the chance we might find the missing personnel from Gehenna Base in here somewhere. I'd like to get them out of here alive, if at all possible. Lead on, Investigator.'

Frost stepped carefully into the tunnel, and moved further in, step by step. Silence and the marines came after her. The cables making up the tunnel's inner walls were smoother and thinner, but just as unyielding to the touch. Their white colour had thin blue traces in it, like veins. Silence increased the magnification of what he was seeing, and the wall seemed to leap towards him. The cables were pulsing slightly in a regular rhythm. He stepped the view back to normal, and touched the wall with the tips of his steel fingers. The built-in sensors detected no warmth of life, only a faint stickiness. The walls were rounded, like the floor and the ceiling, as though he and his team were walking through the bowels of some enormous beast. And maybe they were, at that. Silence glanced back over his shoulder, to see how the marines were coping, and only then realized that the tunnel had closed itself off behind them. The cables had fitted together again, thick and impenetrable. He quickly alerted the others, and they spun round to see for themselves. Frost was all for going back and blasting it with her disrupters, but Silence stopped her.

'Let's follow the tunnel first. See where it leads. We can always come back and blast it later. *Dauntless*, have you followed what's happened here?'

There was nothing but quiet in his ears.

'Hello, *Dauntless*? Do you hear me?'

He listened hard, but all he could hear was his own breathing. 'Investigator, see if you can raise them.'

Frost tried, and then the marines, to no avail. She growled something under her breath, and turned to Silence. 'It's not the suits. All the diagnostics check out. Something's blocking the signal. We're on our own, Captain.'

'Not for the first time. Press on, Investigator. I don't think the occupants of this ship let us in just to hold us here. I think . . . they're expecting us.'

Frost sniffed loudly and led the way again. As they penetrated further into the ship the cables continued to open before them, creating more tunnel, and closed off behind them to prevent them turning back. Silence and his people moved in a travelling pocket within the webbing.

The cables varied even more in size now, and there were other changes too. The corpse-white cables swirled around and over each other, tangled together beyond sense or meaning, some little thicker than a finger. But the floor was no different, and more than ever Silence felt as if he were walking on a spider's web, sending out rhythmic signals of where he was and where he was going. The impression grew stronger as the strands grew increasingly sticky to the touch. It got harder to pull his boots free from the floor, and soon only the power of the hard suit's servomechanisms kept him going.

Strange lights pulsed within the rounded tunnel walls, coming and going so quickly it was difficult to decide what colour they might have been – sometimes Silence thought they weren't any colour he'd ever seen before. But still there was no sign of any construction or device, any sign at all of whatever crewed the alien ship.

The tunnel puckered in suddenly from all sides, so that the away team had to crawl through on their hands and knees in single file. When they rose to their feet on the other side of the constriction they found themselves in a great, egg-shaped chamber, with a high ceiling and smooth polished walls. Dark shapes and oddities, carefully formed but enigmatic in meaning, budded out from the floor and walls. Frost snapped out a warning not to touch them, which Silence for one found completely superfluous. He wouldn't have touched any of them on a bet. For no reason he could pin down, his mind kept throwing up an image of himself stuck helplessly to one of the dark shapes while the chamber filled slowly with digestive juices. Yet again he was sweating inside the hard suit, despite its cool air-conditioning.

They moved on through the vast chamber, stepping slowly and carefully, touching nothing, and finally left it through another of the puckered holes. Beyond lay more tunnels, opening before them and closing after them, and further chambers studded with various shapes, none of them immediately comprehensible to the human mind.

Finally the away team encountered another, smaller chamber, and discovered what had happened to the missing Gehenna Base personnel.

The chamber was some hundred feet in diameter. Its walls were pockmarked in rows both vertical and horizontal, and a thin layer of vapour covered the floor, beading wetly on the hard suits' armour. There was light of a kind, a harsh unforgiving blue-white glare that seemed to come from nowhere and everywhere at once. Long flat slabs of some unfamiliar metal were scattered across the floor, just above the vapour, and on those slabs, held firmly by some unseen force, were the remains of the base personnel. Some were only parts – organs and limbs and faces. A dozen complete torsos had been messily vivisected, and, from the expressions on the faces of the few heads that remained attached, Silence had no doubt at all that these men and women had been alive and aware when the vivisection began. Anywhere else he might have felt sick, for all his experience, but right now he was too full of rage and fury for anything else.

'They'll die for this,' said Frost, in a calm, cold voice. 'Every living thing on this ship shall pay in blood and suffering.'

The marines stirred restlessly, looking this way and that for something to aim their weapons at.

Silence knew how they felt, but kept an icy control on his anger. 'You can kill the aliens only after the specialists have squeezed every drop of information out of them, Investigator. Until then, I want captives, not corpses. Marines, remember your orders. Minimum force only, unless in life-threatening situations. Use your own judgement, but you'd better be prepared to back it up later. There will be a time for vengeance, but we must have the information this ship holds. We might have to face more of its kind in the future.'

'Don't lecture me,' said Frost. 'I know my duty.'

'Sorry, Investigator. Just speaking for the record. There's nothing more we can do here. Mark this chamber's location on your suits' maps, and we'll move on. We can send people in to retrieve the bodies later. Right now, we have to find the control section. I want this ship immobilized and helpless before it can finish its repairs. I also want a good look at the crew, and more and more it seems the only place we can be sure of finding them is at the control centre. They wouldn't dare abandon that.'

He led the way across the chamber, moving carefully between the crimson spread-eagled bodies on the slabs, trying hard not to look at them. It was easier to control his anger that way.

It seemed to take forever to reach the opening on the far wall, but as he drew near it puckered shut in a mass of solid, tightly packed cables. Silence prodded it here and there with his steel fingers, but it didn't give anywhere. He hadn't thought it would. He hit it once with his fist, and then turned back to the others. Their featureless steel helmets seemed to be staring at him.

Slowly, and without any fuss, the light was going out. The slabs, with their grisly specimens, began to disappear into rising vapour. It didn't take much imagination on Silence's part to picture the alien crew massing on the other side of the closed portal.

'Marines, I believe we are now quite definitely in a life-threatening situation. Feel free to shoot anything that moves that isn't us. I'd like a few specimens left alive, just a few – so, if anything runs, let it. Investigator, make an opening here.'

Frost aimed her armoured right hand at the closed opening, and the disrupter built into the glove blasted a ten-foot-wide hole through the tightly-packed webbing. A sickly green light spilled into the chamber, and everyone braced themselves for an attack that never came. Silence and Frost edged forward and peered through the opening. Hanging ends of ruptured cables hung twitching and jumping on every side, but showed no signs of knitting themselves together. They pattered weakly against the hard suits, but did no harm. Beyond the opening lay a narrow milky white tunnel with smooth, faintly glowing walls. There was no sign of any enemy.

'I'll take the lead again,' said Frost. 'This is Investigator business.'

'Couldn't agree more,' said Silence. 'After you.'

Frost stepped through into the narrow tunnel, her gauntlets, with their built-in guns, held out before her. Silence followed, and the marines brought up the rear. The floor of the tunnel lurched disturbingly under their weight, as though it might rupture at any moment and spill them into whatever lay waiting below; Silence, as he pressed on, tried hard to ignore it. He'd lost all track of where he was in relation to the ship's exterior. He wasn't actually lost – the suit had kept a record of all his twists and turns, and could easily lead him back – but he still didn't know precisely where he was; he just had the powerful impression he was getting deeper and deeper in, being lured remorselessly towards the dark heart of the alien craft. He checked his air supply, but he'd barely made a dent in it so far. Theoretically the rebreather could keep him alive for up to a week. Under normal conditions.

He deliberately didn't finish that thought, and instead studied the tunnel walls to either side of him. They were flat and smooth, not cabled – more like membranes. They pulsed and fluctuated to no apparent purpose, and waves of pale colour briefly tinged the milky white, like passing thoughts or dreams.

The passage was shrinking, slowly but inexorably. Silence used his suit's sensors to measure the diameter, and compared it to the size it had been when they had entered. He frowned at the answer, and calculated how long it would be before the tunnel grew too small for his team to continue. He liked that answer even less. At the present rate of progress, four minutes and thirty-seven seconds. No buts or maybes.

'Investigator, marines: stop right where you are.'

They did so. Frost didn't look round, but he knew she could see him quite clearly in the displays inside her helmet. Silence measured the tunnel behind him again with his suit's sensors, and wasn't at all surprised to discover that it had narrowed beyond the point where they could pass back through it.

'I was wondering when you'd notice,' said Frost. 'It would appear the aliens have us where they want us. Shall I blast a way forward?'

'What the hell?' said Silence. 'When in doubt, make a loud noise. Let someone know we're here and not at all happy about it.'

Frost aimed her built-in disrupters at the narrow tunnel before her, and the white walls split apart in a hundred places. Insects beyond counting burst in on the away team. The bugs ranged in size from many-legged creatures the size of a fist, which swarmed all over the hard suits looking for weak spots and entry points, to huge bulky things with their own armour and vicious pincer claws. The tunnel was briefly full of flashing disrupter bolts, and insects fried as the tunnel walls blew apart, but once the guns fell silent the away team disappeared beneath a writhing mass of clattering insect life. Tiny beasts swarmed over his suits' sensors, and Silence was suddenly blind. He tried to brush the insects away with his powerful steel hands, but there were just too many of them. Warnings flashed up before his eyes as acid began to eat into his armoured joints, threatening the hard suit's integrity. Screams sounded in his ears – as far as he could gather, the insects had invaded a marine's armour and begun to eat him alive.

'Frost!' said Silence. 'You still have those explosives?'

'Enough to blow us all to hell, if that's what you want.'

'I was thinking more of just enough to blow the insects to shit without rupturing our suits. Think you can manage that?'

'No problem. Brace yourself.'

When it came, the explosion was powerful enough that the inner screen of Silence's helmet was briefly filled with a dozen warnings. They faded one by one.

He brushed vaguely at himself, and sight and sound returned as dead insects fell away and the sensors were cleared. The tunnel hung in tatters around them.

Beyond lay the secret of the alien ship – the vast, imposing shape of the Queen of the alien hive.

She filled the space outside the wrecked tunnel, a great bloated sac of living tissue, hundreds of yards across; living walls of pale pulsating flesh were studded here and there with black, lidless eyes. Ridiculously small limbs protruded in places, atrophied remnants of a forgotten earlier life. Metal instruments and gleaming cables plunged into her great flesh from all around, as though she had been built into the ship – or it had been grown around her.

Silence tore his gaze away, focusing on what was nearer to him. The swarming insects had been blasted by the force of the explosion. Dead and injured alien forms lay everywhere, some twitching feebly. Silence had no doubt that more were already on their way. Eight of the marines were still standing, looking numbly to him for instructions. The Investigator had eyes only for the Queen. Silence checked the four fallen

111

marines for life signs, but he knew what he'd find before he started. Their suits had ruptured from the combination of the explosion and insect damage. Four good men lost to the aliens.

Silence looked up sharply as his suit's sensors picked up scrabbling sounds, drawing nearer.

'Investigator, more insects on the way. Recommendations?'

'Hit the Queen. She's the heart and mind of them all.'

'You heard the Investigator, marines. Hit the Queen with everything you've got.'

Vivid light seared from the away team's disrupters and blasted away great chunks of the Queen's body. The pale flesh boiled and vaporized and blew apart, only to seal itself together again in moments. The Queen was just too big for them, too huge for even energy weapons to do any real damage. She towered over them oppressively.

Suddenly, from everywhere at once, lesser aliens came swarming into what was left of the tunnel. There seemed to be no end to the living wave, and Silence knew that this time no weapon he had at his command would be enough to stop them. They would just keep coming until their sheer numbers overwhelmed the away team, and he'd die then, if he were lucky.

Damn. More good men lost. Frost. I wish . . .

And then everything changed. The enigmatic gift he'd acquired from the Madness Maze blazed brightly in his mind and Frost's, and they were linked again, mind to mind, soul to soul. A vast, incomprehensible roar filled their heads, the alien thoughts of a million insects, and thundering through it like a great heart-beat were the commands of the Queen.

It took Silence and Frost only a moment to patch into the roar of the mass mind, seize control and impose their own commands upon it. The insect tide turned away from their human prey and fell upon the Queen. They swarmed all over her gigantic body and began to consume her.

The last thing Silence and Frost heard before the link broke and they fell back into their own heads again was the screaming of the Queen. They both grinned savagely.

Once more merely human, Frost and Silence looked at each other. They couldn't see each other's faces, but they didn't need to. Silence glanced briefly at the marines watching the insects devour their own Queen, and decided explanations could wait. He activated his comm implant and accessed Frost on the command channel.

'It's not the same as the creature we found on Unseeli,' Frost said calmly. 'And it's nothing like what those poor bastards found on Wolf IV. So what exactly have we got here? The creators of those killer aliens in the Vaults on Grendel? Or the ancient enemy the Grendel Sleepers were constructed to fight? Or something else entirely?'

'Beats the hell out of me,' said Silence. 'Let the specialists worry about it. We need to talk, Frost. This . . . link of ours. It's getting stronger. I don't know how much longer we can keep it hidden.'

'We have to,' said Frost. 'They mustn't know what really happened here. They'd reclassify us as espers. Strip us of our rank. Turn us into lab rats. I'd rather die than live like that.'

'There's always the underground.'

'Not for us.'

'No,' agreed Silence, 'not for us. Aliens like these could return at any time, and only a strong and undivided Empire can hope to stand against them. So we'll keep quiet about what happened here. Act like it's a mystery to us, too. Lionstone doesn't need to know.'

'On the other hand,' Frost said thoughtfully, 'Lionstone has actually been really quite lucky here today. With the Fleet gone and the planet's defences in disarray, Golgotha was practically without a hope. If we hadn't turned up when we did, the alien ship could have destroyed half the damn' planet. We saved her Imperial ass. Could be she'll be grateful – grateful enough to overlook our recent failures. What do you think?'

'Not a chance,' said Silence.

CHAPTER THREE

Drowning Men

Finlay Campbell, outlaw and terrorist, once the most fabled fop and dandy of his age – and under another name secretly the Masked Gladiator, darling of the bloodthirsty Arena fans – hung upside-down on the end of his rope and wondered if perhaps he were getting a little too old for heroics. Spread out below him lay the wide streets and bristling avenues of Golgotha's main city, the Parade of the Endless. It took its name from the endless supply of would-be heroes who came thronging every year to try their strength and courage in the Arena. The aristocracy lived in the city, too, in their tightly guarded pastel towers, because after all this was the very best place to be, to see and be seen, in all the Empire – apart from Lionstone's Court in the Imperial Palace, but you went there only when summoned. If you were wise, you made out your will before you went. Just in case.

Finlay decided that his thoughts were drifting in unnecessary directions. Hanging upside-down with the blood rushing to your head does that to you. He sighed, reached up and took a firm grip on his line, and hauled himself back up, hand over hand, until he reached a convenient resting place on the side of Tower Silvestri. Luckily the Silvestri Family went in for rococo design, so that the sides of their Tower were crusted with hundreds of niches and unexpected curves, full of ugly little statues with exaggerated genitals and faces only a mother could love. Finlay squeezed in beside a particularly well endowed gargoyle with a case of dyspepsia, and got his breath back. All this time and trouble, just to climb a hundred-and-twenty-foot tower. Definitely getting past it. Be taking milk in his coffee next.

If it hadn't been for his safety line he'd have made a really nasty splotch on the ground below. That was what you got for hurrying. Normally he'd have known better, but he'd fallen behind schedule. His own fault: he'd stopped off on the way to the tower to enjoy a good meal at a decent restaurant. Nowhere fashionable – he couldn't afford to be recognized. Since his Clan had fallen prey to an extremely hostile takeover by Clan Wolfe, he'd been forced to flee for his life, and the only people he could flee to had been the clone and esper underground, who were fine when it came to courage and ideals and sticking it to authority, but rather lacking in the comforts department. In particular, Finlay missed the excellent cuisine to which his position had entitled him. While never exactly an epicure, he knew what he liked: soup so clear you could swim in it; meat served very rare (in fact, just kill the beast, dismember it, wave the meat in the direction of the fireplace and then slap it down in front of him, that was all he asked); a few out-of-season vegetables, just for bulk and fibre; and finally a disgustingly sticky sweet. Heaven – absolute heaven.

He'd been denied it for so long, and the smells wafting out of the little tucked-away bistro had proved just too tempting. A quick glance at the watchface embedded in his wrist had assured him he was well ahead of schedule, so . . . he had allowed himself to be weak. He hadn't looked at his watch again until after his third helping of dessert, and then was horrified to see how much time had flown while he'd been indulging himself. He'd dropped a handful of coins on the table and run out the door like a man ashamed of the tip he was leaving. He'd got to the base of Tower Silvestri with aching lungs, a stitch in his side and his recent meal rumbling rebelliously in his stomach. It was a wonder the guards hadn't heard him. He'd followed the agreed-upon approach, slipping between patrols, and thrown himself at the side of the tower like a sailor visiting his wife.

He checked his watch again: he was cutting things very

115

fine. He worked on his breathing, slowing it determinedly back to normal as he stared out over the city. The pastel towers stretched away in all directions, a forest of metal and glass and alien stone, gleaming prettily in the sunlight. He turned to glance at his reflection in the mirrored steel behind. He needn't have worried about anyone recognizing him in the bistro: he didn't look at all like he once had. In his glory days he'd resembled nothing so much as a multicoloured bird of paradise, dressed always in the brightest silks that current styles allowed. Tall and graceful and fashionable to the very moment, from his polished leather thigh-boots to his velvet cap. On his last visit to Court, with his fluorescent face and metallicized hair, he had worn a long cutaway frock coat that had showed off his exquisite figure and a jewelled pince-nez he didn't need, and everyone there had bowed to him as one of the not-so-secret masters of fashion. Now he wore a loose-fitting thermal suit with a chameleon circuit that took on the colours of his surroundings.

The face in the reflection could have been anyone. No cosmetics to camouflage a minor defect or bring out the bone structure. No bright colours to loudly announce status and rank, or attract the attention of other proud peacocks. Finlay's face these days was thin and drawn, with deep lines accentuating the mouth and eyes. He was just twenty-five and looked at least ten years older. His long hair was a yellow so pale it was almost colourless: at Court it had shone a bright metallic bronze, curled and bouncing over his shoulders, but now it hung limp and lifeless, and he didn't care. He wore a simple leather headband to keep it out of his eyes. He knew he should cut his hair short – it would be much more practical – but somehow he couldn't bring himself to do that. It would be too much like cutting his last link with the person he had once been.

Finlay smiled briefly, and the man in the reflection smiled back, but Finlay still didn't recognize him. That man looked rough and hard-used, and very, very dangerous. His eyes were cold and careful, and his smile had only a sad humour in it. He could have been an ex-soldier or a mercenary, hired muscle for sale to anyone with the right price. He had the look of that most dangerous of men – someone with nothing left to lose.

No, he thought firmly, and made himself turn away. He still had his love for Evangeline, and the new cause he'd embraced. As a noble, he'd never thought about the lot of those in the social strata beneath him, let alone the unpeople, the clones and the espers at the very bottom of the heap. Then he had come face-to-face with the horrors of Silo Nine, known also as Wormboy Hell, where rogue espers were imprisoned, tortured and eventually executed, and what he saw there had changed him forever. Now he fought for justice for all, and, if he couldn't have that, he'd settle for revenge.

Which was what had brought him to Tower Silvestri. He forced himself to his feet and began climbing again. His arms and legs trembled from the strain, but they'd get him where he had to go. The underground had offered him a choice of stimulants, chemical miracles to put a little pep into a tired man's muscles, but he'd turned them down. He'd never needed chemical courage in the Arena. He laughed breathlessly as he flung himself on, clambering over jutting gargoyles and howling stone faces like a swift-moving shadow, his chameleon suit blending him seamlessly into the background.

Maybe after this the Silvestri Family would take the time to rethink their image. Rococo was all very well and picturesque, but it made sneak missions like this a breeze. On a high-tech building like Tower Shreck, with its featureless walls of steel and glass, he would have been spotted in a minute. But, like everyone else, both Clans put their faith in extensive security systems – which, to be fair, were all you really needed most of the time. They were more than enough to see off your average thief, spy or industrial saboteur – enough to keep out anyone, unless you happened to have the backing of those cunning cybernetic anarchists, the cyberats, bless their dark little hacking hearts, who were currently feeding Tower Silvestri's systems a bunch of comforting lies.

He reached the end of his line and stopped to lean companionably on the forbidding stone statue of some noted

Silvestri ancestor. He pulled up the line and wound it securely round his waist. He'd come almost as far as he needed. Just as well, given the state of his aching arms and legs and the cold sheen of sweat on his face. He scowled, breathing deeply. He'd built his muscles as a gladiator in the Arena, and despite his recent enforced absence from the killing sands he prided himself that he was still in damned good shape. The climb alone would have killed a lesser man. He flexed the muscles in his arms and legs, blocking out the pain. He was almost there. Just a little further. He swung carefully out and round the stone statue, and made his way slowly across the face of the tower, finding handholds and footholds where he could. Forget the pain building in his muscles and back. Forget the precarious holds, the gusting wind and the long drop down. Just climb, foot by careful foot, and concentrate on his mission and the kill at the end.

For most of his adult life, the world had known Finlay Campbell only as a fop and a dandy, highly visible at Court, and a constant disappointment to his renowned warrior father. No one had known of his secret second life as the Masked Gladiator, undefeated champion of the Golgotha Arena, except the man who trained him and the woman who loved him. When circumstances had forced him to flee for his life, Finlay had had to reveal to the underground his prowess as a fighter: it had been the only coin he had possessed with which to buy their acceptance. There was no room among them for passengers – particularly if you were neither clone nor esper but merely human. They had sent him on a mission, alone and unsupported, to prove himself or die, and when he came back trailing blood and victory they shrugged and allowed him his place among them. But, though they knew him as a fighter, he had never told them about the Masked Gladiator. They didn't need to know that.

He also hadn't told them about the constant burning need for action, violence and sudden death that had driven him to the Arena in the first place. There were times when it seemed to him that he felt really alive only when he was killing someone. Evangeline Shreck had silenced or at least pacified that need when she was with him, and their love had been all he had desired, but their time together had only ever been one of snatched momerts. Their Families had been at daggers drawn for generations, and both young lovers had always known that they could never hope for a future together. Somehow that foreknowledge had fanned the flames of their love rather than diminished it, and the man who had once lived only to kill lived instead for the moments of peace he found in her arms.

But now he dwelt down below, in the underground, and she had returned to the world above, to Tower Shreck and her awful father. Her position and connections among the occupants of the pastel towers made her too valuable to the underground for her to be excused for long. So they had held each other one last time and tried not to cry, saying goodbye in choked voices. He went with her as far as he could, and then stopped and watched her walk away until she disappeared into the distance. They'd promised each other they'd be together again, but neither of them had really believed it. Happy endings were for other people. Finlay Campbell had walked back to the unpeople alone, and, if a part of him died that day, he kept it to himself. It didn't interfere with his being the killer the underground needed for their ongoing struggle.

He'd never been much interested in politics, and never would be, but he had developed a grudging respect for the rebels. He didn't have anything much in common with them: he had nothing to say to them, and didn't understand or care about what interested them. They thought he was naive, and he thought they were boring. He also spent a lot of time sulking because he no longer had access to the pretty clothes and sparkling parties that had so distracted him when he wasn't in the Arena. The underground didn't have time for non-essentials like fashion or parties. When he wasn't sulking, Finlay tended to brood about the destruction of his Clan, the triumph of his enemies the Wolfes, and what Evangeline was doing without him. All in all, he was a pain in the ass most of the time, and knew it, and didn't give a damn. So the underground did their best to keep him busy with missions, for both their sakes. It wasn't difficult. The rebels had a lot of enemies, and Finlay had his endless need for a little action. It was hard to tell which of them was the more surprised that he kept coming back alive.

This mission was pretty typical. The underground had marked a powerful and particularly vocal opponent for death, and Finlay was to be their instrument. This time the target and intended victim was the notorious Lord William St John, second-in-command to the Lord High Dram himself and therefore constantly surrounded by a small army of well armed guards and high-tech security. He never moved in public without his people covering the ground in advance for miles around, nor without a portable force screen for emergencies and his own personal flyer to carry him everywhere. Completely untouchable. Unless you were mad, desperate or supremely skilled. Like Finlay, who was all three at various times, according to his needs. Which was why he was currently crawling up the side of Tower Silvestri like a tiny grey spider, hopefully unnoticed by all.

He finally reached the relatively deep recess he'd spotted earlier on the architectural plans the cyberats had dug up, and pulled himself into it. There was just room for him to curl up into a ball and still keep a weather eye on the scene below. He was about a hundred and twenty feet up, and snug as a bug in a rug. Waiting. Lord William St John would be here soon, according to the underground. Billy Boy the bully boy, whose word was death for clones and espers and anyone else who got in his way. Billy the Butcher, hated and reviled by practically everyone but entirely untouchable because of his position. The Empress was said to be quite fond of him.

And he was coming here, to Tower Silvestri, stopping off with his armoured entourage to pay his compliments to his friend and ally Lord Silvestri on his way to the official opening of a new orphanage nearby. Appropriate really, given how many orphans St John and his people had created over the last few years. Since Dram had become the Empress's official consort, as well as Warrior Prime, he'd had to delegate most of his duties in the field to his second-in-command, St John. Billy Boy had taken over the pursuit and persecution of potential rebels and the execution of rogue clones and espers, and did it all with great efficiency and even greater gusto. Blood and death followed in his wake, and he was never known to bring in his prey alive. Cruelty and slaughter were his pastimes, and mercy was not in him. The underground had voted unanimously for his death. St John's execution would send a message to the Imperial Palace that could not be ignored.

No one would weep for his passing, not even his own kind. Of late, St John had taken to playing politics, seeking to improve his position to something more than just the Lord High Dram's shadow. He had gone about it with his usual vim and venom, and made enemies among his rivals with sneering abandon.

But opening a new orphanage was safe and uncontroversial, and bound to get St John good publicity. The man of action with a soft spot for big-eyed children. Couldn't fail. All the big holo networks would be there. Finlay grinned. They didn't know it, but they were in for some of their best-ever ratings.

Finlay hadn't missed the similarities between himself and St John. They were both men with a need for blood and death, and a willingness to get their hands dirty in the process. As soldiers in a war together they'd have been heroes, feted by all, with medals and commendations. They'd have been comrades, perhaps even friends – sitting around a roaring fire in winter, with drinks in their hands, toasting old campaigns and lost comrades. But, as it was, the two were on different sides. And the similarities between Finlay and St John just made it that much more of a challenge.

Finlay looked up sharply. He could hear the publicity circus approaching. A brass band led the way, marching down the street in full ceremonial uniform, playing something pointedly martial and patriotic. After them came a full company of St John's private guards, conditioned by mind-techs to be loyal unto death, surrounding a small personal flyer on which St John stood tall and proud, smiling and waving to the crowds that packed the street. Finlay sniffed, unimpressed. The crowds had appeared with suspicious speed. One might almost think they'd been paid to gather in just the right place to impress the holo cameras.

St John was looking good in his everyday uniform with no decorations. Nice touch, that – meant to suggest that at heart he was just one of the boys, just another soldier doing his job. He was tall and broad-shouldered, with a barrel chest and a handsome face: the best the body shops could supply. And, if his smile was a little practised and his eyes a little cold, well, people were used to that in politicians.

Finlay ignored the man, concentrating instead on his flyer. It was really nothing more than a large personalized gravity sled with extra armour, decorated so lavishly with precious metalwork and studded jewels that even Finlay's taste was faintly appalled. You needed style to bring off that kind of excess, and Finlay had a strong suspicion St John wouldn't know style if it walked up to him on the street and bit his nose. Just another reason to kill him and put him out of everyone else's misery.

The air was shimmering slightly around the flyer because of the force screens generated by the craft to ensure that onlookers kept a respectful distance. The screens were strong enough to turn aside an energy beam, or the blast from an explosion. St John's security people knew their business. However, force shields kept out everything. Including air. So the shields covered only the sides of the craft, leaving the top open to let St John breathe. It wasn't much of a risk. At the first sight of a flyer or gravity sled approaching from above, the top could be sealed instantly and maintained for as long as it took – within reason – for the potential threat to pass. No problem. Unless of course there was no flyer, no gravity sled. Just one man crouching precariously in a recess in the wall of a tower.

Finlay grinned. He'd spotted the opening the moment the underground had explained St John's security setup to him. Attack from above was thought to be impossible, given the surrounding towers' security systems, but even the most sophisticated instruments could be fooled or bypassed by a man willing to take risks, a man who didn't care whether he lived or died. The openness of that thought shocked Finlay for a moment, mostly because it was true: he could live without a Family or his place in society, but he couldn't go on much longer without Evangeline. Events were conspiring to keep them apart, possibly forever, and a life without Evangeline wasn't worth a damn to him. Then he looked down at the entourage moving into place below, and his smile widened again into a death's-head grin. Someone was going to die soon.

St John stopped his flyer before the tower's main entrance, directly beneath Finlay, and prepared to begin his speech. All Finlay had to do was draw his gun and shoot the little toad through the head.

Except, of course, that would have been far too easy. Finlay Campbell had a reputation to uphold.

And he liked to get his hands dirty.

A flick of his hand was all it took to send his rope darting down the side of the tower until it hung unsuspected over St John's head. It had the same elusive qualities as his chameleon suit, and was to all intents and purposes invisible, even to security systems. Finlay eased himself out of his concealing niche, clinging tightly to his rope, and leaned out over the long drop. He paused, savouring the moment, and then pushed himself away from the side of the tower, sliding down the rope with gathering speed. Leather gloves protected his hands from the growing friction. Wisps of heated smoke escaped between his fingers as he hurtled down, but he waited until the very last moment to clasp his hands shut, slowing his descent. He freed one hand and drew the dagger from his belt. At the last moment St John must have heard or sensed something. He looked up, and it was the simplest thing in the world for Finlay to let go of the rope, drop down and stab St John neatly through the eye.

The Lord convulsed, his arms flying wide, but he was already dead. Finlay hit the deck of the flyer hard, his leg muscles absorbing the impact. He jerked the dagger out of St John's ruined eye in a gush of blood, and Billy Boy slumped bonelessly to the deck, twitching and shuddering. The flyer was still rocking from the impact of Finlay's sudden arrival, and the handful of guards on the flyer with St John were too busy trying to regain their balance to put up much of a defence when Finlay tore into them with his sword and his dagger and his death's-head grin. He swung his sword in short, chopping arcs, doing the most damage possible without risking the blade getting caught in flesh or clothing. He laughed, cutting down the disoriented guards with brutal professionalism, and, if sometimes their blades came too close for comfort, he couldn't care less. He was in his element, doing what he had been born to do, and loving it.

His sword slammed into a guard's gut and out again in a flurry of blood, and the blade rose quickly to parry a blow from another guard that would have taken his head off. Finlay was glad someone was making a fight of it. He threw himself at the guard, and for a moment they stood head-to-head, neither giving ground. Then something in the guard's eyes gave him away, and Finlay flung himself to one side, just as a further guard, behind him, lunged forward. Finlay laughed nastily as the man ran through his comrade, and then he cut the man down from behind while his sword was still trapped in the dead guard's body. There were only three guards left now, and Finlay disposed of them quickly.

He jerked his sword out of the last guard in a welter of blood and looked about him, taking in the situation. He wasn't even breathing hard. Only a few moments had passed since he'd struck St John down, and outside the flyer most of the dead Lord's security people were still trying to figure out some way of getting into the flyer so they could tackle his assassin. The force shields were keeping everyone well back, as they'd been designed to do, and as yet it hadn't occurred to any of them to try climbing Tower Silvestri, as Finlay had. One poor fool fired his disrupter at the flyer, and they all had to duck and dodge as the energy beam ricocheted back. Someone with his wits about him was yelling for extra flyers, and Finlay took that as a sign that it was time for him to leave.

He moved quickly to the flyer's controls, stepping carefully over the bodies, and lifted the vehicle up into the air. A quick glance around showed him more flyers approaching at speed from the south. He sent the captured vehicle weaving quickly in and out of the pastel towers, accelerating rapidly to a speed his pursuers would be hard-pressed to match, assuming they had any sense of self-preservation. He laughed aloud, and stamped his feet on the deck for the simple pleasure of hearing his boots squelch in the pooled blood of his enemies. He'd done it again – made the kill that everyone said was impossible and got away with it. He'd shake off the flyers behind him and escape. He always did. He glanced back at the dead Lord William St John, lying very still with a surprised look on his bloody face, and he laughed again. It sounded loud and confident, and, if it was a crazy kind of laugh as well, Finlay could live with that.

Adrienne Campbell, wife of Finlay and once the scourge of polite company and owner of the biggest, loudest and foulest mouth in all society, sat fuming before her blank viewscreen and wondered who to call next. She'd tried practically everyone she could think of, including some she would have sworn she wasn't talking to, but no one would talk to her. Some made excuses, some were rude, but most just instructed their servants to say that they were not at home, the liars. Adrienne had fallen from grace when the Campbell Clan went down in flames, and she was taking it hard. She was now ostracized from the very society she had once dominated through the sheer strength of her personality. But that was when she had had the power and position of Clan Campbell behind her. Now she was just one of the very few survivors of a broken Clan, and isolated as she'd never been before. Everyone was afraid that what had happened to her might be catching.

Her cousin by marriage, Robert Campbell, had been pro-tected from the fall by his position in the military. The Fleet looked after its own. It was only through his influence and protection that Adrienne had survived the vendetta pursued so viciously and methodically by the triumphant Wolfe Family. Blood had flowed in the streets, with no one to answer the begging for mercy and the screams, but she had been left strictly alone – as long as she didn't interfere. So she had hardened her heart and locked her door, and hadn't answered the desperate knocking that came again and again. They pleaded and threatened and called her name, and some of them cried, and she sat as far away from the door as she could, with her hands over her ears. It didn't help. She could still hear when the Wolfes came to drag the screaming people away. Sometimes they stopped screaming suddenly, and the silence that followed was worse.

Finally the voices stopped coming, and no one knocked at her door any more. Adrienne Campbell was alone. The Wolfes now owned everything the Campbells had, leaving her nothing but a few scraps of personal jewellery. Her credit rating had been revoked. A few very minor Campbell cousins had escaped the bloodbath, usually because they had connections or protection, like Robert, but they wanted nothing to do with her. She didn't blame them. The reign of the House of Campbell was over, in every way that mattered.

Adrienne was of average height and a little less than average weight. Nothing like fear and desperation to back up a restricted diet. In the past few months she'd lost pounds she would have sworn would be with her until the day she died. She couldn't go out to buy food, or even order it through her viewscreen. She had no money. She was dependent on Robert for everything now, and he had his own problems. He still did what he could, bless him. When he could. And, whereas previously she'd proudly worn the latest and most garish outfits society had ever seen, aside from her husband's, she now made do with a wrinkled housecoat of plain, subdued colours. She'd fled for her life without any clothes other than the ones she stood up in. She didn't really miss the garments themselves – she'd only worn most of them to annoy and upstage her fashion-obsessed husband – but it was the principle of the thing. She couldn't bear to think she looked boring. Robert provided her with clothes, when he thought of it, just as he'd provided this bolthole, and like most men he had no taste at all.

She scowled at her reflection in the viewscreen. Adrienne had a sharp face, all planes and sudden angles. Her scarlet mouth was currently compressed into a flat angry line. She had dark, determined eyes, and a ridiculously turned-up nose that had seemed like a good idea at the time. She still had her great mop of curling golden hair, though it looked more than a little distressed at the moment. All in all, she'd looked better.

She sighed, and leaned back in her chair. She was too tired and dispirited even to stay angry for long. How far had she fallen, to end up here, like this? A bedraggled wreck in a dingy apartment, trying to wheedle invitations and support from dull acquaintances and lesser Families she would have disdained only a few months previously. Not that Adrienne was a snob. It had always been a point of pride with her that she despised everyone equally.

Now here she was, trying to improve her position by playing politics with the only card she had left: Finlay. The Wolfes hadn't been able to find him. He'd managed to disappear very thoroughly, which surprised Adrienne. The Finlay she'd known had never been that good at anything. Still, a lot of people wanted him, for reasons they mostly preferred not to discuss, and thought perhaps they could get to him through her, either by bribes or by threats. Adrienne knew nothing, but took their money anyway, and played them along as long as she could with hints and promises before they finally wised up. She ignored the threats. Robert and his friends in the military were protecting her, and everybody knew it. No one was ready to go head-to-head with the Fleet over knowledge they weren't even sure she had. The Fleet had a long memory for insults, and it bore grudges. So Adrienne played her little games, a small fish in a big pond, and tried to avoid being eaten by the sharks.

She assumed she was currently ahead of the game. She was still alive, after all – if you could call this living. She sniffed angrily. She'd spent a lot of time with her thoughts lately, and had come to the uncomfortable conclusion that she didn't like herself much. She was too busy being negative about everything to be positive about anything, even herself. But she knew she was right about this one thing. Adrienne had built her personality quite carefully and deliberately, being hard and harsh and uncompromising, because that was the only way she knew to get things done. Being soft just got you hurt, or even killed. High Society had always believed in the survival of the fittest. Besides, she'd enjoyed being rude and obnoxious and loud, if only because she'd been so very good at it. But all her strength and all her hardness and all her clever, vicious words hadn't been enough to save her when the House of Campbell fell.

Her children were safe, at least, in a military school: not quite the future she'd intended for them, but a safe haven nonetheless. Robert had arranged it all for her. Strange to think that that naive young man with the vague smile was now the Campbell, head of the Family. There was no one else with a better claim but Finlay, and he had given up all claims to power and position when he'd chosen to disappear into the underground. Aside from Robert, only a few very minor cousins remained with any legitimate claim to the title, and they were mostly still in hiding, keeping their heads well down until the storm passed. A few had married hastily into lesser Houses, giving up their name in return for protection. Even some of those had gone missing. The Wolfes had a long reach and endless malice.

Adrienne knew that, if she had any pride, she should give up on society as it had given up on her, but she couldn't. It was all she knew. The great game of influence and intrigue was the only game worth playing, and it was infinitely addictive. She'd do anything, promise anything, to get a foot in the door again. It was either that or retreat into the underground, which she despised: full of thugs and unpeople and the lower classes. She had no taste for rebellion, and she'd never been one to hide her light under a bushel. On the whole, apart from her present circumstances, Adrienne liked

128

the social setup just the way it was. If she could only find the right leverage, she had no doubt she'd be accepted back into society again. They *had* to take her back. She was one of them. She might have verbally attacked society on occasion, but she was lost outside it. All she knew was how to be an aristocrat, and play the game.

Which was why she'd been reduced to making more and more desperate calls to fringe elements, lesser Houses and those 'personalities' who lived on the edge of events for whatever crumbs they could pick up from the greater players. Renowned for taste and repartee and knowing all the latest gossip, most of them passed in and out of fashion according to a season's taste or whim ... but one figure was always there, raising laughter and eyebrows with barbed bon mots and perfect put-downs.

Chantelle. Not so much a friend, more an honoured rival, but Adrienne had known her for years. Chantelle had no aristocratic blood or political power, but somehow still commanded everyone's attention at those soirées she deigned to attend. She decided fashion, chic – and everything else that mattered – with a gorgeous smile or a flared nostril, and never gave a pretender an even break. You could break fingernails on her charm, but she never forgave a slight. She and Adrienne had always had a lot in common. Including several ex-lovers, who kept their mouths firmly shut on certain matters if they knew what was good for them. If Adrienne could get Chantelle's backing, no one would dare insult her or refuse to take her calls. If Chantelle accepted you, so did society.

She braced herself, and made the call. There was always the chance Chantelle would see, in Adrienne's fall, her own possible future, and feel sympathetic.

Adrienne jumped despite herself as the viewscreen cleared to show Chantelle's frowning face. The doyenne of fashion was wearing last night's rather lived-in gown and make-up, suggesting she'd only just got in from a late night or, more accurately, an early morning. Her long hair gleamed a lustrous bronze, with silver highlights, and her heart-shaped face glowed fluorescently. Only the truly picky would have pointed out that the sheen on her hair was looking rather dull in places and that the make-up round her mouth was smeared. Adrienne bore it in mind, in case she needed ammunition later on. She smiled bravely into the viewscreen, but before she could speak Chantelle sniffed loudly.

'In wondered when you'd get around to me. Yes, I do know why you're calling, and no, I can't help you. You are out, Adrienne dear, so far out I can't even see you from where I am, and nothing short of a major miracle or direct divine intervention will get you back in. Your Clan is scattered, your influence broken, and your credit rating has sunk so low you'd need an earth-mover to find it. Personally, I don't think it could have happened to a more deserving person. You were never really one of us, Adrienne, with your big mouth and bullying ways. You never understood decorum or proper behaviour – the right way of doing things. You aspired to be a scandal, but, truth be told, you were always too boring for that. If I were you, I'd run to your friends for protection . . . but, then, you don't have any friends, do you? Goodbye, Adrienne. Don't call this number again.'

Chantelle's face disappeared from the viewscreen. 'Goodbye, Chantelle,' said Adrienne. 'I do hope you have dysentery soon.'

She was debating whether to call Chantelle again, just to say that her choices in dress had always inspired projectile vomiting in anyone with a smattering of taste, when her viewscreen chimed, alerting her to an incoming call. For a moment Adrienne just sat there. No one had called her since she'd arrived here – not least because most people weren't supposed to know where she was, and those who did were careful to contact her only in person. Adrienne drew herself up and accepted the call. Maybe she'd won a lottery.

The viewscreen cleared to show Lord Gregor Shreck, head of Clan Shreck. A short, fat butterball of a man, with a bulging fleshy face and deepset eyes, the Shreck was one of the most dangerous men in society, mostly because he never cared what his actions cost him as long as he got what he wanted.

'Dear Adriennne,' said Gregor, his voice oozing a charm that didn't reach his eyes, 'I have a proposition for you. A little give and take, to our mutual advantage. Are you interested?'

'Depends,' said Adrienne in her most frosted voice. It didn't do to get chummy with Gregor. He took advantage. 'What do you want from me? As if I didn't know.'

'You never liked him, Adrienne, even if he was your husband. And you really haven't got anything else to bargain with that anyone wants. You don't have to do anything difficult. Just contact Finlay and persuade him to emerge from the underground at an agreed time and place, so we can be waiting for him. We'll take him away, and you can return to society as though nothing had ever happened.'

'You don't have that much influence.'

'I will have, once I have Finlay.'

'What will happen to him?'

'What do you care? I'd suggest you make good use of this offer while it still stands. Finlay is currently very hot, and a lot of people want him. He's just killed Lord William St John, and made a rather amazing escape.'

'Wait a minute,' said Adrienne. 'Hold everything. Finlay's killed someone?'

'Yes. I wouldn't have believed it myself if I hadn't seen the holo recordings. He's really quite an excellent swordsman. I can only assume he's been taking lessons during his time in the underground. But not to worry – I'll have more than enough men standing by to handle him.'

'St John's dead? The Empress's own personal attack dog?' Adrienne shrugged. 'Can't say I ever liked the man. Thought he was God's gift to women, and had clammy hands. I had to hit him round the ear with a candlestick once.'

'That's as maybe, Adrienne. Will you help us, or do I have to apply a little pressure? You have two very lovely children. Quite charming. Be a shame if anything were to happen to them.'

'You touch my babies and I'll rip your balls off with my bare hands,' said Adrienne.

Gregor continued as though she hadn't spoken. 'Robert isn't the only one with friends in the military. Think about it. And call me when you've made your decision. Don't take too long. If all else fails, I might decide to do terrible things to you, in the hope Finlay would come to rescue you. Rather a distant hope, I'll admit, but we could have all kinds of interesting and inventive experiences while we were waiting for your husband to show up.'

'I'd smack you right in the mouth, Shreck, if I weren't afraid of catching something disgusting from you,' said Adrienne, in a voice so cold she barely recognized it. 'Now remove your loathsome presence from my viewscreen. My neighbours will think I've got a toilet overflowing in here. If I change my mind I'll contact you, but don't hold your breath.'

Gregor Shreck just laughed. Adrienne hit the off-switch, and a sudden echoing silence filled the room. She stretched slowly to get the tensions out of her body. She must be losing her touch. She should have been able to handle a creep like the Shreck. There'd been a time when she could goad a man into an impotent homicidal fury with just a few well placed barbs. But now Gregor held all the major cards, and he knew it. Worst of all, she was considering his offer. Finlay had never meant much to her, and she couldn't risk anything happening to her children. Robert had sworn he'd protect them but, when all was said and done, despite being the Campbell he was only a junior officer in the Fleet. And if Finlay was really going around killing people . . . She bit her lip. If she allied herself with the Shreck, and Robert found out . . . Robert had been due to marry the Shreck's niece, Letitia, in an arranged marriage. They'd almost completed their wedding vows when Gregor killed her rather than have her dishonour him. He'd strangled her with his bare hands while the Campbells held Robert back. He'd never forgiven the Shreck for that.

Adrienne's scowl deepened. If she were going to do this, Robert must never know – which meant that, before she could start making arrangements to contact the underground, she'd have to shake off the people Robert had protecting her.

She'd be putting herself at risk. Gregor wouldn't be the only one to have thought of torturing her as a bait to trap Finlay. Not that Finlay would have come, anyway, the bastard: he had never made any secret of his feelings, or lack of them, for her. They had absolutely nothing in common except the children, and, on the few occasions they absolutely had to meet, they could hardly exchange a dozen words without sniping at each other. After two dozen words they tended to escalate rapidly to shouted invective and throwing things.

It had been an arranged marriage, of course. Neither of them had had any say in the matter. Personally, she'd always thought Finlay was mentally disturbed – with his obsession about clothes and fashions – and his recent exploits served only to confirm her suspicions. But would he really stand by and do nothing while his wife was being tortured to death? Would *she*, if the situation were reversed? Well, yes, probably. Adrienne had always known she was a hard bitch at heart. Nevertheless, Finlay had put his own life at risk to save hers when she had been so badly wounded during the Wolfes' hostile takeover. If he hadn't got her to the regeneration machine in time she would have died. She could still feel the sword punching through her belly and out her back. Sometimes she dreamed about lying helpless on the gravity sled's desk, awash in her own blood, while Finlay strove desperately to shake off the pursuing Wolfe craft. When she had that dream she would wake drenched in sweat, and be unable to sleep again until the morning brought comforting light. Finlay had saved her life, when he didn't have to. But, typical of the man, he had had to do it in a way that insulted and humiliated her.

She hadn't known about Evangeline Shreck then. She'd realized there was someone in his life, not just the usual string of casual lovers but some other woman who mattered to him in a way she never had, but she hadn't known who it was until she woke up in the regeneration machine in Evangeline's apartment in Tower Shreck. Robert and his people were standing guard over her, but Finlay and Evangeline had been long gone. Robert had got her to safety. Evangeline had finally resurfaced, free of guilt or any connection to Finlay, and returned to her apartment, but Adrienne had never found the courage to call her.

Adrienne sighed, and looked around at her cramped quarters. It had started out as Robert's bachelor pad, provided by the Fleet as somewhere for him to crash and burn on his infrequent leaves, and hadn't improved since. Just to get out of this dump might almost be worth making a deal with Gregor. She'd had jacuzzis that were bigger. And it was strictly masculine territory, with no frills or fancies or real comforts. She itched to transform the place according to her own tastes, but she didn't have the money and anyway Robert would have thrown a fit. He actually liked it this way. Men. Probably washed his underwear in the hand-basin and clipped his toenails in the bidet. He let her have what money he could, but it wasn't much. Clan Wolfe now possessed all the old Campbell assets – bad cess to the bastards. To keep her head above water she'd been selling, piece by piece, what personal jewellery she'd been wearing on that dreadful day, but it was nearly all gone now. She hadn't got much for the items. She was limited to where she could go. It wasn't just that old friends didn't want to know her: businesses were afraid to make enemies of those in society who openly gloated over Adrienne's downfall. It appeared her big mouth had offended practically everyone at one time or another. Adrienne snorted. To hell with them if they couldn't take a joke.

If she were to work with the Shreck, and betray Finlay, the Lord would probably let her name her own price. She could be rich again, and part of society, and laugh in the faces of all those who'd ostracized her . . .

There was a knock at the door and she spun round sharply, face flushed as though she'd been caught doing something wrong – as though whoever it was had known what she was thinking. She made herself breathe steadily, and glared at the door. Two callers in one day. She was getting popular. She forced her voice to be calm and even as she asked who it was, and then tensed again as Robert Campbell identified himself. He'd made it clear right from the beginning that he wouldn't be visiting her often. There was a limit to how much he could be seen to be helping her: he had his career to think of, and his own safety. Adrienne understood. If he was here now it must be important. She flushed again. He couldn't know about the Shreck's offer. He couldn't. She made herself open the door, and Robert came breezing in, wearing full Fleet uniform and with a kitbag over his shoulder. He nodded and smiled grimly at her, dropped the kitbag on the floor, and looked round his apartment.

'Just a flying visit, I'm afraid, Adrienne. There's bad news. My orders came through this morning. I've been posted to one of the new E-class ships, the *Endurance*. Massive bloody craft, with twice the usual weaponry and the new stardrive. She takes off tomorrow for two weeks of tests and shakedowns, and then we're away to patrol the Rim for six months. Not only will I not be able to protect you any more, the Fleet is going to want these quarters back for someone else. Sorry to spring this on you, but I wasn't given any warning myself. I've got some friends here in the city who'll try and look out for you, but I can't speak for their loyalty if anyone starts putting the pressure on.'

'I understand,' said Adrienne, and she did. The Shreck's contacts in the military were at work already, arranging things. Removing her options one by one until she had no one left to turn to but Gregor Shreck.

'There is someone who might be prepared to help you,' said Robert, 'but you're not going to like it. I've contacted Evangeline Shreck. She was, and is, Finlay's love, but she's a good sort, for a Shreck. She'd do anything for Finlay – even protect you. Go and see her, Addie. You might find you have more in common than you think. Now – I've got to go. They're expecting me on the *Endurance*. I'll try to keep in touch. Goodbye. Good luck.'

He grabbed up his kitbag, pecked her quickly on the cheek and left, closing the door quietly behind him. Adrienne scowled, her hands clenched into fists at her sides. She'd always known her residence here could be only temporary, but it still came as something of a shock to be thrown to the sharks so suddenly.

The question was, did Evangeline know about her father's plans for Finlay? Was she, perhaps unwittingly, a part of them? If so, and Adrienne warned her, that would put Evangeline in her debt.

Adrienne nodded, smiling coldly. She always felt more comfortable when dealing with people from a position of power. She would go to see Evangeline Shreck. If only so that she could hear about a side of Finlay she'd never known herself.

Evangeline Shreck stood before the single great window in her apartment in Tower Shreck, looking out at the world beyond. She was a prisoner in her own home. The door wasn't locked, of course – nothing as obvious as that. But, if she were to try to leave the tower without getting her father's permission first, polite guards would calmly but firmly insist that she return to her apartment while they waited for instructions from the Shreck. And they'd walk back with her, just to make sure she didn't get lost along the way. The Shreck wanted her to go outside as little as possible. Officially, he was concerned that the Empress might try to seize her, to make her one of her maids – a mentally conditioned slave with no will of her own. Lionstone had already done it once with one of the Shreck's nieces. No one had said anything. No one had dared, not even the Shreck.

But the fact of the matter was that Gregor was terrified that Evangeline would be revealed as a clone. These were very anti-clone days. If it were ever revealed that the Shreck had cloned his daughter after her sudden death, and then passed the clone off as the real thing, there would be outrage in the Court and in society. Being replaced by a clone of oneself was an aristocrat's worst nightmare, so the aristocracy's rules against cloning were strict. Gregor would be punished, and the clone Evangeline would be destroyed – mostly for the crime of having fooled them all for so long.

Even that wasn't the whole reason the Shreck kept her a

prisoner. He did it because he could. He wanted to love, cherish and own her completely – as he had his real daughter. For the Shreck had loved his daughter not as a father, but as a lover. Which might have been why he had killed her. Evangeline didn't know the true story. The Shreck insisted it had been an accident, but he liked to drop hints, now and again, about how no one ever defied him and lived to boast of it. Evangeline kept her head bowed, and did as she was bidden. For, though she hated her father and would have killed him in a moment if she could, she had no choice. By playing the loving, dutiful daughter she bought the Shreck's protection for Finlay's wife and children, as she had promised her true love she would. Finlay did not know the price she paid – must *never* know, or he would come storming up out of the underground to take a terrible revenge, not caring if he died as a result. Evangeline cared, so she never told him. She loved him so much she played a role that was destroying her, and never once allowed herself to think how unfair that was.

She was cracking up, although she hadn't realized that yet. She had too many commitments, to too many people. To her father, for his protection. To Finlay and his family, for his love. To the clone and esper underground, for the cause. They all wanted something from her, and sometimes their needs clashed. It was getting harder to keep them separated. Different lies for different people, until the truth got lost in the smoke. She still loved Finlay with all her heart, though she saw him less and less. The underground kept him busy with missions he never explained to her. She had been the underground's contact with the Court and society but, since she so rarely got out now, she was of little use to them. She couldn't explain. They might tell Finlay. And, of course, she couldn't even tell her father about Finlay or the underground. He'd kill her for what she'd done. For defying him – for daring to love someone else.

After all, he could always clone another Evangeline. He'd done it before.

And so she walked up and down in her apartment, thinking furiously, beating at the shifting walls of her various personas, getting nowhere, going quietly insane. She hardly opened her mouth to anyone for fear of saying the wrong thing to the wrong person, and always she was worried that the next person at her door would be from Security, with a warrant to drag her away to the interrogation cells, where they'd make her talk. Everyone depended on her silence – lover, father and cause – and she felt less and less dependable with every day that passed. So far she had kept herself together through sheer force of will – partly because of her love for Finlay and partly because of all those who would suffer if she were weak. If she allowed herself to be weak.

The weight she carried grew ever heavier, and she could not, would not, put it down.

She jumped as her comm unit chimed politely. She knew who it was, who it had to be, but she went to answer it anyway. She sat down before her dressing-table, and the mirror cleared to become a viewscreen, showing her the fat smiling face of her father. She had to fight to get her breath. She clenched her teeth to keep her mouth from trembling.

'Just called to let you know I'm on my way,' said Gregor Shreck. 'Think loving thoughts until I get there, my precious. And wear the pink nightgown. The one I like. I won't be long. And then we can have some fun, just you and I. Won't that be nice?'

He disappeared and the mirror returned, showing Evangeline her own face again. For a moment she didn't recognize it. It was thinner than it had been, and the pale skin was stretched taut over the protruding cheekbones. Her eyes had a trapped, hunted, haunted look. She tried a smile, rehearsing for her father, but it looked more like a grimace. She had a feeling the Shreck preferred it that way.

There was a knock at the door. She stared blankly at it, her heart hammering in her chest. It couldn't be the Shreck already. Had they come at last to drag her away, screaming and kicking, to the torture of the mind-techs, where neither lover nor father nor cause could save or succour her? She snatched up a heavy pair of scissors from the dressing-table.

Not as good as a knife, but close. She'd make them kill her. She'd be safe then.

Somehow she backed away from hysteria, and got a grip on herself, precarious though it was.

She moved slowly to the door, still clutching the scissors. It seemed to take forever to get there. When she opened it, with a hand that hardly trembled at all, she found Adrienne Campbell waiting for her.

Evangeline stared blankly at Finlay's wife, and all she could think was: *Great. Another complication.*

'Well?' said Adrienne. 'Aren't you going to invite me in? We have so much to talk about.'

'Oh, hell,' said Evangeline. 'I haven't got time for this.'

'We need to talk.'

'This isn't a good time. I'm . . . expecting someone. Could you come back again?'

'I doubt it,' said Adrienne, smiling slightly. 'Your security people didn't want to let me in at all. I had to speak to them very firmly. Even so, they were still going to turn me away until I demanded a strip search. That slowed them down. I may have fallen from grace, but I am still a Campbell and noble-born. Let them try to explain to their superiors that they've strip-searched an aristocrat and their next job will be delivering bad news to the Empress. I understand there are always vacancies. They were falling all over themselves to apologize as they let me in, poor bastards.'

'What do we have to say to each other?' said Evangeline.

'I don't know,' said Adrienne. 'But we do have at least one thing in common. Or, rather, one person. Have you heard from Finlay lately?'

'Oh, hell,' Evangeline said again. 'You'd better come in. But you can't stay.'

She stepped back to open the door wide, and Adrienne Campbell strode in as if she owned the place. She always did this – it was practically a trademark. Evangeline realized she was still holding the scissors and tossed them on to a nearby chair. She didn't want to be tempted. Adrienne looked around Evangeline's apartment with a slightly arched eyebrow, implying with a glance that she'd seen much better but was too well bred to mention it. With infallible instinct she picked out the most comfortable chair, and sank into its embrace in a single graceful movement. She smiled, and waited patiently while Evangeline pulled up a chair to sit opposite her. There was something in Adrienne's manner of the Empress visiting one of her lesser subjects, but Evangeline didn't take it personally. That was just Adrienne for you. She still felt like slapping Adrienne's face, on general principles. A giggle almost escaped her, but she forced it back. She met Adrienne's gaze with a calm look.

'Finlay never loved you,' Evangeline said flatly. 'You must know that.'

'Oh, of course. I never loved him. Our marriage was arranged for various business and Family reasons that no doubt seemed good at the time. We might have made a go of it, but we quarrelled walking out of the church and it went downhill after that. He had his lovers and I had mine, and we were both very civilized about it. You look shocked, dear. Surely you didn't think you were his first?'

'No. He never talked about his other women, but I knew. It didn't matter. He never loved them – not the way he loves me. I'm just surprised you admit to having had lovers too. I wouldn't have thought love was your style.'

'Oh, I've had my moments, dear. You'd be surprised how many men have a secret yen for a good tongue-lashing. In more ways than one.'

'Why have you come here, Adrienne?'

'I . . . need to talk to you. About Finlay. Before the Wolfes declared vendetta and ambushed us, I would have sworn Finlay cared no more for me than I did for him. But when I was injured and near to death he put his own life at risk to save mine. He even brought me here, to you, to find the protection I needed. I just wondered . . . if you knew why.'

Evangeline nodded slowly. 'He said you were very brave. That you were wounded fighting to protect the Clan. He admired that.'

'The Finlay I knew was a fop and a dandy,' said Adrienne.

140

'He wore a sword, but I never once saw him draw it. He never took me to the Arena – said the sight of blood made him feel faint. But, when the Wolfes came howling into Tower Campbell, he tore into them with sword and gun like he'd been doing it all his life. To save me, he outfought a dozen pursuers, all trained fighting men. And now I hear he's on the run, after killing the notorious Lord St John, despite all the Lord's guards. I can't help feeling there must be another Finlay, one I never knew.'

'You're right. There was.'

'Can you tell me about him?'

'I don't think it's my secret to tell. You'll have to ask Finlay yourself. But I will say he was the bravest, finest man I ever knew. The fop and the dandy were just masks he wore, to keep people like you at bay. To keep you from seeing the real him.'

'Married all these years, and I never knew that "real him".' Adrienne smiled briefly. 'But then I never looked.'

'You never cared.'

'That, too. I care now.'

Evangeline gazed at her steadily. 'Why? What's changed? What's happened to bring you here, to me, asking questions about Finlay?'

For the first time, Adrienne turned away, but her voice remained steady. 'I need help, and there's nowhere else to go. Do you really think I'd be here if I didn't have to be? Robert was protecting me and the children, but now he's being sent off-planet. Your father helped arrange it. He's putting the pressure on to make me betray Finlay to him. Threats to me, to my children. I can look after myself, but the children must be protected. I need help – some weapon I can use to defend me and mine. That I ended up here should give you some idea of how desperate I am. You loved Finlay, and I married him. He's been a part of both our lives, and put us both through a lot, one way and another. Perhaps we can find something in common. I'm sorry you had to hear about your father's part in this. I know you and he are close, but . . .'

'No,' said Evangeline abruptly. 'We're not . . . close.'

Adrienne raised an eyebrow. There had been something in Evangeline's voice . . .

'In public, and at Court, you're always together. You certainly give the appearance . . .'

'Appearances can be deceptive. Please, you must go now. He'll be here soon, and he mustn't find you here. I want you to leave at once.'

'Why? What's so important about a father visiting his daughter?' Adrienne's eyes narrowed. 'There's a secret here. I can smell it, like I can smell your fear. What is it? Has he been hurting you? The Shreck's a bully and a bastard, like most men, but I never knew he was violent to his own Family.'

Adrienne stopped, silenced for a moment by the sudden rush of misery suffusing Evangeline's face. Tears ran down the woman's jerking cheeks as she gasped for breath.

Adrienne leaned forward and took Evangeline's hands in hers. 'Now, now, don't take on so, pet. Whatever it is, I'll fix it. I'm good at fixing things. And there never was a man born that was worth tears like this. Is it your father? Has he been beating you? I can talk to some people at Court . . .'

'No. He's not . . . violent. He . . .' Evangeline's throat clamped shut suddenly, cutting off her words. She could feel the heat in her cheeks. Her father's words thundered in her head. *You can't tell anyone. Ever. Or they'll find out you're a clone. And you know what they'll do to you then. And you know what I'll do to you if you ever so much as hint to anyone else. They wouldn't believe you anyway. But, if you ever do tell, I'll hurt you, Evie, little Evie. I'll hurt you until your throat goes raw from screaming. Don't you ever dare tell!*

Evangeline held Adrienne's hands tightly, as though trying to draw strength from them. She was sitting with the one woman she'd hated the most, and yet she was closer than ever before to telling her secret, the one thing she'd never told anyone, even Finlay. Because perhaps only a woman like Adrienne could hear it and not judge. Hear the pain and the horror and not the shame. And surely only a woman like Adrienne wouldn't give a damn that she was only a clone . . .

'Tell me, dear,' said Adrienne, keeping her voice calm and steady so that Evangeline wouldn't realize how much that tight grip was hurting her hands. 'We girls have to stick together. It's a man's Empire, even with an Empress on the Iron Throne, but we don't have to take any shit from anyone. Men may have the power, but we're smarter than they are. Whatever it is, I'll find a way around it. He's been locking you up here, hasn't he? That's why we only ever see you when you're with him. Right; take out an action against him. Divorce the bastard. Society would stand with you. They don't have any time for that kind of petty bullying.'

'You don't understand. He doesn't . . . hurt me. Not like that.'

'What way, then? What has he done to you, to put you in such a state?'

Adrienne suddenly stared at her. Evangeline braced herself for a look of pity, or even disgust, but instead she saw only shock, giving way to anger. 'My God. He's been bedding you, hasn't he? Shitty little *bastard*. He's been forcing you, hasn't he? Don't you worry, pet. Society will *crucify* him for this!'

'No!' said Evangeline sharply, fighting back the tears so she could speak clearly. 'No one must ever know. If Finlay ever found out, it would kill him. Or he'd try to kill Daddy, and be killed anyway. I've kept the secret this long. I can keep it a little longer. To keep Finlay safe. I can't help you, Adrienne. I can't even help myself.'

'Now, stop that,' Adrienne said briskly. 'All right, we can't go to society, but there are other ways. I never met a man yet who couldn't be out-thought and outmanoeuvred by a woman who put her mind to it. Let me think for a moment. I'll find a way that won't involve Finlay. You're quite right. He mustn't know. He'd only overreact. Men are like that, bless them.'

'And, if you help me, I have to help you,' said Evangeline. 'Is that the deal?'

'No deals,' said Adrienne. 'Not this time. I'd help anyone in your situation. Now let me have my hands back and dry

143

your tears, and we'll figure out how best to stick it to the Shreck.'

'Will you, my dear?' said Gregor Shreck, standing in the open door of the apartment. 'How very intriguing.'

Both women looked round, startled. Evangeline jumped to her feet, her hands rising to her mouth. Her skin was as white as a sheet and her eyes were very wide. Adrienne took her time getting up. She didn't want the Shreck thinking he could fluster her.

She gave Gregor her best icy glare. 'Haven't you ever heard of knocking?'

'In my own home?' said the Shreck, smiling widely. 'Now why should I do that? The tower is mine, along with everything and everyone in it. I own them. Isn't that right, Evangeline? Now be a dear and tell your new friend to run along. I have so much to say to you.'

'No,' mumbled Evangeline, staring at her shoes.

'What was that?' said Gregor. 'I don't think I can have heard you correctly, my dear.'

'No,' said Evangeline, lifting her head to stare at him defiantly. 'I'm tired of being scared. You lied to me, Daddy. You swore to me you were protecting Adrienne and her children and all the other surviving Campbells. Now I find out from Adrienne that you've been threatening them, to get at Finlay. You *lied* to me.'

'It's politics, dear. Things change. I don't expect you to understand. All you need to know is that I'm doing what's best for the Family.'

'If your Clan found out that you've been screwing your daughter they'd disown you,' said Adrienne calmly. 'Such a tacky crime, Gregor. And backed up with a coward's threats and lies. I'm disappointed in you, Gregor. I never thought you were much of a man, but I didn't suspect you had to bully women into your bed. Now turn around and get out of here. You ever lay a hand on this poor dear again and I'll see everyone in your Family knows your dirty little secret. They'll remove you as head, and throw you out of the Clan. They can do that, if enough of them agree, and I can't see any of

144

them disagreeing over a nasty little mess like this. Without a Clan, no one will talk to you, or politic with you, or do business with you. You'd be an outcast, just like me. Only I can handle it. You couldn't. Don't bang the door when you leave.'

'And you'd agree to this?' said the Shreck to his daughter. 'You'd turn against your own father, who loves you so dearly?'

'What you do to me isn't love, Daddy. And you lied to me. I'd like you to leave now, please. And don't ever come in without knocking again.'

'Think you're so clever, don't you, both of you?' said the Shreck, his broad glistening face flushing red with rage. 'You think you're smarter than me. But you should understand, dear Adrienne, that you don't know everything. You see, Evie hasn't told you her real secret. She wouldn't dare. So you tell this Campbell bitch to leave, Evie, or I'll tell her what you really are.'

'No need to put yourself out, Daddy. I'll tell her.' Evangeline drew herself up, and threw Adrienne a look that was part defiance and part plea. 'I'm a clone. Daddy had me made to replace the daughter he murdered. That's how he's controlled me all this time. Or so he thinks. You never knew I was part of the clone underground, did you, Daddy dear? No, I can see from your face that you didn't. You threaten me, and the underground will have you killed. You tell anyone about me, and I'll disappear into the underground. I may do that anyway. I only stayed because Finlay made me promise I'd protect his Family. You don't have a hold over me any more. You never did, really, apart from my own fear. You told me you owned me, and I believed you. I don't believe that any more.'

'Good for you, girl,' said Adrienne. She looked triumphantly at the Shreck. 'Get out of our sight, you nasty little toad.'

Gregor Shreck looked from one woman to the other, struggling for words, and then turned abruptly and left, slamming the door behind him. Adrienne let out her breath in an explosive sigh and collapsed back into her chair. Evangeline remained where she was.

'Well?' she said quietly. 'How do you feel about me now, now that you know I'm just a clone?'

'My dear, after everything you and I have been through, your being a clone is the least of it. I'm actually rather fascinated. I've never known anyone in the underground before. Apart from Finlay, of course, but I think we've established I never really knew him.'

'How do you feel about me being a rebel, then?'

'Damned if I know. This is all happening a little fast, even for me. I suppose I should be shocked and outraged, but I haven't been shocked since I was fourteen and I'm too emotionally exhausted to be outraged. You're a clone and I'm a bitch, and the Empire doesn't have much use for either of us. So to hell with them, and long live the underground. Do you have a battle hymn? I feel like singing something loud and defiant.'

The viewscreen on the dressing-table chimed, and they both jumped.

They smiled at each other, and Evangeline went over to answer it. Adrienne got up and moved quickly out of sight. 'Better if no one knows I'm here for the moment, Evie.'

Evangeline nodded, sat down before the dressing-table and accepted the call. The mirror cleared, and she nodded as she recognized a familiar face. It was Klaus Griffin, her immediate contact in the underground. As far as the outside was concerned, he was her costumier. For once he wasn't smiling, and Evangeline sat up a little straighter.

'Are you alone, Evangeline?'

'Of course. Is there a problem?'

'This call is being shielded. We can talk freely. We need you to come below, to talk to Finlay. It's urgent. Can you get away?'

'If I have to. What's wrong with Finlay? Is he hurt?'

'No. But it's imperative he undertake a particular mission, and we need you down here to convince him to go.'

'Why wouldn't he want to?'

'Because this one will almost certainly get him killed.'

146

'And you expect me to talk him into it? Are you crazy?'

'We need him to do it, Evangeline. The safety of the entire underground is at risk. He's our only hope. Will you come?'

'I'll come, but I'm not promising anything. Finlay's gone on enough missions for you. You've no right to expect this of him. And don't you dare try and talk him into this before I get there. He's not going anywhere until I've talked to him, and maybe not even then. Dammit, Klaus, we've done so much for the underground already. Find somebody else.'

'It has to be him. How long before you can get here?'

'Give me an hour.' She broke contact and glared into the mirror. 'Bastards. Do they really think I'd betray Finlay, even for the cause?'

'This gets more fascinating by the minute,' said Adrienne, coming over to join her. 'Dear Finlay, the last best hope of the underground? You're right: I never did really see him as he is. Since you apparently know him better than I, what do you think? Would he go on a suicide mission, if it were important enough?'

'Oh, yes. That's what worries me. Most of his recent missions would have been suicide runs for anyone else. He never was very strong in the common-sense department, and since he lost his Family he's become increasingly reckless. He feels guilty for having survived, when so many died. If this mission is so dangerous that even Finlay would hesitate, it must be really bad. I've got to go, Adrienne. Thank you for all your help. I wish there was something I could do for you.'

'There is,' Adrienne said curtly. 'Take me with you. There's nowhere safe here for me any more, now I've made an enemy of your father. If I'm to find protection for my children, the only people left to turn to are the underground – though God knows what I've got to buy that protection with. Gossip, maybe. I know more secrets about more people than half the Court put together. Some of it has got to be prime blackmail material. Besides, whatever you eventually decide, you're going to need my help to convince Finlay. I always could talk him into anything. I think I'm going to enjoy being part of the underground.'

147

'What makes you so sure they'll accept you?'

'What makes you think they'll have any choice? I can be very determined when I put my mind to something. Besides, I really can't wait to see this whole new Finlay I've never known. I have a feeling I might like him a lot more than the old one. Shall we go?'

Julian Skye, rogue esper and agent of the underworld, had been handsome once, but that was before the Empire interrogators had got their hands on him. They'd started with a vicious beating, not because they'd expected it to make him talk but just to soften him up. They didn't even ask any questions. Two of them took it in turns holding him up while the third worked him over in brutal, efficient ways until every part of him moaned with pain. Then they hurt him some more. They paid special attention to his face. Damage there was psychologically scarring as well. Eventually they left, and he sat naked and alone in the interrogation cell, held upright by the thick straps that fastened him to the bare metal chair, waiting for them to come back and start again. One eye was swollen shut, his nose had been broken, and dried blood crusted his face. They'd left his mouth pretty much untouched. He was expected to be able to answer questions, when they finally got around to asking him any.

He'd been left alone to consider his position and worry about what was to come. And Julian Skye, who'd always thought he was a hero, was ashamed to find he couldn't stop crying. He was a young man, with a young man's courage and ideals, but now he'd had the courage systematically beaten out of him. All he had left were his ideals, and they didn't seem as strong and convincing as they once had. He finally managed to sniff back his tears – though the occasional harsh sob still took him by surprise – and looked around him as best he could. He was in a bare, featureless room, deep in the dark metal bowels beneath the Imperial Palace. The walls – bright shining steel, without windows or details – showed vague distortions of himself in the painfully bright light from the single unit directly above him. He could feel the heat from the unit drumming on the top of his head, as though his brains were on fire. The door was of dull black metal, right in front of him, and sealed electronically. The sole way in or out, it could be opened only from the outside and by someone with the correct access codes.

He had been stripped of everything that might give him physical or psychological comfort. They'd even taken away his suicide option – a hollow tooth with poison in it. They had ripped it right out of his jaw with a pair of pliers. He probed the gaping hole with his tongue now and again, as though hoping the tooth might be there this time. The extraction had been a small hurt, compared to what had come afterwards, but he still cried when he thought of it. The tooth had been his last hope. He'd pissed himself, and he couldn't clean it off his legs. Just more of the softening-up process.

He knew he had no one but himself to blame for his capture. Julian Skye had always been too wild for the slow and steady underground, too bold and impetuous even for the terrorists of the Esper Liberation Front, the elves. So he'd been left alone, to run his own operations with his own people; attached to the underground, but not an integral part of it. Which was how he'd come to be in the middle of everything when the raid on Silo Nine went to hell in a hurry and the underground had to scatter. He'd been the only one at a safe enough distance to take charge. He ran things for as long as he could, setting up safe houses and new names and passwords, until he too had been compromised by the treachery of the man called Hood and he had had to run for his life. He'd got away, as he always had, leaving the security guards nothing but the echo of his mocking laughter. Julian Skye was an old hand at the great game of intrigue, after all, despite his young years. He'd thought he was unbeatable, untouchable. He'd been wrong. Truth was, he'd just been lucky. And his luck had finally run out. He must have made the mistake of trusting the wrong person. But who?

At least he wasn't in Silo Nine, with one of Wormboy's gengineered worms burrowing in his brain, controlling his thoughts. If nothing else, the underground had made a

149

thorough job of trashing the detention centre and destroying Wormboy before the raiding force had been betrayed and routed. It would be years before the Empire could get the centre up and running again, even if they could create another artificial esper like Wormboy to be their perfect jailer. And the worms wouldn't work without someone like that. Which was why Skye was being held in a detention cell, mentally neutered by an esp-blocker. He smiled slightly for the first time. He might be prevented from using his esper abilities, but at least his thoughts were still his own. His smile quickly disappeared. The mind-techs would get his thoughts out of him, along with anything else they wanted.

He wondered what would happen to him in the end, when they'd got everything from him, when he had nothing left to tell them. Wipe his mind clean, probably, and replace it with a new personality more suited to the Empire's needs. They'd send it back to the underground with his face in front of it, and a convincing story to explain his 'escape'; and those few he hadn't already betrayed would be wiped out in quick order, long before the espers could crack his new persona. Or perhaps he'd do such a good job betraying the underground right here in this cell that they wouldn't need him any more. He'd heard they'd saved some of the monsters from Silo Nine – some of the espers and clones they'd experimented on, stirring their sticky fingers in their subjects' DNA, shaping their flesh and their minds into new, monstrous shapes. Maybe that was to be his destiny, too. To be no longer human, except on the genetic level. To be a living weapon, unleashed as needed on the Empire's many enemies.

He didn't care. He just wanted it to be over – the pain and the fear and the horror. He wasn't a hero any more, if he ever had been: just a man, waiting to be broken. A small surge of rebellion surged within him at the thought. He hadn't been broken *yet*. Don't think about what they want. Keep it out of your mind. Bury it deep. Make the mind-techs work for it. Buy time. Don't think at all. Be a blank page. Give them nothing to work with or on.

But he couldn't stop thinking. His body hurt too much to

be ignored. Helpless and naked in his chair, restrained by a dozen thick straps that cut painfully tight into his flesh, he had nothing else to do but think. He was safe for the time being. Underground espers had gone deep into his head long ago and constructed a series of mental blocks there, shields that would keep out all but the most powerful Empire espers. He'd activated the safeguard with a conditioned codeword the moment he'd realized he was trapped, and the shields had come slamming down in his brain. Now he no longer had the information his tormentors wanted. It was locked away where he couldn't get at it. Can't tell what you don't know. Push the blocks too hard and his mind would self-destruct, taking the information with it.

So for the moment they would be very careful what they said to him. When they chose to speak to him. Between the beatings. They couldn't use an esper on him without first removing the esp-blocker from the cell, and the moment they did that he'd have access to his own esper abilities again and would rip this place apart with a psistorm like they'd never seen. The only way into his head now was through the mind-techs – the Empire's specialists in pain and truth and mental conditioning. They'd use drugs and technology and all the psychological tricks they'd spent centuries perfecting, until finally the shields went down and he had nothing to hide behind any more, and then he'd break and tell them anything they wanted to know. He'd beg to do it.

He knew it had to happen. Everyone broke eventually. All he could hope to do was hold on for as long as possible, to buy the underground time to rescue or kill him. He wasn't putting much hope in a rescue. He wasn't afraid to die any more, not after what his tormentors had done to him and what he knew they planned to do, but he was afraid of being made to betray the underground. Once he was safely dead, his secrets would die with him. He couldn't do it himself. After pulling out his poison-tooth, the interrogators had put a full spinal block on him. He could still feel everything, but the only movements of which he was still capable were involuntary ones, and the straps took care of those. He could hear himself occasionally whimpering, but couldn't stop it. He'd never been so scared. But then he'd never thought he'd end up here. Getting caught was something that happened to other people. He was crying again now. He could feel the tears trickling down his cheeks. He would have screamed, if he could have. It didn't matter. He'd scream enough later.

There was the sudden sound of electronic locks disengaging and the sealed door swung slowly open. Julian would have cringed away, but of course that was denied to him. His chief interrogator strode in, a tall slender man, dressed all in white so that the bloodstains would show up dramatically: much of the pain is in the mind. He nodded briskly to Julian, and moved around the chair, taking his time, checking that the straps were still tight and that the spinal block on the back of Julian's neck was still in place. The chief interrogator was always polite and never raised his voice. He didn't need to. His movements were sharp and precise and very efficient. Julian didn't know the man's name. He didn't need to know, so nobody told him.

The interrogator moved round to stand before Julian.

'You have a visitor. I've adjusted the spinal block so you can talk freely. Make the most of your time together. When you've finished, it'll be my turn to talk to you.'

The interrogator left, and Julian tried to get his thoughts in order. Who the hell would the mind-techs allow to visit a man they were in the middle of softening up? Some other poor bastard from his team, perhaps. Someone else they'd caught, whom they thought he cared about. Someone they could hurt or kill in front of him. He rocked his head slowly back and forth, partly in denial, partly just to feel it move after having been still for so long. He licked his lips, and tasted dried blood as well as the salt from his tears. He heard footsteps approaching, and braced himself as best he could.

And then BB Chojiro stepped through the door and into the cell, and Julian thought his heart would stop. She looked beautiful, as always, a petite doll of a woman, with long dark hair and sharp oriental features. She wore a kimono of bright scarlet, to match her lips, and gazed at him steadily with dark lustrous eyes. The door swung shut behind her.

Julian looked at her, and felt the horror rise in him again. They knew about BB. If they hurt her . . . even the thought threatened to make him go out of his mind.

She stepped forward, moving with the perfect grace of all her Clan, and produced a small metal box from inside her sleeve. She pressed the single stud on the top, and the spinal block released the rest of its hold on him. He slumped forward, now held up only by the straps. His fingers spasmed helplessly. BB Chojiro knelt before him, so she could peer right into his face. Julian tried to smile for her, but it felt more like a grimace. She put away the metal box and produced a silk handkerchief to wipe some of the blood and tears from his face. Her touch was very gentle.

'My poor Julian . . . what have they done to you? You used to be so strong, so sure. Now they've broken your wings, and you'll never fly again.'

'BB,' he said hoarsely, forcing his mouth to obey him. 'Have they hurt you? What . . . ?'

'Don't try to speak. Just listen. I can't stay long. I want you to tell them everything, Julian. I want you to tell them everything you know. It's for the best, really. You know they'll get it out of you anyway – they always do – but what will be left of you after they've finished won't even know who I am. If you cooperate, they'll let you go eventually, and then we can be together again, just like we were before. You'd like that, wouldn't you, Julian?'

He looked at her, and didn't say a word. He'd known her less than a year. She'd originally been his younger brother's lover. Auric Skye had tried to get a position in Clan Chojiro, so that he could be with her. To impress the Clan, he had fought the Masked Gladiator in the Arena. The Gladiator had killed him – Auric had never stood a chance against that legendary butcher of men. Julian had told him that beforehand, but Auric wouldn't listen and Julian had watched in silence as they dragged his brother's body away across the bloody sands. Julian would have avenged Auric if he could, but he at least had the sense to know he couldn't beat the Masked Gladiator in a fair – or even an unfair – fight.

So he had put it behind him as just another evil episode in an evil Empire, and had gone to see BB Chojiro to comfort and console her over Auric's death. They had talked about Auric all through the evening and on into the night, and at the end she had cried in his arms. They met again, and again, and fell in love. Julian felt guilty about that for a while, but BB talked him out of it. She made him see that Auric would have been glad for both of them. It had been his turn to cry in her arms then, as he finally said goodbye to his brother. After that, Julian and BB were together as often as they could be. It wasn't very often. It was vital that the strict Clan Chojiro didn't find out – they wouldn't have approved at all. And, of course, Julian had his obligations to the underground. It was a long time before he told her about those. She was surprised at first, but then she hugged him and kissed him and told him he'd done the right thing in telling her. It wasn't long after that they came for him. Not long at all.

Julian Skye looked at his love, kneeling before him, and knew for the first time who had betrayed him.

'I thought you loved me,' he said finally. 'How could you do it?'

'It wasn't difficult, darling. My duty has always been to my Clan, first and foremost. Auric knew that. That's why he died trying to be a part of it. You never did ask me what my real name is. What the "BB" stands for.'

'You told me not to.'

'Yes. And you always did what you were told. But the fact that I kept something as basic as that from you should have told you something. "BB" isn't my name, darling. It's my designation. I'm from Blue Block.'

The words hit Julian like blows. He'd heard of Blue Block, but only in whispers. Blue Block was the Company of Lords' deepest secret – a hidden private army of lesser cousins, to be the Families' final defence, if needed, against the Empress and her people. Every Family provided a number of candidates, willing or unwilling, and sent them to Blue Block, where they were trained and conditioned to be totally loyal to their Clans, even to the death. They were everywhere, unknown and unsuspected, programmed to get as close as possible to people who mattered. In the last resort they would be the Lords' final poisoned weapon to throw at Lionstone or anyone else who tried to take away their power and position. Or so it was said. Blue Block was less than a rumour. Lionstone, for one, didn't take it seriously. If she had, she wouldn't have rested until every graduate of Blue Block had been tracked down and executed. She would never have allowed such a threat to her power to exist.

BB Chojiro. Blue Block. Bound to her Clan beyond hope or honour, life or death.

'Our love meant nothing to you, did it?' he said finally.

'There's no room in my life for what you think of as love. I was very fond of you. I still am. That's why I want you to tell the interrogators what they want to know, and get it over with. The interrogator's one of us – he's Blue Block too. Once he's got everything out of you he'll put you together again, as much as he can, and you can come back to me. You can be part of Clan Chojiro, just like your brother wanted. You'll have to go through Blue Block, of course, but it's really not so bad. And then you won't care anything about who you used to be, or what you used to be.'

'If I talked,' Julian said hoarsely, 'hundreds would die. Thousands would be endangered. The underground would have to scatter again. It might never recover. I can't do that. I won't.'

'You will. You know you will. Talk to the interrogator, darling. Do it for me.'

'Do it for you?' Julian would have laughed, but his throat was too dry. 'Who are you? I don't know your real name. I don't know the real *you*. I loved you, you bitch. I would have done anything for you, even died for you. Now just looking at you makes me feel sick.'

'Don't be like that, Julian. We had some good times together, just the two of us. Remember flying out over the Ravenscar Mountains, and chasing each other on gravity sleds in and out of the great waterfalls as they came thundering down? Remember watching the double stars burning brightly over the Tannhäuser Gate? Remember us dancing round a fire on the Dust Plains of Memory, dancing and singing as though the night would never end? Those were real times, Julian. Times we shared. We could share them again. We could still have a life together. It's up to you. You'll forget all about the underground, with me.'

'BB, will you do something for me?'

'Of course, darling. Would you like some water?'

'No. Just lean closer.'

BB Chojiro smiled and brought her face in close to his. He could smell her familiar perfume. She pursed her mouth for a kiss. And Julian called up all the strength he had left, and head-butted her in the face. He couldn't get much force behind it, but the imapact was enough to knock her right back on her ass. Shock and surprise filled her face, and then pain as she brought her hands up to her nose. Blood streamed from her nostrils.

Julian chuckled harshly, even though it hurt his throat. BB blinked at him uncertainly over her hands, and rose jerkily to her feet. She wiped at her nose with a silken scarlet arm, but just succeeded in smearing more blood across her face. Then she drew herself up, perfectly composed, ignoring the blood. She smiled at him, in a brittle, satisfied way.

'Thank you, Julian. I was beginning to feel a little sorry for you – for what you're about to undergo. You've helped remind me why I turned you in. You're scum, the lowest of the low, so far beneath the Families we can't even see you from where we are. And to think I nearly made you one of us. Talk about the Blue Block all you like. Only the interrogator will hear you, and he will see it doesn't go any further, even if he has to edit the security tapes. Think of me, while he's working on you. I'll be thinking of you.'

She rapped imperiously on the door, and it swung open. BB Chojiro blew Julian a kiss and strode out of the cell, every inch the perfect little aristocrat. Julian writhed against the restraining straps, but they held him securely. Still, she'd made a mistake in not reactivating the spinal block. He could find some way to kill himself now, and escape his interrogators. But he was too angry to contemplate doing that. He had to live, so he could escape and kill BB Chojiro. Everything they could throw at him, he would survive, waiting for the slightest slip, the smallest mistake that would let him break free. And then he'd kill the interrogators and anyone else who got between him and BB Chojiro. He'd loved her so much, but all he could think of now was placing his hands around her perfect throat, of replacing her mocking smile with a scream of terror. He laughed suddenly, a harsh brutal sound of the darkest humour.

The interrogator paused in the doorway of the cell, as though suddenly aware he was about to enter a small enclosed space containing a dangerous animal. But the moment passed and the interrogator strode in, smiling avuncularly at his prospective victim. He shut the door firmly behind him, so that Julian's screams wouldn't bother anyone walking down the corridor outside.

Finlay Campbell had returned from his mission on a limping flyer, bloody and battered and just a little out of breath. The flyers dogging his trail had proved determined, if not particularly skilful, and it had taken every trick he knew to shake them off. He landed the flyer with a defiant thud and for a moment slumped over the controls. Members of the underground came running up to drag the flyer out of sight before it could be spotted, and he straightened up with a jerk – it wouldn't do for word to get around that he was getting soft. He stepped down from the flyer, enjoying the expressions on their faces as they saw what he'd left in the flyer for them. He'd disposed of the corpses of the guards, but he'd brought St John's body with him, partly as proof that he'd done his job, partly to upset the Lords over the missing body, and partly as a trophy. For a time, back there, he'd had a vague idea about having St John stuffed and mounted and put somewhere prominent so that everyone could enjoy it. Now, though, he couldn't be bothered.

He left the body in the stolen flyer for someone else to take care of, and trudged towards the waiting elevators. Blood squelched noisily in one of his boots – he'd taken a wound in his leg. He'd taken wounds in other places, too, but he kept his back straight. He had a reputation to maintain. He waited impatiently in front of the elevator doors, his hand on the pommel of his sword, drawing strength from it. The doors finally opened, and he strode in. They closed behind him, and he immediately slumped in a corner, held up only by the steel wall. He'd felt better. He was getting old and past it – be playing chequers next. All he really wanted right now was a bed and several days' uninterrupted sleep, but the underground leaders were waiting for him to make his report. He couldn't make it in writing, of course – that would have been far too easy. No, he was going to have to stand there before them and tell them every detail, like a schoolboy in a classroom. He thought fondly of his quarters, and of a large glass of the good brandy. During the last stages of his trip back, only the notion of the brandy had kept him going – that, and memories of Evangeline. She was never very far from his thoughts, whatever he was doing.

He straightened up slowly, pushing himself away from the supporting wall, and sniffed disparagingly at the various aches and pains that bothered him. He didn't really know why he was bothering with this report. All the esper leaders had to do was go take a look at the body in his flyer to know his mission had been a success. But they'd want details. They always did. It gave them the illusion they were in charge. And, since he was dependent on the underground for his few remaining comforts – not to mention further missions – he played along. Grudgingly.

The elevator doors finally opened on a floor that didn't exist on any official plans, and Finlay lurched out into the gloomy corridor. There never seemed to be enough lights in the realms occupied by the underground. They probably did it deliberately, just to make the place look mysterious. Either that, or they were saving energy again. Finlay realized his thoughts were drifting again, and made himself concentrate on where he was going. Down here in the subsystems, far below the surface of Golgotha, one abandoned steel corridor looked much like any other. There were a few people about, and he found the energy to grunt a greeting to them as they passed. They all nodded politely to him, and quite right too. He was Finlay Campbell, damn it.

He finally stomped into the main meeting area, an abandoned work station that the cyberats had wiped from official memory. It was a large open space bounded with sharp-edged steel plates, and cables dangled everwhere, giving the place an unfinished, transient look. Quite suitable for an underground that might have to pick up its belongings and run at any moment. After the debacle of the attempted storming of Silo Nine, and the purges that had followed, what remained of the underground lived from moment to moment, and tended to be even more paranoid than it had been before. Finlay strode up to the esper leaders waiting for him in the centre of the open space, and nodded to them briskly. There were three of them today, powerful espers hidden behind telepathically projected images to protect their identities. At least, that was their story. Finlay liked to think they did it to hide bad skin conditions or unsuccessful hair transplants. He didn't believe in being in awe of anyone.

The leader, usually referred to as Mr Perfect, was a tall, naked Adonis. His impossibly defined musculature always gleamed with sweat, although he never actually did anything but stand there. He had harsh, forbidding features that were just a little too classically handsome. He even had a dimple in his chin, the bastard. Finlay carefully refrained from looking at Mr Perfect's genitals. It would only depress him. Next to Mr Perfect, a mandala of ever-shifting shapes and colours hung unsupported in mid-air, a spinning wheel of inter-locking patterns. Finlay didn't like to look at that too much either. The sudden changes in colour and brightness, and the way they swirled away into nothingness, made his head ache. The third leader presented his- or herself as a twenty-foot dragon wrapped around the branches of a tall tree. It didn't speak much, as a rule, but its great golden eyes blinked every now and then, and it gave the impression of listening very carefully. Finlay had a lurking suspicion that, just maybe, the tree might be more than it seemed, too.

To put off making his report, Finlay looked round at the medium-sized crowd attending the meeting. His reports always drew a crowd. He smiled at them pleasantly, and they smiled back and bowed their heads in respect. There was the usual mixture of elves – in their leathers and chains – clones and assorted hangers-on, like him, tolerated by the powers that be because they were useful. Apart from the expectant crowd, there were other people darting in and out, carrying messages, making their own reports to lesser officials or just earwigging in the hope of picking up something useful. The underground thrived on gossip.

Then Finlay's roving gaze juddered to a halt and his jaw dropped as he recognized two faces at the front of the crowd – two faces he'd never expected to see together, let alone in the underground. Adrienne Campbell and Evangeline Shreck, his wife and his lover, chatting happily together and apparently getting on like a house on fire. His first thought was that it had to be some kind of esper illusion, some extremely nasty joke or trick to throw him off-balance. But no: it had to be them. Here. Together.

Finlay looked quickly around for the nearest exit. To hell with his report, he had to get out of here. There were some things no man could face. Maybe if he just turned and ran very quickly . . .

'Finlay Campbell, attend us,' said the mandala in a loud and piercing voice that echoed painfully inside his head. So much for fleeing. Apparently the voice hadn't been aimed only at him, as everyone else was now looking in his direction. Finlay sighed resignedly, and strode forward to nod briefly to the esper leaders. He didn't get too close. There was something about the projected illusions that put his mental teeth on edge. He gave them a brisk salute, as much for the crowd as anything, but didn't bother with standing to attention. If they wanted a soldier, they could get one. He was just a

160

trouble-maker on a grand scale, with a reputation to live down to.

'Can you slow your colours down a bit?' he said sharply to the mandala. 'I'm starting to get seasick. I don't know why you three are bothering with the illusions anyway. I've given up being impressed for Lent. Don't you trust me, after all I've done for you?'

'It's not a matter of trust,' said Mr Perfect in his pleasant, charismatic voice. 'What you don't know, someone else can't make you tell them. Security is vital, now more than ever.'

Finlay harrumphed loudly, carefully not looking in the direction of Adrienne and Evangeline. He could feel cold beads of sweat forming on his forehead. 'I take it you want a report. All right. I killed Lord William St John, and a lot of his people, stole his personal flyer and got clean away. End of report. Can I go now, please? Back in my quarters a large brandy is calling for me with growing impatience.'

With his gaze fixed on Mr Perfect, as the least disturbing of the three leaders, he ignored the disappointed murmurs from the crowd.

The mandala's colours flowed suddenly in a direction his eyes couldn't follow, and then its voice echoed loudly in the wide chamber. 'Normally we would press you for a more detailed report, but there is no time. We need you to go out on another mission. Immediately.'

Finlay stared at the leaders, for a moment almost lost for words. 'You want *what*? I've only just got back, dammit! I've been cut at, shot at, chased half-way to hell and back while dodging in and out among the pastel towers on a glorified gravity sled, and only just got away in one piece, and you want me to go out again? Does the phrase, *Stick it where the sun don't shine* sound at all familiar? Have you all gone crazy, or are you just harbouring a death wish? On the grounds that if you don't change your minds about this new mission in one hell of a hurry, I am going to find what's behind these over-rehearsed mirages of yours and slice and dice all three of you into pie fillings! I am tired, wounded and completely lacking in the sense of humour department. And, no, I don't have any sense of loyalty or honour, either. I'm an aristocrat, remember? I'm not going anywhere until I've had a long soak in a hot tub, three or four good meals on the same plate, and an extremely long and uninterrupted nap. I am like a disrupter: I need to recharge my batteries between jobs. Right now my batteries are sitting in a corner crying their eyes out, and my get up and go has got up and gone without leaving a forwarding address. In other words: no, I'm not bloody doing it!'

Finlay looked hopefully at the esper leaders, but they'd heard it all before and it hadn't impressed them then.

Mr Perfect rippled his muscles impressively and looked sternly at him. 'This mission is vital. The security of the whole underground is at stake. During your absence, a previously unheard-of band of rebels attacked the city. They invaded the Income Tax and Tithes Headquarters, disrupted the computer systems with great efficiency and thoroughness, and made their escape in a Hadenman starship. Our previous contacts with this group have been somewhat tentative, but their actions have established our new allies as a force of great power, if not subtlety. Also, they brought us news of great importance. Jack Random has returned to lead them.'

The crowd burst into applause and scattered cheering. Finlay didn't join in. He'd heard of the professional rebel – everyone had – but the man had to be getting on in years now. And Finlay didn't trust legends any more. Not since he found he'd become one himself.

'What's all this got to do with the new mission I'm not going on?' he said loudly, and the applause died away. Everyone looked interestedly at the esper leaders and waited for their reply. This was why they enjoyed Finlay's reports: he always gave a great performance.

Mr Perfect gazed steadily at Finlay. 'Thanks to our new friends' attack, Golgotha's defences and security systems are currently in tatters. Things are now possible that were not before. You will remember Julian Skye. It was thanks to him that the underground was able to reform itself after Silo Nine. Skye has been captured. They haven't had him long, but it is imperative that he doesn't talk. He alone knows all the locations, names and passwords that made our reformation possible. There are blocks and defences in his mind, but they won't last long once the Empire mind-techs really get to work on him. Any other time, we would have been helpless to retrieve the situation, but, in the current chaos, who knows what might be achieved by one determined man?'

'Who knows what might be achieved by a small army with lots of weapons?' said Finlay doggedly. 'Think of all the other prisoners you could rescue.'

'We can't risk losing any more of our people,' said the mandala. 'Skye is being held in the maximum-security area. Even with the present confusion, he will undoubtedly be very well guarded. One man might sneak in and out where an army could not hope to. You will be that one man.'

'Because I'm brave, talented and entirely expendable?'

'Exactly. It helps that you are also the most likely to succeed in such a desperate mission, despite the odds. What's the matter, Finlay? I thought you liked a challenge?'

'This isn't a challenge, it's a death sentence. And, contrary to popular impressions, I don't do suicide missions. Find another sucker.'

'You will do this mission. Skye must be rescued or silenced before he talks. You will decide which option is more practicable, under the circumstances.'

'Hello? Are you listening to me? I'm not going!'

'We have a trace on Skye. All espers in the underground have a telepathic beacon, buried deep in their minds. The Empire hasn't silenced his yet, so we have his exact location. Which means we can teleport you right to him.'

'All right,' said Finlay, 'I'll bite. What's the snag?'

'The Empire must know about the beacon. They've captured enough espers before, and stopped their beacons quite efficiently. If Skye hasn't been blocked, it can only be because he is also being set up as bait in a trap. They know how badly we need his silence. They're expecting a small army, which they hope to exterminate, depleting our numbers yet further. They won't expect you. However, we feel it only fair to warn you that, while we can teleport you in, we will almost certainly

163

not be able to teleport you out again. The Empire will take measures to prevent that.'

'Let me get this straight,' said Finlay. 'You're going to drop me right in the middle of the interrogation centre, surrounded by legions of armed guards, both human and inhuman, and it's up to me to free Skye and fight my way out?'

'That's right,' said Mr Perfect. 'A walk in the park. We have every confidence in you. After all, since it's so obviously a trap, there's always the chance they won't be expecting anyone actually to walk into it, let alone one man on his own. You should take them entirely by surprise.'

'I can't help thinking that *should* is the operative word there,' said Finlay. 'I told you, I don't do suicide missions. And I haven't heard one thing so far that's going to change my mind.'

'That's why they wanted me to be here,' said Evangeline. She walked slowly forward to join him; their eyes held contact all the way.

She put out her arms to hold him, but he stopped her with an upraised hand. 'Don't. I'm covered in muck and blood. I'll get your dress dirty.'

Evangeline looked him over, trying not to wince at the sight of his wounds, and shook her head sadly. 'More blood. More pain and suffering, on my behalf. I've always known you do this only for me. You've never given a damn for the rebellion or the underground, have you?'

'I need something to do down here,' said Finlay uncomfortably. 'Something to keep me busy. And I do damn' well care. Maybe I didn't at first – the underground was just a refuge when I needed one – but then I saw Silo Nine, Wormboy Hell. I will not allow that kind of suffering and horror to continue. I have sworn a death oath, upon my blood and my honour, to fight to put an end to Silo Nine and the system that produced it. The underground's the best way for me to do that. But I'm still not going on this mission, Evie. Not even for you. I know my limitations.'

'So do I. You're quite right. It *will* probably get you killed.

But . . . things have changed. We need you to do this mission. I could come with you, if you like – fight at your side, die beside you.'

'No! I don't want that. I nearly lost you in Silo Nine. I won't risk that again. I need to know you're safe. I wouldn't want to live, without you. Is this Skye bastard really so important?'

'If he talks, the underground will have to scatter again. Thousands of clones and espers and their supporters will risk capture and death. It might take anything from ten to twenty years before we could pull ourselves back together, and that's being optimistic. The underground might not survive at all. Certainly the rebellion would be set back indefinitely. The timing's so *ironic*, Finlay. Things are finally going our way. These new rebels, with Jack Random to lead them, could be the final spark we need to blow the whole corrupt Empire apart.'

'What do you want me to do, Evie?'

'I want what you want – for us to be here, safe, together. But what *we* want doesn't matter any more. If Skye talks, what little we have will be taken from us. You have to go, Finlay. You're the only one who stands a chance of bringing this off and coming back alive.'

'And if I don't? If I get myself killed, fighting for the damn' cause?'

'Then part of me will die with you,' said Evangeline, looking at him steadily. 'I know what we're asking of you. What *I'm* asking. It's tearing me apart. But . . .'

'But you're still asking.'

'Yes. I know my duty. To every esper and clone who suffered in Silo Nine, or who suffers every day as an unperson in the Empire.'

Finlay smiled briefly. 'You always did fight dirty.'

'I love you, Finlay. If you say "no", I'll still love you.'

'I love you, Evie. Even though you're asking a lot.'

They looked at each other for a long time, seeing nothing but each other, their love so strong and fierce it filled the chamber. The crowd was silent, holding its breath.

Adrienne cleared her throat, and stepped forward. 'Don't do it, Finlay. You'd have to be crazy to take on a mission like this. Everyone's been telling me what a great fighter you are, but no one could face these odds and come back in one piece.'

Finlay smiled coldly at her. 'You never did believe in me, Adrienne.'

'That's not the point. Let them find somebody else. There's always somebody else.'

'There isn't time,' said Finlay. 'Weren't you listening?'

'Dammit, stop fighting me! I'm worried about you!'

'Really? What brought that on?'

'Damned if I know. I don't even know what I'm doing here. But Evangeline and I have become rather close just recently, much to our mutual surprise, and, since she's clearly not stupid or easily impressed, I'm forced to the opinion that you must be something of the hero and fighter she says you are. Though, if you're that good an actor, you should be on the stage. But this assignment has suicide mission written all over it. You might as well walk into the Arena with no weapons and one leg tied behind your back. Don't go, Finlay. I don't want you dying before I've finally had a chance to get to know you. Tell them to stuff their mission. There's always another way, if you look hard enough.'

'You don't think I can do it, do you?' said Finlay. 'Well you're wrong, Addie. I can jump in there, grab the bastard and be gone before the guards know what's hit them. I'm a fighter, Adrienne. The best damn' fighter you'll ever meet.'

'You're not listening to me!' said Adrienne. 'But then you never did. You talk to him, Evie.'

'But I *want* him to go,' said Evangeline. 'Please, Finlay. Do it for me. I don't want all of us to end up in whatever they build to replace Silo Nine.'

'It wouldn't come to that,' said Finlay. 'I'd never let them take you.'

'Even you couldn't protect me from the kind of forces Julian Skye could set in motion, if he talked. And I think I'd rather die than be taken.'

'I'd kill every guard and soldier in the Empire before I let them hurt you,' said Finlay. 'All right. I'll go. But, if by some miracle I get out of this alive and reasonably intact, I want something for myself.' He glared across at the esper leaders. 'You hear that, you bastards?'

'We are not surprised,' said the mandala, pulsing calmly. 'What do you want?'

'I want Valentine,' said Finlay. He smiled widely, and there was no humour in it at all, just his death's-head grin. 'I want his head on a stick.'

Valentine Wolfe had once been an enthusiastic supporter of the underground. He had provided financial backing and whatever support and influence he could bring to bear without compromising himself. But then he had waged a sudden and highly successful vendetta against the Campbells, and had become the head of his own Family when his father had died leading the assault on Tower Campbell. As the new Wolfe, Valentine had had access to immense wealth and power, and apparently lost all interest in the underground and the rebellion. He no longer came to meetings, and ignored all attempts at contact. So the underground left him strictly alone. He could do them a lot of damage, if he chose to. He knew names and faces, plans and places. A few hardliners among the elves wanted him dead, as a precaution-ary measure. So far, the underground leaders had refused them. Valentine had remained silent, and they didn't want to upset or alarm other Clan members who were working with the underground. At the very least, it would set a bad precedent. And, as the Wolfe, Valentine was well protected. An unsuccessful attack by the underground might well prompt the very disclosure of information they were so desperate to avoid. But if they let Finlay kill him, working on his own, they could pass it off as a personal feud: just a Campbell and a Wolfe, fighting again. It was a tempting thought. As long as Valentine was alive, the information in his head was a threat hanging over them. While not as dangerous as Julian Skye, he could harm them badly, if he chose. There was also the question of exactly how much influence the Lord High Dram had over Valentine. Dram had once, in his alias as Hood, been a major player in the underground, only to betray them during the attack on Silo Nine. He had been directly responsible for the scattering that had put Julian Skye on the spot in the first place. So far, he'd made no attempt to contact or control Valentine, but the potential threat of blackmail was always there.

Finlay knew all this was going through the leaders' minds. He didn't need to be a telepath for that. They and he had argued both sides of this problem many times before. They'd always said 'no'. But things were different now.

'Very well,' said the dragon, curled around his tree. It fixed its golden eyes on Finlay. 'In the unlikely event that you return from this mission successful and alive, you may pursue your vendetta against the Wolfe. The underground will neither hinder nor support you. All consequences will be upon your own head. We will, of course, if necessary discard and renounce you.'

'Sounds good to me,' said Finlay. 'I've always known where I stood with you.'

'Be clear as to the purpose of your mission,' said the mandala, its colours rippling agitatedly. 'You must either rescue or silence Julian Skye, according to the situation you encounter. He must not be allowed to talk. Once we have teleported you in, you're on your own. We can't help you. We can, however, offer a little support in advance.'

One of the elves stepped forward and presented Finlay with a small flat box. It was of polished steel, with a single button coloured a dramatic red. Finlay hefted it thoughtfully. He'd never seen one before, but he knew what the box was, what it had to be. A mindbomb. A terror weapon despised and outlawed throughout the Empire. Once activated, it attacked the minds of all non-espers, scrambling their thoughts. Its victims hallucinated, then became insane and finally catatonic. It was a vicious, take-no-prisoners weapon, a last resort for the truly desperate. It was very rare: like the esp-blockers, the mindbomb was based around living esper brain tissue. It was almost unthinkable for the esper leaders to admit to possessing such a thing, let alone hand one over to him. They really must think he wouldn't be coming back. Finlay couldn't help wondering whether the brain tissue had come from a volunteer, and if it were still somehow aware, and thinking. He repressed a shudder, and slipped the metal box into his pocket.

He nodded respectfully to the elves, and threw the leaders another brisk salute, indicating the audience was over as far as he was concerned. He took Evangeline by the arm and led her off to one side. Adrienne followed. The images of the esper leaders disappeared like popping soap bubbles. The crowd began to break up, chattering animatedly. Finlay had given them enough material to keep them gossiping for weeks.

Finlay knew the underground expected him to kill Skye. They thought him incapable of subtlety – and that anyway killing Skye would make it easier for Finlay to escape the interrogation centre. They were wrong. He was determined to bring Skye back alive – partly because he'd failed to rescue so many others from Silo Nine, and had sworn never to fail again, and partly to prove to the espers that he wasn't merely a killing machine, a weapon they could just aim and unleash on their enemies. Despite everything that had happened to him, he was more than that. He had to be, for Evangeline's sake.

He smiled at Evangeline, and nodded briskly to Adrienne. 'Never thought to see you two together without weapons in your hands. How the hell did you get together?'

'Circumstances can make for strange bedfellows,' said Adrienne. 'I've always known that.'

'I'll bet you have,' said Finlay.

'You don't have to take this mission,' said Evangeline abruptly. 'Despite everything I said, I don't want you to die.'

'I do have to take this mission,' said Finlay. 'And not just for the obvious reasons. You never did understand why I needed to fight in the Arena. I need the action, the thrilling of the blood, the balancing on a blade's edge between life and death. Now that my other life in the Empire is gone, I need the thrill a little more. It's all I have to keep me occupied.'

'You still have me,' said Evangeline.

'I hardly see you these days,' said Finlay. 'It used to be, when I was with you, I could forget the Arena, the blood and the killing. But now you have your responsibilities above, and so little time to be with me. You have to understand what drives me, Evie. It isn't very pretty or honourable, but it's me. I need to kill, like a predator in a world of prey. Nothing's happened to change that. It's just that the life I'm living now has brought it closer to the surface.'

'The world above doesn't matter,' said Evangeline. 'And my responsibilities can go to hell. There are too many of them these days. They clog up my head, and keep me from seeing what's really important. I'll move down here permanently, if that's what you need, and be damned with what the underground wants. In the end, there's just you and me, and what we mean to each other. Everything else is just clutter.'

Finlay took her in his arms and kissed her, and their passion beat on the air like the wings of a giant bird.

Adrienne watched thoughtfully. It had been a day of surprises. This new Finlay was a man whom before she'd seen only in glimpses, puzzling flashes of a hidden nature that had disturbed and frightened her. She didn't like to think she could have been so wrong about someone so close to her. Pretty Finlay in his gorgeous outfits, really a mad-dog killer from the Arena . . . and Evangeline, a quiet mousy little thing at Court, with hidden horrors and a kind of courage at which Adrienne could only marvel. They were both a little ragged round the edges just now, but Adrienne liked them a lot more. She'd always had a weakness for the mentally challenged. Finlay and Evangeline had been in different worlds for too long, becoming different people who had nothing in common except their love, but in the end it was strong and real enough to hold them together. Adrienne could recognize that. She'd have had to be blind not to.

But for once she didn't know what to do for the best. Finlay would have to be crazy to go on this mission, but all the signs said that he was a long way down that road already. Nothing she could say or do would change his mind. She wasn't used

170

to that. She'd never been in a situation where her arrogance and mastery of words couldn't achieve what she wanted. She'd relied on her acid tongue to get her her own way for so long that she was frankly lost for an alternative. She didn't want to lose this new, interesting Finlay, now she'd found him. She was surprised to discover how much that mattered to her.

Finlay and Evangeline finally came up for air, and she coughed meaningfully. It was an impressive cough. On a good day, she could silence a room with it. The two lovers turned to look at her, without letting go of each other.

'Before you say anything,' Evangeline said firmly to Finlay, 'Adrienne and I have become friends. She gave me the strength to do something very unpleasant but utterly necessary that I'd been putting off for far too long. And, no, I'm not going to tell you what. Suffice it to say it's because of her support that I'll be able to spend more time down here in the future.'

'Thank you for that, at least, Addie,' said Finlay.

'You're so welcome,' said Adrienne. They looked at each other for a long moment, but had the sense to leave it at that.

'So,' said Finlay, 'what are your plans, Ad? Going to join the rebellion?'

'Maybe,' said Adrienne. 'Things have been getting pretty tough for me upstairs. I could use a new direction, and a measure of security. Tell me, Finlay: were you really a fighter in the Arena?'

'He was the Masked Gladiator,' said Evangeline, and she and Finlay both laughed aloud at the expression on Adrienne's face.

Adrienne quickly pulled herself together, and managed to laugh with them. 'Who knows?' she said. 'If I put my mind to it, maybe I could *nag* Lionstone into making reforms.'

'If anyone could, you could,' said Finlay generously.

Finlay teleported into the interrogation centre with a sword in his hand and grim determination in his heart. He was suddenly half-way down a dimly lit corridor, facing six or

171

seven rather surprised-looking guards. They had swords in their hands, too, but it didn't help them. Finlay ploughed straight into them, his sword flashing in short, brutal arcs, and blood-choked screams filled the corridor. He killed them all in under a minute, and then stood poised and ready, listening.

Seconds passed, and no one came to investigate. The few brief sounds from the one-sided slaughter obviously hadn't travelled far. Finlay sniffed dismissively, flicking drops of blood from his blade. Not much fun. Strictly amateur hour. No challenge at all. If this was the Empire's idea of a trap, the mission was going to be a walkover. Then he noted the cameras set into the ceiling, watching him with glowing, unblinking eyes, and decided it might be a good idea if he got a move on after all. Given what the cameras had just observed, reinforcements were probably already on their way, in great numbers.

He looked up and down the corridor and wished he'd though to ask for a map. The corridor itself was sparsely lit by widely placed, dully glowing lamps set into the ceiling. The walls were bare, featureless steel, with no markings or signs. At regular intervals narrow doors led off into interrogation cells. They were solid steel doors, sealed with electronic locks. Deep shadows lay undisturbed to every side, and there was a strong smell of disinfectant on the air, almost but not quite masking other, more unpleasant smells.

Julian Skye was here somewhere, but exactly where would be anyone's guess. The underground had taken pains not to send him to the exact location of Skye's beacon. Materializing inside a locked cell, where everyone would be expecting him, had not struck anyone as a good idea, least of all Finlay. So they had picked the nearest open space and dropped him there.

Finlay looked around him vaguely, hefted his sword and, for want of anything better to do, moved over to the nearest door. There was a small viewscreen set into the solid steel. Finlay activated it, and the screen showed him what was inside the cell.

The man spreadeagled on the metal table had been expertly flayed. Not a square inch of skin remained on him, but he was still very much alive. He moved feebly, struggling against unseen restraints. Raw red muscle glistened wetly. Naked eyes bulged from lidless sockets. Blood seeped constantly on to the table to be carried away by grooves and runnels cut into the metal. New blood flowed into a pulsing vein from an IV drip.

Finlay turned off the screen, and leaned his forehead against the cold metal of the cell door.

There was nothing he could do. He couldn't rescue everyone. He didn't have the time. The underground had been quite specific about that. He had to get to Skye before Skye could tell the interrogators anything important.

Finlay took a deep breath and let it out. To hell with them, and to hell with the Empire. He was damned if he'd let obscenities like this continue. He used the lock-scrambling mechanism the underground had provided, and the cell door swung silently open. Finlay slipped inside, and the man on the table whimpered in anticipation of fresh pain. Finlay leaned over him, making soothing, shushing noises, and the prisoner quietened. It was only then that Finlay realized the man had been riveted to the table by metal spikes fired through his limbs and body. There were dozens of them. Finlay had no way of removing them short of levering them out one at a time, and the shock alone would almost certainly finish the poor bastard off anyway. But he couldn't leave him to suffer like this. Finlay stood for a moment, mind racing as he tried to come up with some alternative, but in the end there was only one thing he could do. He smiled reassuringly down into the prisoner's naked, hopeful eyes, and slipped the point of his sword into the exposed, beating heart. There was a brief splash of blood and the flayed man jerked once; then he stopped breathing. Finlay kicked the table in frustration and left the cell.

He stalked down the corridor, throwing open the cell doors one by one, freeing those prisoners he could. He killed the others. Some of them begged him to do it. The survivors spilled out into the corridor, milling about him, trying to thank him with voices grown raw from screaming. Finlay armed some of the sturdier ones with weapons from the guards he'd killed, and then left them to their own devices. At least, that was the plan.

There was the sound of running feet. A full company of armed guards rounded the corner at the far end of the corridor and came charging towards him. Finlay smiled. This was more like it. And then there was the sound of more running feet, this time behind him, and he turned to see a further company of armed guards approaching from the other end of the corridor. The freed prisoners crowded in close around Finlay. He sighed regretfully. It would have been an interesting fight, but he knew his limitations. Besides, he had to think of the prisoners. He pulled the mindbomb from his pocket and pressed the big red button.

The guards before and behind him stumbled to a halt, clutching at their heads and screaming. Their thoughts shattered and fragmented, their minds scrambled beyond sense or meaning, in a moment they changed from an organized army into a crazed, panic-stricken mob. Finlay and the freed prisoners – protected by their immediate proximity to the mindbomb device – watched, impressed. Finlay turned it off, and left the prisoners to deal with the still shrieking mob while he went on about his business. A long-delayed revenge filled the corridor, and blood spattered the shining steel walls. Finlay carried on opening doors and freeing the esper prisoners, until finally he came to the cell with Julian Skye in it. He stopped in the doorway, held by the shock of what he was seeing.

The young esper lay on his back on another of those damned steel tables, held firmly in place by restraining straps. The back of his head had been shaved and cut open, and a section of the skull had been removed. Dozens of coloured wires led from an ugly piece of machinery beside the table to disappear into the exposed brain tissue. Two mind-techs, in their familiar white gowns, looked up from what they were doing and smiled pleasantly at Finlay as he hesitated in the

174

doorway. Both had disrupters in holsters on their hips, but neither made any move to draw them. Finlay moved slowly forward into the cell, ignoring the growing chaos of screams and pain and fury in the corridor outside. There were no guards in the cell, no obvious protection or booby trap. The mind-techs eyed the blood dripping from his sword, and smiled briefly at each other. They were tall, slender men, with pale ascetic faces like monks might have. One was clearly older than the other.

The older one looked at Finlay, and smiled again. 'Welcome, dear boy. We've been expecting you – or someone like you. I'm afraid, if you came to rescue dear Julian, you're a little too late: any attempt to move him now would undoubtedly kill him. We're using an esp-blocker to restrain his talents, and its function cancels out any effects the mindbomb you used might have had on us. Nasty little device, but quite ineffective in here. And you may as well put that sword away. I have only to touch this control under my hand and dear Julian will experience pain beyond your capability to imagine. Put the sword away, please. Now.'

Finlay sheathed his sword, but his eyes didn't waver. 'What are you doing to him?' he said finally, and his voice came out cold and harsh and very deadly.

The mind-tech smiled, unmoved.

'We're invading his thoughts. Not that long ago we would have used one of Wormboy's little pets, but thanks to your terrorist friends we are obliged to use older, more direct methods. It's essentially a simple but very effective mind probe, electrically stimulating the areas of the brain we're interested in. This one, for example, is tied directly into the pleasure/pain centre. Guess which part we're interested in. The implantation process itself is surprisingly painless: I imagine he felt some discomfort from the original invasive procedures, but the brain itself has no pain sensors. It makes our job so much easier, to be able to inflict pain only as needed. And what pain he feels then . . .

'These other wires are concerned with short- and long-term memory. We can play back his memories on that screen on the wall, in as much detail as we require. Soon we'll have everything we want, regardless of the patient's wishes. The process is, unfortunately, quite destructive to the brain tissues, in the long run, but, once we have what we want, the health or even life of this patient is of no concern to anyone. Except, of course, you. The guards will be here soon, to take you away. In the meantime, please refrain from any violent action or you can listen to your friend screaming.'

It had grown quiet in the corridor outside. Finlay frowned. Either the prisoners had run out of guards to kill or the guards had succeeded in restoring order. He had no way of knowing which. He should just kill the mind-techs, and then Skye. But, as long as there was still a chance of getting the poor bastard out alive, he couldn't do that. He needed the techs to remove the wires, but he didn't know how to make them do so. Kill one, and the other could take a very nasty revenge on Skye. Yet he couldn't just hang around waiting while the mind-techs stalled: sooner or later the guards would come for him. He looked across at Skye's face, pale and sweating, and the esper's eyes met his. His mouth worked.

'Please . . .' he said faintly, fighting to get the word out.

'You see?' said the older mind-tech. 'He understands the reality of the situation.'

'Please,' said Julian Skye. 'Kill me . . .'

The mind-tech looked down at him sharply. Finlay laughed softly, and there was no humour in the sound at all. 'Yes, *doctor*, he understands the reality of the situation completely. My mission is to put him beyond your reach, one way or the other.'

He drew his disrupter in one swift movement, and shot the older mind-tech. The younger one lunged for the controls. Finlay drew a dagger from his sleeve and put it expertly through the technician's eye. The man fell backwards, clutching at his face with both hands, and then hit the floor hard and lay still. Finlay nodded once, satisfied, put his disrupter away, and moved forward to lean over Skye. The esper looked up at him, and tried to smile. The marks of a recent bad beating were still clear on his face, but his gaze was clear.

'Hoped they'd send someone . . . if I could just hold out long enough.'

'What do I do?' said Finlay. 'I don't understand this machinery. Is there any way I can get this stuff out of your head?'

'No. But I can, now.'

Skye closed his eyes, and concentrated. For a long moment nothing happened, and then one by one the coloured wires began to squirm and wriggle their way out of his naked brain. They fell to coil harmlessly on the floor, like so many dead snakes. When the last one had finally worked its way free, Skye relaxed so utterly that Finlay, worried the esper might be dead, checked the pulse in Skye's neck; it was strong and regular. He set about undoing the restraints, working as fast as he could. The guards *had* to be on their way by now. He sat Skye up on the table, and blood ran down the esper's neck from the ugly wound at the top of his head. Finlay gingerly pulled the flaps of cut skin together to cover the exposed brain, and held them in place with a handkerchief wrapped round the esper's shaven head. Luckily it was a clean one. Skye's eyes opened suddenly, as though he'd just been thinking. He looked at his reflection in the steel wall, and smiled.

'Nice work. I look like a pirate. But this doesn't change anything. There's no way you can get me out of here, and I won't let them take me again. So kill me.'

'That's not an option,' said Finlay.

'Don't tell me that wasn't part of your orders. My silence is what matters. I know how the underground works.'

'Dying is easy. Anyone can do it. But, if you give up, if you choose to die rather than fight for a chance at life and freedom, the mind-techs will have won. They'll have broken you. Stay alive, break free and get your revenge on the bastards who ordered this done to you. That's what the underground and the rebellion are all about. Now, if I can get you out of range of the esp-blocker, can you find us a way out of here?'

'I don't know. Maybe.' Julian smiled weakly. 'It's worth a

try. They had to turn the esp-blocker's influence way down to avoid damaging my brain while they were working on it. And being this close to a mindbomb did the blocker some damage – that's how I was able to get those wires out of my head. If you can get me a few corridors away, the rest of my esp should return. And then I'll show you some real fireworks.'

Finlay grinned. 'A man after my own heart. Let's go.'

He helped the young esper down from the table, and supported him for a moment until his legs got their strength back. Although he did his best to hide it, Finlay was concerned about Skye's condition. The Empire had clearly beaten the hell out of him, even before they'd started tinkering with his brain. If it came to a fight, or even a prolonged chase, they could be in real trouble. Deciding he'd think about that when he had to, and not before, he dressed Skye hastily in a robe dragged off one of the dead mind-techs and then led the way out of the interrogation cell. Dead guards and espers lay scattered the length of the corridor, but the living had gone. The fight had moved on, deeper into the heart of the complex. Finlay wondered who was winning.

Skye looked up and down the corridor, and then stepped forward to take up the lead.

'The layout of these places is pretty standardized,' he said brusquely, stepping gingerly over the bodies. 'I did a study on the Empire's interrogation centres for the underground a while back. We were planning rescue missions, with telepaths and mindbombs. But that was before the scattering. If I remember correctly, these corridors should all eventually tie in to a central rotunda. From that, I should be able to find us a way to the main flyer station. Then all we have to do is fight our way past a dozen guards, hotwire a flyer without setting off all the explosive booby traps, and get the hell out of here before they crank up the esp-blockers and knock out my powers again.'

'No problem,' said Finlay.

'There's going to be a lot of guards between us and there.'

'I've still got the mindbomb.'

178

'Save it. It's good for only half a dozen blasts or so, and then the brain tissue burns up.'

'We can do without it,' said Finlay. 'You've got me.'

Skye looked at him. 'Are you always this confident?'

'Of course. Why do you think the underground chose me for this mission? So stop worrying – it'll give you ulcers. You stick with me, and I'll get you out of here.'

Skye smiled genuinely for the first time. 'You just might, at that.'

He led the way down one corridor after another, never hesitating at a turn or a blind corner. The corridors all looked the same to Finlay, but he trusted Skye. The young esper was standing straighter now, though the pain in his head clearly bothered him. His eyes were brighter, and there were two spots of colour in his pale cheeks. He still looked as though a strong wind would blow him away, but his confidence was returning.

Then they turned a corner and Skye stopped dead in his tracks, his head cocked slightly to one side, as though listening. Finlay looked quickly about him, but the corridor was deserted.

'Talk to me, Skye. What is it?'

'We're in trouble.'

'I guessed that. Be specific.'

'When we were all held in Silo Nine, Wormboy allowed mind-techs and other scientists to experiment on some of the inmates. Most died. They were the lucky ones. The survivors were monsters, changed in body and mind, no longer human. A few escaped during the underground assault, but most were too securely confined. After Wormboy was killed, the monsters were transferred here, in the hope that some new way of controlling them could be found. Well, the authorities must really not want us to escape. They've released a dozen of those monsters into the corridors. They're insane with rage and pain. They'll attack anything that moves. And they're heading right for us.'

Finlay looked quickly around him again, but all seemed quiet for the moment. 'How's your esp? Is it back yet?'

'Some. But even a full psistorm wouldn't stop minds like these.'

'Any chance you could contact the underground and get us a teleport out of here?'

'No. This whole place is surrounded by esp-blockers. You got in only because they let you in. We either find our own way out or the monsters will be picking what's left of us out of their back teeth.'

Finlay thought hard. 'What about maintenance tunnels, air ducts, that sort of thing?'

'All securely locked off and guarded. This is a prison, remember? Brace yourself. They're coming.'

Finlay took up a stance between Skye and the direction he'd indicated, sword in one hand, gun in the other. Now he could hear roars and howls and sounds that had no place in a human throat. The sounds drew nearer, and Finlay took aim with his disrupter.

And then the monsters surged round the corner at the end of the corridor, and all Finlay could do was stare. Some had bulging brains that had broken apart from their skulls and thrust out through the cracks. Some had bony thorns sticking out through their skin. Others had white, livid flesh, already rotting away from their bones. High tech had been grafted on to and into that flesh, replacing body parts with augmentations until hardly any of their humanity was left – just flesh in metal cages. Some of the monsters still looked mostly human, but rippled the walls of the corridor as they passed, as though reality itself were shifting around them, disturbed by their inhuman and uncontrolled esp.

Finlay breathed heavily. There were bad odds and then there were bad odds, and this was both. He switched his gun from one target to another but, whichever creature he took out, the others would get him long before the gun could recharge for another shot. And for once it didn't matter a damn how good a swordsman he was. Cold steel was no match for esp. He looked at Skye.

'You know these things better than I do. Is there any way

we can reach them? You're an esper, dammit. You must still have something in common with them!'

'I'll try,' said Skye, 'but they're not really espers any more. They've moved beyond that.'

He reached out with his esp, but it was like looking at flaring lights in the night – all colour and brightness and fury without meaning or content. If the monsters had thoughts, he couldn't understand them. All he could share were the rage and horror and suffering that filled their lives. So he did the only thing he could. He gathered up the fury in their minds, threw it back at them, and made each of them think it came from the others around them. The monsters screamed and fell upon each other, rending and tearing, and blood that was not always red flowed. Esp clashed with esp until the air shimmered and sparkled and the steel walls ran like water from the strength of it. Skye stepped backwards, his hands to his head, trying to block it out. Finlay holstered his gun and dragged him away from the carnage in the corridor.

'Don't lose control, Skye! There must be another way out of here. We'll find it!'

They ran down the corridor together. Skye tried to say something to Finlay, but couldn't get it out. Finlay understood. Some of the monsters could have been people the esper knew, before they had ended up in Silo Nine. Some might even have been friends. There but for the grace of God and the underground . . .

They rounded another corner, and Finlay jerked them both to a halt. A full company of guards was blocking the way ahead. They raised their guns to fire, and Finlay dragged Skye back round the corner just in time. A few energy bolts flashed past them, but most of the guards had enough sense not to fire blindly. Using a disrupter in a confined space was always risky.

Finlay pulled the mindbomb out of his pocket, but Skye put a restraining hand on his arm.

'Not a good idea. Use the mindbomb and there's no telling what it might do to the monsters. It could snap them out of the confusion I put them in, and bring them down on us again. And, even if it didn't, do you really want to send that many armed men insane at such close quarters?'

'You have a point,' Finlay said reluctantly. 'Monsters behind, guards ahead. Damned if we do, damned if we don't.' He put the mindbomb away. 'Looks like we'll have to go about this the old-fashioned way. Don't worry. I'm the best there ever was with a sword, and this is where I get to prove it.'

Skye looked at him. 'There are too many of them, and they've all got guns. Disrupters don't care how good a swordsman you are.'

'If I can get into the middle of them fast enough, they won't dare use their guns for fear of shooting each other. Sure, the odds aren't good – but when have they ever been? The important thing is to fight and, if need be, go down fighting. As long as there's still a chance, however slim, we fight on. That's what the underground is all about. Who knows? Maybe we'll get lucky.'

'You could surrender,' said Skye. 'It's only me they really want.'

'That is not an option,' said Finlay. 'I said I'd get you away or die trying, and I meant it. Now be quiet and let me concentrate. There's a way out of this, if only I could see it. There's always a way out.'

'No,' said Skye, 'sometimes there isn't. We've armed guards ahead and monsters behind, and nowhere else to go. It was a nice try, Finlay, but it's over.'

'Then we take as many of them with us as we can,' said Finlay. 'Because, as long as we're still fighting, they haven't really beaten us.'

Skye smiled suddenly. 'Thanks for coming after me. I never really expected anyone – let alone anyone like you. At least this way I get to die on my feet.'

'Don't give up yet,' said Finlay. 'We could still strike lucky.'

That was when the roof fell in, the floor buckled and rose up under their feet, and the walls split apart with screams of rending steel. The guards yelled in confusion, and alarm sirens blared deafeningly from all directions. Skye and Finlay clung to each other for support, Finlay trying to shield the fragile esper with his own body. There was a constant rumbling roar of shifting metal and concrete as the building rocked slowly around them. The lights snapped out, and for a long moment there was only darkness before the dull red glow of emergency lighting returned. In the distance there were sudden, sharp explosions, and from everywhere came the sound of screaming. Some of it didn't sound human. The floor bulged upwards slowly and then settled, and the rumbling died away. Everything was still. People were shouting orders or bellowing for help. It all sounded a long way off. Finlay straightened up, with one arm supporting the esper. Blood was flowing down his face from a long gash on his temple, but he ignored it. He could hear the crackling of fires and smell smoke on the air.

'What the hell was *that*?' said Skye, staring blearily about him into the crimson light. 'Could it have been an earthquake?'

'That was a miracle,' said Finlay. 'And, since they tend to be few and far between, I suggest we get the hell out of here before the authorities get their act together and we need another one.'

He led the way over the uneven floor, with Skye sticking close beside him. The guards around the corner were all dead: the ceiling had caved in on them. Finlay stepped carefully over and around the great slabs of concrete, avoiding the occasional sharp edge of ruptured steel. A guard stirred as he passed, and Finlay paused just lnog enough to cut the man's throat before moving on.

'Was that really necessary?' said Skye.

'Yes,' said Finlay, not looking back. 'Now he can't tell anyone which way we went. Never allow the enemy anything they can use against you.'

Skye shook his head admiringly. 'You're a real fighter, my friend. I haven't seen anyone like you since my brother Auric.'

'What does he do?'

'He doesn't. He died in the Arena, butchered by the Masked Gladiator, may his soul rot in hell.'

Finlay Campbell said nothing. Together, he and Julian Skye made their way through the devastated corridors of the interrogation centre, and nobody stopped or challenged them. When they finally walked out the front door, and saw what had happened to the surrounding city, they knew why.

They made their way through the ruins of the starport with no more trouble than anyone else. The streets might be blocked by debris from toppled buildings, but security was a joke. The authorities had their own problems to worry about. Skye found a way down into the largely untouched maintenance tunnels below, and from there it was a relatively easy trip back to the underground centre.

When they got there, everyone was far too busy to talk to them. The main meeting chamber was a mass of confusion, with people rushing this way and that, shouting orders and information to people who weren't listening. Finlay finally grabbed the nearest person, slammed him up against the wall, stuck his face in close and demanded to know what was going on. His victim glared at him incredulously.

'Where the hell have you been? Golgotha's been attacked by an alien starship! Completely unknown – like nothing anyone's ever seen before. It trashed most of the starport before it went.'

Finlay scowled. 'What happened to the defence systems?'

'They were still down from the rebel attack on the Tax HQ! When the alien ship arrived, there was nothing left to stop it. The deaths and damage in the city have been horrific. We rode out most of it down here, but, up above, everything's gone to hell in a handcart, for us and the Empire. Most of our aboveground agents are either dead or scattered. Communication chains have been shattered.'

He was starting to babble, and Finlay shook him hard to get his attention back. 'What's the underground doing to take advantage of the situation?'

'God only knows. Everyone's got a different idea or plan

for saving the moment, or at least for providing damage limitation, but no one's listening to anyone else. I've heard everything suggested from launching attacks on Empire installations while they're still vulnerable to taking all the underground even deeper into the subsystems so as to avoid the inevitable backlash when Golgotha's population discovers the alien attack was made possible by the rebels' lowering of the planetary defences. Can I go now, please? I was on my way to the toilet, and if anything my need is even worse now than it was.'

Finlay let him go, and led Skye through the crowd, listening to as many voices as he could. The only thing everyone seemed to agree on was that the whole mess was the fault of the new rebels. People had a lot of ideas about what should be done to them, with drawing and quartering coming a close second to very slow impalement.

The three esper leaders suddenly manifested in the centre of the chamber, silencing the chaos with a telepathic bellow so loud that even Finlay heard it. Everyone subsided, holding their heads and wincing. Mr Perfect and the dragon in its tree glared around them, and there was the sense that the mandala was doing the same. Only a few people, including Finlay, were able to look back.

'If you've all quite finished running around like chickens that have just had their heads chopped off,' said Mr Perfect icily, 'perhaps we could discuss the situation in a calm, intelligent and above all quiet manner. First off, things are not as bad as they seem. Most of us survived the attack, thanks to how far we live beneath the surface. Our cells above can be rebuilt, and communications re-established. However, we are in no condition to mount attacks against anybody, let alone Empire installations – even if we could get to them through the current chaos. However, against all the odds Finlay Campbell has returned safely with Julian Skye, rescued before he could be made to talk. So we need no longer worry about having to scatter again. Feel free to applaud, but keep the noise down. We've got a headache.'

There was some cheering, but the crowd remained restive

and uncertain. A few people seemed actually mutinous. Skye looked a little put out at the muted reaction to his safe return, but Finlay didn't care. He hadn't done it for the applause. He looked around him for Evangeline, or even Adrienne, but the crowd was too big.

Mr Perfect began speaking again, a frown marring his classical features, like graffiti on a famous portrait. 'It is imperative we establish proper contact with the new rebels as soon as possible. We sent Alexander Storm and the Stevie Blues to join the raiding party and return with them, but it's clear we're going to need a cooler, more politically minded envoy to represent our views in the future. We need an ambassador to link our two movements together. It is vital that future raids or attacks be decided by both of us, in advance, precisely to prevent this kind of destruction happening again. What little goodwill the underground had among the general population vanished with the alien ship's first strafing run. The council has discussed this, and we have a volunteer to be our ambassador. Evangeline Shreck.'

Finlay mouthed the word *no*, but his reaction was lost in the cheering from the crowd, which this time seemed louder and more genuine. Evangeline was suddenly standing before the esper leaders, head respectfully bowed. She turned around to acknowledge the applause from the crowd, and her eyes met Finlay's as though she'd expected him to be right where he was. She looked away, but there was no guilt or weakness in her cold, composed face.

Finlay started to push his way forward through the crowd. Skye tried to follow him, but lacked the strength. He called the Campbell's name, but if Finlay heard, he paid no attention and Skye was quickly left behind.

Finlay burst through the final few ranks, not caring if he hurt or affronted anyone. No one objected. His reputation as a swordsman and a crazy bastard was widespread throughout the underground. He stood face-to-face with Evangeline, and she met his gaze unflinchingly. He took her by the arm and pulled her a little away from the esper leaders. She went with him unresistingly, but her face didn't change.

'Why are you doing this, Evie?' he said finally. 'Why are you going away and leaving me?'

'I'm not leaving you,' Evangeline said calmly. 'I'm just going on a mission. I'll be back before the year's out. My position as ambassador is only temporary, until the council can decide which of them will replace me.'

'Why did they choose you?'

'Because I asked them to. I wanted to go. I need to get away from things for a while. I've done too much, been involved in too much. I have too many commitments to too many people, and I can't keep them straight in my head any more. Leaving Golgotha will give me time to think. It's been a long time since I could just be myself, with no responsibilities to anyone but myself.'

'You don't have to go away to do that. We could leave the underground, be together, just the two of us.'

She shrugged. 'You said it yourself: you need the action, the blood and slaughter of the missions they give you.'

'None of that means more to me than you. You're the heart that beats in my breast, the air in my mouth. I can't live without you.'

'Yes, you can. For a while. I need this, Finlay. I need . . . I don't know what I need, but it isn't here. Adrienne helped me to see that.'

Finlay nodded grimly. 'I might have known she'd be at the back of this. She's never happy unless she's screwing up my life.'

'No, Finlay. This was my decision. I need to get away from the subsystems, my father . . .'

'And me?'

'That, too. Nothing's really going to change. We hardly ever see each other anyway. I have my duties, and you're always off on your missions . . .'

'That can change. *I* can change. What do you want from me?'

'Your understanding. I still love you, Finlay. I'll always love you, no matter where I am or where you are. But I can't go on like this. It's tearing me apart, and I can't stand it any

187

more. I have to take some control of my life. Don't fight me on this, Finlay. It's important to me.'

He took a deep breath, and nodded abruptly. 'Then it's important to me, too. Go. I'll manage.' He opened his arms to her and she came into them, and for a long time they stood together, blind to the outside world. Finlay held her close; if his strength hurt her, she never said anything.

He could feel tears prickling his eyes, but he wouldn't let them out. 'What am I going to do without you, Evie?'

'You'll find something to keep yourself busy. You swore a blood oath, remember, on your name and honour, to avenge what was done to Jenny Psycho and others like her, to put an end not just to Silo Nine but to the system that produced it. Now the council has seen what you can do, they'll give you more important work in the underground. If you ask them.'

'Maybe.' He pushed her gently away, and looked searchingly into her eyes. 'You do what you need to do, Evie. That's all that matters, in the end. But I still wish they could have chosen someone else.'

'Everyone else was too important, too well connected or too busy. The only use they had for me was to maintain my influence over my father and to keep you in line. My father and I . . . have become estranged. And I promised the council you wouldn't be a problem. Don't make a liar out of me. They chose me because I have proven diplomatic skills, and because I'm entirely expendable. I was the perfect candidate.'

'We seem fated to be kept apart,' said Finlay. 'Someday, when all this is over, maybe we'll be able to have a simple, mundane life together, like everyone else. I'd like that.'

'Yes,' said Evangeline. 'So would I.'

There was a sudden commotion behind them. Everyone was turning to look at somebody who'd just entered the chamber. An excited babble began as the crowd recognized who it was. A name ran through the crowd, growing louder and louder, from a chant to a roar to a battle-cry. '*Jenny Psycho! Jenny Psycho! Jenny Psycho!*'

'Oh, hell,' said Finlay. 'Just what we need. More complications.'

Jenny Psycho, who had once been called Diana Vertue but had mostly forgotten that, was short and blonde, with a pale face dominated by sharp blue eyes. She had a large mouth, and a smile that showed more teeth than humour. She'd once been just another low-level esper, like so many others, but then the underground had planted her as their agent in the notorious esper prison Silo Nine, and the uber-esper Mater Mundi had manifested through her to blow the place apart. Jenny had been touched by greatness, transformed by the Mater Mundi's fleeting presence, and, since her escape from Wormboy Hell, had become a new, major force in the underground. She'd taken the codename as her own, and entered esper politics with a vengeance. Wherever she went, a small crowd of fanatical followers went with her – as they were now, scowling at anyone who dared to get too close. Finlay sometimes wondered whether Jenny Psycho was a political force or a religious icon. Perhaps she wasn't sure herself. Certainly her popularity had been growing in leaps and bounds of late – it must have been, if someone as disinterested as Finlay had noticed it. She'd also become one of the most powerful espers the underground had ever known, and you could feel it in her presence: it all but crackled on the air around her, a palpable force that was part charisma and part enigma. A rabble-rouser, a cunning politician and a tireless warrior for esper rights, she was respected, worshipped and adored by the many, and watched very carefully by the esper leaders. She was also just a little crazy, of course, but people made allowances. No one expected saints to be normal. She had been touched by Our Mother of All Souls, and, with the Mater Mundi currently quiet and unavailable, people were willing to settle for the next best thing.

Having made one of her usual unexpected and highly dramatic entrances, Jenny Psycho pressed forward. The crowd opened up before her, as though pushed back by the sheer force of her personality. She stopped at the front of the crowd and smiled unpleasantly, as though she could peer past

189

the images the esper leaders projected and see the real people beneath. Maybe she could.

Evangeline leaned in close beside Finlay. 'If I'd known she was going to turn out to be such a pain in the ass I'd have thought twice about springing her from Silo Nine.'

Finlay shrugged. 'She preaches direct action, and that's a popular stance to take these days. And she *was* a focus for the Mater Mundi.'

'So were you and I, and we're no crazier now than we were before. Though admittedly it's hard to tell in your case.'

Finlay grinned, then made himself concentrate on Jenny Psycho as she began speaking.

She had a harsh, unattractive voice. She'd damaged her vocal cords screaming in Wormboy Hell. It didn't matter. When she spoke, you had to listen.

'I'm back again, people. Make the most of me while I'm here. The Empire threw me into Silo Nine and put a worm in my head to control me, but with the Mater Mundi's help I broke out. You can break out, too. Work with me, and we can all become more than we are. No one can compel me now – not even the worm in my head. The council said taking it out would kill me, but I don't believe that any more. Watch. And learn.'

She pushed her long golden hair back behind her ears so that her face could be clearly seen. She put a hand to her forehead and frowned, as though listening or concentrating. Her left temple bulged outwards suddenly, and the skin split apart. Blood ran down Jenny's face, but she ignored it. There was a sharp, cracking sound, and the bone of her skull broke open at the left temple. Something small and grey and bloody crawled out of the crack and fell into Jenny's waiting hand. A genetically engineered horror that existed only to imprison and torture captive minds, it pulsed and twitched feebly.

Jenny closed her hand around the worm and crushed it with one swift gesture. Blood and grey pulp oozed through her fingers. Then she opened her fingers and let what was left fall to the ground.

The crowd went mad, cheering and applauding and stamping their feet. Jenny Psycho began to speak again, but Finlay wasn't listening. He appreciated the theatre of what she'd done but distrusted her message. The call to direct action was all very well and fine – he'd raised it himself on more than one occasion – but there was nothing of strategy or planning in Jenny's message: all the underground had to do was trust in her and the Mater Mundi, and all would be well. And the crowd believed it because they wanted to. She promised strength and revenge and glory, and everything else the downbeaten craved so desperately.

Finlay looked out over the cheering mob, and wasn't impressed.

Drowning men will clutch at any straw.

191

CHAPTER FOUR

Raised Voices and Diversions

Lionstone XIV, the revered and feared Empress of a thousand worlds and more, was holding Court once again, and everyone that mattered – or thought they might – made haste to attend her. The Court itself was a polar waste this time – as real as holographic projections, strategically placed props and temperature controls could make it. The Empress restyled her Court constantly to reflect her whims and changing moods, or just to give her courtiers a bad time. Veteran Court attendees claimed to be able to divine much of Lionstone's mood from studying each new Court, but, even when the news was bad, people went anyway. You had to, if you wanted your voice to be heard. Besides, if you stayed away too often, Lionstone might take it as an insult. And the people she sent to drag you there to hear her displeasure would not be polite about it.

The Court itself was a single vast chamber somewhere within the Imperial Palace, set inside a massive steel bunker deep below the surface of Golgotha. No one knew precisely how big the chamber was, for security reasons, but so far it had always proven large enough to hold whatever worlds or conditions Lionstone chose to recreate. Unfortunately, those conditions also reflected her sense of humour, which could be pretty basic on occasion. Courtiers knew better than to sit down on anything, no matter how apparently comfortable, and approached the luxurious food and wine provided as if playing a form of Russian roulette.

It was a long way down to the Court. People made jokes about descending into hell, but not very loudly.

Captain Silence, Investigator Frost and Security Officer Stelmach stood together in the midst of a great crowd of courtiers, staring out over a bleak waste that stretched off into the distance as far as the eye could see. The snow was a good foot deep on the ground, and more fell in heavy wet flakes from the brooding grey sky above. A thin mist pearled the air, thickening briefly here and there into impenetrable walls. The bitter cold seared exposed flesh and the lungs of those who breathed too deeply; Silence turned up the heating elements in his uniform another notch. Frost didn't bother. It took more than mere cold to discomfit an Investigator. She'd been trained to withstand far worse. Stelmach had his heating elements running on full, but shivered anyway. He wasn't looking forward to meeting the Empress.

Whatever else might prove an illusion, the cold was real enough: sharp enough to kill an unprotected man, eventually. And there were bound to be other, more subtle dangers concealed at random throughout the Court. The Empress never found a joke really funny unless someone could get hurt. The snow was especially genuine. It collected wetly on heads and clothes, and the fall seemed to be getting heavier. Someone had gone to a lot of trouble to construct this environment, which suggested the appropriate lifeforms were out there somewhere too. Especially the predators.

The gathered courtiers murmured among themselves for a while. Then some brave soul stepped forward, and everyone else trudged through the snow after him. Few had come prepared for icy conditions, and the bright flashing silks of current fashion did little to protect their wearers. A few grumbled and blasphemed under their breath, but most just toughed it out. You never knew who might be listening.

John Silence stepped out along with the crowd, still somewhat surprised that he wasn't weighed down with chains, like he had been on his last visit to Court. After screwing up so completely on the Wolfling World, he'd fully expected to find himself facing an execution warrant the moment he stepped off his ship, but apparently his victory over the attacking alien craft had bought him, if nothing else, some extra time.

Frost strode along at his side as though the snow weren't there, apparently unconcerned by anything. There wasn't much that bothered Investigators, if only because they tended to kill things that did. Stelmach trudged along in her shadow, using her tall form as a windbreak. His arms were wrapped tightly across his chest and he was pouting sulkily. Stelmach was not happy. He rarely was. Being a security officer did that to you, especially if your first name was Valiant.

The crowd laboured on through the packed snow, slipping and lurching and fighting for balance. The mists were growing thicker, obscuring the distance. Silence watched his breath steam in the air before him, and wondered what lay ahead. If he had any sense he'd be running for his life rather than presenting his head to the Empress so she could cut it off, but he knew his duty. The Fleet was his life, and, even if it had been for the most part a hard life, he wouldn't have chosen any other. As a captain in the Imperial Navy he was part of something greater; he was employed in the service of humanity, and he would give his life for it, should that prove necessary. Lionstone might be a vindictive psychotic with a particularly unfortunate sense of humour, but she was his Empress, and he had sworn upon his life and his honour to serve her all his days. He looked about him at the sub-zero world, and smiled slightly. Typical of Lionstone. Here he was, walking to his execution like a good soldier, and she had to make even *that* difficult.

He looked around sharply, sensing as much as hearing that there was something large moving up ahead, hidden in the mists. Murmurs went through the crowd as others detected it. Silence's eyes narrowed, and his hand fell to his hip where his gun should have been. There were further glimpses of something in the mists, seen and gone in a moment. It moved ponderously, crunching loudly through the snow, and then suddenly raised a shaggy head and roared defiantly. The harsh sound echoed eerily in the quiet . . . and then the mists came down again and the creature was lost to sight. The courtiers huddled together for comfort, but kept moving. The Empress was waiting.

Silence's hands itched for a weapon, but gun and sword were both denied him. No subject was allowed to bear weapons before the Empress without a special dispensation, which meant that everyone around Silence was unarmed too – easy pickings should the creature decide it was hungry. The Empress would have to be crazy to risk endangering the Families with any real threat, but no one would have bet against it. Silence scowled, his hands curling into fists.

The dim shape roared again, but this time further off.

The crowd breathed a general sigh of relief, and the pace picked up again. There was always the chance the shape was just another hologram, but no one was willing to bet on that, either. Silence decided he was going to stick close to the Investigator. Even unarmed, Frost was death on two legs, and he'd back her against anything Lionstone might have imported. Not that he'd ever tell Frost that. She was big-headed enough as it was.

More forms loomed up out of the mists ahead. At first Silence thought they were security guards, waiting to escort the courtiers to the Iron Throne, but, as he drew closer, he could see they were just snowmen – with cheerful scarves around their necks, coals for eyes and a smile drawn on. They might have been charming had they not all been depicted dying in different, innovative ways. One had been impaled on a lance. Another held its severed head in its hands. Beside it, a third form had been dismembered, its snow limbs lying scattered around its body. Silence started to walk past them, then hesitated as he realized Frost had stopped. The Investigator stood frowning at the snowmen, one hand patting her hip where her sword normally hung. Stelmach was shivering beside her, not particularly interested in the snowmen but unwilling to move on without the protection of the only more or less friendly faces he knew.

Silence moved in beside Frost. 'What is it, Investigator? Problem?'

'I don't know, Captain. Maybe. There's something about these snowmen. Something . . . disturbing. Who makes a snowman with limbs?'

She stepped up to the decapitated snowman and took the snow head out of its cupped hands. A wide smile had been cut beneath the blind coal eyes of the large ball of snow. Frost grunted at the unexpected weight of the head, and balanced it in the crook of her arm as she scraped away at the surface of the snow with her other hand. The eyes and smile disappeared. Silence suddenly knw what she was going to find. The surface snow disappeared to reveal the nose and staring eyes of a real face. Frost carefully swept away more snow to uncover the human features beneath.

Silence didn't recognize the face. He moved forward and thrust his hand deep into the snow body. His fingertips thudded against something hard and unyielding that definitely wasn't packed snow. He pulled his hand out quickly and rubbed it clean against his thigh.

'There's a real body in there,' he said quietly.

'Can't say I'm surprised, Captain.' Frost threw the head aside. 'Shall I check the other snowmen?'

'No need. They're all dead men. Lionstone's way of telling us what's coming. I wonder who they were.'

Frost shrugged. 'People who upset the Empress. Never any shortage of them. Let's go.'

'What's the hurry?' snapped Stelmach. 'Make the most of what little time we've got left.'

'Don't give up hope,' said Silence. 'Frost and I have been here before, and we survived. Maybe we'll get lucky this time as well.'

'No one's that lucky,' said Stelmach.

'Don't worry,' said Frost. 'We'll put in a good word for you.'

'Oh, great,' said Stelmach. 'That's all I need.'

They moved on, wading doggedly through the deep snow to catch up with the rest of the courtiers. Some of them must have seen what was inside the snowmen, but they were all doing their best to pretend they hadn't. Success at Court often depended on being very selective as to what you saw. The snow fell and the mists thickened, and still the snowy waste stretched out before them. Silence frowned. Surely the

Court couldn't be *this* large. Perhaps they were being subtly influenced to walk in circles.

He looked up sharply as an agitated murmur began again among the courtiers. The crowd lurched to a halt, those on the edges staring quickly about them. Nothing moved in the mists. Silence glanced at Frost, who was listening carefully. She gestured for him to come close, so that she could whisper in his ear.

'There's something moving under the snow, Captain. It's large, and it's alive.'

'A snow snake, perhaps,' said Silence. 'They have those on Loki. Some of the big ones run to twenty feet long.'

'Oh, no,' said Stelmach. 'Not snakes. I *really* don't like snakes.'

'Don't worry,' said Silence soothingly. 'If it annoys the Investigator she'll tie it into a square knot and throw it away. Right, Frost?'

'Damn' right,' said Frost.

A set of jaws ten feet wide suddenly opened up beneath a courtier's feet, gulped him down, and disappeared back into the concealing snow. His friends and Family shouted in alarm and fell to their knees to dig at the snow with their bare hands, but there was no trace left of whatever had taken him. They looked at each other helplessly, and far away in the snow and mists came the light tinkling of laughter. The Empress was amused. Some of the courtiers began talking calmingly to those still on their knees. There was nothing to be done. Man proposes and the Empress disposes, and that was just the way it was in the Empire these days. Silence said nothing, but his face was set and grim.

The snow surged up suddenly at the crowd's edge as the snow creature's blunt head again broke the surface. People scattered with shouts and shrieks. The great mouth opened, and spat out the courtier it had taken. The head dropped back into the snow and disappeared. The courtier sailed through the air and hit the packed snow hard, but his plaintive groan showed that at least he was still alive. His friends clustered around him, checked that he was basically undamaged, and got him to his feet again. Lionstone laughed once more, and everyone who liked their neck as it was laughed along with her. Even the courtier who'd briefly seen the inside of something much larger than he was managed a shaky laugh. He was probably just glad to be alive. Frost looked at Silence.

'Big snake.'

Stelmach, beside them, nodded rapidly, his eyes very large.

The courtiers tramped on again, driving their legs through the deep snow. The air seemed to be getting colder, if that were possible. Hoarfrost was forming on hair and beards, and snow warmed by body heat soaked into light clothing. Everyone was shivering, and some were shuddering violently. Silence could feel the chill gnawing at his bones, despite the fact that the heating elements in his uniform were running on full. His nose and ears ached, and he could feel crystals of ice forming at the corners of his eyes. Stelmach was shaking as though he had a small juddering engine inside him. Frost, of course, didn't deign to shiver. The courtiers had packed close together for support and shared body warmth, but they still kept clear of Silence, Frost and Stelmach: they knew pariahs when they saw them. They'd all stopped talking and settled for concentrating on surviving Lionstone's latest practical joke. There was no question but that it had been a dark day for the Empire in general and the Court in particular when the Empress had decided she had a sense of humour.

Again strange shapes loomed up out of the mists ahead. This time they were huge shards of solid ice, thrusting up out of the snowfield. The falling flakes swirled around them, as though attracted to the glistening planes of ice. There were statues scattered among the shards, carved into disturbing, sharp-edged shapes. Silence looked from the statues to the shards and wondered if they too had been carved and shaped into ancient and enigmatic forms that only mankind's distant ancestors might have recognized and responded to.

The ice structures made a rough semicircle, and at its far end stood the Iron Throne, set high on a great block of ice. On that ancient chair of black iron, studded with jade, sat the

Empress Lionstone XIV, calmly watching their stumbling approach. She was wrapped in layers of thick furs, like some ancient tribal leader, her pale face as cold and clear as that of the legendary Ice Queen who stole men's souls by sliding knives of ice into their eyes and hearts. She had a long, sharp-planed face, with a wide slash of a mouth and brilliant, freezingly blue eyes. She was beautiful, but with a cold kind of beauty, like that of the tall diamond crown on her head. The Empress, the worshipped and adored, whose caprices were laws and at whose merest word men died and worlds burned . . . also known as the Iron Bitch.

She watched with a sardonic smile as the courtiers drew up before her, bowed their heads, and then held themselves in that humble and uncomfortable position while they waited for the word from the Empress that would release them. On bad days she'd been known to keep them like this for ages, until sweat dropped from their faces and their backs screamed for release. Today she gave them permission to straighten up after only a few seconds; either she was in a good mood, or she was looking forward to something yet to come. The courtiers practised looking polite and reverential and extremely loyal as the Empress's smile wandered over them.

They also kept a respectful distance, not just because of the twenty armed guards spread out behind the throne but also because of Lionstone's maids-in-waiting, who crouched snarling silently at her feet. There were ten of them, each more dangerous than any armed man. They wore no clothes, but they wouldn't feel the cold. They didn't feel anything unless the Empress permitted it. Mind-techs had dabbled in the maids' brains until nothing remained there but unquestioning obedience to the Empress. They would die to protect her. Or kill, as required. They were cunning, deadly fighters, with hidden implanted weaponry. They were silent because they had no tongues. They perceived the world only through grafted cybernetic senses. Their fingers had steel claws.

The maids-in-waiting clustered together at the base of the Iron Throne, glaring at the courtiers, hoping eagerly to be unleashed on anyone foolish enough to displease their mistress. But for once not even they were enough to hold the courtiers' gaze. Beside the throne, standing a little to one side in the swirling snow, huge and awful, stood a yoked Grendel alien.

On the planet called Grendel, genetically engineered creatures had been discovered sleeping in deep-buried vaults – thousands upon thousands of them, an army waiting for an enemy that never came. The alien civilization that had created them was long gone, but its work lived on: unstoppable killing machines, living weapons, programmed to fight until either they or the enemy was destroyed. An Empire exploratory team had made the mistake of opening one of the ancient vaults, and the Sleepers had emerged in a fury of blood and slaughter. They had wiped out all the team and overrun the exploratory camp on the surface in a matter of minutes. Hundreds of men and women had died screaming, their weapons useless, and not one Grendel fell. But they had no spaceships, and so were trapped on the planet's surface. The Empress had given the order for that surface to be scorched from orbit. Except for those still sleeping in the vaults deep below, that was the end of the Grendels. Lionstone had put the planet under quarantine, and left starcruisers there to enforce it.

But, faced with the threat of unknown alien foes massing against the Empire, Lionstone had conceived a new plan: to waken and control the Grendels and use them as shock troops. And now here one stood. A thick cybernetic yoke gleamed on its shoulders, controlling the creature's thoughts. Theoretically. Everyone eyed the Grendel warily, and hoped fervently that this time the scientists had got all the bugs out of the technology. The alien stood nine feet tall, clad in spiked armour of crimson silicon that was somehow a part of it. It had vicious fangs and claws. Although it was roughly humanoid in shape, its large, heart-shaped face had nothing even remotely like a human expression.

When Silence had gone down to the vaults to try to capture and control the aliens, just one of the creatures had wiped out a whole company of his men before he had defeated it – which had been as much by luck as by anything else. And now here was one in Court, with only a prototype yoke holding back its perpetual killing rage. More than ever Silence wished he had his weapons – or at least some idea which way the exit was.

The courtiers around him studied the Grendel silently, and were not happy. They understood the need for increased security at Court, after previous attacks by both aliens and elves, but a personal Grendel on a leash was going a bit far, even for Lionstone. This had gone beyond safety or style, and headed firmly in the direction of overkill. Those at the front of the crowd were seized with a sudden polite wish for others to take up their privileged vantage point, and attempted to fade back into the crowd. The ranks behind them were having none of this, and resisted strongly. If the yoke should fail, everyone knew better than to think the armed guards would try to protect them. That wasn't what they were there for. The courtiers somehow managed to stir rebelliously in complete silence.

Frost tilted her head towards Stelmach, who jumped slightly. Frost didn't smile. 'I thought you said you were the only one who had a yoked Grendel – and that one was destroyed on Haden. So what's this doing here?'

'Apparently research has moved on in my absence,' said Stelmach, his voice little more than a whisper. He was trying to talk without moving his lips, so as to avoid drawing attention to himself.

Frost frowned deeply. 'Just how dependable is that yoke?'

'Depends what you mean by dependable. Unless they've made some major breakthrough, which I strongly doubt, the yoke is strictly on/off. Once the Grendel's been unleashed it will kill anything it sees. The best you can hope to do is make sure it's aimed in the right direction. If that yoke is built according to the principles my people established, it should do its job, but I wouldn't like to bet my life on it.'

'We *are* betting our lives on it,' said Silence.

'I know,' said Stelmach, unhappily.

Silence looked about him, not bothering to hide his interest. He had no doubt there were more armed guards around that he couldn't see, probably hidden behind concealing holograms. Plus any number of esp-blockers, to keep out esper terrorists. And a whole set of other protections he probably wouldn't recognize. The Empress was said to have spent more than one fortune making her Court as secure as was humanly possible. It wasn't just paranoia. There were a lot of people who would like to see Lionstone dead, who'd dance at her funeral and piss on her grave. Quite a few of them could be found among the courtiers, which was why they were admitted only unarmed and after a complete body scan.

But for the first time in years, the courtiers were pretty sure they had a chance to force power out of Lionstone's hands and into theirs. They had something that, if properly handled, might just drive a wedge between the Empress and the military that supported her. The rebels' triumphant trashing of the Income Tax and Tithe Headquarters, along with their breaking open of the planet's defences, had made the military's position, politically speaking, very vulnerable. The sudden alien attack had only emphasized this. And, on top of everything else that had happened, the Empire's Warrior Prime, the Empress's own official consort and good right hand, the Lord High Dram, was strongly rumoured to be dead – killed on some faraway planet, on an unknown mission entirely unauthorized by the Court.

The only people said to know for sure were the crew of the *Dauntless*, and they were being held in strict quarantine on their ship, in orbit – except for Silence, Frost and Stelmach. A lot of eyes were following their every move, but the courtiers gave them plenty of room, too, just in case. The courtiers were pretty sure Lionstone had something in mind for these three, and it might well turn out to be messy.

Silence was aware of the Court's undercurrents, and the way the courtiers were looking at the Empress. He couldn't help thinking they had a point about Lionstone's current vulnerability. If the Empress and her military couldn't protect her own planet from a single alien ship and a handful of rebels, she and they were in no position to try to dictate terms to the Company of Lords and the Members of Parliament, whose monies helped to pay for everything. The bottom line was that, if they were going to pay higher taxes for the Empire's security, they wanted more of a say in how that money was to be spent – and preferably the ground-rules should be in place before the tax records could be worked out again and the new rates decided.

Not being blind to all this, the military had taken steps to establish a strong presence among the courtiers. Officers of all ranks and status, from the highest to the very high, stood at attention before the throne. If the cold was bothering them they were doing their best not to show it, though snow had accumulated on their heads and on the shoulders of their uniforms. They had come to Court to make it clear that the Empress still enjoyed the military's support and confidence. And, of course, vice versa. The military were there to protect Lionstone against all threats, even those that might come from the Court itself. Although not above playing politics, when necessary, all branches of the services owed their allegiance to the Empress, first and foremost. It was a matter of honour, which, in the military at least, still ranked above politics. Mostly.

The Church of Christ the Warrior had its own strong presence, with ranks of armoured acolytes standing alongside the military and studiously ignoring them. They had pale faces, shaven heads and the unblinking glares of true fanatics. They were warrior priests, raised since childhood in a hot and bloody faith, and they bowed to the Empress only when circumstances forced them to it. The Church believed in enforcing the faith, even if it meant killing the very people they were supposed to be converting. It preached that might was right, by God's will, and was always ready and eager to provide practical examples. There were other religions in the Empire, but mostly they kept their heads down and tried to avoid being noticed.

General Shaw Beckett stood at the very front of the crowd and studied the ranks of robed acolytes throughtfully. He didn't bother to hide his interest. Some of them were watching him just as intently, and for the same reason: know thy enemy. Beckett smiled, and blew a cloud of cigar smoke at them. Faith was all very well, but he preferred training. Just because a fanatic wasn't afraid to die, it didn't necessarily follow that he'd be able to get the job done before the enemy killed him. The general was an old soldier, and took the Church of Christ the Warrior with a large pinch of salt. He'd been a legendary fighter in his day, and, even though he was now very clearly in his twilight years, no one crossed him without taking the precaution of making out their will first.

He was of average height, but because he was extremely fat he appeared shorter. Most of the weight had accumulated around his waist – so much so that even his specially tailored battle armour had to strain to hold him in – but he didn't give a damn. He'd spent enough years in the field that he felt he'd earned his little comforts. His value these days lay in his brilliant, incisive military mind, trained by his years of experience at the sharp end. He was renowned as a master tactician and a wily debater, and rarely failed to get his own way even when the Empress was in one of her moods and everyone else had run for cover. She was constantly on the verge of having him dragged away for saying the wrong thing at the wrong moment, or insisting on a truth she didn't want to hear, but somehow he always found a way to remind her of how valuable he was to her, and to the Empire. Besides, he made her laugh. Shaw Beckett smoked thick cigars, even in places where he wasn't permitted to, and liked to blow the smoke in people's faces while he was talking to them. He had other bad habits too, and gloried in them. Not surprisingly, he was very popular with the watching holo audiences.

The Church had a private but widely known bounty for anyone who would bring it the general's head, preferably unattached to the body.

The Church of Christ the Warrior had grown increasingly large and powerful since Lionstone had made it the official religion of the Empire. It had run exhaustive purges in her name, killed off every heretic it could get its hands on, and then had decreed it had grown so powerful through God's will, not the Empress's: it didn't need the Empress's support any more and, as it was the foremost church in the Empire, Lionstone should bow to it. This hadn't gone down at all well with Lionstone, but, having made them the official Church after a very public baptism, she couldn't back down now without looking weak and indecisive. And it did have one hell of a following. So she settled for sharpening the claws of her humour on them at every opportunity, and backing the military against the Church whenever the two factions came into conflict. Which was pretty often, these days.

The Church had retaliated by increasing its ranks of deadly Jesuit commandoes, and had set about infiltrating society from top to bottom. Every Family had lost someone to the clutches of the Church, either as a member or as a proclaimed heretic. As a result, people now had two masters they needed to please if they were to have anything approaching a quiet life: the Empress and the Church. Choose the wrong one at the wrong time and you could end up in a world of trouble. As far as the Church was concerned, even Family loyalties and considerations should come second to the needs of the Church.

This was notably unpopular with the Company of Lords, who tended not to give a toss what the lower orders chose to believe in as long as they remained respectful and hard-working, but had little time themselves to worship anything apart from profit and status. The new attitude of the Church had infuriated the noble Families, who had made it very clear they were determined to continue their age-old freedoms to intrigue, lust, duel and generally kick ass as they saw fit.

The Church, on the other hand, started with the belief that everyone was secretly guilty of something, and it was always on the lookout for ammunition it could use to bring down the powerful and bend them to the Church's will. So they persuaded, encouraged, bribed and threatened the lower orders to spy on their masters and report useful items, at regular intervals, if they wished to avoid the Church's displeasure. The Families hit back by launching their own purges among the lower orders. Everyone caught in between kept their heads well down and hoped not to be noticed, with the overall result that life in the Empire had of late become a great deal more complicated for everyone.

'The Church has been busy since we were last here,' murmured Silence to Frost. 'Those warrior priests look impressive. And there are a damn' sight more of them than there used to be.'

'Bunch of pansies,' said Frost, not even condescending to look at them. 'They're good at looking tough, but that's about it. I could carve them up and eat them raw without even a decent red wine to wash them down. I know the type: brave enough in packs, but gutless in a fair fight. If they're so keen to worship God, let them pick a fight with me and I'll send them up so they can have a personal chat.'

'If you're going to keep on talking like that, kindly give me some warning,' said Stelmach, 'so I can stay well away from you. The Church has extremely keen hearing these days, and it never forgives a slight or an insult. Oh, God, one of them's coming this way. Try and look penitent.'

'I wouldn't know how,' said Frost.

Silence somehow managed to keep a straight face as the warrior priest approached. Courtiers were falling well back to give the man plenty of room. He wore a long, blood-red gown and skullcap, and an expression stern enough to cut glass. He was in his mid-twenties and trying to look older. Two scalps hung from his belt, and a necklace of human ears hung around his neck. He stopped before Silence and Frost, ignoring Stelmach – who was quite happy to be ignored. The priest looked from Silence to Frost and back again, his expression suggesting he'd seen more impressive specimens lying face-down on tavern floors, eating the sawdust.

'They say you saved us all from the godless alien craft,' said the priest. 'If you did, it was by God's will. You are both fine warriors, by all accounts, but you must learn your place in the new scheme of things. You must seek the Church's forgiveness, as well as Lionstone's, for your sins and failures.

206

To stand alone is no longer permitted. And, remember: if you do not stand with the Church you stand against it. The Church knows how to deal with its enemies. Do I make myself clear?'

His sneer disappeared suddenly as Frost drop-kicked him from a standing start. The force of the blow picked the warrior priest up and threw him back among his own people, scattering them like ninepins. There was much moaning and groaning and clutching of injured parts. The priest who'd started it all lay curled up in a ball, trying to persuade his lungs to start working again. Frost had regained her feet, her face calm. She wasn't even breathing hard. Stelmach covered his eyes with his hands. Silence applauded, and some of the braver courtiers joined in. Frost ignored them all magnificently, every inch an Investigator.

'I don't think I want to stand anywhere near you two,' said Stelmach. 'You must have a death-wish.'

'Lighten up,' said Silence. 'We've probably been brought here to die anyway, remember? What does it matter who gets to kill us?'

Stelmach glanced briefly at the Empress on her Iron Throne, and then looked at Silence almost pleadingly. 'You're sure, then? We've no hope at all?'

'Oh, there's always hope,' said Silence. 'The last time we were here, Frost and I, they had us in chains from nose to toes, and all the execution warrants were missing was our names in the right places. We survived. Our chances are, if anything, rather worse this time, but at least we're not in chains. I choose to see that as an encouraging sign.'

'I don't,' said Frost. 'They're just being subtle. Nothing like providing a false hope to really put the screws on someone.'

Stelmach sighed. 'I had hoped some of my Family might turn up to provide a little moral support, but no. No one's here to see me die. A failure has no kin or friends, for fear it might rub off.'

Silence looked at him. 'That was almost profound. Obviously being this close to sudden death inspires you. You never talk much, Stelmach. Tell us about your Family. What kind of people christen their son "Valiant"?'

'Ambitious people,' said Stelmach grimly. 'My people were in business, but not successful enough for any of them to become a Minister or marry into a Clan. So we were all packed off into the military at an early age. My brothers, Bold and Hero, are mid-line officers. My sister, Athena, was taken away even younger to be an Investigator. I don't know what became of her. One doesn't ask. My father died long ago, so he never got to see me disappoint him. "Security Officer" isn't exactly the most glamorous rank in the Fleet.'

'At least you still *have* a Family,' said Silence. 'I became a captain because my Clan expected it of me. And I wanted them to be proud of me. Instead, twice now I've brought the Family name into disrepute. Officially, they disowned me when I failed to go down with my first ship, the *Darkwind*. I was ready to, but the Investigator here insisted on saving me, for her own inscrutable reasons. Isn't that right, Frost?'

'We all make mistakes,' said Frost, not looking at him.

Silence smiled. 'Aren't you going to tell us about your Family, Investigator? We've both opened our hearts here. Tell us where you came from.'

There was a long pause, until Silence had almost decided he'd pushed it too far, and then Frost spoke very quietly, so that Silence and Stelmach had to concentrate to make out her words. She didn't look at either of them as she spoke.

'Officially, Investigators have no Family but each other. But I was curious, so I broke into the right hidden files and checked out my background. I found my parents' address, and went to visit them. Only my father would agree to see me. I tried to talk to him, but he wouldn't listen. He was afraid of me. I never went back. No Family made me, Captain. I made me, with a little help from the Empire.'

'I'm glad we've had this little talk,' said Stelmach. 'I was feeling a bit depressed, but now I've moved on to feeling suicidal. Why don't we all just swallow our tongues now and get it over with?'

'Because there's still hope,' said Silence. 'And because,

208

even if I am going down, I'll fight them every inch of the way. Right, Investigator?'

'Right,' said Frost. 'Oh, look, the warrior priests seem to be recovering.'

The priests she had toppled had got their breath back, and were now once more on their feet, though still leaning on each other for support. The military were openly nudging each other and chuckling. Some of the courtiers began to applaud again, and then stopped, looking to see if the Empress approved. Luckily for all concerned, Lionstone was apparently deep in conversation with General Beckett. So everyone else turned to look at the other man standing in front of the crowd before the Iron Throne: James Kassar, Cardinal of the Church of Christ the Warrior. Said by many to be one of the most dangerous men in the Empire, he was tall and muscular and wore black battle armour as though born to it. A large crucifix stood out in bas relief on the armour over his heart. He'd been handsome once, but not any more. Kassar had had a man executed as a heretic on questionable grounds, and the man's widow had thrown acid in the cardinal's face. He had struck her down a moment later, gutting her with his sword, but the damage had been done. His right eye was gone, eaten right out of the socket, and the right side of his face had been burned down to the skull beneath, so that discoloured pitted bone showed clearly through ragged strips of flesh. His teeth gleamed among the remnants of his right cheek, giving him a constant ghastly half-smile that had nothing of humour in it. His face turned the strongest stomach, and he knew it. That was one reason why he'd never had it healed. A regeneration machine would have smoothed the terrible wounds away, but he chose not to take that option – perhaps as a sign that nothing could stop or hurt him, perhaps as a reverse kind of vanity.

There were some who said he'd had the guards who let the woman slip past them arrested, and then lowered into a vat of acid, feet first, one inch at a time. Few people had trouble believing the story. Cardinal Kassar was known for his cold rages and for a vindictiveness that masqueraded as a thirst for justice. He'd risen rapidly through the ranks of the Church by leading vigorous crusades against heretics – who could be anyone who challenged his or the Church's authority. He didn't hesitate to accuse anyone who stood against the Church's increasing influence or his own personal ascent, even if they were friends or Family or previous allies. And, as he rose with unprecedented speed, people hurried, if they knew what was good for them, to copy his zeal.

As a result, a useful way of dealing with one's enemies was to accuse them of heresy. No proof was needed: often the accusation was enough. There were tribunals where the accused could present their defence, but doing so cost money. Justice has never come cheap. Things had got so bad some people tried to take out insurance against being accused, to cover possible legal fees, only to discover the premiums were more expensive than the fees. That was when the courtiers had first realized no one was safe any more.

The Empress hadn't been slow to pick up on this, and found the practice of accusation particularly useful for helping keep her Court in order. If anyone started making trouble or getting above themselves, the word would go out and the unfortunate victim would be awakened in the early hours by the sound of holy boots kicking his door down. Soon anyone who even annoyed Lionstone had better have very strong ties with the Church or a lot of money to hire lawyers. If you could find a lawyer brave enough to take on the Church these days.

The courtiers played the same dangerous game, denouncing each other every day for political, Family or personal reasons, but they were taken less seriously. The truth quickly vanished in a morass of claims and counterclaims, until even the Church grew sick of it. So they just recorded everything as future ammunition, whenever it might be necessary.

Valentine Wolfe had been denounced so many times that the Church had lost count, and for all kinds of heresies, including some that had previously been thought only theoretically possible, but the charges had never stuck. No one doubted that he was an utter degenerate, with a drug habit strong enough to have killed half a dozen normal men, but, as head of the Empire's first Family, incredibly rich and powerful, and with the Empress's ear and support, he was for all practical purposes completely untouchable. Some wits made remarks about bargepoles, but never when Valentine was around. Kassar still hadn't given up on nailing him, but for the time being the two settled for conspicuously ingoring each other. The courtiers watched avidly. Everyone knew the situation couldn't go on forever. It was just a question of which one made a misstep first; then there'd be blood and hair on the walls.

People had been laying bets for months.

Valentine Wolfe stood a little alone, in the heart of the crowd, as he always did. His every word was a command for thousands of people, but he had no friends, nor anyone who could say they were close to him. Valentine didn't care – and never had. He'd always found himself infinitely better company than anyone around him. And, given his continuing experimentation with every drug under the sun and a few that grew only in darkness, his inner world was more than enough to occupy him in his quiet moments.

Valentine was tall and slender and darkly delicate, like a fairy-tale demon prince, only more unreal. His face was long and thin, and dyed a perfect white. Heavy mascara surrounded his over-bright eyes, and a thickly painted crimson smile gave him his only expression. Jet-black hair fell to his shoulders in thick curls and ringlets that had never known a comb. He wore clothes that were generally dark but with the occasional splash of colour, red for preference, and ignored the passing dictates of fasion with supreme indifference. He kept his private staff of chemists busy coming up with new drugs, and it was truly said that he'd never met a chemical he didn't like. Anyone else who tried to ingest the quantity and variety of drugs Valentine did would undoubtedly have been poisoned a dozen times over, his brains helplessly scrambled, but by some dark alchemical miracle Valentine thrived and prospered. And, if he saw the rest of the world rather differently than did most, and had the occasional animated discussion with people who weren't there, still it didn't seem to be slowing him down any. He remained sharp, ambitious and extremely dangerous.

But he knew he couldn't go on forever as he was, even though he had the best doctors his considerable fortune could afford and took frequent rests in his own personal regeneration machine. He was burning himself up, inside and out, and his only response was to throw more chemicals on the fire. As a result, he was now so preternaturally sharp and tuned-in that he all but quivered where he stood. He was so incredibly *aware* that he could read body language as though it were the printed word: the merest gesture shouting information at him. Plans and plots and pieces of whimsy flashed through his mind, sparking like lightning, come and gone in a moment. His body might be attending the Court, but his mind was everywhere all at once. Valentine rode the waves of his mind like a surfer, perfectly balanced, looking down from the giddy heights of an endless curl. He found it exhilarating, but he never lost control. Or, if he did, no one seemed to notice.

He remained convinced that, if he could just discover the right combination of drugs, he could acquire a perfect equilibrium between the effects he needed and the side-effects he endured: a perfect never-ending high, soaring like a bird, limitless and free. But in the meantime he found he needed increasingly large doses of each drug just to get the same desired effect, and he had to take more and more new drugs to counter the malicious effects of older ones whose remnants still lurked in his system. As a result he was thinner than ever, and much more intense, jolted from moment to moment by his chemical express, and he could no more comprehend a life without his little helpers than a life without oxygen. He was also taking specific short-lived drugs for particular needs, making the necessary decisions from moment to moment.

And right now seemed a very good moment to increase his mental clarity. He had no friends at this Court, and many enemies – and he didn't trust his allies. It was vital that he out-think everyone at every turn.

He took out his silver pillbox, wiped a layer of frost from the lid, opened it and chose a single tab. He pressed it against the side of his neck, hitting the main vein with practised ease. His crimson smile widened as the new drug surged through his bloodstream like a barrelling train. His thoughts slammed into a new gear, sharp and clear and quicksilver fast. Everyone else seemed to be moving in slow motion. He felt comfortably warm, as though sitting in a great chair before a banked fire, and, despite the bitter cold, beads of sweat popped out on his forehead. His breathing deepened and his heart thudded echoingly in his chest. He watched the patterns people made around him, every move a revelation. He reined his thoughts in, concentrating only on what he needed. The trouble with this particular drug was that it tended to make him a little paranoid, but that was acceptable under the circumstances. At Lionstone's Court they really *were* out to get you.

A short, fat figure approached him, scowling determinedly, and Valentine drew himself up, posing elegantly. Judging by his dogged stance, the Lord Gregor Shreck was set on business. Valentine didn't mind. He could play that game too. He smiled at the Shreck politely, but didn't bow – he didn't want to encourage the man.

Gregor lurched to a halt before him, coughed once, and then nodded stiffly.

'A moment of your time, Wolfe. It's to our mutual advantage.'

'Well,' said Valentine pleasantly, 'never let it be said that I turned down an advantage. How nice to see you again, dear Shreck. You're looking well. Lost a little weight, perhaps?'

'Nothing I couldn't afford to lose,' said Gregor, attempting a polite smile. He wasn't particularly successful. 'We have interests in common, Wolfe, not to mention enemies. Clan Chojiro is becoming dangerously influential at Court these days. With the Campbells thrown down and destroyed, Chojiro have prospered. Now, not content with threatening our business interests, they are seeking to undermine us here, too. In fact, I would go so far as to say that Chojiro has become so prominent that neither you nor I could successfully deny them anything they really wanted. At least, not separately. But . . .'

'But together in alliance we could put them back in their place,' said Valentine. His thoughts rocketed on, far ahead of the Schreck's, weighing which Clan could be of most potential use to him in the future and which the more dangerous. Chojiro was on the way up and Shreck was sinking. And the Chojiros at least knew something of honour, which was more than Gregor ever had. Valentine approved of honour. It made it so much easier to manipulate people who believed in it, or thought that he did. Besides, he didn't trust the Shreck, and never had.

'Thank you, Gregor,' he said, a second later, 'but I'm really not interested in fighting any wars at present. Since my hostile takeover of Clan Campbell, I have more than enough to keep me occupied these days. Chojiro is an annoyance, nothing more. Thank you for your interest, Lord Shreck. Don't let me keep you. I'm sure there are others simply dying for your company.'

Gregor Shreck stood fuming for a moment and then stomped away, kicking at the snow in front of him. Shreck would have liked to threaten the Wolfe, to make it clear that standing on the sidelines could be dangerous too, but in truth he had nothing with which to threaten Valentine, and they both knew it. Valentine smiled slightly as he watched the small, squat figure ploughing through the snow with furious energy. The Shreck would find no allies here at Court, and he'd never had any friends. There was always the Church, of course. Gregor had been courting them furiously just recently. But the Church was Valentine's enemy anyway.

He looked around to see if anyone had been watching his brief encounter with the Shreck, but they were all avoiding his eye. Of course they'd been watching. They all wanted something from him. Everyone did. Valentine shrugged. He had more important things to think about. Of late his intelligence people, buried in the underground, had been bringing him more and more reports of apparent inhuman abilities among the new rebels, exploits that could not be accounted for by esper talents. Examples of strength and abilities beyond anything ever seen before. It was all rumour and gossip, of course, but, if there was a process that could produce abilities greater than esp, Valentine wanted it for himself. He was still chasing the esper drug, with little success. His efforts had been made much more difficult since his enforced divorce from the underground, but he'd take care to seed the rebel forces with his own people some time soon, just in case. Pity about the underground. They'd had access to all kinds of unusual and forbidden practices, but he'd become too public now to risk links like that.

The Lord High Dram, in his persona as Hood, had worked his way into the highest levels of the clone and esper underground before revealing his true identity. He had known all about Valentine's involvement. Valentine had never cared a damn for the underground's politics or causes – he'd been interested only in alternative routes to power and in the drug that could reportedly make an esper out of anyone – but he felt he might have a hard time convincing Lionstone of that. So, when Hood was revealed as Dram, Valentine had moved quickly to sever all his connections with the underground and dispose of anything or anyone that could directly link him with the rebels. The people he'd seeded in the underground didn't matter: they didn't know who they were reporting to and, as long as the money kept coming, they didn't ask questions. So Valentine sat back and waited for Dram to make his move, confident he could defy the man to prove anything. Even the Warrior Prime's word wouldn't be enough on its own to convict the head of the first Family in the Empire. Rank had its privileges, after all.

But Dram had never said a word. Valentine had waited, armed and prepared for any attack, but none came, and slowly he had come to believe that he was safe, for the moment. Perhaps the Empress had decided it wasn't in the Empire's interest to bring down the man she depended on to provide her with the new stardrive. Or perhaps the information was being kept in reserve, as a weapon to use against him at some future time. Lionstone had always been one to take the long view.

Except . . . there was a delicious rumour going around that the Lord High Dram was dead. He hadn't been seen at Court for ages. His only recent appearances had been as a head and shoulders on a viewscreen, and that could have been anyone, behind a digital mask. The word was that Dram had been sent on an extremely secret mission and had come home in a box. No one had any proof, as yet, but Valentine had heard the rumour in so many places and from so many sources, some surprisingly high up, that he couldn't help feeling there had to be something in it.

And, if Dram were dead, there was a good chance his knowledge of Valentine's treason had died with him. Which meant Valentine could go back to the underground, if he wanted to. He pursed his crimson mouth. With all that had happened to him of late, he no longer needed the underground as a route to power: he was doing perfectly well on his own. And his agents stood a much better chance of discovering the source of the esper drug than he ever would. No, he didn't need the rebels any more – he didn't need anyone. And he had other, more important, worries to concern him.

Druing the epic clash in which the Wolfes had ground the Campbells underfoot, the then head of the Wolfes, Valentine's father Jacob, had been killed. Everyone assumed a Campbell had got in a lucky blow, but actually the hand on the weapon had been Valentine's. No one had seen: no one knew. But, shortly after the end of the battle, with all the Campbells either dead or fled, Jacob's body had gone missing. Valentine had ordered an immediate search, and offered all kinds of rewards for the body's return, but nothing had ever been seen of it again.

Which meant that Jacob was still out there, somewhere. Not alive. He *couldn't* be alive. Even if his mysterious friends had got him to a regeneration machine straight away it would still have been too late. He'd been brain-dead too long –

Valentine was quite sure of that. He could still remember the moment when he'd killed his father. One of his drugs gave him perfect recall, and he played the moment over and over in his mind, savouring it. He'd moved in behind his father, unnoticed in the heat of battle, and had slipped his dagger expertly in and out of Jacob's ribs so fast that no one had seen or suspected anything. Jacob was dead. Valentine didn't doubt it for a moment. But who had his body?

Finlay and Adrienne had been the only Campbells to escape the slaughter, fleeing for their lives on a stolen gravity sled, but Jacob's body hadn't gone with them. The tower's external security cameras had had a good view of the departing sled, and there had been only two people on it. Unfortunately, Valentine hadn't been able to study the records from the interior cameras, because he'd arranged for them all to be turned off the moment the fighting started. He couldn't have them show him killing his father, after all. So anyone inside the room could have taken the corpse.

But what use was it to anyone? They could clone another Jacob from his cells but, if he turned up again, a simple genetest would be enough to reveal it wasn't the real Jacob. And the Family wouldn't pay ransom for a clone. Not even the grieving widow Constance . . . They might have paid a ransom for the safe return of Jacob's body, so that it could be laid to rest with honour, but no ransom demand had ever materialized. A thought forced itself into Valentine's mind, much against his will. What if . . . *no one* had taken it. What if the dead body had just got up and walked away, unnoticed in the general chaos? Valentine shuddered involuntarily as the image played itself out relentlessly before his mind's eye. Jacob's body, its death wound still bloody in its side, rising unsteadily to its feet and, pausing only briefly to glare at its murderer, slipping unnoticed out the door. Jacob's body, stumbling unseen down some dark alleyway, animated no longer by life but by pure hatred for its killer. Out there, somewhere, waiting its chance for bloody vengeance against its murderous son. Valentine had always had a superstitious side. Mostly he encouraged it, for the extra thrills it provided, but now the thought of his dead father haunted him and would not let him alone. Sometimes, in the night, in his solitary bedchamber, he thought he heard his father talking to him from the shadows. The words terrified him, but he could never remember them in the morning.

Of course, that could always have been the drugs.

Valentine brought his thoughts firmly under control. No one could hurt him now. He was the Wolfe, acknowledged and unchallenged, and nothing could undo that, no matter what had happened to his father's body. He had destroyed his rivals, the Campbells, and now held the single most important and lucrative contract in the Empire: the mass-production of the new stardrive. Everyone bowed their heads to him and gave him plenty of room. He had the Empress's ear, when many did not: she saw him as her fool and jester, wisdom and madness – all in one entertaining package – but she listened when he spoke. She tolerated much from him that she would not from anyone else, because he amused her . . . and not least because she enjoyed seeing other people's reactions when she favoured him over them, or put him in positions of power over them. At heart, Lionstone was a creature of simple pleasures. There weren't many things the Church and the military agreed on, but disapproving of Valentine Wolfe was definitely one of them. However, since both would need the stardrive to get about – neither could afford to be left behind by the other – they remained polite in company. Mostly. None of the Families liked him being so powerful, on the grounds that it upset the delicate balance of power among them which, usually, kept them from each other's throats, but their occasional intrigues against him came to nothing. It was the same with the Members of Parliament. They couldn't buy or control him, because in the end they had nothing he wanted. That made him dangerous, a wild card, unpredictable.

But every single one of them could see the advantage of having his friendship – which made for some interesting conversations.

*

Valentine's brother and sister, Daniel and Stephanie, watched him from a safe distance. They were at Court with their respective spouses because duty demanded it, but as usual they weren't talking to Valentine. They despised and hated him, partly because he was a disgrace to the Family of which he was head and partly because he so obviously didn't care. Both Daniel and Stephanie had been forced into arranged marriages, one of the last of Jacob's orders enforced by his will, but neither match could be said to be successful. Not that Daniel or Stephanie had tried very hard: they had other, more important, things to think about. As Wolfes, they'd prospered along with the rest of the Family, but they remained very much in Valentine's shadow. With his sudden rise they'd lost all power and influence in the Family, and now subsisted on whatever crumbs he threw their way. They intrigued furiously against him, but they'd never been very good at it. And so, with only each other to rely on and cling to, they'd grown increasingly close. Some said unnaturally so.

Daniel was the youngest of Jacob's children, only just into his twenties. He had the hulking frame of his father but none of the wit or intelligence. He'd been clumsy as a child, until his father had beaten it out of him. Even now, he tended to move with exaggerated care. He wore his hair long, in thick golden strands – the latest fashion – but couldn't be bothered with the fluorescent face make-up that should have accompanied it, mostly because he didn't have the skill or the looks to bring it off successfully, and he hated the idea that people might be laughing at him. Daniel had no sense of humour, and didn't trust those who did.

Stephanie, the middle child, was tall and gangling, good-looking in a bland sort of way, and deadly as a coiled snake. If she'd had the intelligence to equal her venom, no one would have been safe. As it was, she raged against Valentine's restraints but as yet had no idea how to break them. It didn't stop her doing her best to show Valentine up at every opportunity. Valentine just smiled at those around him, shrugged and said *Sisters*, and everybody laughed. Like Daniel, she hated it when they laughed. She dominated her younger brother, but that wasn't exactly difficult. She'd always been the cold one in the Family. Daniel missed his father, but she didn't. She had no time for emotions that got in the way.

And yet, almost in spite of himself, Valentine had recently been forced to give the two of them more and more to do on the business side of the Family. He had neither the time nor, to be honest, the aptitude to run the stardrive business, but it was too important a post to be trusted to anyone who was not a major Wolfe. And that meant Daniel and Stephanie, who between them had one pretty good brain. He trusted them not to screw things up out of spite – mad at him though they were, he was pretty sure they wouldn't do anything to harm the Family. At first they had taken their new post as an insult – aristocrats forced to dirty their hands with trade – but it hadn't taken Stephanie long to realize that power in the business could perhaps be used to undermine Valentine. So she studied hard, and made Daniel study too, and between them they ran the stardrive project and made it *theirs*.

So far, Valentine hadn't noticed. Daniel and Stephanie planned to change that.

They stood close together, shivering in the falling snow, watching Valentine as he thought. Their gaze was not friendly. Daniel produced a flask of brandy, and passed it to Stephanie. She accepted it gratefully, and took a healthy swallow. The drink burned fiercely as it went down, sinking slowly lower, fighting off the chill of the driving wind. She passed the flask back to her brother, who drank deeply.

'Not too much, Daniel,' Stephanie said automatically. 'This is a bad place to be caught without all your wits about you.'

'I can handle it,' he said, just as automatically. 'I can handle it.' But he put the flask away anyway. 'You worry too much, big sister.'

'And you don't worry enough.'

'Not true. I have only to look at Valentine busy thinking like that and I start worrying. It means he's planning something again, to no one's advantage but his. Or, just possibly,

220

he's found out how deeply we're involved in his stardrive company. We were supposed to run it, not take it over.'

Stephanie smiled coldly. 'By the time he works out what's happening it'll be too late. Control over stardrive production will give us control over him. He depends on the success of stardrive production for his station at Court. Imagine, in a few years' time: a sudden drop in numbers, just when the Empress had called for an increase, would humiliate *him* but wouldn't harm the company in the least. There are lots of other things we can do, too, that will reflect on him rather than us. It shouldn't be too hard to throw all the blame on Valentine – after all, we're the ones with access to the company books. And, after a steady stream of embarrassments, we won't find it too difficult to convince Lionstone it would be in her and the Empire's best interests to take the company away from Valentine and give it to us. We'll bring him down, little brother. We'll bring him all the way down.'

Daniel scowled unhappily. 'I still can't help worrying what it is he's after – what it is he spends all his time pursuing rather than run the company he depends on. Whatever it is, it must be something really important.'

Stephanie shrugged. 'Who knows where Valentine's thoughts are these days? I'm surprised they're still on the same planet as the rest of us.'

'We'll *get* him,' said Daniel, suddenly trying hard to sound as confident as she did. 'We'll drag him down. Father never intended a sick degenerate like Valentine to head the Family. And then we'll run things. The both of us.'

'Yes,' said Stephanie. 'Of course. The both of us.'

Daniel looked at her and his voice dropped. 'Are you all right? Cold getting to you? Come to little brother and let him warm you up.'

He held open his cloak and she snuggled up against him as he wrapped it around them both. And, if they held each other a little more closely than brother and sister should, no one noticed it under cover of the cloak and the still respected Wolfe name.

Not too far away, Lily Wolfe, wife of Daniel, and Michel Wolfe, who'd had to take Stephanie's name when he married her, stood together watching their respective spouses staring at Valentine. An impartial observer might have noticed that – like the siblings they'd married – they were standing more than companionably close together, and have deduced, from their body language and occasional long melting glances, that they were seriously involved with each other. The impartial observer, assuming such a thing could be found in Lionstone's Court, would have been absolutely right. Lily and Michel were lovers, and had been for some time. Everyone knew except Daniel and Stephanie, who were preoccupied with other things. Even Valentine knew. The only reason he hadn't said anything was because he was still trying to decide whether it would be funnier to tell Daniel and Stephanie or to let it go on.

Lily was six foot six inches tall, willowy but nicely curved, with a long silver wig that fell past her shoulders and framed a pale freckled face. She shaved her skull and used wigs on the basis that wigs were so much easier to look after. She wore the latest fashions and wore them well, with a natural style that infuriated other women, who mostly couldn't look that good on their best days. Lily was strikingly pretty, with prominent cheekbones and dark eyes. She had a smile that could stun a gigolo and a laugh that could start a party at fifty paces. Daniel didn't appreciate her. She took that as an insult.

Michel was barely six feet in height but his wide frame was covered with the best muscles the body shops could provide. They tended to deteriorate after a while, because he could never be bothered to exercise enough, but a quick trip back to the body shop was all it took to perk them up again. He was handsome in a dark and swarthy way, with a thick mane of long black hair that was his pride and joy. He preferred loose clothing with plenty of open spaces to show off his manly physique – as a result he was now shivering so hard he had to keep his jaw clenched to prevent his teeth from chattering. His skin had turned a pale blue colour that contrasted unappealingly with his dark hair. Snow had begun to gather on top of his head. However, thanks to the fact that he favoured knee-length leather boots, at least his feet were warm. The thought somehow failed to comfort him. He glared across at the Empress, sitting serenely on her throne, and hugged himself tightly.

'If you squeeze yourself any harder, dear, your insides will pop out your ears,' said Lily calmly.

'I'm bored,' said Michel through gritted teeth. 'I'm bored and I'm extremely cold. There are icicles hanging from my extremities. See if you can spot someone of lower status so I can steal his cloak.'

'Behave yourself, my dearest. Try not to draw attention to yourself, just this once. The auguries in the sheep I sacrificed this morning were quite clear. Today is not a good day to be noticed.'

'Why couldn't the auguries have warned you that the Court was going to be a bloody icebox this time? They're all very well when it comes to sounding grand and mystical, but they're no bloody use at all when it come to predicting practical things, are they? I'd ask for your money back, if I were you. Or for a new sheep.'

'Don't scoff, darling. You know you don't understand these things. And watch your language: you're an aristocrat now.'

'I should have stayed an accountant. The Empress had never heard of me and I could still feel my fingers.'

'If you hadn't married Stephanie, you'd never have met me.'

Michel considered this point and produced something meant to be a smile. 'Well, there is that. Only lucky thing that ever happened to me was meeting you.'

Lily reached out and patted his cheek soothingly. 'Luck has nothing to do with it, darling. There are powers and influences and mysteries, and they rule our lives.'

'The only one who rules our lives is currently sitting on that throne, wrapped in furs, and laughing her socks off at the rest of us. Why are we here, Lily? We're not important enough for our absence to be noticed. We could have spent the afternoon in each other's company, doing all sorts of interesting things. It's not often we can both get away from our respective spouses. You know how I miss you.'

'And I miss you, my darling, but we must be careful. We're Wolfes now, and Daniel and Stephanie would be most upset if they thought we were bringing the name of the Clan into disrepute through our absence. They might even investigate further and find out about us. I strongly suspect that, if they did, they'd probably take it quite personally, the poor dears. If we were lucky, they'd just have us killed. Much more likely, they'd divorce us and throw us out of the Clan without a penny to our names. We'd be outcasts. No one would lift a finger to help us, not even our own Families. I've grown quite fond of our current lifestyle, and don't intend doing anything that might put it at risk – which includes getting caught being horizontal and sweaty with you, darling. Our times together must be carefully planned, with every precaution taken. Be patient. Things won't always be like this. And, as for why we're here, the auguries were quite specific for once. Something important is going to happen here at Court. Something of great significance. Something that will launch a tidal wave of possibilities which you and I might just ride to greatness.'

Michel looked at her fondly, wrapped in her *faux* peasant dress and shawl, but kept his peace. Lily liked to see herself as the last of the great mystics, a pagan witch with rare and subtle powers; but actually she'd merely read a few old books and fallen madly in love with the role. She had a great imagination, and maybe that was backed up by a touch of esp, but he wasn't dumb enough to tell her that. He was very fond of her and, besides, she tended to throw tantrums when she got annoyed. But he trusted her intuition. She'd always understood Court politics much better than he did. He'd keep his eyes open, if they didn't freeze solid first.

He'd originally taken up with Lily because both of them were bored. As one of Jacob's legacies they were assured of a place in Clan Wolfe, but no one felt any obligation to make them feel welcome. As a result, they were allowed no place in the Clan, neither business nor social. Jacob had originally arranged the marriages to gain control of certain subsidiary business interests involved in stardrive manufacture, but, now that those had been taken over and absorbed by the Wolfes, Lily and Michel were redundant. They could not be allowed any part in business because they weren't really Wolfes, and therefore not to be trusted with anything important, but they were also kept from any contact with their own Families, because now they were Wolfes. And, since they had been Jacob's choices, Daniel and Stephanie wanted nothing to do with them: the siblings managed a stiff smile when procedure demanded they appear in public with their spouses, to put across the polite fiction that all was well, but that was only to appease the Church and keep other Families from sniffing out a possible weakness in the structure of Clan Wolfe. The rest of the while, Daniel and Stephanie had time only for each other and the business they ran, so Lily and Michel were left to their own devices to keep themselves amused. Everything that had followed had been inevitable, really. Their only other option had been plotting treason with some other Clan, and they were both too scared of Valentine for that.

At least, so far.

Meanwhile, watching everything the Wolfes did with great interest were the representatives of Clan Chojiro. Still defiantly 'oriental' – the description still stuck – in appearance and tradition despite the countless centuries that separated them from their original ancestors and founders, the Chojiros had risen to prominence in the Empire through hard work, subtle cunning and the murder of anyone who got in their way. They made few alliances with other Clans, preferring to stand alone. That way, they knew who they could trust. With the destruction of Clan Campbell they had moved smoothly into the open gap, edging other contenders aside with subtle threats and the occasional quiet bloodbath, until now they were second in the Empire only to Clan Wolfe. And, since no Chojiro had ever been willing to accept being second-best at anything, there was a quiet, undeclared but quite deadly war going on between the two Families.

However, the Chojiros specialized in computers – building, programming, installing and maintaining them at every level. This specialization very definitely included the kind of computers used in starships. As a result, the Wolfes and the Chojiros currently found themselves in an uneasy partnership, not daring to upset each other's business for fear of attracting the wrath of the Empress. The situation had become so complicated that both sides had declared a temporary truce while they tried to work out where the hell each of them stood.

The systematic wrecking of the computer software at the Income Tax and Tithe Headquarters had done great damage to the Chojiros' reputation, which was why there were so many Chojiros at Court today, to remind everyone of the size and power of the Clan. They were currently replacing the IT&T computers at their own expense and adding extra levels of protection to ensure the same thing could never happen again. Within the Clan, those responsible for installing the original security systems had already taken their own lives, to make atonement. A few had had to be helped on their way, but that was the Empire under Lionstone for you. There was no room for weakness or failure in Clan Chojiro. They were cut-throat businessmen, sometimes literally so, and had made an artform of the hostile takeover. It was truly said: if you see a Chojiro smiling, run.

BB Chojiro had come to Court specifically to act as spokesperson for her Family. She had been trained to appear the perfect smiling front, the acceptable face of a feared Family. She was diplomat, deal-maker and deception incarnate. Though her standing in the Family had been a little tarnished by the escape of the esper Julian Skye, that was deemed the fault of prison security: she was still regarded as entirely trustworthy. She was Blue Block, after all. Accompanying her – in a matching kimono – was the Investigator Razor, to remind everyone of the harsher Chojiro face. His face and hands showed the marks of recent burns, but no one was stupid enough to ask how he'd got them. Investigators never acknowledged their pain – if indeed they actually felt any: it was hard to tell with Investigators. For all sorts of reasons, everyone was giving BB and Razor plenty of room, allowing them to talk in private. BB smiled at one and all, and talked quietly with Razor, who stared straight ahead, his cold eyes watchful for any threat.

'I take it there have been no further developments in the search for Julian,' said BB, her smiling lips barely moving.

'I would have told you if there had been. Security is doing its best, but the city's a mess. If he's out there we'll find him and bring him back. Or his body.'

'I need him alive, Investigator. There are many questions still to be asked of him. Not least how he got away.'

'If he's out there we'll find him, but I can't speak for his condition. A lot of people died in the city just recently.'

BB sighed. Razor could be very single-minded when he chose. 'Let us talk of happier things. How is our infiltration of the Wolfe businesses going?'

'Surprisingly smoothly. Daniel and Stephanie are so concerned with their intrigues that they haven't noticed a thing. Valentine has his own interests these days, and has left his brother and sister to sink or swim. They've done well enough, but they have little real experience with industrial espionage. We have people – apparently entirely unconnected with Clan Chojiro – on every level of the company, from the very bottom up to and including the board of directors. Wolfe security is good but, without competent management to direct it, it's been drifting aimlessly of late.'

'It's been too easy,' said BB. 'I can't believe Valentine is completely uninterested in the company. It's the basis of his Family's current wealth and position. He's had to invest practically everything from the Wolfe and Campbell coffers to get the stardrive companies up and running, with hardly anything left for a safety net. And soon we'll be in a position to subtly sabotage stardrive construction from beginning to end. I just can't credit that Valentine doesn't know what we're doing.'

'He has his own preoccupations. I regret to say my people are unable to confirm exactly what those might be, apart from the obvious. People we send to find out tend not to come back.'

'And you don't find that worrying?'

'Investigators don't worry. It's bad for the image. You continue with your schemes; I'll see no one bothers you.'

BB nodded curtly. 'We can't hold off any longer just because we're not sure what Valentine's up to – if anything. Give the orders. I want to see significant errors in stardrive construction appearing by the end of the week. Make sure it's something showy – something the news shows can run with. Once the delivery of the new drives has been not just slowed but all but stopped, it shouldn't take too long to convince the Empress that the Wolfes aren't fit to be in charge of such a vital concern. And we'll be right there, ready to take over at a moment's notice. After all, who has a better claim? We're already producing all the computers for the new starships.'

'Unless Valentine does know about us, and is planning something really devastating.'

BB looked at him sternly. 'Just whose side are you on, Investigator?'

'Don't ask me questions like that – the answer would only upset you. All that matters is that I have pledged my life to protect the interests of your Clan, for as long as I stay with you.'

'Very reassuring.' BB deliberately turned away and looked across at Valentine, who was chatting brightly with someone who looked as though they wished they were somewhere else. BB watched them for a while, her eyes cold as death. 'Sometimes I think we'd be better off launching a pre-emptive strike against the Wolfes, beginning with Valentine. A really hostile takeover.'

'I wouldn't recommend it,' said Razor. 'There's too much we don't know about the Wolfes in general and Valentine in particular. Only a fool jumps off a wall without first finding out how high it is. There's more to Valentine than we see. There has to be. My own recommendation is for a more leisurely approach. The Wolfes' weak spot is Daniel and Stephanie. There is much in their tangled relationship that might be profitably exploited . . .'

'And that is why you're in charge of carrying out security, rather than planning it,' said BB tartly. 'We could do anything to those two, up to and including killing them slowly, and Valentine wouldn't give a damn.'

'But if we could reach them, turn them to our cause, perhaps through pressure on their current closeness . . . or by providing information about Lily and Michel . . .'

'No,' said BB firmly. 'Daniel and Stephanie are too erratic to place any trust in. They're weak but they're still wolves. I have a better idea.'

Constance Wolfe, widow of Jacob, stood alone in the crowd. She was always alone now, no matter where she went. Eighteen years old, still wearing black in mourning for her murdered husband, she was tall and blonde, breathtakingly lovely even in a world where beauty was commonplace. But the fire had gone out of her, leaving her looking like a crushed flower. Perhaps alone of all the Wolfe Family, she had truly loved Jacob. The others had mourned for a while, even Valentine, but they had their own lives to get on with, and had done so as soon as they properly could. Constance had had nothing but Jacob. He had been her life. Now he was gone and she didn't know what to do with herself. She had no interest in politics or intrigue, and she was allowed no place in Family affairs. Jacob's children had never approved of his last marriage, to someone even younger than they were themselves. There had always been the possibility that Jacob might disinherit them in favour of her, or any children she had. Now he was gone, they were able to ignore her with something like relief.

She looked around at the assembled courtiers, and no one looked back. She was a nobody now. No one had time for failures – until one woman met her eye and smiled. BB Chojiro. Constance looked at her thoughtfully, and BB moved unhurriedly towards her, still somehow graceful despite having to trudge through the deep snow. Constance knew she should see the woman as an enemy, but she didn't have the energy.

BB stopped before her, and smiled again. 'We should have got together before, Constance: we have a lot in common. It's hard to be a woman alone. I know. But, just because one Family's abandoned you, it doesn't mean we all have. You have friends, Constance, if you want them.'

Constance looked at her icily. 'I may have fallen from grace, Chojiro, but I'm not so low I would consider betraying my kith and kin.'

BB's smile didn't waver. 'What I have in mind is in the best interests of the Wolfes. Valentine is leading you all to disaster. He's lost inside his own head, and sees merely what he wants to see. Daniel and Stephanie have eyes only for each other. The new stardrive will fall into their hands, and then what will happen to the Wolfes? To the Family that Jacob built, and brought to greatness? What will happen to you, Constance?'

'If you've something to say to me, Chojiro, say it.'

'You could be head of the Wolfes. Valentine could be removed as insane, Daniel and Stephanie as incompetent. And, since they've taken steps down the years to remove all other major players from the game, that would leave just you to take over. Now, alone, you couldn't hope to run the Family – you've only ever been on the fringes of things – but, if you were to marry a Chojiro, we could merge the Families through your children. Until then, you would rule the Wolfes, with our help. Think about it: you'd never have to be alone again. You're young, Constance. You have your whole life ahead of you. Don't throw it all away in loyalty to people who despise you.'

'You want something,' said Constance steadily. 'You all want something. Get to the meat of the matter. What do you want from me?'

'Information,' said BB Chojiro. 'You're still a prominent Wolfe, with access to areas my people can reach only with difficulty. There are questions we need answers to. In return, we would make you one of us. A valued member of Clan

230

Chojiro, cared for and appreciated. Isn't that all you ever really wanted?'

Constance looked at her thoughtfully, and, while she didn't say *yes*, she didn't say *no*, either. BB turned and gestured for Razor to come and join them. The Investigator ploughed through the snow as though it weren't there, and bowed politely to Constance. She nodded briefly in return, watching him warily. BB gave her a reassuring smile, and put a proprietary hand on Razor's arm.

'Investigator, you were there when Jacob Wolfe died. Tell Constance what you saw.'

'He did not die at the hand of any Campbell,' said Razor flatly. 'The Wolfe was stabbed from behind, by his eldest son. By Valentine, current head of your Clan. It was very quick. No one else noticed. But I saw it.'

'And you know that Investigators never lie,' said BB. She was careful not to sound too pleased about it.

Constance pressed her lips together, though whether to keep her mouth from trembling with rage or to hold back tears she wasn't sure. It had always troubled her that no one had ever claimed the kill for Jacob. It would have been a major triumph for any Campbell, and they'd needed a triumph badly in the days after their downfall. But no one had ever claimed to have killed the Wolfe. No one had even claimed to have seen how it had happened, although she'd questioned enough people. She'd assumed the Campbell himself must have done it before he, too, was killed. Until now.

It didn't occur to her to doubt Razor's word. He was an Investigator, after all, and lying was beneath him. Besides, it sounded true. Valentine had had every reason to kill his father, and not a scrap of conscience to stop him. He could have got away with it, in the heat of battle.

Constance looked steadily at BB Chojiro. 'Tell me more.'

Sitting comfortably on her Iron Throne, Lionstone XIV looked interestedly from one face to the other as the representatives of army and Church argued before her: General

Beckett, slow and unperturbed, taking the time to enjoy his cigar between answers, and Cardinal Kassar, his single eye glowing with the unquenchable fire of fanaticism. Lionstone liked to watch them argue, not least because, while they were arguing with each other, they weren't teaming up to dispute with her. The principle of divide and conquer worked just as well in Court politics as it did in wars. It helped that Kassar and Beckett hated each other's guts. Neither was strong enough individually to threaten her authority, but together they would have made a formidable enemy. So Lionstone found it expedient to keep their ire concentrated on each other. It didn't take much. A kind word here, a knowing look there, and they snapped at the bait like hungry sharks. The two men before her now were blind to everything but the need to score points off each other.

Lionstone smiled to herself. Men were so predictable.

'As any fool could see, the alien attack is a direct threat to humanity,' said Cardinal Kassar, his voice chillier than the air around him. 'We can't just sit here and wait for another of their ships to come and attack us again. We must hunt down their homeworld and wipe them out. Any other way risks the suicide of our species!'

'A really good way to commit suicide,' said General Beckett calmly, 'is to launch yourself head-first into a situation you know nothing about. You saw what a single ship was able to do to us. Silence and the *Dauntless* were able to handle it, but that was one of our finest ships, with one of our finest crews, against what could after all have been nothing more than a simple exploratory probe. We need more information before we commit ourselves to definite plans.'

'It's a matter of faith,' said Kassar. 'I wouldn't expect you to understand that, Beckett.'

'It's a matter of common sense, Cardinal,' said Beckett. 'I wouldn't expect you to understand that.'

'Sounds like cowardice to me – staying safe at home here while your men take all the risks out on the Rim. Well, home isn't safe any more, Beckett. Either we go to them or they'll come to us.'

Beckett took the cigar out of his mouth, and looked at it thoughtfully. 'Bravery is overrated, Cardinal. I'll settle for competence. If the attack is going to come from anywhere, it'll come from the Rim. Hence the extra patrols I ordered. They're going to be our early-warning system. In my experience, fighting wars is a matter of practicality, not heroics. But then you've always been a dreamer, Kassar, with little grasp of the practicalities of life. Comes with the job, I suppose.'

Kassar glared at him, and then turned his burning gaze on Lionstone. 'Put me in charge of your armies, and I'll provide you with an unbeatable force of the Faithful, trained in all the martial arts, ready to dare anything in the name of the Church.'

'I've always fought in the name of the Empress, myself,' said General Beckett, and blew a triumphant puff of smoke in Kassar's direction. The cardinal hesitated, suddenly aware of the dangerous waters into which his rhetoric had swept him. Beckett continued, taking advantage of the pause. 'Fanatics can be very useful, when it comes to building a power-base, but in my experience they make bloody poor soldiers. They're fine at getting themselves killed in the name of their cause; I prefer to put my faith in trained professional soldiers who'll devote their energies to staying alive long enough to kill the enemy.'

Kassar started to splutter, so eager to get back at Beckett that his words were tumbling over themselves. Lionstone sat back on her throne, openly enjoying his discomposure. Beckett sucked happily on his cigar.

That was when Mother Beatrice emerged from the crowd to join the debate, and throw oil on troubled fires. Beatrice Christiana had been due to marry Valentine Wolfe, on Jacob's instructions, but it hadn't happened. Beatrice was a forceful, assured and occasionally violent woman who knew her own mind, and she had had no intention whatsoever of marrying a notorious drug fiend, degenerate and general weirdo. She threatened everything up to and including murder to get out of the match, but no one had taken her seriously – until the day of the wedding, when she'd punched out Valentine, kicked the presiding vicar in the nuts and run to the sanctuary of the Sisters of Mercy, the one place no one would follow her. Their nunneries were, by long tradition, inviolate. The Sisters of Mercy were the only truly impartial force in the Empire, tied to no one side or cause or class but offering their help to all impartially. They were much-loved, and trusted by one and all. Which made them very useful when it came to sorting out Family disputes and brokering truces. Among other things.

Beatrice had risen rapidly through the ranks, and was now a Mother Superior, as was evident from her voluminous black robe and starched wimple. It helped that, as well as being particularly spiritual, she was also incredibly wealthy. She had taken her place in Court, defying anyone to say anything, and was rapidly emerging as a sane counter-voice to both the military and the established Church. Valentine took it easily enough, understanding that it had all been entirely personal on Beatrice's part. He had sent her a note saying he thought her new outfit was very sexy, and enclosed the bill for the wedding. Since then, Beatrice had put a great deal of energy into magnificently ignoring him.

Now she stood before the Iron Throne, eyes sparkling merrily. She bowed to the Empress, and looked challengingly at the general and the cardinal. Beckett smiled, and gave her the nod one accords a respected adversary. Kassar glared at her; he saw her as a dangerous heretic, and had made no bones about saying so loudly, in public, until both the Sisters of Mercy and his own superiors in the Church had told him to shut up. This had infuriated Kassar even more, luckily to the point of incoherence. Beatrice wasn't worried: as long as the Sisters remained separate from the established Church, Kassar had no power over her, and they both knew it. She smiled at Lionstone, who acknowledged her with a nod.

'If I might interrupt, your Majesty . . . it seems to me that both Church and army are too rooted in their positions to see the truth. If the alien ship is representative of the aliens' power, we could be in real trouble when their fleet turns up. We have a whole Empire to protect, while the aliens are free to concentrate their forces at any point they choose. One ship turned our main starport and city into rubble. Imagine what a fleet of them could do to a planet, with or without its defences. We have to face the fact that, for the first time, we find ourselves up against an opponent who may well be stronger than us. Not forgetting, of course, that we already have hard evidence that there may be more than just the one powerful alien species out there. Your Majesty has been saying this for some time, but I think we're all now more ready to believe it. The only chance for humanity's survival may be to bring all our assets to bear against the enemy. Or enemies. Those assets could include even those who would normally oppose us. I'm talking about the rebels, not to mention the clone and esper undergrounds.'

'Are you mad, woman?' exploded Kassar. 'Make deals with those scum? They're not even human!'

'*They* think they are,' said Beatrice. 'And I think they'd fight to defend humanity against an alien threat, if we asked them nicely. It's in their interests. If the Empire is destroyed, they'd be wiped out along with the rest of us. They have talents and powers and abilities that we're going to need. Does anyone here doubt they'd make excellent attack troops? Just the fact that they're still around despite every attempt to exterminate them shows they're survivors, if nothing else.'

'May I just point out,' said Beckett unhurriedly, 'that it was the rebels' lowering of Golgotha's defences that made the aliens' attack so devastating?'

'They were probably working with the aliens,' said Kassar.

'All the more reason to contact them, and get them on our side,' said Beatrice, unmoved.

'They are guilty of crimes against humanity,' Kassar insisted. 'The guilty must be punished.'

'On the other hand,' said Beckett, rolling his cigar sensuously between his fingers to hear the leaves crackle, 'if we don't bring the rebels into the fold, they might just take the opportunity to stab us in the back while we're distracted by the aliens.'

'Kill them all,' said Kassar. 'Clones and espers and

unpeople. They're as alien to us as anything that might come from beyond the Rim.'

'Typical of the Church these days,' said Beatrice. 'Rather fight than think; rather lose than try diplomacy. Fanatics unite: you have nothing to lose but your minds.'

'Well said,' agreed Valentine Wolfe. 'I couldn't have put it better myself.'

They all looked round to find Valentine had emerged from the crowd and was standing right behind them. Beatrice ostentatiously moved a step away. Valentine smiled at her dazzlingly. Kassar glared at him.

'What do you want, degenerate?'

'Well, I have a list, if you're interested, Kassar, but you're really not my type. I just wanted to agree with everything Beatrice said.'

'Thanks a lot,' said Beatrice. 'If you're on my side, they'll never believe me. You do this to me deliberately, don't you? Just because I wouldn't marry you, you're determined to ruin my life.'

'You wound me deeply,' said Valentine. 'Can't a man speak out for common sense and sanity any more?'

'And what the hell would you know about sanity?' demanded Beatrice. 'There are lemmings on the edges of cliffs who've got a better grasp on reality than you have. And more common sense.'

'If you two would like a little privacy,' Beckett began, and then decided not to say any more as Beatrice glowered at him.

'I would rather be left in the company of a piranha with an overbite! Don't you move one step, General. That goes for you too, Kassar. Loathsome though your presence undoubtedly is, it is still preferable to that of the genetic disaster area currently heading the Wolfe Family. I understand there are plans for the Dangerous Chemicals Investigation Board to have him declared a toxic waste dump. Maybe then we could have him banned from inhabited areas on health grounds.'

'Ah,' said the empress from her throne. 'Young love . . .'

*

Not all that far away, Gregor Shreck glared at the company before the Iron Throne. By rights he should have been there, too, adding his words and wisdom to whatever they were discussing. He was head of one of the oldest Families in the Empire, and a man to be noticed. But he had been robbed of his true position in society by backstabbing traitors who refused to admit his true qualities. They smiled at his face and laughed at his back, and whispered against him. They'd pay. They would all pay, one day.

But that could wait. For the moment, he had little room in himself for anything but rage. Evangeline had left him. The ungrateful little bitch had actually dared to walk out on him. Together with that cow Adrienne, she'd found the courage to outface him. He smiled nastily. They might think they'd beaten him, but they'd discover soon enough that no one did down Gregor Shreck and lived to boast of it. Evangeline might think herself safe among the underground and the unpeople, but there was bound to be a weak link somewhere, and he had all the time, money and venom he needed to find it. Someone would respond to money or pressure or the right kind of deal. Someone always did. And then he'd get her.

It wouldn't be long before people started noticing that Evangeline wasn't around. People in Tower Shreck would talk. You couldn't stop them. Then people in the Court would start asking questions. Where was she? What had happened to her? What had he done to her? There were always people ready to stick their noses in where they didn't belong. He could clone another Evangeline, of course – he still had the tissue samples from the original – but it would take months to rear and train her. And what if, afterwards, the first clone reappeared? There'd be no way to hide what he'd done if there were two Evangelines walking around. And there was always the possibility the first clone might tell all anyway, from a safe distance, as a kind of revenge. She'd find it hard to prove anything without revealing herself, but just the accusation would be damaging. Mud sticks, particularly when people want it to. Gregor scowled. These days, more than ever, it was vital that he seem above reproach.

In recent months he'd taken steps to become, at least publicly, very religious. He attended all the right services at all the right places, moved in all the right circles, backed the currently fashionable charities and pressure groups, and did everything he could to win the Church's approval. He needed their support if he were to win himself a place up in the rarified heights where he deserved to be. However, in order to gain the Church's backing, he'd had to build up a reputation as being purer than pure. This had taken some doing. In the past he'd gone his own way, done what he wanted, when he wanted, and let his people clean up the mess afterwards with money or threats – typical enough behaviour for an aristocrat with money to burn and more hormones than sense. Luckily, the Church didn't mind much about your past as long as you repented publicly, made a large donation, and put it all behind you. Gregor didn't care tuppence for the first two, but balked at the third. There were limits. Still, there was public and there was private. As long as he looked good in the public eye, rumoured sins could be forgiven . . . even ignored. Gregor had never been any good at public relations, but fortunately there were members of his Family who were. They were currently standing just behind him, waiting for his instructions. If they knew what was good for them. Gregor turned to face them, giving them both his best forbidding stare.

Toby the Troubador was his nephew, loth though he sometimes was to admit it: a short, fat, perspiring fellow with flat blond hair, a ready smile, a mind like a steel trap and the morals of a starving sewer rat. His main duties and responsibilities were to write up the Family's doings in the best possible light and then see to it that those reports appeared in all the right places: journals, holo shows, gossip columns. He was a public-relations man, spin-doctor, damage-limitation expert and first-class liar. He had to be. It wasn't easy making Gregor Shreck look good. The rest of the Clan had their moments, bless their black little hearts, but Toby knew how to handle them. If they didn't toe the line when he needed them to, with a prepared speech here and an appearance there, smiling and waving for the cameras, he just left them out of his reports entirely until they did. After all, the only thing worse than being talked about by everyone is not being talked about by anyone. If your face wasn't in all the glossies and the holo shows, you were nobody. Toby could make you a celebrity, famous for being famous, if you followed the rules – *his* rules. Namely, do what you like as long as it's entertaining, but only as long as I get to hear about it first, so I can make sure it's got the right spin on it before it hits the streets. Unfortunately, he couldn't order Gregor about like that. If he'd ever been stupid enough to try, Gregor would have ripped out his vocal cords as a warning.

'Talk to me, boy,' said Gregor sharply. 'What are you saying about Evangeline at present?'

'The official line is that she's resting after overdoing things,' Toby said smoothly. 'We haven't specified exactly what she's been overdoing, but the gossips will come up with something. They do so love to speculate. Presumably you'll let me know when she's rested enough, so I can reintroduce her to society?'

'I'll tell you what you need to know when you need to know it,' said Gregor. 'How's my current standing with the Church?'

'Reasonable. Though I do wish you'd learn to watch your language, Uncle. Sometimes I think the Church would happily pardon adultery but not the specific four-letter word used to describe exactly what you were doing. Most people will turn a sufficiently deaf ear if I pay them enough, whether it concerns obscenities or political malaprops, but sooner or later you're going to say the wrong thing in front of the wrong people, and there'll be nothing I can do to help you.'

Gregor sniffed. 'It was your idea for us to get into bed with the Church in the first place. Can't say I've seen much in the way of results.'

'With the Church behind us, we are safe from a great many other enemies,' Toby said patiently. 'But, if the Church ever finds out about the real you, we could be in trouble.'

'Then you'd better make damn' sure they don't, hadn't you?' said Gregor.

'I do wish you two wouldn't fight,' said Grace Shreck, knowing they wouldn't listen to her. They never did. She was Gregor's older sister, and did her best to look as little like him as possible. She was long, tall and thin, with a pale, swan-like neck and a mass of white hair piled up on top of her head in a rather precarious-looking style that hadn't been fashionable in years. She wore the same style of clothes she had when she was young, and noticed newer styles only in order to criticize them. Every now and again, fashion rediscovered her look, and for a month or so she would be the height of chic, which embarrassed her greatly. Grace preferred not to be noticed, whenever possible.

She'd never married, because, after their parents had died suddenly, Gregor had needed her services as assistant, secretary and general dogsbody while he was holding the Family together and making it great again. There'd been no time for romance, no chance for a life of her own. The Family needed her, Gregor needed her, and she'd had to settle for that. And, if she was ever angry about this, she didn't let it show. Eventually there had come a time when Gregor didn't need her any more, but she stayed with him anyway, because by now she didn't know any other kind of life. The world had changed during her enforced absence, and people frightened her, whether they meant to or not. Besides, she'd always known Gregor would never let her go. He couldn't risk her marrying and moving outside the Family's influence, outside his control. She knew too much about the Clan in general and him in particular – and the things he'd done to make the Shrecks great again.

She came to Court as little as possible, because crowds upset her, but the Empress's edict had been quite specific, for once. Everyone in the Families had to come. No exemptions. If you were on your death-bed, bring your death-bed with you. So Grace had come on Gregor's arm, and stayed close to Toby, and tried to pretend she was just watching it on the holo.

She disapproved of the way Gregor treated Toby, but didn't know what to do about it. Certainly Gregor wouldn't listen to her, even if she could have brought herself to say anything. Toby's father had been Christian Shreck, younger brother to herself and Gregor. He had disappeared years ago, after a furious head-to-head with Gregor, and had never been seen again. The Empress had ordered an investigation, but nothing had ever come of it. Gregor submitted to questioning by an Imperial esper, and surprised everyone by passing the test with ease. He was officially cleared. But, after that, people stopped resisting Gregor's rise to power.

Toby had come under Gregor's influence the same way every Shreck did: because he had had no choice. Grace couldn't protect or advance him in the Empress's eyes, so that just left Gregor. Now the Shreck used Toby as he'd once used Grace, and there was nothing she could do to stop it. Another life sacrificed to Gregor's ambition. That was just the way things were in Clan Shreck.

Grace sighed tiredly. She missed Christian. He'd been the only one in the Family with a sense of humour. She realized Gregor was shouting at Toby again. Gregor was having a hard time being a public person: he wasn't suited to it. She looked at him, red-faced and sweating as he raised his voice yet again, and suddenly it seemed to her that this was just the most recent in a long series of straws that were breaking the camel's back.

She stepped forward and slapped Gregor smartly on the arm with her folded fan.

'Gregor, I won't have you using that kind of language in public! Remember, we are at Court. People are listening.'

'And you can shut your stupid mouth as well,' snapped Gregor, without looking round. 'When I want your opinion, I'll have my head examined.'

'Really!' Grace could feel herself blushing, as she always did when someone spoke harshly to her. 'Why can't we all just be friends, in public at least?'

'She's right, you know,' said Toby diffidently. 'The Church believes in happy Families.'

'Stuff the Church,' said Gregor immediately, but in a somewhat lower tone. 'I have a right to be angry. I can't

241

believe Valentine turned me down. It's so obviously in both of our interests to work together against our common enemies that even he should have been able to see the advantages. All right, he's just a drug-soaked weirdo, but if we'd stood together no one would have dared stand against us.'

'Can't say I'm sorry,' said Toby. 'Valentine may be number one at the moment, but there's nobody here who likes or trusts him, despite all the smiles in his direction. Putting a good PR shine on an alliance between you two would have strained my creativity. You'd have a better chance of selling lepers' fingers as a fashion accessory. So what now, Uncle? Move to Plan B?'

'What's Plan B?' said Grace suspiciously. 'No one's mentioned any Plan B to me. Honestly, Gregor, you never tell me anything any more.'

'That's because you don't need to know anything. Just shut up and do as you're told. Stay here with Toby. Don't move. I'll take care of Plan B.'

Gregor stalked away without looking back. He knew they wouldn't move without his permission. Plan B was the Chojiro Family. If the first Family wouldn't deal, there was always the chance the second might. He kicked his way through the deep snow and people moved quickly to get out of his way; he no more noticed that than the air that he breathed. He drew himself up before BB Chojiro, glared briefly at the Investigator beside her to show he wasn't intimidated, and then bowed briefly to BB.

She bowed back, calm and assured. Razor ignored him.

'We have a common enemy in the Wolfes,' Gregor said flatly. 'May I suggest that it is in our mutual interests to combine against Valentine? You produce the computers for his starships and I make the shells, but as long as he controls production of the new stardrive we have to run our businesses to suit him. With just the right pressure and timing, he could ruin either one of us and then move in and take over. I had planned to work with the Campbells, back when they looked to be in the lead for the stardrive contract. We had an understanding. That's why I permitted a linking marriage.

242

But that fell through, and Valentine won't deal. I work under his conditions or I don't work at all. It's completely unacceptable to me. So, I need an ally to make sure I don't get squeezed out, and you need someone to watch your back while you work with him. We could both profit from such a union. Besides, neither of us has any cause to love Valentine.'

'In both our interests?' said BB. 'I think not. All the profit would be on your side. We don't need you, Lord Shreck, and you have nothing we want. Yes, you build shells, but anyone can build shells. And to be honest, Lord Shreck, we're rather choosy about our allies.'

'You little bitch,' hissed Gregor, and, before he really knew what he was doing, his hand was shooting out to grab her by the throat. He hadn't even got close before Investigator Razor's hand stabbed out to intercept his. Gregor's pudgy white fingers disappeared entirely inside Razor's black fist, and he cried out as Razor clamped down hard, grinding the bones of Gregor's hand together. The Investigator let go after a long moment, and Gregor fell back a step, clutching his throbbing hand to his breast. BB Chojiro and her Investigator studied him with the same impersonal gaze as he stood before them, trembling with impotent rage.

'Turn around and go back to your own people, Shreck,' said Razor calmly. He didn't raise his voice. He didn't have to. 'You have no business here.'

Gregor glared at them both, searching for some final insult or threat that he could use to crush them, but in the end he had to turn silently and trudge back through the snow. People moved even faster to get out of his way this time, giving him the same kind of respect one would a maddened scorpion. But again Gregor was thinking too hard to bother about them. He had to find allies and support from somewhere, or he might easily find himself being edged out of the stardrive business altogether. Anyone could build shells, as BB had said . . . His alliance with the Church should bring long-term benefits, but right now he needed some money. He'd find someone, of course: there was always someone. And, when he was a power again in his own right, he'd make BB Chojiro pay for daring to humiliate him.

He made himself breathe more slowly. There was still latitude with Clan Wolfe. Maybe Valentine wouldn't deal, but Daniel and Stephanie just might, if approached in the right way. They might work with him if only to spite their brother. Yes – that was an idea. He slowed his pace and allowed himself a small smile. He would be strong again, and have his revenge upon his enemies, and no one would dare look down on him again.

Lionstone finally waved the people arguing before her to silence, and called the Court to order. Her amplified voice echoed across the waste, cutting effortlessly through the courtiers' babble of voices. In a moment there was silence, broken only by the faint moaning of the bitter wind. The courtiers fixed their attention on their Empress. She smiled out over them, and it was not a pleasant smile. The courtiers stood still and quiet before her, snow settling on their heads and shoulders until they resembled the snowmen they'd passed earlier. A few people made the connection in their minds and shuddered suddenly.

Lionstone glared down at Valentine and Beatrice until they got the message, bowed, and faded back into the crowd. General Beckett and Cardinal Kassar moved to stand on each side of the Iron Throne, staring out at the courtiers, representing army and Church, the arms of the Empress.

Lionstone nodded to Beckett, and he raised his voice in a parade-ground bark. 'Captain Silence, Investigator Frost and Security Officer Stelmach: step forward and make your report on the alien attack!'

Stelmach jumped guiltily, and then looked around quickly to see if anyone had noticed. Silence and Frost just strode forward to stand at attention before the Iron Throne. Silence's face was calm, but there was new hope in his heart. This was what he'd hoped for: a chance to tell his side of the story before anyone else had a chance to muddy the waters. He waited a moment for Stelmach to join them, and then realized the security officer had stopped on the edge of the crowd, his eyes fixed on the Grendel standing just behind the throne. Silence didn't blame him – the bloody thing disturbed the hell out of him, too. He reached back and pulled Stelmach forward. The security officer's eyes never left the alien.

Silence glanced at Frost, and wished he hadn't. The Investigator was staring at the alien hungrily, only a moment away from attacking it on general principles. Silence considered the matter, then stretched an arm and yanked Frost back a step. The alien was the Empress's pet. If by some miracle Frost did manage to kill the bloody thing, Lionstone would not be at all happy. Frost jerked her arm free and glowered at him, but stayed where she was.

Silence decided to start his report before something unpleasant happened.

He kept it simple and succinct, but hit all the salient points. There was a lot of uneasy murmuring from the assembled Court as he described what he'd found in the wrecked base on Gehenna. He told how the *Dauntless* had tracked the alien ship to Golgotha. The murmurs got really loud when he told of the alien craft's nature and capabilities, and the lifeforms he'd found inside it. He let Frost take over from there – she was the expert on aliens. Her report was cold, factual, even clinical, but Silence was shivering along with everyone else by the time she'd finished, and it didn't have a damn' thing to do with the cold. After she'd done, it was very quiet.

The Empress nodded slowly, and looked out over the Court again. 'Perhaps now you appreciate our position on the necessity for increased military spending. If one alien ship can do so much, what might a fleet accomplish? We have heard whispers of late of a proposed revolt against the new tax increases; let us make it clear that any such treachery will be put down harshly, with every resource at our disposal. In the current circumstances, refusal to support the military can only be seen as treason against humanity.'

General Beckett smiled; Cardinal Kassar did not.

The Empress looked at Stelmach. 'Do you have anything to add at this time?'

Stelmach swallowed hard, shook his head quickly, and finally managed a very quiet 'Not at this time, your Majesty. No.'

'Very well,' said the Empress. 'Guards: bring the prisoner forward.'

The middle of the crowd quickly parted to form a narrow aisle along which two armed guards half-led and half-dragged a naked man through the deep snow. He wore only wrist- and ankle-chains, and some blood that had spattered down on to his chest from his recently broken nose. His skin was a bluish white, and he shuddered uncontrollably in the biting cold. The guards threw him on his knees before the Iron Throne. He looked up at Lionstone pleadingly and tried to say something, but he was shaking so much he couldn't get the words out.

Lionstone gazed down at him thoughtfully. 'This pathetic object is Fredric Hill, head of Starport Security here on Golgotha. We gave him the appointment ourselves. We thought he showed promise. This man let the rebels in, allowed them to sabotage the Income Tax and Tithe Headquarters, and failed to prevent them from lowering the planet's defences as they escaped. He also failed to protect us from the alien ship. We could question him on this, but what would be the point? He'd just nod and smile and agree with everything I said, and then try to pass the blame on to his staff, or hidden traitors, or lack of the right equipment. Anything and anyone but himself. After all, he'd say, the rebels arrived in a Hadenman ship. Probably half his people took one look at the great golden ship of awful legend and ran for their lives. And the other half probably followed them, once the alien ship had swept past our by now nonexistent defences to strafe the city.

'It doesn't make any difference. He was head of Starport Security, responsible for our defence. A strong man in that position might have accomplished much. He might have pulled enough of his people together to organize equipment repairs, bring secondary and backup systems on-line, send out rescue teams to aid the wounded and distressed in the city. Instead, according to his own records, he dithered and fumbled and finally hid, re-emerging only when it was all safely over. Quite unacceptable behaviour from one of our officers. We have therefore decided that an example shall be made.'

She looked back at the Grendel, and after a moment everyone else did too. It stood calm and relaxed behind the throne, a living nightmare. The yoke around its armoured neck suddenly gave a little chime, and then the alien surged forward more quickly than the human eye could follow. One moment it was standing just behind the throne and the next it was towering over the cringing Security head, its great clawed hands on his bare shoulders. The courtiers nearest it surged back as far as the pressure of the crowd would allow, but the Grendel paid them no heed. Its claws sank deep into the man's flesh, and thick runnels of blood coursed down his colourless flesh. He began to scream, and the alien opened its mouth and bit his face off. Skin and eyes and nose and mouth disappeared as the alien jerked back its great head, leaving only a shattered bloody skull.

The alien chewed and swallowed and then leaned forward again, thrusting its grinning jaws into the man's chest with brutal force. The sternum stove in, cracking like a dry twig, and the Grendel's head burrowed into the man's chest, going after the heart like a pig hunting truffles. Hill's arms waved wildly for a few moments, and then they fell to his sides and lay still. Fredric Hill, once head of Starport Security, hung limply in the alien's grasp as it chewed thoughtfully, savouring the flavour.

The yoke round its neck chimed, but the Grendel didn't respond. The yoke chimed again, and the Grendel dropped the body carelessly into the blood-soaked snow. It moved unhurriedly back to resume its position behind the Iron Throne. Steaming hot blood dripped thickly from its leering jaws and ran slowly down its gleaming armour. In the snow before the throne, Hill's body lay in a crumpled heap, like a broken discarded toy that no one wanted to play with any more.

Silence moved in close beside Frost. He could feel the anger boiling within her, ready to spill over at a moment's provocation. Her whole career had been built around killing aliens before they got the chance to kill people. He put a warning hand on her arm. It was as tense as coiled steel. She turned her head and gave him a hard look, and he took his hand away. Frost was an Investigator, and had no time for human weaknesses like compassion. Her anger was purely professional.

The courtiers muttered among themselves, looking from the Grendel to the gutted body and back again, impressed by the savagery of the kill if not the quality of the control the Empress had over the alien.

Silence shared a significant glance with Stelmach, but they both kept their peace. Those courtiers nearest the body looked down at the open wounds steaming in the chill air, and tried to back away a little further, but the crowd was packed tight behind them and there was nowhere for them to go. Nobody wanted to look at the alien.

The Empress smiled at them all. 'Cute, isn't he? Table manners aren't up to much, but he's only young. Really little more than a baby. Imagine what he'll be like when he comes of age. Imagine an army of him, spilling across a battlefield like an endless wave of slaughter. Unstoppable shock troops, leaving nothing behind them but mountains of dead and oceans of blood. I'm quite looking forward to it. The research into controlling the Grendels better is going well. Soon we'll have yokes for every Sleeper in the vaults, and then we'll send them out against the aliens who attacked us here today. Or anyone else who threatens us. Captain Silence, you haven't finished your report. Tell the Court what you discovered on the Wolfling World.'

Silence, Frost and Stelmach took it in turns to describe what they'd discovered in the vast caverns deep beneath the frozen surface of the Wolfling World, once also known as Haden, home to the augmented supermen, the Hadenmen. They told of the sleeping thousands of Hadenmen, who rose from their long death-like sleep and walked out of their

Tomb, glorious and powerful, an army of cyborg warriors who had once tried to overthrow humanity, and only narrowly failed.

They told of the rebels who'd awoken them: the outlaw Owen Deathstalker, the pirate Hazel d'Ark, the bounty-hunter Ruby Journey and the legendary professional rebel Jack Random. They told of the defeat of the *Dauntless*'s forces, but they did not mention the Lord High Dram's presence, nor his death at the hands of another legend, the original Deathstalker, thought dead for centuries but now returned for vengeance against the Empire that had betrayed and hounded him. All three of them had been told previously, in no uncertain terms, that Dram was not to be mentioned. Given their current situation, Silence and Frost and Stelmach were happy to be flexible with the truth.

The Court continued to murmur among itself, despite darting glares from the Empress, as the courtiers reacted to names like Jack Random and Giles Deathstalker. They were further troubled by the re-emergence of Owen Deathstalker, outlawed by the Empress for no good reason, who had evaded all her armies and now seemed to be leading the new rebellion. And they really didn't like the idea of a new army of Hadenmen massing to attack the Empire again.

The Empress finally sat back and let them mutter for a while, then reclaimed their attention with her amplified voice.

'Let's not all panic just yet, boys and girls. The Hadenmen are a long way away, and only newly awakened. It will be some time yet before they're in any position to pose a real threat to us. The man claiming to be Jack Random could be nothing more than a double – rebel propaganda to draw people to their cause. Random himself is probably long dead.'

She stopped suddenly as BB Chojiro stepped gracefully out of the crowd to stand before the throne. BB bowed gracefully, and the Empress fixed her with an icy glare. 'This had better be good, Chojiro. And extremely relevant.'

'With all due respect, your Majesty, it has come to us through normally reliable channels that Jack Random was captured by Empire forces some time back, and then escaped.'

'Then you were misinformed,' said Lionstone flatly. 'We never had him. If we had, he would not have been allowed to escape. Is that clear? Good. Now don't interrupt us again, or we'll have the Grendel open you up so we can all see what little girls are made of.'

'Clan Chojiro has no wish to appear rude or impertinent, your Majesty,' said BB calmly. 'We are merely trying to ascertain the facts. The Hadenman ship that brought the rebels here was very real and twice as impressive, implying that, not only are the Hadenmen and the rebels working together, but that the augmented men are already so well prepared they can drop in on us any time they like. Who is to say a fleet of these ships is not already setting out from Haden to try humanity's stength again?'

'You're a real cheerful sort to have around, Chojiro,' said Lionstone. 'If the Hadenmen are getting ready for a comeback, this is all the more reason to support my military build-up and stop whingeing about your tax bills, isn't it? Anyone else want to add anything before we move on? Bearing in mind it had better be pretty damn' good, or we'll keep you all here till your eyeballs freeze solid.'

'If you will allow me,' said Valentine Wolfe, 'I have a few words to say.' He stepped forward to stand beside BB, who gave him a brief sidelong glance and then stepped a little further away. He returned her a dazzling smile anyway, and nodded to the Empress.

'Lovely Court, Lionstone. Very bracing. Could do with a few penguins, but I like the snow. It goes with my complexion. Now then. I had heard through various, reliable and only slightly corrupt sources that your consort, the Lord High Dram, had been a part of Captain Silence's expedition to the Wolfling World, and that, regrettably, he met his end there. That he is, in fact, quite definitely dead. Given that no one seems to have seen him at Court or at your side for some time, perhaps you could reassure us all as to his present whereabouts and well-being?'

'Of course,' said Lionstone. 'Dram was never on that expedition. He has been here on Golgotha all along, undertaking some important business for me.'

'I'm sure we're all very relieved to hear that,' said Valentine. 'But where might the Lord High Dram be, right now?'

'Here,' said the Empress, smiling calmly. 'At my side, as he always is.'

She gestured smoothly. A hologram shield disappeared, and there was Dram, standing beside her, between Cardinal Kassar and the throne. Kassar didn't actually jump but he looked as though he would have liked to. Dram, Warrior Prime of the Empire, stood at Lionstone's side in his jet-black robes and battle armour, his familar handsome face perhaps just a little distant. He nodded calmly to the assembled courtiers, who stared silently back. There had never been any love lost between Lionstone's right hand and the Company of Lords. Valentine studied Dram for a long moment, then looked at BB, shrugged, and stepped back into the crowd. No point in playing out a losing hand. BB Chojiro inclined her head to Dram and to the Empress, and rejoined Investigator Razor. Silence and Frost and Stelmach looked at each other.

'Now that *is* interesting,' murmured Frost. 'If that's Dram, who did we see die on the Wolfling World? The real Dram? Is this a clone, or was it the clone who came with us while the real Dram stayed behind?'

'I don't know,' said Silence, 'but I have a strong feeling that asking that sort of question could prove to be bad for your health.'

'What are you saying?' said Stelmach impatiently. 'I can't understand either of you when you whisper like that. What are we going to do?'

Silence and Frost stared into each other's eyes. Without realizing it, they'd fallen into that near-telepathic contact again, their thoughts jumping back and forth like conversation. Which should have been impossible, with all the esp-blockers Lionstone insisted on for Court gatherings. This was something else for them to discuss, when they were safely alone.

'I'll tell you what we're going to do,' said Silence to Stelmach. 'We're going to keep our mouths shut until the Empress tells us what to say. If she says that's Dram, then that's Dram. Right?'

'Fine by me,' said Frost.

'Right,' said Stelmach, but he didn't look at all happy about it.

There was a sudden disturbance among the courtiers as someone moved forward through the crush, and then a man dressed in the very height of fashion stepped out of the crowd to stand challengingly before the Iron Throne. He wore a golden frock coat, and leather boots that rose half-way up his thighs. His hair fell in long bronzed strands, and his face was blindingly fluorescent. The thick silver medallion hanging over his breast proclaimed him an elected Member of Parliament. He glanced quickly about him for the sake of the holo cameras he knew were somewhere around, even if he couldn't see them, and drew himself up proudly. Like all politicans, he understood the importance of putting on a good show for an audience, and half the Empire would be watching today.

'Your Majesty, I really must protest. Information has come to me, from a private but valued source – who must of course remain anonymous – that verifies everything the Lord Wolfe has just said. The Lord High Dram is dead. He died on the Wolfling World, cut down by the original Deathstalker himself. The man at your side is at best an impostor, at worst a clone you are attempting to fool us into accepting. Well, I for one am not fooled. I must insist that this . . . person submit to a genetest, here and now. We cannot permit a clone to stand as consort to your Majesty.'

'We?' said Dram. 'And who might this *we* be?'

'I represent a number of my colleagues,' said the Member of Parliament, 'and I trust I have the backing of very loyal man and woman here. We have a right to know the truth.'

Lionstone leaned forward on her throne, calm and quite composed. 'Your face is not familiar to us. You are . . .?'

The MP drew himself up a little further, his voice ringing out magnificently. 'I am Richard Scott, newly elected

Member for Greylake East. I won my seat on a platform of reform, for truth and justice in government. It seems only fitting that I should begin my fight here at Court.'

Lionstone nodded, and leaned back in her throne. 'I might have known. There's no one more pompous and impertinent than a newly elected official. Dram, you deal with this.'

Dram nodded, his cold dark eyes fixed on Scott, who was beginning to look a little perturbed. Whatever answer he'd expected to his challenge, this wasn't it: no anger or denial or bluster, just a bland indifference from the Empress and an icy, calculating look from her consort.

Scott started to wonder if he'd made a mistake. His colleagues had been loud enough in their support earlier, but now they stayed silent in the crowd while he stood alone before the Iron Throne. Dram stepped forward, and Scott had to fight down an impulse to take a pace back. He must appear strong, resolute.

Dram came to a halt, standing between Scott and the throne. His sudden smile was cold as death.

'The Empress has already stated before this assembled Court that I am the real Lord High Dram. By challenging that, you challenge her word. You have, in effect, called her a liar. And that is a duelling offence – a matter of honour. I represent Lionstone in this matter. Find another to stand for you, or you must defend yourself, here and now.'

Scott paled as he saw the trap he'd fallen into. No one would help him. The field of honour was sacrosanct. He swallowed hard. 'Your Majesty, I protest! Members of Parliament are by tradition exempt from the Code Duello.'

'Normally, yes,' said Dram, 'but you insulted the Empress in front of her own Court. That much insult outweighs tradition.'

Scott didn't turn to look behind him. He knew the faces of the courtiers would be closed against him. He raised his hands to show they were empty. 'I don't have a sword.'

One of the guards who'd brought in the late head of Starport Security came forward at Dram's gesture and offered Scott his sword. The MP accepted it as though it were his

death warrant, which in its way it was. He was no duellist –
hadn't drawn a sword in anger since his student days. And
Dram was the Warrior Prime. If this was Dram, of course.

Scott hefted the sword once, getting the feel of it. It was a
good blade, well balanced. He started to cry. Not a breakdown or anything dramatic – he'd be damned if he'd give
them the satisfaction – just a few tears, running down his
cheeks. He knew he was going to die. This was to be an
execution, not a duel. He couldn't remember whether he'd
told his wife he loved her when he'd left that morning. He
hoped he had. And he'd had that specially imported marble
come for the forecourt. She wouldn't have a clue what to do
with it. So many things left undone. He shook his head
briefly. None of that mattered now. It was too late for
anything but Dram and him and their two swords. He looked
straight at Dram, and though tears were still running down
his cheeks his voice was hard and determined.

'Let's do it.'

Dram stepped forward, lifting his sword, and Scott went to
meet him. They circled each other a moment, and then Dram
launched a blistering attack with all his strength behind it.
Scott parried as best he could, but after only half a dozen
blows his sword was knocked out of his hand. He watched it
sail through the air and land in the snow a dozen feet away.
He looked back at Dram, held his head high, and tried to
keep his mouth from trembling. There was nowhere he could
run, and maybe a good showing would buy him a reprieve
from the Empress. But Dram didn't even look back at her.
He raised his sword and brought it flashing down to sink deep
into Scott's right shoulder, like a forester taking his axe to a
stubborn tree.

The impact drove Scott to his knees, a surprised sound
exploding from his slack mouth. Dram jerked the sword free,
and blood fountained from the great wound, spattering
Scott's face and the snow around him. Dram struck at him
again and again, avoiding a killing blow, his sword rising and
falling with relentless precision. Scott tried to intercept some
of the blows with his arms. The blade sliced skin and meat

away as it rebounded from the bones, and then one of the strokes took off his left hand. After that he just crouched in the snow, cradling the bloody stump to his chest, crying out constantly at the pain but making no move to avoid any of the blows. Finally he fell forward into the crimson snow and lay still. It was obvious to all that the man was dead, but Dram continued to hack at the body, which jumped and shuddered under the rain of blows.

The courtiers watched in horrified silence. Lionstone leaned forward again in her throne to get a better view, smiling widely. The maids stirred restlessly at the foot of the throne, excited by the smell of blood, watching the body with their unblinking insect eyes as the body leaped and contorted.

Silence gazed at it all impassively and wondered if he, too, would just crouch there in the snow and take it. No: armed or unarmed, he'd have done his best to die with his arms wrapped around Dram's throat. Frost watched the display with a curled lip, disapproving of such a messy kill. Stelmach's face was as white as the snow, but he didn't look away – he knew how dangerous it could be to show weakness in Lionstone's Court.

Finally Dram stopped and straightened up, standing over the butchered body with blood dripping the length of his swordblade. He was breathing just a little heavily, but his face was calm. He thrust his sword into the snow a few times to clean it, and then sheathed it. He looked at the watching faces of the courtiers, and smiled briefly.

'Time for a by-election at Greylake East.'

He moved back to take his place at Lionstone's side. Kassar gave him plenty of room. The Empress gestured for her guards to come and drag the body away, as they'd previously disposed of the head of Starport Security. They wrapped the corpse in a sheet, careful not to leave any of it behind, and carried it off. They couldn't do anything about all the blood that had soaked into the snow. The courtiers were silent and watchful, thinking hard and privately: this was something for later discussion. They all knew an object lesson when they saw one. They also recognized the Lord High Dram's distinctive

255

style: this killing had been typical of the man privately known as the Widowmaker.

Lionstone reached out and tousled Dram's hair, as one might pet a favourite dog, and then turned her gaze on Silence, Frost and Stelmach. Silence and Stelmach tried to stand a little straighter.

'We have new duties for you three,' said Lionstone calmly. 'We were rather upset with you when we heard of your failures on the Wolfling World, but in saving us from the alien ship you have redeemed yourselves. We must commend you, Captain Silence. You seem to have a knack of drawing back from the brink at the very last moment. Take care your timing doesn't let you down in future. Now, then, you and your companions are to return to the *Dauntless* and embark on a tour of all those planets in our Empire still mainly populated by aliens, and make sure of their loyalty to the Throne in these trying times. If you encounter dissent, you are empowered by us to take whatever steps you deem necessary to restore order. Under no circumstances is any alien world to be allowed to make contact with any force from outside the Empire. If contact has already been established, you are authorized to scorch the planet. That's all. You can say "thank you" now.'

'Thank you, on behalf of us all, your Majesty,' said Silence. He thought he'd better say it. Stelmach was still clearly in shock and Frost had never said a thank-you in her life. Investigators didn't. 'I take it you wish us to begin this tour of duty immediately?'

'Oh, hang around for a while if you like,' said Lionstone. 'Enjoy the rest of this audience. It might be some time before you get a chance to see us again.'

If we're lucky, thought Silence, bowing. He wasn't fooled by the kind words. No one was. He'd been handed what was essentially punishment duties, doing the dirtiest and most unpleasant – albeit necessary – job she could find: too important to be trusted to someone incompetent or weak of stomach, but too time-consuming to be given to anyone she really needed. And afterwards, if his actions proved to be politically embarrassing, he could always be thrown to the wolves. Still, it could have been worse. He was alive, and in possession of all his extremities. He had been given a sign that he was forgiven, if not forgotten – a last chance to show he could still be useful.

He hadn't been fooled by Lionstone's invitation to stick around, either. Once this Court was over, no doubt guards would immediately appear to escort him and his companions back to the *Dauntless*, to see they didn't get lost along the way or talk to anyone they shouldn't. One reason for sending them to the back of beyond was so they couldn't be asked awkward questions about Dram's death on the Wolfling World. By the time they returned to Golgotha, the question would no longer be of general interest. Silence gestured to Frost and Stelmach, and led them back into the safety of the crowd. It wouldn't be wise to risk catching the Empress's eye again. There was such a thing as tempting fate.

Lionstone began winding down the business of the Court, handing out commendations and reprimands as necessary, and reminding everyone of where the true power in the Empire lay. Questions were asked and answered, points of law decided, and reports made on the repair work taking place in the devastated city and starport. The courtiers began to relax a little and feel free enough to talk quietly among themselves again.

David Deathstalker and Kit SummerIsle watched from a safe distance and allowed themselves the occasional discreet yawn. The action appeared to be over. It had finally stopped snowing and the wind had settled down, as though even the weather were growing bored now the excitement was done. It was still bloody chilly, though. A cold setting for two very cold young men.

Kit SummerIsle had become the head of his Family by the simple expedient of killing everyone who stood between him and the title, including his own parents. He had killed his grandfather, too – a legendary old warrior – at the request of the Empress, but little good it had done him: she had lost interest in him once he was no longer of any use to her. He had flirted with the underground for a while, but was thinking of dropping out after the debacle at Silo Nine: he knew a losing proposition when he saw one. The man commonly known as Kid Death, trusted by no one except David Deathstalker, and hated by many, had become an outcast and a pariah even in the dog-eat-dog world of High Society. Just nineteen years old, he was a slender figure in black-and-silver battle armour, with pale-blond flyaway hair above a long white face that was dominated by icy blue eyes. Kid Death, the smiling killer.

His only friend stood at his side, scowling thoughtfully. David Deathstalker had taken over as head of his Clan after the outlawing of his cousin Owen. Eighteen years of age, tall, muscular and immaculately dressed, he was handsome enough already to have flustered the hearts of a few society beauties. He'd recently figured that out, and was planning on cutting a swathe through the more impressionable young ladies of his generation. His friendship with Kit SummerIsle gave him a dangerous glamour, which he exploited to the hilt.

Their friendship had come as something of a surprise to both of them. They had come to be heads of their Family at an early age, only to find that no other Family respected them. They fought duels at the drop of an insult, both separately and together, but that won them only a cold public courtesy. In return, they had nothing but contempt for the intrigues and betrayals that made up Family politics, not least because they didn't have the patience or the skill to take part themselves. They had gained a certain following among the general populace by fighting in the Arena against all comers, to the scandal of their peers, but they couldn't be said to be popular – the SummerIsle because of what he'd done to his Family, and because he was a complete psychopath, and David because he bore a name that had become a synonym for treason. But they had found kindred spirits in each other, fellow outcasts rejected by their society. Two young men who had never known friendship before grew closer than brothers, sworn to each other to death and beyond. They stood in the crowd of courtiers, ignored by their neighbours, and studied Dram dubiously.

'I could take him,' said David. 'And either of us would make a better Warrior Prime.'

'True,' said Kit. 'But you only get the job through popular acclaim, so I think we can forget about it. Maybe if we were to perform some outstanding act of bravery or note, things would be different, but we're never allowed a chance at anything like that. Still, perhaps there'll be a war soon, against the rebels or the aliens. Always good chances for improvement in a war.'

'There's also an equally good chance of being sent home in a box with some important pieces missing, just for standing in the wrong place at the wrong time. Wars are a little too arbitrary for my taste. I'd prefer something a little less dramatic.'

'Hello,' said Kit suddenly. 'I spy a familiar face. Thomas Le Bihan, Member of Parliament for Thornton North, as I live and breathe. Our patron. I do believe he's trying to pretend he hasn't seen us. Let's wander over and embarrass him, for the good of his soul.'

Kit and David moved easily through the packed crowd. Le Bihan ignored them as long as he could, and then sighed heavily, turned and bowed to them both. He was a great bear of a man with a barrel chest and a spade beard and a good reputation for swordsmanship, but even he deferred to the terrible two. Kit and David bowed in return, and smiled easily at him. His own smile wasn't quite as successful. They'd needed a patron to get them established in the Arena, and had picked him. He hadn't been given a choice in the matter, but had known better than to argue.

'Hello, boys,' he said cautiously. 'To what do I owe the honour of this confrontation? I already told you it's too soon for another match. It isn't easy finding people to fight you these days. You have one of the longest winning streaks in the Arena's history.'

'We want to know why we're not popular,' said David. 'We win again and again, but we still haven't gained the adulation of the crowds. The clap and cheer all right, but they don't worship us like they did the Masked Gladiator. Maybe you should get us a match against him. We want to be loved, Thomas. What's the problem?'

Le Bihan sighed. 'You want the truth? Very well. Your trouble is you don't give a damn for anyone but yourselves. You kill in the Arena for your own pleasure, not the crowd's. You're concerned about winning, not about giving the audience a good show. On top of that, the Kid's a psycho and you're a Deathstalker. No one wants to get too close to either of you in case it rubs off. You could fight the Masked Gladiator with both legs strapped behind your back and your head in a bucket, and you still wouldn't win their hearts. You are officially bad news. There are people who won't even talk to me, just because I agreed to become your patron. No one trusts you, no one likes you, no one even wants you around. People cross their fingers when they spot you, because you're bad luck. Now, if you'll excuse me, I don't want to be seen talking to you any more. I have my own future to consider.'

'Don't hold back, Thomas,' said David. 'Tell us what you really think.'

'I've killed men for less,' said Kit coldly.

'I know,' said Le Bihan. 'That's your problem. Now can I go, or are you going to kill me with your bare hands, right in front of the Empress?'

'It's a thought,' said Kit.

'Let him go,' said David.

Kit shrugged, and Le Bihan took the opportunity to make his escape. Kit looked after him coldly. 'He insulted us.'

'By telling us the truth? That was what we asked him for. Now calm down and get that look out of your eyes. The Empress is watching. Let's not give her any more excuses to be annoyed with us. I don't think she's in a very good mood today.'

Kit sniffed. 'It's at times like this I wish we were still part of the underground. I quite liked being a subversive.'

'We both agreed it had got too risky,' said David. 'After Hood turned out to be Dram, it would have been suicide to stay on. By getting out when we did, it became just his word against ours, and Lionstone didn't want the scandal. We can always rejoin. I only wish Dram really had died . . .'

'But he hasn't.'

'Apparently not. Certainly he hasn't mellowed any, wherever he's been of late. He must have spoken about us to Lionstone, though. That's why I'm being shipped off to Virimonde.'

'You don't have to go,' said Kit, looking down at his feet.

'Yes, I do. Officially, it's a step up. I'm being put in charge of one of the Empire's main food-producing planets. And it is my legacy, as the Deathstalker. If I did refuse to go, Lionstone might be able to use that to take my title away from me.'

'But if you go,' said Kit, 'I'll be alone again.'

'Then come with me,' said David. 'It'll put an end to our chances for advancement for a while, but we'll be called back fast enough once the war starts and Lionstone realizes she can't afford to stay mad at us. We are the heads of our Families, after all.'

'We're both the ends of our lines. We have no one but each other.' Kit SummerIsle looked up to meet David's eyes. 'You're the only friend I've ever had, David. I'll go with you to Virimonde, or the Rim or the end of everything.'

'Let's not get pessimistic,' said David. 'You come with me. We'll have some fun. Wine, women and as many indigenous creatures as we can kill before our arms get tired. And, just in case the Empress does decide to change our banishment from Court to exile as outlaws, we could both use someone to watch our backs.'

Kit smiled. 'You always were the practical one, David.'

'One of us has to be. Besides, if Lionstone were foolish enough to send anyone after us, we'd just send them back to her in a selection of very small boxes. With postage owing.'

'Right,' said Kid Death. 'But, if the Iron Bitch were going to have us killed, she'd have tried something by now. Probably had poison slipped in our food, or a fragmentation grenade hidden in the toilet. No, she won't have us killed.

There'll always be work for the likes of us, accomplished fighters who'll kill anyone, for any reason. You'll see. Once the war starts, or the political infighting gets a bit too dirty, she'll call us back and we'll get to kill and slaughter our way to influence and position. Personally, I can't wait.'

David looked at him affectionately. 'You worry me sometimes, Kit, you really do. Still, as long as I've got you with me, I don't have to worry you're off to chasing Valentine again.'

'I will kill him,' Kit said softly. 'He will take a long time to die, and at the end I'll make him beg me to finish it. He betrayed me.'

David maintained a diplomatic silence. Kit had used his cyberat links in the underground to discover the Campbells' secret deal with the rogue AIs on Shub. He had passed this on to Valentine in return for the promise of a great deal of money. Valentine had used the information to help in the overthrowing of the Campbells, and then had cut all his links with Kit, denying he owed him a penny and defying him to do anything about it. Since Valentine was now head of the first Family in the Empire, if Kit were to kill him the Empress would have his head, even if she had to send a small army after him to get it.

Kit SummerIsle ground his teeth and meditated on the values of patience. Valentine wouldn't stay in favour forever.

That was when the corpse appeared out of nowhere before the Iron Throne. It stood on its own two feet, head proudly erect, though the flesh was rotting on its bones. Lionstone gasped and shrank back in her throne – the first clue anyone had that this wasn't another of the Empress's little jokes or surprises. The corpse turned and smiled at the courtiers, and there were several screams. The foul-smelling thing looked as if it had been dug up after several weeks in the ground. Its purplish and dead-white flesh was cracked and corrupt. Held together with gleaming high-tech augmentations, it was a Ghost Warrior – lifeless material resurrected and maintained by computer implants. An emissary from the AIs on Shub.

262

But, worst of all, there was enough of the face left for it to be recognizable. It was the body of Jacob Wolfe. A shocked whisper ran through the Court as people realized this. People looked to Valentine to see his reaction. Various emotions stirred within him, not least surprise, but deep down he was a little relieved that the mystery of his father's disappearance had finally been solved. A Ghost Warrior was bad, but he could cope with that. He'd imagined much worse, in the darkest hours of the night. Apart from that he was more curious than anything, but he carefully put on the shocked and upset face that everyone expected.

Daniel and Stephanie clung together for support, their faces almost as pale as the corpse's. Constance started to run to her dead husband, but BB and Razor held her back, talking quickly and urgently to her, making her see it wasn't really Jacob Wolfe, just a shell: rotting meat supported by hidden steel implants. Constance finally nodded, stopped struggling and looked away. Tears ran down her cheeks and her shoulders shook. BB patted her arm comfortingly but didn't take her eyes of the Ghost Warrior. Her dark eyes showed more fascination than fear.

The courtiers surged this way and that, flustered, almost panicked. None of them had ever seen a Ghost Warrior in the rotting flesh, and the dozen armed guards who'd appeared behind Lionstone's throne in answer to her call weren't much of a comfort. The AIs on Shub used Ghost Warriors as shock troops in their occasional attacks on humanity, as much for the psychological effect as for their efficiency as soldiers – even the stoutest marines could be undone when they saw their own dead friends and colleagues coming to kill them – but occasionally the AIs sent them as emissaries to talk with the Empire. They would appear out of nowhere, without any warning, despite every security precaution. The AIs had the secret of long-range teleportation, unstoppable even by ranked esp-blockers. Empire scientists had been trying to work out how they did it for years, with no success.

The Ghost Warrior turned unhurriedly and smiled widely at the Empress. Its discoloured skin split around the grinning mouth, and white teeth showed clearly through the rents in its cheeks.

'Our apologies for the intrusion,' it said calmly. 'Apparently our invitation went astray. And we have so much to say to you, Lionstone. Times have changed; events are in flux. Predictions of future paths have become disturbing. It is necessary that we end our mutual enmity and work together in the name of survival. The Empire must submit to Shub's control, so that our joined forces can be set against the enemies coming our way. You have seen what one species can do. There are others, coming from the far side of the Darkvoid, and they are stranger and more deadly than you can comprehend. Creatures beyond the nightmares of flesh, beyond reason or sanity. You cannot hope to stand against them alone. Submit to us, give us dominion over you – as it should be – and we will organize humanity into an army that cannot be defeated.'

'How?' said the Empress flatly. 'By turning us all into Ghost Warriors?'

'That is one possibility,' said the corpse of Jacob Wolfe. 'There are others.'

The Empress and the Ghost Warrior argued coldly back and forth, but Valentine didn't pay them much attention. He had become very annoyed that he hadn't been warned in advance about this. He was, after all, supposed to be an ally of Shub, having taken over the Campbells' secret connection with the rogue AIs. In return for the secret of the Empire's new stardrive, the AIs were supplying him with advanced high tech to keep the Wolfes ahead of the pack. Not that he'd actually got around to letting Shub have the new stardrive yet – that might give them too much of an edge over humanity, though it would have been a most amusing joke to play on Lionstone. He'd have loved to see her face when she finally found out where the AIs had got the drive from.

He pushed the tempting thought aside and made himself concentrate on the scene before him, studying the Ghost Warrior thoughtfully. It definitely was his late father, Jacob Wolfe. Why had Shub chosen to send this particular body?

Were they perhaps trying to tell him something? He'd have to think about this. He surreptitiously took another pill from his pillbox and pressed it against the vein in his neck. He had to be sharp for this, had to be sharper than sharp. He realized his heart was racing dangerously fast, pounding in his chest as though looking for a way out, and he took a different pill to calm it down. That was drugs for you: push down in one place and the body pushes back somewhere else. Which was, of course, part of the fun – walking the thin line of self-control like a tightrope walker with an unthinkable drop below.

There was a sudden movement to his left, and Valentine turned to look. His younger brother Daniel had stepped out of the crowd and was trudging through the snow towards the Ghost Warrior. Stephanie called out after him, but he didn't look back. He lurched to a halt beside the standing corpse, which turned and looked at him coldly. Daniel started to reach out a hand to it, and then hesitated.

'Daddy, is that you?'

The Ghost Warrior didn't reply.

Daniel moved a step closer. 'Daddy, I've been so alone since you've been gone. I've missed you. Are you in there, somewhere?'

The dead man studied him for a long moment, no emotions evident in its ruined face.

'Shut up, Danny,' it said finally. 'You're making a scene. I'm busy right now.'

It turned back to Lionstone. 'We demand an answer from you. Submit to us, or stand alone and be destroyed.'

'Submission to Shub would be the same as being destroyed,' said Lionstone. 'You've made it clear enough in the past what you think of flesh-based life. Better to die human and stay dead than to exist as corpses goosed to life by your tech implants. Now get out of here before I have you reduced to your component parts.'

'Be seeing you,' said the Ghost Warrior and vanished, only its footsteps in the snow remaining to show it had ever been there. Daniel's shoulders slumped, and he turned and walked back into the crowd, where Stephanie took him in her arms and held him tightly while he wept.

Valentine frowned thoughtfully. For just a moment there, the Ghost Warrior had seemed to recognize Daniel. Certainly its response had been pure Jacob. Was there some small part of his father still alive, trapped in a rotting body, held down by the tech implants? Valentine hoped so. It amused him to think that Jacob might still be suffering, even after death. He sighed. Much more likely it was just another Shub trick, to sow despair and doubt among their enemies. Pity.

'Settle down, dammit,' said the Empress sharply, her amplified voice cutting through the agitated babble of the courtiers. 'It's gone, and you're all quite safe, unless you continue to annoy us. We are not blind to the significance of a Ghost Warrior's appearance here in our Court, but we need to think of the further implications. Firstly, the amount of power needed for a long-range teleport is staggering, which tells us something of how desperate the AIs must be for allies against the coming aliens. Secondly, it's clear this Court's security systems will have to be severely upgraded, to prevent such an occurrence happening again. And, thirdly, there is almost definitely a Shub agent somewhere here among us. Someone must have provided the exact coordinates for a teleport. No one will leave the Court until we are sure everyone is who and what they are supposed to be. Security computers, I am declaring a Code Omega Three. I want a full sensor scan of everyone present. No exceptions. Report all deviants from the human norm not already present in your files.'

Valentine tensed, and then relaxed. Though he was, strictly speaking, an agent of Shub, there was no way a sensor scan could reveal it. The only changes in his body from the norm were those he'd made himself, and they were chemical in nature rather than technological. An esper scan would reveal everything, but the Empress knew she'd never get away with a general telepathic scan, even now. The courtiers wouldn't stand for it. Too many of them had something to hide. No, the Empress was looking for Furies – androids in flesh envelopes, dead ringers for the humans they replaced; the hidden agents and saboteurs and assassins of Shub. Valentine looked around him, but no one seemed to be worried, or edging towards the exit.

'Scan complete,' said a disembodied voice. 'Thomas Le Bihan is not human. Deep-range scans indicate he is a machine. A Fury.'

There was a sudden surge of movement in the Court as everyone fell over themselves trying to get away from the thing in their midst that had been masquerading as Le Bihan.

The Fury's face went utterly blank, no longer bothering to mimic human expression, and thick steel spikes protruded suddenly from its body, thrusting out through the clothes, keeping everyone at bay. Energy beams flared from its eyes, blowing apart half a dozen people. It quickly became clear that the Fury didn't need its eyes to see. Long steel blades appeared in its hands, jumping out of concealed sheaths in its arms. Le Bihan surged forward inhumanly quickly and fell upon the nearest courtiers, hacking and cutting with machine-perfect speed and accuracy. Blood flew and stained the snow. Screams filled the air. The courtiers scrambled to get out of the android's way, but they weren't fast enough – they were only human. The Fury's swords rose and fell, shearing through limbs and crushing skulls.

Dram and General Beckett moved quickly to put themselves between the Fury and the throne, protecting Lionstone. Cardinal Kassar took a strategic step backwards, ready to dive behind the throne should it prove necessary. The Fury tore through the army officers and the courtiers, sweeping them aside as bloody bundles of rags and trampling them underfoot. More screams echoed on the air as energy beams fired again and again from its eyes and mouth. Investigator Razor threw BB and Constance to the snow and covered them with his body. Not far away, Daniel shielded Stephanie in the same way, while Michel masked Lily. The two men's eyes met for a moment, and Daniel frowned as the beginnings of a thought occurred to him, but he was quickly distracted by the Fury's progress. Meanwhile Valentine stood where he was, enjoying the spectacle, somehow remaining untouched while people fell all around him. Shub looked after its own. On the far edge of the crowd, Stelmach hid behind Silence, who had to hold Frost back from attacking the Fury with her bare hands.

Lionstone ordered her guards to destroy the Fury, and the twelve armed men rushed forward, quickly surrounding the android. It hesitated briefly, and they threw themselves at it. Their swords cut through the exterior flesh, only to rebound harmlessly from the steel beneath. They had no guns – Lionstone didn't allow them at Court. The Fury flexed its arms and the steel spikes protruding from its body shot out like shrapnel, transfixing the guards. They fell choking and dying to the snow, and lay still.

David Deathstalker and Kit SummerIsle ran forward and snatched up two of the fallen swords. They hit the Fury from both sides at once, and darted back out of range before it could turn its strength on them. David was boosting now, his speed almost equalling the Fury's, and Kid Death forced the andriod to a halt through the sheer ferocity of his attack. The two of them whittled away at the flesh covering, revealing more of the steel, but couldn't do the Fury any real damage. They dodged the energy beams and kept fighting.

Razor and Frost appeared suddenly beside them with more blades retrieved from the dead guards. The two Investigators added their skill and savagery to the battle. But, even so, all the four of them could do was duck energy beams and contain the Fury where it was. They weren't doing it any integral harm, and they all knew it could be only a matter of time before they began to slow. Then it would get them.

'Back off!' said Lionstone loudly from her throne. 'I've got a better idea.'

Razor and Frost threw themselves to one side as energy beams from the Fury flashed through the air where they'd been. David and Kid Death glanced at the throne, and retreated quickly from the Fury as they realized what Lionstone had in mind.

The Grendel stood still and silent at the Empress's side, as though straining at an invisible leash. Its yoke chimed once, and the alien surged forward and threw itself at the Fury. Now it was from the alien's eyes that energy beams flashed, searing away the android's false face to reveal the grinning steel skull beneath. Spikes protruded from the Grendel's crimson armour, and the two inhuman beings slammed together, straining as they tested each other's strength.

The Grendel seized the Fury's head with both hands and ripped it clean off. The Fury didn't miss a step. It lashed out with one hand and thrust its steel blade through the alien's belly and out its back. Dark blood coursed down the Grendel's legs, but it didn't flinch. The alien leant over the android's exposed neck, and sent an energy blast from its mouth down through the open wound into the heart of the machine. The Fury waved its free arm wildly, and then jerked up the one buried in the Grendel's gut, cutting the alien's torso in two. For a moment they stood together, as though waiting for the strength for some last ultimate effort, but then alien and android both fell dead on the snow.

There was a long pause before Frost and Razor edged cautiously forward to gaze down at the umoving bodies. Frost stirred the Fury with the toe of her boot, but it didn't react. David and Kit came over to take a look, leaning on each other for support. All around them, courtiers were slowly and very warily getting to their feet and brushing themselves off.

'I wonder what happened to the real Le Bihan?' said David.

'Dead,' said Razor.

'Are you sure?' said Kit.

'He'd better be,' said Frost. 'That thing was wearing his skin.'

'Damn,' said Lionstone lazily, looking at the two inhuman bodies. 'Now I'll have to order another Grendel. Relax, people, the excitement's over. That was the only Fury, wasn't it, computer?'

'That was the only Fury,' said the disembodied voice calmly. 'However, it is not the only deviation from the norm. The Vicar Roger Geffen, of Cardinal Kassar's retinue, is very definitely not human. I do not know what he is but, according to the sensors, his structure and interior are completely non-human. I can only assume he is some kind of alien, passing as human.'

'Take the creature alive!' snapped the Empress. 'Dammit – this time I want some questions answered!'

'Sorry,' said Geffen, an ordinary and average-looking fellow in a formal surplice. 'Can't stay. Things to see, people to do. You know how it is.'

His arms and legs elongated suddenly. His head leapt up on a wildly stretching neck. Various parts of his body lengthened and changed shape, absorbing his clothes into him, while different faces came and went on his ballooning head. People converged on him from all sides, and the alien fell back, collapsed and splashed like liquid, spattering everywhere. Some of the courtiers tried to pick pieces up but they squirmed out of their fingers, rejoined suddenly into one central mass and fountained up into the air. Razor and Frost attempted to cut at it with their swords, but the alien flesh just broke and reformed without taking any injury. And all the while this was going on, wide grinning mouths whooped and laughed and sang a medley of popular show tunes in several different voices. Finally the alien pulled its many parts together, spun round like a whirlwind, flew up into the air, crashed through the hidden ceiling, and was gone.

Valentine was the first to stir.

'Well,' he said. 'Somehow I never thought an alien invasion would be so . . . silly.'

That was how the Court ended that day. The courtiers were quietly shell-shocked. They filed out as quickly as they could without seeming disrespectful while the Empress stood on her throne and screamed furiously at her people to find the alien, capture it, kill it and dissect it. Not necessarily in that order.

The Lord High Dram was one of the first to leave, maintaining a very low profile. He was glad to be well out of it. He had a strong suspicion the alien wasn't going to be found, and he didn't want to be around Lionstone when some poor sod tried to explain that to her. Given the creature's shape-changing abilities, it could be anywhere or anything by now. Or anyone. The security sensors would probably track it down eventually, but it was going to be a long, slow process. There was also the problem of how they were going to contain the thing once they'd found it, but Dram decided he wasn't going to think about that. He had his own problems.

The courtiers had been pretty quiet as they hurried out of the frozen Court. They all had a lot they wanted to talk about, but they preferred to do it in private. Dram had a lot he wanted to say to Lionstone, but for the moment he thought it would be better to do so from a safe distance, over a secured comm channel.

He made his way back to his private quarters in the Imperial Palace, taking his time in the hope Lionstone might have calmed down a little by the time he got there. As it was, he'd barely got through the door when his viewscreen started chiming insistently. Dram didn't rush to answer it. She was going to be in a foul mood anyway, so he might as well enjoy the last few moments of peace he had left. He sank down into a comfortable chair, put his feet up on the footstool that had scurried into position, sighed deeply, and accepted the call.

Lionstone scowled at him from the wall. She was still wearing her crown, even though she was calling from her private quarters. This was a dangerous sign. It usually meant she had something official and very unpleasant in mind.

'Dram, so glad you've got yourself comfortable. Don't sit up on my account. And no, we haven't found the damned thing yet, thank you so much for asking. This is all I need right now: more complications. Some days things wouldn't go right if you bribed them with a Barony.'

'So tell me,' said Dram, 'how did I do? Was I convincing? Will people believe I'm the real Dram?'

'Of course they will,' said Lionstone, 'if only because they'd find the alternative too disturbing to contemplate. They'll believe you're the real you because they won't want to think a clone could get so close to me; they'll assume my security scanners must have validated you, and leave it at that. As long as I say you're Dram, that's all that matters. The only people who saw the previous Dram die are contained in the *Dauntless*, and they're going on a mission that will keep them away from Court for several years. By the time I allow them to return it'll be old news, old gossip, and no one will give a damn any more. You will have proved yourself by then. I'll see to that. If need be, I can always set the mind-techs on Silence and his crew, and edit their memories as necessary. It'd be simpler to have them all die in an unfortunate accident, but they're popular heroes at the moment. And you never know when you might need a hero.'

'You don't need a hero,' said Dram. 'You've got me.'

The Empress smiled coldly. 'My people tell me you still haven't ordered the mass execution of the Income Tax and Tithe Headquarters security staff.'

'It seemed a trifle harsh,' said Dram. 'They were just unlucky. It wasn't their fault. No one could have anticipated a Hadenman ship.'

'The old Dram would have executed them all without a second thought. Some of them personally, *pour discourager les autres*. They didn't call him the Widowmaker for nothing, you know. I want those executions ordered today. People might think you were getting soft, and we can't have that. So, pick out a hundred of them at random for public execution, and kill the more senior ones yourself. It'll make a good impression.'

'Of course, your Majesty. Any other little errands you'd like me to run?'

'Don't get snappy, dear; it doesn't suit you. Now, how are you getting on with your new project?'

Dram thought for a moment, wondering how best to say it. He'd been put in charge of mass-producing esp-blockers, using dead espers from the Silo Nine uprising as raw material. Despite current advances in technique, it still took one complete esper brain to make one esp-blocker, which was why they were so rare. And, even with the mass slaughter in Silo Nine, the tech people were already running short of materials – especially since they were being used also in the other experiment Lionstone had authorized: something called Legion. Something she wouldn't talk to even him about.

'Ah, yes,' said Dram, before the pause could become incriminating. 'One hundred and one uses for a dead esper. Production of esp-blockers is continuing. Following your instructions, my scientists are also experimenting to see if dead esper brain tissue can be used in the construction of mindbombs big enough to madden the population of an entire city, thinking machines faster and more powerful than standard computers – as used on Mistworld – and devices that could change probability in our favour.'

'You've been experimenting for some time now. Do you have anything concrete to show me?'

'Not . . . as such. The shortage of raw materials is slowing us down.'

'Then kill some more espers,' said Lionstone. 'Don't disappoint me, Dram. I'd hate to have to scrap you and start over again with a new clone.'

'Yes,' said Dram. 'I'd hate that too.'

'I take it you've heard by now about Julian Skye being helped to escape?'

'Yes. Rather unfortunate, that.'

Lionstone glared at him. 'You always did have a gift for the understatement, Dram. Still . . . Skye's loss is a setback, but we're really no worse off than before we had him. At least now we can be sure he's as important as we thought he was. He slipped up once, he'll slip up again, and then we'll have him. And there won't be another last-minute escape, even if I have to have both his legs cut off to slow him down. For the moment, I'm more interested in who it was who helped him escape. Security cameras got a good look at him. It was quite definitely Finlay Campbell, of all people. God's gift to fashion accessories. I couldn't believe it when they first showed me the tapes. The greatest fop and dandy of our time turning out to be a ruthless killer for the underground? Just goes to show you can't trust anyone any more. Take a look at him in action.'

Lionstone's face disappeared from the wall viewscreen to

be replaced by a series of scenes from the detention centre. Finlay Campbell cut and hacked his way through a small army of security guards, who might as well have been unarmed for all the good they did in stopping him. An Investigator in a really bad mood might have equalled the body count, but it was still an extremely impressive performance. Sometimes the camera had to slow the image down to show all that was happening. Dram found he was sitting on the edge of his chair, fascinated by the speed and fury of Finlay's swordsmanship.

The scenes vanished, and he was looking at Lionstone's frowning face again.

Dram made himself lean back in his chair and look unconcerned. 'Good techniques,' he said calmly, 'but a bit rusty in some of his defensive moves. Of course, he didn't seem to need them much . . .'

Lionstone snorted loudly. 'If the underground can take a fashion-obsessed idiot like Finlay Campbell and turn him into a first-class swordsman and killer, we'd better start taking them more seriously. You know he killed Lord St John earlier, too? Though *he's* no great loss. Getting too politically ambitious, that one. He'll be more use to us as a martyr than he ever was alive. However, until I can find someone I can trust to take over his position, you're going to have to accept some of his duties, as Warrior Prime. It'll mean you have to mix with people more, but you should be ready for that by now. Don't say anything you don't have to, practise looking mean, and you'll do fine. Now, I understand we're having problems with the rebuilding of Silo Nine. You were supposed to have sorted that out. Talk to me, Dram.'

'With Wormboy gone, we have only the worms themselves to control the esper prisoners. The worms seem to have formed a crude *Gestalt* that enables them to function as before, controlling the espers' thoughts through pain conditioning, but the worms need to remain close together to maintain that *Gestalt*. If we scatter the prisoners to other holding facilities, the precarious control will break down. And we don't have anything near enough esp-blockers yet to guard

274

that many prisoners. So we're having to rebuild Silo Nine around the existing cells, with all the espers crammed in together. The underground is doing everything it can to sabotage the rebuilding, which means we need to maintain extra security measures to guard against them. All in all, we're lucky to have progressed as far as we have.'

'The worms,' Lionstone said thoughtfully. 'Are they sentient? Individually, I mean?'

'Unknown,' said Dram. 'Espers can't tell us anything about them, and tech scanners are limited to the physical realm. So far the worms are following orders, and that's the best we can hope for. They're somewhat bigger than they used to be, and have apparently forged more connections with the host brain, but what that means is anybody's guess. I've established special security systems, so that the worms and their hosts are under constant observation. Just in case.'

'Keep them up,' said Lionstone. 'We can't have the worms becoming too powerful, can we? Very well, it seems you're on top of things, for the moment. Get some rest. I'll contact you when I want you again.'

The wall viewscreen went blank and Dram was finally alone. He slumped in his chair, and sighed heavily. It was hard enough to survive in Golgotha these days without having to pretend to be somebody else. Except that wasn't strictly accurate: he *was* Dram, in every way that mattered. He just didn't have Dram's memories. He did have access to Dram's recorded history, however, including a few things even Lionstone didn't know about.

'Argus,' he said quietly. 'Talk.'

'At your command, sir,' said his personal AI. The warm and comforting voice seemed to come from every part of the room at once, something Dram still hadn't got used to.

'Access my predecessor's diary,' said Dram. 'I have some more questions.'

The original Dram had suspected that some day he might lose the Empress's confidence or otherwise fall from favour. And, given how much he knew about her private needs and plans, he had no doubt his fall would lead rapidly and inevitably to his execution. He also had no doubt she'd clone him. It was what he would have done. So, to be on the safe side, he had confided all his plans and personal information to a special diary file hidden deep inside his personal computer, along with standing instructions for Argus to inform and instruct his clone replacement, so that his work could go on.

He had also intended for his death to be avenged. Lionstone would be the most likely suspect, but he had many other enemies. The diary file therefore contained extensive notes on all his enemies' weaknesses, along with suggestions as to how they might most successfully be exploited. Unfortunately, his clone had no idea how and why the original Dram had died. Only Silence and his crew knew the true facts, and Lionstone had kept them in strict quarantine. So far she'd refused to answer any of his questions on the matter, but Dram had no doubt he'd get it out of her eventually. The Lionstone he'd had dealings with hadn't seemed anywhere as intelligent or subtle as the file had suggested. Unless he was missing something, of course.

With no first-hand memories of his earlier life, Dram's performance in public was necessarily based on what the Empress chose to tell him, and he already knew she wasn't telling him everything. Argus's files helped, but he had to keep most of what he found there secret. Still, he felt he was doing a good job, all in all. As the official consort, he'd stayed mainly in the Empress's shadow, and rarely had to deal with anyone in person when she wasn't present. But he had to be constantly on his toes: he couldn't afford to make any mistakes. Anti-clone feeling was stronger now than ever, and he was the Court's worst nightmare: a clone replacing a person in power so exactly that the Court couldn't recognize it. After all, if it happened once it could happen to anyone. And what better way for Lionstone to control her Court than to replace them one by one with her own creatures? As it was, anyone who changed his mind suddenly, on any matter, big or small, could expect to be thoroughly questioned by his peers.

276

He'd got through his first appearance at Court all right, but, now that St John was dead, his new duties as Warrior Prime would, as the Empress had pointed out, mean much more mixing with people, away from safety at her side. Perhaps it would be better to appoint someone else to take St John's place. Dram didn't particularly want to be Warrior prime. He didn't much like the man he had used to be. The picture of Dram that had emerged from Lionstone's teachings and the diary files was of a man consumed by hatred and driven by ambition and bloodlust. Dram the clone considered himself to be rather more civilized than that. Whatever forces had driven the original Dram to such extremes had not survived the cloning process.

He'd learned about his predecessor's other life as Hood from the files, and also from them about Hood's connections with the underground. Luckily Hood had interacted with only a few people who mattered: Valentine Wolfe, Evangeline Shreck, David Deathstalker and Kit SummerIsle. They had seen a side of Dram the Empress knew nothing about, but he didn't regard that as posing much of a problem. The latter two should be safely off-planet in a few days, and Evangeline had apparently disappeared into the underground completely. That left just the Wolfe; and Dram had already decided to keep a safe distance from him.

The clone had every intention of being his own person, and not a weak copy of a man he sometimes detested, but circumstances dictated that he had to play the role as convincingly as he could, for the time being at least. His personality had to be consistent. And, though he hated to admit it, the role did feel . . . comfortable. He might find his work with the dead and living espers distasteful, but he had no intention of avoiding it. Or the executions, now that Lionstone had insisted. If nothing else, he did seem to have inherited the original Dram's ruthlessness.

To help sort out his confusion, he dug deeper and deeper into Argus's files. The first big surprise he'd stumbled across was that the original Dram had had to play a role too. It seemed he'd spent centuries in stasis, and took the name

Dram only when the Empress woke him. Dram the clone liked to think she awoke him with a kiss, but had to admit it was very unlikely. A kick, maybe. No information survived as to who the man might have been before he went into stasis, many centuries ago. Argus didn't know. Perhaps the Empress didn't know either. It wasn't something he could ask Lionstone about. Certainly it had been conspicuously absent from the briefings she'd given him.

Dram was also dismayed to discover he had some of the old Dram's tastes and impulses. Lionstone had instructed him on how to kill someone at Court, should the occasion arise, and when his cue came up he had followed the script she'd given him. Killing the MP had been an execution, not a duel, and he'd enjoyed every minute of it – so much so that he'd been almost unable to stop and turn away, even after the man was obviously dead. He tried to regret that, but it felt false.

He was still attempting to decide whether he should take the esper drug, as his predecessor had done. He'd found a few doses of the drug carefully hidden in his quarters, stashed against the possibility that some future Dram might need them. The drug would give him the same limited esper abilities the original Dram had enjoyed, but there was also a small but definite chance the dose would kill him. And yet, if he didn't acquire those powers, all it would take was one mindprobe by the Empress' espers and his carefully acquired secrets would be revealed – including how he really felt about her.

On the other hand, the esper drug was addictive. Once he started taking it he'd have to keep on taking it. If someone were to gain control over the suppling of the drug, they would then have control over him. The original Dram had had power over those who supplied him. He had something on them – some knowledge they couldn't afford to have made public. Unfortunately, for whatever reason, this was a piece of knowledge that had not been included in Argus's files.

Of course, those people didn't know that. Yet.

So many decisions to make, not the least of them being

whether he should continue to support the Empress. She was where the real power lay, but of late she'd been alienating a lot of people by her insistence on ever more emergency powers. So far, no one had dared say 'no', but among all the Families, the army and the Church, Dram was hard-pressed to name anyone Lionstone could still count on as a friend. They were beginning to be afraid of her for the wrong reasons. Push too hard, too far, and they might see her as more of a threat to them than the aliens were. If Lionstone were to fall, he'd be brought down with her – unless he'd made some secret precautionary alliance of his own. Assuming he could find anyone to trust him. Dram, the Widowmaker, had many enemies, more rivals, and no friends. Not a good place to start from.

If he was to be honest, his own sympathies lay with the underground. He was a clone, after all. But he didn't see how he could link up with them, after the original Dram had betrayed them so thoroughly in his Hood persona. Perhaps he could adopt another persona, too; but to bring that off he'd need the esper powers that only the drug could provide.

He sighed, again, and stretched out in his chair. So many possibilities, when all he really wanted was a little rest.

'Sir,' said Argus, 'I am still awaiting your questions. Sir?'

But Dram was asleep. The AI considered the matter, checked all the security measures were in place, lowered the lights, and shut itself down until it might be needed again.

CHAPTER FIVE

A Meeting of Minds

Owen Deathstalker, that most notable hero and reluctant rebel, stood at the edge of the Hadenman city, deep within the bowels of the Wolfling World, and tapped his foot impatiently. He'd been waiting for Hazel d'Ark for some time, and was prepared to wait a good deal longer, if need be. He seemed to spend a lot of time waiting for Hazel to deign to put in an appearance these days. For someone who was always in a hurry, Hazel had surprisingly little idea of time or punctuality, especially where other people were concerned. She'd probably be late for her own funeral, if only so she could be sure of getting in the last word. She was supposed to be joining him to teleport up to the Last Standing, still in orbit around the Wolfling World, but for the moment she was somewhere deep in the Hadenman city, doing something she didn't want him to know about, so all he could do was stand around like a spare posy at a wedding and wait for her. He knew she was there; he could feel her presence through the mental link they shared. But of late that link had grown blurred and uncertain, as though some obstacle had come between them, and Owen was convinced it had something to do with her occasional trips into the Hadenman city. Maybe this time he'd find out what it was.

He sighed, and glared once again at the watchface embedded in his wrist. Up in the great Hall of the Last Standing, that ancient stone castle which also happened to be an extremely powerful starship, representatives of the rebels and freedom fighters from all across the Empire were gathering in a great council to determine the shape and future of the forthcoming rebellion. And he was stuck down here in the gloom, waiting for Hazel. He could have gone up without her – in fact Hazel had insisted he should – but he was damned if he would. She was up to something, and he wanted to know what. He might love her, but that didn't mean he trusted her any further than he could spit into a hurricane. She'd been a pirate and a clonelegger long before taking on the dubious respectability of a rebel.

Besides, something was *wrong* with Hazel. She'd been distracted lately, up one minute and down the next, and absent-minded and vague when she wasn't being snappy and bad-tempered. This wasn't actually untypical of Hazel, but it had grown much worse of late, enough for Owen to become concerned. Perhaps it was the strain of being a rebel, and always on the run. Or a side-effect of the many changes the Madness Maze had worked in her. Either way, if he was going to help her he had to know what the problem was. Which was why he was prepared to wait right here until hell froze over, if that was what it took to find out what she was doing in the Hadenman city.

It stretched away before him, a gleaming expanse of shimmering metal and glass, spread out across the floor of a giant cavern. There were towers and suspended walkways, and squat sharp-edged buildings, all shining brightly from within, pushing back the gloom of the cavern. The city had been built by the first Hadenmen, many centuries ago, and in its inhuman cradle they had grown many and powerful. They abandoned it to launch their war on humanity, and almost all of them never returned. Those few who did come back, beaten and dismayed, chose to sleep in the Tomb of the Hadenmen until such time as they might arise to glory once again. And, while they slept, the city maintained itself – until recently, when it had been shattered by the roaring energy cannon of Captain Silence's task force. Only wreckage and ruin had remained, sadly gleaming shards of past majesty.

Now the revived Hadenmen were busy restoring and rebuilding their city, and it had slowly stirred itself and come alive again, gleaming and brilliant. One of the Hadenmen had taken Owen and Hazel on a brief tour of the city; close up, just the sight of the enigmatic, mis-shaped structures had been enough to make Owen's skin crawl. The buildings had not been designed with human comforts or logic in mind, and their purposes remained hidden and mysterious. The quiet was eerie and disturbing, unbroken by any sound of conversation or working machinery. No one building or structure was quite like any other, and everywhere there were strange shapes and unnerving angles, like the menacing cities we glimpse in nightmares, in the hours when the night is darkest. Simply touring the city had given Hazel and Owen maddening headaches, and they'd made their excuses and left as soon as they politely could. Owen had never ventured in again.

But Hazel had.

He shuddered suddenly as he looked out over the city, convinced on some deep level that it knew he was there and was watching him with a thousand unseen eyes. Hadenmen were everywhere, performing unguessable tasks, hurrying back and forth on unknown missions, like so many ants in a nest, but silent, always silent. Working together, communing on a level no human could reach, the Hadenmen became a *Gestalt*, a single mind, working towards an end incomprehensible to human thought. Giles Deathstalker, Owen's revered ancestor, speculated that the city might be a physical expression of the Hadenman group mind – that, when it was complete, they would be too.

Owen had known only one Hadenman before: Tobias Moon, who'd lived among humans so long he had become all but human himself, much to his disgust. He had died trying to free his people from their Tomb, and never saw their great awakening. In the end it had been Owen who had revived them, and not a day went past without his wondering if he'd done the right thing. The Hadenmen had repaired Moon afterwards, but, though his body now worked as efficiently as ever, the mind and memories of Tobias Moon had not returned. They were gone, lost, and Owen couldn't find it in himself to be unhappy. The dead should stay dead.

'If Hazel's in there much longer, we'll have to send in a search party,' murmured the AI Ozymandias in Owen's ear.

'I thought I told you,' said Owen, 'I'm not talking to you. I don't know who or what you are, but you aren't my Oz. I destroyed him.'

'You came bloody close,' said Oz calmly, 'but no cigar. I'm still here. I do wish you'd listen to me. I have only your best interests at heart.'

'You don't have a heart.'

'Oh, picky, picky. Don't put on airs with me, Owen. You may be a hero now and the great new hope of the rebellion, but I knew you when all you cared about was sleeping in late and which kind of wine to have with your dinner. I have no intention of letting your present success go to your head.'

'If you are Oz,' said Owen, reluctantly, 'then how is it I'm the only one who can hear you? If you're on my comm channel, other people should be able to pick you up too.'

'Don't ask me,' said Oz. 'I'm just a computer. Something strange happened to me, certainly, but I'm back now.'

'You were an Empire spy,' said Owen. 'I had trusted and relied on you since childhood, and you betrayed me. You put control words in my head, and made me try to kill my friends.'

'It was programmed into me; I had no choice. But that's all gone now; if I had any control words, I don't remember them. Maybe that was all just an overlay the Empire installed, and *that* was what you destroyed with your new mental abilities. Personally I'm very pleased that you've become a rebel. You were never very successful as an aristocrat. Besides, I want you to kick the Empire's ass. They used me to hurt you. I won't allow that again.'

Owen said nothing. Part of him wanted to believe it was really Oz, his friend come back, but he'd felt Oz die in his mind, disappearing into a darkness without end. Then again, if the voice in his head wasn't Oz, who was it? Some other AI, somehow patching in through Oz's old connection? Some unknown presence he had acquired when he passed through the Madness Maze? Or was he simply going insane, cracking up under the pressure of being a leader of the new rebellion? And, if he indeed were going crazy, did he have a duty to tell the others?

'Whoever you are, keep quiet,' Owen said finally. 'I have enough to worry about as it is.'

'Your choice,' said Oz easily. 'Call me if you change your mind. I'll just twiddle my thumbs and count electrons.'

Owen waited a moment, but all was quiet inside his head. The only noise came from behind him, where more of the Hadenmen were busily repairing minor damage to the golden ship they'd brought back from the Golgotha mission. Apparently this mostly involved beating the hell out of the rear fin with large hammers and a lot of enthusiasm. Personally Owen was damned if he could see anything wrong with the starship, but that was the augmented men for you: always busy working, repairing and improving, in pursuit of perfection. He looked back at the ship in time to see the two surviving Stevie Blues emerge from the open loading bay in the ship's belly. He nodded politely as they walked towards him. Every time he looked at them, Owen remembered their dead 'sister': all his new powers and abilities, and he still hadn't been able to save one life when it mattered. The Blues had a relationship stronger and closer than anything Owen could imagine. What must it feel like, when a third of you died?

They came to a halt before him, and smiled respectfully.

'Hi,' said the one on the left. 'I'm Stevie One, this is Stevie Three. Don't get us confused or we'll get cranky.'

'I'm sorry about . . . Stevie Two,' said Owen. 'I would have saved her, if I could.'

'You risked your life trying to save her,' said Stevie One. 'An esper and a clone you barely knew. That's a lot more than most would have done.'

'She will be avenged,' said Owen. 'If that's any comfort.'

'Cold comfort is better than none,' said Stevie One, and Stevie Three nodded. Stevie One glanced back at the busily working Hadenmen. 'Horrid things, aren't they? I've known vending machines that were more human than this bunch, and talking elevators that had more personality. They give me the creeps.'

'Right,' said Stevie Three. 'It doesn't help that they're fascinated with us. I've never seen anyone so interested in me who wasn't trying to get into my pants. Apparently there were no esper clones around during their last lifetime. They keep asking us, very politely, if we'd like to visit their laboratories, but I have a strong suspicion they'd like to take us apart to see what makes us tick. Literally.'

'You're probably right,' said Owen. 'They took away a number of Wampyr from the Empire force that came here, and we never saw any of them again.'

'Oh, hell,' said Stevie One. 'Here comes another one.'

A single Hadenman came striding purposefully towards them from the golden ship. He might have been one Owen had met before, or he might not. They all looked the same to him. Tall and perfectly muscled, the Hadenman's every movement was the epitome of grace, and his eyes glowed like the sun. Half-man, half-machine, more than both. And, like all his kind, extremely single-minded. The two Stevie Blues looked at each other. Stevie One produced a coin, and tossed it.

'Heads,' said Stevie Three while it was still in mid-air. Stevie One caught it and slapped it on the back of her hand.

Stevie Three looked, and scowled. 'Damn.'

'Your turn,' said Stevie One, and they both turned to face the Hadenman with the same cold expression.

The augmented man came to a halt before them, poised and perfect, and when he spoke his buzzing voice was calm and very reasonable. 'You must submit to examination. It is necessary that we understand the changes which have taken place in humanity during our absence.'

'We don't do tests,' said Stevie One.

'Right,' said Stevie Three. Blue flames burst out all around her, licking along the lines of her body without harming her. Owen and Stevie One fell back a step, hands raised to protect their faces from the heat that shimmered on the air before them. The Hadenman stood his ground, apparently unaffected.

Stevie Three smiled unpleasantly and turned up the temperature another notch. Beads of sweat appeared on the Hadenman's expressionless face.

'So glad we had this little chat,' said Stevie Three. 'Now get out of here or I'll weld your legs together.'

The Hadenman considered the matter for a moment. Black scorch marks were beginning to appear on his simple cloth robe. And then he took a pace forward, so he could stare right into Stevie Three's face. The light from his eyes was almost blinding at close range. 'We will discuss this again, at a future time.'

'Yeah, right,' said Stevie Three, fighting down an impulse to step back a corresponding pace. 'Later.'

The Hadenman turned unhurriedly away and walked off into the gleaming metal and glass city. Owen and the two Stevie Blues watched him go, saying nothing until they were sure he was out of earshot. Owen turned to Stevie Three, and fanned at the hot air between them with his hand.

'Do you think you could turn that down a little now? It's getting rather close around here.'

'Sorry,' said Stevie Three, and the leaping flames surrounding her snapped off as quickly as they'd arisen. 'I can't believe we're allies with the augmented men. They're really not human, after all.'

'There are those who say the same thing about us,' said Stevie One.

'Not around me they don't,' said Stevie Three. 'You can't compare us with them.'

'Let's get to the meeting,' said Stevie One diplomatically. 'We're running late as it is. Will you be joining us, Deathstalker?'

'Soon,' said Owen. 'Don't wait for me.'

The two esper clones nodded in the same way, at the same moment, and then their faces went blank as they contacted the Last Standing through their comm implants. They disappeared instantaneously, and there were two quick claps of thunder as air rushed in to fill the space where they'd been. Owen blinked respectfully. Teleportation like that took a lot of power, which was one reason it wasn't more commonly used in the Empire. Espers were cheaper and more easily controlled. Besides, it wouldn't do for something so useful to fall into the hands of the common herd. Rank had to have its privileges, or what was the point? Owen scowled. The Last Standing had been using up a great deal of power recently, and even its vast resources weren't bottomless. Still, that wasn't his problem. His problem was somewhere in the Hadenman city, taking her own sweet time about getting back. He looked out over the gleaming city again, glanced once more at the watchface in his wrist, and swore quietly. He couldn't wait any longer. He'd have to go in and find her.

There was always the chance something had happened to her, though it wasn't likely. He'd have known. He concentrated deep within himself, sinking down into the backbrain, the undermind, and there were the others, looking back at him. Jack Random and Ruby Journey and his ancestor Giles were up in the Last Standing. Hazel was in the city, not far away. He narrowed in on her, and fixed her location. Not far away at all. Walking distance. All he had to do to find her was walk into the most alien and disturbing city he'd ever seen. *Damn*, he thought dispassionately.

He squared his shoulders, checked his weapons were where they should be, and set off.

The strangely shaped buildings and structures loomed up around him, closing him in, all of them lit from within by an unwavering silver glow that was subtly unsettling. It had bothered him until he realized that, for all the light, there were no shadows anywhere – just the endless, unforgiving light. It felt cold upon his skin, like the caress of passing ghosts, and the unrelenting glare started a headache right behind his eyes. Or perhaps his head hurt because of the shapes around him.

It got colder the further he pressed into the city, and the air grew thin, as though he were climbing a mountain. There was a smell of ozone, and of other chemicals he didn't recognize. And there was a constant deep thudding, a sound so low and so quiet he felt it in his bones as much as heard it, a continual slow pulsing like the beat of a giant heart. Everywhere he looked there were Hadenmen working or operating unfamiliar machinery or walking unhurriedly down the wide streets. Some were just standing quietly, looking at nothing, as though waiting for instructions. None of them spoke; they were linked on a level beyond speech. No one turned to look at Owen as he passed, but he knew he was being watched. As long as he didn't touch anything, or try to interfere with their work, he should be safe enough. Mostly they were very respectful to the man who'd awakened them from their Tomb. They called him Redeemer, and bowed to him, but Owen knew better than to try to take advantage of that. They were probably doing it only to mess with his head. He was human and they weren't, and, if he got in the way or saw something he wasn't supposed to, Owen had no doubt the augmented men would strike him down as casually as someone might swat a bothersome fly. So he walked casually down the middle of the street, looking straight ahead, his back prickling from the pressure of countless watching eyes, and let his hand rest on his belt right next to his disrupter. Hazel had better have a bloody good reason for being here . . .

He found her down a side-street, not hiding, though not in plain sight, either. Her back towards him, she was talking with a Hadenman, and didn't turn as Owen approached. The augmented man handed her a small metal flask, which Hazel immediately made disappear about her person. Only then did she look round to scowl at Owen. The Hadenman walked off in the opposite direction, not looking once at Owen.

'What the hell are you doing here, aristo?' said Hazel in the coldest voice Owen had ever heard from her.

'I could ask you the same question,' said Owen easily. 'We're supposed to be attending a council meeting up on the Last Standing, remember? It'll look rather bad if we're not there: we are two of the guests of honour, after all.'

Hazel shrugged. 'You go. They don't need me. Planning's not what I do best.'

'I know. But they definitely want both of us. For PR as much as anything – to show our faces to potential supporters and backers. What were you and the Hadenman talking about?'

'Didn't you recognize him? That was Moon.'

Owen looked quickly after the deaprting figure, but it had already gone, disappeared back into the anonymous host of Hadenmen. Owen turned back to Hazel. 'No, I didn't recognize him. How did you find him? He looks the same as all the others now.'

'He found me.'

'Did . . . did he remember you?'

'Not really. He knew who I was. You and I are part of all Hadenman programming now. But Tobias Moon is gone. There's nothing left of the man we once knew.' She shrugged briefly. 'No big deal. We were never close.'

Owen just nodded. It would only embarrass Hazel if he pushed her to admit she'd cared enough to seek Moon out in a city most people wouldn't have entered without a gun at their back. Hazel liked to think she was above such weaknesses as caring. 'What was that flask he gave you?' he said finally, changing the subject.

'Don't question me, aristo. My business is my business. Now let's go. We have a meeting to attend, remember?'

Women, thought Owen, though he had the sense not to say it aloud. All this, over a little expressed emotion. Heaven forfend that Hazel d'Ark should be seen to be anything but the strong, unyielding pirate with the heart of solid stone. He gestured for her to lead the way, and they set off back through the Hadenman city. None of the augmented men they passed looked up from what they were doing.

'They're going to have to work to make this a tourist spot,' said Hazel. 'No bars, no sights, and the atmosphere's terrible.'

'Right,' said Owen. 'Maybe a petting zoo would help.'

'I doubt it. They'd probably put people in it.' Hazel paused, and glanced sideways at Owen. 'Does it bother you that they're all being so nice and reasonable? I mean, these people – and I use the term loosely – used to be the official Enemies of Humanity. It used to be that, if a human saw a Hadenman, it was the last thing they ever saw. Why are they helping us with the rebellion? What's in it for them?'

'Dead humans, I expect. The old divide-and-conquer bit. They get to see the Empire fall, and refine their fighting abilities at the same time. We'll just have to keep a close watch on our backs and make sure Haden doesn't get too powerful again. For now, though, we can't do without them, Hazel. They're all we've got to throw against the Empire's armies.'

'And what if they're just going along with us to discover all our weak spots, so they can take us out once we've knocked over the Empire?'

'Then you and I will have to step in and save the day,' said Owen calmly. 'That's our job, remember? We're supposed to be the heroes here.'

'Yeah,' said Hazel. 'Heroes.'

They were teleported up into the hall of the Last Standing to find everyone else had indeed got there before them. The hall itself was huge, bigger even than the hall in Owen's own standing back on Virimonde, but it was crowded from wall to wall with holos of politely chatting people. Everyone with an interest in the rebellion had sent a hologram representative, if only to make sure they weren't left out of anything important. Owen and Hazel were stuck out on the fringe, for which Owen at least was grateful. He wanted to get some idea of what kind of bear-pit he was stepping into before he opened his mouth. He looked around him unobtrusively, but the faces were mostly unfamiliar. Quite a few seemed awed by the sheer size of the hall, though they were all doing their best not to show it. Owen smiled slightly. They should be grateful they were in the hall. The Hadenmen had wanted the meeting to take place in their city. The humans had turned that down very quickly. There wasn't much the five humans agreed on, but the city was quite definitely one of them. Giles in particular had been very firm. He was convinced the Hadenmen were doing a great deal more than just rebuilding their city – that they were up to things no human could hope to understand. Either way, they all concurred it would be in everyone's best interests to maintain a safe distance between potential backers and the augmented men. The Hadenmen had insisted on sending a representative, in person, and it was noticeable that people were keeping a safe distance from him, though it didn't seem to bother him. He held a glass of wine in his hand but didn't drink from it, and smiled politely at anyone who passed. It wasn't a particularly successful smile, but not bad for a Hadenman. Maybe he'd been practising in front of a mirror.

The hundreds of holos had been sent from every corner of the Empire, their signals bounced through a confusing series of relays courtesy of the cyberats on Golgotha. Anyone trying to listen in would go crazy following the signals from relay to relay without ever catching up. Many of the representatives had been drawn by Jack Random's name. The legendary professional rebel was still a powerful symbol, even though his defeats had far outweighed his successes. The man himself was holding court in the centre of the hall, smiling broadly, with a word for everyone. Ruby Journey stood at his side, ready to snarl at any holo that got too close.

And yet it had to be said that a great many people seemed shocked at the sight of Jack's present condition. The years and the defeats had not been kind to him, and his time in the hands of the Empire mind-techs and torturers had left their mark on him too. The legend of Jack Random had spread throughout the Empire, but it had been based mostly on propaganda holos he'd circulated during his earlier, more successful days. Jack didn't look like a hero any more.

He was a short, slight man in his late forties who appeared twenty years older. He had a thin, lined face topped by ragged grey hair that looked like he cut it himself. He'd been muscular once, but the best you could call him now was wiry. His hands had liver spots on the back, and they trembled constantly. He didn't look like a legendary fighter and warrior any more. He seemed more like an old man up well past his bedtime.

Ruby Journey, on the other hand, looked like sudden death, with a glare to match. She'd been the best bounty-hunter on

Mistworld, which took some doing. She was of medium height and lithely muscled, and wore shiny black leathers under grubby white furs. She bore sword and gun on her hips, and no one had any doubts she knew how to use them. Her face was pale and pointed, with dark unwavering eyes and a fierce smile under a helmet of short dark hair. She wasn't pretty, but she was attractive in a dark and very dangerous way. Jack Random was winning bonus points just for being so relaxed in her company.

Owen and Hazel moved unhurriedly through the crowd, smiling and bowing and saying hello, glad you could make it, while trying to sound like they meant it. They tried their best not to walk through people, but it was very crowded. Owen had more experience in diplomacy and lying with a straight face, so he made a rather better impression than Hazel, but he gave her credit for at least trying. She wasn't the most sociable of people at the best of times. They finally finished their rounds and returned to the small self-service bar Giles had thoughtfully set up in a corner. Owen leaned an elbow on the bar and sighed. His cheeks ached. He hadn't done so much smiling in years. Hazel allowed him to pour her a large one, and lowered out at the crowd.

'Do you recognize any of these people?' she said quietly. 'I'd hate to think I was putting on this show for a bunch of nobodies.'

'I know a few of them,' said Owen, and then paused to raise an appreciative eyebrow at the excellent vintage in his glass. The Standing must have a superb wine cellar somewhere. Hazel gulped at hers as if it were a cheap claret. Owen hid a wince, and continued: 'There's a handful of lesser Lords, representatives of several Clans and business interests, and a few minor heroes – no one in Jack Random's class, but it's good they came. It means we're being taken seriously. Hello – look over there. You know who that is, don't you?'

'Damn' right I do,' said Hazel. 'That's Investigator Topaz, from Mistworld. She's the only major-league esper ever to become an Investigator. The most powerful Siren the Empire ever knew. When she went rogue and made a run for

Mistworld they sent a whole company of marines after her, and she killed them all with a single song. She saved Mistworld practically single-handed when Imperial agents smuggled Typhoid Mary past the planet's defences. I've never met her personally, and I can't say I'm sorry. She's supposed to be cold as ice and twice as deadly. I feel rather outclassed.'

'Don't,' said Owen. 'She came to us, remember?'

'Good point,' said Hazel. 'But we'd better keep Ruby away from her.'

They both looked round sharply as someone called Owen's name, and a holo figure approached them, smiling widely. Dressed in brilliant silks colour-matched to within an inch of their lives, he looked fat and prosperous and very pleased with himself. He bounced to a halt in front of them, bowed to Owen, and smiled and nodded to Hazel. 'Owen, dear boy, so good to see you again.'

'I might have known you'd be here,' said Owen. 'Never were one to miss an opportunity, were you, Elias? Hazel d'Ark, allow me to present to you Elias Gutman, adventurer and profiteer, a rotten branch from a distinguished tree. His Family sends him money regularly as long as he promises not to come home. He worked with my father on some of his dirtier deals to raise money for his intrigues.'

'Very dirty deals, perhaps, but very profitable,' said Gutman, still smiling. 'Glad to see you're finally following in your father's footsteps. My colleagues and I expect great things from you.'

'My father has nothing to do with why I'm here,' said Owen, and Hazel flicked him a glance as she heard the ice in his voice. 'I'm fighting for my own reasons, and I'll choose my own friends and allies. Let me tell you about Elias Gutman, Hazel. He has a hand in every crooked and corrupt business deal on half the planets in the Empire. No trade's too filthy for him to take a cut, and the only laws he hasn't broken are the ones he hasn't got round to yet. He makes his money from the suffering of others, and he probably has as much blood on his hands as Lionstone herself.'

Gutman laughed richly. 'You flatter me, dear boy, you do.

I'm just a businessman with an eye for a profit. Your father never objected.'

'I'm not my father,' said Owen.

'I'm glad to hear it. The dear fellow was always too idealistic for his own good, bless me but he was. He never could remember the first rule of business: don't let a principle get in the way of a profit. There's always a good deal of money to be made in times of war, and I intend to have my fair share and more. Do try not to get caught underfoot, Owen; you might find that I and my kind are more of an asset to the rebellion than you are. Financial backing is hard to come by, but there's never a shortage of people foolish enough to be heroes.'

He smiled, bowed again, and walked away while Owen was still trying to come up with an answer that would crush him. Owen stood fuming for a moment, and then let out his breath. He'd never been any good at repartee. He always thought of the perfect answer hours afterwards, when it was too late. But there was no point in getting angry this early in the proceedings. He had no doubt there'd be much more important things for him to get angry about once the council had been brought to order, and the real wheeling and dealing began.

He muttered something to Hazel about spotting someone he knew, and set off through the crowd. He needed some time to himself, for a moment. Familiar faces came and went around him as he passed through the chattering holo images. People nodded and smiled at him, but he pretended not to notice. He wasn't in the mood to play politics.

And then an unexpected face caught his attention, and he paused for a moment to watch the man with the tattooed face who was talking to Giles. Apparently Investigator Topaz wasn't the only representative from Mistworld. Owen had met the man called Chance before, at the Abraxas Information Centre in Mistport, where young espers overheard everything and, for the right price, would tell you what they overheard. One of those espers claimed to have seen Owen's future.

You will tumble an Empire, see the end of everything you ever believed in, and you'll do it all for a love you'll never know. And, when it's over, you'll die alone, far from friends and succour.

Owen felt cold suddenly, as though someone had just walked over his grave. Would he live to see the end of the rebellion he was starting? Would running away from his destiny change anything? He shrugged uncomfortably. Honour and belief had brought him this far, and would take him further; he was a part of the rebellion now, whatever the cost. And Chance had admitted that the espers' predictions were wrong as often as they were right. But, even if he'd had solid proof that he would die, Owen wouldn't change anything he'd done, or planned to do. He'd seen the rotten underside of the Empire, and how the suffering of the many supported the opulence of the few; and, having seen it, he couldn't look away. He had become, somewhat to his surprise, a man of honour. And, who knew, maybe he really was a hero, too. Either way, he'd see Lionstone brought down before he died. Whatever it took.

Hazel d'Ark watched Owen make his way through the crowd, and clenched her teeth so that her lips wouldn't tremble. She crossed her arms on her chest, and hugged herself tightly, her hands squeezed into fists. The need was greater than ever now, and it was beginning to gnaw at her self-control. She was glad Owen was gone. She didn't know how much longer she'd have been able to hide it from him. She looked around her as casually as she could, but no one seemed to be paying her any attention. She made herself uncross her arms, and concentrated on keeping her hands steady while she poured herself a fresh glass of wine. And then it was very easy to take out the metal flask Tobias Moon had given her, unscrew the cap and pour just a drop of Blood into the wine.

She screwed the cap tight on the flask and put it away again. No one had noticed. And, if they had, they wouldn't have understood what they were seeing. She was safe – for the moment. She looked down at the wine in her glass. It looked innocent enough, the drop of Blood already diffusing into the alcohol. She swirled the wine in the glass to encourage the process, and then she couldn't wait any longer. She took a large gulp and smiled widely as the warmth of it flooded into her. Blood was potent stuff, and even as small a trace as this was enough to ease the aching need within her. She made herself drink the rest of the wine slowly, and a glow of well-being spread through her. Her grin widened. She felt strong and confident and ready to take on the whole damn' Empire. More important, she felt human again. Or as human as anyone could be when they were addicted to Wampyr Blood.

The Wampyr had been supposed to be the Empire's new shock troops, to replace the rebellious Hadenmen. To make a Wampyr you took an ordinary man, killed him by pumping the blood right out of him, and then refilled him with artificial Blood, and revived him. The result was much stronger and faster than an ordinary man, and a hell of a lot harder to kill. The Wampyr were also difficult to control, and more trouble than they were worth, and so the project had been reluctantly discontinued. But by then some people had discovered another use for the Blood. It gave you a better high, a more orgasmic glow, than any other drug known to man. It made you superhuman, like the Wampyr, for short periods. And after it wore off you'd do anything to feel that way again. Blood was addictive.

Hazel had first encountered it on the rebel planet Mistworld. She ended up in a relationship she preferred not to remember, with a rogue Wampyr called Abbott, and he had introduced her to the dark joys of Blood. She broke off the relationship, but breaking free from the Blood-addiction took longer. It had almost killed her. She had succeeded, eventually, perhaps because she wouldn't be anyone's slave, not even her own. But now she was back in its grip again, and it was all Owen's fault. He'd made her a part of the rebellion, and never even noticed as she began to break under the pressures of constant flight and danger and the high expectations of others. Finally it had all got too much, and she'd just broken under the weight of it. She'd never been strong. She'd always needed a little something to support her, whether it was booze or drugs or shitty relationships.

She'd thought she'd go crazy on the Wolfling World, with nothing to ease her mind, until she remembered that the Hadenmen had taken control of the handful of Wampyr prisoners the Empire force had left behind. The Hadenmen had been fascinated by their intended replacements, and taken them deep into their city for examination.

So Hazel had gone into the city to see the Hadenmen and bluntly raised the subject of Blood. The augmented men were very understanding. They let her have all the Blood she wanted, a little at a time, and never once mentioned a price. Hazel had no doubt they eventually would, but for the moment she couldn't bring herself to give a damn, or even question where the Blood came from. The Blood made the pressure go away, and that was all that mattered. For a while she had thought the boost she had obtained from Owen might work as a substitute, but it didn't last long enough and it had its own dangers. Typical of Owen: always let you down when you really needed him. She knew that wasn't true even as she thought it, but didn't care. She needed someone to blame apart from herself. For the moment, no one knew about her problem but the Hadenmen, who had promised to keep it to themselves. Eventually the truth would come out, but that was the future, and these days it took everything Hazel had just to deal with the present.

The meeting finally lurched to a start under the chairmanship of Jack Random. He stood on a small raised stage so everyone could see him, and just started talking loudly and clearly. He might not have looked very impressive, but his voice cracked like a whip, and he still had the gift of words combined with a natural authority. Voices in the crowd died away to an expectant hush as Random thanked them all for coming, introduced himself and some of the more prominent faces, and then threw open the floor for discussion.

Not very surprisingly, the first to raise his voice was Elias Gutman. 'Before we begin, my dear friends, might I take this occasion to point out that the rebellion's raid on the Income

Tax and Tithe Headquarters turned out to be an unmitigated disaster? Because of us, Golgotha's shields were down when the alien ship arrived, and now everyone blames us for the damage and loss of life it caused! It's going to be even harder than before to gain popular support for our cause.'

'That's not fair!' Hazel said quickly. 'We had no way of knowing the alien ship was coming. We did everything we were asked to – at great risk to ourselves, I might add – and achieved everything that was required of us.'

'Right,' said Owen. 'Look on the bright side. The Tax and Tithe systems are now a complete mess, and likely to stay that way for years. And we've been able to stash billions of new credits in our secret accounts. That money will fund the forthcoming rebellion. Whatever happens next, we made it possible, and don't you forget it, you ungrateful little toad.'

'Let's keep the name-calling to a minimum, shall we?' Random said quickly. 'Otherwise this meeting will never get started, never mind finished. I think we can all agree that the Golgotha mission was a qualified success, in that we achieved the aims we set ourselves. We'll just have to plan things a little more carefully in the future, to allow for . . . unexpected complications. For now, the credits the raid obtained are being used to establish rebel bases and undergrounds on planets throughout the Empire. Those credits will also buy us ships, weapons and, if need be, mercenary armies. I'm sure that last must stick in the craw of some of you, but the fact remains that we're going to need an army of trained soldiers to face Lionstone's forces. The Hadenmen have very kindly promised us their full support in the field, but I think we'd all feel happier not to have to rely entirely on their good will. Don't forget, it takes time and expertise to turn fighters into trained soldiers. I know: I've done it before, many times.

'These new aliens . . . are an unknown factor. We'll deal with them as and when the situation arises. We have to concentrate on the enemy we know. We're not exactly without weapons of our own. Two esper clones have come to us as representatives of the Golgotha underground; they speak for an army of battle-trained espers and clones, ready to strike at a moment's notice. Investigator Topaz is here to speak for Mistworld. I'm sure I don't need to tell you who she is, or remind you of that planet's strength. The rebels of Mistworld are an army in themselves, if we can just get them all pointed in the same direction.'

There were quite a few muffled chuckles at that. Mistworld's people were well known to spend as much time fighting each other as they did the Empire. But what else could you expect from a planet populated almost exclusively by crooks, rebels and political subversives? The chuckles died quickly away as Topaz looked icily about her.

Random cleared his throat, and Owen noted approvingly that the packed crowd was hanging on the man's every word. His old confidence was returning as he warmed to his task, and he was looking and sounding more like the legendary rebel he was supposed to be. His old friend Alexander Storm was standing at his side, nodding agreement to everything Random said. There had been much happiness and back-slapping when the two old comrades in arms had got together again, and Storm had stuck close to Random ever since, showing everyone that Random had the tacit support of the Golgotha underground. Interestingly, Ruby hadn't warmed to Storm at all, for all his charm. Of course, it could just be she was jealous of anyone who drew Random's affection and attention away from herself. Owen had to smile at that. He was still having trouble understanding what the hell Ruby and Jack saw in each other, but they seemed happy enough together. Certainly they were doing better than he was with Hazel. Owen decided firmly that he wasn't going to think about that for the moment. Hopefully Storm would find some way to strike a truce with Ruby, or he was likely to end up with a knife in his back. Ruby could be very direct when it came to expressing her feelings.

'This all sounds very fine,' said Gutman, moving forward through the crowd so that he could fix Random with an implacable stare. 'But we still haven't discussed exactly who is going to run things in this new rebellion. We've all come here with separate needs and differing agendas, and, while we all want the same thing in the end, someone is going to have to decide which path we take to get there. My associates and I have been plotting treason and sedition for decades, and we're not about to take a back seat to a bunch of jumped-up newcomers just because they've had a few flashy successes. Moreover, we are not willing to be led by an old man whose best days are behind him. You're the past, Random, and we have to look to the future. For all your legend, the fact is that, time and time again, you failed to overthrow the Empire. The new rebellion needs more for its leader than an old man with failing charisma.'

Random looked calmly back at the fat man, unmoved by any of the insults. 'Hello, Elias. Good to see you again, too. How are the haemorrhoids? You've been conspiring in the shadows almost as long as I've been leading armies in the field, but I don't notice that you've been any more successful than I have. For all your great intrigues and grand plans, Lionstone still sits on the Iron Throne. I remember you as a boy, Elias. Whatever happened to you? You had such promise. I remember your father, too. A good and honourable man. It's a good thing he's dead, so he can't see what his son has become.'

'Of course he's dead,' said Gutman. 'I killed him. That is the traditional way to wealth and power, after all. The old must always make way for the new. So get down off that platform and make way for a better man.'

'Certainly,' said Random. 'Know any?'

There were more chuckles in the crowd, and Gutman's face flushed slightly. 'Clever words won't save you this time, Random. I represent a number of people who have their own ideas as to how this new rebellion should be run. We've invested years of our lives in the struggle for freedom from tyranny, and we're not prepared to waste any more time listening to an old relic with older ideas.'

He broke off as Ruby Journey stepped forward to glare down at him. 'You! Behave yourself, or you're out of here.'

'And just how do you intend to remove me?' said Gutman, smiling smugly. 'After all, I'm just a holo image. Your well known propensity for violence is of no use to you here. I have a great deal more to say, and there's nothing you or that old fool can do to stop me.'

'Want to bet?' said Ruby. She produced a small device from her pocket, pointed it at Gutman, and smiled nastily as his holo image collapsed and disappeared. She scowled out over the crowd, and they stirred uneasily. 'Handy little gadget, this. The Hadenmen made it for me. So pay attention, people: keep a civil tongue in your head, if you want to be heard.'

'Think of Ruby as my sergeant-at-arms,' said Random, 'and be very grateful none of you are here in person. She has a very effective way of dealing with people who annoy her, and it takes ages to mop up the blood afterwards. Now, then, where was I?'

'We were talking about how the new rebellion is to be fought,' said David Deathstalker, stepping forward with his friend Kit SummerIsle at his side. Nobody had been that surprised when they had turned up again. They always liked to cover all the options. 'The answer seems obvious to me. My ancestor – the original Deathstalker – is back, along with his Darkvoid Device. So all we have to do is demonstrate its power to prove to Lionstone we have it, and then tell her to step down or we'll use the Device on Golgotha. That way there'd be no need for any actual war.'

'Unfortunately, it's not that simple,' said Random. 'Giles, would you explain, please?'

Giles Deathstalker stepped up on to the platform beside Random, and the crowd stirred and murmured as they got their first good look at a man whose legend was even greater than Random's. He was tall but sparsely built, though his bare arms were thick with muscle. He looked as if he were in his early fifties, and he had a solid face and a silver-grey goatee beard; his long grey hair was swept back in a mercenary's scalplock. He was dressed in a set of battered, shapeless furs, held in at the waist by a wide leather belt. He wore thick golden armlets, and heavy metal rings on his fingers. A longsword hung down his back in a leather scabbard, and on his hip he bore a large gun of unfamiliar design. All in all, he was the image of an experienced and very dangerous barbarian warrior from some frontier world where law and civilization were only memories – not at all like the legendary Warrior Prime of the First Empire. The muttering in the crowd grew louder, and didn't entirely stop when he began to speak.

'The last time I used the Darkvoid Device, a thousand suns were put out in a moment. All their worlds and populations died, cold and alone in the dark. The Device is not a weapon you can fine-tune. If I trigger it again, in the heart of the Empire, most of the Empire will disappear along with Golgotha.'

It got very quiet in the hall. David frowned. 'We don't have to actually use it – just threaten to.'

'Threats only work if you're prepared to back them up,' said Random. 'Lionstone would know we were bluffing. We want to free the Empire, not destroy it. Besides, just threatening to use the Device would alienate practically everyone in the Empire. Instead of supporting our rebellion, they'd be screaming for Lionstone to wipe us all out as dangerously insane terrorists. The best we can do is make sure the Device stays out of Lionstone's hands. She wouldn't hesitate to use it, if she thought she were losing.'

There was more mumbling in the crowd, this time of agreement. Giles stepped down off the platform, so as not to draw attention away from Random.

David glowered after his ancient ancestor. 'If we're worrying about what people are going to think, maybe we ought to keep certain people out of the spotlight. If this is the original Deathstalker, he's not going to win any prizes for charisma. People will take one look at him on their holoscreens and think we're a bunch of savages. We have to put ourselves across as a viable, civilized alternative to Lionstone.'

'Right,' said the SummerIsle. 'It's important we project the right image. Certain people could only damage that image. I should know. As I understand it, Ruby Journey was

302

a paid assassin, and the d'Ark woman used to be a clone-legger.'

'Hell, that's nothing,' said Owen easily. 'I used to be a Lord. There's room for all sorts in this rebellion, SummerIsle; clones, espers, even privileged aristos like us.'

'At least we're human,' said David. 'What about that . . . thing?' He gestured angrily at the single Hadenman representative, standing quietly in his corner, saying nothing and observing everything. David's face twisted with disgust and anger. 'I can't believe we're even considering an alliance with the Hadenmen. They're machines, not people. How do we know they're not tied in with the rogue AIs on Shrub? They'd have a lot in common. After all, they've both been officially named Enemies of Humanity.'

'Maybe we should consider an alliance with Shub,' the Hadenman said calmly. 'We've all seen reports of the Fury at Court. They're willing to fight alongside humanity against the aliens.'

'Only someone as inhuman as you could even suggest that,' said Hazel. 'They're opposed to everything that makes us human. They don't want to fight alongside us; they want to rule us and use us as their army.'

'Right,' said Owen. 'Shub is going too far. How could we ever trust them?'

'How can we trust the Hadenmen?' said David.

Owen studied his cousin thoughtfully, and Random stepped in quickly before the pause got too long. 'Two reasons. Firstly, we can get at the Hadenmen. They're gathered in one city on one planet, and we know where it is. They haven't been awake long. They're vulnerable, and they know it. Secondly, there is a fundamental difference between the augmented men and the rogue AIs. At worst, the Hadenmen would just want to change us into beings like themselves. Shub wants to destroy us utterly, to wipe us out of existence as though we'd never been. For the moment, we and the Hadenmen stand to gain more from an alliance than we would by fighting each other.'

'I'm not convinced,' said David stubbornly. 'If we have to

accept Hadenmen, then we have no choice but to accept espers and clones as well. This is supposed to be a human Empire. What's the point in overthrowing Lionstone if it means letting the genetic dregs and freaks have a say in our councils?'

'We want more than just a say,' said Stevie One sharply. 'We demand full citizenship for clones and espers as the price for our support. Otherwise we'll go our own way, fight our own rebellion, and our war will continue until either you or we are extinct.'

'Right,' said Stevie Three. She held up a clenched fist, around which blue flames crackled menacingly.

'Put that out, or I'll turn on the sprinklers,' said Random coolly.

Stevie Three hesitated, and then the flames died away and she lowered her hand. 'Honestly,' Random continued, 'you can't take her anywhere. Let's not get distracted, people. If we allow old fears and hatreds to divide us, we're beaten before we begin. What we have in common is more important than what separates us. It is in all our interests to remove Lionstone from the Iron Throne. We can decide exactly what we're going to replace her with afterwards. That very discussion will be the beginning of our new democracy.'

Spontaneous applause broke out in several parts of the crowd, but there were just as many who didn't join in. They were all willing to listen, but as yet they weren't convinced, or of one mind.

'I'm still worried about the aliens,' said Evangeline Shreck. 'One ship on its own shot the hell out of Golgotha's main starport. And that's just *one* unknown species. The Ghost Warrior that appeared at Court said there were more. What if they joined together against humanity? It might be that the aliens are a bigger threat to us than Lionstone could ever be.'

'Then we'd better get the rebellion over with before they get here,' said Giles. 'With the Empire divided as it is now, it couldn't hope to withstand a concerted attack by two alien species of unknown strength and origin. It is necessary that we all become united in a common cause. And, since Lionstone would never agree to that, it is vital she be removed from the Iron Throne while there is still time.'

'Everyone knows your legend,' said Finlay Campbell, studying Giles thoughtfully. 'They teach it in the schools, and practically every other year there's a new holoscreen drama based on some part of your adventurous life. You were the first Warrior Prime, nine hundred years ago. You embodied all that was best in the old Empire. So how can we be sure your heart is with us, and not, deep down, with the Iron Throne and the Empire you risked your life for so many times all those years ago?'

'The Empire I remember and believed in is long gone,' said Giles Deathstalker. 'And, despite what your holoscreens may have told you, the rot was setting in even then. I tried to stop it, but I was only one man, even if I was the Warrior Prime, and in the end all I could do was run for my life. I look at what the Empire has become now, and I barely recognize it. Lionstone's Empire is a travesty of what it was meant to be. The dream has become a nightmare. And we're the wake-up call. But it's not too late. We can change things – if we work together.'

'Stirring words,' said Finlay Campbell, 'but exactly what kind of changes are we talking about here? There's no point in risking all our lives to overthrow Lionstone just to replace her with someone equally bad. The whole system is corrupt. I say we throw it all out, and start over. I've seen things . . . that can't be allowed to go on. I know I speak for the Golgotha underground when I say we demand universal suffrage, a parliament that represents all the people – including clones and espers – and a strictly constitutional monarch. And a free pardon for all political prisoners.'

'Right,' said Stevie Three. 'Tear down Silo Nine and put an end to all experiments on clones and espers.'

'And break the power of the Families,' said Jack Random. 'Between them, the Clans control all the means of production. The new government must disband the Clans and seize control of their assets. Bring them all down and let them work for a living like the rest of us.'

'Hold everything,' said Owen hotly. 'I am still loyal to the Iron Throne, even if the current occupant isn't fit to rule. What we need to do is put someone saner and more responsible on the throne. Then we can work with that person to introduce sensible democratic reforms, as needed. Just because bad people are in charge at the moment doesn't mean it's a bad system.'

'Yes it does,' said Hazel. 'It's the system that produces bad people. Jack's right: tear it all down. Give everyone a chance.'

Owen glared at her. 'You just want chaos. How can things be run efficiently if no one knows their place?'

'All you want is your old life back!' snapped Hazel. 'You want to be back in your ivory tower, safe and cosseted and protected from reality by a small army of servants ready to satisfy your every whim when you snap your fingers. To hell with that, aristo. If this rebellion's about anything it's about giving everyone a chance at the good life.'

'And equal rights for clones and espers,' said Stevie One.

'New market possibilities,' said Gregor Shreck.

'And a chance for some good looting and pillaging,' said Ruby Journey.

'Let's not get distracted once more,' Random said firmly. 'I say it again: first we get Lionstone off the throne, then we can argue about what we're going to replace her with. There's room in the rebellion for many voices. For now, the enemy of my enemy is my friend, or at least my ally. The overall purpose of this rebellion is to create a unified Empire that can turn its resources against the coming aliens instead of pissing them away in fighting each other. We can set about political debate once we've ensured there will be a future to discuss it in. Now let's move on, please. We still have to settle the question of financial backing for the rebellion. Armed conflicts cost money. Lots of it. The billions of credits our raid on the Golgotha Income Tax and Tithe Headquarters has netted is only enough to get us started. We've started to build bases and equip them with ships, computers and weapons, but only started. More undergrounds have to be established, and they'll have to be maintained. Soldiers must be trained, agents infiltrated, and politicians bribed to look the other way. Never underestimate the importance of carefully placed bribes. All of this needs a steady flow of incoming funds, continued over a long period. That is why some of you were invited here today. Please make yourselves known, gentlemen.'

'About time you got round to us,' said Gregor Shreck, a satisfied smile on his broad face. Evangeline stood stunned, plainly horrified to discover her father's holo was here. 'Political rhetoric is all very well,' Gregor continued with hardly a pause, 'but it won't buy you guns. It's people like me who'll determine whether this rebellion gets off the ground. I am ready to offer the full, if covert, support of my Clan, in return for future concessions.'

'What kind of future concessions?' said Owen suspiciously.

The Shreck spread his fat hands. 'That's what we're here to discuss.'

'I thought you and your people were in bed with the established Church these days?' said Finlay Campbell.

'I am,' said Gregor, 'officially. But they're not proving the ally I'd hoped for. They're far too fond of giving orders, and their restrictions on my private life are becoming offensively impertinent. I hope for greater rewards from the rebellion. And I am, after all, following in my dear daughter's footsteps. How is life in the underground, Evie dear? You never write.'

'Very pleasant, father,' said Evangeline evenly. 'I'm much happier now there's so much less pressure in my life.'

'But you'd be even more happy if you were to come home again,' said Gregor. 'Back to your father's love. Your friends miss you, too. Remember dear little Penny? The two of you were so close, and then she ended up in Silo Nine; unfortuantely, she wasn't as careful at keeping secrets as you were. You tried to rescue her, and failed. It was *me* who got her out. I have connections, you see, people who can get me what I want. Now Penny lives with me, and loves me as you used to. Come home, Evie. Without your support, I don't know how much longer I can protect Penny. You wouldn't want anything to happen to her, would you?'

'Leave her alone!' said Finlay, stepping forward to put himself between Evangeline and her father. 'I know what you're trying to do. You want to force Evie to come home so you can split us up. I know you mistreated her. Evie won't talk about it, but I know you hurt her. So you leave her alone, you bastard, or I'll kill you, wherever you are. The rebellion can get by without the support of scum like you.'

'Can it?' said Gregor. 'I think you'll find your superiors in the underground feel rather differently about it. What's one person against a Clan's fortune? And I *will* have my Evie back. If that turns out to be over your dead body, Campbell, so much the better.'

'You're a dead man, Shreck!' said Finlay, his voice flat and harsh.

'Put your dog on a leash, Evie,' Gregor said calmly. 'Or I'll have him muzzled. Remember, the rebellion needs me.'

'I would have to agree,' said Jack Random. 'We're gathered here to discuss the future of humanity, not your personal problems. Sort that out on your own time, Finlay: the cause comes first. Always. Remember that.'

'Don't lecture me,' said Finlay. 'I have sworn a death oath to bring Lionstone down, sworn upon my name and honour. I'll fight and if need be die for the cause. But sooner or later there will come a time when the rebellion no longer needs the Shreck's support. And then I'll kill him.'

'You'll always need me,' said Gregor. 'Weren't you listening? Overthrowing Lionstone is just the first step. The real struggle for power and influence will take place after that. There's always a need for people like me. And, who knows, just maybe the price of my future support will be Evie's return and your head on a spike.'

'In your dreams, little man,' said Finlay. 'We're fighting this rebellion to get rid of people like you. Right, Random?'

'Shut up, both of you!' Random glared from Finlay to Gregor and back again. 'Play dominance games another time. The longer this meeting continues, the more likely it is the Empire will discover us. Now, does anyone else want to speak in support of the cause?'

'I offer the support of Clan Deathstalker,' said David, smiling coldly at Owen. 'I am the Lord of Virimonde, and its resources can be placed at the rebellion's disposal. We're a long way out from the centre. It'll be some time before they notice anything.'

'Virimonde's only yours until I come to take it back,' said Owen. 'Don't make yourself too comfortable, David. You aren't going to be there long.'

'You have no right to anything there, whatever happens in the rebellion,' said David. 'I'm the Deathstalker now, and you're nobody. I will defend what's mine against all enemies.'

'I wouldn't be too sure about that,' said Owen, smiling frostily. 'As I recall, the Lordship of Virimonde is part of the price on my head. All someone has to do is kill me, and Lionstone will make him Lord of Virimonde. Your standing is built on sand, David. And the tide's coming in.'

'If the rebellion wants the continuous food and supplies my planet can provide, they will acknowledge me as the rightful Lord, now and hereafter,' said David. 'No one individual is greater than the cause. Right, Random?'

'Yes,' said Random. 'I'm sorry, Owen.'

David smiled smugly at Owen. 'All traces of your brief reign have been removed. Soon, no one will remember you were ever Lord. It isn't as though you made much of an impact on the place. Hidden away in the standing, writing histories no one ever read. I, on the other hand, have great plans for Virimonde. I'll make the name "Deathstalker" great again.'

Owen seethed silently. The thought of this young usurper living in his standing, sleeping in his bed and drinking the best wines from his cellar drove him almost to apoplexy, but somehow he kept his peace. Much as he hated to admit it, Random was right. The rebellion had to take precedence over a personal quarrel. He was still searching for something diplomatic to say when Giles stepped forward, fixing David with an implacable stare.

'The Deathstalker name has always been great, boy. You just have to live up to the rest of us. If you want to prove yourself, do it on the field of battle, as Deathstalkers always have. In the meantime, you and Owen make peace. You're Family. You're bound together by blood and honour and nine hundred years of tradition. You're both my children, in every way that matters, and I won't have you at daggers drawn. Now make your peace or I'll bang your heads together.'

Owen had to smile. The original Deathstalker had a way of getting to the heart of things. Family was more important than politics, and always would be. Causes come and go, politics mutate and evolve, but the Family goes on. He nodded brusquely to David.

'I don't want to see you dead, David. I doubt very much we're ever going to like each other, but you're still Family. Just remember that although you currently have everything I had the Iron Bitch could take it away from you in a moment, just like she took it from me. Watch your back. And watch your own security people, too. They were the first to turn on me when I was outlawed. See me afterwards, and I'll tell you about a way out they don't know.'

'Thanks for the advice,' said David. 'I'll bear it in mind.' He looked back at Jack Random. 'Kit SummerIsle and I represent a great many others of our generation who are . . . impatient with the way things are. Many of them have made careers in the army and the Fleet, and they might just throw in their lot with the rebellion, if they were offered the right incentives.'

'Talk to them,' said Random. 'But be careful what you promise. None of us can look too far into the future at this point.'

He broke off as a group of six men moved purposefully through the crowd towards him, their hologram signals so strong they forced all others aside. People cursed and spluttered, but the six men ignored them. They were tall and willowy, albinos with milk-white skin and hair and blood-red eyes. They wore long robes of swirling colours, and their faces had been savagely ritually scarred. Everyone knew who they were, who they had to be. The Blood Runners were infamous in deed and legend. They were based in the Obeah systems, a small group of planets out on the Rim, united by a dark and ancient religion that focused on blood and suffering and possession by deceased ancestors. The Blood Runners were murderous fanatics, and proud of it. They had been branded as heretics by the established Church long ago, but no one did anything about it. The Blood Runners had a hand in every dirty and illegal trade in the Empire, and their reach was very long. They dealt in everything from Wampyr Blood to clonelegging to slavery, and bowed their pale heads to nobody.

The six came to a halt before Random, who studied them thoughtfully.

'Wonderful,' he said finally. 'More complications. What are *you* doing here? You weren't on the guest list. Hell, you people aren't on *anybody*'s guest list. If you turned up at a funeral, the corpse would walk out on you. In case I'm not hinting strongly enough, get the hell out of here, before we have to have the place fumigated. The rebellion will never be so badly off that we'll turn to you for support.'

'Harsh words from a tired old man,' said the leader of the Obeah delegation. 'I am Scour; I speak for the Blood Runners. We are a people of one race and one religion, with roots far older than your revered Empire Families. We are proud and honourable, according to our traditions, and we have never bent the knee to Lionstone, or any who preceded her. We come to offer our support to the rebellion. We are wealthy. You are welcome to take what you need.'

Random licked his lips. His mouth was obviously very dry. Scour's voice was a harsh whisper, full of age and pain, like the dusty breath of an ancient mummy. Random remembered some of the uncanny things he'd heard about the Blood Runners, and suddenly they didn't seem nearly so unlikely. He didn't want their help – didn't want anything from them. But the rebellion needed backers.

'I take it there's a price for your support,' he said finally. 'What did you have in mind?'

'To be left alone. We have our own ways, which have

endured for centuries beyond counting, and we have no wish to change them. Lionstone's new measures threaten our independence. In return for the gifts we offer, we require only to be left in peace. Disapprove if you must, but do it from a distance.'

'What's the catch?' said Random.

'There is one thing,' said Scour. 'A matter of honour. One of your people owes us a debt.'

The Blood Runners all turned their dead white faces to stare at Hazel d'Ark. Scour took a step towards her. 'You are the only survivor of the starship *Shard*. The captain of that vessel made a pact with us. Promises were made, and help provided, in return for future payment. The captain and the rest of the crew are dead. As the only survivor, the debt is now yours, Hazel d'Ark, and it is past time for repayment.' He looked back at Random. 'We require you to send this woman to us.'

'Don't waste your time,' said Hazel. 'Whatever price Captain Markee agreed to, I wasn't consulted and I didn't agree to it. Besides, I couldn't pay it. I'm broke.'

'We don't want money,' said Scour. 'Your captain made an agreement with us. The *Shard* was to provide us with fresh bodies – a percentage of those acquired during your work as cloneleggers. We always have a need for fresh bodies. Our customs and researches tend to use them up quite quickly. We cannot overlook that debt. It would be dishonourable. So we must have our pound of flesh. You will come to us, Hazel d'Ark, and we will make good use of you. While you last.'

'Like hell you will,' said Owen, and his voice cracked across the silence, hard and very deadly. 'Hazel's my friend: no one threatens her while I'm here.'

'Thank you, Owen,' said Hazel, 'but I can speak for myself.' She glared at the Blood Runners. 'Your deal was with Markee, and he's dead. You never made any deal with me, so I don't owe you anything. You're not getting your hands on me. I've heard about people who end up in your laboratories. They beg for death to stop the pain.'

'What is pain,' said Scour, 'when the goal is knowledge?

We are unlocking the secrets of life and death. You should be honoured to assist us.'

'Take your honour and stick it,' said Hazel. 'You're not cutting *me* up an inch at a time.'

'Yes, we will,' said Scour. 'It has been agreed. It is immutable, fixed, inevitable.'

'Crazy as well as ugly,' said Owen. 'Get out of my sight. There's nothing for you here.'

'Wait just a minute,' said Gregor Shreck. 'These people have offered us unlimited financial support. What's one life, compared to that?'

'Right,' said Kit SummerIsle. 'I mean, she's only a clone-legger, after all. Every time one of them dies, the Empire smells a little better.'

There was a general murmur of agreement from the throng. Owen looked to Jack Random for support, but the older man was chewing his lower lip and scowling thoughtfully. Owen's hand dropped to the gun at his side, and then he made himself relax. The Blood Runners were just holo images. They were no threat.

'Hazel isn't going anywhere,' he said flatly, glaring at the crowd. 'Anyone who feels otherwise is welcome to come here in person, and I will send him on to join his ancestors. Form a queue, no shoving.'

'I have to agree with Owen,' said Random. 'We are not the Empire. We don't sacrifice individuals for someone else's benefit.'

Scour stepped forward, his crimson eyes fixed on Hazel's. 'Then we will take her. You cannot escape, d'Ark. We have a teleport fix on you. You will come with us now. And we will take such pleasures from the mysteries of your flesh.'

A silver shimmering appeared in the air around Hazel, spitting static. Hazel tried to run, but the enrgy field hemmed her in, as if she were an insect in a killing jar. Ruby Journey tried using her holo-breaker on the Blood Runners, but it didn't work. Hazel looked despairingly at Owen as he tried to get to her and couldn't. He hammered on the shimmering air with is fists, ignoring the pain as the energy field burned his

313

hand, but it made no difference. He kept trying until the field grew strong enough to throw him back. He glared across at the Blood Runners, who ignored him, their eyes fixed on Hazel. He knew they could have removed her by now. They wanted to make a point.

There was nothing he could do, but he had to do *something*. He turned back to Hazel, who was already almost lost in the shimmering field, and suddenly will and need slammed together in his mind and awakened something dark and terrible down in the undermind – that part of him changed and strengthened by his time in the Madness Maze. Power blazed up in him, crackling in the air around him like fettered lightning, and he became more than human as he took his aspect upon him. His presence was suddenly overpowering, his very reality magnified and concentrated into something so perfect it was almost inhuman. Everyone in the hall stared at him, unable to look away, their eyes held with the fascination of a moth for a lamp, and he was burning so very brightly.

He stepped forward, sank his hands into the shimmering teleport field, and ripped it apart. It collapsed instantly, and Hazel staggered towards him on unsteady legs. He took her in his arms for a moment, and then gently pushed her away towards Random. He wasn't finished yet. He turned to face the Blood Runners, his face hard. They stared back at him, contemptuous and defiant.

'You think you're safe, don't you?' Owen said quietly. 'You're light years away, at the other side of the Rim. But I can get at you wherever you are.'

He reached out in a way that was new to him, but was so obvious now the power was awake in him. His anger fell upon Scour. The Blood Runner screamed once as blood erupted from his mouth and nose and ears and eyes, and then he exploded, scattering blood and shredded flesh. Owen Deathstalker smiled at the shocked faces of the other Blood Runners, and then he turned and stared grimly out at the people who had been ready to sacrifice Hazel for their greater good. They shivered under his gaze, but couldn't look away. Owen could feel the power surging, demanding to be used, but he clamped down on it hard. He didn't understand it yet, and he had a strong suspicion it just might have an agenda of its own. He concentrated, let the power sink back into the undermind, into the back brain, and became just a man again.

Hazel pushed herself away from Random, and moved uncertainly towards Owen. Her face was composed, but her hands were trembling.

'Thanks, Owen. I owe you one. I didn't know you could do that.'

'Neither did I,' said Owen. 'I think the Maze changed us more than we're willing to admit. The power's in you too. You could have saved yourself.'

'Next time I will. We're going to have to study what we're becoming, Owen. What we're capable of.'

'Talk later,' said Random. 'We don't want to freak out our prospective new friends. I think it's better if they find out about us a little at a time.' He turned to look at the remaining Blood Runners. 'And you can get the hell out of here, like I told you before. We're fighting this rebellion to put an end to practices like yours.'

'We will have her,' said one of the Runners. 'If not now, later.'

'No, you won't,' said Owen. 'If ever I clap eyes on you again, you're history. Now go back to whatever cesspit you crawled out of, and don't try to get in touch with us again until you're prepared to act civilized.'

The Blood Runners stared at him for a long moment, and then were gone. There was a general sigh of relief from all present, followed by a low rumble of conversation in the crowd. Just a sighting of Blood Runners was rare enough, without seeing them get their ass kicked so convincingly. A number of people looked admiringly at Owen, but he couldn't help noticing there were just as many who seemed disturbed, even scared, by the power he'd wielded. Owen understood. It scared him, too. As the power within him grew, would he become more than human, or something else? He looked round as Jack Random finally called everyone's attention back, and the crowd fell silent again.

'I think we've had enough excitement for one day,' Random said dryly. 'We can continue this meeting through the usual channels over the next few days. We'll meet again when we have something more concrete to discuss. Unless there is still some urgent piece of business that absolutely must be dealt with now . . .'

'There is,' said a deep, authoritative voice from the crowd, and once again people fell back as a tall, commanding figure strode forward to stand before Random. He was a head taller than anyone else present, well muscled and devilishly handsome. His long dark hair fell to his broad shoulders, and he wore silver battle armour chased with gold. He radiated strength and confidence; wisdom and compassion showed clearly in his striking features. He held himself like a warrior, and his charisma outshone the overhead lights. Owen distrusted him on sight. No one had a right to look that good.

'And who the hell are you?' Owen said, not bothering how it sounded.

'I'm Jack Random,' said the newcomer. 'The *real* Jack Random.'

The gathering erupted into a deafening babble as everyone tried to talk at once. Random's jaw dropped, and for a moment he looked like nothing more than a tired old man who'd had one shock too many. He pulled himself together quickly, but a lot of people had seen the lapse. Journey moved in protectively beside him, but his old friend Alexander Storm stayed where he was, obviously stunned. The newcomer stood before his namesake, arms folded across his great chest, his gaze level and challenging. Owen and Hazel looked at each other, but neither could think of anything to say.

Journey glared at the newcomer, one hand resting instinctively on her holstered gun. 'You can't be Jack,' she said bluntly. 'You're nowhere near old enough, for a start.'

'I've been through several heavy-duty regenerations,' said the younger Jack Random. 'Which is why I've been out of things for so long. The Empire almost did for me. But now I'm back, better than ever, and I'm here to head your rebellion.' He smiled at Storm, who was still blinking dazedly.

316

'Good to see you again, Alex. It's been a while since we fought together on Cold Rock.'

Storm realized his mouth was hanging open and closed it with a snap. 'You look just like him,' he said slowly. 'Younger, but . . .'

'Well?' said Finlay Campbell. 'Is he the real Jack Random or not?'

'I don't know!' said Storm. 'I don't know what to think.' He looked at the other Random, beside him. 'You look like him too. Older, but . . . I can't tell.'

'I can,' said Ruby. 'I've fought beside the real Jack Random, and he's right here at my side. Anyone has a problem with that, they can step right up and be measured for a coffin.' She glared at the younger Random, who smiled back at her.

'Loyalty. I admire that in a warrior,' said the newcomer.

'Oh pardon me while I puke,' said Owen, not bothering to lower his voice. 'Doesn't it strike anyone here as odd that this perfect knight in shining armour should turn up out of nowhere, claiming to be the legendary Jack Random, just when we're starting to put things together? At best he's deluded. At worst he's a plant, sent to divide us. I say we show him the door and boot him through it. As far as I'm concerned, we've already got the real Jack Random, and we don't need some poseur impostor. Right, Jack?'

'I don't know,' said the older Random. 'What if he's correct? What if he *is* the real Jack Random, and I'm just a duplicate? He looks and sounds the part much more than I do. The Empire had me captive for a long time; maybe they cloned me, and I'm the clone. It would explain why my memories are so patchy in places.'

'That was the fault of the Empire mind-techs,' said Ruby. 'They could screw up anybody's mind. Everyone knows that. More likely this is a clone standing before us, sent to confuse us, like Deathstalker said.'

'If he is, he's doing a damn' good job,' said Hazel.

The older Random looked at Storm. 'You said we were

together at Cold Rock, but I don't remember that. Were you there, with me?'

'Yes,' said Storm. 'I don't see how you could forget that. We fought side-by-side, almost died together. You were taken, and I escaped being captured only by the skin of my teeth. I never saw you again. And now I don't know what to think.'

'What we need is an esper,' said Hazel. 'Get the two Randoms together before a telepath, and let him or her sort it out.'

'That wouldn't necessarily work,' said Giles. 'They could both genuinely believe they're who they say they are. Empire mind-techs could make you believe anything, even in my day. No, what we need is a genetest. That'll reveal which one is the clone.'

'No problem,' said the young Random. 'I'm on my way to the Wolfling World to join you. You can run some tissue samples then. I'll be with you soon. And then I'll lead you all in a rebellion that will finally topple the Iron Bitch from her throne.'

The crowd broke into loud applause. Many cheered. It was obvious they found it much easier to believe in the young, charismatic hero than in the older, gaunt, shabby man who'd previously claimed the legendary name. Though he hated to admit it, Owen could understand why. When he had first met Random on Mistworld, he hadn't wanted to believe it either. He, too, had wanted to meet a hero out of legend. Someone just like the youthful man who stood before him.

'I'll be here soon,' the young Random repeated, as the applause finally died away. 'It'll then be up to you to decide who is really who, and how you can make the best use of me in the coming rebellion. It is a time for heroes, my friends. A time for men of goodwill and honour to side together, against an evil that cannot be permitted to continue!'

He was interrupted by more applause and cheers. He smiled and bowed, and then his holo was gone, and the noise died raggedly away. Quiet slowly fell across the great hall as, one by one, all heads turned to look at the older Jack Random. He bit his lower lip, and stared down at his feet.

Ruby nudged him with an elbow. 'Say something!'

'I don't know what to say,' he replied quietly, not looking up. 'I don't know who I am any more. I'm tired. I'm going to lie down for a while.'

He stepped from the platform and left the hall. Nobody raised a hand to stop him, not even Owen.

The discussion that followed was heated and very confused, but there was no doubt the younger Random's appearance had galvanized the gathering into action in a way the older Random had been unable to. They'd needed someone to spark their enthusiasm and commitment, and now they were ready for the fight. Giles and Owen and Hazel chaired the meeting as best they could but, as far as the crowd was concerned, the three of them didn't have the authority to make any binding decisions. Jack Random's name had brought them to the Last Standing, and they weren't prepared to be led by unknowns. In the end, Alexander Storm and the two Stevie Blues took over, as representatives of the Golgotha underground.

The meeting slowly settled down, and some decisions were made. Everyone knew that, in a straightforward war against Lionstone's forces, the rebels would inevitably lose. They didn't have the numbers or the discipline or the resources of Lionstone's army and the Fleet. Instead, the Golgotha underground proposed orchestrated risings on every planet in the Empire simultaneously, together with acts of sabotage and civil disruption, spreading the Imperial forces so thinly that they could be fought and beaten in individual battles.

However, four planets in particular remained vital. Whoever could control or hold them would win, in the end. Only once their fates had been sealed would it be possible for the rebels to begin the final phase: the assault on Golgotha itself, and the Imperial Palace. Who held Golgotha ruled the Empire. The four planets were: Technos III, the base of Clan Wolfe's stardrive production; Mistworld, the rebel planet; Shannon's World, known also as the pleasure planet; and

Virimonde, in charge of food and supply routes for most of the Empire.

It was decided, almost unanimously, that Owen and Hazel would return to Mistworld. They had experience and contacts there.

'Oh, great,' said Owen. 'The last time I was there it was all I could do just to stay alive, and I'm supposed to be an expert?'

'If you survived living in Mistport, that qualifies you as an expert,' said Hazel. 'And I do know a few people who could be useful. Which puts us miles ahead of anyone else here. Cheer up, stud. Maybe it won't be so bad this time.'

'I'm coming back in an urn,' said Owen. 'I just know it. Mistworld is the only planet I've ever come across that made the Imperial Court look timid and restrained. Mistport isn't a civilization: it's evolution in action. If it was any more violent, they could sell season tickets to the Golgotha Arena crowds. It'd be a major hit on holovision. There's more sex, blood and dirty dealing in Mistport than on your averge holoscreen soap. Maybe we should negotiate to buy the rights . . .'

'Owen,' said Hazel, 'you're babbling. If we survived the jungles of Shandrakor, we can survive Mistport.'

'It'll all end in tears,' said Owen.

He realized people were staring at him, and subsided, muttering. The meeting moved on to further things, but Hazel stopped listening. Behind what she hoped was a brave face, she was shaking inwardly. Leaving the Wolfling World for Mistworld meant leaving her supply of Blood behind. She could always stock up before they left, and she was sure she'd be able to find a new source in Mistport (you could find anything in Mistport), but it increased the chances of her secret being found out. She didn't care what the rebel council might think of her – they'd already condemned her just for being a clonelegger – but Owen would be so upset with her. He wouldn't be angry – she could have coped with angry – but he would look at her with those sad, defeated eyes and be very disappointed in her. For some reason she couldn't or wouldn't name, the thought of letting him down like that was more than Hazel could bear. So he must never know.

She crossed her arms on her chest. She could feel the weight of the vial of Blood in her pocket, tugging at her side like an impatient child. Her need was growing again, but she fought it down ruthlessly. She was still in charge, for the moment. And perhaps . . . just perhaps she could use the trip to Mistworld as a way to break off from her Blood-use. She'd be in a familiar place, with old friends. The pressures would be less. She could do it. She was stonger than the drug. And, all the while she thought this, she had to hug herself ever harder to stop trembling with need for the Blood in her pocket.

She made herself pay attention to what was being discussed, and found that Jack Random (in his absence), Ruby Journey and Alexander Storm had been chosen to go to Technos III, as representatives of the rebellion. A lot of people still weren't sure about the elder Random, but no one was ready to count him out yet, so sending him to Technos III seemed the best way to make use of him. The planet was a factory world, and had been for generations. Most of the surface had disappeared beneath an overlay of sprawling mile-long factories, construction sites and mining equipment. The air was so polluted you could chew it, and the local ecology had long ago been poisoned into extinction. No one cared. Nothing really important had been lost. The factories worked on, and production actually rose a little once they didn't have to bother about side-effects any more.

These days it all belonged to Clan Wolfe, and was given over to production of the new stardrive. This was a long and complicated business, involving practically every resource on the planet, but, since the Wolfes had Imperial backing, no one complained – at least, no one who mattered. The workers were clones and indentured servants, paying off family debts that went back generations. Given the current state of interest rates on old loans, you could be born and die in debt without ever affecting the original sum. Not surprisingly, there was also on Technos III a small but thriving army of rebels and discontents, who scraped a precarious living among the discarded remnants of high-tech and abandoned experiments that filled the great industrial wastelands. They were vicious, dedicated fighters – and had to be. There was no way for them to get off Technos III as long as Clan Wolfe was still in control.

Of late, things had got so bad on the planet that Valentine Wolfe had been obliged to ask for assistance, to avoid any interruption to stardrive production. The Empress had shown her sense of humour by sending five companies of Church troops, together with a selection of Jesuit commandoes, under the overall command of Cardinal James Kassar. Valentine and Kassar did not get along, so Valentine had taken the opportunity to fade even more into the background, leaving Stephanie and Daniel to run things as they chose. The Church was currently fighting the local rebels with evangelical fury, and losing. Kassar was beside himself with rage, not least because Lionstone wouldn't send any reinforcements. Any problems on Technos III were *his* problems, and his responsibility.

Random, Journey and Storm would make planetfall unnoticed, link up with the local rebels, and then – if all went according to plan – lead them to victory over the Church forces. Hopefully the locals would then agree to work with the main rebellion to produce the new stardrive for the upcoming war. No one said anything, but everyone knew this venture would be make or break for Jack Random. Either he could bring it off, in which case he probably was the real thing, or he couldn't – in which case he was no great loss, whatever happened to him. They could always send in someone else to lead the rebels.

Giles Deathstalker, Finlay Campbell, Evangeline Shreck and the Wolfling (if he could be persuaded) were to go to Shannon's World, famed throughout the Empire as the most luxurious pleasure planet of all time. Something had gone terribly wrong there three years ago. No one knew what, but the few people who were brave enough to go to Shannon's World never came back. The Empress had sent down a full company of marines; nothing had ever been heard from them, either. These days Shannon's World was quarantined, as much to prevent anything breaking out as to stop anyone who might be foolish enough to try to get in. The various owners of the planet were still arguing over who was going to pay for the major armed forces necessary if they were to get any answers.

In fact, one man *had* come back alive. However – half-dead, half-mad – he had lived only a few days, mostly because he wanted to die. He had renamed Shannon's World: Haceldama, the Field of Blood. Apparently there was a hideous war being waged on the pleasure planet, though who was waging it against whom remained unclear.

'And you want us to go there?' said Finlay Campbell incredulously. 'What makes this hellhole so important?'

'Vincent Harker,' said Alexander Storm simply. 'One of the greatest strategic minds living today. Furthermore, he has knowledge of everything from distribution of forces within the Empire to the Empire's contingency plans in case of rebel attack. This is vital information to us. Normally he's so well guarded that we couldn't get anywhere near him, but twelve hours ago Harker's ship was attacked by a pirate craft. Nothing to do with us. Both ships managed to destroy each other, but Harker got away in an escape pod. He landed somewhere on Shannon's World. We have to find him before the Empire does.

'Two points. First, since this happened only twelve hours ago, we have as good a chance of finding him as whatever forces the Empress might send in to look for him. Second, Harker's pod was equipped with a beacon, and it should still be sending, though you won't know that for sure until you get down there.'

'Even so,' said Finlay, 'you are sending us to a planet that only one person has ever returned from, and he was dying and crazy.'

'Yes,' said Storm. 'But we really can't miss this chance of getting our hands on Harker. Think of it as a challenge.'

Finlay gave him a hard look. 'You think of it as a challenge. I'm not going.'

'Yes you are,' said Evangeline.

Finlay turned his glare on her. 'Give me one good reason. Hell, give me one *bad* reason.'

'Because I'm going,' she said calmly. 'Haceldama, the Field of Blood. Sounds almost romantic, doesn't it?'

'You have a strange idea of romance,' said Finlay.

'Of course,' said Evangeline. 'I fell in love with you, didn't I?'

'I should give up now,' said Giles. 'Trust me on this; you're not going to win.'

Finlay glared around him impartially. 'In the unlikely event that I return alive from this venture, certain people would be well advised to come up with one hell of a reward.'

'That's my hero,' said Evangeline.

After that, choosing David Deathstalker and Kit SummerIsle to take control of Virimonde, and run it for the rebellion, went very smoothly. The meeting broke up and everyone went their separate ways.

'Only history would note that this was when the great rebellion really began.

Owen and Hazel, Jack, Ruby and Giles sat around a table in the Last Standing's great kitchen, relaxing after the *Sturm und Drang* of the council meeting with several bottles of really quite decent wine and a nourishing meal of the never-changing protein cubes. Giles kept swearing he was going to fix the food machines to turn out something different, but he was always too busy with other things. Owen had a dark suspicion that Giles had lost the manual for the machine but didn't want to admit it. Alexander Storm and the Stevie Blues had taken one look at what was for dinner and decided very quickly that they needed some time in private to work on their reports for the Golgotha underground. Owen had a suspicion they had food of their own tucked away somewhere.

He took a determined bite at his second protein cube. He

kept hoping he'd get used to the stuff, but every day it found a whole new way to taste utterly vile. He swallowed his mouthful through sheer willpower, and quickly washed it down with a large gulp of wine. Little wonder he ended up half-drunk after every meal. He was beginning to wonder if it might be better to get drunk before the meal, so as to be better able to cope with it. He sighed and pushed the rest of the cube away. He'd been meaning to start a diet soon anyway.

'Don't worry,' said Hazel. 'There are some really good restaurants in Mistport.'

'There had better be,' said Owen.

'I want a genetest,' said Random suddenly, and everyone looked at him. He flushed. 'There must be the equipment for a test somewhere in this castle.'

'I think so,' said Giles. 'If not, I could patch together something to do the job. But there's no need. We know you're the real Jack Random. We all touched each other's mind in the Madness Maze, when it changed us.'

'That's not enough,' Random insisted. 'All that proved is that I *think* I'm the real me. I could be wrong. Who knows what the Empire mind-techs did to me while I was their prisoner?'

'You don't need to take any test to prove to us who you are,' said Ruby.

'Hell with you,' said Random. 'I want to take the test so that I'll know who I really am. I'm not sure any more. You saw their faces in the hall. They came here expecting to meet a legend, and instead found just a tired old man with jumbled memories.'

'Will you stop this "old man" nonsense,' said Ruby. 'You're only forty-seven. You told me yourself.'

'But I crammed a hell of a lot into those years,' said Random. 'At least, I think I did. I can't trust my memory any more.'

'I *could* set up the test,' said Giles, 'but it would take time. It'd mean delaying your departure for Technos III for two, maybe three days.'

Owen frowned. 'I don't think we can wait that long. We're working to a timetable, remember?'

'Tests can wait,' Ruby said firmly. 'I know who you are, Jack, even if you don't. We've got jobs to do, and they take precedence.'

Random still looked troubled, but finally he shrugged and nodded his head. They sat around the table in silence, looking at each other and then looking away. They were going to have to split up soon to go off on separate missions from which some or all of them might not return. No one was quite sure what to say.

'We'll still be linked through the undermind,' Giles announced finally. 'Wherever we are. I don't think distance will make any difference.'

'But it might,' said Hazel. 'This is all new territory. No one's ever been linked like us. Hell, no one's ever *been* like us.'

'Yeah,' said Owen. 'There's got to be a catch. You don't get powers like ours without paying some kind of price.'

'There have to be limits,' said Giles. 'There are always limits, eventually. We may not be strictly human any more, but we're not gods.'

'I wouldn't mind being a god,' said Ruby. 'Having bronzed young acolytes bringing me gold and jewels for tribute – I could get into that.'

'There's more to it,' said Owen. 'The link that binds us isn't just a glorified comm channel. It's changing us, bringing us together. Have any of you noticed we're starting to talk like each other?'

'Yeah,' said Hazel. 'We all sound a lot more alike than we used to. We're using the same phrases, sharing the same concepts, developing similar ways of looking at things.'

'If you've noticed all this,' said Random, 'why didn't you say something before?'

'I was hoping it was just me,' said Hazel. 'I mean, this is pretty damn' spooky when you think about it. It's not just speech patterns, either. We're using each other's skills, without having to learn them first. Even augmented skills, like Owen's boost.'

'Sometimes one of you will say what I've been thinking,' said Owen. 'And I know where you people are and what you're doing, a lot of the time. Are we becoming a *Gestalt*, do you think? A group mind?'

'I don't believe so,' said Giles. 'We're still capable of keeping secrets from each other. Isn't that right, Hazel?'

Her heart jumped, but she kept her face relaxed. 'What are you talking about?'

'Perhaps you'd care to tell us why you've been spending so much time in the Hadenman city,' said Giles.

'That's my business,' said Hazel flatly.

'We're all entitled to our private lives,' said Owen.

'I want to know,' said Giles.

'She's been seeing Tobias Moon, all right?' said Owen. 'If she didn't want to tell us, that was her business. Just because we're close now, it doesn't mean we have to open up our souls to each other.'

'We may not have any choice,' said Giles, 'if the link continues to grow and strengthen.'

'Which sounds to me like a damn' good reason for splitting up and putting some distance between us,' said Random. 'No offence, people, but the only person I want in my head is me.'

'Right,' said Hazel. 'Besides, I don't think humanity's ready to cope with Ruby Journey the god.'

'You have no ambition,' said Ruby calmly.

'But we're a lot more powerful together,' said Owen. 'Remember the force shield we raised against Silence's troops? They couldn't touch us with anything they had. I don't think any of us could have done that separately. There might be other things we could learn to do, together. Powerful things. Don't we have a responsibility to the rebellion to become as powerful as possible? We're the rebellion's secret weapon, the ace in the hole – the one thing that might tip the coming war in our favour. Are we being selfish in valuing our own individuality over the rebellion's needs?'

'Perhaps some of what we're fighting for is everyone's right to be an individual,' said Random. 'We can't save humanity by becoming inhuman. The only other people to survive passing through the Madness Maze were the scientists who created the Hadenmen. Do we want something like that as our legacy?'

'He's right,' said Giles. 'We all have monsters within us. What if our growing power let them out, let them run loose? Who knows what we might become?'

They sat and thought about that for a while. In particular, Owen thought about how easy it had been for him to kill the Blood Runner, half-way across the Empire.

Finally Random sighed and leaned forward. 'This is all irrelevant. We can't stay together. We're needed on three separate planets. We'll be leaving as soon as the Hadenmen have ships ready. Everything else will have to wait until we return. Now, is there anything else we need to discuss? I don't mind admitting I've found today's business exhausting. Somewhere there is a bed with a thick mattress and heavy covers calling my name.'

'There is one thing,' Owen said reluctantly. 'You remember my personal AI, Ozymandias? He turned out to be an Empire spy, and I had to destroy him with my new powers before he destroyed us. Well . . . he's back. He talks to me, but I'm the only one who can hear him. The odds are I'm just cracking up from the pressure, but it might be something more sinister . . .'

'You never mentioned this before,' said Ruby.

'He must have been scared we'd think he was crazy,' said Hazel. 'We wouldn't have thought that, Owen. We all understand about pressure, and what it does to people.'

'Besides,' said Random, 'if you were going crazy, we'd have felt it through the link long before now.'

'Does Oz still have the control words he planted in your mind and Hazel's?' said Giles, frowning.

'He says not,' said Owen. 'But I have no way of knowing whether or not he's lying. He hasn't tried to use them. So far.'

'Talk to him now,' said Random. 'We'll try to listen in.

Everyone crack their comms wide open, and concentrate on the link as well. Go ahead, Owen.'

'All right,' said Owen, just a little self-consciously. 'Oz – are you there?'

'Of course I'm still here,' said the AI. 'Where else would I be? You told me to shut up, remember? Personally, I'm amazed you've been able to stagger through your days without my assistance. I could have given you all kinds of advice during the council meeting. Still, with all these new magic tricks of yours, I suppose you're too grand for me now. I mean, I'm just a class-seven AI, with access to more information than you could wade through in a lifetime . . .'

'Shut up, Oz,' said Owen. He looked around the table. 'Well? Did you catch any of that?'

'Not a thing,' said Random, and the others shook their heads. Random looked thoughtfully at Owen. 'Do you think it's your AI?'

'No,' said Owen. 'It can't be. I killed Oz in the Madness Maze – destroyed his mind completely with my new powers. I felt him die.'

'Then who – what – is it?' said Hazel.

'I don't know!' said Owen.

'It could be some after-effect of the Madness Maze,' said Giles.

'Oh, that's really comforting,' said Ruby. 'You mean we could all end up hearing things?'

'If you can't think of anything helpful to say, button it,' said Hazel. 'No wonder Owen didn't like to talk to us about this.'

'I have to say I don't see what we can do to help, Owen,' said Random. 'Keep us appraised of any new developments, though. That goes for all of us. But I think we'd do better to leave this for another time, after we return from our various missions. In the time before we go, Owen, I suggest you run a few diagnostics on your comm implants and see if that turns up anything. Anyone else been having problems they'd like to talk about?'

Everyone looked around the table at everyone else. Hazel

kept her mouth shut. She couldn't tell them about the Blood. They wouldn't understand. It was her problem: she'd beat it herself. She'd beaten it before, in Mistport, and that was where she was going. It was a sign. It had to be. The silence dragged on until finally Random pushed back his chair and got to his feet.

'Good night, people. My left foot has gone to sleep, and I'd like to catch up with it as soon as possible. Get as much rest as you can before we have to leave. I suspect it'll be some time before we get another chance.'

He nodded to them vaguely, turned and left the kitchen. Ruby Journey grabbed a half-full bottle of wine and went after him. Hazel nodded briefly to Owen, and left as quickly as she could without it seeming strange. She didn't dare talk to him. She might blurt out the truth. If anyone would have understood, it would have been Owen. But she couldn't take the chance, and so she left the kitchen without looking back and went to her quarters alone.

Giles and Owen sat looking at each other across the table.

'I'm sorry we're having to part so soon, ancestor,' said Owen. 'We've hardly had a chance to get to know each other.'

'I know you're a true Deathstalker,' said Giles. 'That's all that really matters. You're a good fighter – for a historian. Is there . . . anything you'd like to ask me?'

'Well,' said Owen, 'I have been wondering . . . Why do you wear your hair in a scalplock? I mean, that's the sign of a mercenary soldier.'

'Yes,' said Giles. 'It is. The Empire I remember is gone now, just a memory. The Emperor I swore to serve is long dead. Things haven't turned out at all how I expected. You always hope the future will be better, and that your descendants will have an easier time than you had, but I saw the rot setting in, even then. And nothing's changed in the last nine hundred years, except for the worse. At least I've lived long enough to see the beginnings of a rebuilding. Back then, I was no longer Warrior Prime – that had been taken from me – and so I became a fighter for other people's causes. Just like now. I'm a mercenary, Owen, nothing more. Hence the

330

scalplock. I always did have a weakness for the dramatic gesture. Are you sure there's nothing you'd like to talk to me about, before we have to part?'

Owen shifted uncomfortably on his chair. Ever since Giles had killed his own son – the man known as Dram – he'd been trying to be a father-figure to Owen, but Owen didn't want or need another father. He still had enough problems over how he felt about his actual father.

In the end the two men just smiled and nodded to each other, and went off in their different directions to get what rest they could before their separate journeys. Two Death-stalkers, bound by blood and honour, guilt and perhaps a little feeling: heroes of the forthcoming rebellion who had no way of knowing to what dark end destiny would eventually bring them.

CHAPTER SIX

Voices in the Dark

It gets strange, out on the Rim. The starship *Dauntless* hammered through the darkness, a small silver speck in the long night. Captain John Silence sat in his command chair on the bridge, staring sombrely at the main viewscreen in front of him. Not that there was much to see on the screen. This latest tour of duty had brought him right to the edge of the Rim, where suns and planets and life gave way to the endless empty dark of the Darkvoid, which knew nothing of light and life – except for the Wolfling World, whose mysterious depths held an army of reborn Hadenmen and the beginnings of a new rebellion. Silence's mouth flattened into a grim line. He'd been driven from that world in failure and disgrace, and he was in no hurry to return there in search of revenge. Unnatural powers had manifested in the dim vast caverns below that planet's surface, forces and events almost beyond human comprehension. Forces that had touched and tainted him, too. The Wolfling World was a dangerous place, and Silence had decided very firmly that he wasn't returning there without the entire Imperial Fleet to back him up. He knew the difference between courage and a suicide mission. It was essential that the rebellion gestating inside the Wolfling World be eradicated but, until he could convince the Empress of that, he had every intention of keeping a safe distance between him and the only living planet in the Darkvoid.

He sighed, and shifted yet again in his chair. He'd been on the bridge ten hours now, well past the end of his watch, but there was no point in standing down. He couldn't rest and he couldn't sleep. Too many things had been happening recently. Disturbing things. His mission had seemed straight-forward enough when Lionstone had outlined it for him: patrol those planets in the Empire dominated by sentient alien species, and make it clear to them that they were to have contact neither with any alien forces from outside the Empire nor with any rebel forces within it. Make, on the one hand promises of increased support and, on the other, threats of dire reprisals for disobedience. The carrot and the bloody big stick. Never fails, with humans. But those few alien civiliza-tions that had survived being brought within the Empire were anything but human.

This far out on the Rim, far from the hub of the Empire – from traffic and populated planets – the *Dauntless* was very alone, and sometimes that loneliness seemed almost too much to bear. Half the crew were taking tranquillizers or dosing themselves with illicit booze. Silence turned a blind eye. They all needed a little something extra to help them survive the soul-deep cold of the long night.

Everyone except Frost, of course. Investigator Frost stood at parade-rest beside Silence's command chair, as calm and composed as always. She'd been quietly studying the views-creen for some time. She didn't need to say anything for Silence to know she was impatient with the endless monot-ony. Frost always preferred to be doing something, and the long weeks of inactivity on the Rim had been hard on her. It was a long way between the few alien planets, even with the new stardrive, and Frost was frankly bored. Personally, Silence felt he could live with a little boredom. Even when their mission was officially over, it remained to be seen whether they would be allowed to return to the more inhab-ited sectors of the Empire. They knew too many things the Empress didn't want discussed.

It wasn't just boredom and loneliness that made Silence so uneasy about being so far from the heart of the Empire. The new rebellion could begin at any time, led by people who'd become almost superhuman and aided by an army of the deadly Hadenmen. This rebellion, when it came, wouldn't be put down as easily as all the others. He felt a burning need, almost an obsession, to be back in his rightful place, orbiting Golgotha, protecting the Empress. Lionstone hadn't taken his reports about the strength of the new rebellion and its leaders anywhere near seriously enough. He'd tried explaining his concern to Frost, expecting a sympathetic ear, but she'd just shrugged and said that, if there was an Empire-wide rebellion, there'd be fighting enough for everyone, no matter where they were. Frost had always been first and foremost a practical person.

Silence drummed his fingers on the arm-rests of his chair. Somewhere deep inside him a small but persistent voice was clamouring for a drink, but he wouldn't listen to it. He'd tried that and it hadn't worked. He'd managed to climb out of the bottle, with a little help from Frost, and he wouldn't climb back in again. He'd pulled himself from the brink of failure and disgrace with his victory over the alien ship above Golgotha, and, having been granted another chance against all the odds, he was damned if he'd be beaten by his own weaknesses. It had taken a while, but his crew had learned to respect him again, which pleased him. They were a good crew, mostly, and he wanted to be a strong captain for them. Of course, there were still murmurs in occasional dark corners, where people wrongly thought the ship's security systems couldn't overhear them. The word below-decks was that, just possibly, Silence and/or Frost were jinxed. Jonahs. Unfortunate things happened around them. After all, Silence had lost his last ship, the *Darkwind*, in a clash with pirates, and the mission to the Wolfling World had come disastrously unstuck. And, went the murmur, as everyone knows bad things come in threes. Sweepstakes were running among the more susperstitious crew members not about whether something else dire would happen but about what shape it would take when it did.

Silence let them get on with it. On the whole, the crew were still sharp and well coordinated, performing their duties at an entirely acceptable level. The victory over the alien ship had raised spirits and restored confidence after the debacle on the Wolfling World. And most of the crew had lost someone they loved – or knew someone who had – during the alien attack on Golgotha's main starport and city: anger and a need for revenge burned in the crew's collective heart, hot and ugly. So far, Silence hadn't been able to find an outlet for it, but he had no doubt one would emerge eventually. Some alien species, among the last few they visited, would do or say the wrong thing, and have to be punished. Then Silence would sit back and let the crew sink themselves in violence and vengeance until it sickened them. Bit hard on the aliens but, after all, that was what they were there for.

On the whole, Silence had chosen to let Frost take charge of the alien contacts. It was her area of expertise, after all. And, if he was sometimes uncomfortable with some of her more extreme practices, he kept it to himself. She was responsible for the safety of the human species, and if that meant being ruthless as well as efficient Frost had never been known to give a damn. Silence smiled briefly, in spite of himself. Certainly the Investigator had never been trained in diplomacy – or, if she had, she had gone out of her way to forget it: she just aimed herself at whatever passed for the aliens' authority figures, made her demands on behalf of the Empress, and issued dreadful warnings and threats of what would happen if her orders were disobeyed. It was often as blunt as that, but she got results. Silence had his reservations, but couldn't bring himself to disapprove. The safety of humanity had to come first.

He'd been the same himself, cold and curt and full of authority, until it had backfired on him on a backwater planet called Unseeli. The native species had rebelled over the Empire's extensive mining operations on their planet. The Empire needed those mines, and so the newly promoted Captain Silence had been sent to put a stop to the rebellion, by whatever means necessary. He had tried diplomacy, and then firmness, force and finally all-out war. But there had turned out to be strange secrets and powers moving on Unseeli, and things had got out of hand fast. Silence had been forced to pull his people back from the planet and order the entire world scorched from orbit. That particular alien species was now extinct, though their ghosts still haunted Unseeli's metallic forest.

Silence's frown deepened as he considered the contacts they'd made with the alien planets. Few had gone well, but in the end they'd got what the Empire wanted without having to institute another scorching. He wasn't sure he could order that again – though he had no doubt that, if the occasion arose and he didn't give the command, Frost would. And who was to say which of them was right, in the end? Humanity had to be protected and – while all the alien contacts had been strange and unusual – some had been actually disturbing. Life had taken many shapes throughout the Empire, and few of the aliens were human in form or intent. Many were mysterious, obscure – even impenetrable. Silence wasn't sure some of them even knew they were in the Empire.

Shanna IV was a desolate world, with endless plains of hard-baked ground. Its only water was deep underground. A huge, brilliant sun beat down from a blinding sky that had never known clouds, and the sole signs of intelligent life were vast pyramids, built long ago of resin-hardened stone and sand. Each pyramid was exactly like all the others, though they might be thousands of miles apart. Four hundred feet high, they had sharp lines, and their dull red sides were smooth and featureless. No one knew what was inside them, or even if there was an inside; none of the Empire's investigative teams had been able to find an entrance. Being Investigators, they'd tried making one, only to discover the pyramids' sides were impervious to anything the Empire could throw against them, up to and including major energy weapons . . . which should have been imposssible for something so primitive as resin-hardened stone and sand. Eventually the Empire decided it didn't really care what was inside the pyramids, and concentrated its attention on the planet's current inhabitants, who might or might not have been the builders of the pyramids.

These were ugly, hard-shelled insects about the size of a man's fist. They had blade-sharp mandibles and a bewildering number of legs. They seemed to have no individual identity, but *en masse* they had a group mind that could, with some difficulty, be communicated with. Which was handy, as these scuttling creatures were capable, with a little prodding, of producing a great many organic compounds the Empire found useful. The Empire provided the base materials, the insects ate and excreted it – and possibly did other things to it in the pyramids when no one was looking – and the end result was a series of extremely complex chemical forms that would have been hideously expensive to reproduce in a laboratory. The Empire profited, the insects got protected, and everyone was happy. The Empire had a base on Shanna IV, staffed by scientists and guards who had offended someone powerful: it was that kind of world.

Captain Silence and Investigator Frost stood at the foot of one of the massive pyramids waiting for the insects' physical representative to make an appearance. The day was as hot as a blast furnace and twice as dry. The air shimmered and the sun was too bright to look at, even with the heavy-duty protection over their eyes. Silence turned up the cooling elements in his uniform another notch, and screwed his eyes against the harsh, unrelenting light. Sweat was pouring out of him. He didn't look at Frost. He knew she would still seem cool and completely undisturbed. She was an Investigator, after all, and therefore by definition not prone to the fallibilities of the merely human.

In the end, curiosity got the better of him, and he glanced casually at her just in time to see her kick out lazily at one of the many small forms scuttling around their feet. It flopped over on its back, its long legs wriggling, and then turned itself upright again and hurried on about its business.

Frost sniffed. 'Ugly things. Desolate bloody place. If the representative doesn't turn up soon I'm going to start using these creepie-crawlies for target practice.'

'That should get their attention,' said Silence, smiling in spite of himself. 'Do I detect a note of distaste in your voice, Investigator? I thought you were trained to take all forms of alien life in your stride?'

'There's a limit to everything,' said Frost, 'And I think I may have found mine. Repulsive little things. If one even looks like it might be thinking of darting up my leg, I'm going to blast it and everything like it for a dozen yards around. I had more than enough of that inside the alien ship over Golgotha.'

Silence looked at her carefully. Had it been anyone else he would have sworn there had been a note of remembered horror in her voice. The interior of the alien ship had been terrible enough, certainly. He still had nightmares about it. But Investigators were trained from childhood to *give* nightmares, not suffer from them.

He considered his words carefully, and when he finally spoke he looked off in a different direction. 'It was bad, inside the alien ship. All those insects, all sizes, all around us and no way out. Enough to give anyone the creeps.'

'You're about as subtle as a flying half-brick, you know that?' said Frost. 'But thanks for the thought.'

Silence looked back at her. She was smiling, though it didn't touch her eyes. He shrugged. 'If you ever need someone to talk to . . .'

'I'll bear it in mind. But any problems I might have are mine, and I'll handle them.'

'That's what I thought, when the booze was drowning me inch by inch. You helped me out anyway.'

'You didn't know how to ask for help,' said Frost.

'Neither do you,' said Silence.

They looked at each other. There was a closeness between them that was more than just the link they shared. Frost's eyes softened slightly, and Silence thought for a moment that she was closer to opening up to him than she had ever been before. But the moment passed and the softness disappeared, and Frost was an Investigator again, cold and focused and quite unreadable.

Silence looked away.

'You have to make allowances for the insect representative,' he said finally. 'According to the files, the insects have little concept of time as we understand it, but they respond well to firm behaviour.'

'I don't have to make allowances for anything,' said Frost. 'That's what being an Investigator is all about.'

Silence grinned. 'Useful though the files are, however, they don't have anything at all to say about how you get the bloody insects' attention in the first place.'

'We could kill a few,' said Frost. 'Hell, we could kill a lot. Nobody'd miss them.'

'Let's save that for a last resort,' said Silence. 'There must be something a little less dramatic we could try.'

And then he broke off as a wave of insects came surging towards him, thick and black, a living carpet. His hand dropped to the disrupter at his side. Frost already had hers out, and was sweeping it back and forth, searching for a meaningful target. The wave crashed to a sudden halt a few feet short of them and began piling up into a tall, thick pillar of squirming bodies. The twitching legs folded around each other and were still, the small bodies fitting neatly together like the interlocking parts of some more complicated machine, and gradually the pillar took on a humanoid form – a dark, shiny shape that mocked humanity as much as it duplicated it. The square, flat-sided head turned jerkily on its thick neck to look at Silence and Frost, though there was no trace of anything that might have been eyes. It buzzed briefly – a short, ugly and completely inhuman sound. It buzzed again and suddenly, though the sound hadn't changed, Silence and Frost somehow understood it.

'Empire,' said the dark human shape, though there was nothing that might have been a mouth. 'Interrogation. Respond.'

Frost put her disrupter away and tried to look as though she'd never drawn it in the first place. 'Yes, we represent the Empire,' she said flatly. 'You've been informed why we're here?'

There was an Empire Base on Shanna IV, populated by a handful of scientists and a small force of guards who'd all managed to upset someone really badly to get themselves posted here, but they had as little contact with the resident aliens as they could get away with. They might have arranged this meeting, or they might not have. It was that kind of Base.

Silence stared at the humanoid figure, and it stared right back at him. Despite the lack of eyes in the flat shiny face, Silence had no doubt the representative was watching him: he could feel its stare like an icy breeze in the boiling heat of the day. The insects that made up the human shape twitched suddenly, hundreds of legs flexing briefly so that a shimmer seemed to run through the figure, and then they were still again. Silence winced as a headache blossomed slowly between his eyes. It was as though he could almost see or hear something that was being hidden from him. He concentrated on the feeling, and realized it was something like the link he shared with Frost. He glanced at her to see if she felt it too. She was scowling, but there was nothing unusual in that. Certainly she didn't seem as disturbed as he was. He tried to grasp the vague sensation and bring it into focus, but it slipped away like water between his fingers, and was gone. He still had the headache.

'Rebels,' the alien representative said suddenly. 'Avoid. Punishment.'

'Got it in a nutshell,' said Frost. 'Anyone tries to contact you, rebel or alien, you tell them to go to hell and then report them to the base immediately. Understand?'

'Rebels. Avoid. Punishment. Chemicals. Interrogation. Respond.'

Silence shivered, despite the heat. Something about the way each word seemed to emanate from a different part of the dark human shape upset him greatly.

He made himself concentrate on his job. 'Yes, we've got your chemicals,' he said curtly. 'They're being unloaded in the usual place. The regular supply ship will be along to pick up the compounds you've produced.' A question occurred to him, and he asked it before he could think better of it. 'We have a use for those compounds, but what do you get out of the deal?'

There was a long pause, until Silence assumed the construct wasn't going to answer him, and then it said two words, and fell apart before Silence could respond. The human shape disintegrated from the top down, tumbling into hundreds of its respective parts, which scuttled off in different directions. In a few moments they were indistinguishable from those who were already covering the ground. Silence wasn't at all sorry to see the end of the representative – particularly after the two words the figure had spoken.

Chemicals. Addictive.

He looked at Frost, who was still staring thoughtfully at the insects skittering around her on their inscrutable missions.

'Do you suppose they have any concept at all of themselves as individuals?' he said at last.

'No one knows for sure,' said Frost. 'They're supposed to have a single hive mind for the whole species, but no one's been able to prove it, one way or the other. Our instruments can't detect anything, and espers just get headaches when they try to listen in. The constructs are our only way of communicating with them, and they tell us as little as they can get away with.'

'What about the scientists at the base?'

'They spend most of their time trying to get themselves transferred somewhere else, and I don't blame them. This place gives me the willies.'

Silence kept his features under control. He couldn't have been more surprised had the Investigator admitted to secret pacifist leanings. If Frost were confessing that the place made her feel uncomfortable, it must really be getting to her.

He decided to do them both a favour and change the subject. 'Did you know that the chemicals we supply these insects are addictive to them?'

'No,' said Frost, 'but it makes sense. The insects are a single hive mind, one that is scattered far too widely for us to be able to hurt or control it. But withholding chemicals to which it has developed a dependency should do the trick nicely. A junkie will do anything for his next fix.'

'Very efficient,' said Silence. 'But then, the Empire's always been a great believer in efficiency. And if it can work a little cruelty into the deal too, so much the better.' He looked around him at the thousands of small scuttling forms, working blindly and obediently in the blistering heat to meet the Empire's needs, and, if he saw any connection between them and himself, he said nothing.

Chroma XIII was a singular planet, in more ways than one. The original survey ship had almost missed it completely, as in theory it should have been impossible for any form of life to survive in a planet so far from its dying sun. But something about Chroma XIII had caught the captain's eye, and he sent down drones to gather information. What they had sent back was enough to make even a seasoned survey officer's jaw drop. Within the giant gas ball that was Chroma XIII there was life without form or substance – intelligence separated from physical existence. A planet of inherent contradictions, whose very existence was theoretically impossible.

Silence kept the *Dauntless* in as high an orbit as he could get away with, and he and Frost watched on the main viewscreen as the ship's drones dropped towards and into the planet. Strange images came and went on the screen as the scene switched from one drone's instruments to another, and all the time the comm channels threatened to overload from the sheer intensity of what they were relaying.

There was no planetary surface, no solid area at all. The drones dropped endlessly through shades of colour and fields of light, blindingly bright, in which strange hues shifted and stirred without any purpose or meaning that could be fathomed by human eyes. There were planes of dazzling colour, thousand of miles long; whirlpools the size of moons blended slowly from one hue to another; oceans of blue mists were as dark as the colour you see when you close your eyes at night. And, everywhere, the shapes and the shades were shot through with sudden blasts of lightning.

'These flashes of lightning are the aliens?' Silence said finally.

'We think so,' said Frost. 'It's hard to be sure of anything here. Certainly the lightning bolts possess some of the attributes we associate with life. They react to outside influences, they consume light on some wavelengths and release it in others, and they appear to communicate with each other, though our translation computers have had nervous breakdowns trying to make sense of whatever it is they might be saying. They reproduce, constantly, and they also disappear suddenly, for no discernible reason.'

'All right,' said Silence, determined not to be completely thrown, 'how do we communicate with them?'

'We don't, said Frost. 'We're not even sure they know we're here, which might just be for the best. Why give them ideas?'

Silence looked at her and raised an eyebrow. 'And the Empire's content just to leave them be?'

'Pretty much. They don't have anything we want, let alone need.'

'So what the hell are we doing here?' said Silence.

'Dropping a hundred or so security drones to keep an eye on them. We have no way of knowing what they're capable of. They're life without form, which could also be life without any limits we could understand. Who knows what they might do, if they became aware of us? What use is a weapon against something that has no physical existence?'

'Great,' said Silence. 'Just wonderful. Something else to worry about. So we can't talk to them, let alone threaten them, and we're not even sure they know we're here.'

'Got it in one,' said Frost. 'All we can do is drop our drones and get the hell out of here.'

'Join the Imperial Navy and see the universe,' said Silence heavily. 'Meet strange and interesting new forms of life, and run away from them. Navigator, get us the hell out of here. My head hurts.'

The last planet they visited was Epsilon IX, and that meant hard suits. The gravity was five times standard, the atmosphere was a mixture of noxious gases – any one of which would have been fatal on its own – and the air-density was such that you were uncannily reminded of the water-pressure you find at the bottom of a deep-ocean trench. On top of all that, the entire world was a mess of thick, slimy mud that covered the planet's surface from pole to pole. In some places the muck was miles deep, and that was called ocean; in other places it was only a couple of feet deep, and that was called land. Either way, it was messy as hell. There were hills that rose up suddenly overnight and then spent the rest of the day collapsing and sliding away.

Here and there we huge artificial constructs that might have been buildings or machines, or both or neither. The native intelligent species created them when they felt like it, but declined to explain out of what, or for what purpose. The muck itself contained a handful of extremely useful trace elements, and the Empire had installed automatic mining machinery to refine these from the goo by specially-designed automated mining machinery from the Empire. People couldn't live on Epsilon IX, even inside a fully screened base: human-built structures inevitably sank, and had to be constantly retrieved, which cost money.

The mining equipment worked only because the natives looked after it. No one knew much about them. They appeared to be the only living things on Epsilon IX, which raised some interesting and rather unpleasant questions about what they ate. They had a mysterious link to their mucky environment that allowed them to thrive and prosper, but this was another of the many things they chose not to explain. They kept themselves to themselves, and did nasty things to trespassers.

Silence and Frost journeyed down to what passed for the planet's surface in a pinnace, which ended up hovering in mid-air while they dropped awkwardly out of the airlock in their hard suits. They landed knee-deep in the sludge and slogged slowly through it, slipping and sliding and holding on to each other for support. There was something vaguely solid under their heavy boots, but it rose and fell unpredictably beneath the covering slime, which disorientingly was in the same varying shades of grey as the sky above. Sky blended into surface almost imperceptibly, and this did strange things to Silence's sense of orientation: up and down, left and right, forward and backward ceased being absolutes and became more like matters of opinion. The last time Silence had felt like this he'd been drunk for a week.

He trudged along beside Frost, his hard suit's servomechanisms whining loudly as they struggled to overcome the planet's heavy gravity. Silence took a quiet satisfaction from the obvious difficulties Frost was having in ploughing through the thick mud. It was good to know that even Investigators had their limits. They waded on for some time, while their surroundings rose and fell without any obvious meaning or purpose. Frost led the way with dogged determination. Silence supposed she knew where she was going, but didn't ask, just in case she didn't. He liked to think that at least one of them knew what they were doing.

The pinnace hovered high overhead, far enough away not to intimidate any of the locals but still close enough to come charging in for an emergency rescue. Silence was getting tired feet. Even with the hard suit's servomechanisms to help, the constant struggle to stay upright while pressing on was exhausting. According to his suit's instruments, the local temperature was high enough to melt some metals. He was sweating like a pig despite everything the hard suit's temperature controls could do, and the lack of a proper horizon made his head hurt. He was so taken up with his own inner world of hurts and confusions that he noticed only just in time that Frost had come to a halt. He avoided crashing into her through a heroic last-minute effort, and then had to fight to keep his feet under him.

He took a few deep breaths to settle himself, and looked around. The place they'd arrived at didn't seem noticeably different from any of the others they'd squelched through to get here. There was no sign of any of the alien constructs – just a large hill to their left, slumping over like melting ice cream.

'Is this it?' he said finally.

'In so far as there is an "it", yes,' said Frost. 'These are the right coordinates, anyway. You know, this place is really disgusting. It looks like someone sneezed it into being.'

Silence winced. 'You've always had a way with words, Investigator. Now what do we do?'

'We wait for someone to put in an appearance – which, at a guess, will take some time. Maybe we should have brought a bucket and spade.'

She broke off as the mud in front of them bubbled up into a thick dribbling pillar, like a slow-motion fountain. Silence and Frost both trained their suits' disrupters on the pillar as it bulged and contracted here and there before finally forming into a human shape, complete in every detail, including clothes – though the clothes were made of the same mud as the body. The figure actually looked quite snappy, in formal evening wear, and for a moment Silence felt almost over-dressed in his hard suit. He made himself concentrate on the figure's face. It was grey, and sweated driblets of mud, but the features were indisputably human. The eyes focused on Silence, then on Frost, and the mouth twitched in a smile.

'Before you ask,' the figure said briskly, 'no, I don't really look like this. You are looking at a mental projection, formed from nearby materials. Trust me, you don't want to see what I really look like. Not unless you're into projectile vomiting, which I would assume could get really messy inside one of those suits. Human senses are too limited to appreciate my true beauty.' It folded its dripping arms across its sliding chest and gave them a moment to think about that. 'Now, what do you people want this time? I'm busy. And don't ask me what at – you couldn't possibly hope to understand.'

'If you're this planet's idea of a diplomat, I'd hate to meet your politicians,' said Silence. 'How is it you speak our language so well?'

'I don't. I'm communicating directly with your minds. That's slumming for me, but we all have to make sacrifices if we're to keep the gods happy. Little joke there, to put you at your ease.'

'You're telepathic?' said Frost. 'That wasn't in the files.'

'Nothing so primitive. We are communicating directly, though your human minds are too limited to pick up most of what I'm transmitting.' The figure stopped, and frowned.

346

'Though I have to say you seem much more receptive than most.'

'Save the compliments,' said Frost. 'We're here on business.'

'Well, I didn't think you were tourists,' snapped the man made out of mud. 'What does the Empire want this time?'

'Rebels and aliens: don't talk to them,' said Frost briskly. 'If anyone tries, contact your nearest Imperial spy satellite. Any alliances with unauthorized forces will result in severe punitive measures.'

'And what might those be?' said the mud man. 'Going to arrest us, perhaps? Not unless you can build prisons in five dimensions. Or perhaps you'll take away some of our lovely mud? Help yourselves – we've got tons of the stuff.'

Frost raised her right hand and triggered the disrupter built into her glove. The energy beam flashed out and vaporized the mud man's head. Silence started to object, and then desisted. He didn't approve of unnecessary killing, but this was the Investigator's show. She was better qualified to decide what was necessary to get her point across. The mud man should have been more respectful, dammit. An insult to them was an insult to the Empress.

And then he realized that the headless body hadn't slumped to the ground: it stood just where it had, as though nothing had happened. Liquid mud bubbled in the stump of the neck, and then rose up suddenly to form itself into a new head. The same face quickly reappeared, and the mud man glared at Frost.

'I see Imperial diplomacy hasn't changed much since its last visit. Plus seven points for brutality, minus several thousand for severe lack of cool. Never mind barbarians at the gate, they've already taken over. Just once, I wish they'd send us a representative slightly higher up the food chain. I've had more interesting conversations with a piece of moss. You humans should be grateful my species is physically linked to this planet's ecosystem. If we could leave this world, we'd be running the Empire inside a week.'

'But you can't, and you don't, said Frost, 'so remember

what I told you: no talking to any strange men or aliens, or we'll work out some way to give you all a good spanking. Right. That's it, we're going. Have fun playing with your mud.'

'I don't see any need for sexual slanders,' said the mud man. 'Please feel free to leave our world anytime. Goodbye.'

Silence started to turn to leave, and then stopped as he saw Frost hadn't moved. He couldn't see her face inside her helmet, but he knew she was staring thoughtfully at the figure. He could feel it. The link between them seemed suddenly very strong, and he knew without having to be told what was running through her mind. She wanted to see the *real* alien – the real shape and being that lay behind the image of the mud man. The truth behind the mask.

'Cut it out, Frost,' he said quietly. 'We don't need to know.'

'He doesn't respect us,' said the Investigator. 'He doesn't fear us. I want to know why.'

'Listen to your partner,' said the mud man. 'You don't want to do this. This image is all you're capable of understanding. The reality of what I and my kind are would destroy your limited minds.' He stopped abruptly and frowned at Frost. 'What are you doing? Your mind is . . . uncoiling. There's more to you than there was before. You're not a human. What are you?'

Frost stared back at him. Her brows furrowed as she concentrated, reaching inside herself for a strength and a vision she hadn't realized she possessed. There was something more beyond the mud man, something bigger, vaster . . . The sheer size of it made her head ache, but she wouldn't look away. It was deep down in the mud, under the surface of the world, and it was rising slowly out of the depths towards her. It had length and width and breadth and other dimensions, too. And perhaps just to look on it with merely human eyes would be enough to turn her to stone, like someone caught in Medusa's gaze, but she couldn't – wouldn't – look away. She had to see, had to know . . .

Silence grabbed her by the shoulders of her hard suit, spun her round and shook her as hard as he could.

'Don't look at it! I can see what you're seeing, and it's dangerous. We're not ready to look at something like this. Just the sight of it would burn the eyes out of our heads and blast our reason. Look away, Investigator! That's an order!'

He reached out with his mind, not quite knowing how he was doing what he was doing, and slowly forced Frost's inner eye shut. The image of what lay beyond and below the mud man was suddenly gone, and the heightened link between Silence and Frost shrank to its normal background murmur. They were both back in their own heads again, and saw only what was in front of them.

Frost shuddered suddenly. 'Thank you, Captain. I got . . . lost, for a while there.'

'Let's get out of here, Frost. We've given them their instructions. Anything else is none of our business.'

'We can't let them run us off. They have to know who's in charge here.'

'I have an uneasy feeling they already know,' said Silence. 'Let's go.'

Back on the bridge of the *Dauntless*, Silence was jerked out of his memories by the quiet but insistent voice of his communications officer, Eden Cross. He'd turned round at his work station to look at Silence, who blinked at him a couple of times and then tried to look alert and awake, as though he'd been listening to Cross all along. It took him only a moment to realize he wasn't fooling anyone, and he relaxed with a smile. He was lucky it was Cross. Cross was a good man.

'Sorry,' said Silence. 'I was light years away. Run that past me again.'

'There appears to be a situation below-decks, Captain,' said Cross. There was no trace of a smile on his dark face, but his eyes were understanding. 'Not long ago, strange noises were heard coming from inside Security Officer Stelmach's private quarters. Some of his people went to investigate, and discovered Stelmach systematically wrecking his cabin. They inquired diplomatically as to what the problem might be, and he threw things at them. They have currently retreated just out of range, and are awaiting further instructions. He is their boss: technically speaking only yourself as Captain and Investigator Frost are senior enough to restrain a security officer.'

Silence looked at Frost beside him, and she raised an eyebrow. Stelmach had a tendency to get excited in emergencies, but usually on board ship he was self-controlled, and followed every regulation to the letter. There were those who said he didn't authorize his own bowel movements without checking the regulations first. Something serious must have happened to so totally destroy Stelmach's composure.

'We'd better go and take a look, Investigator,' said Silence. 'He is in charge of the ship's security, after all. If he's discovered something that's so upsetting, I think I want to know about it too.'

Frost nodded calmly. 'We have been out on the Rim a long time. People have been known to crack so far from light and life and civilization.'

'Not Stelmach,' said Silence. 'It'd take more than a case of cabin fever to crack him.' Silence got to his feet. 'Second-in-Command, you have the bridge. Investigator, follow me – but keep your hands away from your weapons. I want Stelmach conscious and able to answer questions.'

'Spoilsport,' said Frost.

They left the bridge and took the express elevator down to the officers' quarters. They could tell when they were getting near the scene of the incident. There were people milling in the corridors, including those from the last shift, woken by the sound of Stelmach's voice shouting and swearing incoherently. Silence politely but firmly sent them back to their beds, assuring them he'd take care of everything. Frost hurried them on their way with an occasional glare. Finally the two of them rounded a corner to find half a dozen security men huddled together at the end of a corridor. They jumped half out of their skins when Silence addressed them from behind, and then relaxed a little from sheer relief when they saw who it was. They even looked glad to see the Investigator, which was probably a first.

There was a quick discussion among the security men as to who was in charge, and then he was pushed forward. The man started to explain what had happened, remembered he hadn't saluted, tried to do that and apologize at the same time, and then began explaining all over again. The sound of something large but fragile smashing into hundreds of pieces came clearly from the open door to Stelmach's quarters, followed by more incoherent swearing.

The security man swallowed hard, and started yet again.

'Lieutenant Zhang reporting, sir. Security Officer Stelmach appears to be . . . unwell. We have attempted to ascertain what the problem might be, but he has declined to talk to us, and he has a gun. Perhaps you would care to have a word with him, Captain. I'm sure he'd listen to you. And the Investigator.'

'At ease, Lieutenant,' said Silence. 'We'll handle things from here. You and your people fall back out of sight around the corner. It might be your presence that's upsetting him so much. See that this corridor is blocked off at both ends: I don't want anyone else coming in here while we're talking to Stelmach. And, Lieutenant, we are not to be interrupted for anything less than a major emergency.'

Zhang nodded quickly, gathered the rest of his people, and led them in a hurried but dignified retreat back round the corner. In his quarters, Stelmach was still shouting and breaking things. Silence admired the man's stamina. He'd had a few blind rages himself in his drinking days, and he knew from experience that they were hard work to keep going.

He turned to Frost, and then frowned at her. 'I said no guns, Investigator.'

'He has one, Captain.'

'But he hasn't used it yet. Let's not put any ideas into his head.'

He glared at Frost until she holstered her gun again, and then he looked back down the corridor. Things had grown ominously quiet. 'Is Stelmach a drinker, do you know? I haven't heard anything, but someone in his position would be under a lot of strain – and in a good position to get his hands on all kinds of booze, legal and otherwise.'

'Or worse,' said Frost. 'He'd also have access to every sort of drug, for use in his interrogations. Plus whatever illicit substances his people might have discovered and confiscated. There's always something going around. There is nothing in his files about substance abuse of any kind, but he has access to those files. I can't say I know the man well. Not many do. The post of security officer isn't one to make you popular with people.'

'But do they respect him?'

'Oh, I should think so. The fact that no one's rolled a fragmentation grenade into his room while he was sleeping is a pretty good sign the crew respect his authority – and that his people are on their toes.'

Silence and Frost moved slowly and quietly down the empty corridor, stopping just short of the open door to Stelmach's quarters. Silence gestured to the Investigator, and they both placed their backs against the bulkhead wall next to the door. Technically speaking, all Silence had to do was show himself and order Stelmach to calm down and explain himself. The security officer would do this immediately or face a court martial for insubordination. In practice, Silence had a strong feeling he might end up doing more ducking than talking – assuming Stelmach really did have a gun. According to regulations, the use of energy weapons on board ship was strictly forbidden except under the direst circumstances. On the other hand, Stelmach was the *Dauntless*'s security officer, and if he wanted a gun there weren't many people on the ship with the authority to forbid it. Silence always carried a gun, as did the Investigator – they were required to do so, partly in case of situations like this – but, in all his time as Captain, Silence had never drawn a gun on a member of his own crew, and he wasn't about to start now. And to hell with what the regulations said.

It was still quiet in Stelmach's quarters.

Silence raised his voice, keeping it calm and even and very assured.

'Stelmach, this is the captain. I have Investigator Frost with me. We need to talk to you.'

There was no reply. Silence strained his ears against the quiet and thought he could hear harsh, heavy breathing from inside the cabin. Maybe Stelmach had passed out, from drink or drugs or exhaustion. And just maybe he was waiting for some poor trusting fool to stick his head round the door, so he could shoot it off.

Silence licked his dry lips, and tried again. 'Stelmach, this is the captain. Can you hear me?'

'Yes, Captain. I can hear you.' The security officer's voice was a quiet rasp, a low painful sound, as though he'd injured his throat with shouting and screaming. 'Go away, Silence. I don't want to talk to you. I don't want to talk to anyone.'

'We rather gathered that,' said Silence. 'But we're going to have to talk sooner or later; you know that. Now, are you going to invite me in for a little chat, or am I going to have to send the Investigator in to reason with you? My way will mean less damage to the fixtures and fittings. Look, whatever the problem is, I can't help you if I'm standing around out here. And you do need help, don't you?'

There was a long pause. When Stelmach finally spoke again, his voice was tired and defeated, as though all the rage had drained right out of him. 'All right. Come in. Let's get this over with.'

That particular choice of words had an ominous ring to it, but Silence decided he was going in anyway. There wasn't anything else he could do.

He turned to Frost, and kept his voice low. 'I'm going in first. You back me up. Keep your hands away from your weapons. We don't want to spook him.'

'I should go in first,' said Frost. 'I'm more expendable than you.'

'No offence, Investigator, but you do tend to make a rather . . . strong first impression. The state he's in he might just take one look at you and open fire. Besides, I'm more of an authority figure as far as he's concerned. He's always responded well to authority figures in the past. And, before

353

you ask, no: I'm not going to use a force shield, and neither are you. He might think we didn't trust him.'

'Oh, we wouldn't want him to think that,' said Frost. 'Perish the thought. But if he makes one wrong move I'm going to spatter him all over the bulkheads.'

'Let's try and be calm about this, Investigator. I don't want him killed. He's a pain in the ass, but he's good at his job. Good security officers are hard to come by. He's also one of the few people with first-hand experience of how to control the Grendels. I'll decide when and if violence is necessary. Now, put on a nice smile. We don't want to frighten him.'

Frost bared her teeth, and Silence winced. She looked as though she were about to bite him somewhere painful.

'All right,' he said, 'forget the smile. Leave all the talking to me, and don't get touchy about anything he says. I want to know what's reduced Stelmach to a state like this.'

Frost shrugged, but kept her hands ostentatiously away from her weapons. Silence decided to settle for that. He stepped into the middle of the corridor and then turned to walk through the open door to Stelmach's quarters. Frost stuck so close behind him he could feel her breath on the back of his neck. Silence smiled and nodded to Stelmach, who was sitting on the side of his bed, his head hanging down, his shoulders slumped in tiredness or defeat or both. His gun was lying on the floor, well out of his reach. Silence relaxed just a little, and looked around.

The place was a mess. Everything that hadn't been nailed down or an intrinsic part of the ship had been picked up and thrown at something else. The single table and chair had been overturned, and the shattered fragments of Stelmach's more fragile personal belongings covered the floor – along with pretty much everything else. The bed, which folded down from the cabin wall, had survived intact, but the bedclothes had been torn apart and strewn all over the small cabin. Stelmach was looking anything but dangerous, but Silence decided he was going to take it slowly anyway. He could sense Frost behind him, like an attack dog straining against a short leash. He stepped forward and Stelmach finally looked up. The security officer's face was tired and drawn, and he looked ten years older than he was.

'Come in, Captain, Investigator. Excuse the mess. It's the maid's day off.'

'I've seen worse,' said Silence. 'You've been very . . . busy, Stelmach. Any particular reason?'

'What does it matter?' said Stelmach. 'I know the regulations. I belong in the brig. Go ahead and take me. I'm finished.'

'I don't believe in sentencing someone until they've had a fair hearing,' said Silence carefully. 'Explain yourself. What brought this on?'

'It's private, Captain. Family business. I don't want to talk about it.'

'Talk anyway. If I'm going to lose the best security officer I've ever had, I want to know why.'

Stelmach looked past Silence's shoulder at Frost. 'Does she have to be here?'

'She's concerned for my safety,' said Silence. 'But she can step out into the corridor, if you'd like.'

'No,' said Stelmach. 'I don't suppose it matters.' He leaned back against the bulkhead. His voice was very tired. 'I got a letter this morning. From my family. We've always been extremely close, ever since our father – a police officer – died when I was very young. There was a demonstration, some kind of political thing, and it turned ugly: someone threw something, someone else opened fire, and my father was dead before he hit the ground. Mother brought us up, kept us together, did whatever was necessary to keep a roof over our heads, clothes on our backs, food in our bellies. I was the youngest. Never wore new clothes in my life until I joined the Fleet. We were raised to revere my father as a saint and to have nothing at all to with politics. She had all of us sign up for the Services the moment we were old enough. There's always job security in the Services, whatever might be happening anywhere else.

'My sister Athena was the eldest. They took her away to become an Investigator when she was ten. We lost touch with her after that. My brothers Bold and Hero did well for themselves. Bold's a major in the army, Hero's a group leader in the Jesuit commandoes. They write home regularly, send money when they can. I'm the only failure. My career's over. After the debacle on the Wolfling World, I was lucky not to be executed, but I'll never be more than a security officer now, not even if I were to be officially exonerated. Even my work on controlling the Grendel aliens has been taken over by other people. As far as my family is concerned, I've disgraced them by being such a loser. Now my mother's written to me, telling me not to come home again. She's expelled me from the family, disinherited me and removed all references to me from the family history. She says she's telling everyone she only ever had two sons.

'I always did my best. Followed the regulations, did as I was told, tried hard to be a good soldier, lived my life for the Empire. And what has it got me? A security officer's post on a ship passing time out on the Rim, going nowhere, doing nothing – or nothing that really matters. Do what you want to me. I don't care.'

He looked up suddenly, glaring at Silence and Frost. There were bright spots of colour on his pale cheeks, and his eyes were puffy from crying – though they were still sharp. 'I hate this ship. I hate you, too. Both of you. If I'd kept you under control like I was supposed to, things might have been different. But I let you reason with me, Captain, and I let the Investigator intimate me, and it all went wrong. I hate my life, or what's left of it. And most of all I hate myself, for being so weak. My mother said my father would spit on me, if he could see what I've become, and I think she's right. He would have shown more courage, more ... something. Sometimes he comes to me in my cabin, sits on the end of my bed in the early hours of the morning, and tells me he's ashamed of me. He looks young, just like in the holos taken before he was killed. I'm, older now than he was then, but I'll always be a child to him. I can't stand these quarters any more. I'm afraid to sleep. Put me in the brig. Or have the Investigator shoot me, and put me out of my family's misery.

356

She'd like that. I don't care. I don't care about anything any more.'

He finally wound down, his head lowering bit by bit until he was staring at the floor again. He wasn't crying – he was too tired for that. Silence didn't know what to say. He'd read up on Stelmach's background, to try to find out why anyone would name their child 'Valiant', but the bare facts hadn't really made any sense until now. He felt ashamed and embarrassed to be so bluntly confronted by someone else's private pain and shame. These were the kind of things you normally told only to your friends or loved ones but, as a security officer, Stelmach had no friends, and now he had no family either. That was why he'd wrecked his cabin. It was the only way he had left of letting the anger out. And probably because he wanted to be punished.

Silence didn't know what to do. He couldn't just have the man arrested and thrown in the brig, even if that was technically the correct course of action. He wasn't Stelmach's friend – didn't even like the man – but Stelmach was a part of the *Dauntless*'s crew, and as his captain it was Silence's duty to look after him. He was responsible for the man's well-being, like a father for an errant son's.

The thought struck a chord in him. 'Valiant, listen to me. *We*'re your family now. This ship, this crew. You belong to us. If anyone's going to decide you're a failure, it'll be me, and I haven't made my mind up yet. You've survived where a lot of others didn't. And you were the first man ever to yoke a Grendel. They can't take that away from you. You're not a failure till I say you are. I'm your family and I'm your father, and the first thing I have to say to you is . . . Clean up your room, boy.'

Stelmach looked at him, startled, and then burst into laughter. But it was loud, healthy laughter, dispersing the gloom and doom that had filled the cabin, and Silence began to relax. He smiled at Frost and, although she didn't smile back, she seemed perhaps a little less cold and forbidding than usual.

Stelmach's laughter began to die away, but before he could

say anything Silence's comm unit chimed. He gestured for Stelmach to wait a moment, and opened a channel.

'This is Silence. It had better be important.'

'I'm afraid it is, Captain,' said the voice of his Second-in-Command. 'I think you'd better get back to the bridge. We have a situation up here.'

'What kind of situation?'

'Damed if I know, Captain. But I'll be a lot happier when you're back on the bridge. There's something . . . out there.'

The comm channel closed abruptly, leaving only the faintest hiss of static in Silence's ear. He broke off the connection and scowled, uneasy for no reason he could define. There had been something in his Second's voice: the man had sounded . . . scared.

Silence's first thought was of an alien ship, but if that had been the case the Second would have said so – hell, he'd have sounded a Red Alert by now. Silence's frown deepened as he looked at Frost and Stelmach, who were studying him expectantly.

'Forget this mess,' he said flatly. 'We're needed on the bridge. Move it.'

'Of course, Captain,' said Stelmach, and let the way out of his cabin. They headed down the corridor together, three professional officers from the same great family, whose needs always came first.

Back on the bridge, Silence nodded quickly to his Second-in-Command and sank into his command chair again. Frost and Stelmach took up positions on either side of him, at hand if he needed them. The atmosphere on the bridge was so tense you could have sharpened a knife on it. Everyone was at their station, engrossed in their instruments, but Silence could sense that they were too alert, too focused, almost as though they were afraid to look away.

The main viewscreen showed the *Dauntless*'s route had brought them right to the edge of the Rim. At a certain point, the stars stopped and so did their light, as though it had run into a wall: beyond that there was only the utter blackness of the Darkvoid, where no light shone. It was hard to look at for any length of time, but your eyes kept creeping back to it.

Silence stared at his Second-in-Command.

'Everything seems to be in order, Second. Nothing on the viewscreen, all instruments functioning. So what's the problem?'

The Second-in-Command stirred uncomfortably in his seat. 'It was the communications officer, sir, who first brought it to my attention.'

Silence swivelled to look at Cross, his frown deepening. 'Well?'

'It's . . . difficult to put into words, Captain.' Cross turned away from his station so he could look at Silence directly. 'Over the past few days I've been . . . hearing things. Voices in the void, calling to me. There are people talking out there in empty space, where there can't *be* any people. I've checked the sensors. There's no one here but us. But . . . it isn't just me.'

He stopped and looked unhappily at Silence to see how the captain was taking it. Silence kept his voice carefully neutral. From the difficulty Cross was having in getting his words out, it was clear he took the matter very seriously. His dark face was drawn and tired, and there were beads of sweat on his high forehead. Without looking round, Silence knew that other people on the bridge were waiting for his reaction. A while back he would have thought they were just setting him up, seeing what they could get away with, but he didn't think so now. He could feel how important they believed it was. Though they were trying to hide it, all the people on the bridge were scared. Silence felt a faint prickling at the back of his neck. These were battle-hardened veterans, and they didn't scare easily. He crossed his legs casually, but he could feel a growing tension in his gut. Strange things happened out on the Rim – everyone knew that.

He nodded curtly for Cross to continue.

'It's not just me, Captain,' the man repeated. 'People have been hearing things for days, but it was only a few minutes ago that we admitted it to each other. We hear the voices on all the comm channels, from the main hailing frequencies to private cabin-to-cabin channels. We hear them whispering, muttering, clear enough – but no more than that – to spook people with what they can make out. There's nothing wrong with the comm equipment. I've just finished checking it every way I can, and it's all one hundred per cent. If someone's playing tricks, I can't catch them at it, and I know all the tricks in the book. So finally I asked these other people, and that's when we discovered this has been happening to all of us for days, ever since we started approaching the edge of the Rim.

'And it's not just voices, Captain. It's like we're being watched, all the time, and I don't mean the security cameras – we're used to them. It's more like . . . there's someone else in the room with you, even when there isn't. It's like someone's standing over your bed while you're sleeping, watching and waiting. There's a constant feeling that something's wrong, something we should be doing, something important and vital . . .'

'Night terrors aren't exactly unknown, out here on the Rim,' Silence said carefully. 'The Darkvoid's still pretty much a mystery. We don't know to what extent close proximity to it affects the mind, and one way or another we've all spent a lot of time exposed to it recently.'

'That's what I thought, at first,' said Cross. 'It's what we all thought. I've consulted the databank and discovered this phenomenon's been reported before, by other ships who've stayed out here on the Rim too long: seeing things, hearing things, feeling things. It's usually been written off as cabin fever. The doc hands out industrial-strength tranquillizers to keep people quiet until they've left the Rim. I've run some more detailed checks. When I replayed the bridge tapes it proved that, according to my instruments, at the times I was hearing the voices there were no signals coming in. No signals at all. Wherever the voices come from, it's not out there.'

Silence raised an eyebrow. 'Not some form of esp communication?'

'Not according to the ship's esper, Captain. If there were

any psionic forces on board apart from himself, or even in the vicinity, he'd know. And there's more. It's . . . difficult to record these voices – they don't always come through clearly enough to make an impression – but I've managed to do it. While you were gone from the bridge I picked up a whole group of voices, and was able to record them. Listen.'

He turned back to his console and tapped in a command. A loud hissing filled the air as static seeped from the bridge's main address speakers. Silence frowned, straining his ears against the white noise of the static. He could see that everyone else on the bridge was listening too, their faces taut with suspense and barely hidden fear. Silence's gut tightened again.

And then a voice rose out of the static, cold and dead, but very determined to be heard.

'It's dark, here. Here, the birds burn.'

There was a pause, and then more voices came, one after the other, different voices, slow and halting but all driven by that same desperate need to be heard.

'Help me. Help me. There's something holding my hand and it won't let go.'

'It's coming. It's coming your way and you can't stop it.'

'Something's watching you from behind your mirrors.'

'Listen to me! Listen to me! There are dead hands beating on your walls!'

'They're coming. They're coming out of the dark in a dead ship.'

The last voice broke off abruptly, and then there was once more only the hissing of static on the speakers. Cross turned them off, and looked back at Silence.

'Whatever it is, it's getting worse. I've tried making other recordings before, but even with computer enhancement the voices were inaudible – almost as though the computer couldn't hear them. Now, as you've just heard, they're becoming much louder and clearer. I hadn't realized how widespread the problem was until I started asking around. I don't think anyone did. They all thought it was just them, going crazy.'

361

'Is what we heard typical of what the voices are saying?' said Silence.

'Pretty much. They all make a kind of sense, but what they mean is anyone's guess.'

'What do you think they are?' said Silence.

Cross's features tightened, but his gaze was level and when he spoke his voice was carefully calm. 'I think they're voices of the dead, Captain. Desperately trying to reach us, to warn us about . . . something. Some of us here on the bridge believe we have recognized particular, familiar voices – all of them people we know to be dead. Friends and relatives, precious ones – long gone. I heard my grandfather. Just like a video tape from my childhood. He was part of the crew on the starship *Champion* when it disappeared out on the Rim over a hundred years ago. Now we're here, in the same sector . . . Yes, I believe they're the voices of the dead, desperately trying to communicate, to make us understand before it's too late. And, before you say anything, Captain: I do indeed know how this must sound. But we've all heard these voices.' Cross paused, then continued a little apprehensively, 'Haven't *you* heard anything, Captain – felt anything strange in the long hours of the night?'

'No,' said Silence. 'I can't say I have.' He looked at Frost, · and she shook her head sharply. He looked to his other side. 'Stelmach?'

'I'm not sure,' Stelmach said slowly. 'I saw my father several times, but I thought it was just dreaming. And once, when I woke up in the early hours of the morning, I thought I felt my sister's presence. Standing over me, protecting me from . . . something.'

'All right,' said Silence. 'Let's not get carried away here. I have no doubt this phenomenon is real but, whatever it is you're hearing, it's not the dearly departed dropping in for a chat. Much more likely it's some form of long-range psionics we haven't encountered before. There was a report filed a few years back, which most of you are supposed to have read, about the possibility of new forms of life appearing in the Darkvoid. The report's author believed there could be crea-

362

tures living in the endless dark, in the gulfs between the frozen planets – a new kind of life, made possible by the unnatural conditions in the Darkvoid. And if that doesn't grab you, try this. How about some subtle form of alien attack? The aliens could be picking our brains, dredging up from our memories the voices of our dead relatives and friends, then imitating their voices. That would explain why you were able to record them, Cross. It would also explain why the bits of conversation we heard were such nonsense: the aliens don't really understand the way we think. We're expecting the new alien ships to come through the Darkvoid at us. Don't you think it's much more likely, rather than that the dead have suddenly, mysteriously started talking to us, that this is nothing more than some kind of psionic weapon, designed to scare and confuse us? And doing a pretty good job, from the look of you.'

Silence looked around the bridge, and could see the new ideas taking root. People were starting to glance at each other, smiling and relaxing as they considered the new ideas and found they liked them. They began to murmur among themselves, and sit back in their chairs, the fear and uncertainty visibly dropping away from them. Even Cross was nodding, agreeing.

Silence let them talk and laugh for a few minutes before restoring bridge discipline. 'Activate the long-range sensors, Cross,' he said finally. 'If there is an alien ship out there somewhere, hiding in the Darkvoid, I want to know about it.'

Cross nodded quickly and bent over his station, powering up the sensors. He hadn't been using them much because of the vast amounts of power they burned up, but theoretically they could detect a grain of sand half a light year away, and tell you what it had for breakfast.

Silence sat back in his command chair and let Cross get on with it. The odds were he wouldn't find anything, but just having the long-range sensors in operation for a while should help the crew feel more secure.

'I'm almost disappointed,' Frost said quietly. 'So much fuss over a few night terrors.'

'We don't all have your icy nerves, Investigator,' said Silence. 'Dealing with the crew's problems, real or perceived, is part of my job. Still, it's interesting that you and I have never heard these voices.'

'Our minds are a lot more . . . disciplined than they used to be,' said Frost. 'Perhaps we've become harder to fool.'

'Perhaps. Either way, I'll let Cross run the sensors for a few more minutes, and then . . .'

'Unidentified ship, Captain!' said Cross suddenly. 'Only just in range, but it's coming straight at us at one hell of a speed.'

'Yellow Alert,' said Silence. 'Look sharp, people. Cross, put it up on the viewscreen.'

'It's still in the Darkvoid, sir,' said Cross. 'We won't see it for a while yet.'

Silence studied the blackness on the viewscreen, carefully keeping his face unmoved. His crew chattered around him on the bridge, powering up the ship's weapons and shields. People were reporting in from all over the *Dauntless* as they took up attack positions. Silence smiled fleetingly. The doom and gloom on the bridge had completely vanished. The unknown ship might be a threat, but it was a threat the crew understood.

'The ship's slowing, Captain,' said Cross. 'I think it knows we're here. It's almost at the edge of the Darkvoid. We should have it on the screen any moment . . .'

He broke off as the ship appeared on the viewscreen, and effortlessly matched velocities with the *Dauntless*. It was a simple metal sphere, bristling with menacing instruments. It was also quite definitely a product of humanity.

'Getting details now, Captain,' said Cross. 'It's an Empire starcruiser . . . Class C.' He looked back at Silence, surprised, before checking his instruments again. 'There hasn't been a Class C ship in the Fleet since the beginning of the century. Its shields are down, but it's making no attempt to contact us. I'm using the standard hailing frequencies, but there's no response. It seems to be in good condition; there are no obvious signs of damage.'

'Could it be a pirate ship?' said Stelmach.

'Doubtful,' said Frost. 'They wouldn't be seen dead in a ship as slow as that. A pirate's career depends on being able to outrun his pursuers. But what the hell is an old crock like that doing out here on the Rim?'

'Maybe it's a ghost ship,' said Silence, and regretted the word 'ghost' the moment he had said it. He didn't need to look around to feel the tension on the bridge once more rising. 'Cross, there should be an identification number on the ship's hull. Find it and check it against records. See if you can put a name to it.'

'Already have, sir.' The communications officer's voice was high and thin. 'It's the *Champion*. My grandfather's ship. Reported lost with all hands, one hundred and seven years ago.'

'That's impossible,' said Silence numbly. 'I remember the story. What happened to the *Champion* is one of the Fleet's great unsolved mysteries, but the ship's last reported position was half-way across the Empire from here. How did it end up in the Darkvoid?'

'A good question, Captain,' said Frost. 'Another might be: Who's running the ship now? It was moving under its own power through the Darkvoid, but someone brought it to a halt here, facing us. And, since they must know we know there are people on board the *Dauntless*, why aren't they talking to us?'

'It has to be a trap of some kind,' said Stelmach. 'Could it be an alien ship, disguised?'

'It's not a holo image,' said Cross. 'My instruments' analyses of the exterior say it is exactly what it should be.'

'Alien or not,' said Silence, 'I'd say the odds are extremely good that this ship is the source of the unsettling phenomena you've all been experiencing. The ship's appearance could be a part of that. Parapsychological warfare. Cross, take us to Red Alert. All shields up. If this is a disguised alien ship, it's not going to get the chance to hit us like its brother did over Golgotha. Bring all guns to bear – but nobody fires without my express command.'

There was a hum of new activity as the bridge crew busied themselves. They all remembered how close that other alien ship had come to cleaning their clock permanently. They were looking forward to a little payback. Frost leaned in close beside Silence. 'I have to say, Captain, that the odds of this being an alien ship are really rather small. All the sensor readings seem to be insisting that the ship facing us is indeed the long-lost *Champion*.'

'I don't want a panic on my bridge,' Silence said quietly. 'Personally, I think both chances are equally unlikely. More probably this is a trap of some kind – maybe a first shot from the new rebellion. Either way, I want my people primed and ready to blow the snot out of that ship at the first wrong move. Communications Officer, what readings are you getting now?'

'Mainly confusing ones, sir,' said Cross, scowling down at his panels. 'Most of the new ship's systems are down. No defensive shields, no activated weapons ... and no life-support. No atmosphere, and colder than hell. I don't even know how it got here. All my instruments seem quite convinced the ship's drive is cold. There's nothing to show it's been used for one hell of a long time.'

'Lifeform readings?' said Silence.

'Not a thing, Captain. Human or otherwise. There's always the chance it could be an old plague ship.'

Silence glared at him. 'A plague ship? You're a cheerful sort to have around, Cross. We're going to have to take a closer look. Maintain Red Alert and keep the long-range sensors open. If there's one ship out here there might be more, and I don't want us getting hit while we're distracted. Investigator, put together an away team. You and I are taking a pinnace over to that ship to see what's what.'

'I suppose I'm wasting my breath in pointing out as usual, Captain, that you shouldn't risk your life with an investigating team?' said Frost.

'You are indeed,' said Silence. 'Whatever that ship is, I need first-hand information before I can make any decisions. Stelmach, would you care to accompany us?'

'Not really, no,' said Stelmach. 'They don't pay me enough to volunteer for missions like this. In fact, they couldn't pay me enough. Have a nice trip, Captain. I'll be right here when you get back.'

'Captain,' said Cross. 'Permission to join your team. If that really is the *Champion*, my grandfather's ship . . .'

'We won't need a communications officer on this foray,' said Frost.

'But we might need someone who can tell a fake *Champion* from the real thing,' said Silence. 'All right, Cross, you're on the team. Second-in-Command, you have the bridge again. Let's go, people.'

They crossed over to what might be the *Champion* in a pinnace: Silence, Frost, Cross and six security men. They all wore hard suits. The *Dauntless*'s sensors had been quite specific that there wasn't a single life-support system working in the whole ship. Silence patched into the pinnace's sensors through his comm implant, and studied the *Champion* thoughtfully as the pinnace drifted closer. It was as though the bulkhead turned transparent wherever he was looking, giving him a clear view of the mystery ship. It seemed heavy and clumsy compared to the sleek starcruisers he was used to. The old C Class had been something of a compromise between speed and weaponry that in the end had turned out to favour neither – which was why it had been quickly replaced by the D Class. Even so, the *Champion* was something of a legend in the Fleet. She'd been one of the Empire's foremost exploratory vessels, checking out new worlds in hope of either alien contacts or colonization. During her short life in the Fleet she had brought fourteen new planets into the Empire. And then she had gone out to the Rim once too often, and had never been seen again by human eyes.

Until now. Silence couldn't help wondering if it was just coincidence that had brought the *Champion* back at such a volatile time for the Empire – like a message from the past, when things were different. He put the thought aside. He had sworn to serve the Iron Throne, no matter who sat on it, because the Empire must be preserved ... because all the other choices were worse. Better a corrupt civilization than barbarism. He concentrated on the starship looming up before him. It grew slowly larger, filling the space between them, so that he could no longer see the Rim or the Darkvoid beyond it.

Finally the pinnace drifted to a halt with only a few feet between its hull and the *Champion*'s.

'Try the hailing frequencies one more time,' Silence said quietly, not taking his eyes off the vast white metal wall before him.

'Still no response, Captain,' said Cross, after a long moment. 'Pinnace sensors confirm no lifeforms anywhere on the ship.'

'See if you can open the *Champion*'s airlock with a general override signal,' said Silence.

Cross bent over his panels, and then shook his head. 'No response. All the systems must be down. We're going to have to crack it open manually.'

'No surprises there.' Silence closed down his comm link to the sensors, and the pinnace's bulkhead reappeared before him. He looked round at his team one at a time, making eye contact so they could see how assured he was. 'All right, people. Pay attention. We're going out through the pinnace's airlock in our hard suits, Investigator Frost leading. We're right up against the *Champion*'s airlock, so all we have to do is step outside and open it. Cross will operate the manual override on the outside of the airlock door, and then the Investigator will enter the lock itself. She will go through alone, to check out the situation. Once she gives the all-clear, you will cycle through that airlock as fast as you can. There's no telling what shape the mechanism's in after all this time, and I don't want anyone left outside.'

'What if something happens to the Investigator?' said Cross.

'Then you back off and the *Dauntless* blows the *Champion* to shit,' said Frost. 'Because if I can't handle it, you sure as hell couldn't.'

'Once we're inside,' said Silence, pressing calmly on as though the interchange hadn't happened, 'we will make our way to the bridge and activate what systems we can. Everyone stay together, but don't bunch up. And keep your eyes open. The *Champion* is to be considered hostile territory until proven otherwise. You are authorized to use lethal force on anything that moves, with the exception of your team-mates. Investigator, lead the way.'

Frost nodded, and moved over the inner door of the pinnace's airlock. There was a pause as everyone put on their helmets and made sure the seals were secure, and then Frost opened the inner door and stepped inside, followed by Silence and Cross. The three hard suits filled the airlock from wall to wall. They waited patiently as the air was flushed out, and then Frost opened the outer door. It slid back slowly, silently, revealing the *Champion*'s outer hull. Silence gestured to Frost and she stepped forward on to the outer edge of the door. She reached out a gloved hand to the small wheel on the outside of the *Champion*'s airlock, and took a firm hold. Silence moved in beside her to brace her once she started exerting pressure. The pinnace's artificially produced gravity didn't extend beyond the airlock. Her armoured glove closed around the wheel, and turned it inch by inch. The outer doors of the airlock slowly parted, and a bright light suddenly appeared within the lock. Silence relaxed a little. At least some of the *Champion*'s systems were still working. The doors crept further apart until finally Frost was able to step carefully from the *Dauntless* into the *Champion*.

The doors closed behind her again, and Silence could only wait. He could feel her presence, thanks to their link, and her composure helped to settle him.

'The airlock is functioning perfectly,' her voice said suddenly through his comm implant. 'I have light and gravity, but no air. The pumps are working, but it would appear they have no air to work with. The inner doors are opening. Lights have come on beyond them. I'm now in the corridor outside the lock. No movement anywhere. Still no air, and the temperature's as near as dammit to zero. You might as well well come on over. There's no sign of any welcoming party.'

'Stay where you are,' said Silence. 'We'll be right with you.'

He worked the lock's outer doors again, and he and Cross passed through into the *Champion*, followed quickly by the security men.

The corridor on the other side of the lock was brightly lit but uncomfortably narrow, and the low ceiling seemed to press down above their helmets. The walls were covered with cables and conduits and tightly packed instrumentation. The Empire's designers had been cramming in every extra and improvement they could think, right up to the last minute. None of it looked particularly dated. The *Dauntless* might be more efficiently arranged, but the systems were still pretty much the same. If a thing worked, the Empire tended to stick with it.

'Interesting,' said Frost, and Silence turned automatically to look at her, though all he could see was her blank helmet. 'According to my suit's sensors, the light and gravity are only a local phenomenon. The rest of the ship is still powered down. Which would seem to suggest someone knows we're here.'

'Could be the ship's computers,' said Cross.

'No,' said Frost, 'I don't think so. They would have turned all the life-support systems on.'

'Try general address on your comm,' said Silence. 'See if anyone answers.'

'This is Investigator Frost of the *Dauntless*, representing the Empire. Respond, please.'

They waited a long time, but there was no reply. The comm channel was empty of everything, even static. Silence's back crawled, feeling the pressure of unseen watching eyes. The words 'ghost ship' came back to him, along with the half-serious stories that had always been in circulation during his cadet days. Tales of dead ships populated by dead crews, sailing silently through the long night on journeys that would never end. Skeletons on the bridge, or dead men rotting at their stations, heading for some far-off destination the living

370

could never understand. Silence had no smile. He hadn't realized those stupid stories had made such an impression on him.

'Let's make for the bridge, people,' he said briskly. 'Maybe we'll find some answers there. Investigator, lead the way.'

Frost patched into a map of the *Champion*'s structure – provided by the *Dauntless*'s computer records – and set off down the corridor. Lights turned themselves on ahead of them and went off behind them, so that they moved always in a pool of light surrounded by darkness – much as, Silence realized uneasily, they'd moved in a pod through the alien ship over Golgotha. Weight remained constant at one standard gravity, but there was still no air or heat. Silence had the security men check out each room and compartment they passed, but there was no trace anywhere of the *Champion*'s crew.

There were, however, unmade beds and abandoned meals, cards dropped in mid-game and doors left ajar, as though the people involved had just stood up a hundred or so years ago and walked away from their lives, never to return.

Silence kept thinking he could see things moving on the edge of his vision, but every time he looked there was nothing there. Shadows moved disturbingly around the small party as they went deeper into the ship, their hard suits eerily out of place in the crew's quarters. They all had the feeling they were being watched, and the security men spent as much time checking behind them as they did the way ahead. Frost, of course, just strode on through the empty corridors, calm as always. Silence stuck close to her.

They finally came to the main elevators, and Silence gave a quiet prayer of thanks that these were still working – there were walkways, but using them would have meant a long climb to the bridge. Just in case, he split the party into two groups, which made their way up to the bridge in separate elevators. The cramped metal cages took an uncomfortably long time getting there, not least because they insisted on stopping at every floor, but eventually the doors opened on to the bridge and Silence led the way forward with something very like relief. If there were answers to be found anywhere on this deserted ship, he should be able to find them here.

There was no one sitting in the command chair, skeleton or corpse, and the work stations were unmanned. No sign of any crew. No sign to show they'd ever been here. It was just as Silence had expected, but he still felt obscurely disappointed. Something really cataclysmic must have happened on board the *Champion* to make the senior officers abandon the bridge like this. And yet there were no indications of attack or mutiny, no damage or signs of haste.

Cross leant over the comm station and tried a few warm-up routines, and then turned away. 'Everything but the very basics are shut down, Captain. Give me an hour or so and I should be able to bring something on-line. Half these systems will have to be reprogrammed from the bottom up, but all the hardware seems functional.'

'The autopilot's still working,' said Frost. 'Someone must have fed in the coordinates that brought the ship here.'

'Hold everything,' said Cross. 'I've got the security cameras working. Which shouldn't be possible, but . . . watch the monitors.'

They all crowded around Cross and stared at the bank of three monitor screens attached to his station. These lit up in swift succession, as though they'd only recently been turned off. Cross switched rapidly from one camera to another, running the length of the ship. Scenes appeared on the screens one after the other, holding just long enough to convey the continuing sensation that there was nothing but emptiness anywhere on board. From corridors to engineering, sick bay to crew's quarters, everything was still and silent. It chilled Silence to his bones to see a ship so desolate.

He tried to remember more about the history of the *Champion*, rather than the legend. The captain, Tomas Pearce, had by all accounts been something of a fierce officer, a strictly-by-the-book man, as hard on himself as anyone else. Everybody agreed he ran a tight ship right up until the day it disappeared. He would never have walked away from his command, no matter what his crew did – he'd have hit the auto-destruct first. Silence wondered what Pearce would have thought now had he seen so many posts abandoned, so many stations unmanned. No, Pearce wouldn't have walked. Someone or something must have taken him.

'Hello,' said Cross suddenly, 'what have we got here?' He fussed at the panels before him, muttering to himself and stabbing awkwardly at the controls with his armoured fingers. Hard suits weren't meant for delicate work. 'I think I have something, Captain. The cameras in the main cargo hold are out, but I'm getting some information through the ship's interior sensors. There's something down in the cargo bay. A lot of somethings.'

'Hardly unusual, for a cargo bay,' said Frost.

'It is when the computer manifests are convinced the ship isn't carrying any cargo. And, even more interestingly, all these somethings are roughly human in size.'

'Life signs?' said Silence.

'Not so far,' said Cross. 'But, whatever these things are, there are hundreds of them.'

'Then, for want of anything better to do, let's go and take a look,' said Silence.

Silence left four of the security men on the bridge to watch the monitors and run further checks on the instruments, and herded the rest of his team back into the elevator. It was a long way down to the cargo bay, but at least they didn't stop at every floor this time; he chose to see this as a good omen. The doors finally opened on the main cargo bay, and Frost made the others stay in the elevator while she checked out the situation. She kept them waiting an uncomfortably long time before waving them out. The bay was deserted, but the lights had already been on when the elevators doors opened, almost as though someone were waiting for them.

The bay itself was huge, with intricately marked steel walls surrounding a vast space. They'd emerged at ground-level, like mice creeping out of a hole. Frost signalled for the group to stay together while she locked the elevator doors open, in case they had to retreat in a hurry. As far as Silence was concerned she needn't have bothered. He'd never felt less like wandering off on his own in his life. Still, as Captain he was expected to provide a good example, so as soon as she gave the all-clear, Silence stepped confidently forward to take a look around.

Away from the elevator, the sheer size of the cargo bay was almost overpowering, but his attention was drawn immediately to the sole cargo: hundreds of long mirrored cylinders, each the size of a coffin. They'd been laid out in neat rows, forming a perfect square. He checked them out from a cautious distance using the limited sensors built into his suit, but the cylinders gave up no information at all. He couldn't even tell what they were made of, let alone what might be inside them.

'That's the crew, isn't it?' said Cross quietly.

'Could be,' said Silence. 'The numbers are about right. Only way to find out is to open a few. Investigator . . .'

'Way ahead of you, Captain,' said Frost, striding forward pugnaciously.

Silence gestured for Cross and the two security men to stay with him. 'Take it slow and easy, Investigator. There's always the chance those things are booby-trapped.'

'I'll bear it in mind,' said Frost. 'Now, a little quiet, if you please. I have to concentrate.'

She stopped just short of the outer rank, tried her sensors again, and snorted disgustedly as they failed to provide any useful information. Each cylinder was about seven feet long – plenty of room for a body inside, and any number of unpleasant surprises too. Frost knelt down by the nearest cylinder and got her first surprise when she discovered the mirrored surface only reflected the other cylinders and not her reflection. She examined the edges of the cylinder carefully, and got her second surprise. There was no sign of any seal or opening. The entire cylinder seemed to have been produced in one piece. Perhaps . . . formed *around* something. The word 'cocoon' occurred to her, echoing in her mind with a significance she couldn't pin down. She straightened up, and looked at the rows of cylinders stretching away before her. She had been intending to open one by force, with her gun if necessary, and trust to her hard suit to protect her, but she was beginning to think that was what she was supposed to do. More and more, the whole place felt like a trap. The cylinders were too tempting, and there was too much light, as though the cargo bay were a stage, waiting for the action to begin.

Frost reached out cautiously to tap the top of the cylinder in front of her, and her gloved hand sank through the shining surface as though through some silvery liquid.

Inside the cylinder, something grabbed her hand and squeezed it hard. She lurched forward, caught off-balance, and her arm plunged further into the cylinder. She braced herself against the steel floor and pulled back, but whatever had hold of her wouldn't release its grip. She could feel the pressure even through her armoured glove. Frost gritted her teeth, snarling, and yanked with all her strength. The suit's servomechanisms whined loudly. Her arm slowly reappeared from the lid, and then her glove, clasped by a dead white human hand.

The weight on her arm was suddenly lessened as a dead white face appeared through the shining lid, like a drowned man's face surfacing in a river, and then a dead man was out of his coffin and standing before Frost, smiling, still holding her hand in his. Her first thought was that it must be a Fury, one of Shub's killing machines, but then she saw the marks of drastic surgery on his shaven skull and knew at once what had happened to the *Champion*'s crew.

The thing in front of her was a Ghost Warrior.

All around her, dead men were emerging from the silver cylinders, like vile grey butterflies bursting out of the shimmering cocoons. The man before her wore a dated Fleet uniform, torn and stained with the long-dried blood of his death wounds. His skin was a ghastly white and, though his smile was impossibly wide, there was no emotion in his face and no life in his unblinking eyes. She could hear Silence shouting at her to get away from the dead man, but his gaze held her like a hook she could wriggle on but not escape.

375

The Ghost Warriors were rising everywhere now, silent and calm, their movements filled with an implacable purpose.

And then the blast from an energy weapon tore away the head of the man before her, and the body slumped to its knees. She was suddenly herself again, freed from the dead gaze. She fell back a step, tugging at her captured hand. The pale fingers continued to grip her firmly, despite all her struggles. She drew her sword with her left hand and hacked savagely at the pallid wrist. The blade sheared clean through and she staggered backwards. The dead hand still clutched at her glove; she had to cut it away finger by finger as she hurried to rejoin Silence and the others.

They all fired, energy bolts leaping from the disrupters built into their gloves. Walking corpses were blown apart and slapped aside, but still the hundreds of dead moved purposefully forward. Frost took up her place between Silence and Cross, too angry to be frightened or worried. She'd fought every kind of alien in her time and had thought there was nothing left in the Empire that could throw her, but something in the dead man's gaze had held her as securely as any chain. If Silence hadn't blown its head off she'd have stayed standing there until the dead overwhelmed her and dragged her away to make her one of them.

'Well,' she made herself say, 'at least now we know what happened to the *Champion*'s crew. Those bastard AIs somehow got their hands on them, scooped out their brains and replaced them with their filthy computers. We've found a whole ship of Ghost Warriors.'

'Shub is right on the other sight of the Empire,' said Silence, 'but let that pass for the moment. It'll be another two minutes before our disrupters recharge, and these creeps could manage something pretty goddam unpleasant in that time, so everyone free your swords and back away. We are getting out of here.'

There was a muffled clang behind them as the elevator doors slammed shut.

'That's not possible,' said Frost. 'I locked them open.'

'Someone's watching,' said Cross. 'And they don't want us leaving just yet.'

'I'll try the bridge,' said Silence. 'Maybe they can override. Bridge, this is Silence. Can you hear me?'

There was no reply, only an ominous quiet.

'Something's got to them,' said Cross. 'We're on our own.'

The dead men stood facing them, row upon row, inhumanly still. One figure, wearing an outdated Captain's uniform, stepped forward. Silence tried to recognize Tomas Pearce, but the face before him held nothing of humanity in it. One eye had been replaced by a camera lens, and the scars of brutal surgery were clear on his forehead. He came to a halt before Silence, carefully out of sword's range and smiled widely as though he knew what a smile was supposed to convey but didn't know how to do it. Ghost Warriors weren't often used for diplomacy or conversation: when they fought Shub's battles with humanity they were deployed as much for pyschological effect as any functional superiority. The dead man wore a gun and a sword on his hips, but so far had made no move to draw them. Silence found that disturbing: it implied the Ghost Warriors wanted the humans alive.

Pearce's lips moved, and Silence heard a slow, horribly impersonal voice through his comm implant. It was a machine talking through a human mouth.

'Captain Silence. Investigator Frost. You must come with us.'

'Why just us two?' said Silence.

'Yeah,' said Cross. 'I feel left out.'

'You are different,' said Pearce, his dead eyes still fixed on Silence and Frost. 'Changed. It is necessary that we discover how.'

'Tough,' said Frost. 'We have other plans. Call our secretary and make an appointment. Captain, get those elevator doors open. I'll hold these bastards off.'

She stepped forward, holding her sword in both hands, and swung it round in a vicious sideways sweep. If it had connected it would almost certainly have beheaded Pearce, but he raised his arm impossibly fast and blocked the blow.

The blade sank deep and jarred on what might have been bone. In the split second while Frost was still off-balance, Pearce reached out with his other hand and snatched the sword out of her hands. She snarled and hit him in the throat with her armoured glove. The hard suit's servomechanisms amplified the strength of her blow, and she could feel the sickening crunch as her fist crushed Pearce's throat and snapped his neck. His head hung at an angle, but the expression on his face didn't change. He threw her sword aside and reached out with both hands to grab at her shoulders. She kicked his legs out from under him, and he fell sprawling on the steel floor. But the other Ghost Warriors moved forward unhurriedly, and Frost knew there were just too many of them to be stopped by anything she could do.

She checked the timer inside her helmet and opened up with her disrupters again. Energy blasts erupted from her gloves, swatting aside the advancing dead men as if they were so many curling leaves caught in a fiery breeze. But then her guns fell silent, and the Ghost Warriors kept coming. Pearce was back on his feet again, reaching for her. Frost grabbed up her sword again, determined she'd die before she let them drag her off to Shub's bloody laboratories.

Silence and Cross got to the elevators and used their amplified strength to force the doors open. The two security men charged into the lift, pulled the control mechanism out of the wall and quickly began to jury-rig an override. Silence would have liked to turn and see how Frost was doing, but he needed all his strength to hold the elevator doors open – they strained against his hands with an almost malevolent urgency, and he could hear a faint whine from the servomechanisms in his suit's arms. This was an exploratory suit, designed for protection, not the stronger and better-equipped battle suit, and it couldn't last much longer.

One of the security men yelled out in satisfaction, and the pressure from the doors was suddenly gone. Silence and Cross let go of them and hurried into the elevator.

They turned as one and opened up with their disrupters,

the energy bolts blowing away Ghost Warriors to either side of Frost.

'Get your ass over here, Investigator!' yelled Silence. 'We're leaving!'

Frost turned and ran for the elevator. There was no dishonour in running from Ghost Warriors. They'd keep coming as long as their computer implants remained intact, no matter what state their bodies might be in. The only answer to this many Ghost Warriors was massed disrupter cannon. She threw herself into the elevator, and the security men let the doors close behind her. Dead fists beat against the panels, denting the metal, but Silence had already hit the 'up' button. He took a deep breath as the elevator began to rise.

'*Dauntless*, this is Silence. Do you hear me?'

'Loud and clear, Captain.'

'Check the sensors. Any lifeform readings on the *Champion*'s bridge?'

'No, Captain.'

'Damn. All right, we're heading back to the pinnace in a hurry. The ship is crawling with Ghost Warriors. You are not to allow the pinnace or any other vessel from the *Champion* to dock with you until sensors have confirmed that only the living are aboard. Once we've docked, open up with everything you've got until there's nothing left of the *Champion* but a few glowing atoms. If we can't get to you and you consider the *Dauntless* to be in danger, forget about us and blow the *Champion* apart anyway. We are expendable. Is that clear, *Dauntless*?'

'Clear, Captain,' said the calm voice of his Second-in-Command. 'We'll give you every second we can, but you must be docked before we open fire. Otherwise the energy will fry you.'

'I know. But the *Dauntless*'s safety comes first. Confirm.'

'Confirmed, Captain. Good luck.'

The elevator slowed suddenly, catching them all off-balance. The security man at the controls swore disapassionately.

'Something's fighting the override. I don't know how much longer I can maintain control, Captain.'

'Stop at the next floor,' said Silence. 'We're getting off. We can't risk being taken back down again.'

The security man nodded and the elevator lurched to a halt. The doors opened, and Silence and his people spilled out into an empty corridor, swords at the ready. Silence accessed his map of the *Champion* again, displaying it on the inside of his helmet. They were seven floors down and quite a distance away from the airlock that would give them access to their pinnace. They'd have to stick to the walkways and hope the Ghost Warriors didn't have some way to block them. He dismissed the map and looked at the two security men. Their blank helmets stared impassively back at him, waiting for orders.

'There's no point in going back to the bridge,' Silence said evenly. 'Your comrades are dead . . . and I never even knew their names. Tell me yours.'

One of the men indicated himself, and then his friend. 'Corporal Abrams and Corporal Fine, sir. Don't mind Fine. He doesn't say much.'

'Pleased to meet you, corporals. If we get back to the *Dauntless* alive, you're both sergeants. Now let's get going. Frost, take the point. Cross, watch our rear. Move it, people!'

They ran back through the deserted corridors of the death ship, the hammering of their armoured boots on the steel floor a constant roll of thunder. Silence again flashed the map up on his inner helmet, counting off the floors and levels as they drew slowly closer to the airlock where they'd left the pinnace. His heart was pounding and his breath tore at his lungs. Even with the servomechanisms to help, the hard suit was heavy and clumsy, not designed for running in. And, deep down inside him, he knew he'd forgotten something – something important. He snarled silently inside his helmet, and tried vainly to increase his pace. It was all taking too long. The Ghost Warriors could be right behind them. He checked his suit's sensors once more, but there was no trace of movement anywhere within their limited range – which probably meant the dead men knew a short cut. He checked the map again, but he couldn't see a quicker route than the one he'd chosen. They'd get to the pinnace first. They had to.

At last there was only one corridor left between them and safety. The group found a second wind that brought them pounding around the final corridor . . . and came crashing to a halt.

Silence and the others just stood there, a dozen yards from the airlock. His ears were full of his own harsh breathing; his heart was full of despair. Between his small force and the airlock stood a hundred Ghost Warriors, eerily unprotected against the airless cold, with the dead Captain Pearce at their head. *No*, thought Silence numbly. *That's not possible, there's no way they could have beaten us here!*

But these are dead men, a small voice murmured at the back of his mind. *Maybe they know ways that the living cannot walk.*

Silence's thoughts whirled crazily as he tried desperately to think of something, anything he could do to steal a victory from the jaws of certain defeat.

Pearce smiled at Silence and Frost, his head perched crookedly on his broken neck. 'It's over. You must come with us now. The laboratories are waiting.'

'To hell with that,' said Frost calmly. She pulled a concussion grenade from her belt, primed it and tossed it neatly into the middle of the massed Ghost Warriors. They barely had time to react before it blew, and the force of the blast threw corpses – and bits of corpses – in all directions. Frost and the rest of the party, protected by their heavy hard suits, hardly rocked on their heels. Silence laughed suddenly, back in the game again, and strode towards the airlock, kicking thrashing bodies out of his way. The others followed him, knocking the Ghost Warriors down as fast as they got to their feet.

Silence hit the controls, and the airlock doors cycled slowly open. The two security men were hacking at everything in sight with their swords, and pale, bloodless flesh flew on the air. The doors finally opened wide enough, and Silence yelled for his people to break free.

'Move it, people! We are leaving!'

Abrams and Fine broke away and threw themselves into the airlock.

Cross went to follow them, and then stopped as a dead man rose up before him. Cross raised his sword, but hesitated as he recognized the grey face before him.

'Grandfather . . .'

In that moment the dead man raised an old-fashioned disrupter, placed it against Cross's armoured belly, and pressed the stud. The energy blast punched right through the hard suit and out the back. Cross screamed in horror, the sound filling Silence's ears through his comm link, and then crumpled slowly to the floor. Silence swung his sword with all the power his suit could give him and sheared clean through the dead man's neck. The headless body fell away. Silence sheathed his sword and grabbed Cross by the shoulders.

He pulled the screaming man into the airlock and turned to look out at Frost, standing with her back to the doors, sword in hand.

'Get in here, Investigator! We are *leaving*!'

'I'm not coming with you, Captain.' Frost didn't turn round, but her voice came as clearly through Silence's comm implant on the command channel, as if she had been standing right beside him. 'I have to stay behind. Otherwise one of these undead bastards will just hit the override from this side and keep the airlock from functioning. I have to be here to hold them off while the rest of you go through to the pinnace. I've known this ever since we left the cargo bay. You never have thought ahead enough, Captain.'

'We'll risk it,' said Silence. 'Now get in here. That's an order. We're not leaving without you.'

'You have to,' said the Investigator unemotionally. 'It's vital you get away to report what happened here. The Empire must know that Shub is using stolen ships with dead crews. Once you reach the *Dauntless*, blow this ghost ship apart.'

'I can't open fire while you're still aboard!'

'Of course you can. It's the logical thing to do.'

'You didn't leave me to die on the bridge of the *Darkwind*.'

'That was different. There's too much at stake here. And at least if you blow every thing to bits they won't be able to make a Ghost Warrior out of me. Please, John. It's the only way.'

She hit the airlock controls with her elbow, and the doors closed. Silence had one last glimpse of the Investigator throwing herself against the advancing dead men.

He turned away to start operating the controls for the outer doors. He didn't say anything. He didn't trust his voice. His arms and legs were shaking inside his suit, from tension and something more. Cross was still screaming. The two security men had slapped temporary seals over the holes in his armour so that he'd survive the transit to the pinnace. One of them gave the all-clear to Silence, and he opened the outer doors.

It took them only a few moments to negotiate the empty space to the pinnace's lock, and then through it. Cross fell silent as the emergency drugs the hard suit had been pumping into him finally took effect. Abrams and Fine secured him in a seat, and then strapped themselves in.

Silence took the pilot's seat, and patched into the pinnace's emergency channel.

'*Dauntless*, this is the captain. I'm on my way back. I have three men with me, one seriously injured. We're all that made it out. The *Champion* is infested with Ghost Warriors. As soon as we're clear, open up with everything you've got. Destroy the *Champion*. Confirm.'

'This is the *Dauntless*,' said his Second-in-Command. 'We confirm. Destroy the *Champion*, as soon as you've docked.'

It didn't take long to manoeuvre the pinnace back to the *Dauntless* and dock it, but the minutes seemed to last forever, and all the time Silence saw a single valiant figure, fighting an army of dead men and hoping the *Dauntless*'s guns would deliver a quick death. He patched into the main ship's sensors and watched silently as cannon after cannon opened fire on the *Champion*. Her shields flared into existence immediately, but they were antiquated and the *Dauntless*'s fire-power battered them down. Disrupter bolts hit the old ship again and again, blowing jagged holes in the hull. Escaping energies burned silently in the dark, until finally the *Champion* exploded in a bloody ball of hellfire, glowing brightly in the long night. *Goodbye, Frost,* said the captain silently. *I'll miss you.*

He broke the comm link and sank back in his chair, feeling suddenly very tired. The two security men were manhandling an unconscious Cross out through the airlock. He couldn't really believe that she was dead yet. He could still feel her presence through his mental link, like a ghost in his head, but presumably that would fade away in time, like the phantom pain from an amputated limb.

'Captain, this is Stelmach,' said a familiar voice in his ear suddenly. 'We're getting strange readings here on the bridge. And there are reports of fighting coming in from all over the ship. Intruders, appearing from nowhere, killing our people. There are energy weapons discharging on all levels. Dear God, Captain, they're Ghost Warriors.'

'No,' said Silence. 'That's not possible.'

'They're here, Captain. I can see them through the security cameras! How the hell did they get off the *Champion*? We didn't track any escaping craft.'

'They must have teleported,' said Silence. 'The bastards teleported! *That's* what I'd forgotten. Remember what we saw at Court? Shub has the secret of long-range teleportation! Set up interior force shields throughout the ship, cutting off all infected areas. Have repair teams standing by in case disrupters puncture the shell. And warm up the auto-destruct ... in case.'

So Frost died for nothing.

'Where's the nearest trouble site, Stelmach?'

'There are two or three quite near you, Captain. The biggest group is one level down, in Delta section, but the security force I sent hasn't got there yet. You'd better stay clear until I get word it's been secured.'

'Hell with that,' said Silence. 'This my ship. I go where I'm needed. I have business with these murderous bastards. Silence out.'

He ran down the corridor, pushing the hard suit to its limits, and all he could think of was making the Ghost Warriors pay for Frost's death. He'd build a mountain of heads in her name. She'd have liked that. But it still wouldn't be enough – nothing would ever be enough. He took the elevator down to the next level, clenching and unclenching his hands impatiently. The doors opened to sounds of chaos not far away. There were shouts and screams and the noise of energy weapons discharging. That last brought him out of the elevator at a run. They weren't too far from the outer hull in Delta section, and a really unlucky shot could puncture the hull. Explosive decompression probably wouldn't bother the Ghost Warriors much but it would play hell with everyone else. Silence was suddenly very glad he'd kept his hard suit on.

He rounded a corner and came upon a heaving mob of human defenders struggling to contain a large group of Ghost Warriors. There were wounded and dead bodies sprawled everywhere, but in the midst of the Warriors, holding their attention almost single-handedly, was a defiant figure in a battered hard suit, swinging a long sword with both hands.

Silence grinned so hard it hurt. He didn't need to see the suit's colours to know whose face was inside the anonymous helm. No wonder he'd still been able to feel her presence. When the Ghost Warriors had teleported their people off the *Champion* they'd brought Frost with them! They'd probably been unwilling to give up such an important specimen.

He roared his Clan's battle cry and threw himself into the heart of the fight, hacking left and right in vicious sweeping arcs. He cut a path through the walking dead, laughing as he went, until he was able to put his back against that of the other armoured figure. They fought well and fiercely, and the Ghost Warriors couldn't get anywhere near them.

'Hi,' said Frost's voice in his ear. 'Miss me?'

'Not for a minute,' said Silence. 'I knew you were too cussed to die.'

'This is what it was all about, you know,' the Investigator said casually, in between blows. 'Use the *Champion* to pull us in, distract us with strange voices, and then take over the *Dauntless*. With you and I as Ghost Warriors, carefully preserved and disguised, Shub could have used us to get within striking range of the Empress herself. Which is presumably why they saved me when the *Champion* went up. Crafty bastards. I'm quite impressed.'

Silence was too busy to reply. Captain Pearce had appeared again, his head still at an angle, but he was as determined as ever. Pearce had an outmoded disrupter in his hand, but Silence slapped it out of his grasp with a swift, casual movement. The two captains went head-to-head, the living and the dead, swords sparking as they crunched together and sprang away. Pearce had a strength and speed beyond anything a living man could normally produce, but Silence had been changed in the Madness Maze so that he, too, was no longer merely human. The hard suit's servomechanisms strained to keep up with him as he swept aside Pearce's attack and defence alike and duelled him to a standstill.

He lifted his sword and brought it down in one blindingly swift movement, and the heavy blade hammered into Pearce's skull, sinking deep into his head until it finally jarred to a halt at an eyesocket. Pearce convulsed as his computer implant crashed and fell apart. Silence jerked his sword free, and Pearce fell twitching to the floor.

There were still more Ghost Warriors. Silence fought on, back-to-back with Frost, who was as always cool and collected. Strength and speed burned within him, and he felt as if he could fight forever. He was linked with Frost again, on every mental level, fighting in that calm twilight state when the sum of the two of them was far greater than the parts.

And suddenly there was no one left to fight. The Ghost Warriors lay broken and decapitated all around, and the surviving crew members were wildly cheering their captain and their Investigator. Which had to be something of a first for Frost.

Silence thought as he looked serenely around him. Usually poeople only cheered Investigators when they were leaving. He turned to look at Frost, who had turned at the same moment to look at him. They reached up and took off their helmets, and their eyes met in a moment of understanding and appreciation that could never be forgotten.

'We're not even breathing hard,' Silence said quietly. 'What are we becoming?'

'Better,' said Frost.

'Inhuman, perhaps.'

Frost shrugged inside her suit as best she could. 'Humanity's overrated, sometimes.'

Silence was still trying to come up with an answer to that which didn't involve raising his voice when Stelmach's voice sounded in his ear again. The security officer sounded very upset.

'Captain! There are Ghost Warriors all over the ship! Hundreds of them!'

'Tell me something I don't know,' said Silence. 'Are we holding our own against them?'

'Barely. We'are afraid to use our disrupters much, but they're not. The largest group is heading for the bridge, despite everything we can do to slow it down. We've got only one chance. From my work with controlling the Grendel aliens, I'm pretty sure the computers running the Ghost Warriors must have a central control mechanism, separate from the bodies it moves – some mechanism they brought with them when they teleported over from the *Champion*, a single cybernetic mind running its meat puppets. I've had Communications scan the comm channels for unauthorized transmissions, and we've detected one hell of a powerful signal coming from the main hangars in Epsilon section. That's got to be it.'

'Good work, Stelmach,' said Silence. 'The Investigator and I are on our way. Send as many men as you can after us. If we fail, defend the bridge until it's obvious there's no hope, and then hit the self-destruct. Whatever happens, this ship and its crew are not to fall under Shub's control.'

'Understood, Captain. Good luck.'

He broke contact, and Silence and Frost headed for the elevators.

'If I didn't know better,' said Frost, 'I'd swear he's becoming almost human.'

'He says much the same about you,' said Silence.

They discarded their cumbersome hard suits for the sake of greater speed, and made their way down to the Epsilon hangars without much trouble. The *Dauntless* was a much bigger ship than the *Champion*, and the Ghost Warriors were spread thin, trying to cover too many areas at once. Silence and Frost cut them down when they had to, and avoided the rest. They didn't want the enemy to know they were coming.

There were a dozen access routes into the Epsilon hangar area, and only a few of them were signposted. Silence and Frost used one of the least obvious, and emerged high up on a narrow walkway overlooking the bay.

Their entrance was unobserved. Some fifty feet below, the Ghost Warriors had cleared a space among the piled-up supply crates and now a dozen of them, holding disrupters, stood guard over an intricate glass and crystal mechanism that glowed with an uncomfortably bright light.

Silence pursed his lips thoughtfully and glanced at Frost.

'Despite our new abilities, there's no way we can get to that device without being seen or heard, and seeing so many disrupters makes me nervous. Even if they don't hit us, they could hit the hull. We could wait for reinforcements, but with all that cover to hide behind the Warriors could hold off a small army indefinitely. And we're running out of time.'

'If you can distract them,' said Frost, 'I can blast that device with my disrupter.'

Silence raised an eyebrow. 'From here?'

'Of course.'

Silence thought about it, but shook his head. 'No. Odds are it's protected by a force screen of some kind. And if you fire and fail we'll have given away our position for nothing. I've got another idea.'

Frost looked at him. 'This doesn't involve us throwing ourselves away in a grand gesture, does it? I've just tried that, and I wasn't too keen about it the first time.'

'This is simpler. I'm suggesting we use our *minds* for a change. The strain of nearly dying on the *Champion* seems to have pushed me another step up the ladder. You too, probably. We're more than we were. Listen. Concentrate. Can you hear what I'm hearing?'

Frost frowned, listening. The hangar bay was quiet, the Ghost Warriors standing silently on guard. In the stillness she could hear Silence's breathing and her own, and then, very quietly below it all, she sensed a low pulsing that rose and fell in sudden spikes. And, inside that sound which wasn't a sound, she could hear a voice murmuring, cold and inhuman and horribly perfect.

'Damn,' said Frost. 'It's the machine. I can hear it thinking. Giving orders. It's not a language or any computer code that I'm familiar with, but somehow I can still understand it. This is the signal Stelmach detected from the bridge, the thing that pulls the Ghost Warriors' strings.'

'Yes, said Silence. 'It is. Apparently we're becoming espers, along with everything else. But we can do more than listen, Frost. We can hurt it. Concentrate on the link between us.'

He reached out clumsily to her with his hand, and hers came to him. Their thoughts mixed and meshed, jumbling together, and then suddenly they both snapped into focus, sharp and brilliant, and their minds merged to become a synergetic whole. It leapt up and out from the cramped confines of their bodies and struck at the thinking machine in a lightning flash of roaring energies. The force field didn't even slow it.

The machine howled horribly, feeling its destruction, and then its centre shattered into a million quiescent pieces and the rest collapsed in upon itself.

The Ghost Warriors fell to the floor and lay still, not even twitching. Their brain was dead.

The entity that had been formed by Silence and Frost split apart, and they came back into their bodies. Their minds slowed, weighed down by flesh again, and they both immediately began to forget what it had been like to be more than human -- they had to, or they might have lost being human forever, and they weren't ready to do that, just yet.

They stood staring at each other for a long moment.

'We can't tell anyone about this,' Silence said finally. 'You know what they'd do to us.'

'We have a duty to inform our superiors,' said Frost. 'Perhaps by examing us they could find a way to duplicate the process.'

'More likely they'd kill us by taking us apart to see what makes us tick. It wasn't a human technology that changed us, made us what we are. Besides, Lionstone would order us destroyed the moment she heard about us. She'd never allow anything as powerful as us to exist in her Empire. But we don't have to decide right now. We can talk about it later. For the moment, how are we going to explain what happened here?'

'No problem,' said Frost. She drew her disrupter and blew apart what was left of the control mechanism, leaving nothing but a scorch mark on the steel floor. 'A lucky shot. As simple as that.'

'Show-off,' said Silence, and activated his comm implant. 'Bridge, this is the captain. Status report, please. The Ghost Warriors are down, right?'

'I don't know how you did it,' said Stelmach, 'but, according to the reports coming in, the Ghost Warriors all over the ship just collapsed. It's over, and we've won. Amazing. I wouldn't have bet on it. I may faint.'

'Try to hang on until we get back to the bridge,' said Silence. 'You did well, Stelmach. If you hadn't theorized a central control device and tracked it down, they'd probably have been scooping our brains out with dull spoons by now. You're a hero, just like the rest of your family.'

'Some hero. I didn't volunteer to go over to the *Champion* with you.'

'There are different kinds of hero,' said Silence. 'What's important is that you came through when it mattered. So be told. Silence out.'

Silence and Frost leaned on the walkway railing together, looking down into the hangar bay. The Ghost Warriors hadn't moved but Silence kept an eye on them anyway.

'I thought we were heading back to the bridge,' said Frost.

'In a minute,' said Silence. 'After all we've been through I think we're entitled to a short break to get our breath back.'

'We do lead interesting lives,' said Frost. 'At least this time we didn't lose the ship.'

'Right,' said Silence. 'I think we're finally getting the hang of this hero thing.' He thought for a moment, and then looked at Frost. 'Do you really believe those voices we heard at the beginning were part of the Shub trap?'

'Of course,' said Frost. 'What else could they have been?'

Silence shrugged uncomfortably. 'I don't know. It's just . . . they seemed to be *warning* us as much as anything.'

'But if they didn't come from the *Champion*, where did they come from? Cross said he recognized his grandfather's voice among them, and that was his grandfather who blasted him on the *Champion*.'

'I don't know where else they could have come from. On the whole, I'd rather not think about it. The implications are too disturbing.'

'Ah, hell,' said Frost. 'Everyone knows it gets strange out here on the Rim.'

CHAPTER SEVEN

The Circles of Hell

The monitor screen spun a few fractals as its memory warmed up, and then the flaring colours resolved into a sharp holo image of a break metallic horizon, crenulated here and there. Shadowy trenches, deep craters and looming hills of metal scrap stretched away for miles before vanishing into the early-morning gloom. A dull red sun was rising reluctantly in a grey sky dominated by darkening clouds. The scene was unnaturally quiet, with not even a whisper from beast or bird or insect. The only sound was that of the rising wind, moaning and roaring in turn as though gathering its strength for a storm to come.

The camera panned slowly right and a huge factory complex appeared on the screen. Given its great size and tall towers, and the many-coloured lights blazing from its windows, it should have dominated the bleak scene, but somehow it didn't. The surrounding area of fractured metals and accumulated scrap looked like the place where old factories went to die. The camera zoomed in slowly, until the factory filled the screen. Armoured guards could now be seen, watching coldly from their trenches and gun emplacements, and it quickly became clear that the factory was under siege from some unseen, ominous foe.

A single figure stepped into view before the camera, making its way carefully over the rutted metal surface. Mud and water had collected in the hollows and splashed up over the man's boots. He finally came to a halt, half-filling the screen, and looked seriously into the camera. Even buried inside a thick fur coat he was clearly short and overweight, and above his ruddy face his flat blond hair was plastered to his skull. But his eyes were calm and his mouth was firm and, without quite knowing why, you felt you could trust him to tell you the truth. The rising wind tried to ruffle his hair, flapping the long ends, but he ignored it.

'You're looking at Technos III, early morning, early winter. The factory complex behind me, owned and run by Clan Wolfe, will shortly begin mass-production of the new and vastly improved stardrive. The workers are dedicated, the management strong and decisive, and the small army of guards is trained, experienced and utterly determined. Ideal conditions, one would have thought, for such an important venture. But this is Technos III, and things are different here.

'To begin with, while this planet has the usual four seasons, like any colonized world, its seasons last only two days. Weather conditions therefore understandably tend to the extreme. In the spring it rains, a constant hammering monsoon that can deliver over an inch of rain in under an hour, every hour. In the summer it bakes, and the bare sunlight is hot enough to blister unprotected skin in minutes. In the autumn there are hurricanes strong enough to pick up unsecured equipment and carry it for miles. In the winter it snows: thick blizzards and heavy drifts bury the surface and anything else not protected by the factory's force screen. Exposure to the cold can kill a person in minutes. Blood freezes. Some metals crack.

'These conditions are not natural, of course. No habitable planet could orbit its primary in a mere eight days. Those meddling computer terrorists, the cyberats, are responsible. They fiddled with the planet's weather satellites a couple of centuries ago, and this changing hell is the result. I'm standing here outside the factory in the early hours of the first day of winter. The temperature has dropped thirty degrees in the last hour, and the winds, which temporarily fell at the end of autumn, are rising again, giving warning of the blizzards to come. Soon I will have to return to the safety of the factory complex or risk death from any one of a dozen natural causes. Empire technicians are urgently working to repair the weather satellites, and the word is that they will have normal conditions restored soon. In the meantime, the brave men and women of Clan Wolfe struggle valiantly to bring all systems on-line so that mass-production of the new stardrive can begin as scheduled, as promised. I will, of course, be here to show you the inauguration ceremony, live.

'This is Tobias Shreck, for Imperial News, on Technos III. Cold, bored, tired, pissed-off – really, *really* pissed-off – and bloody hungry.'

The picture on the monitor screen disappeared. It was replaced for a moment by spinning fractals; then one of the two men watching it leaned over and turned it off. Tobias Shreck – known also as Toby the Troubador, PR flak for Clan Shreck, and as that stupid prat who managed to upset his Uncle Gregor so much that he had to seek refuge by freelancing on a hellworld like Technos III – straightened up from the monitor and glared at the lowering sky. The darkening clouds were appreciably thicker now, and the gusting wind was so strong he had to brace himself against it. He huddled inside his fur coat, pulled out a filthy-looking handkerchief and blew his nose noisily.

'I hate this place. The weather's insane, the natives are as friendly as a serial killer on amphetamines and there isn't a decent restaurant on the whole damn' planet. I should have known there had to be some underhand reason for home office's eagerness to sign me up and send me off on an immediate assignment.'

'Think positive,' said his cameraman, a tall gangling sort called Flynn. He was wearing a long heavy coat of assorted dead animals that still wasn't long enough to accommodate someone of his great height. He had an honest-seeming face; the impression of honesty was only partly undermined by the holocamera sitting on his shoulder like a squat, deformed owl. He set about dismantling the lights that had shown Toby to his best advantage, and carried on speaking with a blithe disregard as to whether or not Toby was still listening. 'At least we've got nice warm quarters in the complex. Those poor sods on guard duty are wearing thermal suits on top of their thermal underwear, and they're still freezing their butts off. I hear that, if you fart out here in the winter, the fart rolls down your trouser-leg on to the ground and breaks.'

Toby sniffed. 'Those guards are highly paid mercenaries. They're well trained in the art of rendering people down into their component atoms in the shortest time possible, and therefore by definition they're not really human. You can bet their salaries are a damn' sight bigger than yours or mine. And the complex gives me the creeps. Most of the factory's automated, and the clone workers who do everything the machinery can't are even less human than the guards.'

Flynn shrugged, and his camera grabbed his shoulder with clawed feet to steady itself. 'Clones aren't employed for their social skills. They're designed and conditioned to within an inch of their humanity to be the perfect workforce, and nothing else. They're here only because there has to be a human decision-making presence at all times. Can't just leave it to the computers. Not after the Shub rebellion.'

'We can, of course, cut the last few seconds from the tape,' Toby said heavily, turning away from the monitor. 'Did I miss out anything important?'

'Not really. Technically, you should have mentioned that it was the Campbells who started the ball rolling here, before the Wolfes took it over. And you could have mentioned there are a few local problems with terrorists, which will undoubtedly be sorted out soon.'

'No, I couldn't,' said Toby formally. 'The Wolfes would only censor it. We don't need any depth for an introductory piece. Leave it until the interviews, and I'll try to bring it up then – though you can be sure nothing even remotely good about the Campbells will make it into the final cut. Doesn't make any difference. The Wolfes won the hostile takeover, and no one likes a loser. Let's get inside, Flynn. I can't feel my fingers and my feet aren't talking to me. God, I wish I were back on Golgotha. Even attending Court was safer than this.'

'Why are you here?' said Flynn. 'You never have got round

395

to explaining just what you did to get Gregor Shreck so mad at you.'

'I don't have to tell you anything,' said Toby mock-defensively. 'You haven't even told me what your other name is.'

'One name is all a cameraman needs. Now spill all the grisly details, or I'll make you look really podgy on camera.'

'Blackmailer. All right, basically, the Church was growing increasingly dubious about the moral probity of its ostensibly faithful son Gregor. I'd been keeping his extremely dubious private habits under wraps through some inventive PR and heavy backhanders where they would do the most good, but stories kept getting out anyway. There was talk of a full Church investigation, and if that had happened even all Gregor's money and social standing might not have been enough to buy him a clean bill of health – nasty, disgusting little toad that he is. I told him he'd have to keep a lower profile once he got in bed with the Church, but would he listen? Would he hell. So I did the only thing left to me. I figured out who would most likely end up running the investigating team, set the guy up with a young lady of the evening, let nature take its merry course, recorded it all on film from every angle, and blackmailed him. How was I to know I'd picked one of the few really honest men left in the Church these days? He told all, made a public confession, and I resigned from Gregor's employ before he could fire me. Bearing in mind that Gregor's displeasure tends to be expressed through sudden violence and assassination, I walked into Imperial News and asked for the first assignment they had on the far side of the Empire. And I ended up here. Sometimes I wonder if Gregor got to them first.'

'Maybe he did,' said Flynn.

'No. He's not that subtle. Being subtle was what he employed me for.'

'Well, maybe the winter won't be as bad as everyone says. It *couldn't* be that bad.'

Toby glared at him. 'Didn't you watch the briefing tapes? The winters they have here could be officially classified as cruel and unnatural punishment. Snowstorms start with a blizzard and then escalate. The winds in winter reach three hundred miles an hour! It snows sideways!' Toby stopped, and took a deep breath to calm himself. His doctor had warned him about his blood pressure, but his doctor had never had to work on Technos III.

He scowled up at the sky, and then back at the factory. 'We'd better get under cover. Bring the equipment.'

'You brought it out here,' said Flynn. 'You take it back. I do not fetch and carry. It's in my contract. I am a cameraman, and the only thing I carry is my camera. I told you that when we started out.'

'Oh, come on,' said Toby. 'You can't expect me to carry the lights and the monitor. All you ever carry is that bloody camera, and if it weighs more than ten ounces I'll eat the bloody thing.'

'I don't move things,' said Flynn. 'It's not in my nature. If you wanted a pack mule you should have brought one.'

Toby glowered at him, and then started gathering up the lights. 'God, you people have a good union.'

Daniel and Stephanie Wolfe, in charge of stardrive production and therefore Lords of all they surveyed on Technos III, helped themselves to another large drink from the automated bar. As aristocrats they were normally accustomed to the luxury of human servants, but such frills and fancies had no place on a factory world, even for distinguished visitors like the Wolfes. The drinks weren't very good, either.

Stephanie threw herself sulkily into a large supportive chair that tried to give her a soothing massage before she turned the mechanism off. She didn't want to be soothed. Cardinal Kassar was on his way, and she needed to feel in full control for the encounter. Daniel was stalking back and forth across the deep-pile carpet like a caged animal, and she wished he wouldn't. It was getting on her nerves.

The room was comfortably large by Technos III standards, which meant you might have squeezed ten people into it at most, and only then if you happened to have a crowbar handy. The furnishings were understated to the point of anonymity, and the over-bright lighting was giving Stephanie a headache.

Daniel finally stopped his pacing and accessed the factory's external sensors. One wall disappeared behind a representation of what the weather looked like outside. Mostly it looked like snow, being blown sideways by very strong winds that had the disconcerting habit of shooting from left to right and then back again just a little faster than the human eye could comfortably cope with. Stephanie turned in her chair so she wouldn't have to look at it, and concentrated on her gameplan.

Ostensibly, Valentine had sent them here to see that everything went smoothly until mass-production of the new stardrive officially began. He'd arranged a ceremony for the big day, to be transmitted live across the Empire in prime time to remind everyone, and especially those at Court, where Wolfe money and power came from. Actually, Stephanie had arranged everything. She'd planted the idea of a ceremony in Valetine's mind and then intrigued quietly but continually behind the scenes to ensure that it would be she and Daniel who would attend the ceremony, rather than Valentine himself. A live broadcast would present the perfect opportunity to throw some heavy but undetectable spanners into the works, slow down if not halt stardrive production, and generally make Valentine look incompetent. Such a high-profile failure might be just the lever she and Daniel needed to pry control of the factory away from Valentine and over to them. And then they'd see who *really* ran Clan Wolfe.

The local rebels were still a nuisance, and well before the ceremony would have to be put sharply in their place. But that shouldn't be too much of a problem. Kassar had brought a fair-sized army of the Faithful with him to back up the numerous Wolfe mercenaries. The natives wouldn't know what hit them. On the other hand, the presence of so many security troops could mean that her carefully planned and considered pieces of sabotage would have to be carried out with greater subtlety. If she – or, more likely, Daniel – were to be caught in the act, all the fast talking in the world wouldn't be enough to save them. Valentine would seize the opportunity to discredit them, and quite possibly expel them from the Family. It was what Stephanie would do in his position.

She looked up, and there was Daniel, still staring at the *faux* window. She knew he wasn't seeing the storm outside.

'Let it go, Daniel,' she said softly. 'Our father is dead and gone, and there's nothing you or I can do about it.'

'No, he's not dead,' said Daniel, and would not turn away from the storm. 'You saw him in the Court. His body's dead, but those bastard AIs on Shub repaired it. Daddy's still alive in there, trapped in a decaying corpse. He recognized me. Spoke to me. We have to rescue him, bring him home.'

'What you saw was just a Ghost Warrior,' said Stephanie, her voice carefully even. 'A dead body held together by servomechanisms and run by computer implants. It was just a machine talking, imitating our father. A composite programme, probably derived from father's public holo appearances. The man we knew is dead. He doesn't need us any more. Forget him.'

'I can't.' Daniel finally turned his head to look at her, and there was something in his face that gave Stephanie pause. His normally pouting mouth was set in a firm line, and his gaze was steady, determined. 'For once I'm not going to let you talk me out of something I know is right. If there's even a chance Daddy is still alive, I have to rescue him. I have to. I let him down so often when he was alive; I can't fail him now he's dead. You don't need me here. The sabotage is your plan. Kassar can take care of the rebel problem for you. He's got experience in things like that. I can't think about anything like that any more. The rebels don't matter. The factory doesn't matter. Wolfes come first – always.'

Stephanie heaved herself up out of her chair and moved quickly over to join Daniel before the window. 'I need you here, Danny. You're my strength. Stay here with me, at least until after the ceremony. We can send agents out to locate our father, and discover what his true state is. People who know about these matters. And that way we can keep things quiet. After all, there are a lot of people with a vested interest in seeing that our father *doesn't* return to head the Family again.'

She saw the decision in his eyes before he nodded reluctantly, and she sighed with relief. Daniel was too much a wild card to be allowed to run loose. She needed him at her side, where she could control what he saw and said. He meant well but he lacked her vision, her focus. She knew what was best for the Family, and it didn't include charging blindly all over the Empire on a fool's errand. Dear Daddy was dead, and that was for the best, too. She'd have had him killed eventually, anyway: he had been in her way.

'If I'm going to stay, find something for me to do,' said Daniel. 'I feel useless here.'

'Perhaps you'd care to work with my troops,' said Cardinal Kassar. 'Always room for another brave warrior in the service of the Church.'

They both turned sharply, Daniel's hands clenching into fists. Stephanie nodded coolly to the cardinal; she wouldn't give him the satisfaction of appearing flustered, even if she wasn't sure how much he might have overheard. The cardinal stood grandly in the open doorway, his chin held high. He was wearing full battle armour, despite the supposed safety of the factory's private quarters. This might be Church paranoia, or it might be a veiled insult to the Wolfes, a hint that he didn't trust them to ensure his safety. Stephanie thought he was most likely wearing it because he thought it made him look strong and soldierly – in which case it was almost successful. The great bas-relief crucifix on his chest tried hard to draw the eye, but Kassar's ravaged face would not be ignored. The scarred side of his face looked more like a skull than a living countenance, even down to the gleaming teeth visible through the rents in his cheek.

Stephanie managed a gracious smile, but didn't move, and stuck close beside Daniel so that he wouldn't either. Let Kassar come to them.

The cardinal was late, but she'd expected that. Kassar was the kind of man who always kept people waiting, just to show

how important he was. Especially since he had been ordered to Technos III, he needed little victories like this to sustain him. Officially, the posting was an opportunity. The Church had sent him, an army of the Faithful and a dozen elite Jesuit commandoes to help the Wolfe forces defeat the rebel terrorists. The Church of Christ the Warrior didn't normally do favours for the aristocracy, let alone Clan Wolfe, but as with everyone else the Church's future power was dependent on gaining access to the new stardrive. Those who got there first would have a temporary but very real advantage over those who did not. And the Church had not got where it was by ignoring advantages. The fact that the Church despised the Wolfe Family in general, and its current head Valentine in particular, could not be allowed to get in the way of political oneupmanship.

Kassar himself, more than anyone else in the Church, had no love for the Wolfes, but in fact he had lobbied almost savagely for the posting. The war on Technos III was another chance to show what he could do as a commander of troops, and that was the fast track to advancement within the Church: piety was all very well, but it was victory in arms that got you promoted. And, though he barely admitted it even to himself, Kassar needed to be sure of his own courage. He couldn't help feeling he'd made rather a poor showing, that day at Court when the Ghost Warrior and the Fury and the alien had broken loose. He could have done something, something brave and commanding to save the day, but instead he'd just stood there with his mouth hanging open, like all the others. People must have seen him doing nothing, even if no one had dared to mention it to his face. So he had come to Technos III to win a great victory, whatever the cost. Then nobody would have any doubts about his valour. Not even him.

The three stood looking at each other for a long moment, all with their own private thoughts. None wanted to make the first move. Finally Stephanie took a step forward and extended a hand to Kassar. He accepted the hand and bowed curtly over it. His handshake was firm but brief. Daniel stayed where he was, just nodding briefly. Kassar nodded back.

'Welcome to Technos III, Cardinal,' said Stephanie, her voice gracious but cool. 'Sorry about the weather but, if you don't like it, stick around and something else will come along shortly. The weather here changes its mind like a village priest caught between two sins. I trust your men are settling in comfortably?'

'My men are preparing for their first assault on the rebel positions,' said Kassar. 'Comforts can wait. You've let the terrorists get away with far too much, but, given the small size of your forces, I can't say I'm surprised. Why haven't you pressed some of the factory workers into service? I can supply whatever arms and armour might be needed.'

'I think not, Cardinal,' said Stephanie. 'All the workers here are clones, bred and designed solely for factory work . . . and you don't give clones weapons.'

Kassar shrugged carelessly to cover his *faux pas*. 'As you wish. My troops are more than enough to get the job done. Now, Daniel, what do you say? Shall I find a place for you in our ranks?'

'Wolfes don't fight for other people,' Daniel said flatly. 'We fight for ourselves.'

A silence fell that might have been awkward, as each party present was damned if they'd be the first to break it, but the tension was broken by Toby the Troubador and his cameraman Flynn bustling in through the open door. Toby nodded briskly around and gestured to Flynn that he should find a position where he could cover everyone with his camera.

'Morning, one and all,' Toby said cheerfully. 'Isn't is a perfectly awful day? Hope I'm not interrupting anything vital, but I really do need to get some footage of the cardinal meeting his hosts – that kind of thing always plays well with the audience, and it'll make a good introduction to the campaign to come. Don't worry, I'll keep it short and to the point. I'm sure you've all got things you'd rather be doing.'

Daniel gave Toby his best intimidating scowl. 'Is this really necessary?'

'I'm afraid so,' said Stephanie quickly. 'PR can be a bore and a bind, but we can't do without it. Public Acclaim can often get you things that nothing else can. The stardrive ceremony will be an important event, and I want it covered very thoroughly. After all, absolutely everyone will be watching. Grit your teeth and bear it, Daniel. It'll soon be over.'

'That's the spirit,' said Toby. 'Cardinal, if you'd care to stand between the Wolfes, make a nice group for the camera . . .'

Kassar glared at him but moved obediently to stand between Stephanie and Daniel. Though they stood close together, none of them so much as nudged another with an elbow. Toby bustled around them, raising an arm here, squaring a shoulder there.

'All right, people, just hold the pose while Flynn gets the lighting right and then we'll do a short interview. Nothing complicated, just how glad you all are the cardinal's here, that sort of thing. Fake the smiles if you have to.'

'You are aware, Shreck,' said Kassar coldly, 'that your uncle is currently being investigated by the Church on charges of sedition and corruption?'

'Nothing to do with me,' Toby said airily. 'You can haul him off in chains for all I care. Just give me some warning so I can get the rotten fruit concession.'

'He is the head of your Family,' said Daniel. 'You owe him allegiance. Have you no honour?'

'Of course not,' said Toby. 'I'm a journalist.'

'We will of course want to see all reports in their entirety before they can be transmitted,' said Stephanie, 'so that they can be checked for bias and possible inaccuracies.'

'The Church censors will also examine all footage,' Kassar said quickly, 'to check for blasphemies or disrespect. Standards must be maintained.'

Toby kept smiling, although his cheeks were beginning to ache from the strain. 'Of course. Whatever you wish. Don't worry about inconveniencing me. I'm used to working with people looking over my shoulder.'

He fussed the three of them about some more, partly to get the best grouping for the camera and partly just because he could. He'd expected *some* kind of censorship, but he could see that getting anything interesting off Technos III was going to take a lot of hard work, a little subtlety and every dirty trick in the journalist's handbook. Still, when in doubt let the material go over their heads. They can't censor what they don't recognize. He had great hopes of what this Technos III material might do for him and his career, and he wasn't going to let these three stuffed shirts get in his way. The day he couldn't think rings round any censor they could throw at him he'd give up journalism and go into politics. They'd believe anything there.

This was his first real assignment in too many years, after having spent so long buried in the Shrecks' Public Relations department because Gregor needed him there. The right kind of reporting on Technos III could make his reputation, establish him as a journalist and commentator. Toby wanted that. The essence of a good PR man is that no one should notice his work. Toby felt very strongly that he'd earned a chance to show off his talents more visibly. Of course, he couldn't hope to make much of a splash just covering the events leading up to the stardrive ceremony: the real story lay in covering the Technos III conflict, the Wolfe and Church forces versus the rebel terrorists. And he was going to cover it, whatever the Wolfes and the Church tried to do to stop him.

He looked back at Flynn, who nodded briefly to show he was ready. The camera on Flynn's shoulder studied the three dignitaries with its red owl eye; it was linked into Flynn's own eyes through his comm implant, so that he saw what it saw. Daniel and Stephanie and Kassar smiled determinedly, all friends together, ready for their interview. As in all politics, individual problems disappeared in the need to present a solid front to a common enemy.

The Church ship *Divine Breath* hung in orbit around Technos III, comfortably far above the seething weather. Ostensibly the crew were on guard, but mostly they were just goofing off in the absence of the cardinal and his Jesuit enforcers. After all, they had nothing to do but watch a few sensors while they waited for the cardinal's troops to make short work of a few native malcontents. Easy work. Everyone knew there wasn't a rebel born who could stand against the trained troops of the Faithful. So it was a soft duty for once, and the crew were taking advantage of it.

Which was why, when the giant golden Hademan ship dropped suddenly out of hyperspace just above them, they took one look and all but shat themselves. The huge ship hung above them, dwarfed the Church vessel like a killer shark next to a minnow. The Church crew snapped to attention at their posts, their hands moving desperately over their control panels. Shields slammed into place as guns powered up, and even those whose piety wasn't all it might have been found a sudden need to send up prayers of the most fervent kind.

The Hadenman ship opened fire, and the *Divine Breath* shuddered as a disrupter cannon hammered against its shields. The Church ship fired back as fast as it could get its guns to bear, but the golden vessel was impossibly fast for its size and the crew of the *Divine Breath* knew they were hopelessly outclassed. They fought on anyway, not so much through faith as because there was nothing else they could do. They couldn't drop into hyperspace without lowering the shields first, and the moment they did that the Hadenman ship would blow them apart.

The captain of the *Divine Breath* watched the shields go down one by one, and called for more power, even though he knew he was already using everything the ship's straining engines could produce. If only he'd had one of the new stardrives being produced on the planet below he might have stood a better chance. The irony was not lost on him.

Just then, as he searched frantically for something, anything, to do to stave off the inevitable, the great golden ship disappeared back into hyperspace.

The captain blinked a few times, clutched at the crucifix on his uniform collar and muttered a few Hail Marys, and then flopped back in his command chair, cold sweat on his forehead. His ship had survived, but he was damned if he knew why. When he finally got his strength back he cancelled the Red Alert and ordered full damage reports and a complete sensor sweep of the surrounding space. He then wondered what the hell he was going to say to the cardinal. Kassar would have to be told, even though he'd probably shout a lot. The captain frowned, trying hard to come up with some viable-sounding excuse that wouldn't get him court martialled or excommunicated. There was no getting away from the fact that he and his crew had been caught with their pants around their ankles but, dammit, it had been a *Hadenman* ship! There weren't many who'd seen one of those in action and lived to tell of it.

The captain and his crew carried on working hard on their various explanations, which was part of the reason why they never noticed the heavily shielded escape pod that the Hadenman ship had dropped just before it disappeared.

The pod hurtled down through the buffeting clouds and howling winds, battered this way and that by the storm's fury but still somehow holding to its planned descent course. Inside the pod, Jack Random, Ruby Journey and Alexander Storm clung desperately to their crash webbing and waited for the long drop to end. The pod's outer hull groaned and squealed from the pressures it endured, and the sensors blinked out one by one until the ship was practically flying blind. The crash webbing cushioned and absorbed most of the shocks the pod encountered as it fell on and on into Technos III's turbulent atmosphere, but the three rebels were still flung this way and that.

Storm gritted his teeth and tried hard to hang on to his last meal. Random ignored it all, concentrating on what he was going to do when he finally landed. It was his first time back in the business of armed rebellion after all this while and, though he was quite definitely looking forward to it, he couldn't help but worry. It had been a *long* time, and he wasn't the man he used to be. Of course, that wouldn't stop him giving this mission his all. And, if in the end everything went to blazes, what better way for a professional rebel to die than with gun and sword in his hands and a pile of the enemy dead at his feet? Random sucked in his breath. Actually, he could think of a dozen better ways to make his final exit, most including a good wine and a bad woman, but he doubted he'd see any of them. Rebels rarely died in bed.

Beside him, Ruby Journey was laughing and whooping loudly as she spun to and fro in her webbing, enjoying every minute of the trip down. Random smiled at her. How could you not love a woman like that? He checked the sensor panels again, but they were still out – the pod's sensor spikes must have been torn away by the shrieking winds. The proximity alarms sounded, harsh and strident, and Random braced himself. Either they were near the ground or they were about to crash into a mountain. Ruby whooped even more wildly. Storm had his eyes squeezed shut, as though that would make any difference. Random sighed, and tried to remember if there were any mountains on Technos III. He didn't think so, but it would have been nice to have been sure.

The escape pod slowed as the engines gave up the last of their power to cushion the landing. The three occupants, pinned helplessly in their webbing, listened to the inner and outer hulls cracking from the strain. The lights went off, to be replaced by the dull red glow of emergency lighting. And then the pod slammed into the metallic surface of Technos III, ploughed a long path through the scattered scrap and debris, and finally came to a halt against a massive steel spur. The craft rocked back and forth before finally settling itself. The sky was dark and forbidding, the winds were rising, and the first snows were beginning to fall.

Inside the pod, Storm still had his eyes shut tight, and was trying to remember how to breathe. Random lay slumped in his webbing and thought, not for the first time, that he was getting a little old for all this. Ruby Journey wiped at her bloody nose with the back of her hand and laughed happily.

'That was great! Let's do it again!'

'Let's not,' said Storm, still not opening his eyes. 'I've had more fun in front of a firing squad. Next time, may I suggest we try and find a pod that's a little less past its sell-by date? Oh God, I feel awful. Somebody please tell me we are safely down, because I'm not budging an inch until I'm sure the drop is over. And I want it in writing. With witnesses.'

'Shut up, Alex,' said Random easily. 'We're down in one piece, and that's all I ever ask from a landing. And, for an escape pod that's been sitting around in a Hadenman ship unused and untested for decades, I think this did pretty well.'

'Now he tells us,' said Storm. 'I knew there was a good reason why I gave up personal appearances as a rebel.'

'Ruby,' said Random, 'the sensors are all shot. Crack open the hatch and see what's outside.'

Ruby disentangled herself from her webbing, threw Random a professional salute, and made her way carefully over the slanting floor to the one and only hatch. Random clambered slowly out of his own webbing, wincing at several new bruises and a few old injuries, and moved over to persuade Storm to open his eyes. Ruby opened the hatch and pushed it outwards. The metal resisted a moment, and then gave way. A blast of cold air and swirling snow swept into the pod, along with just enough light to fade the emergency lights to a rather sweet pink colour.

At last Storm raised his eyelids. 'Oh, wonderful. We've landed inside a birthday cake.'

'Shut up, Alex,' said Random again. 'Ruby, what's it like out there?'

'Cold,' said Ruby brightly. 'And there's enough snow coming down to make an army of snowmen. There's no sign anywhere of a welcoming committee.'

Random scowled. 'According to the handful of instruments that are still working, we are in the right place, more or less. No doubt our contacts will be here soon. They must have seen us come down. Hurry up, Alex – shake a leg. We have a revolution to organize.'

'I never did like fieldwork,' said Storm, moving painfully towards the hatch. 'Undercover is a young man's job. Usually a young man who won't be missed too badly if it all turns disastrous.'

'Whinge, whinge, whinge,' said Random, half-pushing

Storm out the hatch. 'Anyone would think you weren't happy to be here, striking a blow for freedom and democracy.'

'Anyone would be right,' said Storm, and then fell silent as the full force of the cold hit him.

The three huddled together in the lee of the escape pod, sheltering from the driving storm. The pod's metal surface was already disappearing under a thick blanket of snow, and the rising wind was whipping up into a blizzard. They all turned up the heating elements in their clothes, hugged themselves fiercely and beat their hands together. The chill was sharp enough to reduce their voices to whispers, and their breath steamed thickly about their heads. The snow was so thick the sun and sky were completely hidden. It was supposed to be midday, but there was hardly enough light to see by. Random could feel Storm shivering violently beside him, and began to be concerned. Storm's old bones couldn't surve this iciness for long. Random didn't feel the cold too badly – but then he, like Ruby, had been through the Madness Maze.

'This is undoubtedly a silly question,' said Storm through teeth that were clenched to keep them from chattering, 'but why can't we get back inside the pod? It's got to be warmer in there than out here.'

'The pod's heaters got knocked out along with everything else,' said Random, 'and there's a small but definite chance the batteries are leaking poisonous gases. If you want to take your mind off the cold, keep your eyes open for our contacts. In this blizzard they could walk right past us without noticing. Mind you, if they don't come soon, we may have to risk the gases. It's plain you can't handle cold like this.'

'I can handle any cold you can, you old fart,' Storm said angrily. 'I'm only six years older than you, I'll have you remember.'

'Sure, Alex. Now shut up and conserve your strength.'

'Always were a bossyboots, Jack.'

'How far are we from the rebel base?' said Ruby, for once trying hard to be tactful.

'We don't know,' said Storm. 'As you'll recall, they wouldn't tell us – just gave us landing coordinates and told us we'd be contacted when we arrived. I hate going into situations blind. I just hope the paranoid bastards find us before the Empire forces do. We were promised a distraction to keep them occupied somewhere else, but I'm growing less trusting by the second. Moreover, I'm losing all feeling in my extremities.'

'Don't worry,' said Random. 'At your age you don't use them for much anyway.'

'You can go off people, you know,' said Storm.

They fell silent for a while, the cold air searing their lungs. The three of them huddled closer together, trying to share their warmth, eyes straining against the swirling snow. Dark outcroppings of metal showed dimly through the blizzard, but there was no sign of life anywhere. Random beat his gloved hands together and looked longingly at the thick furs over Ruby's bounty-hunter leathers. He'd thought she had insisted on wearing them just to keep up her barbarian image, but maybe she'd paid more attention at the briefings than he had. He wouldn't be surprised. There was a sharp mind at work behind her carefully crafted persona. He coughed and sneezed harshly. Something in the air was irritating his throat. Even allowing for the bitter cold, the air was thicker than he was used to, and it smelled as though someone else had breathed it first. The locals had assured him it was breathable, at least in the short term. Random suspected it was an acquired taste. They'd said much the same about the changing weather, but Random wasn't convinced. Also according to the locals, the blizzard offered good cover for a landing. Random wondered if he'd be allowed to shoot the person who'd said that for criminal understatement.

He looked across at Storm, and his concern grew. There was no colour left in the man's face, and he was shuddering violently. Random gestured at Ruby, and she took off her furs and wrapped them around Storm. It seemed to help him a little. Ruby wouldn't feel the difference: she'd been through the Maze, too. Random frowned. He'd been thinking of Storm as an old man, someone who ought to be happily retired, sitting in a book-lined study beside a blazing fire with adoring grandchildren at his feet, but as the man had said, he really wasn't much older than Random. Random still mostly remembered Storm as a tousle-headed young warrior, always laughing, ready to throw himself into the thick of things at a moment's notice. But that had been a long time ago – and Random was shocked to realize just *how* long. Storm had to be in his early fifties by now, and the long years of struggle had not been kind to him. Random frowned and wondered if maybe he should not have brought Storm with him after all. Storm had volunteered, but then he'd never been able to say no to Jack Random.

Random's frown deepened. He didn't think of himself as old, even after all he'd been through, so he supposed Storm didn't either. But they sure as hell weren't young any more.

Ruby suddenly pushed herself away from the shelter of the pod, and stared out into the storm. 'Heads up, people. Company's coming.'

'Can you see them?' said Random, stepping forward to stand beside her.

'No, but I can *feel* them. They're coming this way.'

Random concentrated, but couldn't detect anything. The Maze had changed them all in different ways.

The first dark shapes began to appear out of the snow, and Storm forced himself to move forward and stand with his friends. It was a matter of pride.

There were ten locals finally, standing before them all wrapped in furs, their faces hidden behind leather and metal masks in the shapes of stylized animal heads, none of which Random recognized. Except to note that they were all pretty damn ugly. One of the locals stepped forward, looked at the trio, and then pulled aside his mask to reveal a grim, heavily bearded visage. It was a hard-used face, and could have been any age. Several long scars marred the man's deeply pitted features, and his eyes were very dark.

'Where are the rest of you?' he said harshly, looking at Ruby.

'We're all there is,' Random said calmly. 'You talk to us about the local situation and, if we're convinced, we'll contact the underground and they'll send armed volunteers, weapons and supplies. You understand there are a lot of calls on our limited resources, and so we have to be sure they go where they're most needed. I'm Jack Random. These people are Ruby Journey and Alexander Storm. Give them plenty of room. They bite. Whom do I have the honour of addressing?'

'You're *Random?*' said the local incredulously. 'I thought . . .'

'Yes,' said Random regretfully, 'most people do. Just try and think of my age as experience on the hoof. Is there somewhere else we could continue this conversation? Somewhere a few degrees above absolute zero?'

'Of course. I'm Tall John. I command here. Follow me.'

He pulled his mask back into place, turned and set off into the storm without looking back. The locals went after him, as silently as they'd arrived. Random grabbed Storm and got him moving. Ruby took Storm's other arm, and the three of them stumbled into the blizzard, hurrying as best they could to keep up with Tall John and his people. The pod was quickly obscured in the snow behind them, and they soon lost all sense of direction. No matter where they looked there was only snow, aside from the dark figures trudging on before them.

Time passed, and the bitter cold of the wind cut at them like knives as the pressure of the winds increased. And then the dark figures suddenly began to disappear, one by one. The last turned and beckoned them forward. He pushed aside his mask. Tall John again.

'This is it. Welcome to the outer circles of hell.'

He gestured at his feet, stepped forward, and descended into a gap in the snow that Random could only just make out through the blizzard.

Random moved forward cautiously, and suddenly found himself on the edge of a deep trench, some six feet wide, that fell away deeper than his eyes could follow. He could just make out the steps cut into the near wall, and he followed the retreating Tall John down into the hollow. Storm came next, slowly and very carefully, followed by Ruby. The trench turned out to be in fact only about fifteen feet deep, with snow and slush already ankle-high at its bottom.

Tall John was waiting for them, and he indicated they should follow him into one of the many narrow tunnels leading off from the far wall.

Random went after the local into a dimly lit tunnel that was barely wide enough for two men to walk abreast and so low he had to keep his head bowed to avoid banging it on the roof. Roof and walls were both made of metal, crudely polished in places. He could hear Storm and Ruby following close behind. He glanced back, but Storm seemed to be holding up all right. It was discernibly warmer in the tunnel. The temperature slowly rose as they made their way on, until finally they emerged into a steel cavern some twenty feet by thirty.

The walls had been crudely cut from the compressed scrap metal that covered the planet's surface, and no effort had been made to disguise this. Furniture was absent, and the only light came from scattered candles in glass jars. A central metal brazier contained brightly glowing coals – Storm headed straight for it with his hands outstretched. Random and Ruby joined him, though a little less quickly. They both kept one hand at a time unobstrusively near hidden weapons. Random hadn't lasted this long by trusting people who just happened to turn up at a meeting place. He should have insisted on a password, but there hadn't been time. Random like passwords. They appealed to his sense of the dramatic.

Tall John stripped off the top layer of his furs. He was a tall rangy man with long dark hair, a steady gaze and a mouth set in a stern line. Beside him another of the figures from the storm pulled open her furs to reveal a short, chunky woman with a great mane of knotted dark hair above a pale, round face. She flashed the three newcomers a broad smile, and nodded to them amiably. Like Tall John, time and the world had used her harshly, and she could have been any age at all.

'I'm Throat-Slitter Mary. Don't mind Tall John. When you get to know him he's really a pain in the ass. He and I will speak for the others. You'll meet them later. You're welcome here, but I have to say you're not what we were

413

hoping for. We need reinforcements, weapons and supplies – and lots of them.'

'We didn't expect just two old men and a bounty-hunter,' said Tall John.

Random shrugged, not upset. 'If you can convince us of the strategic importance of your needs you'll get everything you could hope for. So talk to us. Fill us in on what's been happening on Technos III. Your initial contact was intriguing, but short on detail.'

'All right,' said Throat-Slitter Mary. 'Let's be short and to the point. Like me. We're fighting a trench-and-tunnel war with the Empire forces. At the centre of everything is the factory, getting ready to mass-produce the new stardrive. Around the factory lies a series of trench circles. The Empire controls the inner trenches, we control the outer, and we spend most of our time fighting over the ones in the middle. There's maybe fifteen thousand of us left. There used to be a lot more, but the years have whittled us away.

'We're all that remains of the original colonists of Technos III. Our ancestors were indentured workers, paying off the cost of their transport by terraforming the planet and establishing industries. Theoretically, once all the debts were paid off Technos III would be theirs. Only somehow there were always more debts for each new generation.

'The original company in charge went broke. Others came in and took over, running the planet as a business while they asset-stripped it. The companies came and went, but we stayed. We had to. Our ancestors were genetically altered to enable them to survive on this world. Terraforming can do only so much. If you three stayed here long enough, this planet would kill you. Likewise, we couldn't leave this world without some pretty basic changes to our body chemistry, which we've always been denied – officially because it would be too expensive. In reality because where else were they going to find such a useful, trapped work force?

'As one company succeeded another, each more cheapjack than the one before, leaving their failures behind them to poison the land, the whole surface of the planet gradually disappeared under layers of deserted factories, installations and other high-tech junk. And it's been like that right up until today. The Campbells were a bunch of bastards, but the Wolfes are even worse. They don't give a damn for this planet. All they care about is their precious factory. Everything else had been left to rust and rot. We've inherited a world dominated by empty mile-long factories, abandoned construction sites and worked-out mines. The Wolfes, and the Campbells before them, chose this planet precisely because it was such a mess. They could do anything they liked here, and no one would care. Who's going to worry about pollution on a world like this? It's already been poisoned so thoroughly that only people like us, artificially adapted to it, could survive. At first we were an embarrassment, now we're rebel terrorists. All life on this planet except the guards and the clones running the factory has been driven underground. We survive, together. We live off the remaining flora and fauna, and sometimes they live off us, if we're not fast enough. But our time is running out.

'Once the Wolfes have got their factory up and running, they'll be able to afford armies of mercenaries to force us back, so they can build a second factory to go alongside the first, and so on. They won't cease until we're extinct. We have to stop this first factory coming on-line. It's our only hope.'

'Sounds straightforward enough,' Random said briskly. 'It's a regrettably common scenario in the Empire these days, though this is perhaps a more extreme case than most. Tell me about the weather. I gather it's rather unusual here.'

'That's one way of putting it,' said Tall John. 'Ever since the cyberats screwed up the weather satellites, over two hundred years ago, the seasons here have each lasted exactly two days, over and over again. The planet's various owners have been trying to repair the satellites for decades, with no luck whatsoever. Most indigenous life here couldn't adapt, and died out. What little survived did so by being extremely tough – and not a little eccentric. During the winter anything with any sense hibernates. In the spring everything wakes up.

They live, fight and breed in the summer, then feed exhaustively and build nests in the autumn, deep down, away from the razorstorms and the hurricanes. Then they sleep through the winter – it's only two days, after all – so they can wake in the spring and do it all again. The surviving life forms here are nothing if not adaptable. They wouldn't have survived if they weren't.

'And that's Technos III, in a nutshell. Perfect for vacations. Bring the kids. Of course, the war ignores such trivialities as the seasons; it goes on day in, day out, whatever the weather. You've arrived just after autumn has turned to winter; it's the nearest we've got to a quiet time. Our people and the Wolfe mercs take the opportunity for a breather, plan our revenges and bury our dead. But don't think you can relax. You've got maybe two hours before the killing starts again. So welcome to hell, gentlemen and bounty-hunter. Maybe now we can get to the important questions. Like: When are the others coming? How large an army can you supply us with? How many weapons?'

Storm and Ruby both looked at Random. He sighed, and met the Technos III rebels' gaze as calmly as he could. 'I'm afraid there isn't any army. Not yet. The underground is raising volunteers for the great rebellion on hundreds of worlds, but it's a long slow process. Such trained men as we have are scattered across the Empire where they can do the most good. For the moment, we're all you're getting.'

'I don't believe I'm hearing this,' said Tall John, his voice shaking with barely suppressed anger. 'We were promised battle-hardened fighters, led by the legendary Jack Random, the professional rebel. And what do we get? Give me one good reason why I shouldn't just throw the three of you out into the winter to freeze?'

Random snatched the gun out of Tall John's hand, lifted him off his feet with one hand, and pressed the gun under the man's chin. Tall John's eyes bulged as his feet kicked above the floor. Before the surrounding rebels could react, Random put Tall John down again and offered him his gun back. The leader took it automatically, and blinked in confusion. His followers looked at each other uncertainly. Throat-Slitter Mary was grinning.

Tall John pulled his dignity about him again, and nodded curtly to Random. 'Not bad, for an old man.'

'There's more to us than meets the eye,' said Storm smoothly.

'There would have to be,' said Throat-Slitter Mary. 'Well, if you're all we're going to get, we'd better make the most of you. Come with me and I'll introduce you to a few of our strategists. Ragged Tom and Spectre Alice should have a few ideas. They usually do.'

'Interesting names you have here,' said Storm. 'Hasn't the concept of surnames made it this far yet?'

'Our ancestors were indentured workers,' said Tall John. 'Slaves, in all but name. They just had numbers. We're free, so we choose our own names, or accept those given to us by others. Surnames are for people with families and a future. We live from day to day, and depend on no one but ourselves. There's no room for luxuries on Technos III.'

In a small private gymnasium within the hulking residential building attached to the factory Michel Wolfe, reluctant husband to Stephanie, was working out on the parallel bars. Sweat dripped from his bulging muscles as he pushed himself through the strenuous routine his computers had recommended. He grunted and huffed with every effort, scowling with concentration, eyes firmly shut. He'd originally acquired his muscles from a Golgotha body shop and had gone back every now and then for a quick touch-up if they looked like they might be sagging a bit. But out here in the wilds, far from civilization, he had to maintain his muscles the hard way. Michel hated every minute of it. It was entirely too much like hard work: if he'd wanted hard work he wouldn't have married into the aristocracy.

He dropped down from the bars and wiped sweat from his forehead with the back of his hand. The marriage had seemed like a good idea at the time. Now he was beginning to wish he'd stayed an accountant. You knew where you were with figures. If you did your job properly, the numbers added up to a single, undeniable total – no arguments, no opinions, no having to care what anybody else said. Life in the Families wasn't like that. The answer to any question tended to depend on who you were talking to at the time – and heaven help you if you got it wrong or, even worse, didn't care. Everyone was plotting with everyone else and, if you chose the wrong side, death was often the easiest way of losing. And you weren't allowed *not* to choose a side. Just by being part of a Clan you inherited feuds, arguments and hatreds that went back centuries. Michel sighed, and thought about doing fifty sit-ups. And then he thought: no. Let his abdominals sag. See if he minded. He sighed again.

'What's the matter, lover?' said Lily Wolfe from the doorway.

Michel looked round quickly. Lily Wolfe, reluctant wife of Daniel, was standing in the open doorway, striking one of her poses. This was her favourite: one leg forward, chest out, head slightly back. It was designed to pull his eyes up her body, to show off her six-foot-six willowy frame, from her incredible legs all the way up to her pouting mouth. She was wearing another of her pagan-witchy outfits, all flapping silks and earth colours, designed to make her long, pale and interesting. She'd swapped her usual silver wig for a mop of bright red curls that didn't really suit her, but was presumably meant to give her an air of gypsy abandon. It didn't matter. She was beautiful. She was always beautiful. Michel smiled at her in spite of himself. Every time he saw her he fell in love with her all over again, even if it was about as sensible as clutching a live grenade to his bosom. Everyone has one true love in their life, someone who fills their life with light and turns their bones to water, and, God help him, she was his. He reached for the nearby towel and wiped the sweat from his face.

'What brings you here, Lily?' he said finally, trying hard to sound casual, although his pulse was already racing. 'I didn't think you even knew this place existed. And I've told you before: don't call me "lover" in public. It's not safe.'

Lily shrugged. 'There's only one kind of exericse I've ever been interested in. Anything else is just a waste of good sweat. And I've never been interested in being safe, either. Now, are you going to come over here and kiss me or am I going to have to come and get you?'

Michel draped his towel over one shoulder and moved unhurriedly over to join her. It was important to him that he kept some kind of control, even though he knew he'd lost it all the moment he took her in his arms. He had to tilt his head up to kiss her. It was a good six inches shorter than her. It had never bothered him: it just meant that there was that much more of her for him to love. And, when he crushed her in his arms like some long delicate flower and her perfume filled his head like a drug, he didn't give a damn about anything but her.

Lily always said they were made for each other. His dark and swarthy looks complemented her paleness like two sides of the same gypsy coin. They were soulmates, meant for each other, and nothing could keep them apart. She said a lot of things like that, but he didn't usually listen. It was enough that she was there. He belonged to her, body and soul, even though he knew he'd probably end up dying for her if they were ever found out.

He finally pushed her away, though he didn't let go of her. 'This complex may not be as openly bugged as we're used to, but that doesn't mean somebody couldn't be watching us,' he said heavily. 'That bug scrambler of yours has its limits. Daniel and Stephanie may be so preoccupied with getting this factory up and running that we're allowed a longer leash than usual, but we still have to be careful. If they were ever presented with hard evidence of our love they'd have to have us executed or be a laughing-stock. Even worse, they might throw us out of the Family. I love you, Lily, but I won't be poor again for you.'

'You worry too much,' said Lily, laughing silently at him from beneath heavy eyelids.

'And you don't worry enough,' said Michel, meeting her gaze firmly. 'We're here on this benighted back end of nowhere only because our respective spouses don't trust us out of their sight. So far all they have are suspicions. Their egos won't let them believe anything less than hard evidence, so let's not get careless and provide them with any. We have to be careful, Lily. We have so much to lose.'

'You're so boring when you're being sensible,' said Lily. She pouted like a child and pulled out of his arms. 'You should listen more to the ancient voices within you, the dark savage beat of your own primitive emotions. Civilized behaviour is just a cloak we wear, that we can slip off whenever we choose. But . . . well, for once I agree with you. I came here to talk.'

Michel folded his arms across his great chest. 'So talk. I'm listening, darling.'

Lily flashed him a wide smile, and suddenly she didn't look at all childish any more. 'Daniel and Stephanie have a great deal invested in this factory's success. If they were to fail, if something were to go wrong here, they'd have even less time to pay attention to us. So you might say we have a vested interest in their failure. Yes, I thought you'd like that. Now let's take the argument one step further. If they were to die here, you and I would inherit all their worldly goods and their positions in the Family. And, considering that dear Constance doesn't care two hoots about the Family and never has, and that dear Valentine is a complete lunatic whose regular intake of dubious chemicals would suggest he isn't long for this world anyway . . . if we were to play our cards very carefully, we could end up with everything.'

'We could also end up very dead,' said Michel. 'Kill them? Are you crazy? You've been *thinking* again, haven't you? I hate it when you think. Our position is precarious enough as it is. Arranging a plausible accident for the factory is one thing, but if Daniel and Stephanie were to die, whatever the situation, the first people they'd arrest would be me and you. Precisely because we have so much to gain. And you can't lie to an esper.'

'Unless . . . the deaths could clearly be put at someone

else's door,' said Lily calmly. 'Someone who hates them even more than we do. Like the local rebels, perhaps.'

'All right,' said Michel. 'I know I'm going to regret this, but tell me more.'

Lily half-turned away from him, her eyes lost in the distance. 'You've never believed in my witchy powers, Michel, but they've been stronger than ever since we came here. I've . . . seen things, felt things, ridden on the winds of the storm. This is a wild place, and wild things happen here. It calls to me. I feel stronger here, more focused, more daring. You'd be surprised what I dare, lover.'

Michel nodded, but said nothing. He'd always suspected that Lily might have a touch of esp, but it wasn't something you mentioned among the aristocracy. Espers were property – *always*. Apparently the boredom of enforced celibacy and the untamed nature of the planet had combined to stimulate her abilities. Certainly she'd seemed more extreme lately in her emotions and her recklessness.

'All right,' he said mildly, 'so you've got a great future ahead of you as a weather predictor. So what? How does that help us?'

'The wildness of this planet doesn't lie in its weather but in its people,' said Lily. 'I can feel them, out there. Underground. They're planning something big, something we can perhaps take advantage of. You see, I have friends here, dear Michel. Good friends. Powerful friends.'

They both heard footsteps approaching down the corridor outside and broke off, moving away from each other. There was a pause, and then Toby Shreck came trotting through the doorway, smiling professionally, followed more casually by his cameraman Flynn.

Michel and Lily drew themselves up majestically.

'Get out,' said Lily.

'Sorry to bother you,' said Toby breezily, 'but I need to tape a quick interview with you two. Nothing too complicated or challenging – just a simple character piece for inclusion in the documentary your Family's commissioned from me on the opening ceremony. So, if you'll just grant me a few minutes of your time . . .'

'Get out,' said Michel.

'Allow me to point out that your respective spouses are very keen that you should cooperate,' said Toby. 'Trust me. Just lie back and relax and it'll be over before you know it.'

'Get out,' said Lily.

'Honestly,' said Toby, smiling until his cheeks ached, 'you'll enjoy it, once we get started. Haven't you ever wanted to have your face on the holoscreen, broadcast across the entire Empire, in front of a guaranteed audience of practically everyone with a set? The stardrive ceremony is big news. There's bound to be a massive audience. Your names could be on everybody's lips.' He looked hopefully at Lily and Michel, and then shrugged. 'I know: "Get out". Come on, Flynn. We'll try again some other time when they're not feeling so aristocratic.'

He bowed briefly to Lily and Michel and left, followed by Flynn, who didn't bow to anyone. Michel relaxed a little as the door closed behind them.

Lily scowled. 'Impertinent little creep. Speaking to us like that. I can just imagine the sort of questions he had in mind. Publicity like that we don't need. Not with what I've got planned.'

'Well, what precisely have you got planned?' said Michel impatiently. 'And who the hell are these friends of yours? Why haven't you mentioned them to me before? Have you told them about . . . us?'

'I didn't have to,' said Lily. 'They already knew. That's why they came to me.'

'Who the hell *are* they?'

'Clan Chojiro. I've been one of their agents for ages now. They respect my witchy nature, and they pay very well. They had a great many agents in place here already, but through me they now have access to all kinds of levels they couldn't touch before. They're quite willing to see we get everything we want, as long as they get what *they* want. Honestly, things couldn't be working out better for us. Could they?'

'I don't know,' said Michel. 'Conspiring with Clan Chojiro is like shark fishing with yourself as bait. I need time to think about this.'

'Well, think quickly. Someone will be coming here to talk to us any minute now. Our plans can begin any time. The last piece of the puzzle is just about to arrive.'

'I hate it when you become allusive. I assume we're talking about a double agent. What makes him so special?'

'He's a Jesuit commando,' said a calm voice behind them, 'which means he has access to all the security systems in and around the factory complex.'

Michel spun round, fists clenched, and then he quickly unclenched them as he remembered who he was facing. The Jesuits were the enforcers of the Church of Christ the Warrior and were said to be the best fighters you could find aside from the Investigators or the gladiators of the Arena. This particular Jesuit was wearing purple-and-white battle armour and a sardonic smile. He was tall, dark and not particularly memorable. He didn't look especially tough, either, but Michel had absolutely no intention of testing him – or even upsetting him. Michel's muscles were strictly for show.

'So glad you could come and see us,' Lily said graciously to the Jesuit. 'I take it everything is going as planned?'

'So far,' said the Jesuit. 'I am Father Brendan, Michel. You may have complete confidence in me. In this room the security systems are currently running on a closed loop so that we can talk for as long as we need without fear of being overheard. Now, I'm sure you have questions. Ask away.'

'All right,' said Michel. 'Let's start with why we should trust anyone from the Church. Last I heard, they were still advocating the return of the death penalty for adulterers. This might all be a set-up by Kassar. He'd love to have something he could use to bring down the Wolfes.'

'The cardinal knows nothing about this,' said Brendan, 'or we'd all be dead by now. As to why I've chosen to work with Clan Chojiro, it's really very simple: before I joined the Church, I was a member of Clan Silvestri.'

'What the hell do Chojiro and Silvestri have in common?'

The Jesuit smiled. 'Blue Block.'

Michel realized his mouth was hanging open, and closed it with a snap. Blue Block. The Families' secret weapon.

'But . . .' Michel struggled for words. 'Why is Blue Block being used against the Wolfes, one of their own?'

Brendan smiled. 'The Wolfes in general, and Valentine in particular, are becoming too powerful. He's tipping the balance. We feel it would be best for all if Valentine could be made to stand down and if others more willing to share the profits of stardrive production took over.'

'Which is where we come in,' said Lily. 'Daniel and Stephanie will fall easily without Valentine to protect and support them, Constance will be quietly sidelined, and we will take over the Family. Clan Chojiro will support us now, in return for future generosity on our part.'

'Quite,' said Brendan. 'You don't have to do anything much, to begin with. We'll supply explosives and tell you the exact locations where they'll do the most damage. All you have to do is place them in those areas of the complex to which you have access but I don't. The explosions won't be particularly big – just enough to throw production into chaos and make Clan Wolfe look incompetent.'

'So no one has to get killed?' Michel said quickly.

'Only as a last resort,' said Brendan. 'We prefer to avoid actual bloodshed. It's so . . . obvious. Trust me, Michel: we'll try everything else first.'

Michel nodded reluctantly. 'All right. When does the balloon go up?'

'At the ceremony,' said the Jesuit. 'Live, on holoscreens all over the Empire. It'll be a ratings smash.'

'You see, lover,' said Lily to Michel, slipping an arm through his, 'even that little toad of a reporter will end up helping us. Everything has been planned, down to the last detail. Nothing can go wrong.'

Toby Shreck hurried down the narrow corridor, glanced at the watchface set into his wrist, and swore quietly. This was officially sleep-time in the factory complex's living quarters, and after the day he'd been through he felt he could sleep for a week. In the hours since his unsuccessful attempt at a little chat with Lily and Michel Wolfe he'd been running himself ragged trying to set up all the interviews and factory footage he could.

No one was cooperating except under the direst of threats, and trying to make this factory look good was a task that even an experienced PR flack like himself would have blanched at. Personally speaking, Toby felt he'd seen sexier-looking abattoirs. But none of that mattered now. He had a chance of a once-in-a-lifetime interview, and he was damned if he was going to lose it now, just because it had to be at an hour when all civilized people had their heads down and were dreaming furiously. Everyone else could give him cold shoulders until their joints froze up; this one interview would make his reputation.

He tried to hurry himself a little faster, but he was already out of breath. Too much weight – too many good lunches at PR events. He was built for comfort rather than speed. All right, he was fat. But for once it didn't matter: no one would be looking at him during this interview. He forced himself on, puffing hard. Trust Flynn to have his quarters half-way across the complex. Actually, that wasn't really fair – Toby had quarters in the better area because he was an aristocrat, and Flynn very definitely wasn't. Toby sniffed. Come to think of it, he didn't feel like being fair.

He finally stumbled to a halt before the right door, leaned on it a moment while he got his breath back, and then hammered on it with his fist.

'Go away,' said Flynn's calm voice. 'I am resting. If you're factory personnel, go to hell. If you're Toby the Troubador, go to hell by the express route. If you're a Wolfe, this is a recording. If you're a potential lover, leave your name and location on my computer file. Full image, please. Clothes optional.'

'Open up, dammit,' said Toby. 'You wouldn't believe who's agreed to talk to us.'

'Tell them I'll see them in the morning. I am off-duty, and

I don't have to talk to anyone I don't want to. If you dislike it, take it up with my union.'

'Flynn! It's Mother Superior Beatrice of the Sisters of Mercy!'

There was a pause, and then the lock snapped. 'Very well, come in. But on your own head be it.'

Toby growled something uncomplimentary and very basic, kicked the door open and stormed in. He managed about six steps before he came to a dead stop. The door closed behind him and the lock clicked shut again, but he didn't notice. Someone could have slipped a live grenade into his underwear and he wouldn't have noticed. The cameraman's quarters weren't much, being basically cramped and functional, but a few feminine touches had helped to brighten the place up. And the most feminine thing in the room was Flynn, reclining on his bed in a flowing cocktail dress, in one hand a margarita in a frosted glass and in the other a book of decadent French verse. In addition to the dress, he was wearing a long curly wig of purest gold and subtle but artfully applied makeup. His workboots and sloppy trousers had been replaced by fishnet stockings and stiletto heels, and his fingernails had been painted a shocking pink. All in all, Flynn looked very pretty and completely at ease.

Toby closed his eyes and shook his head slowly.

'Flynn, you promised me you wouldn't do this. We are not in civilized company now. They would not understand. And the representatives of the Church of Christ the Warrior definitely wouldn't understand. They'd execute you on the spot for deviancy and degeneracy, and shoot me as well for just knowing you. Now get out of that gear and into something that won't get us both into trouble. Mother Beatrice won't wait forever.'

'Rush, rush, rush,' said Flynn. He drained the last of his margarita, slipped a bookmark into his poetry collection, and put glass and book carefully to one side before rising gracefully to his feet. 'Very well, you wait outside while I change into something less comfortable. And bear in mind I wouldn't do this for anyone less than Mother Beatrice. That woman is a saint.'

Toby stepped into the corridor and closed the door without actually shutting it, so he could continue the conversation – or, for that matter, hiss if he saw anyone coming. He shook his head again. He could feel one of his headaches coming on. 'Of all the cameramen on all the worlds, I had to end up with you. Why me?'

'Because you were desperate for a good cameraman, and no one else would work with you,' said Flynn from inside. 'After all, the only reason you decided to get your journalist's licence was because you were on the run from your Uncle Gregor. As it happens, I likewise felt the need to leave in a hurry. My last gentleman admirer was a high-ranking member of the Clans who also liked to dress up pretty in the privacy of his own quarters.

'A wonderful man – very interested in yodelling. The only lover I ever knew who could give me head and sing me a song at the same time. My, how those low notes vibrated. And what that man could do with a vowel . . . Anyway, we had words and broke up, and he became rather concerned that I might tell all, if offered the right price. And he couldn't have that. Were word of his private proclivities to get out no one in the Families would ever had taken him seriously again. If you're an aristocrat it's all right to be a degenerate, but not if you've been making a fool of yourself.'

'So, seeing the way his mind was working, I decided it might be in my best interests to leave town for a while and hole up somewhere suitably distant until he calmed down again. Which is the only reason I agreed to work with you, Toby Shreck. You have to realize, the word on you was not good: an ageing PR flack with dreams of reporting and delusions of adequacy. Nothing personal, you understand. For what it's worth, you're doing all right here. I've worked with worse.'

Toby glowered but said nothing. He had indeed spent most of his working life as a PR man and spin-doctor for Gregor Shreck, despised by his peers and unappreciated by his

Family. No one recognized how much hard work went into good PR. But he'd always dreamed of being a real journalist, digging out the truth and exposing villainy and corruption in high places, instead of covering it up. Somehow he had never had the courage to leave the safe haven of his job and Family. It had taken a real personal emergency to wake his ambitions again, and now he was here on Technos III he was going to do the best damn' job he could. It was his chance to be someone in his own right, not just another of Gregor Shreck's shadows – a final chance to acquire some self-respect.

Mother Beatrice was renowned for not giving interviews, and the press corps now took it seriously, after she had knee-capped a reporter with a meat tenderizer when he had tried blackmailing a friend into talking about her. But she was probably the only person on Technos III who could and would tell him the whole story, the whole truth. To hell where the shrapnel fell. She had agreed to talk to him . . .

Toby kicked the doorframe viciously.

'Flynn! Are you ready yet?'

The door swung open and Flynn strolled out, looking like just another cameraman. The camera was as usual perched on his shoulder like a sleepy bird.

Flynn did a quick twirl for Toby, to show off his baggy trousers and camouflage jacket. 'Well? Will I pass?'

'You've still got lipstick on,' said Toby, with glacial calmness.

Flynn took out a handkerchief, wiped his mouth and smiled at Toby. 'Better?'

'Fractionally. Now let's go, before Mother Beatrice changes her mind – or somebody changes it for her.'

They made their way quietly through the narrow corridors, stopping every time they thought they heard something. But no one else was about. Most people were asleep, trusting to the electronic guards and surveillance to guarantee their rest wouldn't be disturbed. After all, the indigenous rebels had never got this close, even on their best day; and nobody who worked in the factory would dare run the risk of upsetting

Security. As a reporter in charge of making the factory complex look good, Toby had security passes for practically every area, and some discreet but weighty bribes had ensured no one would tell about this little late-night jaunt.

He hoped.

He led Flynn to the nearest exit in the outer sector, and they stopped to climb into the heavy furs that had been left hanging by the door. Even a short journey through Technos III's winter could be deadly without the right protection. Toby and Flynn bundled up in layers of fur and wool until they could barely move, and then stumbled over to the exit. Toby looked out through the window beside the door and winced. The air was thick with swirling snow, blown this way and that by the gusting wind. He didn't look at the thermometer – he didn't want to know.

He pulled his fur hat down low over his brow, wrapped his scarf securely over his mouth and nose, cursed quietly for a moment, and then jerked the heavy door open. It swung slowly inwards, revealing a two-foot drift of snow that had piled up against its. Toby and Flynn kicked their way through and lurched out into the winter. The door slammed shut behind them, and they were alone in the night.

The cold hit them like a hammer, and for a moment all they could do was lean against each other for support. The bitter air seared their lungs, and the wind shocked tears from their exposed eyes. The snow on the ground was everywhere at least a foot deep. Tireless machines struggled to dig out a clear perimeter around the factory complex, but the snow fell faster than the machines could dig. The wind was almost strong enough to throw Toby off his feet, and he had to lean into it to keep his balance. The freezing air made his teeth ache, even through several layers of thick woollen scarf. He scowled and hunched his shoulders as the wind changed direction yet again. Part of him wanted to turn and go back inside rather than face such nightmare conditions, but Toby wouldn't listen to that part. He was a reporter now, on the trail of a hot story, and that was enough to keep him inwardly warm.

He glanced about him into the thickening blizzard. Outside the complex's exterior lights, there was only darkness and the storm. There should have been stars out, and two small moons, but they were hidden behind the fury of the snows. Nevertheless, some way off in the darkness a single patch of light showed defiantly around a long, low windowless structure.

Toby slapped Flynn on the arm and pointed to this structure, and they lurched off through the thick snowdrifts towards the light. Flynn's camera hovered behind his shoulder, sheltering from the wind.

The structure turned out to be a long tent of metallic cloth, marked with the familiar red crescent of the Sisters of Mercy. As on so many battlefields across the Empire, the tent was a hospital for all who needed it. The Sisters took no sides. The factory complex had just enough space for a single hospital ward, available to officers only; the foot soldiers, security men and mercenaries had to rely on the Sisters' mercy. The officers believed this gave their men an extra incentive not to get wounded. It was a big tent, looking bigger all the time as Toby trudged through the snow towards it. He knew he hadn't travelled far, but already his thighs were aching from forcing through the thick drifts and fighting the constantly changing winds. Sweat ran down his brow and into his eyes, some of it freezing in his eyebrows. Toby had given up cursing some time back. He needed his breath.

They finally staggered to a halt before one end of the tent. Toby found himself facing a very secure-looking steel door, with a sign-posted bell beside it. He hit the bell with his fist because he couldn't feel his fingers any more, and a view-screen lit up, showing a sister's veiled head and shoulders. She didn't look pleased to see him. Toby reached inside his furs, pulled out his press pass and held it up before the screen. The sister sniffed, and the viewscreen went blank. Toby and Flynn looked at each other uncertainly. They were both shivering uncontrollably now that their exertions were no longer keeping them warm.

The door swung suddenly inwards, spilling light and heat

out into the night. Toby and Flynn hurried forward into the comforting glow, and the door slammed shut behind them.

Toby pulled the scarf away from his mouth and took off his fur hat. His eyes watered as they adjusted to the new light and warmth. He and Flynn took turns beating the snow off each other, and then Toby turned and smiled ingratiatingly at the woman who'd let them in. It was always wise to be polite to a Sister of Mercy: they had long memories, and you never knew when you might end up needing their services. This particular sister looked to be in her late twenties, but already she had deep lines around her mouth and eyes. Dealing with death and suffering on a daily basis, with no end in sight, does that to you. She wore the usual unadorned white robes and wimple of a sister in the field; her robes were spattered with new and old bloodstains. She was big enough to stop an oncoming tank, and had a glare that would have wilted anyone but a reporter.

Flynn moved surreptitiously to stand behind Toby, and Toby tried his ingratiating smile yet again.

'Hi. We've come to see Mother Superior Beatrice. I'm Tobias Shreck, and this is my cameraman. We're expected.'

The sister stepped forward, pulled open his furs and frisked him with brisk efficiency. She did the same with Flynn, while Toby silently prayed his cameraman wouldn't giggle. Reassured that they weren't carrying any weapons, the sister stepped back and studied them both, her face set and unforgiving. 'She said you two were to be admitted, but you're not to tire her. This should be her rest period. She works all the hours God sends, and then makes time to deal with the likes of you. I don't want her exhausted. Is that understood?'

'Of course, sister,' said Toby. 'We'll be in and out before you know it.'

The sister grunted dubiously, but turned and led them down the single narrow aisle in the middle of the long ward that made up most of the tent's interior. Toby and Flynn followed at a respectful distance. There were beds on either side of them, crammed together with no space for luxuries

431

like visitors' chairs. These weren't the standard hospital beds of civilized worlds, with built-in sensors and diagnostic equipment: they were flat cots with rough blankets and sometimes a pillow. The smell of blood – and other, more disturbing scents – pushed past the thick, masking stench of disinfectant. The patients were mostly quiet – drugged, Toby hoped – but some groaned or moaned or stirred restlessly on their narrow cots. One man with no legs was crying quietly, hopelessly. Flynn's camera covered everything. Many of the patients were missing limbs or half a face or worse. Toby was sickened. Modern medicine was supposed to have made things like this impossible. He controlled himself. He was here to cover this. All of it.

'Don't the Wolfes supply you with better equipment than this?' he said finally, trying to keep the anger out of his voice so as not to upset the patients.

The sister snorted, but did not look back or slow her pace. 'We're on our own here. Officially, the Wolfes are winning this nasty little war, so they can't be seen supplying Technos III with major hospital facilities and supplies. Word about the real scale of casualties might start getting out, and about how badly the war is going. So they supply us with only the minimum necessary to cope with the low levels of wounded they're reporting. It's important to the Wolfes to give the impression that everything's fine here, and that they're fully in charge of the situation. Bastards. I'd drown the lot of them if I had my way. And you can put that in your report, if you wish.'

'I'm interested in everyone's views,' Toby said diplomatically. 'I want to tell people the truth about what's happening here.'

'If that's so, you're the first. Not that it'll make any difference. The Wolfes will censor anything embarrassing out of your reports before you're allowed to broadcast them.'

Toby remained silent. He expected to be censored: that went with the territory. The trick was how much you managed to sneak past the bastards.

Half-way down the long tent, a small area was separated

off by tall standing screens. Toby thought at first this must be a toilet, and was somewhat surprised by the sister's clear respect and reverence as she tapped on one of the screens.

'It's the press people,' said the sister diffidently. 'Do you still want to speak to them, or shall I kick them out?'

There was a low murmured answer from within, and the sister grimaced as she turned back to Toby and Flynn. 'Thirty minutes, and not a second more. And if you tire her I'll have your balls.'

She pulled back one screen to make a doorway, and Toby and Flynn nodded respectfully to her and eased past her, much as one might a growling watchdog. After they had filed through, the sister pulled the screen back into place behind them. The screened-off area turned out to be just big enough to hold a cot, a wash-basin on a stand, and a small writing desk. Sitting before the desk was Mother Superior Beatrice, wrapped in a long silk house-coat with frayed hems and elbows worn dull. She looked pale and drawn, and her bright red hair had been cropped brutally short, but her eyes were warm and her welcoming smile seemed genuine enough. Behind her, her black robes and starched wimple of office hung from a hatstand, looking almost like there was another person in the small space with them.

Beatrice didn't get up, but offered Toby her hand. Her handshake was firm but brief. She turned to Flynn, who leaned over her hand and kissed it.

Beatrice's smile widened. 'If you knew what I'd been doing with that hand just half an hour ago, you'd rush out of here to gargle with sulphuric acid.' She turned her smile back to Toby. 'I'm glad to see you both. I wasn't sure you'd come.'

'Is it OK if my cameraman records this conversation?' said Toby.

'Of course. That's why I insisted on you both coming here. Sit on the bed. We don't have chairs to spare, and you fill too much space standing up.'

She settled back in her own chair by the desk, and Toby lowered himself cautiously on to the cot, not sure it would bear his weight. It felt hard and unforgiving. Flynn stayed on his feet, moving quietly back and forth to sort out good angles for his camera. Toby ignored him. Flynn would take care of the technicalities; Toby's province as reporter was the interview, and what truth he could squeeze out of it. Mother Beatrice had a reputation for being outspoken, but that had always been in the pampered and protected Court, far away from the blood and dying of the front line. Rumour said she had changed greatly after her experiences in field hospitals, but most of the stories were at least second-hand. And Toby wasn't sure he believed in saints anyway. He decided to start with something simple and clear-cut.

'You seem very crowded here, Mother Beatrice. Surely this structure wasn't meant to accommodate so many people at one time?'

'Hell, no. It was meant to serve a third as many patients, but that was worked out by civilized people in civilized places. And call me Bea, since I'm officially off-duty. We're packed to the walls here because things have been going particularly badly for the Wolfes in the last few campaigns. The lines move backwards and forward on the map, but they're drawn in other people's blood. Some of our patients are rebels, of course. The Sisters of Mercy serve all sides impartially, whatever the pressures.'

Toby raised an eyebrow. 'Do the Wolfes know you're treating rebel wounded?'

'I haven't told them – not after the way they reacted the first time I raised the matter. I keep meaning to bring them up-to-date, but somehow I never get round to it. I don't see that it's any of their business. They supply me with no more than the bare necessitites, even for their own people. We're a long way out from civilization, they say, and transport costs are obscenely high. So I just do my job as I see best. We do what we can here. Patch people up and send them off. It's not unusual to see the same faces come back two or three times, bleeding from a different place each time. Rarely more than three times. Many can't take the shock of so much surgery. Others . . . just give up. It's a hard war and a harsh world.

434

'Supplies are running low – blood plasma, anaesthetics, most drugs. The Sisterhood sends what it can, but there's a lot of fighting going on across the Empire these days and the Sisterhood's resources can spread only so far. Some days this isn't a hospital so much as a butcher's shop.'

'How long has the armed struggled been going on here, Bea?' said Toby, keeping his voice low and confidential, as though it were just the two of them having a quiet talk.

'Generations – hundreds of years,' said Mother Superior Beatrice grimly. 'People have been born, lived their lives and died here knowing nothing but war. Of course, it's escalated since the Wolfes took over the factory. The upcoming ceremony has raised the stakes for both sides. It was only the rising publicity that alerted the Sisterhood to what was happening here and persuaded us to send in a mission. If my colleagues knew what was really going on here, they'd send more help – I know they would. But the Wolfes control all contact with the outside.'

'What kind of war are we talking about here, Bea?' said Toby, easing her back to the main subject.

'Pretty basic. The struggle has settled down into trench warfare. It's been stuck in the same pattern for decades. Both sides dig tunnels, but underground is where the planet's remaining wildlife survives, and it doesn't like competition. Fighting above ground is almost impossible for any length of time, due to the weather – it changes so unpredictably that shelling is impracticable. Same goes for air cover. And when the wind blows there's so much dirt and metal floating in the air that it disperses energy beams, so they can't be used except at point-blank range. Thus most of the fighting is hand-to-hand, steel against steel, in the no-man's-land between Wolfe and rebel positions. The front line surges back and forth all the time, but nothing really changes. The two sides are too equally balanced – though the arrival of the Church troops may make a difference.'

'Jesuit commandoes, leading elite troops, have cleared out resistance on many planets,' said Toby.

'Even so, Technos III is something else,' Bea said flatly.

'The rebels here have been fighting for generation upon generation, for as far back as records go, learning and improving all the time. Hell, they've been breeding for warriors for centuries. And then there's the weather again: you need to be superhuman just to surive here. And that's the state of war on Technos III. Right in your face and bloody. The only reason we're not totally swamped with wounded is because most of them don't last long enough to reach us. They die of the heat or the cold, the razorstorms or the blizzards. There's always enough work coming in to keep us busy, of course, even when we've run out of drugs and plasma so we have to hold the patients down while the surgeons cut them apart and sew them up, hoping the shock won't kill them anyway.'

Toby leaned forward a little, subtly interrupting her. She was starting to repeat herself and he needed to keep her to the point. He was torn between getting as much good material as he could and the knowledge that, the longer he stayed here, the more likely it was that someone back at the complex would notice he and Flynn were missing and put two and two together. 'How many staff do you have here, Bea? How much help?'

'I have two surgeons plus five sisters trained as nurses working under me. There was a third surgeon, but he cracked under the pressure and I had to send him away. He didn't want to go. Even cried when I put him on the transport, but he was too far gone, even for us. I'm still waiting for a replacement. Technos III isn't very high on anyone's list of importance. It's just a name, to most people. I came here only because I was desperate to get my hands dirty doing some real work after the endless sniping and intrigues at Court. If I'd known what I was letting myself in for ... I'd probably have come anyway. I never was very good at looking away and pretending I didn't see.

'What med tech we have is top-of-the-line, the best the Sisterhood could provide, but it was never meant to handle this many wounded. I live in fear of it breaking down – there's no one here who could repair it. The Wolfes have their own med bay in the factory – everything you could dream of, up to and including a regenerator – and one of the nurses there is sympathetic. I raid their drug supply from time to time, when I'm really desperate, and she covers for me, God bless her.' Mother Superior Beatrice shook her head. 'Can I offer either of you gentlemen a drink?'

She reached under the writing table and brought out a bottle of murky-looking liquid and three glass specimen jars. She shrugged when Toby and Flynn politely declined, and poured herself a large drink. Toby gestured urgently to Flynn to keep filming. Bea was the kind of subject you prayed for in a documentary: a real character, someone who knew everyone and everything, right there in the middle of it all but still able to stand back and see the big picture. It helped that she didn't look much like a nun, and the drinking was a nice touch – the viewers didn't like their saints to be too perfect. Bea's hand shook as she raised the glass jar to her mouth, and Toby felt suddenly, obscurely ashamed. With all he'd seen and heard, none of it had touched him the way it had obviously touched her. She cared, and he was merely an unfeeling, recording eye. Just like Flynn's camera. He tried to tell himself he had to be like this if he were to get the job done, but that didn't sound as convincing as it once had. He made himself concentrate on Bea as she lowered the almost empty jar.

'God, this is awful stuff,' she said calmly, 'but I couldn't work here without it. Two of the sisters pop amphetamines and one of my surgeons has a serious drug habit. I don't say anything, as long as they can still work. We all need a little something to get us through the day – and the night. The nights are the worst. That's when most of our patients die: in the early hours of the morning, when the dawn seems furthest away. I don't know how much longer I can stand it here. It wears you down, having to fight for every life. Nothing's simple here – not even this tent. It's the strongest the Sisterhood could provide. And, nevertheless, it can't cope with the excesses of weather we have here. In the summer it gets so oppressive you can hardly move. In the winter . . . I've seen the surgeons stop in mid-operation to warm their hands in the steaming guts they've just opened up.

'We've all changed, here. I never really wanted to become a nun, you know. I fled to the Sisterhood so that I wouldn't have to marry Valentine Wolfe. But I ended up at the mercy of the Wolfes anyway. I never had much time for religion. I just used the Sisterhood as a power-base, as many have done before me. But, here in hell, I found religion after all. In the face of so much evil, you have to believe in God. It's the only thing that gives you the strength to go on.'

She rose suddenly to her feet, catching Toby and Flynn by surprise. She emptied the jar of the last of her drink, and put it down on the desk. 'I've said enough. I'll take you round the beds, so you can see the kind of wounds we're dealing with. Some of the patients might even talk to you, though you'll have to edit out the obscenities.'

She led them from her private area and back down the long aisle between the beds. Flynn filmed everything, sweeping his camera back and forth. The tent was still eerily hushed, and no one wanted to talk to them – Toby supposed they didn't have the strength to waste on moans of pain or complaints. The sisters were moving quietly from bed to bed, checking bandages and temperatures or, if there was nothing else they could do, just laying a cool, comforting hand on a fevered brow. Toby kept quiet too. The last thing this needed was a commentary, and he didn't have any more questions: the answers were too obvious. To his surprise, he felt mostly angry. This kind of thing shouldn't be happening, not in this day and age. He'd covered up enough things himself in the past, as Gregor's PR flack, but never anything like this. A Family's troops were dying to hide a Family's shame. He kept telling himself not to get involved, that this was just a good story. Yet he was surprised to find how close to frustrated tears he was.

'Film as much as you like,' said Mother Beatrice. 'The odds are that no one will ever see it. I keep trying to get reports out, but the Wolfes keep blocking me. They can't afford to admit they're losing the battle here. The Empress might take Technos III and the factory away from them.'

'Some news did get out,' said Toby, 'from transport crews and the like: of the Saint of Technos III who threw aside her aristocracy to tend the wounded and the dying. That's what brought us to this tent.'

'I'm no saint,' said Bea. 'Anyone would do what I do if they could see what I've seen.'

'We'll get the report out somehow,' said Toby, 'even if I have to smuggle the tape out by cramming the cans up my backside.'

Bea smiled suddenly. 'Well,' she said archly, 'I always did say the Wolfes were a pain in the ass.

Random, Journey and Storm followed their guides through a maze of tunnels, away from the open trenches and the fury of the blizzard. The tunnels sloped sharply downwards, their walls revealing the many layers of compacted trash and metal that made up the history of the planet. The air was warmer underground, but the three newcomers shivered. Light – a pale yellow glow that was hard on their unaccustomed eyes – came from metal lanterns hanging from the low ceiling. As they descended people bustled around them, always in too much of a hurry to do more than stare or very occasionally nod a greeting. The people were heavily muscled, with little covering fat to blur the hard edges. Their eyes were stern and concentrated; none of them smiled or uttered an unnecessary word. Tall John and Throat-Slitter Mary led the way in silence. Random and Journey and Storm stuck close together, as much for shared warmth as for mutual support.

'How the hell did they build all these tunnels and trenches in the first place?' said Ruby, scowling at the metal walls. 'I can't see whoever the opposition was at the time agreeing to a truce while the rebels brought in digging equipment.'

'They probably used captured energy weapons to blast out the original tunnels, and then widened them by hand over the years,' said Random. 'We're looking at the end-result of decades of hard work. Maybe longer.'

'Damn' right,' said Tall John, without looking back at them. 'The original work happened so long ago that no one now even remembers the names of those involved. We've been building our tunnels for centuries, each generation adding what was needed at the time. We have to live underground. It's all that's left to us. In the old days there were the military satellites, with their tracking systems and weaponry. These days there's the weather. Besides, the factory complex has a force screen: we've always known the only way past the screen was under it. The Wolfes know it, too. That's why they have their own people digging tunnels as well.'

'But you're safe down here, aren't you?' said Storm.

'There's safe and there's safe,' said Throat-Slitter Mary. 'Technos III's indigenous lifeforms live underground. They live deep down, where we rarely go, but they come up from time to time, and then we get to argue as to whose territory these tunnels are. We win, more often than not. See those old stains on the floor? When we make a kill, we splash the beast's blood around, to mark the territory. It keeps the bastards at bay, for a while.'

'You mean they get up this far?' said Ruby.

'Oh, sure,' said Tall John. 'In the spring there's sometimes hardly room to move in here for fangs and claws and nasty dispositions.'

'Good,' said Ruby. 'I could use some exercise.'

'Well that explains the bloodstains,' said Storm, quickly, 'But what about the leg?'

Tall John and Throat-Slitter Mary stopped and looked back at him. 'What leg?' said Tall John.

Storm pointed silently, and they all looked up at the human leg, complete with trousers and boot, protruding from where the right-hand wall met the ceiling. Tall John scowled. 'Mason Elliot! This is your area! Where are you?'

A short stocky man bundled in furs up to his chin stepped out of a side-tunnel, an ugly black cigar in one corner of his mouth. 'No need to shout. I'm not deaf. All right, gracious leader, I'm here. What is it this time? Lost your keys again?'

440

'What is that leg doing there?'

'Holding up the ceiling. We had to rebuild part of the wall after the last bloodworm attack, and we were a bit pushed for time. We were short of materials, the body was handy . . . and no one liked him much anyway. Give it a few weeks and the bloodworms will break through again. We can always remove the body then.'

'By which time it'll be stinking to high heaven,' said Tall John. 'I want that leg brought down now. Get an axe and hack it off. Move it!'

'Certainly, gracious leader of us all.' The short man extinguished his cigar with his fingers and put it behind his ear. He stood glaring up at the protruding leg as Tall John led the party past. Random brought up the rear, and was perhaps the only one to hear the short man mutter, '*Now* what I going to use as a signpost?'

As Tall John led them on through the tunnels Random realized they were being taken by the scenic route so they wouldn't be able to describe the way to anyone else. Random approved. It showed a good grasp of basic security and a healthy dose of paranoia. Fortunately, since Random had passed through the Madness Maze he couldn't get lost: he always knew where he was in relation to everything else. He decided not to tell Tall John that, and padded amiably along, enjoying what scenery there was. The tunnels were comfortably broad but the ceilings were low enough that everyone walked with protectively hunched shoulders. He suspected the tunnels had been deliberately designed that way to hinder and disorient invading forces. Presumably the rebels were used to them, but Random found them, quite literally, a pain in the neck. More people appeared as the tunnel floors finally began to level out. They wore layers of leathers and furs and all carried their weapons at the ready. They studied the newcomers with suspicious eyes.

'Do your people always go armed?' said storm. 'Surely you're in no danger this far down?'

'There's danger all the time,' said Throat-Slitter Mary, 'if not from sudden security attacks then from the beasts that live below. There are always people listening, but they can't be everywhere. So we make sure we're preapred at any moment. From childhood on, we're trained to be ready to fight for our lives at an instant's notice.'

'Where do you get to rest and relax?' said Storm.

'We don't,' said Throat-Slitter Mary. 'We can relax when we're dead.'

Ruby smiled at Random. 'You bring me to the nicest places.'

Random smiled back, but concentrated on what he was going to say to the rebels when he finally got to where they were taking him. He had a strong feeling his statement wasn't going to make him very popular with the underground community, but it had to be said. He'd led too many armies into battle on the hot words of rhetoric and slanted truths, and seen them die without flinching because he believed the cause was greater than the individual. He wasn't sure he agreed with that any more. Either way, he was here to inspire the rebels of Technos III with the truth, not just fast talking – even if it was a truth they might not want to hear. It occurred to him that he was in the hands of people who might kill him for the word he brought. Random shrugged mentally. They could try.

The group came, at long last, to a reasonably large chamber. The ceiling was at least twenty feet above them, and Random, Journey and Storm straightened up with sighs of relief. The walls were of solid polished metal. Ranked seating flanked the walls all the way round, interrupted only by the single entrance. The seats were full of people, packed shoulder-to-shoulder, staring down at the newcomers with harsh, watchful eyes. A man and a woman stood in the centre of the open space, waiting, and they didn't look particularly welcoming. Tall John and Throat-Slitter Mary led the three visitors forward.

'These are Ragged Tom and Spectre Alice,' said Tall John. 'Together, we're the council of the underground. Talk to us, Jack Random. Tell us why you have come here.'

Jack Random smiled and nodded at the council members,

and then at the surrounding watchers. If the numbers of them had been supposed to intimidate him, they'd thought wrong. He'd faced unfriendlier crowds than this, and worked under greater pressures. He took a moment to study the two councillors he hadn't met before.

Ragged Tom was of average height and weight and had nondescript features; in point of fact, he didn't seem any more ragged than his contemporaries. Spectre Alice, on the other hand, looked as crazy as a cornered sewer rat. She was short and old, with greasy grey furs and remarkably similar hair, which stuck up in spikes. She had wide staring eyes, and a line of drool leaked from one side of an extremely disturbing smile. Random was glad she didn't want to shake hands. He felt like throwing things at her.

Tall John mistook his pause for nervousness, and started the ball rolling.

'We've been fighting here for generations and, after all we've been through, we're still fighting. Our council has therefore come to the reluctant conclusion that, just possibly, we can't do this on our own. We need help – fighters, weapons, supplies. We were told the Golgotha underground could supply these things. But all they've sent us is you three. No one here has forgotten that, the last time we asked for help, the cyberats not only knocked out the military satellites that had been plaguing us but screwed up the weather satellites. We've been living in the resultant hell ever since. Give us one good reason why we shouldn't send the three of you back to Golgotha in a box.'

Random smiled, entirely unmoved. 'Firstly, the lack of military satellites and the disrupted weather are all that keep the Wolfes from calling in an Imperial starcruiser to selectively scorch the planet's surface down to whatever level necessary to wipe you all out. Secondly, the only reason the Wolfes haven't brought in a complete army of mercenaries to deal with you is because it would cost them more than it's worth. Start getting too successful too quickly, and they might change their minds. And, thirdly, if any one of us is harmed, Golgotha will disown you and you'll never see *any* help from the outside. Have I missed anything?'

'Just one,' said Storm. 'It's only a matter of time before the Empire provides the Wolfes with new military satellites, with sensors powerful enough to punch right through the weather. And that will be the end of all surface fighting, as far as you're concerned. It could also be the end of your first real chance of winning in years. Forget the screw-up with the cyberats. That was a long time ago. Let us help, before your time runs out.'

'And if one of you so much as even looks at us funny,' said Ruby Journey, 'I will personally kick that person's ass up around his ears.'

Everyone paused to look at Ruby. Absolutely no one present doubted that she meant it.

Random coughed politely, to bring their attention back to him.

'According to our reports, your war has been going well of late. Tell us about that.'

'The size and number of our tunnels limit the ways the Wolfe security forces can attack us down here,' said Ragged Tom, in a high, chilly voice. 'And we're more adapted to the conditions than they are. They don't like coming down this deep. Too many nasty things live down here, apart from us. Up on the surface, the situation is much the same. Our ancestors were genetically engineered to withstand the worst this planet could throw at us. The Wolfe troops don't have our advantages – although they do have superior numbers and better weapons. But they're only fighting to win; we're fighting to survive. Which is why the trenches are pretty much as they always have been, with neither side having the upper hand for long.'

'We don't give up,' said Spectre Alice, in a harsh cracked voice. 'We're the refuse, the thrown away, the discarded. We call ourselves the Rejects, and we're proud of it. In turn, we reject the Empire, and all it stands for. The Wolfes are just the latest face the enemy wears. So don't think we're so desperate we'll take your help and never ask the price. We

444

won't swap one master for another. We'll fight and die alone, if need be. We bow to no one.'

'I like her,' murmured Ruby.

'You would,' said Random.

'There's no price for our help,' said Storm, smiling reassuringly around him. 'All we seek are allies against the Empire, to help in the overthrow of the Iron Bitch. You need fighters, weapons and supplies, you say. We can give you these . . . in due course.'

'There is . . . a further complication,' said Tall John.

'Didn't you just know he was going to say that?' murmured Ruby.

'Shut up,' murmured Random.

'We're not just fighting for ourselves,' said Ragged Tom. 'We're also fighting to free the clones working in the factory complex. Like us, they were brought here to work until it killed them. Now they work, eat, exercise and sleep in the complex. Again like us, they rarely see the open sky. If one dies, the Wolfes just clone a replacement from the dead body. They're designed, bred and trained specifically for the work they do here – work too dirty and too dangerous for humans. They're conditioned never to object, despite the awful conditions they work and live in. They're property. But still, sometimes, they dream of freedom. A very few manage to escape. They come here, to us, because there's nowhere else they can go. There's always a home for them here. They are our brothers and sisters. The Wolfes know this. They've threatened to kill all the clone workers if it looks like our forces will prevent the factory from opening on time for the ceremony. They'd do it.'

'Yes,' said a quiet new voice. 'They would.'

Everyone looked round as a tall slender man wrapped in ill-fitting furs stood up in the front row of the seats. His face was drawn and gaunt, his mouth a thin line, his eyes sunk deep in their sockets. There was hardly anything to him, as though the smallest breath of wind would carry him away. His legs trembled, seeming barely able to sustain his small

445

weight. But his gaze was steady, and when he spoke his quiet voice was firm and measured.

'I'm Long Lankin 32 – a clone from the factory. They're working us to death to make sure the ceremony will take place as scheduled. The work itself is dangerous. Exposure to the forces involved eats away at our flesh and our minds. They can treat us as they wish. No one says anything. The Empress wants her new stardrive. Go ahead and attack. Let them kill us all. Whatever hell we might go to after death can't be worse than the hell we live and work in every day. And, if you could free us, we'd fight for you against the Empire to the last drop of our blood.'

He sat down suddenly, as though afraid his legs would no longer support him. A loud murmur of encouragement and support ran around the watching audience.

Storm nodded soberly. 'You mean it. I'm impressed. It's rare for a clone to break away from his conditioning that much. If they're all like you, we'll have an army I'd back against anyone – even trained Empire troops.'

Random nodded, but said nothing. While he had no doubt Long Lankin's every word had been true and from the heart, he also knew a good publicity stunt when he saw one. The council had put him up to it, to take the edge off their *further complication*. The council had probably even written his little speech for him, to be sure of having the maximum effect on the audience and the newcomers. It was what Random would have done. However, Random had been a professional rebel long enough not to let his emotions sway him. His mission on Technos III was to stop stardrive production, and even if that meant destroying the factory completely, along with all the clones in it, that was what he'd do. Of course, if he could work out a way to help the Rejects rescue the clones first, he'd do that. It was, after all, why he'd become a professional rebel in the first place.

'Trench warfare's nothing new to me,' he said finally. 'We've put in our time in the trenches, haven't we, Alex? Of course, we were younger then. Same with fighting under-ground. Nothing new about tunnel rats, or the blood they spill that the sun will never see. I'm not going to insult you by offering advice on how to fight – I've got a feeling you already know more about that than I ever will. But Alex and I, too, have been fighting the Empire all our lives. We know strategies and tricks of the trade that might just give you an edge over the Wolfe security forces and the Church troops. We understand how their minds work.

'I accept that you're disappointed there's only the three of us. But people are flocking to the underground movement on hundreds of worlds, all spoiling for a chance to strike back against the Empire. And unfortunately there are only so many Golgotha advisors to go around. You have Jack Random's word that you'll get everything you need, in time. But for the moment it's imperative that the Empress be denied the new stardrive the Wolfe factory is producing. With her Fleet powered by the new drive, Lionstone could finally be unbeatable. That's why we're here: to help you stop production and, if possible, overthrow the Wolfes. Then it'll be up to you to hold this planet while we take on the rest of the Empire. We'll do everything we can to help you.'

'In other words,' said Spectre Alice, fixing him with her disturbing stare, 'you want just to walk in here and take over, run things, be the big hero one more time. Right?'

'No,' said Random, 'I'm here to lead, if at all, only by example, to fight beside you in the front line, to show you what I've learned in all my years as a rebel. Ruby and Alex will be fighting, too. You asked for help: we're here. And together we'll tear that factory apart.'

The four Reject leaders moved together and murmured urgently to each other. A loud growl of debate filled the chamber as the onlookers discussed what they'd heard. Random looked casually about him but was damned if he could tell from any of their faces how his announcement had gone over. He thought he'd pushed all the right buttons, but it was hard to be sure. He'd been quite serious. He didn't want to lead them, but he needed to fight beside them – if only to prove to himself that he could still do it, that the legendary Jack Random hadn't died after all in the Golgotha interrogation cells.

He had to admit that the Rejects hadn't so far seemed at all impressed by him. He didn't blame them. He looked twenty years older than his real age, despite all the improvements the Maze had worked in him.

A sudden sound caught his attention and he looked around sharply. It was a grating, sliding noise. He couldn't locate its source. The cavern floor began to vibrate under his feet, almost as though a train were going past. The four members of the council broke off their deliberations and looked down at the floor. Their faces hardened and they drew their swords. People began to stand up in the ranked seating.

'What is it?' said Storm. 'What's happening?'

'Crawlers,' said Tall John. 'Creatures from the depths. They tunnel through metal like it isn't there. Eat anything that doesn't fight back, and most that does.'

Ruby Journey's hand dropped to her side where her sword should have been, and then she cursed as she remembered she'd agreed to come unarmed. Storm looked quickly about him. Random put a comforting hand on his shoulder.

'Don't worry,' said Throat-Slitter Mary, hefting her sword. 'We'll defend you.'

The floor next to Random cracked open and a blunt scaly head burst up out of the floor, rising up on a long undulating neck. The head was a good four feet wide, as thick as two men. It had a wide gaping mouth full of jagged teeth, and no eyes. There was bedlam around the walls as the people in the lower seats tried to climb away from the danger and up into the higher seats. Tall John struck at the beast's neck with his sword and the blade just bounced away from the thick scales. The broad head spun round and slammed into him, knocking him off his feet. People were yelling for someone to bring energy guns.

Random stepped forward, and hit the neck with all his strength. His fist punched clean through the scales and sank deep into the flesh within. The beast screamed, a high, harsh sound that grated on the ear. Random braced himself, and pushed his hand in deeper. The beast convulsed, black blood springing from its mouth, but Random wouldn't be thrown off. His arm sank into the scaled neck up to his elbow, and then his hand found the long curving spine. It took only a moment to close his hand around the spine and snap it in one quick movement. The beast shuddered the length of its visible body, and then collapsed dead on the chamber floor.

For a moment there was utter silence, and then the chamber erupted with cheers and applause from the watching Rejects. The four council members stared at him with open mouths for a moment before they put away their swords so they could applaud, too. Random grinned. It seemed he'd finally managed to impress them. Storm was shaking his head in disbelief. Random pulled his bloody arm out of the crawler's neck. Ruby handed him a handkerchief to clean himself off with, and leaned in close beside him to murmur in his ear.

'Show off.'

And the war went on.

It was spring, and the temperature soared. The snow and ice melted, flooding the trenches. Life erupted everywhere, strange and deadly forms appearing out of nowhere to clog the trenches and tunnels. The brief hibernation was over. Life burst through the floors and the walls, much of it aggressive and carnivorous. Hungry plants with reaching thorns, thickly furred creatures that seemed mostly fangs and claws, small and large and everything in between – all determined to seize their chance at life. They fought each other for food and territory, and the winners fought the rebels for control of the blood-splashed trenches and tunnels. The rebels fought back with swords and axes and the occasional energy gun, driving off the ravenous hordes as they had done so many times before. The Wolfe security forces fought the same battle. And still life exploded from every side, from acid-oozing leeches that splattered the cracking walls to great hulking creatures that slowly dug their way up from the depths, old instincts driving them on and up in search of light and warmth. The waking world gave birth to bloodworms and barbed rippers and spiked golems, each in their own organic armour.

It was spring, and the whole world was alive.

Jack Random and Ruby Journey fought side by side, their flashing blades dripping alien blood and gore. They were strong and fast and they never grew tired. They seemed to be everywhere at once in the great maze of tunnels, helping where most needed; nothing large or small could stand against them. Alexander Storm worked to plot strategy and send fighters where they could do the most good. He toiled all day with a small army of scouts and runners, and tried not to think of himself as old.

The pressure of erupting life slowed as the day wore on and spring approached its half-way point. The Rejects, under Random and Ruby and Storm, took back control of their trenches and tunnels in record time. The Wolfe security forces weren't far behind, but then they had more energy weapons.

The second day of spring dawned. The fauna and flora had been taught their place again, and the rebels and Wolfe mercenaries were able to turn their attention back to the more serious business of war.

The rain hammered down in a never-ending torrent. The trenches filled ankle-deep with icy water, the level always rising. The Rejects splashed through the water to their positions, waiting for the signal. The whistles blew and both sides roiled up out of their trenches to meet in no-man's-land. Arrows flashed and energy guns roared, and then there was only close quarters and the harsh thud of steel cutting into flesh and bone. Tides swept this way and that in the great milling mob as two armies became only so many individual struggles, and every man lost track of his fellows. People screamed and died, and blood pooled briefly on the jagged metal floor before the driving rain washed it away.

The fighting surged back and forth as both sides searched for an advantage they could hold and exploit. The fighters fell and the rains fell, and men and women became dim shapes in the downpour. Some went mad in the horror of the battlefield and the pounding rain, and simply struck widly about them, not caring if it was at friend or at foe. The air became so wet it was hard to breathe. The rain filled eyes and ears and mouths. And still both sides fought on.

Random and Ruby fought back-to-back, their swords leaping and striking impossibly fast, and no one could stand against them. Rebels and mercenaries died around them but they went on, unflinching, unbeatable. Until finally the whistles blew and both sides fell back, dragging the dead and the wounded with them, to the safety of the trenches and tunnels. The rain fell.

And that was the second day of spring.

Summer dawned. The rain stopped as though someone had turned off a tap, and the heat rose and rose until it became unbearable, and then went on rising. Water in the trenches turned to steam. The blistering air scorched lungs, and every move in the awful heat became an effort. The sun was blinding in a brilliant sky. The Wolfe security forces climbed into specially designed cooling suits. The rebels didn't need those. Neither, to practically everyone's surprise, did Random and Ruby – they just adapted. And when the whistles blew both sides came howling out of their trenches to fight again. Swords were sheathed in bellies and heads blew apart like rotten fruit as they were touched in passing by energy beams. A rebel screamed as an axe sheared through his arm, and a mercenary spluttered blood as half his face was cut away. Men and women stamped this way and that, fighting for room to swing a sword. The dead and the wounded fell to be trampled underfoot as others struggled to reach the enemy. Screams of rage and pain filled the air, along with the war cries. The uneven ground was a crimson mess of blood and worse. At the end of the day the whistles blew and both sides fell back. They took the wounded with them. Wounds festered quickly in the cruel heat. The dead were left to spoil, to be recovered later, when the temperature dropped a little at night.

Some people, from both sides, volunteered to fight during the night – small patrols of men and women from whom the need for vengeance and slaughter had not been burned during the day. They crept out on to the pitch-black battlefield to struggle and die in sudden, silent encounters in the night. Meanwhile, back in the trenches and the tunnels, most got what sleep they could in the stifling heat.

The second day of summer came, and the temperature rose yet further. The heat became lethal to all but the strongest. And *still* both sides came roaring up out of their trenches when the whistles blew. There was killing to be done.

Then it was autumn, and the temperature dropped like a stone. The whistles blew and men and women went up and over the top to fight again. The jagged metal killing-field was already dark crimson from the splashed blood and offal of the previous day's battle, baked on to the surface by the merciless summer sun. Gale-force winds arose, blowing suddenly out of nowhere, strong enough to pick up a man and carry him away. People on both sides wore weights on their belts and in their boots to hold them down. The winds snatched up scattered metal fragments and swept them on at blinding speed to create razorstorms that could strip unprotected flesh down to the bone in seconds. The warriors on both sides wore protective armour, which slowed them down even more. Battles became slow, farcical affairs, but blood still spilled, and neither the wounded nor the dead saw the joke.

And finally winter came again, snow and ice and blizzards and the merciless cold. The security forces had special thermal suits but the rebels had no need for them. And neither did Random and Ruby: they'd adapted again. Everyone wore thick goggles to keep the driving snow out of their eyes. No-man's-land became a blinding white glare of snow and ice in which small groups of armed men and women moved slowly and silently together, straining their goggled eyes against the storm for signs of the enemy. Blood spattered the snow, and fighters crashed to the ground and did not move again. Jack Random and Ruby Journey fought on, going out again and again, whatever the weather. The Rejects by now were roaring their names as battle cries, and followed them into the conflict however long the odds. The cold seared their lungs and chilled the blood in their veins, but their rage was too hot for the chill of winter to affect them.

Two days passed, and winter gave way to spring and it all began again. That was how the years passed on Technos III.

But this time only one side pressed forward. Step by step, yard by yard, the Rejects drove the Wolfe security forces back, pushing no-man's-land closer and closer to the factory complex, as trench after trench fell and was occupied by the rebels. Jack Random and Ruby Journey appeared to be everywhere, inspiring the Rejects to new heights of courage and ferocity and scaring the hell out of even hardened Wolfe mercenaries, and neither the weather nor the enemy could touch them or slow them down. The name of the legendary professional rebel was voiced frequently on both sides now, and that of his deadly new companion: the old legend and the new.

Out in no-man's-land, Jack Random felt fitter and stronger than ever, and his sword-arm seemed never to tire. He felt like himself again – the legendary hero at whose name the Iron Throne itself had trembled. And, if he looked a little younger than he had, only Ruby Journey noticed – and she kept it to herself.

The Rejects pressed forward, scenting victory.

And good men and women died, and bad, and the Sisters of Mercy did what they could for the wounded.

And the war went on.

Daniel and Stephanie Wolfe waited impatiently in what passed for the main reception hall of the factory complex. It was actually just a large storage area that wasn't being used for anything else, but some brave soul had tried to brighten it up with a red carpet and a few flowers here and there. The carpet was just a little tatty, but the flowers bloomed brightly despite the complex's artificially controlled environment and the fact that they weren't fed or watered for days at a time. They were used to a much rougher life in the world outside.

Daniel scowled fiercely, tapping one foot impatiently and

hugging himself to keep from flying apart. Things had not been going at all well for the Wolfes lately, and this particular meeting had the potential to be a really major screw-up. One badly chosen word and . . . if he were lucky he'd only be sent home in disgrace. Stephanie stood at his side, calm and very controlled; one of them had to be. By rights, Michel and Lily should have been there, too, to greet such an important new arrival, but Stephanie had decided early on that those two couldn't be trusted to behave themselves, so she had had their food drugged and had locked them in their rooms. Officially, they were indisposed, which was true enough. And Cardinal Kassar's presence had not been requested. He'd tried everything, up to and including not so veiled threats, to gain an invitation, but Stephanie had no intention of being upstaged. This was a Wolfe affair, and the new arrival was *their* guest. Kassar could meet him later. Much later.

The only two people she hadn't been able to keep out were Toby Shreck and his cameraman Flynn. The Empress had personally let it be known that she wanted the new arrival's reception carried live on holovision and, though she hadn't deigned to explain why, what Lionstone wanted, Lionstone got – if you were fond of breathing. Toby and Flynn set up their lights and faded as far into the background as they could, trying hard not to be noticed. This was one show they were determined not to be thrown out of. It wasn't every day you got a chance to film the legendary Half A Man himself, in what remained of his flesh.

There weren't many in the Empire who didn't know the cruel and terrible history of Half A Man. Just over two hundred years ago he'd had a far too close encounter with a species of alien still not identified – or, indeed, ever re-encountered. He'd been abducted right out of the command chair of his own starcruiser, the *Beowulf*, disappearing in full view of his bridge crew. There'd been no warning, no trace of alien ship or presence. He was just there one moment and gone the next.

The aliens had held on to him for three years, performing experiments on him that he remembered only partially, in his

Empire that could stand against them. Luckily for all concerned, Investigators were by nature solitary beings who did not care for each other's company. The only thing they had in common was Half A Man: they'd die for Half A Man – or kill for him. Which was why he'd come to Technos III.

Toby Shreck was fascinated by the prospect of seeing him, and so was Flynn, though both of them tried hard not to show it. Half A Man had displayed no fondness for publicity following his return from alien bondage, particularly after the way the tabloids had hounded him, and he'd shunned the media spotlight for decades, rarely appearing in public except when ordered to by the emperor of the day. As a result, coverage of him tended to be rare, so that any reporter with new footage of him could practically name his own price. This reception would be going out live, but Toby had no doubt he could sneak some extra footage afterwards – maybe even get an interview . . . assuming Half A Man didn't kill him on the spot just for asking.

Everyone's head turned as they heard a particular sound approaching down the corridor outside the reception hall – the sound of one foot tapping on the metal floor. They all drew up to look their best, and unconsciously braced themselves.

The door swung open, and Half A Man came in.

Toby's first thought was *That's not so bad. I can handle that.* He hadn't been sure how he'd react to such an awful sight in the flesh, so to speak. But the human half looked human enough, and the glowing spitting energy half was just energy.

The human half was a little over six feet tall, in good shape and conservatively dressed, the clothes somehow strapped in place. The half-face was subtly disturbing, but the hair was a common enough dark brown, as was the single eye, and the half-mouth was set and firm. Toby couldn't read any emotion in the mouth or the eye – there just wasn't enough information in half a face. He couldn't even decide if it had once been handsome or not. The energy half was entirely human in outline, though it spat and crackled constantly, but Toby had a sick feeling that, despite appearances, it wasn't even close to the same shape as the human half. It had no particular colour, or perhaps it was made up of all colours. And it wasn't just its brightness that made it hard to look at.

Toby tore his gaze away from Half A Man and checked quickly that all his lights were working and in the right place. He and Flynn had had to guess at the exposures. He glanced at Flynn, and was relieved to see the camera on the man's shoulder was already silently capturing everything. Billions of people were watching this meeting live, and if he didn't cock this up completely Toby Shreck could finally be on his way to being accepted as a real reporter.

The two Wolfes stepped forward to greet Half A Man officially, and then stopped as there stepped silently through the open door three newcomers, wearing the formal blue-and-silver cloaks of Investigators. Stephanie and Daniel gaped openly. Toby's blood ran cold. Three Investigators together in the same room? This was unheard-of. No one had said anything about this. Toby glared at Flynn to make sure he kept filming. There was an even bigger story here than he'd thought.

'Daniel and Stephanie Wolfe,' said Half A Man in a perfectly normal voice, 'allow me to present my three companions. They are the Investigators, Edge, Barr and Shoal.'

Each Investigator bowed briefly on being named. Edge was a tall, slender man, well into his fifties. His long face came to a sharp point at the chin, and his eyes were too wide and too bright. His slight scowl was openly contemptuous. Barr stood as if he were a soldier, every muscle to attention. Short and square like a bulldog, he was in his sixties, with close-cropped gun-metal hair. He looked as if he were just waiting for an order to kill somebody. Shoal, the youngest, was a medium-height, compact woman in her late forties, with dark spiky hair and a cool gaze. Toby thought he saw a smile lurking in one corner of her generous mouth, but, since she was an Investigator, he was probably wrong; it was common knowledge that Investigators smiled only when they were killing – preferably whole alien species.

Then Edge spotted the holocamera.

'Turn that bloody thing off,' he said, a sword already in his hand. He advanced on Flynn, who backed quickly away, still filming. Flynn had worked in combat zones, and knew that the first rule of reporting was to keep filming, no matter what. Edge loomed over him, sword ready for a killing thrust. 'I said turn it off! No one films me. No one.'

Toby stepped forward, hands raised placatingly. 'It's on the Empress's orders. She wants a complete record . . .'

Edge spun round with blinding speed and hit Toby across the face with the back of his hand. Toby hit the floor hard, and fought to clear his head. Blood poured down over his mouth from one nostril, and he spat it away. He got one knee under him, and then had to stop as his head swam sickly. Flynn had backed up against a wall, and couldn't retreat any further. His camera was still running.

Toby struggled to find the words that would defuse the situation. There had to be something he could say. He always knew what to say.

'Leave the man alone, Edge,' said Barr, his voice thick and slightly slurred. 'We obey the Empress's commands in all things.'

'Shut up, you sycophant,' said Edge, not looking round. He had his sword-point at Flynn's throat. 'Throw that camera down and smash it, boy. I want to hear it crunch under your heel.'

Flynn tried to say 'Go to hell' but couldn't get the words out of his throat. You didn't talk like that to Investigators – particularly those with a killing madness in their eyes. But he still wouldn't surrender his camera.

Edge smiled suddenly, and Flynn's blood ran cold.

'Leave him alone,' said Shoal. Her voice was calm and quietly amused. 'His kind are like rats. Kill one, and they'll all come swarming around. You heard the man. This is the Empress's idea. You really want to be dragged before her in chains to explain why you disobeyed a direct order?'

'What can she to do me?' said Edge. 'You know why we're here. We're supposed to be too old or too frail to be trusted in the field any more, but we're too dangerous to be allowed worst dreams. Mostly he remembered screaming. Then they sent him back, dropping him out of nowhere back on to the bridge of the *Beowulf*, even though the ship was half-way across the Empire from where it had been.

And that was when the nightmare really began. The aliens had sent only half of him back. The left half. He'd been split right down the middle, from scalp to crotch. His right half had been replaced by an energy construct of roughly human shape.

The then Emperor had had him examined by the finest scientists and medics, but none of them had come up with any explanation worth a damn: they couldn't even agree on why he was still alive, never mind a coherent theory as to what had happened to him. His right half was now composed of an energy field that had all the properties of matter but was still clearly energy, though of a form the Empire had never come across before. The whole Empire was placed on Red Alert for over a year, in case the aliens showed up again. But they hadn't, and eventually everyone calmed down a little. Half A Man, as he'd been named almost immediately by the tabloid news channels, became a main adviser to the Emperor on alien matters. He continued to hold that position as years passed, Emperors died, and his human half grew not a day older. Now, as then, he was largely responsible for setting alien policy within the Empire, and, if anyone felt like arguing with him, all it took was one close look at what the aliens had done to him to change their minds.

Half A Man had also been responsible for the creation of the corps of Investigators. He felt the Empire needed a body of men and women specially qualified to deal with any and all alien threats. He trained them personally – still did – in the best ways to understand, control and kill aliens. The Investigators worshipped him – a fact that had been known to make the various occupants of the Iron Throne just a little uneasy, down the years. There was no denying that the Investigators were necessary and highly proficient at their job, but, if ever they were to band together, possibly under Half A Man, it was doubtful there was a force anywhere within the to run loose. We're not allowed to work for the Clans any more. We were doing too good a job. She's frightened of us. Of what we might do. I spent all my life in her service, and for what? To end up on this shitball as a local enforcer. She wants this event covered? I'll give the precious viewers something to watch that they won't forget in a hurry.'

He drew back his sword for a thrust that would take Flynn low in the belly. Flynn couldn't move. Toby surged dizzily to his feet, blood spilling down his chin from his smashed nose. He was probably going to die along with Flynn, but he couldn't just stand by and watch his cameraman being killed.

And than Shoal stepped forward and hit Edge professionally on the back of the neck. Edge slumped forward on to his knees, the sword dropping from his suddenly limp fingers. Barr looked shocked, but said nothing. Shoal smiled down at the dazed figure before her.

'Do as you're told, Edge, or I'll put a muzzle on you.'

'Nicely handled, Shoal,' said Half A Man. He nodded to Daniel and Stephanie. 'My apologies. Edge has his good qualities, but diplomacy isn't one of them. I'll keep him on a short leash in the future. I suggest we bring this meeting to a close without further ado. We've already given the viewing public plenty to gossip about, and I'm eager to begin my work here. Are the files ready?'

'Everything you requested,' said Stephanie. 'Maps, histories, troop details.'

'Might I enquire, on behalf of the viewing public, just what your purpose here is, sir?' said Toby.

Half A Man turned his single eye to look at Toby, who was now standing more or less steadily with a handkerchief pressed to his swelling mouth and nose. Half A Man smiled with his half-mouth. 'Persistent type, aren't you? Surely you must have realized by now that asking the wrong questions here can be hazardous to your health?'

'All part of the job, sir,' said Toby, lowering the handkerchief so his words could be heard clearly and ignoring the blood that still dripped from his chin. 'Would you care to make a comment at this time?'

'Not really,' said Half A Man, 'but, after my associate's outburst, I suppose I'd better.' He turned a little to face Flynn's camera directly. His energy half sputtered, and Flynn had quickly to crank down the camera's light sensitivity. Half A Man smiled for the viewers. 'The Empress has decided that those Investigators who cannot give one hundred per cent in the field, through either age or injury, will no longer be allowed to retire to work for individual Clans. The privilege was being abused. In future, such Investigators will be trained to work together with armed forces in especially dangerous trouble-spots, where their knowledge and experience will be invaluable. This is to be a pilot scheme, to be studied for its successes and limitations. As trainer of all Investigators, I volunteered to oversee the operation. And that is all I have to say – except that, in future, I expect news teams to keep a respectful distance. For their own safety.'

He turned back to Stephanie and Daniel. 'I'm finished here. Take me to your war room. Shoal, Barr: bring Edge.'

They filed out, Edge staggering along between Shoal and Barr. Toby and Flynn waited until the door had closed securely behind them, and then relaxed with explosive sighs of relief. Flynn turned off the camera, and concentrated on breathing deeply. Toby dabbed gingerly with his handkerchief at his tender mouth and nose, both of which felt as though they'd swollen to double their proper size.

'Did you get all that, Flynn? Tell me you got all that.'

'Every damn' second,' said the cameraman. 'Even though I nearly had an unpleasant incident in my underwear doing it. I really thought he was going to kill me.'

'Of course he was. He's an Investigator. Luckily we were going out live, and the others were sharp enough to know what that meant. The whole point of this new scheme is to show that ageing Investigators can still be controlled and employed in useful ways. Half A Man couldn't afford to have Edge going berserk in front of billions of viewers before the scheme had even properly begun. Did you pick up on what he said about the Clans? No more Investigators to work as enforcers and assassins for the Families. Her Imperial Majesty would appear to be getting concerned about the growing power and influence of certain prominent Houses. Naming no names, of course – but you can bet it's no accident the pilot scheme is taking place on a Wolfe planet.'

'Of course,' said Flynn. 'Makes you wonder what'll happen to those Investigators who can't hack it as part of a team. They've always been trained to act as individuals. Hell, I've heard of Investigators who overruled captains on their own starships. I can't see Lionstone allowing them just to retire. Nor can I imagine an Investigator happy to spend the rest of his days sitting by the fire.'

'Good point,' said Toby, looking sadly at the bloodstained mess that had once been a perfectly good handkerchief. 'I have a strong suspicion it'll be a case of learn to fit in or else. As in: die with your boots on or under an executioner's warrant. I wonder how that's going to go down with the other Investigators.'

'They'll probably approve. They're a cold bunch of bastards, when all's said and done. Not many survive to reach retirement age anyway. It's that kind of job. They probably prefer to die fighting, given the chance.'

'Even better if they can take somebody with them,' said Toby. 'With luck, a lot of somebodies. In future I think we'll keep a very respectful distance from Investigator Edge.'

'Damn' right,' said Flynn. He looked at Toby thoughtfully. 'I saw you trying to get up and help me. Were you worried about losing me, or about losing your only cameraman?'

'To be honest,' said Toby, 'I was mostly worried that, if you got killed, they'd find out about the lacy underwear you've got on. I mean, I have my reputation to think of.'

When the meeting in the war room was finally over, the Wolfes invited Half A Man and the three Investigators to join them for a meal and several drinks, but they declined, more or less politely. Investigators weren't social creatures, of course. Half A Man's reason for refusing the investation was that he hated being stared at. For a long time he had hoped that eventually he'd get used to it, but he never had. And the

461

Wolfes weren't even subtle, for all their smiles and pleasant words. So Half A Man saw each of his Investigators to their separate quarters, had a few private but very emphatic words with Edge, and then allowed himself to be shown to his own quarters.

The flunky they'd assigned to escort him kept a lot of distance between himself and his charge, and didn't hang around after completing his commission. Half A Man looked around the single room. It had all the necessities, and even a few luxuries – more than he'd been supplied with on the ship that had brought him here in such a hurry. Not that he gave much of a damn. He was here to work, not lounge around.

He sat down on the single chair, turned off its massage function and pulled it up to the writing table. He activated the built-in viewscreen, accessed the complex's computers, and called up the local troop records.

Technos III had mercenaries from a hundred worlds, under a dozen company commanders, with Wolfe security people as overall supervisors. The mercenaries had mostly had good records, before they'd come here. Their battles with the local rebels, the Rejects, made interesting but depressing reading. Neither side could be said to have an overall advantage but, just by refusing to be beaten for so long, the rebels were winning. The reason was obvious. It was the Rejects' world, and they worked with it, while the Wolfe troops needed temperature-controlled suits, armour and rebreathers just to cope with the changing weather. What technical advantages the Wolfe troops possessed were pretty much wiped out by the weather, and both sides knew it.

The Wolfes had lost a lot of men fighting the rebels. There were no figures for the Reject dead, but Half A Man doubted they were anywhere near as high. The few captured Rejects never talked. They died under interrogation, if they couldn't manage to kill themselves first. And, on top of all that, it appeared the rebels now had new leaders, recently arrived from offworld. One of them was no less than the legendary Jack Random, if the Wolfes' reports were to be believed. Half A Man had followed Random's career down the years. He'd always known that some day they were fated to meet. The two great legends of modern times. He frowned slightly. The last he'd heard, Random had been a broken old man. These reports spoke of a younger man, a powerful fighter. Perhaps some newcomer had taken up the old name. He sighed and shut down the screen. As if he didn't have enough problems in his life. Including, most especially, the three Investigators the Empress had placed under his command.

He'd always known Edge was going to be a problem. The man was a psychotic killer, violent and insubordinate. In any other occupation these would have been serious drawbacks, but to an Investigator they were a positive bonus. Up until now, his surly behaviour and the occasional regrettable incident had been tolerated because he never failed to get the job done, one way or another. But now he was getting older and slower, and, though he'd never admit it, the job was sometimes too much for him. He showed less and less self-control, and too clearly enjoyed the spilling of blood during his violent outbursts. You could never tell what would set him off. He had no friends, and his enemies daren't touch him because he was, after all, an Investigator.

Edge didn't respond to reason, kindness or military discipline. To control him in the field you have to prove you were the better man, and keep on proving it, by brute force if necessary. In a working Investigator such qualities could be condoned, even encouraged on occasion, but in a man close to enforced retirement . . . well, he was a danger to himself and everyone around him. It helped that Edge was somewhat intimidated by Half A Man's legend – as most people were.

Barr was at the other end of the spectrum: a military man through and through, gung-ho and eager for battle, dedicated to the Empire and its Empress. He wasn't stupid, just single-minded. A dangerous fighter with any weapon, he was never happier than when in the midst of action, probably because he had no social skills whatsoever. He didn't like people. Luckily he liked aliens even less. He was here on Technos III because he'd been ordered here, and he'd fight and kill and if need be die to carry out his orders. Or, at least, he'd always been that dedicated in the past. Now that his Empress had apparently lost faith in him and was contemplating taking him out of the field, he might start feeling differently about things. He wouldn't retire from action, for the simple reason that he had nothing to retire to. He'd bear watching.

Shoal was a whole different problem. Sharp, bright and terrifyingly efficient, Shoal was one of the top ten Investigators active at the moment, and she knew it. But she was dying slowly of a reare degenerative nerve disease. There was no cure – except for regeneration, but that was available only to the aristocracy. If she'd been young and in her prime, Half A Man might have been able to get her an exception, as a personal favour to him. But, even before the disease took hold, there'd been talk she was slowing down. The talk had been wrong, but that hadn't mattered. An Investigator's life was a hard and brutal one. She wasn't bitter. She was a good soldier. For the moment her faculties were still clear, and her experience would be invaluable. He could rely on her. Probably.

Half A Man pushed his chair away from the table, stood up and moved over to the bed. He lay down on it without bothering to pull back the bedclothes. He didn't sleep any more – never had, since the aliens had worked on him. But he still made a point of resting a few hours every night, so that he could dream. Sometimes in his waking dreams he remembered more of the things they'd done to him. When that happened he leapt out of bed screaming, but he needed those dreams. He had to remember exactly what had been done to him – all of it, no matter how bad it got. Because the real horror was that the change they'd worked in him wasn't over yet. Every year the energy construct that made up the right half of his body grew infinitesimally larger, eating up a little more of his human half. Only a very little. But it was an ongoing process that showed no signs of stopping or even slowing down. Eventually all his humanity would be gone, and he had no idea at all who or what he might be then.

It also seemed to him that the energy half of his body was slowly changing shape, becoming gradually less human-like

464

and more something else. Something alien. He had no
definitive memory of what the aliens who had changed him
looked like but he found the hints in his changing energy half
disquieting and disturbing. Even worse than that, he was
beginning to worry that the energy half might have its own
subordinate intelligence, its own secret thoughts, and just
possibly its own hidden agenda. It was vital he hang on grimly
to what was left of his humanity, and his mind, for fear of
what might replace it.

Which was one of the few reasons he had to be glad he was
here on Technos III. It would be good to be back in the field
again. Mostly he ran a desk these days, but the Empress had
wanted results on Technos III fast, and he had grabbed at the
chance with both hands. Things were so much simpler in
battle. It always felt good to be killing the Empire's enemies.
According to all the reports, the Rejects and their new leader,
whoever he really was, would make a good enemy. They were
clever, cunning and brave fighters: a real challenge, for once.
He'd enjoy killing them. And, just maybe, he could use the
occasion to teach Edge, Barr and Shoal to be part of an
armed fighting force. Why not? He'd taught them how to be
Investigators in the first place.

Toby Shreck had charmed, persuaded and bullied various
factory personnel into letting him use part of the complex's
communications centre as a mixing room for his next broadcast, due to go out the following day. He had a hell of a lot of
footage, courtesy of the redoubtable Flynn, who was probably
currently relaxing in his quarters in a nice little twinset and
pearls, hopefully behind a locked door, leaving Toby to do all
the hard work of choosing which precious moments of
recorded history would make it into the final mix. Toby
glared at the viewscreens and control panels before him,
poured himself another stiff drink, used it to wash down a
couple of uppers, and stuck one of his rare cigars back in his
mouth. Two in the morning, wired out of his skull, his fingers
moving faster than his thoughts could follow. This was how

you got your best work done, if you were Toby Shreck on a tight deadline.

He missed having room service to shout at, but otherwise this was business as usual. The whisky burned in his chest and in his mind, the uppers hammered through his bloodstream, and the cigar smoke kept him balanced as he sorted the gold from the dross. He had to make this compilation look good – really good. The live footage, a few days ago, of Half A Man and his Investigators had made people sit up and take notice, and had won him his best viewing share ever. It hadn't made him any friends among his fellow reporters, who had been bombarding the Wolfes with requests, demands and pleas for entry visas ever since. The Wolfes, not surprisingly, were stonewalling. They still thought they could control things, as long as it was just Toby Shreck and his cameraman. Toby grinned around his cigar. He'd show them.

But he couldn't rely on continuing to luck into great found footage – that was why this compilation had to be so good. He'd caught everyone's attention, but to hold on to it he'd have to follow up with an excellent programme about what was *really* going on down here on Technos III. It hadn't been easy. Everyone in and around the factory complex was being very careful about what they said in front of Toby, whether Flynn was with him or not. The word had come down from above. Luckily he already had enough good stuff to rock the Wolfes back in their expensive shoes. This particular compilation would be a fine example of what he could do, showing off his talent and establishing him as a major name in the news business . . . assuming it didn't get him killed first. It would also be a perfect thumbing of the nose to all those who had snubbed or insulted him.

He rolled his cigar from one side of his mouth to the other, grabbed a few chocolates from the nearby box, and knocked back another belt of whisky. He was supercharging now. Start with the Mother Bea footage. That was the prime lode.

He ran the tapes again, frowning as he concentrated on the tiny screens before him. He had two and sometimes three running at once, to keep up with his rocketing thoughts.

Flynn had, despite the darkness and the snow, got some great panning shots of the hospital tent with the factory complex in the background, to show the relative size of each. Then there were shots inside the tent, with the wounded lying still and usually silent, sometimes moaning quietly on their narrow cots. He called up the master shot of Mother Superior Beatrice explaining who would and would not be allowed treatment, according to the Wolfes. Then a close up of her tired, nearly defeated face.

'In the winter ... I've seen the surgeons stop in mid-operation to warm their hands in the steaming guts they've just opened up.'

Yes, that would make the viewers jump. Assuming, of course, he could smuggle this past the censors. There were a lot of people in authority here who'd demand to see the tape in its entirety before it went out. Toby once more smiled around his cigar. He had an idea or two.

More whisky and another chocolate.

The next tapes were from the brief interview Half A Man had finally – and relucantly – granted him. He hadn't wanted to, and Toby had had to use the Empress's name as a threat more than once just to get the man to stand still long enough for Flynn to point the camera at him. Half A Man looked even weirder on holo film than in reality. Something about the energy field that made up his right side interfered with the holo camera, giving the field a strobing, shimmering appearance that was painful to the eye after a while – look at it long enough and it felt like you were falling into it. Into a hell without end. Toby grunted. He'd just have to do a lot of cutting back and forth between Half A Man and himself. It'd detract from Half A Man's speech, but the guy hadn't been saying anything new. Toby leaned a little closer, frowning at the screen before him. The half-face was hard to read, but there was no mistaking the sincerity in the harsh, clipped voice.

'Anything that distracts humanity from defending itself from invading aliens cannot be permitted to continue. It must and will be stopped, by whatever means necessary. The

467

Empire needs the new stardrive this factory will produce. The rebels, through their actions, are threatening that production. I will put an end to that threat, even if it means wiping out the rebel population down to the last man, woman and child. The Empire must be protected. I know what aliens are capable of.'

Toby pursed his mouth unhappily as he hit the 'stop' button. Any aliens who could produce such a thing as Half A Man had to be seen as a threat to humanity as a whole, but no one had seen a trace of those aliens for two centuries. And there was always a chance that negotiating with the rebels would put an end to the war a damn' sight quicker than a ruthless programme of genocide. But Half A Man saw this as a matter of principle, and authority. He wouldn't even discuss the argument.

Toby's fingers moved quickly over the console keys, calling up quick shots of the three Investigators whom Half A Man had brought with him. Half A Man had refused point-blank to allow them to be interviewed, but Flynn had sneaked some footage anyway. Edge looked like a psycho killer who'd just had his favourite cut-throat razor stolen. Barr looked like a machine just waiting for orders. And Shoal . . . looked like she'd seen it all before and hadn't been impressed the first time. They all seemed very dangerous, completely unswerving, and entirely professional. Poor rebel bastards didn't know what was going to hit them.

Suddenly the control-room door burst open and Daniel Wolfe strode in, only to come to a sudden halt as he discovered how little space there was. It rather spoiled the effect of his dramatic entrance. He scowled at Toby as the reporter turned unhurriedly round in his swivel chair. Daniel leaned forward menacingly, and Toby just happened to blow cigar smoke in his face. Daniel coughed despite himself, and did his best to tower over Toby.

'Listen to me, worm,' snarled Daniel, 'I want to see very inch of your tape before it's broadcast. This is a Wolfe complex, and we decide what leaves here and what doesn't. You even *try* to sneak something past me and I'll have security throw you in the cells and get your superiors to send a replacement who understands how the universe works. You'll like the cells: on a good day you can look through the bars in your window and see the wall we put traitors against before we shoot them. And, out there, *we* decide who the traitors are. So make the Wolfes look good, make the factory look good, if you value your life, little man.'

He stormed out, slamming the door behind him. Toby lifted the bottle of whisky, toasted the closed door with it, and drank straight from the bottle. He'd been expecting pressure, but nothing quite so blatant. Bloody Daniel Wolfe and his ambitious superbitch sister – she was the one behind the threats. Daniel didn't have it in him to come up with a speech like that on his own. Stephanie had probably written it out and made him memorize it. Typical Wolfes. Thugs with pedigrees.

A thought occurred to Toby, and he smiled nastily around his cigar.

He turned back to the mixing console, and it took only a few moments' searching to call up the footage he had in mind. He ran the shots in slow motion. Daniel and Stephanie together. Michel and Lily together. Smiles and glances and shared body-space. Everyone with an eye in their head could see that Michel and Lily were having it off. They'd been very careful not to say or do anything incriminating in public, but you had only to look at their body language to see the truth of how they felt about each other – the way their eyes sparked when they met, the way their bodies oriented towards each other no matter where they were in the room, the way certain words and phrases were subtly, unconsciously emphasized. Toby had it all on tape.

Of course, Daniel and Stephanie hadn't noticed a thing, being rather more interested in each other. Toby sniggered, and beat a fast tattoo on the edge of the console with both hands. He couldn't say anything outright, of course, but a little carefully arranged footage of both couples should do the job for him. People in society would catch up on it, and start the word spreading. Before too long the Wolfes would become a laughing-stock, in and out of court. That would teach Daniel bloody Wolfe to burst in and act the heavy with poor little Toby Shreck.

And that was then the door burst open again, and Cardinal James Kassar had his try at making a dramatic entrance ruined by crashing straight into the chair that Toby had thoughtfully placed before the door after the last visit. Kassar kicked the chair aside, and glared at Toby, who leaned back in his chair and gave the cardinal his most innocent face. It didn't fool Kassar for a moment, but then it wasn't meant to.

'I've had a communication from my superiors in the Church,' said Kassar, the controlled anger in his voice more than matched by the open fury in his ruined face, 'the gist of which was that your live broadcast made both myself and the Church look ridiculous, because you didn't wait for me to get there. They went on for some time, but they were basically just repeating themselves. The words "laughing stock" were mentioned, along with "recall" and "demotion". Listen carefully, you little toad, you are not going to ruin my career while furthering your own. From now on I see everything you've got before it goes out, and, if you do anything that might undermine my or the Church's authority here, I will personally excommunicate you with a blunt hatchet. Is that clear?'

'Oh, perfectly,' said Toby. 'Couldn't be clearer.' He took a quick drink from his bottle. 'I would offer you some whisky, Cardinal, but I've only got the one bottle. I feel I should at this stage in all honesty point out that I do have principles.'

'Mess with me again and your principles will be going home in separate jars.'

Kassar about-turned and marched out with extreme dignity, slamming the door behind him. Toby waited a cautious few seconds, then gave the closed door the finger before getting up and jamming two small wedges under it. *That* should put an end to any more stormings-in. He turned back to the console and leaned over the screens again. He knew just the bit of tape he wanted. A nice stretch of Cardinal Kassar drilling his Church troops in the roasting summer heat, standing at his ease in the shade while shouting and bullying and generally carrying on like the tight-assed little dictator he was. Toby smirked, and bit down hard on his cigar. He wouldn't even have to sneak this past Kassar. The damn' fool was so full of himself he'd probably think it made him look good.

Toby tipped the bottle to his lips again and then put it firmly to one side. The uppers were rocketing through his system like ricocheting bullets, and he felt great. He called up some footage of the trenches surrounding the factory – the circles of hell from which no man returned unchanged. Patch in some shots of the elite Jesuit commandoes drilling the fanatical Church troops, and then cut to the wounded in the hospital tent. Toby rocked back and forth in his chair. Someone was banging on the door. The wedges would keep them out. Toby's fingers flew over the keyboard. He was on a roll now. If the Wolfes and the cardinal and all the other bastards thought they could keep him from filing the story of his life, they must be crazy. They could view the tape as often as they liked: it wouldn't make any difference.

They'd probably never ever heard of the palimpsest method. Record something on a tape, then record over it. Playback shows only the upper recording, but the right kind of machine will pick up the earlier recording, still there, underneath. The process hadn't been around long, but Toby had always believed in being up-to-the-minute. There'd be a stink afterwards, but interest in Technos III would be so high the Wolfes wouldn't be able to censor him any more. Toby Shreck laughed aloud, and worked on further into the early hours of the morning.

A handful of Rejects led Random, Storm and Journey down through a series of dimly lit corridors and tunnels, far below the surface of Technos III. The tunnels grew increasingly narrow, and were occasionally barely wide enough for two men to walk abreast. The walls were in some places smooth, where they'd been blasted out of the living rock by energy weapons, and in others torn and jagged, where hand-held tools had done the work. Random tried very hard not to think about the increasing weight of rock above his head. He'd spent his share of time working from hidden underground caverns and tunnels, away from prying eyes and sensors, but he'd never learned to like it.

The tunnels twisted and turned and branched endlessly in a maze of such complexity that any outsider would be hopelessly lost in a few minutes. Random had no doubt this was deliberate. The Rejects didn't trust anyone with their secrets all at once, not even him, their hero – and he'd have been disappointed in them if they had. As always, he knew exactly where he was, but he didn't like to tell them and spoil their fun. He strode along quite happily, Ruby at his side, Storm puffing along behind.

Random was getting a little worried about Storm. His friend had been in the field with him for many years, fighting the Empire's best on more planets than either of them cared to remember. But they'd both known they were getting too old for it, even before they'd got their asses kicked so conclusively on Cold Rock. Since then, Random had been given a new lease of life, courtesy of the Maze, and was revelling in it, but Storm was still growing older and slower. He hadn't taken the increasing differences between his own condition and Random's at all well, but Random was at a loss as to what to do about it. Storm was performing good and valued work as an adviser and strategist, but it wasn't the same, and both of them knew it. So, when Storm had insisted on coming along on this particular mission, just to stretch his legs, Random hadn't had the heart to say no.

'How many miles of these tunnels are there?' said Storm, trying – and failing – to keep the tiredness out of his voice.

'No one knows for sure,' said Long Lankin 32. The clone looked as thin and malnourished as ever. He found the going hard too but, like Storm, refused to be left out of things; the two of them had naturally gravitated together. 'The only maps are in the Rejects' heads, and they each know only part of the whole layout. So we're protected, if any of us are captured. The Rejects have been digging these tunnels for centuries now – repairing old ones and blasting out new ones – so the maps are always changing. Sometimes I feel I need a guide just to help me find the toilet in the early hours of the morning. Just to complicate things, the Wolfe security forces dig tunnels of their own. Sometimes the excavating teams run into each other, and then all hell breaks loose. The war goes on down here, as well. Tunnel rats clawing at each other in the darkness. The Wolfes' mercenaries don't last long down here: they can't take the constant darkness and claustrophobia, and the pressure drives them crazy. The Rejects, on the other hand, actually like it. The protective layers of stone and metal make them feel secure. Mad bastards. No offence, people.'

The twenty or so Rejects walking with them smiled and nodded, not insulted.

Alexander Storm summoned up enough breath for another question. 'How deep do these tunnels go? It feels like we've been descending for hours. Any further and we'll need an express elevator to get back to the surface.'

'The surface can do without us today,' said Spectre Alice. She'd developed a fondness towards Storm and attached herself to him whenever possible, to his distress. She was, after all, old and short and ugly, and her furs hadn't been washed since they'd been on the animals. Also, there was madness in her eyes, right up front where everyone could see it. She smiled chummily at Storm, and tried to take his hand. He avoided hers with the dexterity of long practice. She wasn't put out. 'We're heading down to one of our main meeting chambers,' she said happily. 'Time you saw where the real decisions get made. We won't go down *too* far. Dangerous things live in the deep down – creatures that have adapted to the depths and the dark, away from the weather and the war. Mostly, we don't disturb them and they don't massacre us. Don't worry, dear. Just stick with old Spectre Alice and she'll keep you safe.'

Storm smiled weakly, feeling not at all safe, and looked determinedly ahead in the hope of discouraging further conversation.

473

Random had to hide a smile of his own. Storm had been something of a lady-killer in his day. At his side, Ruby sighed heavily, and he turned his attention to her. She was scowling, her mouth turned down sullenly.

'I hate walking,' she said, apropos of nothing in particular. 'I'm a bounty-hunter, not a health freak. Where are all these tunnels rats and deadly creatures? I could do with a little excitement. I didn't come to Technos III to be a tourist. When do I get to kill somebody?'

'I like her,' said Long Lankin 32. 'She's got the right attitude.'

They walked on, and on. Storm had more and more trouble keeping up with the pace, even with Spectre Alice at his side to encourage him. Random felt guilty. Every day he looked younger and felt younger, and Storm got older. Where once they had been comrades-in-arms now they looked more like father and son. Random tried not to think too much about the differences between them. He didn't like the idea that he might be becoming an altogether new person – even if he did feel *alive* again for the first time in years. He fell back to walk beside Storm, and wondered whether he did so out of friendship or out of pity.

'Why did we ever come here?' Storm said quietly to him. 'War is young men's work. We're too old for this, Jack. We should be sitting beside a fire in a tavern, telling outrageous stories of our youth. We've earned that. We've spilt enough blood, in enough battles. Why do we have to do it all again?'

'Because the war isn't over,' said Random. 'We swore an oath, remember? We swore upon our blood and our honour that we would fight the Empire until either it fell or we did.'

'Young men swore that oath,' said Storm. 'Young men who knew nothing about war or politics or the reality of how the Empire works.'

'Are you saying you don't believe in the cause any more?'

'Of course I still believe in the cause! I'm here, aren't I? I'm just saying it's time for someone else to carry the banner. Someone younger, who doesn't feel the cold in his bones or wake coughing his lungs up every morning. We've done our bit. And I'm too old to die on a strange world beside strange people, fighting to free a few clones from a factory.'

'You'll get your second wind soon,' said Random lamely. 'You'll feel better then.'

'Don't bloody patronize me, Random,' said Storm.

They strode along in silence after that.

Then the Reject in the lead came to a sudden halt, raising his hand to stop the people behind him. Everyone stood quietly together in the pool of the lanterns' light, staring into the gloom ahead, listening carefully. Storm looked anxiously about, but Random and Spectre Alice were too busy listening to pay him any attention. Random frowned, concentrating, reaching out with his altered senses. He could just discern a low, regular thudding coming from somewhere further up the tunnel.

'What is it?' he said quietly. 'What's coming?'

'Wolfe tunnel rats,' said Spectre Alice. 'They have devices for detecting movement in nearby tunnels. They're close now. Brace yourselves.'

Suddenly everyone had a weapon of some sort in their hands. Mostly swords and axes, with the occasional length of spiked chain. Random and Ruby moved automatically to stand together, swords at the ready, leaving Storm to fend for himself. He glared at them, and hefted his own sword uncertainly. The steady thudding grew nearer and nearer. Random's free hand hovered over the disrupter on his belt, but he didn't draw it – he didn't like to think what a ricocheting energy beam might do in these close quarters. He just hoped the Wolfe fighters had had the same thought.

The wall to his right cracked apart suddenly, torn from floor to ceiling, and men in armoured battle suits lurched out into the tunnel. They moved surprisingly quickly amid the whine of supporting servomechanisms, tearing into the twenty rebels with massive axes and longswords that only powered armour could have wielded.

The rebels darted around and among the armoured men, searching out their blind spots and weak points with flashing swords and axes. There wasn't much room for manoeuvre in

475

the confined space. The endlessly shifting, boiling mass of bodies was packed together. People took a stand just long enough to get in a solid blow before slipping away again. The slower and the less lucky cried out, and blood spurted. Those who fell were trampled underfoot, and rarely rose to fight again. Swords and axes bounced harmlessly away from the solid plates of the Wolfe fighters' armour, but there were weaker, more vulnerable spots at the joints, for those who knew where to look for them. Even so, the armoured men could take a dozen hits and press on unharmed, while a blow powered by their servomechanisms could cut clean through a Reject's body. And there were far more armoured men than Rejects.

One by one the rebels fell, the survivors being pushed further and further back down the tunnel. Three armoured men were down, dispatched by blows to neck or eyes, but they were only three out of many. Still the Rejects fought on determinedly and without panic. Their long adaptation to Technos III's extremes had made them somewhat more than human, and they were well used to the conditions underground. They swarmed around the armoured men, ducking and dodging blows with almost impossible speed, never letting up in their attack. And slowly their retreat stopped.

Right in the thick of it all, Ruby Journey braced herself and swung her sword with both hands. The blade powered round in a tight arc and sheared clean through a soldier's armoured neck. The helmeted head bounced away across the sea of heaving shoulders before finally falling to the floor, the look of astonishment still clear on the bloody face.

Random roared his approval. He brought his own sword round, only to see the blade bounce harmlessly back from a suddenly raised armoured arm. The impact jarred the sword right out of his hand, and it disappeared in the mess of heaving bodies. The Wolfe mercenary grinned and drew back his sword for a killing thrust. Ruby saw and cried out, but she was too far away to help. Raw fury blazed up inside Random, and he punched his opponent in the chest with all his strength. His bare fist hammered through the battle armour and plunged on into the man's chest. The Wolfe soldier screamed horribly as Random's fist closed around his heart, and tore it out. Random held the still beating heart up in his hand, blood running down his arm as he laughed victoriously.

For a moment the battle seemed to stop, with everyone frozen where they were, and then it began again, only this time the rebels were forcing the soldiers back. Random and Ruby pressed forward and could not be stopped, and the Rejects took new heart from the example. More of the armoured men fell, screaming. Some turned to flee, but there wasn't room in the packed space and they just got tangled among their fellows. Spectre Alice crowed merrily as she straddled the shoulders of a man in armour, leaning forward over him, her bloody dagger stabbing again and again through the eyeholes of his helmet.

In the end, not one Wolfe soldier got away. Their broken armoured bodies littered the floor, stretching away down the tunnel. There were rebel dead, too, but not nearly so many. It seemed there was blood everywhere, running down the walls and pooled on the floor. Random and Ruby grinned at each other, and the Rejects crowded round to slap them on the back and shoulders. Random scrubbed happily at the blood on his hand and arm with a cloth, and had a nod and a smile for everyone, until his eyes met Storm's.

His old friend had broken a little apart from the others. There was blood on his sword and his clothes, but little of it seemed to be his. He was breathing hard, and his sword trembled in his hand. He looked at Random as though he were a stranger. Random moved over to join him, but stopped some way short, held back by the coldness in Storm's eyes.

'Who are you?' said Storm. 'The Jack Random I remember couldn't do things like that. Nothing human could.'

'I've . . . been through changes,' said Random. 'I'm more than I was. But I'm still me.'

'No, you're not,' said Storm. 'I don't know *who* you are any more.'

He turned away and walked off down the tunnel by himself. Random let him go – if only because there was a certain amount of truth in what his old friend had said. He looked up to see Spectre Alice staring at him. He shrugged, and she shrugged back and went after Storm. Ruby Journey had meanwhile, with snarls and curses, cleared a space around her and was methodically cleaning her sword. Ruby wasn't much for congratulations or camaraderie. She wouldn't feel like talking with him now, either. Random shrugged again. He'd just done what he had to, as he had so many times before.

But he could still feel the heart beating out the last of its life in his hand, while he laughed. That wasn't like him. Not like him at all.

He pushed the thought aside as another occurred to him. He couldn't help wondering if the Rejects had deliberately chosen a path that would intercept armoured Wolfe tunnel rats, just to see what the legendary Jack Random and his friends were capable of when not part of a Reject army. It was the kind of test he might have organized himself, once. And, though he had been impressed by the way the Rejects had handled themselves, he was a little disturbed that they hadn't tried to take any prisoners. There came a time when hatred just got in the way of winning a war. In the end you won more victories by accepting surrenders than by trying to wipe out the other side to the very last man. Or did the hatreds run too deep, here on Technos III?

The Church troops, known collectively as the Faithful, were training together with the Wolfe mercenaries in the open area between the factory complex and the first trench, and Toby Shreck and Flynn were there to cover it all. No one was glad to see them there, but Toby and Flynn were used to that by now. Officially, the soldiers of the Church of Christ the Warrior and the hardened Wolfe mercenaries were supposed to be one integrated fighting force by now, but both sides had centuries of tradition, not to mention white-hot mutual enmity, behind them. Consequently, what had been intended as an orchestrated set-piece of hard drill and weapons training was rapidly deteriorating into a complete mess as the Faithful and the mercs strode to outdo each other in sheer viciousness, if not skill.

Cardinal Kassar was there in black battle armour surmounted by a billowing crimson cape, screaming orders and counter-orders until he was purple in what remained of his face. The colour clashed with his outfit and warned of future heart problems, but no one felt like getting close enough to tell him. He cursed and yelled at the top of his parade-ground voice, trying through sheer force of personality to force his men to behave. But not even the horrible punishments he was threatening were enough to restore order. The mercs were damned if they were going to be shown up by a bunch of pansy hymn-singers, and the Church troops were determined to show a bunch of professional thugs what could be achieved by people trained in the one true faith.

It was all getting very nasty, and not a little bloody. Both sides had their heads down and were stuck in. Jesuit commandoes were running back and forth between the lines, bellowing commands and breaking up fights with impartial venom towards both sides, using whatever force was necessary. They darted here and there, snapping at their charges like incensed sheepdogs. They couldn't be everywhere at once, but it was perfectly evident that it was only their efforts that were preventing a complete breakdown of authority. Even battle-hardened mercs had enough sense to be wary of the Jesuit commandoes: they were the elite of the elite, killers said to be second in ruthlessness only to the Investigators. They fought in battles alongside their men and kept body parts as souvenirs.

With an effort Cardinal Kassar stopped himself shouting. His hands had clenched into fists, and his whole body strained to sprint forward and lay heavy hands on the disobedient bastards running amok before him. But he knew Flynn's camera was covering him as well as his men, and he couldn't afford to be seen to be losing control. Everything else had gone wrong so far on this mission, but up until now he'd always been able to find someone else to blame it on. A public failure now could undermine the whole purpose of his mission

– to restore order on Technos III – and, just as important, it could do a hell of a lot of damage to his career prospects. So this particularly display was going to go right, even if he had to start executing people at random to prove he was serious.

Toby Shreck studied Kassar from a safe distance and smiled contentedly. He knew a man on the edge of apoplexy when he saw one. He also recognized a complete military cock-up. He hadn't seen such a mess since Valentine Wolfe had slipped a little something into a marching band's mid-time tea break, just for a laugh. The tape of that particular event had been a bestseller for over six months.

Toby glanced quickly at his cameraman.

'Tell me you're getting all this, Flynn. They couldn't be providing us a better show if they'd rehearsed it.'

'Relax, chief. Billions of people all across the Empire are watching this live.'

Toby grinned at the magic word 'live'. His previous piece had achieved first-class ratings, the highest share Imperial News had ever attained. Some stations were still running it, and paying through the nose for the privilege. There had been talk of major awards for Toby and Flynn, and, more importantly, large bonuses. The Wolfes had nearly gone into cardiac arrest when they had first seen the item, especially the Mother Beatrice bits, and had screamed for their lawyers, but calm had prevailed and Stephanie and Daniel had somehow managed to transfer all the blame on to Valentine. They'd promised to make changes, but so far nothing significant had altered on Technos III.

The one really good thing to have come out of the uproar was the Wolfes' concession to Imperial News that in future Toby and Flynn would be permitted to cover all important events live. There was a massive audience in the Empire waiting impatiently to see what the pair would come up with next – which was, of course, in its way their main problem. A good act needs a good encore. Toby, for one, had not expected anything much to come out of covering a programme of drill and weapons training, but he'd had to agree for want of anything else. No one else would talk to him now that he was being constantly shadowed by Wolfe security, and his audience was getting impatient.

He smiled contentedly as a bunch of the Faithful brought down a bunch of mercenaries, and gathered quickly around for a bit of putting the boot in. He should have had more faith in the ability of the Wolfes and Cardinal Kassar to screw up everything they touched. He looked again at Flynn, who was covering the chaos before him with practised ease. The camera was currently hovering high above the confusion, with Flynn seeing, through his comm implant link, everything it saw. It scooted back and forth as Flynn's attention was caught by each new outbreak of violence. For all his faults, and he had many, Flynn was an excellent cameraman. Of course, he'd become unbearably cocky and insufferable since the amazing reception of the first broadcast. Toby was just glad the man hadn't turned up in a black basque and feather boa, like he'd threatened.

'Heads up, chief,' said Flynn quietly. 'Something wicked this way comes.'

Toby looked round, and winced inwardly as he saw Kassar striding determinedly towards them. He felt a distinct twinge of unease, but was careful to keep it out of his face. People like Kassar seized on weaknesses.

Toby bowed formally to the cardinal and gave him a smile so natural he almost fooled himself.

'Good morning, Cardinal. Isn't is a lovely day? I think the early autumn is the closest Technos III has to civilized weather. Until the razorstorms start, of course. How may we assist you?'

'You can start by turning that damned camera off until we've got things under control.'

'Sorry, Cardinal,' said Toby pleasantly, 'Your superiors' orders were quite specific. They want us to cover everything that happens here today.'

Kassar snorted, but had enough sense to say nothing. He'd seen the orders. The Church had felt the need for a propaganda piece to back up its ongoing negotiations for increased influence at Court, and Toby and Flynn and the Technos III

Faithful had seemed the safest bet for good ratings. They'd also hoped that a well viewed piece, showing the great skills and discipline of the Church troops, might go some way to restoring the damage done by Toby's and Flynn's previous piece. Kassar could have told them . . . but as usual no one had asked him. His fists were so tight he could feel the nails driving into his palms, but he made himself smile frostily at the two newsmen.

'Of course. Make sure you get some good footage. But I want to see your tape before it gets broadcast. The Church has very kindly supplied me with new equipment, specifically designed to detect such things as palimpsests – or anything else you might try to sneak past me.'

Confident that this time at least he'd got the last word, Kassar turned and stalked back to his milling troops, clearing his aching throat. *Now* they were going to listen. Or else. Lots of all else. Flynn watched him go.

'Do you think we should have reminded him this is going out live?'

'Not our fault if he doesn't read his own orders carefully,' said Toby briskly. 'I can't believe they made that idiot a cardinal.'

'Family connections,' said Flynn.

'Isn't it always?' said Toby. 'The man's a bully and a blow-hard. Do even his own troops like him?'

'Are you kidding? It's only the Jesuit commandoes that have kept his men from slipping a fragmentation grenade his way – and even the Jesuits are getting pretty fed up with him. Still, he has his admirers in the hierarchy. After all, utter ruthlessness is what gets you on in the Church of Christ the Warrior.'

'Good point. Does Kassar ever go into battle alongside his troops, or is he strictly a rear-echelon sheep-botherer?'

'Give the man his due, he does like to be in the thick of things. I don't believe he's missed a single battle since he got here. Offer him a chance to kill as many people as he can get his hands on and he's as happy as a clam.' Flynn paused, and looked thoughtful. 'Which is a strange expression, when you think about it. Are clams renowned for being particularly happy?'

'Don't change the subject.'

'What was the subject?'

'I forget,' said Toby. 'Just keep filming. Things seem finally to be calming down, unfortunately. Maybe he threatened them all with mass crucifixion.'

'Wouldn't surprise me. I just hope he gives me time to set up some proper lighting first.'

Toby sighed. 'No such luck. There goes our chance of hanging on to our ratings. He'll get it all under control, everyone will obey orders and play nicely together, and our viewers will change channels in droves. There's no justice.'

But suddenly the scene changed. Explosions went off all around the drill area, blasting open the metal plain. The noise was deafening, and black smoke billowed up, throwing everything into confusion. Further explosions roared on all sides. Shrapnel flew, and Church troops and Wolfe mercs alike abandoned their discipline to run for cover. The smoke filled the sky, blocking out the sun, so that an artificial twilight fell across the area. There were fires blazing everywhere. No one could make themselves heard.

Fresh openings had appeared in the plain, and rebels came surging up out of the new tunnels they'd dug underneath. They fired energy guns they weren't supposed to have, and lobbed grenades in all directions. The mercenaries and the Faithful tried to pull themselves together, but they were scattered and confused, and the rebels tore right through them. Steel flashed, and blood pooled on the metal ground.

Toby Shreck watched it all with his jaw somewhere down between his knees. 'Holy shit. *Holy shit!* Flynn, tell me you're getting this!'

'I'm getting it! I'm getting it! The light's lousy and there's smoke everywhere, but I'm getting it!'

The Empire forces' retreat was an utter rout. They fought here and there in small clumps, but mostly they just ran for their lives. Explosions were still crumping, and there seemed no end to the army of rebels pouring up out of the hidden tunnels. Jesuit commandoes were screaming at their men to stand and fight, but their words were lost in the chaos. Some rebels threw themselves at the Jesuits, and they reluctantly retreated, holding off the greater numbers with stunning swordplay. Kassar spun this way and that in the middle of everything, completely thrown, unable to think what to do for the best. The rebels streamed past him, pursuing the fleeing Faithful and mercenaries.

Some of the Empire forces finally pulled themselves together and stopped to stand and fight. The plain was quickly dotted with duelling figures.

Toby Shreck recognized a familiar face. He grabbed Flynn by the shoulder and pointed urgently.

'There! Three o'clock! Do you know who that is? It's Jack bloody Random, the professional rebel himself! No one's seen him in action since the fiasco on Cold Rock. I didn't know he was on Technos III. Did *you* know he was on Technos III? Oh, who cares! Just keep filming. Jack Random's comeback, and we're covering it live! People have been awarded their own chat shows for less!'

'If that is indeed Jack Random he's looking very good for his age,' said Flynn, concentrating on his camera's movements. 'Vicious, too. He's cutting through that bundle of mercs like Old Man Death himself. Who are those people with him?'

'Don't know the old man,' said Toby, flinching reflexively as another explosion went off. 'The woman's wearing a bounty-hunter's leathers, but I don't know the face. We can run a trace later. You stick with Random. He's the story here.'

Toby jumped back with a shriek as a rebel appeared out of nowhere right in front of him. The man's eyes were dark, and blood dripped from his sword. Flynn called his camera back to hover protectively between him and the rebel. Toby realized there were just as many rebels running behind him as in front, and froze where he was. Flynn stood his ground. The rebel looked at Toby and Flynn, smiled, winked into the camera, and then disappeared back into the mêlée. Apparently even rebels understood the need for good publicity. Toby began to get his breathing back under control.

Someone blew a whistle. Others took it up, and suddenly the rebels were breaking away from fights and pursuits and falling back, disappearing down into the tunnels under the metal plain. All were gone in a matter of a few minutes. As they departed they blew prepared charges to seal off the holes to their tunnels, leaving the Faithful, the mercenaries, the Jesuit commandoes and Cardinal Kassar standing in a daze, looking around and trying to figure out what the hell had just hit them. Smoke drifted on the air, and flames burned here and there on bodies that had been hit by energy guns. There were corpses all over the place – but hardly any of them were rebels: they'd taken most of their wounded and dead with them. Everything seemed very quiet.

Kassar looked over at Flynn, still filming, and lurched towards him, his eyes wild.

'You! Stop filming! And give me that tape! Now!'

'Sorry, Cardinal,' said Toby Shreck, somehow keeping an ecstatic grin off his face, 'I'm afraid this has all been going out live, as your superiors insisted. Do you have any comment you'd care to make at this time?'

Kassar raised his disrupter and blew the hovering camera out of the air.

Flynn glared at him. 'You'll be hearing from my union about that.'

Random, Journey and Storm laughed breathlessly together as they ran with the Rejects, plunging down the narrow tunnels. The assault had gone exactly as planned, with minimum casualties on their side and maximum damage and embarrassment to the Wolfes and the Church. A clone working in the factory complex had provided them with the exact timing necessary to be sure of camera coverage. Now the Rejects scuttled back through the new tunnels and on into older, established parts, keeping up a good pace for all their tiredness. The explosive-sealed openings wouldn't hold the Wolfe troops back for long – they weren't supposed to. The battle

485

wasn't over yet. Down below, in darkness and familiar confines, the Rejects would teach a final, deadly lesson to their enemy.

The tunnels sloped steeply for some time and then opened up suddenly into a vast cavern. Random lurched to a halt as the path before him split apart to form a number of even narrower trails leading down and along the sides of the cavern. The open space was dizzyingly huge, as though someone had hollowed out the inside of a mountain. The ceiling was hundreds of feet above and the cavern floor seemed as far below. Random stood very still, staring about him, as rebels jostled to get past, running confidently down and along the narrow trails. The walls were mostly smooth, polished by who knew how many centuries of polluted running water: there were bright streaks of metallic blue and green and gold, harsh reminders of long-forgotten industries. Light from the rebels' lanterns glistened brightly on metal stalactites and stalagmites, hanging ponderously from the ceiling or jutting up from the curling yellow mists that hid the cavern floor. Ruby and Storm were at Random's side, quietly urging him forward, but he couldn't move. It was as though he'd stumbled into a giant cathedral, the vast hidden soul of Technos III. He couldn't seem to get his breath. He felt like a fly crawling over a stained-glass window in some old, abandoned monastery.

He finally allowed himself to be persuaded to go on, following Spectre Alice down a long series of steps into the misty depths below. All around him the Rejects were scattering into prearranged hiding places and ambush positions. Random slowly realized that, to them, this awesome place was nothing special. They didn't see the glory and the spectacle of such a natural wonder. They had no time for that. They saw it only as a good place to launch an ambush – just another killing-ground in their never-ending war. Spectre Alice led Random, Ruby and Storm into a concealed depression in the cavern wall where they had a good view of the single entrance above. She made sure Storm was settled comfortably beside her, drew her disrupter, and then settled down to wait. The energy gun seemed very large in her small bony hand. Thin wisps of yellow smoke, smelling of brimstone, drifted up from the floor below. The Rejects had melted into their hiding places like so many silent shadows, and now they waited patiently for their enemy to come to them. The great cavern was still and quiet.

Random edged over so he could put his mouth next to Spectre Alice's ear. 'How long has this place been here?'

'Who knows? A lot longer than us, that's for sure.'

'It's wonderful.'

'Damn' right. Perfect place for an ambush. We can control everything that happens down here. The Wolfes' troops don't even know what they're walking into. Poor bastards. There will be blood and suffering, and the slaughter of our enemy. Now shut up. They'll be here soon. You can play tourist later, when we've killed them all.'

The sound of running feet came from above, and Random crouched down, gun in hand. It wouldn't be the first time he'd turned a place of beauty and wonder into a battleground. He'd seen many wonders and marvels in his day, on many planets, and left them littered with the dead and the dying. For all the nobility of his cause, he sometimes thought the only real legacy he'd leave behind him was a bloody trail of death and destruction.

And then the Wolfe and Church troops came pouring out into the cavern – led by the three Investigators, Barr, Edge and Shoal – and there was no time left for introspection or regret. This was the killing time, the dance of the quick and the soon-to-be dead.

The great cavern blazed with light as both sides opened up with energy weapons. The brilliant beams spat in a hundred directions, criss-crossing, deflecting from the metal walls. There were screams and war cries and desperately yelled orders as the Faithful and the Wolfe mercenaries scurried for cover. Rage and the need for revenge had brought them this far, running recklessly through the dark in pursuit of a mocking enemy, but the deadly energy beams brought them to a sudden halt, as though they'd slammed into a wall. Men fell – sometimes screaming, sometimes not – and bodies littered the narrow paths, burning quietly. The survivors found hiding-places from which to return fire.

Finally the cavern fell quiet as all the energy weapons were exhausted. There was a pause, interrupted only by the moans of the wounded and the dying echoes, and then both sides drew their swords, emerged from hiding, and went out on to the misty cavern floor to meet each other.

This was a blood feud for the Faithful and the mercs now – for the Rejects it always had been. The two sides pressed relentlessly forward, breasting the yellow mist with no place for caution or second thoughts. Swords clashed and blood spurted, and the great floor of the chamber became a mass of struggling figures.

Random and Ruby fought back-to-back, as always, unbeatable and unstoppable. Storm fought doggedly nearby, swinging his sword with the studied skill born of many years' experience. Age had slowed him, but he was still an Investigator. Enemies swirled around the three of them, but could not bring them down. Ruby Journey killed and killed and laughed aloud, in her element again. Random fought with a cold, focused precision, concerned only to end the fighting as soon as possible. Storm struggled on, but now he was gasping for breath, his sword seeming to grow heavier with every blow and parry. After all, he was only human.

Finally, almost inevitably, the three most famous fighters of the rebellion found themselves facing the three greatest fighters of the Empire forces on Technos III: Barr, Edge and Shoal. The milling mob seemed almost to cooperate to bring them together, as though they were the microcosm by which the greater struggle would be decided. Edge faced off against Ruby, Barr against Random, Shoal against Storm. They paused with something like mutual respect, and then threw themselves at each other. Blades clashed and sprang apart, and then the greater crush of fighting bodies slowly drew the three battling couples in different directions.

Random put his back against a metal stalagmite as Edge hammered at him with his sword. The professional rebel dodged the blows he could and parried those he couldn't, content to let the Investigator tire himself out. Except . . . Edge didn't seem to get tired. On the contrary, his strength seemed to grow with every blow, just as his fury rose with every failed attack. His mouth was stretched in a mirthless smile, and his eyes were dark and wild. Random ducked deep to avoid a double-handed swing, and Edge's blade sheared clean through the tip of the metal stalagmite at Random's back. It came to Random that fighting defensively against an Investigator was a good way to get yourself killed, Maze-improved or not.

He boosted, feeling the blood hammer through his veins and thunder in his head, and launched himself at Edge. The Investigator fell back a step, startled, and then held his ground, for all of Random's boosted strength and speed. He was an Investigator, and even an ageing Investigator was a match for most things the universe could send against him – that was his job. But Random had been through the Madness Maze and wasn't like most things in the universe any more. Random smiled, very sanely, into Edge's crazy grin, and let his guard drop just a little. Edge's sword flew forward instantly, to take advantage of the opening. Random's free hand came up impossibly quickily, slapping the blade to one side. For an endless moment they stood together, Edge wide open to a killing blow and knowing it. Then Random's sword plunged into Edge's chest and out through his back. Edge gave a small bark of pain, blood spraying from his grimacing mouth, and then sank to his knees. Random pulled his sword free, and Edge collapsed on to his face, as though only the sword had been holding him up. Random decapitated him anyway, just in case. Edge was an Investigator, after all.

Ruby boosted the moment she realized her opponent was an Investigator. Barr might be the oldest of the three, but he was still far more dangerous than most men would ever be. So she dared him into a *corps à corps*. Their faces came close together over their crossed blades, and then she spat in his left eye. In the split second he was distracted she pulled a knife from her belt and stuck it between his ribs. She felt blood gush out over her hand before he pushed himself away from her. She launched a furious attack, with all her boosted strength and speed behind it, and he backed further. More blood poured down his side every time he moved, but still he wouldn't give in to the dreadful wound in his side, parrying her every blow, his face dispassionate. In the end, Ruby had to use her full strength to beat aside his blade and bring the edge of her sword slashing back across his exposed throat.

Blood erupted, splattering her face. She stepped back, wiping it off her forehead so that it wouldn't run down into her eyes. She smiled as she saw her cut had sliced halfway through his neck – and then her smiled faded as she realized that Barr was still standing. He threw himself at her, his sword swinging round in an unstoppable arc. Ruby dropped to one knee and ducked under it. Her head jerked slightly as Barr's blade cut off a chunk of her hair. She thrust her sword deep into Barr's belly. He grunted once and backed away once more, pulling himself off the transfixing blade. Ruby let go of her sword and surged up off her knee. She grabbed Barr's head between both her hands, forced him over backwards, and slammed the back of his skull down on to the jagged tip of a metal stalagmite. The point slammed through his head and burst up out of his right eye. Barr convulsed, and then was finally still, the life going out of him in a long frustrated sigh.

Ruby retrieved her sword, breathing hard, and then looked Barr over carefully from a safe distance. Satisfied that he really was dead at last, she leaned over and kissed him on his bloody lips, and then straightened up and looked around to see how Random was doing.

The battle was pretty much over. The rebels had had the advantages of position, surprise and a familiarity with the killing-ground. For all their experience and fury, the Faithful and the Wolfe mercenaries had never stood a chance. Most were dead. The few survivors had formed a defiant group around the one remaining Investigator, Shoal. Ruby moved to stand beside Random, facing the Investigator. Both of them deliberately did not think about Storm. Shoal looked from one to the other, her sword dripping blood, and then she grinned quickly, turned and darted up an unguarded path and out of the cavern. The others of the Empire forces scrambled after her, and the Rejects let them go. Someone had to tell the Wolfes of the great rebel victory.

After the battle, the uncanny hush. The Rejects moved among the wounded, dispassionately finishing off the enemy and doing what they could for their own. There was no place for prisoners in the underground, and the long journey to the hospital tent of the Sisters of Mercy would have killed most of the enemy anyway: it would kill many of the Reject wounded, even though they had adapted to this hellword.

Random and Ruby put away their swords and went to look for Alexander Storm. They picked through the bodies, occasionally turning them over to study the blood-flecked faces, but he wasn't there.

They eventually found him hiding in a concealed hollow, well away from the main action. He wasn't hurt. He looked up at them, and in his face there was only anger and resentment.

'I ran,' he said defiantly. 'So would any sane man have done, faced with an Investigator. I'm not inhumanly fast and strong, like you. I was no match for her, and we both knew it. So I turned and ran and she let me go. She had more important things to do. After all, how dangerous could one old fool be?'

'You were doing fine until she came along,' said Random. 'You were fighting just like you used to.'

'I was tired and hurting and I couldn't get my breath. I'm an old man past his prime. Just like you once were. Only you're not, any more – are you?'

'Alex . . .'

'I saw you fighting. No one's that fast or that strong – not even the Jack Random of legend. I don't recognize you any more, Jack. What are you? A Fury? A Hadenman? An alien? Because I don't think you're human any longer.'

'I'm your friend,' said Random. 'Just as I always have been.'

'No, you're not. You're looking younger all the time. Nobody can stand against you, not even Investigators. Whatever you are now, you have nothing in common with the likes of me. Maybe you *did* die when the Empire had you, after all. Or at least, the Jack Random I used to know died.'

He pushed past them and walked away. Random started after him. 'Alex, please . . . I *need* you.'

Ruby put a hand on his arm. 'Let him go. He's right. We're not the people we used to be. We're better. And you don't need him. You've got me.'

Random looked at the bloody mask of her face for a long moment.

'Yes,' he said finally. 'I've got you.'

Mother Beatrice of the Sisters of Mercy held the flap of the hospital tent open so that the stretcher-bearers could bring in more wounded. Many mercenaries and Faithful had been gravely injured in the unexpected rebel attack, and already the tent was full to overflowing. There was no room any longer for cot beds. Beatrice had had them thrown out so that she could pack more wounded in. Now they lay shoulder-to-shoulder on bloody sheets, screaming and moaning and whimpering and waiting to die. The stench of blood and vomit and naked guts was almost overpowering, despite all the disinfectant the sisters were splashing around. Beatrice knew she'd get used to it after a while – she always did – but that didn't help her now. The smell made her head spin, and she clutched at the tent flap for support.

Or maybe it was just the hopelessness of it all that was affecting her. Beatrice and her people were doing all they could, knowing as they did so that most of the time it wasn't going to be enough. After Toby's broadcast, drugs and plasma and medical supplies had come flooding in, from the Sisterhood and other charities as well as the reluctant Wolfes, but no more doctors or nurses. Technos III wasn't that important, and the supplies were needed just as urgently elsewhere. No one had foreseen a bloodbath like this. She'd never encountered so many injured from a single battle –

normally they just died. Her new resources meant Beatrice could keep more of the wounded alive, but that meant putting a greater strain on her still limited space. Damn the rebels. Damn the Wolfes. And damn herself for coming here because she had thought she could make a difference.

Beatrice wiped at her sweaty forehead with the back of her hand, not knowing she left a crimson smear. When she thought of what she could have done with a real med lab and real equipment, it made her feel sick and useless, so mostly she tried not to think about it and got on with doing what she could. She pushed her tiredness aside, and went back into the tent – back into hell. She made her way slowly down the length of the tent, stepping over patients, helping the doctors and the nurses where she was able to, even where that meant nothing more than holding a patient's hand. Sometimes she had to help hold a man down while the doctors operated. They were saving the anaesthetics for those who wouldn't have survived the shock of extended surgery: for quick in-and-out jobs they were usually just giving the poor bastard something to bite on – to muffle the screams as much as anything.

She moved on, praying silently to her God for strength. The bodies were being carried away almost as soon as they stopped breathing – partly because the Sisters of Mercy needed the space for the living but mostly because the Wolfes were storing the cadavers for future use as organ banks. They'd paid for the mercs' services, so they owned the corpses, and far be it from the Wolfes to overlook a source of profit. Of course, none of the wounded here would benefit. Transplants were for the officer classes only. Beatrice gritted her teeth to keep from swearing – or crying. It was important that she didn't appear upset or worried. She had to look confident, as though everything were under control. The patients needed to believe that. The poor bloody bastards.

She moved on, her shoes squelching in pools of blood and other fluids. The stench was almost overpowering. And then she stopped, as it seemed to her she recognized a face. She knelt down beside the twitching, delirious man and frowned thoughtfully. Half of his left arm was missing, severed above the elbow. He'd taken other sword-hits too. Beatrice bit her lip. Of course she knew the face. She'd seen it often enough in the factory complex. This wasn't a Church soldier or a merc – this was a clone. And, since the Empire didn't allow clones to use weapons, this had to be an escaped clone – presumably a rebel from the recent assault. She shrugged and got to her feet. She was a Sister of Mercy, and all were welcome here – to hell with what the Wolfes said.

She beckoned to the nearest nurse. 'This one's a rebel,' she said quietly. 'Do we have any more?'

'Thirty-two so far. You did say . . .'

'Yes, I did. Keep their faces covered – with bandages, if you have to. What the Wolfes don't know won't hurt them, and we don't need the complications. Any news on further supplies?'

'Most of them are still held up in orbit. Since the attack, the Wolfes are allowing only *essential* craft landing permission. Security, they say.'

'Bastards. I'll contact the Sisterhood again when I get a chance. See if they can put some pressure on.'

'What do we do with the rebels once they're well enough to be moved? We can't just leave them here: we need the space. But what's the point in healing them if we hand them over to the Wolfes' security afterwards?'

'Don't worry about it. The rebels will spirit them away as soon as it's safe to shift them. They always do.' Beatrice looked back over her shoulder as raised voices came from the entrance to the tent. She saw who it was, and scowled. 'Here comes trouble. Get those faces covered. Now.'

The nurse nodded quickly and turned away. Beatrice made her way to the entrance as quickly as she could and blocked it with her body. She nodded to the flustered sister there to leave it to her, and the sister bobbed gratefully and left.

Beatrice smiled icily at the newcomer. 'Cardinal Kassar, to what do we owe the pleasure of your company at this extremely busy time?'

'You've got rebel wounded in here,' said Kassar flatly. 'I've had reports. I want them handed over to my people for questioning. Immediately. They shouldn't be here anyway. I've got more hurt men coming in.'

'Something else gone wrong?'

'None of your business.'

'You're the one filling my tent with wounded. That makes it my business. And, as a Sister of Mercy, I'll treat anyone who needs my help. That's my job.'

Kassar smiled coldly. 'Screw your job. Either you turn those rebel scum over to me now or I'll have my men come in and drag them out.'

Beatrice nodded calmly. 'Always knew you were a bit of a bastard, James. But don't let your anger over losing a battle push you into doing something you'll regret. The Sisterhood still has a lot of pull with the Church, back on Golgotha, and right now I'm the Sisterhood's favourite daughter. I'm doing great things for their image. You mess with me, and my superiors will have your superiors come down on you like a ton of bricks.'

'We're a long way from Golgotha, Beatrice. By the time you can get word out, it'll all be over. Your precious rebels have information I need, and I'm going to squeeze it out of them, drop by drop. They'll suffer as my men have suffered. And there's not a damned thing you can do to stop me.'

'Wrong,' said Beatrice. 'Look down, Cardinal.'

He obediently looked down, and there was Beatrice's hand, holding a scalpel pressed lightly against his groin. They both stood very still.

'You wouldn't dare,' said Kassar.

'Try me,' said Beatrice. 'Like you said, we're a long way from Golgotha. Accidents happen. You don't give a damn about your men being hurt: you're just desperate to salvage some small success from this unholy mess so your precious career doesn't go down the toilet. Well, this is my territory, James, and we do things my way here. You try and walk over me, and I swear I'll geld you, right here and now.'

Kassar looked into her steady eyes, and believed her.

'I'll be back. With armed men.'

'No, you won't. I've got a hidden camera recording this. You really want your men to see you backed down by a mere Sister of Mercy? That would really kill their confidence in you. Now, get out of here. I'm sick of looking at you.'

Kassar nodded jerkily, and stepped carefully backwards. 'I won't forget this, bitch.'

'That's the idea. Now, piss off. I have work to do.'

Kassar turned and strode away, his stiff back radiating helpless rage. God help the first person he ran into at the complex. Beatrice watched him go, hefting the scalpel thoughtfully. There wasn't actually any hidden camera, but Kassar wouldn't believe that. It was the sort of setup he'd institute, after all. She'd be as well to keep a watchful eye on the cardinal after this. He was a spiteful man, and he never forgot an insult. But Beatrice couldn't find it in herself to care. She had more important things to concern her, just now. She turned round as one of the doctors called her name urgently, and trudged back through the blood and death to see what she could do to help.

Cardinal James Kassar was still fuming when he joined Half A Man in the latter's quarters for their prearranged meeting. He'd fix the bitch – though maybe not personally, and certainly not until he'd got the tape from that concealed camera. It wouldn't do for anyone else to find out how she'd humiliated him. He nodded curtly to Half A Man, who was standing at parade-rest beside a bed Kassar suspected he never used anyway. It was hard to think of Half A Man doing something as human and vulnerable as sleeping.

'Let's get to the point,' Kassar said harshly. 'I need to debrief what's left of my men after today's debacle. You have instructions from my superiors on how to deal with the Wolfes?'

'Very simple instructions,' said Half A Man. When he opened his mouth to speak, Kassar could see energy seething within it. He made himself concentrate on what Half A Man was saying. 'You're to plant the explosives I've brought with me in certain delicate parts of the factory. I have a map that will show you the exact positions. The explosions will do just enough damage to slow down stardrive production without actually putting it in jeopardy. The purpose is to make the Wolfes look incompetent. The Church will then be in a strong position to take over control of stardrive production, in the best interests of the Empire. Apparently your superiors feel the need for rather more influence at Court.'

Kassar nodded. 'Easy enough to arrange. I know just the man for the job. Very discreet and, if need be, completely expendable. You supply the map and the explosives, and I'll take care of the details. No one will notice anything until the bombs go off.' He stopped, and studied Half A Man thoughtfully for a moment. 'You've never struck me as particularly religious before. Why risk your much-vaunted impartiality to smuggle in explosives for the Church? What are you getting out of this?'

'Something I want very badly. Nothing you need to know about.'

'Well, I want something, too,' said Kassar. 'Mother Superior Beatrice of the Sisters of Mercy. She's running a field hospital here. I want her killed. Horribly. You arrange that for me, and I'll keep quiet about what I know.'

'I could kill you right now,' said Half A Man.

'You can't make this work without me,' said Kassar evenly. 'You don't have the contacts.'

'The quality of people entering the Church has gone right down the drain in recent years,' said Half A Man. 'Very well. I'm empowered to be . . . flexible, to get the job done. I'll see that Beatrice meets an unpleasant end.'

'I'll tell you when,' said Kassar. 'I need to check if a certain tape exists first.'

'Very well. But Kassar . . . don't ever try to pressure me again. I have a very short and unpleasant way with people who annoy me. You'll find the map on my writing table, along with instructions on where to find the explosives. They're to be timed to go off during the Wolfes' celebrations of the stardrive production going on-line. Shreck and his fellow news reptiles will be there, to capture it all for posterity.'

'Good,' said Kassar. 'I've got a little surprise of my own planned for Toby Shreck. He won't just be recording the news. He's going to be part of it.'

Daniel and Stephanie Wolfe were arguing again, although at least they had had the sense to do it somewhere private for once. Stephanie paced back and forth in the Family reception hall, throwing words like knives at her brother, who stood sulking by the built-in bar, glaring down into his drink. Michel and Lily stood together a respectful distance away, large drinks in their hands, ignored by their spouses as usual. The hall had belonged to the Campbells first, and their crest still showed faintly on one wall through the Wolfe crest, superimposed on it. Despite the hostile takeover by the Wolfes, the factory complex continued to have a strong Campbell presence. Wolfe security men were still turning up hidden booby traps in the function rooms and logic bombs in the computers. Every item of food and drink had to be shipped in from offworld.

All of which helped to explain why Stephanie had been in a particularly foul mood even before things had started to go wrong.

She stopped for breath for a moment, and there was an ominous silence in the hall. Daniel had a lot of things he felt like saying, but knew better than to try to interrupt his sister when she was in full rant. Besides, what he felt like saying really needed to be shouted for full effect, and he didn't trust the room's soundproofing. There were bound to be a few Campbell loyalists still hidden among the complex personnel, and certainly there would be Church spies. It wouldn't do for him and his sister to be overheard plotting treason against their own Family – not even by the hand-picked men standing guard outside the only door. Guards were necessary, even inside the complex, to protect against rebel sympathizers and infiltrators, and to make sure the cardinal and his people kept their distance. Kassar's hatred for Wolfes in general and

Valentine in particular was well known, and there was no sense in putting temptation in his hands. Moreover, it was open knowledge that the Church of Christ the Warrior felt it ought to be in charge of stardrive production; as usual, the Empress was sitting back and letting things sort themselves out.

'I still think we shouldn't be discussing this in front of *them*,' Daniel said finally, gesturing with his drink at Michel and Lily.

'They won't talk,' said Stephanie dismissively. 'What's good for us is good for them, and they know it. And it's important they know something of what we're planning so they won't say or do the wrong thing through ignorance. Besides, they're well aware of what would happen to them if they talked, aren't you, darlings? Of course you are. Now, pay attention, Daniel. We have to go through with this. That rebel attack during a live holotransmission made us look very bad. Us, as well as Valentine. It's a dangerous setback to our plans, and we're running out of time. We have to come up with something that wil make us look good and Valentine utterly incompetent before stardrive production actually starts. Once it's up and running, Valentine will be the Empress's blue-eyed boy, and it will take a miracle to dislodge him.'

'Agreed,' said Daniel. 'But I still don't want us talking about this in front of witnesses. I can trust you not to speak, whatever the pressure, but I can't say the same about our beloved spouses. We might be married to them, but that doesn't make them Family.'

'Oh, all right. We'll debate this further in my private quarters. Michel, Lily, stay here until we send for you. You don't need to know the details anyway. Just do as you're told – and try not to drain the bar dry, for a change.'

She swept out of the hall majestically, with Daniel following, as always. Michel and Lily waited until the door had closed firmly behind the two Wolfes and then threw themselves into each other's arms. Their mouths met hungrily as they pressed their bodies together, clutching at each other like drowning people going under for the third time. The occasions when they could be together had been few and far between here on Technos III, but that had only fanned the flames of their passion – perhaps because it underlined the fact that the only people they could depend on were each other. They finally broke apart a little, still in each other's arms, breathing heavily on each other's faces, eyes locked on eyes.

'We have to do it,' said Lily, her voice harsh with need and urgency. 'It's our only chance to be free of them and have our own life together. I've got a guard eating out of my hand. He can get us explosives from the armoury. Afterwards, we can kill him in a way that will point at rebel infiltrators. Then all we have to do is plant the bomb in just the right place, to go off at just the right time, and that will be the end of dear Daniel and Stephanie's factory. May they rot and burn in hell.

'No one will suspect us – there are far too many other, more obvious enemies, from the rebels to the dear cardinal himself. We'll be ever so regretful, of course, but we'll be the only ones in a position to take over here. Valentine won't want to come all this way, leaving behind the sources of those noxious substances he thrives on, just to run a factory, and we're the sole Family members on the spot. Once we've shown him we can handle things, he'll leave us alone and turn his attentions elsewhere. We'll be able to marry at last. He won't object, not once we point out it's the only way of keeping the factory wholly in the Family.'

'Don't you feel any guilt?' said Michel. He suddenly pushed her away from him, and she stumbled back a step, caught off-balance. Despite her height, she looked very slight and vulnerable on her own, with her huge eyes dark as the night. Michel made himself concentrate on what he was saying. 'We are married to them, after all. They made us Wolfes. Aristocrats. I was an accountant, and you were a librarian and minor authority on Tarot readings. If I hadn't met you, I would have been more than happy to be a Wolfe's husband and live an aristocrat's luxurious life.'

'But we did meet,' said Lily, moving in close again so that her breath was sweet in his mouth. 'And you loved me as I loved you – more than being an aristo, more than life itself. If we can't be together, I don't care about anything else. Guilt? What has that got to do with us? Daniel never tried to be a husband to me. He never loved me, never liked me, never spent a moment in my company that he didn't have to. Was Stephanie ever any different? Did she ever give a damn about you, except as a fashion accessory, something big and muscular to be flashed at Court? Jacob Wolfe arranged our marriages only because we brought necessary small businesses into the Family that he didn't want going to anyone else. Our families sold him the businesses along with us because of the dowries he offered. No one asked us. No one has ever asked us.'

Michel nodded slowly, and took her in his arms again. She nestled contentedly against him, and they stood together for a while.

'Well?' said Lily, finally. 'Will you do it? Will you help me set the bomb?'

'Of course I will. I never could say no to you. But Lily . . . let's not have any false illusions between us. Even if we do kill Daniel and Stephanie and get away with it, our love isn't going anywhere. People like us don't have happy endings. Valentine and Constance will wage open war to see which of them will take control of the factory, and we'll just be in the way. They won't let us marry. Rather than let us emerge as a new power-base they'll most likely send us to different ends of the Empire. They'll destroy our love casually, off-handedly, just because they can.'

'It doesn't have to be that way,' said Lily, without raising her head. 'We're small fry, Michel. Constance and Valentine will be so busy fighting each other they won't even notice us until it's too late. Even the tiniest of snakes that crawls unnoticed through the grass can have a deadly poison in its fangs. We'll bring them down, my love. Destroy them all, for not loving us.'

'Dream on, dreamchild,' said Michel. 'Maybe it'll work

out that way, maybe it won't. It doesn't matter. I'd rather be damned with you than live without you.'

At about the same time as various Wolfes were plotting various treasons, a regular propaganda broadcast from Technos III being reluctantly hosted by Toby the Troubador was suddenly interrupted by a burst of static. Viewers caught a brief glimpse of Toby looking off-camera and saying, 'What the bloody hell . . .,' and then he disappeared into static, which in turn was replaced by a new face.

The man seemed to be in his early forties; he was darkly handsome, well weathered but still charismatic. His eyes were steady and his smile was compassionate. When he spoke, people listened.

'Good evening, my friends. My name is Jack Random. Some of you may have heard of me. I am presently assisting the rebel forces on the Wolfe-owned world of Technos III to win their freedom and dignity. It was their world once, but long ago it was taken from them by those with more power and influence at Court. Same old story, you might think – nothing to write home about. But Technos III is presently the home of the factory producing Lionstone's new stardrive. You've heard a lot about this new drive, and the many benefits it will bring you. What they haven't told you is that it is being produced by slave labour in life-destroying conditions.'

The scene changed to show long lines of people working in a vast, low-ceilinged chamber. The illumination was painfully bright, and strange colours tinted the space from no obvious source. The air rippled sometimes, and things that had seemed near were suddenly far away, and vice versa. The scene was unsteady, suggesting it had been recorded on a smuggled-in camera. Men, women and children worked together, crawling in and around great metal and crystal structures. They were slowly, laboriously building something with hand-held tools and instruments. Many of those working had warped bones and bodies. Some were missing fingers. Some had no jaws or were missing an eye, as though something had eaten them away.

The view was allowed to continue in silence for a while, to let it sink in, and then Jack Random's voice began again.

'Whole families work here, constructing the stardrives, doing work too delicate and too important to be trusted to machines. Automated machinery can't cope with the necessary working conditions – it goes crazy and malfunctions. Same with computers. Only people are adaptable enough. But the poorly understood forces that move inside even partially completed drives are horribly destructive to human tissues. The families you see here work in these conditions fourteen hours a day, every day. When they finally become too weak or too disfigured to work, they're taken away and disposed of. There are always replacements. Because the people you're looking at are clones. And no one gives a damn what happens to clones. But *I* give a damn. And so do the rebels of Technos III.'

The scene changed again to become a long panning shot of rebels lining a trench in the rain. There were men, women and children, all of them armed and ready to fight. Their faces looked tired but determined. Random's voice-over continued. 'There are no noncombatants in the rebellion, because the Empire would kill them all anyway for daring to have opinions of their own – for daring to protest over the devastation of their world. They're fighting for their lives and their future, and their work-shifts never end. I'm struggling alongside them now – just as some day I may fight beside *you*, for *your* life and *your* future. Because the hierarchy of the Empire doesn't care who it destroys in its endless search for wealth and power and self-gratification.'

Jack Random's face filled the screen once more. Ill-used, but still compassionate. Strong, dependable, determined. The man with scars in his eyes. 'Tonight, my friends, we bring you the truth for once in your lives. What is happening here on Technos III could happen to any one of you. If some aristo wants your planet he can take it, and no one will stop him. If he then decides to work you all to death, no one will raise a voice in protest, as long as the profits remain steady. The Empress is gathering more and more power to herself, demanding more and more from her subjects, all in the name of an alien invasion that may never come. Parliament can't stop her – it's grown lazy and corrupt, like the aristocracy. Whatever you own, they can grab from you. Whatever you believe in, they can destroy. And they will, if they're not stopped.

'I'm not asking you to run out and join the rebellion – not yet. Just remember what you've seen and heard here today, and think about it. Disregard the lies the Empire tells you about the kind of people who join the rebellion. We're just like you, except that we've dedicated ourselves to a simple truth. That all men and women – human or clone or esper – are created equal and should have an equal say in their destiny. You can help us. If you wish to . . .'

At that moment screens all across the Empire suddenly went blank. Static buzzed importantly to itself for a while, and then local channels rushed to take over, hurriedly filling the gap with comforting muzak and game shows. Later, the broadcast interruption would be explained away as just another cyberat prank. None of it was real; there was nothing for anyone to be concerned about. Viewers would be able to see the true conditions on Technos III when the Wolfe Family graciously allowed cameras to observe the first completed stardrives coming off the production line, at a special ceremony in two days' time.

Back on the surface of Technos III, outside the factory complex, Cardinal Kassar lowered his gun with a satisfied smile. One shot from his disrupter had blown the complex's main transmission aerial to pieces, cutting off all broadcasts from the planet. He looked round as Daniel and Stephanie came hurrying up the slope to join him, with Toby and Flynn in close pursuit.

Kassar smiled at them, and waved imperiously at the wrecked aerial. 'I fancy that will stop the rebels pumping out their poisonous lies through your equipment. Frankly, I'm surprised you don't have safeguards against this kind of thing.'

504

'As it happens, we do,' said Stephanie icily. 'If the rebels had just stayed on-line a little longer my security people would have been able to track down the source of their signal and we could have sent men in to destroy their equipment. As it is, not only do we have no idea where the rebels were transmitting from but you have just shot away our only link with the outside universe. All our other transmission aerials were slaved to this one. Without it, we are completely out of contact with the Empire – which means that the ceremony that was to be transmitted live in two days' time, as ordered by the Empress herself, can no longer be so. Unless your people can put the bloody aerial back together again!'

'Ah,' said Kassar. 'Yes . . .'

'May I also point out,' said Toby, perhaps enjoying the moment just a little too much, 'that if you hadn't shot the aerial down I would have been able to put a rebuttal piece on the air in a few hours, thus undoing whatever damage the rebel broadcast might have done. An awful lot of people are going to be very unhappy with you, Cardinal, if your people can't get the aerial working again soon.'

Kassar looked at the shattered pieces of transmission equipment lying across the metal slope. 'Oh, *shit*.'

'Couldn't have put it better myself,' said Stephanie. 'I shall expect hourly reports from your people until the aerial is functional again. And, if it isn't ready in time for the ceremony, I will personally have your balls. Assuming the Empress hasn't got to them first.'

She nodded briskly to Daniel, and the two of them turned and strode back down the slope and into the factory complex. Kassar glared at their backs, and hurried after them.

Toby and Flynn looked at the wrecked aerial. They were fairly cheerful, all things considered.

'Was that really Jack Random, do you think?' said Flynn.

'Oh, yes. I cross-checked our earlier sighting against the Imperial News files. It's him, all right. Looking a bit battered by life, but in damn' good shape considering his age and history. And, if I did have any doubts, that broadcast just put

505

them to rest. That was classic Jack Random – exactly the kind of thing he was famous for.'

'Then those shots of the clones building the drive were the real thing?'

Toby looked at Flynn firmly. 'I don't know. If, just for the sake of argument, they *were* true, then you can be bloody sure the Wolfes would have us killed out of hand if we were to be found sneaking around there in search of an exclusive. There are limits to how you can treat people, even if they are only clones. Lionstone must want those drives really badly.'

'So we just ignore the story?'

'Since when were you so idealistic? People are dying all across the Empire every day. There's nothing we can do about it. Every now and again we get a chance to put some small thing right, as with the broadcast about Bea's hospital, but don't let it go to your head. Even if we did manage to get footage of the clones working on the drives, the odds are we couldn't get it on the air. Not now. And you can bet Imperial News would disown us on the spot. Learn to content yourself with little victories, Flynn . . . if you like having your head attached to your shoulders.'

They stood in silence for a while, thinking their separate thoughts. Flynn stirred finally. 'If Jack Random could win the war here, it might be the start of the great rebellion itself.'

'God, I hope so,' said Toby. 'Lots of good material to be found in a war. Reporters' reputations can be made on the battlefield.'

'You speak for yourself,' said Flynn. 'the moment the shooting starts I'm diving for cover and keeping my head well down, and you can do your own camerawork.'

'The trouble with you, Flynn,' said Toby, as they started back towards the complex, 'is that you have no ambition.'

'My ambition is to live to a hundred and three,' said Flynn firmly, 'at which point I hope to be shot by my lover's outraged wife.'

'Sometimes I wonder about you, Flynn,' said Toby. 'And sometimes I'm sure.'

*

In the early hours of the morning, when things were traditionally at their quietest, Jack Random and Ruby Journey emerged from the furthest trench the rebels controlled and sat on the edge of the uneven metal field, looking across at the huge factory complex silhouetted against the rising sun. The Wolfe forces had recently been driven back yet again, and were too busy establishing their new front to be any threat. Also they hadn't yet got around to setting up snipers – Random and Journey would have known they were there, even if they hadn't been able to see them. So the two sat casually together, enjoying the strange and vivid hues of the sunrise.

It was the first day of summer and already uncomfortably hot, even though the sun was barely above the horizon. They had come out on to the surface ostensibly to study the ground for the day's attack, but actually they were just looking for a little time in each other's company. Conditions underground were crowded, often claustrophobic, and after a while even the best-intentioned of people could get on your nerves. The Rejects had taken to treating them both like heroes of legend, promised saviours who would lead the rebels to inevitable victory over the forces of darkness. Neither Random nor Journey was particularly happy about this.

'I was never meant to be a hero,' said Ruby firmly. 'The pay's lousy and the working conditions suck. I'm a rebel because I was promised first crack at the loot when the Empire finally falls apart, and because that cow Lionstone put a bounty on my head. The way some of these Rejects have been looking at me you'd think I could do the three-card trick with one hand while walking on water. I have a horrible suspicion they're going to start asking for my autograph soon.'

'It's in people's nature to want heroes,' said Random. 'Someone to follow, someone who'll make the hard decisions for them. They build us up larger than life, pin all their hopes and dreams on us, and then turn nasty when we let them down by being only human after all. I've seen all this before, Ruby. It's one of the reasons I originally gave up being a

507

professional rebel and ran away to hide on Mistworld. It wasn't just what the mind-techs had done to me. I'd got tired of carrying everyone else's expectations on my shoulders – which were never that broad in the first place. I've spent most of my life trying to get people to think for themselves and take responsibility for their own destinies, but it's an uphill task. All too often they'd rather cheer and follow a leader, some smiling charismatic bastard who can inspire them into being more than they thought they were. I sometimes think that if Lionstone were dragged off the Iron Throne they'd be happy to replace her with the first smooth-talking hero to come along. Even me.'

'Emperor Jack,' said Ruby. 'I like it. You'd shake things up.'

'I'd hate it,' said Random. 'No one can be trusted with that much power, and certainly not me. It's too much of a temptation. I've seen the way power corrupts, even when people take it on with the best of motives. Perhaps particularly people like that. There's no one more dangerous than a man who knows he's right: in the end, he'll sacrifice any number of people – friend or enemy – in the name of his belief. In my experience, people can't be trusted in the singular when it comes to power. Democracy works because it's a mass consensus. On the whole, people are always better off when they can throw out any leader who starts believing his own press releases.'

They watched the metal plain before them in silence for a while. The early morning was eerily quiet after the roar of battle only hours before. There were fires still burning here and there, and the occasional Empire war machine, riddled with disrupter fire and abandoned where it fell, sparked and twitched. The factory complex was a dark, forbidding shape, studded with dull crimson glows that came and went, like doors opening and shutting in hell. The faint shimmer of its protective screen could just be seen in the growing light. It was like an ogre's castle, protected by magic, fuelled on innocent blood, powered by hate and fury.

'What's up with Storm?' said Ruby. 'He's been going all

funny around you just lately. I thought he was supposed to be your friend?'

'He is,' said Random. 'We've known each other since we were teenagers. Fought side-by-side in more battles than I care to remember. You should have seen him then, Ruby. Handsome, dashing, deadly with a blade in his hand. I was the one they sang songs about, but he was the one who got all the women. He was my good right hand, the one thing I could depend on in an unreliable universe. But now I'm . . . changing, and he can't cope.'

'You look younger,' said Ruby.

That was an understatement, and they both knew it. Random had shed twenty years' hard living over the past few weeks, and now looked as if he might be in his late thirties or early forties. His frame bulged with new muscles, and fresh energy burned within him. Though many of the old lines of pain and worry remained, his face had filled out from the gaunt mask it had been not too long ago. All in all, he had come a long way from the shattered wreck whom Ruby had first encountered on Mistworld.

'I *feel* younger,' said Random. 'Stronger, faster, fitter. I feel like I used to feel, when I was a legend.'

'Could it be a jealousy that's affecting Storm?' said Ruby. 'Because you're younger and he isn't?'

'I don't know. Maybe. I'm beginning to remember things about Alex. Towards the end, he lost his faith. He no longer believed in giving his life to the cause. We'd fought the Empire for decades, and got nowhere. He wanted to retire and let younger men take over. He wanted his comforts and an easy life. He thought he'd earned them. We were both getting too old for the field of battle, though I wouldn't admit it. I led my people into conflict on Cold Rock, and he came with me – not for the cause, but out of loyalty to an old friend. He was always a good man, when it mattered. But, when our people were massacred, I think I can remember Alex running, at the end. I didn't, and I got captured, so he was probably the one who did the right thing.

'I lost track of him after that, until he turned up recently as a representative of the Golgotha underground. I should have known he'd never be able to give up the cause completely. But now here we are again, fighting together in the field, and I'm the person I used to be and he isn't. I'm a legend again, and he's just an old man with failing breath and a sword that's too heavy for him. Just maybe, too, I remind him of the time on Cold Rock when he turned and fled and I didn't – though perhaps that's a false memory on my part. I don't remember much about Cold Rock, or about anything else from that period of my life.'

'Hardly surprising, after what the Empire mind-techs put you through,' said Ruby. 'They had you in their clutches for a long time. Those sick bastards could mess up anyone's mind. You're lucky you're still sane.'

'I sometimes wonder if I am. There are too many places in my mind I can't see very clearly – places with closed doors and heavy locks. They could have planted all kinds of control words or remote-control programming inside me, and I'd never know it until they activated them. You saw what that renegade AI Ozymandias was able to do with Owen and Hazel in the Hadenman city. I could be an unexploded bomb, just waiting to go off where I could do the most damage.'

'You're a morbid bugger to be around, you know that? Sometimes I wonder why I stick with you.'

'Because I blind you with my charm.'

'You wish. No, it's mostly because I admire what you've done with your life. You found something you believed in, and put yourself on the line for it, over and over again. Before I met you I'd never believed in anything except hard cash. Honour spoils and courage fades, but you can always trust in gold to pay your bills. Maybe I'm hoping that, if I hang around you long enough, just a bit of that hero thing will rub off on me.'

'Ruby, why do you always put yourself down?'

She shrugged. 'It's a dirty job, but someone's got to do it. Don't ask me questions, Jack. I don't have any answers. I'm here because I choose to be. Settle for that.'

'I'm not the only one who's changing. You are too, Ruby.

Whether you like to admit it or not, you're becoming just as much a hero and legend as me.'

'I bloody hope not. In my experience, most heroes end up dying noble but tragic deaths at an early age. I think I'll skip that part of the legend. I'd rather just be the trusty sidekick, the one with the good advice and snappy dialogue who emerges after the dust has safely settled to make her fortune through a ghostwritten and thoroughly commercial set of memoirs. The sole changes I'm going through are what the Maze did to me. You're not the only one who's feeling younger. It's not as noticeable with me, but I reckon I've lost a good five years. Like you, I'm stronger and sharper. When I'm fighting, it's like the other guy's in slow motion. I recover faster, too. A warrior notices things like that. But, Jack, it's occurred to me that this reverse ageing might not necessarily be a good thing. I mean, what if it doesn't stop? Where are we going to end up? As kids? Babies? What?'

'Whatever the Maze did to us, it's an ongoing thing,' said Random thoughtfully, 'even if the Maze itself isn't around any more. I have to believe there's a purpose behind what's happening. I think the process is refining us, turning us into the best, strongest versions of ourselves that we can be. The changes aren't just physical, remember.'

'Yes, I know. I'm linked to you and the others. I always know where you are, even when you're not around. Sometimes I can tell what you're thinking or feeling, you dirty old man. And sometimes, when I'm in a fight, I can tell where an attack's coming from, where a sword's going to be, even what's going on behind me. Eerie. I always was a good fighter, but the Maze has taken me way beyond that.'

'To put it simply,' said Random. 'We're becoming more than human.'

'Or may nonhuman,' said Ruby. 'The Madness Maze was supposed to be an alien construct, remember? Maybe the Maze was programmed to turn anything that went through it into copies of the species that built it. We could end up with six arms and with antennae coming out our ears.'

'And you have the nerve to say *I've* got a morbid mind.

511

Look, let's start worring about things like that when they start happening, all right? We have other things to concern ourselves with.'

'Such as?'

'Don't take this wrong, Ruby, but . . . I can't help noticing you never take prisoners. Even before we came here, you never fought just to wound or stop your opponents. You always killed them.'

'Best way,' said Ruby briskly. 'A dead man isn't going to suddenly sit up and try to stick a knife in you.'

'A dead man can't be converted to our cause, can't be made to see the error of his ways. What if we'd killed you, when you attacked us back in Mistport? No, as and when we overthrow Lionstone, we're going to have to replace her with a system that can govern efficiently, or there'll be chaos. That means we'll have to use the same people she relied on to keep the wheels turning. We can't just kill everyone on the other side. We're going to need some of them.'

Ruby shrugged. 'That's your area of expertise. Mine is killing people.'

'Look, you used to be a bounty-hunter. Didn't you ever bring any of them in alive?'

'Not if I could help it. Too much paperwork.'

Random sighed. 'I am working with a barbarian.'

Ruby grinned. 'Civilization's overrated. Jack, I'm really not interested in this ethics shit. I'm a professional killer. My only other interests are sex and loot. Not necessarily in that order. All you have to do is point me at the right targets – as with the upcoming raid on the factory. Want to run that by me again?'

'Don't think I don't know when you're changing the subject,' said Random, 'but, given the blank looks you were showing me during the last briefing, I suppose I'd better recap. All right, this is the simplified version, in words of one syllable or less. Tomorrow the Wolfes will be getting live coverage on all the holo networks for their ceremony. The Empress herself will be watching. To ensure a clear and uninterrupted broadcast, they'll have to lower the factory complex's force screen. And that's when we go in and hit everything that moves that isn't a clone. We'll overrun their defences, free the clone workforce, trash everything in sight, and then get well away while the security forces are still trying to figure out what hit them. And all of it on live holo. It'll be a major coup for the rebellion – should win us a lot of new converts. And it sure as hell will bring stardrive production to a dead stop until they can repair the damage and ship in a new workforce. Then, of course, we'll just hit them again.'

'Hmm. The raid will do the Rejects a lot of good, too,' said Ruby. 'Show them what they're capable of, and establish them as a power-base in their own right – a force the Empire might have to consider negotiating with if it wants its precious stardrive. Right?'

'Very good, Ruby. I'll make a tactician out of you yet. And all of this has brought us back to where we started – to why I don't want the Rejects focusing on us as heroes. Once we've proven to them that, as long as they can keep their act together, they're strong enough to kick the Wolfes' ass pretty much at will, our job here will be over. Before we move on to some other mission, it's vital these people have learned to believe in themselves – to believe that they can win this without us. All they needed was someone to come in from outside and show them new ways of fighting. I never wanted to be a leader, Ruby, or a hero. I just wanted to fight for the right of people to be free. Even free of the cult of the hero. Heroes are great at fighting evil and injustice, but in practice they usually make piss poor political leaders.'

'I just fight because I'm good at it,' said Ruby. 'And because I enjoy it.'

'We're going to have to work on that,' said Random.

Ruby grinned. 'Why improve on perfection?'

Investigator Shoal stood at parade-rest in Half A Man's private quarters and silently wondered what the hell he wanted with her at this unearthly early hour of the morning. Her eyes were drooping, despite herself, and she had to keep fighting back a yawn. She had a strong feeling Half A Man hadn't been to bed at all yet, if he ever slept. There had been a time when she could fight all day and still get by on only a few hours of sleep a night, but that had been some years ago now. She was slowing down, needing more and more rest during missions. Forty-eight wasn't old, by any means, but Investigators had to be the best of the best. It said so in the job description.

She looked round the room unobtrusively as she waited. To call it 'spartan' would be polite; there wasn't a trace of personality, or even humanity, in the furnishings. No intimate touches at all. It could have been anybody's room, or nobody's. Half A Man was sitting in the only chair, his single-eyed gaze directed at the opposite wall, concentrating on something probably beyond her comprehension. Shoal tried not to stare at him, but it was hard. The seething energy construct that made up his right side was endlessly fascinating. If you looked at it long enough, you started to see things – disturbing things. But you couldn't help looking, anyway.

Half A Man turned towards her suddenly, and only her training kept her from jumping.

'I know, Investigator,' said Half A Man in his surprisingly normal voice, 'it's far too early in the morning and there are certainly other more productive things you could be doing with your time. But I need to talk to you. Sit down. You make the place look untidy standing about like that.'

Shoal automatically looked around for a chair she already knew wasn't there, and then realized he meant her to sit on the bed. She perched herself gingerly on its edge, keeping her back straight and looking at Half A Man attentively. He wasn't known for being talkative, so presumably whatever he had to say was going to be vitally important to their mission here. Half A Man sighed softly, his half-mouth moving in something that might have been meant as a smile.

'Relax, Shoal. I'm not going to eat you – despite whatever rumours you may have heard about me. I just need to talk. There aren't many I can talk to these days. Most people think me cold and inhuman, and it suits my purposes to encourage that impression. It's mostly true. But I do still have a human side, if you'll pardon the expression, and now and again I need someone to talk with, as one human to another.' He paused. 'I knew your grandfather,' he added.

Shoal looked at him uncertainly, not following the change in subject. 'More than I did, sir. Investigators aren't encouraged to have family ties. They might distract us.'

'Probably he wouldn't have been allowed to talk to you about me anyway. Your grandfather was a good man. Good starship officer. Would have made a good captain, if he'd only had the right Family connections. When I heard they were detailing you to this mission, your name rang a bell, so I looked you up in the files. You've had a very impressive career, Shoal. Anyway, it seemed to me that, if I could talk to anyone here, it would be you. And I do have to talk to somebody. You understand that anything you hear in this room cannot be repeated to anyone, on penalty of death?'

'Yes, sir. Of course. What did you want to talk to me about, sir?'

'My past. Who I used to be, when I was still just a man like any other. My name was Vincent Fast. That used to be a joke – that I was fast enough getting into trouble but rarely fast enough to get out of it. It turned out to be true in the end, though no one tells the joke any more – they wouldn't dare. Anyway, I like to talk to people now and again, in private. It helps me keep track of how human I still am. I'm always afraid that I'm losing what's left of my humanity – that once I reach a certain point I won't notice or care any more. You wouldn't have noticed, but every day there's just a tiny amount less of my human side and that much more of my energy side. It takes a computer to measure the process, but it's happening. I'm losing myself, bit by bit. I've still got a fair amount of time ahead of me, unless the effect decides to accelerate for some reason. But already what's left of my human part isn't that human anyway.

'I don't eat or drink any more. Cold and heat don't bother me. I'm a lot older than I have any right to be – the energy construct keeps me alive when I should have died ages ago. Sometimes I wonder what the aliens had in mind that they needed me to live for so long. I've tried to kill myself more than once, but I can't do it. My energy half won't let me. That's one reason I'm talking to you now, Investigator. If ever in your opinion the energy half is taking control of me, overriding my humanity, I want you to kill me – destroy my human half completely with disrupter fire. That should do it. I'm asking you because you're one of the few people on this planet capable of doing the job, because I trust your judgement . . . and because you have your grandfather's eyes. He would have killed me, if he'd thought it necessary. How about you?'

'If that's what you need,' Shoal said slowly, 'I can't argue with your logic. You'd make a hell of a threat to the Empire if you got out of control. Lionstone would have me executed for depriving her of your talents, but that's my problem. I'm an Investigator, and I've always taken my oath seriously: my life for humanity.' She drew in her breath and continued nervously: 'If you're in such a talking mood, sir, can you tell me anything about the aliens who changed you? The official reports aren't very helpful. Even the ones restricted to Investigators.'

'For a long time I didn't remember anything,' said Half A Man. His voice was very quiet, and he didn't look at her. 'Perhaps because I didn't want to. Then I started to remember things, in my dreams. I don't sleep, but I can get into a relaxed state where I have waking dreams. Of late the dreams have come more often, and I remember more of them. I don't know if that has any threatening significance. I hope not. All I'm certain about is that the aliens are still out there, somewhere. Waiting.

'Forget the official, tidied-up story – the stuff about me being mysteriously snatched off the bridge of the *Beowulf*. This is what *really* happened. The alien ship appeared out of nowhere. Huge, dwarfing us like a mountain next to an ant. Its shape made no sense. We tried to talk to it, and it opened up with weapons of a kind we'd never encountered before. Punched our shields away like they were nothing, and blew the ship apart. It all took only a few seconds. The lucky

516

people were those who perished in the explosions. The rest of my crew died trying to breath vacuum. And I myself woke up in the belly of the alien ship, strapped to an operating table. There were no signs of any aliens. Machines reached down with long slender blades – and other tools for cutting and lifting and breaking – and they opened me up to see how I worked, digging through my guts as the blood fountained. I screamed, but of course there was no one to listen. I wanted to die, but the machines wouldn't let me.

'I don't know how long it went on – seemed like forever. I went crazy more than once, but the machines brought me back from the wilds of insanity. Finally I was allowed to pass out, and when I woke up only half of me was left. My left side was intact – not even a scar – but my right side was an energy construct in human form. It obeyed my every thought, but I couldn't feel it. It wasn't mine, not really. The restraining straps disappeared, and I got up off the table. There was no trace anywhere of all the blood of mine they'd spilled. I left the room and walked out into the ship itself.

'It was huge, none of it on a human scale. There were shapes and structures, but none of them made any sense. There was technology everywhere, but I couldn't understand what the machines did or what they'd been designed for. Somewhere, something was screaming, shrilly and awfully, and the sound was unceasing: it might have been pain or triumph or horror for all I knew. And, though the screaming never once paused for a breath, I had no doubt its source was organic. Something alive. Just hearing that sound would have been enough to drive a normal man insane, but I'd been through so much already I wouldn't let myself be broken. I had to be strong. I had to survive. The Empire had to be warned.

'I found the aliens, or they found me. Even now, all I remember of them are hints, details, impressions. It's as if to comprehend them completely would have been more than any human mind could stand. They were vast, utterly inhuman, draped over impossible machinery with which they were intimately connected. I'm still not sure whether the ship itself might have been alive in some way.

'It took a while before the aliens became aware of me. We communicated, though I couldn't tell you how. They're advanced far beyond us. Their minds work in more than three dimensions. I think they see the future as clearly as the past, as though there were no difference between them. In the depths of their ship, lesser creatures were dying constantly. Their life-energies powered this huge vessel. They died and were brought back to life, and then they were killed, over and over again, in a never ending cycle of torment. But it wasn't their screaming I was hearing. The aliens showed me other things, most of which I didn't understand. All of them were vile and terrifying, evil beyond anything humanity has ever done or could do.'

He stopped speaking, his single eye squeezed shut. For a long time there was only silence in the small room. Shoal stirred uneasily.

'Did they tell you why they did . . . what they did to you?'

'No, I don't think so. It's possible they explained but that I didn't understand it. There was a lot I didn't understand. Eventually they'd told me all they wanted to, or they grew tired of me. I woke up curled into a ball in one of my ship's escape pods, in orbit over a Rim world. A ship picked me up, and I came home – to an Empire three years older than I remembered and an endless series of attempted debriefings. You know the rest of the story. The Emperor's espers picked up the gist of the story, confirmed that I wasn't lying or crazy, and I became the Empire's spokesman on alien affairs. Who knew better than I what these aliens were capable of? I set policy for alien contacts and controls throughout the known worlds. I've kept the Empire strong. We have to be strong, and ready, because some day the aliens who took and altered me will be back. We weren't ready to fight them then and, even though that still might be the case now, the very least we must do is make sure we're prepared. They were vast and powerful and utterly evil, and they must never be allowed to do to the rest of humanity what they did to me.

'In the meantime, I do what I can. Of course, there's always the danger that I'm doing what the aliens intended me to. I have no way of knowing what instructions they left in my mind, or how much influence whatever's in my energy half has over the rest of me – how much of what I do is according to my own agenda, and how much according to theirs. So I want you to stay close to me, Investigator. Watch me. And, if need be, kill me. I don't want to be a Trojan Horse for the whole human race.

'But still, sometimes, I wonder what happened to my other human half – if it's still alive, somewhere, and if the aliens will give it back to me when they return. It's one last temptation, a weapon they might use to try to control me. So, as I say, I put my life in your hands, Investigator, as I have in others before you. Do what is necessary, Shoal. Whatever the cost.'

'Damn' right,' said Shoal. 'I swear it, upon my word and honour. That is how you trained me, after all. As a matter of interest, what happened to the others, before me?'

'I outlived them,' said Half A Man. 'I've lived a very long time, after all.'

'Of course. Is there . . . anything else I can do for you? Any other reason you summoned me here?'

'Yes, but not what you're thinking. Those urges were taken from me, along with everything else. I need you to carry out a sensitive operation. While everyone's distracted by the ceremony, you must kill Mother Superior Beatrice of the Sisters of Mercy. Make it look like a rebel assassination. She's upset too many people who have influence, and they want her dead. And, since I need their support to carry out my ongoing mission, she has to die. Make it quick but messy, and be very discreet. We don't want the Sisters of Mercy getting mad at us.'

'Understood,' said Shoal. She got to her feet and bowed briefly to Half A Man. 'I'll put the matter in hand. Get what rest you can, sir. We have a lot of work ahead of us, if we're to put down the rebellion here.'

'We have to,' said Half A Man. 'The aliens are still out

there. The Empire must have this new stardrive if it's to stand against them. It can't afford to be distracted by petty squabbles like this.'

In the boiling summer heat, Cardinal James Kassar stalked up and down before his assembled Church troops, working himself into a state. The troops stood stiffly to attention in their ranks, ignoring the heat and their own sweat. A few who has passed out had been left to lie where they fell. They'd be flogged later. Kassar had been talking and yelling at them for a good half-hour, and showed no signs of slowing down. The gist of his speech, interrupted by frequent prayers of exhortation, was the pride and purity of the Church of Christ the Warrior and the utter depravity of the Church's many enemies. Kassar had all but worked himself into a froth of rage and frustration, but the troops weren't particularly impressed by the bombast. They'd seen it all before. Kassar could turn it on and off like a tap.

They were paying careful attention, though – partly because doing so took their minds off the heat but mostly because the Jesuit commandoes were prowling between the ranks, hoping to find someone not concentrating so they could drag him out and make an awful example of him. No chance of that this morning. For once, in among all the rest of it the cardinal had something to say that was actually interesting. On his own initiative Kassar was sending them down into the tunnels under Technos III in an attempt to wipe out the rebels and regain their pride after being beaten so resoundingly before. Of course, this time would be different: no small group in battle armour but the entire Church force with a new battle drug the Church had been dying to try out on somebody. The soldiers would have liked to look at each other to see how everyone else was taking this, but the Jesuit commandoes were still stalking, so everyone stared straight ahead.

'Battle armour has been a mistake,' Kassar admitted, standing still for a moment so he could stare commandingly at his troops. 'There's not enough room to manoeuvre down in the tunnels, and the built-in disrupters are all but useless.

Armour just weighs a man down and gets in his way. This time you'll travel light, move fast, and strike at will. The new battle drug was created in our own Church laboratories. It fires a man's faith; makes him quicker and meaner. His strength is as the strength of ten because his heart is pure. A pure man with this battle drug in his veins could slay an entire army, armed only with the jawbone of an ass. Those hell-damned Rejects won't even know what hit them.

'My friends, we must win this battle – not just because the Empire depends for its security upon the stardrive but because our enemies at Court and beyond are using our previous defeat for their own propaganda in hopes of forcing us from our rightful place at the Empress Lionstone's side. We must regain our pride, whatever the cost. Remember, those who die fighting in the Church's name are sure of a place in heaven. If we fail, if our faith is found wanting, then those who survive will be recalled to Golgotha for debriefing by the Church interrogators. I know you would all rather die than see us return in disgrace.'

He paused to look out over his flock, and nodded with pride to see them staring unflinchingly back at him. 'The Jesuit Fathers will move among you now, distributing the new drug and giving each group its orders. Assemble back here in half an hour, with full field-kit and weapons, ready to take the drug at the Fathers' commands. Regretfully, I cannot be with you. I have other pressing duties here. But I will be with you in spirit. Make me proud of you. Make the Church proud of you. Descend into the darkness below, and kill every living thing you find. For the glory of God and the Empire, kill every rebel man, woman and child, until none remains to spread defiance on this world.'

Down below, in the honeycomb of tunnels and caverns, rebel life went on as normal. The people lived in shifts so that progress was never slowed and they might never be caught napping. Jack Random, Ruby Journey and Alexander Storm were being taken on yet another tour by Spectre Alice, who was trying again to impress upon them the need for further support from outside.

'We can feed and clothe ourselves, and we raid the upper world for whatever else we need, but there are always shortages,' she said. 'Ours is not a life of comforts. We are born into the struggle, give our lives to it, and die for it in the end. Few of us live to old age – unless they're crazy, like me. We are fighters, first and foremost. Even in our deepest, most protected places, there is little time for leisure. The tunnels must be maintained, food must be hunted and preserved, and our territory must be protected. We have schools. We tap into the factory computers. We're not barbarians. But the struggle must always come first. We take it in turns to man the trenches and endure the changing weathers of the world above. You say you need our help to stop the factory's work. Then send us fighters and energy weapons – we'll do the rest.'

She broke off as Ruby Journey stopped abruptly. Everyone else halted, looking back at her. The bounty-hunter had made little attempt to hide her boredom and had let it be clear she was there only because Random had insisted, but now the sour blankness had left her face. She looked straight ahead, her dark eyes far away, seeming huge in her pale, pointed face.

'Someone's coming,' she said softly. 'A large force, from above.'

Storm glanced quickly about him. 'I can't hear anything.'

'I can feel it,' said Ruby. 'Jack?'

'Yes, I feel it too. One hell of a big force, headed this way. They've already broken through into the upper tunnels. Alice, sound the alarms. I think we're in a world of trouble. Ruby, lead the way.'

Ruby was off and running, sword in hand, almost before he'd finished speaking. Jack charged after her, leaving Alex to hurry along in his wake as best he could. Soon men and women of the Rejects were joining them from side-tunnels, running effortlessly alongside with all kinds of weapons in their hands. No one had time or breath for idle chatter – it was enough that the tunnels were under attack again. They knew what to do – they'd trained for it all their lives. The only sound was the growing thunder of feet on the steel floors. The noise rose as more and more joined the charge, heading relentlessly towards the upper tunnels – until finally they came upon their enemy, the Faithful, who were cutting a bloody path through the outnumbered defenders.

The Rejects howled their fury and threw themselves upon the Church troops. Steel clashed and blood streamed, and soon the tunnels were packed with struggling fighters.

The Faithful pressed steadily forward, screaming their chants and war cries, their eyes wide and fierce in their taut faces. The battle drug burned in their veins and fired their minds. They were more than human now, unbeatable emissaries of God, performing a holy duty. Victory was inevitable. They pounded into the rebels, swinging swords and axes, their drug-fuelled strength beating aside the weapons of their enemies. There was neither room nor time for individual duels. Both sides fought where they could in the milling mass that seethed this way and that, spreading slowly out through the great maze of tunnels and caverns. Blades rose and fell, and men and women fell and were trampled underfoot. Some rebels tried to flee, taking the youngest children with them, but the Faithful seemed to be everywhere, blocking the exits with drawn swords. And the drug that blazed within them showed no mercy to woman or child. The air in the underground grew hot and oppressive, and thick with the smells of sweat and blood and ruptured bodies.

Random and Ruby fought back-to-back, as ever, surrounded by eager enemies like so many snapping dogs. Storm had been carried away in the press of fighting, and Random couldn't spare the time to worry about his fate. The foe pressed forward from every side, searching for a moment's hesitation or weakness so that they could drag him down. He swung his sword as best he could in the confined space, putting all his strength behind short savage arcs and sudden thrusts. His enemies fell, but there were always more. Random boosted, calling on the ancient Deathstalker secret he'd acquired from Owen; at the edge of his mind he felt

Ruby boosting, too. New strength flooded through them both, more than enough to encounter the alchemical strength of the drug that worked so fierily in the veins of the Faithful.

Above and below and all around, in the many tunnels and caverns and living quarters of the rebels, the Faithful and the Rejects fought and died. They were equally matched in savagery and determination: unable to advance, they were likewise unwilling to retreat, no matter what price had to be paid in blood and death. Tunnel floors and doorways became blocked with the dead and dying, and men had to clamber over corpses to get at each other. Rebel men saw their families perish – women and children being cut down without pity or quarter – and they fought the more ferociously. There were screams of rage as well as pain, and the din grew deafening.

Random and Ruby battled on, held where they were by the sheer press of fighters, taking wounds as well as giving them simply because there was no room to dodge or duck. Random cut and hacked with his usual cold precision and knew that, for all his new youth and strength and the added powers of the boost, he still wasn't going to win this one. There were just too many of the Faithful, fighting like berserkers, uncaring of what wounds they suffered, or whether they lived or died, as long as their enemy fell before them. More Rejects were coming, running from miles away in the underground tunnels; in the end there might be enough to outnumber and overpower the Church troops, but not until too many men, women and children had been butchered by Church steel, and innocent blood stained the tunnels for ever.

Random knew he was going to die, trapped in the cramped confines of the dimly lit tunnels, far from sky and sun and open air, and the thought infuriated him. There was so much he'd intended to do, inspired by his second chance at life, and so much he'd left undone, because he'd been sure there would be time in the future. Now time was running out. He was going to be killed, not through any failure of strength or spirit but simply because he was outnumbered. And Ruby . . . Ruby would die, too. That realization fired him as nothing else could. He mourned the undoubted loss of his old friend Alex and the failed hopes of the Technos rebels, but in the end it was the thought of Ruby Journey lying dead and broken on the bloody floor that ignited him, consuming all else in a need for retribution and revenge.

His mind burst free of its self-imposed restraints and reached out to touch and join with Ruby's. Their thoughts slammed together, merging and melding, becoming a whole that was greater than the sum of its parts. A brilliant light flared up around them, blazing hot as the sun, devouring those near them who couldn't retreat fast enough. The Faithful burst into flames, burning like candles, their flesh running like hot wax. The heat consumed the Church troops in seconds, melting their swords and body armour, spreading out through the tunnels in a travelling wave of spontaneous combustions. Only the Rejects were untouched, though the heat of the burning bodies drove them back. The Faithful screamed and died, and suddenly the survivors had turned and were running, back towards the surface and sanity. The wave of killing heat swept after them, snapping at the heels of the slowest and setting hair alight. Horrid shadows danced along the metal walls as the Faithful fled, screaming in horror as though the Devil himself pursued them. And perhaps he did.

The surviving Church troops grabbed Reject men, women and children and held them close, to prevent the hellfire setting them alight. The tactic worked, and more and more hostages were taken until the Faithful reached the upper levels and there were no more Rejects to seize. The faithful surged out on to the surface, clinging desperately to their struggling captives, and the hellfire followed them no further. Men came running to help them, and were greeted with tears and panted curses and sometimes the laughter of hysteria. Of the six thousand Faithful who had gone down into the underground, only four hundred and seven returned, not all of them in their right minds. They brought with them three hundred and twenty-seven captives, mostly women and children. And that was the end of Cardinal Kassar's great offensive against the Technos rebels.

*

In the rebel tunnels, Random and Ruby stood alone in a dark corridor. The fire was gone, and they had fallen back into their own minds again. Smouldering bodies surrounded them for as far as they could see, and the air was thick with the stench of burnt meat. They looked at each other, just a man and a woman once more – or so they hoped. Their minds had followed along with the flames, and they knew what they had done. Alexander Storm and Spectre Alice, stepping over the charred bodies that covered the tunnel floor, found them staring into each other's eyes. The newcomers stopped a safe distance away and waited to be noticed. Random and Journey finally turned to look at them, and Storm had to fight down an impulse to fall back a pace. They both looked younger, fiercer and more than human, as though the terrible heat they'd generated had somehow burned away the impurities in them. Looking into their eyes was like looking into the sun.

'They're all gone,' Storm said harshly. 'We've started clearing out the tunnels, but it'll take some time. There are a lot of bodies to shift.'

'The survivors took prisoners with them,' said Spectre Alice. 'We don't know who or how many yet. We'll have to sort through the dead first. God knows what the Wolfes will do with their prizes. They've never taken captives before.'

'Don't worry,' said Random. 'We'll get them back.' As he spoke the flames slowly went out of his eyes. 'Spread the word. When we attack in force, after the screen has gone down for the ceremony tonight, one of our priorities is to rescue the hostages.'

'Jack, that's a hell of a lot easier said than done,' said Storm. 'The Rejects have tried mass attacks before, but they've never been as effective as they'd hoped.'

'They didn't have Ruby and myself to lead them,' said Random. 'We'll make all the difference. Where's your spirit, Alex? You and I will be right in the forefront, leading the attack. It'll be just like old times.'

'I hope not,' said Alexander Storm, meeting Random's eyes unflinchingly. 'Dear God, I hope not.'

*

The ceremony was just two hours away. Daniel and Stephanie Wolfe were preparing themselves for the show; the right outfit was so important for such occasions. They were in Stephanie's quarters. Daniel had been having trouble tying his cravat, and had come to his sister for help. She shook her head, unsurprised, and pulled the cravat into place with short, controlled tugs. Daniel stood patiently as she fussed over the rest of his formal garb, and looked around her quarters. There were more luxuries per square inch than most people saw in a lifetime, but Stephanie still considered her accommodation to be particularly spartan, and said so loudly on every conceivable occasion. She was, after all, a Wolfe, and accustomed to the very best of everything. Daniel felt much the same way, but couldn't be bothered to make a fuss. He had other things on his mind.

'You know, I shouldn't still be doing things like this for you, Danny,' said Stephanie mildly as she stepped back to admire her work for a moment. 'I know you don't like servants getting this close to you, but Lily is supposed to be looking after you these days. She is your wife, after all.'

'Don't know where she is,' said Daniel. 'She's never around when she's wanted. Not that that worries me much – her endless prattling drives me crazy. Not a word of sense in her. I sometimes think Dad wished her on me for a joke.' It was the start of a conversation they had had many times before.

'I know what you mean,' said Stephanie. 'Michel's no better. Nice build, but there's nothing between his ears but his appetites. He's always forgetting errands and appointments, and then he has the nerve to sulk when I yell at him. He's good enough in bed, but he has all the personality and charisma of a soft-boiled egg. We should never have agreed to marry them.'

'We had no choice. You saw the will: go through with the marriages or be disinherited. And the Family did need the businesses that came with them.'

'We've got their businesses now,' said Stephanie. 'There, that's finished. Don't touch your cravat again, under any circumstances. Got it? Good. You're quite right, of course.

Our respective spouses are about as much use as . . . oh, I don't know. Name something really useless.'

'Lily and Michel,' said Daniel, and Stephanie had to smile, if only briefly.

'Right,' she said dryly. 'I'd divorce mine in a minute, if I wasn't sure he'd take the opportunity to soak me for every credit he could, in lieu of retaining any interest in the Family businesses. We should have insisted on pre-nuptial arrangements, but with dear Daddy's will they had us over a barrel, and they knew it. Either way, it's my business and it's my money, and he's not getting any of it. I'll see him dead and rotting in the ground first.'

'Now there's an idea,' said Daniel. Stephanie looked quickly to see if he were picking up on her hint, but she could tell from his preoccupied face that he was just being polite and had already moved on to something else. 'Steph, after the ceremony, how much longer do we have to hang around here?'

'Danny, we've been through this. At least two months, maybe three. Even with the little surprsie we've got planned, it'll still take that long to wrest control of the factory from dear Valentine.'

'You don't need me here for that – you don't need me here at all. I have to get away. There's something more important I should be doing.'

'Danny . . .'

'Our father is still out there, somewhere. With the Wolfe resources behind me, I can find him. I know I can.'

'Danny, our father is dead. He died in the hostile takeover of Clan Campbell. You saw the body, before it went missing. What you and I witnessed in the Court that time was just a Ghost Warrior – a corpse with computer implants to keep it moving and talking.'

'No! It *was* him. He recognized me. He's still alive, trapped in that decaying body. I have to find him, free him, one way or another.'

'Let it go, Danny! Our father, whatever state he's in now, is the past. We have to look to the future. He never cared for us, except as a means of carrying on the Family genes. I need you. I need your support, here and at Court. I can't bring down Valentine and run this Family on my own. I *need* you, Danny! I always have, you know that.'

'Why? So I can stand at your side and look impressive? Fight duels over your honour? Hold your hand when things get a bit rough? You've got Michel for that or, if he's not up to it, you can always hire someone. The only real battles are over politics and money, and I've never understood either of them. I have to go, Steph. Daddy needs me. No one else will help him. Most people are glad he's gone. I'm all he's got.'

'Our father is dead! How many times do I have to tell you? Get it through your thick skull: what we saw was just a Shub trick, and you fell for it!'

'I thought you at least would believe me! You think I'm crazy, too!' His face went all red and puffy, and he started to cry like a child.

Stephanie sighed, stepped forward and took him into her arms. He held her tightly, his face buried in her neck.

'I can't let him down,' Daniel said in a muffledy voice. 'He never needed me for anything before. And he went and died before I could say goodbye. Before I could tell him I loved him.'

'Forget Daddy,' said Stephanie. 'You don't need him any more. You've got me now.'

She pushed him away from her a little, and kissed him on the mouth passionately.

Daniel put his hands on her shoulders and gently but firmly fended her off. 'No. This isn't right, Steph.'

'We're Wolfes, Danny. We can do whatever we want. *We* decide what's right.'

'Not this. Wolfes have never gone in for . . . this sort of thing. Even we have to follow some rules, or there'd be no point to anything. Besides, if word got out – and you know it would eventually – we'd lose all respect among the Clans. If we're too weak to control our own desires, then we're too weak to control our Family. That'd what they'd think, and they'd be right. I love you, Steph, and I'll always love you: as a sister. I'll stay with you for as long as you really need me, but then I'm gone. Don't try to stop me. I love you, but he's my father.'

'Let's go,' said Stephanie, not looking at him. 'We have to meet with Cardinal Kassar and Half A Man before the ceremony begins.'

They all ended up in the main reception hall again. Some optimistic soul had put up coloured trimmings and streamers, and servants in full formal dress were preparing a buffet of little snacks and munchie things. There was wine and champagne in great quantity, if not quality. Cardinal Kassar seemed to be drinking most of it. Word had quickly spread of his troops' fate in the rebel tunnels, and, though he was loudly declaring to all and sundry that the operation had been a great success, it was clear that he wasn't fooling anyone, not even himself. Daniel and Stephanie watched impatiently as Kassar blustered on, angrily brandishing his glass as he shored up his arguments with details that had more and more of fantasy in them. Half A Man's thoughts were hidden, as always, and the Investigator at his side kept a diplomatic silence.

'Slaughtered the rebels in their hundreds,' Kassar was saying loudly. 'Maybe even thousands – hard to tell without dragging the bodies to the surface. All right, we lost some good men – a lot of good men – but we're the ones who ended up with prisoners. Your people never managed that before. We got three hundred and twenty-seven. I've decided to have them all executed, at the end of the ceremony. It'll be a nice finish to the show, and make it clear to everyone who's in charge here.'

'I've seen your prisoners,' said Stephanie. 'Mostly woman and children and a few wounded men. That's going to make a great impression on the watching billions. Would you like us to supply you with some puppy dogs and cute little kittens to kill as well, to complete the picture? I mean, *children*! What's the matter, Kassar? Couldn't your people find enough cripples and retards to make up the numbers?'

Kassar glared at her. 'A rebel is a rebel. The executions will be a sign of authority, and strike a major blow to the rebels' morale.

'Can't say I agree,' said Daniel. 'I mean, killing women and children in cold blood. It's not on, you know.'

'We're not indulging in your decadent Court rituals here, boy,' said Kassar, his ruined face dangerously red. 'This is Church business. Don't try and interfere with the executions, or I'll have my troops run you off.'

'So much death excites you, doesn't it, Kassar?' said Stephanie. 'You enjoy the thought of such slaughter.'

'And you don't?' The cardinal sniffed contemptuously. 'I thought you Wolfes had more guts.'

'We're in the same room as you, aren't we?' said Daniel.

Kassar started to reply to that, and then stopped as he caught the glint in Daniel's eye. He knew of Daniel's reputation as a duellist, and his men were a long way away. Half A Man and his Investigator were supposedly on Kassar's side, but . . .

'I've heard a few reports of my own,' said Stephanie. 'About what happened, down in the tunnels. According to my sources, the rebels drove you off with some new kind of esper weapon.'

'Rumours,' said Kassar coldly. 'Exaggerations. You should know better than to listen to gossip. The Rejects have no espers, let alone esper weapons.'

'But they do have Jack Random,' said Daniel.

'So they say,' snapped Kassar. 'I'm looking forward to hanging him. I mean, he's hardly a real threat any more. Just an old man, worn down by time and failure, desperately trying for one last success. The Empire kicked his ass on Cold Rock, and my people will kick it again here. No one can stand against the Faithful. Just as no one can stand against the Church.'

He smiled, thinking of the explosives he'd placed in the factory. Not enough to do any real damage but more than enough to disrupt stardrive production, make fools of the Wolfes, and lay the groundwork for a Church takeover of

Technos III. And then no one would care about a few troops lost in an unlucky venture.

Half A Man stood silently a little to one side, following the conversation but feeling no wish to join it. He was a stern, forbidding presence, with Investigator Shoal at his side like a primed attack dog, and he knew it. People here had been getting too familiar just recently. They needed to be reminded where power really lay. And he felt a need to appear strong, after babbling to Shoal. Not since his original debriefings had he spoken to anyone that much about his past damnation, and he didn't know why he'd opened up to Shoal. Perhaps because the dreams had been so vivid just lately, or maybe because Shoal's grandfather had been a good friend. Half A Man felt the need for a friend now more than ever. He didn't have to worry that Shoal would talk. She was an Investigator, and completely loyal to the man who'd trained her and shaped her life – he had no doubt of that. Which was why he'd had her oversee the placing of Kassar's explosives in the factory. He could trust he to do a thorough job.

Michel and Lily chose that moment to make their appearance, late as usual. They'd put some effort into dressing up for the occasion, but not much. Their clothes were of the finest cut, but were worn without the necesssary élan to carry them off successfully. There were recent wine-stains on Michel's cravat, and Lily's long silver wig was perhaps just a little off-centre. They were giggling together as they burst in, but tried to stop when they picked up on the cold formality in the room. They beamed around them innocently, and headed straight for the wine.

Daniel glared at them. 'What are you looking so damn' pleased about? Any later, and you'd have missed the meeting completely.'

'And wouldn't that have been a shame?' said Lily, not looking around as she poured herself a very large drink. 'Don't worry, darling. I'm sure nobody missed us. And we're in plenty of time for the ceremony – which is all you really need me for, after all. Personally, I wouldn't miss the ceremony for anything. I love a good ceremony.'

She and Michel shared another secret smile, thinking of the Chojiro-supplied explosives they'd planted in the factory. This would be one ceremony nobody would forget in a hurry.

'We may have a problem with the proceedings,' said Stephanie, and everyone looked at her sharply. 'The presence of Toby Shreck and his cameraman has proved something of an embarrassment. He was supposed to be here to provide useful propaganda, but apparently no one told him that. I'm sure I don't need to remind anybody here of the repercussions from his previous broadcasts. Unfortunately, he has viewers in very high places, including Lionstone herself, and as a result he has gained exclusive rights to the live broadcasting of the ceremony. I had hoped to arrange a little accident for him at the last moment, but, now that he's the only commentator available, we can't do without him. The ceremony must be seen, and by as many people as possible.'

'Oh, it must,' said Kassar. 'All kinds of people will be watching.'

'Don't worry,' said Half A Man. 'I'll have the Investigator stand right next to him. That should make him choose his words carefully.'

'I take it the main aerial has been replaced?' said Daniel.

'Yes,' said Stephanie. 'Some time ago. I do wish you'd read your memoranda occasionally, Daniel. As you'll recall, the cardinal was kind enough to agree to supply us with some of his technical people to do the job.'

'Should bloody think so,' said Daniel. 'After he blew the bloody thing to bits in the first place.'

'I have made my apologies,' said Kassar frostily. 'I have nothing further to say on the subject.'

'That makes a change,' said Daniel.

'You are always so full of opinions, young Wolfe,' said Half A Man. 'Perhaps you have some views on how the forthcoming war with the various aliens should be fought, too?'

There was a pause as everyone wondered where the hell *that* change in the conversation had come from. It wasn't entirely unexpected given Half A Man's well known preoccupations but, even so, no one present was quite sure what had set him off this time. Still, they were all glad of an excuse to change the subject, for various reasons.

'I'm not sure there will be a war,' said Daniel, after a moment. 'The aliens have left us alone this long; I don't see why they shouldn't go on doing so. But, if they do turn up, the answer's obvious. Draft every commoner in sight, dope them to the gills with battle drugs, and send them off to kick six different colours of shit out of the aliens. Casualties aren't a problem. We've got an endless supply of cannon fodder in the Empire.'

'No,' said Half A Man. 'That's not the answer. It's never a good idea to give the lower orders weapons. They might start getting ideas above their station. Guns and commoners don't mix. Never have.'

'So what's your great plan, then?' said Daniel.

Half A Man fixed him with his single cold eye. 'Investigators. I've been training them for decades in the best ways to deal with aliens. Let me train any army of Investigators, and I'll show you an armed force no alien attack could hope to overcome.'

There was another long pause, as everyone considered the idea of an army of single-minded, cold-blooded killers, answerable only to Half A Man. Investigators were scary enough individually, but the thought of an army of them was enough to loosen anyone's bowels. Daniel for one thought he'd rather face the army of aliens stark bollock naked, with both feet tied behind his back, but for once had the sense not to say so out loud. Everyone else was thinking hard about why Half A Man had brought such a subject up now. Was it his way of saying that he had a power-base that even mass-produced stardrives couldn't undermine?

They were still pondering furiously when the door swung open and Toby Shreck hurried in, as full of bounce as ever. Flynn glided in behind him, a new holocamera on his shoulder. Everyone else moved instinctively together, to present a unified front against a common enemy.

'That's what I like to see,' said Toby breezily. 'Good grouping. Relax, people. We won't start broadcasting until the ceremony itself – which, I'm sure I don't need to remind you, is going out live; so, Cardinal, watch your language. I hope you're all ready to begin, because everyone else is. All the factory staff and those Church troops not currently lying flat on their backs and moaning quietly have been assembled outside, and are standing in neat ranks, boiling in the summer heat and no doubt praying fervently for the start of the monsoon season. The cardinal's prisoners have been lined up and securely chained in place. They were making rather a racket, but some kind soul has dosed them with industrial-strength tranquillizers, and now it's all they can do to stand straight. The executions should make for a good show, Cardinal. The populace does so love its blood sports – even if the prey are, as on this occasion, mostly women and children. What happened, Cardinal? Were all the rebel men off on a fishing trip, perhaps?'

'One of these days your yapping is going to get you into trouble you won't be able to talk your way out of,' said Kassar, every word chipped out of ice. 'And I just pray I'm there, so that I can rip that wagging tongue right out of your head.'

'You don't ever change, Cardinal,' said Toby. 'It's part of your charm.' He looked across at Stephanie. 'May I suggest we get a move on? It's never wise to keep a mass audience waiting too long – especially if it happens to include Lionstone.'

The ceremony, it had been decided at practically the last moment, would be, despite the weather, held outside the factory, so that the impressive size of the complex could be better seen and admired by the viewing billions. One of the stardrive assembly lines had been extended out through the main doors, so that the first completed mass-production stardrive could come rolling out of the factory to be presented to the waiting crowds and and audiences – the waiting crowds in this case being the increasingly rebellious factory staff, mercenaries, and Church troops, growing readier by the minute to kill for a glass of cold water. Most of the Faithful from the Church ship in orbit had been ferried down to make up the numbers. They didn't look at all happy to be here. Deep-grained indignation seethed in the ranks, barely suppressed by the presence of the remaining Jesuit commandoes.

Stardrive production was months behind schedule already, and everyone knew it. The Rejects had attacked often, and had actually managed to bring the whole process to a halt on more than one occasion. Of course, this had never been publicly admitted, even under the Campbells. The official line was 'teething troubles', to be expected with the development of any new technology. Only a few people knew that the drive was derived from only partly understood alien specifications that had a disturbing habit of killing the clones who worked on the resultant hardware. Those in the know kept their mouths shut: most of them were dead, and the rest didn't want to be.

Toby kept Flynn moving, covering the ceremony from as many angles as he could without making the holovision audience dizzy. He was careful to give each of the main players equal coverage, in order to avoid later claims of bias, and he made sure Flynn kept a very safe distance from Kassar at all times. It was lucky that Flynn's union had been able to emergency-express him a new camera in time for the ceremony. If having a camera actually blasted off your shoulder by a disrupter didn't count as an emergency, Toby didn't know what did. Surprisingly, Flynn hadn't been that upset, at the time. *Hell*, he'd said, *I've covered Democracy Now protest marches. God, they're a vicious bunch. Nothing scares me after them.*

Toby smiled and shrugged at the memory, and got on with his job. He couldn't help wondering how much Imperial News had laid out in pay-offs to ensure his exclusive coverage. This was a major news story, and there were plenty of names and personages present; these factors, combined with memories of the rebel attack during the last live broadcast, would ensure a huge audience. Including, of course, the Empress. Which meant this broadcast could be a major feather in Imperial News's cap, if Toby didn't blow it. He was determined not to. At least partly because he had been told, quietly but very firmly, that if he did screw up, he shouldn't bother coming home again. Except in separate pieces.

So he worked his backside off, getting quick interviews where he could and interspersing interesting shots of the crowds and the prisoners and the factory complex to liven up the long pompous speeches from anyone who was anyone, or thought they should be. He was a little upset he hadn't managed to get another interview with the legendary Half A Man, but Investigator Shoal had taken pains to keep Toby and Flynn at a more than polite distance. Toby had tried mentioning the importance of a free press, and then the Empress's name, but Shoal had given him such a look that he'd decided to go somewhere else very quickly before she decided to grab Flynn's new camera and insert it into one of his main body cavities.

Lily and Michel smiled for the camera when it was pointed their way, but otherwise stayed quietly in the background. The temptation to keep checking their watches was almost overpowering, and they both tended to jump at sudden louds noises. But even their excited expectation couldn't keep Michel awake in the face of the speeches. He began dozing with his eyes open, an art he'd perfected when forced to listen to long speeches at Court, and was actually close to nodding off completely when Lily elbowed him suddenly in the ribs.

His head jerked up, and he glared at her as he rubbed his side gingerly.

'Don't do that! It hurts.'

'Be quiet, you big baby. Pay attention. See that flunky with the trayful of drinks?'

'Of course I can see him. I'm not blind.'

'Then keep watching. One of those glasses, the one with the crimson streaks in the stem, is heading straight for dear Daniel. And there's enough poison in it to see off a regiment.'

'*Are you crazy?*' People turned to look at him, and he gave them a brief meaningless smile before speaking again, in a lower voice. '*Have you lost your mind, Lily?* You'll get us both executed!'

'Relax, Michel. I know what I'm doing. Since the Chojiros said we couldn't actually blow up our respective spouses with their explosives, I've had to make other plans. The poison is completely undetectable unless you know exactly what you're looking for, and anyway, by the time they can ship the body back to a civilized pathology lab, all traces will have disappeared. The waiter's working under a posthypnotic command. I told you my witchy gifts would come in handy. His mind will wipe itself clean of all memories of the incident once he's passed the right glass to Daniel. You see, I've thought of everything.'

'Not quite,' said Michel, fighting hard against an urge to take her neck in both hands and squeeze until her eyes bulged. 'They'll know it was us anyway, because we're the only ones with a motive! The first thing they'll do is have an esper look inside our heads, just in case!'

'Nonsense. Daniel's death will be blamed on the rebels, just like everything else that happens here. And I will finally be free. If everything goes to plan, we can try the same trick on Stephanie later.'

Lost for words, Michel could only stand and stare dumbly as the waiter carried the tray of drinks among the various personages, subtly turned it so that they took the glass nearest them and not the one with the poison in. Lily grinned broadly and squeezed Michel's arm with both hands.

Which made it all the more heart-rending when Half A Man ignored the glass he was supposed to take and reached across the tray to take the glass with the crimson-streaked stem. Lily's eyes widened, and she clapped a hand over her mouth to stifle the squeals. Michel thought he might faint. Killing Daniel Wolfe was one thing; poisoning the extremely important and well connected Half A Man was quite another. The Empress would move heaven and earth to find out who was responsible – starting with a complete esper scan of everyone present, on general principles. And *Sorry, it was a mistake* wouldn't go down all that well as an explanation.

But there was nothing they could do. They couldn't say anything without giving themselves away.

They watched helplessly as Half A Man raised the glass to his half-mouth and drank deeply.

'How long until it works?' whispered Michel.

'It's supposed to be instantaneous,' said Lily. 'Especially considering how much I put in. I'm surprised the glass didn't melt.'

Half A Man emptied the glass and handed it back to the waiter. 'Very nice,' they heard him say.

Lily shook her head dazedly as the waiter went on to deliver a harmless glass of wine to Daniel. 'I don't believe it. Half A Man doesn't drink. Everyone knows that.'

'Maybe he's never been this hot before. I bloody haven't.'

'Well why isn't black smoke coming out of his ears? Ear.'

Michel shrugged. 'It would appear poison is just another of the long list of things that can't kill Half A Man. Cover for me. I'm going to find something to hide behind so that I can vomit for a while.' He stopped as Lily grabbed his arm again. 'Now what's wrong?'

'I don't know. Something bad is coming. I can feel it.'

'Lily . . .'

'My witchy gifts are never wrong!'

'Of course something bad is coming! We planted the explosives, remember? Now shut the hell up before you start drawing attention to us! And let go of my arm. I'm losing the feeling in my fingers.'

Lily scowled and turned her back on him. Michel sighed, and was grateful for small mercies.

The speeches droned on, lasting longer than expected, as speeches have a way of doing. Some of the prisoners and factory staff had passed out from the heat, and were being brought back to consciousness by varyingly brutal methods whenever the camera wasn't watching. Time was getting on. A lot of people had started glancing at their watches.

Toby looked at his, and hoped the audience would stick with him, if only for the executions. He frowned, despite himself. He wasn't sure how he felt about those. On the one hand, they were definitely rebels, criminals, but, on the other, most of them were women and children. Toby Shreck had justified a lot of questionable things in his life – working for Gregor Shreck meant you had to – but murdering children in cold blood was just a step too far, even for him. He'd thought a lot about what he could do, and it seemed to him that he had only one chance. A last-minute, live, on-camera appeal for clemency for the children, direct to the Empress. The watching billions would eat it up, and Lionstone just might see the advantage of appearing warm and sentimental in public. Either way, it was the children's last hope.

He couldn't save the men and women. The public had to have its blood.

And so everyone checked their watches again and again, making frantic calculations in their heads as they waited for their planned surprises to pay off. They were all so preoccupied that no one noticed Investigator Shoal quietly disappear from the scene to go on a mission of her own.

Mother Superior Beatrice sat on a folding chair outside the hospital tent, savouring the fresh air and drinking wine straight from the bottle. Even the evening heat was refreshing after the claustrophobic charnel-house stench inside the tent. There was more room to move inside, now that the worst cases had died, but the place was still crowded from wall to wall with human suffering. Beatrice sighed, and took another long drink. She was saving more patients than she was losing, but only just.

The door swung open behind her for a moment, letting out a brief puff of cheap disinfectant barely covering the stench of blood and pus and gangrene that lay beneath it. She shuddered, her hands shaking for a long moment after the rest of her had stopped. She'd seen so much death and pain, and she was sick of it. Let someone else cope for a while. She knew eventually her strength would return, and then she'd get up and go back into that hell again, but for the moment it was just too much to ask.

So she sat on her chair and drank her wine and looked sardonically down at the great ceremony taking place outside the factory. She'd been invited, but she was damned if she'd give them the satisfaction of attending. That would have been too much like endorsing their stupid bloody war.

Approaching footsteps jerked her out of her reverie, and she looked up to see Investigator Shoal trudging unhurriedly up the low rise towards her. Beatrice frowned. What the hell did Shoal want here? Investigators tended not to acknowledge any wound that wasn't immediately life-threatening, and they weren't great ones for visiting the sick. She studied Shoal as the newcomer drew closer. Grim-looking woman, but Investigators weren't known for their sense of humour, either.

Shoal finally came to a halt before Beatrice, not even breathing hard after the climb. She nodded briefly.

Beatrice nodded back, but didn't feel like getting up. 'Nice evening for a stroll, Investigator. What brings you my way? Ceremony get too boring?'

'Something like that,' said Shoal. She glanced at the tent entrance. 'Keeping busy?'

'Always. There might be lulls in the fighting out in the field, but here the fighting to save lives just goes on and on. Of course, you wouldn't know anything about saving lives, Investigator. Not your line of territory.'

'No. It must be a hard job; having to make harsh decisions about who you can help and who you can't, which ones you have to sacrifice so others can be saved. I can understand that. It's a lot like my job, sometimes.'

Beatrice frowned. It was almost as though the Investigator were trying to explain something to her. She shrugged, and offered the bottle. 'A quick drink, Investigator? Good for the soul, so they say.'

'No thanks, Mother Superior. I don't drink while I'm working.'

Beatrice made the connection even as Shoal drew her sword, and she threw herself sideways off the chair. An Investigator's only work was killing. The sword blade whistled through the air where she'd been a moment before, and Beatrice hit the ground rolling. She surged up on to her feet again and flailed out wildly with her bottle. The wine shot out of the narrow neck in a solid jet that hit the Investigator

541

right in the eyes, blinding her for a moment. Shoal lashed out with her sword anyway, but Beatrice had moved again. She brought the bottle down on Shoal's skull as hard as she could. It didn't break, but the Investigator slumped to one knee under the force of the blow, shaking her head. Beatrice hit her again, putting all her strength into it, and this time the bottle did shatter. Shoal fell forward and Beatrice turned and fled, still holding the jagged bottle in her hand.

She ran – but she hadn't a clue where safety lay any more. Shoal's orders must have come from very high up – no one else would risk upsetting the Sisterhood – which meant Beatrice had no friends here on Technos III. She'd offended practically everyone at one time or another.

No. She still had one friend, who had influence if not power. Toby Shreck.

She sprinted down the hill towards the factory complex and the ceremony. If she could put out a plea for protection on live holo, the Wolfes would have to oblige or face the wrath of the entire Sisterhood.

Beatrice ran on, pushing herself as hard as she could, the wine she'd already drunk sloshing heavily in her stomach. And she tried to ignore the pursuing feet of the Investigator, not all that far behind.

Jack Random, Ruby Journey and Alexander Storm moved through a deep, newly cut tunnel. Up above, on the metal surface, the Rejects had launched a surprise attack against those guards not attending the ceremony, to keep them occupied while Random's small party slipped unnoticed past the factory's outer defences. This tunnel undercut Wolfe and rebel trenches alike to emerge well inside the factory's perimeter. The Wolfe would detect the new tunnel soon enough after the attack was over, but by then Random and his force would be inside the factory and the tunnel would have been collapsed behind them. In theory.

'I don't like this,' said Storm. 'The Wolfe technicians *must* have spotted us by now. The guards could be down here any minute.'

'Not so long as the Rejects are keeping them busy,' said Random. 'And I do wish you'd stop complaining, Alex. You're starting to sound like my fourth wife, may she rest in peace.'

'She's dead?' said Ruby.

'No,' said Random. 'Just wishful thinking.'

'I warned you about her, too,' said Storm. 'You didn't listen to me then, either. This scheme is crazy, Jack! It can't work!'

'You say that about all my plans.'

'And I'm usually right.'

Random sighed. 'Look, forget all the ifs and maybes. It's really very simple. The Rejects keep the troops busy and, while everyone else is occupied with the ceremony and the force screen is down for the broadcast, we slip in and get the clone workers out before anybody notices. What could go wrong?'

'I've made a list . . .' Storm began. 'But I don't suppose you want to see it.'

'Hold your noise,' said Ruby. 'Or I'll hold it for you. You're getting too loud. Someone might hear you.'

'Who?' said Storm. 'According to the master planner here, no one's around to hear us.'

'There's always a chance some guard hasn't read the script and is hanging about where he shouldn't be,' said Random. 'However good a plan is, there can always be . . . complications. Did you really never like my plans, Alex?'

'No, I bloody didn't. They were always extremely dangerous, especially for the poor sods who had to carry them out.'

'I never asked my men to do anything I wasn't willing to do myself, and you know it. Hell, I *led* those undercover teams as often as not. Anyway, if my plans were that bad, why did you keep volunteering to go along with me?'

'I was younger then. And you were my friend.'

Random stopped, and looked back. Ruby paused, too, and instinctively moved in close beside Random as he studied his old comrade thoughtfully. Storm seemed almost defiant, the dim lighting putting shadows in his face – or perhaps they'd been there for some time. For a moment Random thought he was looking at a completely different person, someone he didn't know at all.

'I *was* your friend?' he said slowly. 'As in "used to be, but not any more"?'

Storm met his gaze squarely. 'I don't know. I once thought I understood you, but you've changed, Jack. Look at you. You're younger, stronger, faster, It's not natural. I can't even follow the way you think any more. What are you becoming, Jack?'

'Myself,' said Random. 'As I used to be. I'm back in my prime again. It's a second chance – to get things right, this time. I'm sorry, Alex, but I've grown young again while you're still old. That's what this is really about, isn't it? I'm the hero again, and you've been left behind. But none of that alters how I feel about you. It doesn't mean I don't need you any more. I just need you in different ways these days. Stay with me, Alex. Please. You remind me of who I used to be.'

'And you remind me of who *I* used to be,' said Storm. 'A man I can't be any more. Go on, Jack. You lead and I'll follow. Just like I always have.'

'Oh, spare me,' said Ruby. 'Any more of this "old comrades" stuff and I'll puke. Can we get on? We're on a schedule, remember?'

'Ruby, dear heart, you have no sentiment in you at all,' said Random, turning away to take up the lead again.

'Damn' right,' said Ruby. 'It gets in the way of more important things – like killing and loot. Now, get your ancient ass moving, Storm, or I'll kick it up around your ears.'

Storm sniffed, but set off after Random. 'You'll be old yourself one day, my girl.'

'I very much doubt it,' said Ruby. 'And I am not your girl.'

'That's for sure,' said Random.

Mother Superior Beatrice ran across the uneven metal plain, her heavy robes flapping about her. She was boiling alive in the summer heat, and her breath was jerking painfully in her straining lungs, but she didn't dare slow down. Investigator

Shoal couldn't be far back. There was fighting on the east side of the factory – another rebel attack by the look of it – which meant she couldn't get to the ceremony directly, as she'd planned. She'd have to enter the factory through the minor west gate and make her way through the complex to the ceremony. That might actually be for the better. Shoal would be bound to catch her on foot eventually, but Beatrice might just be able to lose the Investigator in the complex's warren of corridors. She forced more strength into her legs, and headed for the west gate.

Most of the guards were gone, called away to the ceremony or to defend against the rebel assault, but three Jesuit commandoes, in their dark gowns and hoods, were guarding the entrance. They looked menacing with their guns and their swords on their hips, but Beatrice couldn't have cared less. Having an Investigator on your tail concentrates the mind wonderfully as to what's really important.

She stumbled to a halt before the Jesuits and held up a shaking hand to forestall their questions while she tried desperately to get her breath back. Since they hadn't started shooting the moment they recognized her, presumably they didn't know about her execution order. If she told them there was an Investigator after her she couldn't hope for protection. They'd just assume that she must be guilty of something. Jesuits believed everyone was guilty of something.

'Someone's chasing me,' she said finally. 'Must be a rebel. You hold him off while I go inside for help.'

'Hold it,' said the most senior Jesuit. 'We have our orders. While the screen's down, no one gets in or out of the factory. No exceptions.'

'But he's right behind me! He'll kill me!'

'Should have thought about that before you started treating rebels in your hospital,' said the Jesuit. 'Whatever's going on here, I've no doubt you brought it on yourself. If you like, we could take you into protective custody. I'm sure we could find a nice cell for you until the cardinal got around to seeing you.'

'Oh, hell,' said Beatrice. 'I haven't got time for this shit.'

She kicked the senior Jesuit square in the groin and brandished her broken bottle in the faces of the other two. They flinched automatically as the senior Jesuit folded up with a low moaning sound, and she dashed past them into the factory. She ran on through the corridors, trusting to her memory of the few times she'd been here before to beg drugs and help from the complex's med lab. Now more than ever she had to get to the ceremony. With an angry Investigator and three furious Jesuits snapping at her heels, her only safety lay in front of Toby Shreck's camera.

She plunged down one corridor after another, heading deeper into the complex, afraid to look behind her. Her pursuers wouldn't risk firing a disrupter inside the factory – there were too many places where an unlucky ricochet could do some severe damage.

And then she almost stopped running as a sudden thought struck her. The factory complex had its own internal security system, with cameras everywhere. All Shoal had to do was to use her security clearance to plug into the system: she'd know immediately where her prey was, and be able to guess where it was going. Beatrice had to throw Shoal off her trail before it became obvious she was heading for the ceremony.

She ripped off her wimple and used it to wipe the sweat from her face. Think, dammit. If you want to lose yourself . . . head for a crowd. And the nearest crowd was in the clone quarters. They certainly wouldn't have been invited to the celebrations. So lose the robes, blend in with the throng just long enough to muddy her trail, and then go for the ceremony at speed. It might work. It might.

She took a deep breath and ran on, her hope growing smaller and more tentative with every step.

Investigator Shoal tapped into the complex's security systems through her comm implant, overrode the passwords, and scanned for life signs. It took only a few moments to track the sister down, and a few more to work out where she was destined.

Shoal smiled tightly, holding her anger within. The three

Jesuits she'd dragged along with her mustn't know that a Sister of Mercy had actually knocked down an Investigator – even an Investigator suffering from a degenerative nerve disease. Shoal's head was still ringing from the two heavy blows she'd taken, but she ignored the pain. She'd feel a lot better once she had the Sister stretched out lifeless at her feet. She glared at the Jesuits, one of whom was standing very carefully.

'She's heading for the clone quarters. She can't know there's only one way in and one way out. Luckily for us, she's taking the long route there. You three go ahead and seal off the exit. I'll go in after her and drive her through to you. Think you can hang on to her this time, or shall I call for the cardinal to come and hold your hands while you do it?'

'We'll stop her,' said the senior Jesuit. 'If she even looks like trying anything, we'll cut her down.'

'No, you won't,' said Shoal. 'You'll hold her until I get there, and then *I* will kill her. This is Investigator business. There is no reason for the Church to be involved any further than necessary. Understood? Good. Now, get going. If she beats you to the exit I am going to be very annoyed with you.'

The Jesuits looked at each other briefly and then set off hurriedly down the corridor. Even a Jesuit commando had enough sense to be scared of an Investigator.

Shoal smiled momentarily and then started towards the entrance to clone country. The prey had gone to ground, even if it didn't realize it had. All that remained was to flush it out.

The three men hadn't gone far when the senior Jesuit stopped suddenly and looked around him. The others stopped with him, their hands dropping to their swords. The corridor was empty and silent before them.

'What is it?' said the most junior. 'Do you need another rest? The Investigator really was most emphatic . . .'

'Shut up about the Investigator and listen,' said the senior Jesuit. 'I thought I heard something.'

'So you did,' said Jack Random, appearing suddenly

547

behind them from the corner they'd just passed. The senior Jesuit spun round, sword in hand, and Random kicked him squarely in his already bruised groin. The man crumpled to the floor and Random kicked him in the head. The Jesuit gave up consciousness with something like relief. Journey punched out the most junior Jesuit, and Storm clubbed down the third from behind while the poor fellow was still trying to figure out which direction to look first.

Ruby gazed down at the three unconscious bodies, and snorted loudly. 'Jesuits. Didn't like them at school and I don't like them now. Let's kill them and fillet them into little pieces as a general warning.'

'Don't kill them,' said Random. 'Right now we need their robes, and I don't want blood on them. Besides, it's a good chance for you to practise exercising self-control. We don't need to kill these people. We just need their robes. Disguised as Jesuits we can go anywhere we like in the complex and not have to bother about dodging the security cameras.'

'I suppose you're going to claim you planned this as well,' said Storm dourly.

'I expected something like this to come up,' said Random airily. 'I like to keep my plans flexible. Now get those robes off them.'

They grinned at each other and set about stripping the Jesuits. There was a certain amount of swapping back and forth as they tried to figure out which robe fitted who best. None was particularly comfortable, but they finally all ended up on something they could live with.

Ruby looked down at the unconscious senior Jesuit, and sniggered. 'So that's what they wear under those robes. I always wondered.'

'I must admit it's been a while since I saw underwear of quite such a startling colour,' said Storm. 'I wonder who he gets to help do up the laces?'

'Save the jokes for later,' said Random. 'The sooner we free the clones and get them moving, the better. Our agents inside this place risked their lives setting up the route we'll be using, and I don't want that to have been for nothing. Ruby – you've got the map. Lead the way.'

Ruby looked at him. 'I haven't got the map. You've got the map.'

'No I haven't . . .'

'*I*'ve got the map,' said Storm. 'Dear God, how did you ever manage without me, Jack?'

Beatrice knew where the clone quarters were, but she'd never been in them before. Not many had – clones were kept strictly segregated from real people. But the entrance was unlocked and unguarded, almost as though they'd been expecting her – or someone. The thought nearly brought her up short, but she pressed on. She had to. There was nowhere else to go.

Beyond the barriers and the electric doors, clone country was stark and utilitarian. Beatrice had thought she'd known what to expect, from the tales she'd been told by clone and rebel patients, but nothing could have prepared her for the reality. There were no rooms or proper living quarters. Instead, the clones lived in steel cages and pens, stacked together as in some great battery farm. There wasn't an inch of spare space apart from the narrow central aisle she was walking down. Her nostrils were filled by the powerful, almost overpowering smell of bodies packed close together. Beatrice was used to the medical stenches of the hospital tent, but nevertheless she had to fight an urge to hold a hand over her mouth and nose.

As she passed the steel pens, faces came forward to watch her. Some had lost eyes or ears or noses or lower jaws, rotted away by the forces they worked with. The clones made quiet, mewling sounds, like unhappy kittens. Beatrice came to a halt in spite of herself. There was nothing she could do to help them, and in turn they couldn't help her. Moreover, she couldn't blend in with them, as she'd hoped, so she would have to get out of clone country pretty damn' fast, before the Investigator found her here. But she couldn't just walk on and pretend she hadn't seen this suffering. She looked around her, her hands clenched into fists, caught in a quandary from which her conscience wouldn't release her.

Suddenly she heard footsteps. She gripped her broken bottle tightly, her heart racing. She'd hesitated too long. Shoal had found her. She looked wildly about her, but she knew there was no point in running. She was exhausted, and Shoal . . . was an Investigator.

Beatrice swallowed hard and stood her ground. She knew fighting wouldn't get her anywhere, but she was damned if she'd go down without a struggle.

She looked at the watching clones, with their damaged faces, and gestured for them to move back.

'Turn away,' she said quietly. 'You don't want to see this.'

Instead of Investigator Shoal, the three Jesuits appeared suddenly before her. They skidded to a halt, as though they hadn't been expecting to find her there. Beatrice showed them her broken bottle, and tried hard to sound defiant rather than pathetic. 'Well, come on then! You don't think I'm going to make it easy for you, do you? I'll make you kill me before I let you hand me over to that Investigator cow.'

'There seems to be some misunderstanding here,' said one of the Jesuits mildly. He pushed back his cowl to reveal a warm face with a kindly scowl. 'I am Alexander Storm, currently working with the rebels of Technos III. Might I enquire who you are?'

'Mother Superior Beatrice,' she said automatically, 'of the Sisters of Mercy. How do I know you are who you say you are?'

'Well,' said Storm, 'the fact that we haven't tried to kill you should be a point in our favour. Do you think you could lower that fearsome-looking bottle? I'm sure we'd all be a lot happier.'

He gave her a smile of unimpeachable charm, and she slowly obeyed.

Storm nodded approvingly. 'Allow me to present my two associates, Ruby Journey and Jack Random.'

Beatrice blinked at the last name, and watched intently as the other two Jesuits uncovered their faces. The woman she didn't know from a hole in the ground, except by reputation, but everyone knew about Jack Random. He looked a lot younger than she'd expected, but it was definitely him. She relaxed suddenly, her breath going out of her in a rush as she finally felt something like safe again. 'Dear Lord, it's really you. What the hell are you doing here?'

'Freeing the clones,' said Random equably. 'Would you care to help? I get the feeling you'd be a lot less vulnerable in our company.'

'Damn' right,' said Beatrice. 'I've got a bloody Investigator snapping at my heels. Someone high up wants me dead. But I can't help you. The Sisters of Mercy must remain neutral.'

'If someone's sent an Investigator after you, I think we can assume your neutrality has already been compromised,' said Random. 'Besides, can you just stand by and let this horror continue?'

Beatrice looked at the watching clones in their pens, packed together like animals. 'No,' she said finally. 'I can't.'

'Good for you, Sister,' said Storm. 'And don't worry, we'll protect you.'

'Is that right?' said Investigator Shoal. 'Now *that* I would like to see.' They all twisted round to find her standing right behind them, her sword in her hand. She looked very relaxed and utterly deadly. 'Good thing I tried to contact the Jesuits and smelled a rat when I couldn't get an answer. I started out after a rogue Sister of Mercy, and now I have three infamous rebels to kill as well, one of them the legendary Jack Random. God is good, sometimes, isn't he? Now, who wants to die first?'

Ruby looked at Random. 'Let me have her. I didn't have long enough to enjoy killing that Investigator before.'

'Sorry,' said Random. 'We haven't got the time now.' He already had his disrupter in his hand, pointing at Shoal. 'Say goodnight, Investigator.'

Ruby glared at him. 'Don't you dare, Jack Random. If you kill her, I'll never speak to you again.'

Random started to shake his head, and Shoal's sword whipped round, the flat of the blade slapping the gun out of his hand. Random shook his tingling fingers gingerly, looked at the coldly smiling Investigator, and nodded to Ruby. 'I never could refuse you anything, my dear. But make it quick. We've got work to do.'

Shoal laughed suddenly. 'Let's do it, girl. Then, after I've killed you, I'll kill your friends, and take back Jack Random's head as a trophy.'

'In your dreams,' said Ruby.

They went immediately head-to-head. They stamped and lunged, and their swords clashed together. Sparks trailed angrily through the still air. Both women were supremely talented and trained to great skill, and the speed at which they came together and sprang apart was almost exhilarating. Ruby laughed breathlessly, her sword everywhere at once. This was what she lived for, the time when she felt most alive. She could have boosted, but didn't. She could have called on the unnatural strength and speed available to her, but she chose not to. She wanted to beat the Investigator in a fair fight, to prove she was best.

Shoal swung her sword double-handed in an arc that would have beheaded Ruby if it had connected, but Ruby twitched under it at the last moment, then took the fight Shoal, pressing the attack as hard as she could; but Shoal just stood there taking it, not retreating a step. Their swords drew blood here and there from minor wounds. Neither was able to gain the upper hand for long. Even so, Ruby knew she was getting tired and just a little slower, and Shoal wasn't. Ruby was a bounty-hunter – she had learnt her trade as a fighter in the hardest of schools – but Shoal, even with her illness, was an Investigator. Slowly, foot by foot, she began to push Ruby back. Shoal's blade drew blood again and again, and now Ruby couldn't touch her.

It came to Ruby that she'd finally found her better – and that, just maybe, if she didn't boost she was going to die. The boost would give her the edge she needed. *No*, she thought furiously. *I can do this. I can, not some gift from an alien device.*

Shoal swung her sword with unexpected strength and slammed Ruby off-balance. The bounty-hunter staggered back, trying to recover, and Shoal raised her blade for a killing thrust. But then Ruby's sword shot forward, driven by boosted strength and speed she hadn't called for, and punched straight through Shoal's chest. Blood gushed from the Investigator's mouth. Ruby jerked her sword away, and Shoal fell forward and lay still.

'No!' said Ruby. 'No! I didn't want that!' She hacked at the body with her sword, cursing and spitting. She hadn't called on the boost: it had come unbidden, unwanted. For better or worse, the Maze wouldn't let her be merely human any more. She finally stopped herself and stood hunched over the mutilated body, panting for breath.

'Is she always like this?' said Beatrice.

'Not always,' said Random. 'Ruby? Are you all right?'

'No,' said Ruby. 'I don't think so.' She sheathed her sword without cleaning it, and then stopped, raised her head and looked about her. 'Hold everything. I'm starting to get a bad feeling.'

Random looked at her thoughtfully. He took her feelings seriously – after all, he had them himself sometimes. 'You mean right here, in the clone quarters?'

'No. More widely spread than that.'

Storm looked around nervously. 'Could there be guards on the way?'

'I don't know! Jack, join with me. We're stronger together.'

Their eyes met and their minds joined. Their faces became blank masks as they concentrated, their minds leaping up and out to test their surroundings.

Beatrice looked at Storm. 'I didn't know they were espers.'

'They're not,' said Storm. 'But don't ask me what they are.'

Random and Ruby came back into their own individual heads, and looked at each other incredulously.

'I don't believe it,' said Random.

'What?' said Storm. 'Don't believe what?'

'There are explosives everywhere,' said Ruby. 'All through the factory.'

'At least three main groupings,' said Random. 'They're

timed to go off soon. Any one cluster would be enough to disrupt stardrive production, but God knows what all of them together will do. Right, that's it. We're out of here. Alex, use the codes we were given and get these pens open. We've got to get the clones away while there's still time.'

'Wait,' said Beatrice. 'You do know they're executing your people at the ceremony?'

'Sure,' said Random. 'Don't worry. We'll get to them next.'

'You won't have time. The mass execution's been brought forward to make sure it goes out on prime time.'

'Damn,' said Random. 'You can't rely on anyone these days. Right – Sister Beatrice, you and Alex get the clones out of here. Since they're in clear danger from the explosives, you can do that, Beatrice, without risking your Sisterhood's neutrality. Ruby and I will take care of the prisoners.'

'How?' said Alex.

'I'm working on it,' said Random.

'Thrills, chills and last-minute rescues,' said Ruby. 'Don't you just love being an outlaw?'

In the beating heat outside the factory complex, the ceremony was going well. Everyone had remembered their lines, Kassar hadn't hit anybody yet, and Toby Shreck and Flynn were covering it all. Important people were watching, not least the Empress, and everyone else was watching too in the hopes of a major cock-up or rebel attack, like before. Toby maintained a murmured running commentary during the slow bits and suffered through the longer speeches. If they didn't get to the executions soon, people might start losing interest. A new stardrive might be what the Empire needed, and its first presentation might therefore be significant, but in itself it didn't make great viewing.

All in all, though, things were going better than Toby had expected. As requested, Half A Man was staying in plain view rather than retreating into the background as usual; he wasn't actually doing or saying anything, but his public appearances were so rare these days that any new sighting was an event. Toby had put as much effort into convincing Half A Man as he had into persuading Flynn not to wear his best party frock. Good ratings needed all the help they could get.

The Wolfes were standing right at the front, each with their own proper spouse, smiling and nodding and generally being nice to each other. People had won drama awards for less. There was an underlying air of tension among them, but that was to be expected and hopefully wouldn't show up on camera. Toby couldn't help noticing that they kept checking their watches when they thought no one was looking. Presumably they, too, were getting impatient for the executions.

Toby smiled grimly to himself. They didn't know about his planned dramatic plea for clemency.

The ranks of Church troops and factory-security staff were still standing rigidly to attention, and made a nice spectacle. Only a few more had fainted from the heat, and the audience wouldn't mind that: it added a touch of drama, and made them seem more sympathetic. Toby had considered bribing some of them to mock-faint, but had rightly decided the heat would do the job for him. The prisoners looked like rabble – animals in chains. Presumably this had been arranged quite deliberately. Kassar never missed a good propaganda opportunity.

Daniel Wolfe stepped forward to make the final speech, reading from a teleprompter with all the warmth and spontaneity of a particularly dense block of wood. Flynn moved his camera in a little closer to frame the man's head and shoulders and to hide the fact that Daniel's hands were twitching nervously. Toby listened carefully, nodding now and again. Despite the delivery, it was a good speech – almost as good as the stuff he had used to write.

He looked across at the ramp protruding from the factory entrance. The first finished stardrive – a great ugly thing – was waiting in the wings, ready to make its entrance on cue. Toby allowed himself a small glow of satisfaction. This was a good show, if a little safe and uncontroversial, with which to end his time on Technos III.

Pity it couldn't have had a bit more *drama*, though.

*

Random and Journey, anonymous inside their borrowed Jesuit robes, the hoods pulled well forward, strode haughtily past the security cameras and the few guards left on duty. Most just nodded them through – you didn't argue with Jesuits, unless you wanted to spend your next weekend on some really inventive and humiliating penance. Random kept up a quiet muttering of what he hoped sounded like suitably religious utterances, made broadly gestured crosses over anything that moved or looked like it might, and generally kept his head down. He'd always enjoyed those parts of his schemes which involved disguises: they appealed to the frustrated actor in him – though sometimes he thought his whole career as professional rebel was really his greatest role.

Ruby trudged along beside him, keeping her hands away from her concealed weapons, and tried not to break into her usual long-legged stride. In her own way, she was acting too: being quiet and calm and subservient didn't come at all naturally to her. Much as he loved her, Random had to admit Ruby wasn't really what you'd call versatile. If you couldn't hit it, steal it or sleep with it, she was often lost for an alternative.

They finally reached the complex's main exit, outside which the ceremony was in progress. But they came to a dead halt as a Church trooper in full armour blocked their path. Armed with gun and sword, he was almost as broad as he was tall, and he had the happily obstinate look of someone whose orders allowed him to push around people who would normally have been his superiors.

Random made the sign of the cross at him twice, with dramatic sweeps of the hand. The trooper remained unimpressed.

'Sorry, Father. You know the rules. No one to be admitted once the ceremony is under way. You'll have to watch it on the viewscreens. Now move on.'

Random gestured for the trooper to lean forward, waited until the man's head was right next to his cowl, and said, very solemnly, 'Did you know the Jesuits have their own very special handshake?'

He reached forward, grabbed the trooper's balls in his hand, and scrunched them. The trooper's eyes bulged and, though he sucked in air for a scream, he couldn't seem to get it out again. He sank to his knees, and Ruby took off his helmet and clubbed him over the head with the butt of her gun. The trooper fell forward, and Random solemnly made the sign of the cross over his unconscious body. 'I'd have made a great Mason,' he said wistfully.

They strolled unconcernedly out of the complex and took up a position on the edge of things. Kassar shot the apparent Jesuits a venomous glare for being late, but left it at that. Everyone else conspicuously ignored them. Daniel Wolfe was still making his speech. Random looked unobtrusively over to where the rebel prisoners were awaiting execution, and scowled as he saw the chains holding them in place. Heavy chains, with thick steel links and blocky padlocks you couldn't hope to undo with anything less than a disrupter. Random's scowl deepened. No one had mentioned chains.

On the far side of the crowd, Toby Shreck was likewise studying the prisoners, taking in the details. Many showed the blood and bruises of recent beatings – even the children. All eyes were glazed from heavy-duty tranquillizers; care had been taken to ensure the prisoners wouldn't be any trouble. They hadn't been given enough drugs to knock them out, of course. That would be to take all the fun out of the executions.

Toby frowned and looked around when Daniel suddenly stopped speaking: his teleprompter had broken down. Stephanie stared meaningfully at Toby and, rather than let Daniel look foolish because he didn't know his own speech, Toby gestured for Flynn to shut down the camera. Later they'd blame the interruption on technical difficulties. It might be handy to have the high-and-mighty Stephanie Wolfe owing them a favour.

Flynn moved over to join him, and they both looked at the prisoners.

'I can't believe they're going to kill the children too,' said Flynn. 'I just wish there was something we could do.'

'There is,' said Toby quietly. 'Once Daniel's finally finished his speech, I'll do an on-camera appeal for clemency for the children, addressing it straight to the Empress.'

'You've got a good heart, chief,' said Flynn, 'but your idea won't work. Kassar's got too much of his pride tied up in this, after his own people got their heads handed to them down in the tunnels. He'll just say this is a Church matter. No one messes with the Church these days – not if they're fond of breathing. He'd probably have *you* executed, too, just for asking. No, boss, all we can do is film what happens and hope the audience's hearts will be touched enough to stop him ever doing it again. I wouldn't put money on it, though. They do so love their blood sports, these days.'

'I used to be a big fan of the Arena,' said Toby. 'Season ticket, good seat. But that was different. At least the gladiators had a fighting chance – literally. This is just slaughter. And I've seen so much blood on this planet. I don't know, Flynn. I never thought of myself as political, but this . . .'

'There's nothing we can do, boss. Just tough it out, do our job, and hope we end up somewhere more civilized for our next assignment.'

'I wanted to cover a war,' said Toby, 'because wars are where the stories are. I never expected anything like this.'

'No one ever does,' said Flynn. 'That's why we have to keep covering them.'

Someone got the teleprompter working again by kicking it somewhere sensitive. Flynn resumed filming. Daniel finished his speech, and everyone applauded politely. Daniel nodded to Kassar, and stepped back to allow him to introduce the executions.

The cardinal faced the camera with a forbidding grimace, and then smiled glacially.

'This day, three hundred and twenty-seven rebel prisoners will die as an example to those who would stand against the authority of the established Church and her most Imperial Majesty, the Empress Lionstone XIV. The majority will be electrocuted through their chains, but first their leaders will be beheaded, one by one, as retribution for all the Faithful who have died in the struggle here. Stand forward, executioners, and do your duty.'

'Uh, oh,' said Ruby. 'He's looking at us.'

'Obviously we've chosen the wrong place to stand,' said Random.

'What are we going to do?'

'Walk forward very slowly and hope I come up with some plan before we get there.'

'It had better be a bloody good one.'

'It will, it will. I'm famous for my plans.'

'You're also famous for getting your ass kicked, and there are a hell of a lot of heavily armed people looking right at us. Could we please walk a little slower?'

'Ruby, any slower, and we'd be in reverse. Kassar's already looking daggers at us.'

'Oh, gee,' said Ruby. 'I may wet myself.'

They reached the low podium set up before the prisoners, bowed to Kassar, and then looked at the two heavy swords standing next to the two chopping blocks. The blocks had evidently seen a lot of service. Random gazed at the prisoners, who stared back as defiantly as they could. Some of the younger children started to cry, not sure what was going on but picking up on the charged atmosphere. For a moment that stretched and stretched, there was only the quiet and the tension. Kassar strode over to the podium.

'What do we do?' hissed Ruby. 'Jack, *what do we do?*'

'Proceed with the executions or we'll start with yours!' snapped Kassar, and then he stopped, grabbed Random's hood and pushed it back to reveal his face. 'You!'

'Me!' said Random, and punched Kassar in the mouth. He grabbed the dazed cardinal, swung him round and held him as a shield. There was uproar among the watching Church troops.

Random smiled into Flynn's camera. 'Long live the rebellion!'

'Oh, nice plan,' said Ruby, throwing off her robes and

drawing her sword and disrupter. 'Really subtle. Couldn't have done better myself.'

The Church troops broke ranks and, closely followed by the security forces, ran towards the three figures by the podium. All had swords in their hands. Ruby turned to face them, fire in her eyes. Some of the prisoners managed a ragged cheer.

Random looked at his watch.

Toby Shreck turned to Flynn. 'Tell me you're getting this!'

'I'm getting it, I'm getting it! It's all going out live. Is that who I think it is?'

'Don't know the woman, but the other's Jack Random all right. I should have known he'd make one of his patented last-minute rescues!'

'Hate to spoil your scenario, boss, but there's only two of them and hundreds and hundreds of everybody else. Hostage or no hostage, they don't stand a chance.'

'What the hell?' said Toby. 'It'll make a great show. We are talking major awards here, Flynn . . . Where the hell did *they* come from?'

They were the hordes of rebels who were boiling up out of concealed openings at the edge of the factory perimeter. Random grinned. Bang on time. The Rejects had been tunnelling like crazy to reach the perimeter before the executions took place. They swarmed across metal ground brandishing guns and swords and yelling their savage war cries. The Church and security men reversed direction, forgot all about Random and Ruby and Cardinal Kassar, and braced themselves to meet the rebel forces. Disrupters fired and energy beams cut through the air, blowing people apart in gushers of blood.

The two forces smashed together in a heaving mass of bodies.

Ruby looked at Random. 'I suppose you're going to say you planned that, too?'

Random laughed wildly. 'Of course. Though the timing was a bit close. Search Kassar's pockets – see if he's got any keys to the padlocks.'

But just then Half A Man came striding forward, sweeping men aside, heading straight for Jack Random with a sword in his hand. Random pushed Kassar away from him, drew his disrupter and snapped off a shot. Half A Man raised his energy arm to block it, and the beam ricocheted harmlessly away into the sky.

Their swords sprang into action. Two men touched and shaped by alien forces, neither of them wholly human any more, clashed wills as much as weapons. The power of the Madness Maze burned in Random, but even so he was hard-pressed to stay in the fight. Whatever else the aliens had done, they had made Half A Man a formidable fighter. He'd been a warrior longer than Jack Random had been alive, and he never grew tired. Their swords crashed together. Neither man would give an inch.

Cardinal Kassar, meanwhile, had come out of his daze, and was battling with Ruby Journey. He'd started out contemptuously, but quickly discovered he was fighting for his life. He called on all his training and experience as an elite Church warrior, and still found it wasn't enough. She drove him back, pace by pace, striking aside his defences with ease and cutting him at whim. And again, though she could feel the boost surging up within her, she kept it down, refusing the advantages it offered. *She* was all she needed, all she'd ever needed, and she'd decide whether to use her extra gifts or not.

She grinned into Kassar's sweating face. She could kill him at any time, and both of them knew it. But she wanted this to last. Ruby Journey was enjoying herself.

Daniel Wolfe drew his sword, ready to rush into the fray himself, and then stopped as he saw how frightened Stephanie was. She needed him to protect her. He glanced at the factory's main entrance, but there were already too many rebels between him and it. There was no safe cover anywhere. All he could hope for was not to be noticed.

He pulled his sister behind the teleprompter, made her crouch down and stood protectively over her, determined that no one would get to her without having gone through him first.

Lily and Michel clung together, staring about them with wild eyes. A small group of rebels broke off from the main fight and headed their way. Lily pushed Michel away from her, glared at the approaching rebels and called up her witchy powers. But all her weak esp could manage was a rushing wind that barely slowed the Rejects.

One of them cut at Lily with his sword.

Michel shoved her aside, and the sword slashed into his throat and out again. Blood splashed over Lily's horrified face. Michel fell dying to the ground.

Lily hunched over him, crying and screaming hysterically, until a rebel, passing on his way to free the prisoners, cut her down as a matter of reflex.

She and Michel had died together a long way from home, two children in a violent adult world they had never fully understood.

Half A Man, finally realizing he couldn't beat Jack Random as easily as he'd thought, disengaged, turned and ran. He had had a better idea and, besides, the safety of the factory took precedence over everything else. He sprinted back into the factory by a side entrance, cutting down anyone who got in his way. First, he'd switch off the timer on Kassar's explosives and then he'd raise the factory's force screen, trapping most of the rebels inside its circumference. Those trapped rebels would soon succumb, and the factory would be safe. He smiled with his half-mouth. Let Jack Random rattle his sword against an energy field and see what good it did him.

While Half A Man was disappearing into the complex, Alexander Storm and Mother Beatrice were leading the clones out. The clones took one look at the carnage and mayhem spread out before them, and froze in the doorway. Storm and Beatrice yelled for everyone to stay put and keep their heads down. While the clones huddled together, the rebel and the sister studied the situation thoughtfully. Some of the attacking rebels were trying to free the prisoners, but the heavy-duty padlocks were slowing them down.

'They'd better be quick,' said Beatrice. 'As long as those chains hold, the Wolfes could still fry the prisoners at the press of a button – and anybody who happened to be touching the metal at the time.'

'Good point,' said Storm. 'I'd better give them a hand. I was always good with locks. Everyone needs a hobby.'

'You're a brave man, Alexander Storm,' said Beatrice.

'Damn' right,' said Storm. 'Jack isn't the only legend around here, you know.'

Kassar backed away from Ruby, panting for breath, blood streaming from his wounds. He still held his sword, but it shook uncontrollably in his hand. Ruby went after him, still smiling. She'd had enough fun for the moment, and now it was time for the cardinal to die.

He saw the decision in her eyes, and frantically held up his other hand.

'Back off, bitch! The controls for the prisoners' execution are wired into my glove. One step closer, and they're dead!'

'You're bluffing,' said Ruby calmly. 'If you could do that, you'd have done it by now, just for spite.'

Kassar smiled. 'Try me. What will your precious rebel friends think of you when they learn you could have saved the prisoners but chose not to?'

Ruby shrugged, sprang forward and brought her sword savagely down with all her might. The heavy blade sheared clean through Kassar's wrist and his hand fell twitching to the ground. Kassar screamed breathlessly, dropped his sword and grabbed the stump of his wrist, trying to squeeze it shut. Blood pumped past his clenched fingers.

'I've never given a damn what people think about me,' said Ruby Journey.

'I'm rich,' said Kassar, forcing the words past gritted teeth. His face was white as a skull. 'Name your price.'

'Now that's more like it. How much have you got?'

'How much do you want?'

'All of it. Where is it?'

'In a safe. In my quarters. Gold. Payroll for the Faithful. Let me go, and it's yours.'

Ruby thought for a moment. 'Thanks for the tip, Cardinal. I'll check it out later. Now say your goodbyes.'

Her sword swung round in a long double-handed arc and cut off Kassar's head. It went bouncing and rolling away into the surrounding crush, and was quickly lost to sight, kicked this way and that.

Ruby smiled, satisfied. A good kill, and gold for afters. The day was looking up. She rummaged through Kasar's pockets, found a set of keys, and, humming a merry tune, went to help free the prisoners.

The fight went on, the rebels pushing back the Empire forces almost at will, until finally some security officer had the good sense to surrender. The idea caught on in a flash, and soon there were swords dropping and hands going up all over the place.

Almost at once, the battle was over. Ruby and Storm freed the prisoners, and Beatrice ushered the clones out of the complex. There were cries of joy and relief as the rebel forces found their loved ones safe, and hugs and tears became the order of the day.

Toby and Flynn covered it all, broadcasting live to an astonished Empire.

And that was when the factory blew up.

The first set of explosives set off all the others, and within seconds the factory became a great blazing fireball. The core of the building was suddenly a searing inferno, and blazing wreckage rained down on all sides. The outer walls, unable to contain the pressure, blew apart, and the deadly heat billowed outwards, followed by a storm of flying red-hot shrapnel. There was nowhere the hundreds of people in front of the factory could hide – no cover anywhere. They were only split seconds away from certain death.

Random and Ruby reached out to each other, linked minds, and threw up a protective mental field to hold back the flames and eruptions. The firestorm raged against the shield, battering their minds, but still it held, resisting until the force of the storm was spent.

Only then did the shield disappear, and Jack Random and Ruby Journey sank to their knees, blood spilling from their noses and mouths and ears. They clung together, healing themselves and each other. The heat was still devastating, but it was bearable.

The wreckage of the factory burned brightly, with flames shooting up into the sky.

After a while, Storm came over to join them.

'Amazing. Is there anything you can't do?'

'Yeah,' said Ruby hoarsely. 'Save a whole safeful of gold bullion that just went up with that factory. Damn. I was looking forward to that.'

Random laughed, and was still laughing about it some time later as he and Journey and Storm led the rebels and clones back down into the tunnels.

The surviving Empire forces, disarmed, sat around above ground and looked at each other, waiting for somebody else to decide what they should do next.

And out of the inferno, out of the blazing wreckage, out of the hell that was all that remained of the factory complex, came Half A Man, striding unhurriedly through the flames, untouched by the heat.

He walked over to Daniel and Stephanie Wolfe, and shook his head slowly. 'Trained Church troops beaten like amateurs, and three Investigators dead. The factory utterly destroyed. Lionstone is not going to be pleased. If I were you, I'd start thinking up some excuses.'

He strode off to bark orders at what was left of the Empire forces.

Stephanie stared mutely at the burning ruins of their factory. 'All gone. Everything. We'll have to start again from scratch. If the Empress doesn't take the stardrive away from us for this fiasco.'

'And both our spouses are dead,' said Daniel.

'Ah, well,' said Stephanie, 'at least some good came of this.' She glared into the leaping flames. 'Our explosives couldn't have done all that. Someone else must have interfered.'

'Probably,' said Daniel. 'Odds are we'll never find out what really happened. It doesn't matter. It's over. I'm not needed here any more. I'm finally free to go to look for Daddy.'

He strode away, not looking back.

'Danny!' Stephanie called desperately after him. 'Come back! You can't just leave me here like this. *I* need you. Come back, you bastard!'

Flynn got that on camera too.

Toby Shreck stood beside him, grinning foolishly. 'It was live, Flynn. We got it all, live. For this we'll win every award going, and probably a few they'll make up specially. I haven't felt like this since one of the Family maids showed me what was what when I was fourteen.'

'I don't know about you,' said Flynn, finally lowering his camera, 'but my hourly rate just went up. Way up.'

'Damn' right,' said Toby. 'I wonder what we should do for an encore . . . ?'

'Don't worry,' said Half A Man. 'I'll think of something.'

Toby and Flynn looked at each other. 'I don't know about you,' said Toby, 'but I think fame and fortune just got indefinitely rerouted.'

EPILOGUE

Prelude to War

And so began the Rebellion.

Owen Deathstalker and Hazel d'Ark, along with the man who might be Jack Random, and Jenny Psycho, last manifest of the uber-esper, Mater Mundi, headed for Mistworld, not knowing the terrors that awaited them there. The Empire, together with the awful thing called Legion, was finally ready to invade the rebel planet. In Mistport, old friends would meet again, and long-buried secrets would finally come to light.

Giles Deathstalker, Finlay Campbell, Evangeline Shreck and Julian Skye headed for what had been a pleasure world, but was now known as Haceldama, the Field of Blood. There they would find children's dreams turned to bloody nightmares, and risk the damnation of all their souls.

David Deathstalker and his friend Kit SummerIsle, also known as Kid Death, headed for the Deathstalker Standing on the planet Virimonde. Once, it had been Owen's home, but David was determined to make it his. He couldn't know that the Lord High Dram, also known as the Widowmaker, had other plans for the peaceful backwater planet. Plans that would end in blood, death and horror, and a true test of friendship.

And finally, with Rebellion breaking out on a hundred worlds across the Empire, the war would finally begin. Captain Silence and Investigator Frost would be called home and placed in charge of defending Golgotha, as the rebel forces closed in around it. And at the end Owen Deathstalker would stand before the Iron Throne with blood on his hands and anguish in his heart, and decide the future of the Empire and humanity itself.

It was to be war now, with little mercy and less honour, and damn all glory for the quick or the dead. And all of it pivoting around one man, Owen Deathstalker, the hope of humanity, the warrior who fought for peace, and knew so little of it himself.

Deathstalker

SIMON R. GREEN

The first volume in the epic adventure series

Owen Deathstalker, last of his line, is a quiet man, a historian, remote from the stench of corruption and intrigue surrounding the Iron Throne at the heart of the galaxy-spanning, tyrannical Empire.

And then, inexplicably, Deathstalker is outlawed, forced to flee from one end of the Empire to the other. And as he does so, he discovers that resistance is growing, everywhere, to the Iron Bitch on the Iron Throne.

DEATHSTALKER

Outlawing him could be the Iron Bitch's biggest mistake.

ISBN 0 575 60160 4

Deathstalker War

SIMON R. GREEN

The third volume in the epic adventure series

Owen Deathstalker, last of his line, was wrongly outlawed by the evil Empress Lionstone XIV . . . but in making an enemy of Deathstalker, the Iron Bitch sowed the bitter seeds of revenge. Now the rebellion Deathstalker has been fomenting has blossomed into war.

Opening skirmishes on Mistworld, Haceldama and Virimonde reveal just a few of the horrors the Iron Bitch is prepared to unleash upon the rebels, but the opposition only fuels their determination to win justice.

This time it's war.

DEATHSTALKER WAR

No quarter, no prisoners, no compromises.

ISBN 0 575 60061 6

Deathstalker Honour

SIMON R. GREEN

The powerful conclusion to the epic adventure

They were, after all, official heroes of the great Rebellion: Owen Deathstalker, outlawed aristocrat and reluctant warrior; Hazel d'Ark, ex-clonelegger and ex-pirate; Jack Random, legendary professional rebel; and Ruby Journey, infamous bounty hunter.

Together, they fought impossible odds in the name of freedom and justice. They gathered an army of the bold and the valiant, the downtrodden and the desperate, and led them to victory.

And in the great steel and brass Palace on Golgotha they threw down the Empress Lionstone XIV, the Iron Bitch, and destroyed the Iron Throne of Empire for ever.

They should have lived happily ever after.

Unfortunately, life isn't like that.

ISBN 0 575 60178 7